RICHARD HOWARD OMNIBUS

Bonaparte's Sons
Bonaparte's Invaders

RICHARD HOWARD OMNIBUS

Bonaparte's Sons
Bonaparte's Invaders

RICHARD HOWARD

A *Time Warner* Paperback

This omnibus edition first published in Great Britain by
Time Warner Paperbacks in 2004
Richard Howard Omnibus Copyright © Richard Howard 2004

Previously published separately:
Bonaparte's Sons first published in Great Britain in 1997 by
Little, Brown and Company
Published by Warner Books in 1998
Reprinted 2000, 2002
Copyright © Richard Howard 1997

Bonaparte's Invaders first published in Great Britain in 1998 by
Little, Brown and Company
Published by Warner Books in 1999
Reprinted 2002
Copyright © Richard Howard 1998

A CIP catalogue record for this book
is available from the British Library.

ISBN 0 7515 3641 5

Printed and bound in Great Britain by
Clays Ltd, St Ives plc

Time Warner Paperbacks
An imprint of
Time Warner Books UK
Brettenham House
Lancaster Place
London WC2E 7EN

www.TimeWarnerBooks.co.uk

Bonaparte's Sons

PROLOGUE

Alain Lausard peered up at the dull grey light of dawn creeping through the bars of the cell and sighed wearily. The arrival of a new day promised nothing for him. It would be a day like any other. A day of monotony spent alone in his eight-feet-square cell. A day indistinguishable from all those he had already endured and he knew it would continue until those who chose to keep him captive decided otherwise. The soul-destroying predictability would only be interrupted by the arrival of a few slops pushed through the slot at the bottom of the wooden cell door; and these would only come if someone on the other side could be bothered to ladle gruel into the wooden bowls that passed for eating receptacles. Sometimes the meagre meals never even arrived.

Lausard got to his feet and took two paces across the cell to the window. Two strides was all it took to cover the cramped confines of the enclosure. He was a powerfully built man and even the lack of good nourishment for so long had done little to diminish the impressiveness of his physique. His hair was long and badly in need of a wash; lank strands hung down as far as his shoulders, framing a square and somewhat cold face. His appearance was made all the more daunting by piercing blue eyes which fixed on things with unwavering concentration. That gaze now settled on the droplets of moisture running down one wall of the cell, chasing each other like dirty tears over the pock-marked stonework. The floor of the cell was covered with straw rotting in the damp, the stench of which he'd found intolerable at first but now the rancid odour seemed to belong. In fact, looking around the cell, Lausard felt as unfeeling and unforgiving as the rock which hemmed him in. But if there was nothing *inside*, then the world beyond the bars and the walls offered just as little. The world outside was, in its own way, as unforgiving as the place he now called home. The streets and gutters of Paris could be as harsh as any prison, as he had found during the past two years.

Sometimes he forgot how long he'd been scrounging a living on those streets. Time seemed to have lost its meaning even *before* he had been arrested, before his world had been condensed into four damp walls and a floor of rotting straw.

Standing beneath the barred window set about six feet up in the wall, he watched the dawn light creep unwillingly across the floor as if it too were reluctant to enter this place.

Further down the corridor, in one of the dozens of cells identical to his own, he could hear snoring. Someone, at least, was managing to ignore the discomfort and find escape in the oblivion of sleep. Lausard both envied them and resented them for that ability. He himself was rarely that lucky. When the cell was transformed into a black hole by the onset of night, he managed to get only a little sleep, during which time he was momentarily free of the hungry fleas which infested his clothes and hair. He could feel one on the nape of his neck now. He picked it away and crushed it between his thumb and forefinger.

Another day of waiting and wondering. Of languishing in this stone box which imprisoned him with nothing to look forward to but the opening of that one door which led to the outside. Deep in his heart though, Lausard knew that should that door be opened, and the guards finally come for him, then his journey would be one way and it would be final. He waited like the others in the prison with him for release in only one form.

He sat down against one of the damp walls and gazed at the wooden door, almost willing it to open but knowing that if it did, he faced a meeting with the guillotine. His crime carried the death penalty, as did most transgressions in the city. He knew the time would come. All he could do was wait.

He continued to stare at the door.

CHAPTER 1

Captain Nicholas Deschamps reined in the magnificent bay he was riding and patted the animal's neck reassuringly, glancing around at his companion.

Sergeant Legier brought his own mount to a halt and glanced around the prison courtyard, waiting until his superior swung himself from the saddle before he too stepped down. He winced slightly as his booted foot connected with the cobbles beneath. Having injured his hip a couple of days earlier it was still painful.

The Conciergerie was one of the largest of twenty-eight prisons currently in use in Paris. It held over six hundred prisoners and had been home to Marie Antoinette before her execution. Only Bicetre was larger. Some of the jails held as few as thirty captives; Maison de Coignard and Prison Luxembourg boasted thirty-five and thirty-three respectively. Nearly five and a half thousand unfortunates were currently held within the walls of these prisons, charged with crimes ranging from forgery to rape, stealing to heresy. Three years earlier, on Jean Paul Marat's orders, more than one thousand four hundred prisoners throughout the city had been butchered in the space of five days. A year later, Marat himself was dead, stabbed to death in his bath by Charlotte Corday.

The political climate in the city, and in France itself, seemed to change on a daily basis. Those who were enemies on Monday were allies by the Tuesday and sometimes dead by the Wednesday. Any man or woman branded a member of the wrong political party could expect swift and summary treatment. 'The Patriotic Shortener', as the guillotine became affectionately named by the masses, began to work overtime.

When Robespierre came to power, the blade of the killing machine was rarely still. The Jacobin leader had overseen the mass blood-letting known as 'The Terror' before he too had finally come to rest his neck beneath the sharpened steel.

The early morning breeze which whipped across the courtyard was icy but neither Deschamps nor Legier felt its sting. They were both dressed in the green uniforms of dragoons, with thick woollen tunics faced with white lapels, cross-belts and bleached breeches tucked into knee-length boots. As Deschamps walked, his sabre bumped against the polished leather and the breeze whipped the horsehair mane of his brass helmet around his face. He was a big man, close to six feet tall. His colleagues had always joked that his size made him a bigger target and his collection of wounds would seem to bear that out. There were several scars on his face, the worst of which had been acquired during the battle for the Heights of Abraham during the Seven

Years War. A sabre cut had left him with a split upper lip and another wound gave him the appearance of wearing a perpetual smirk, with one corner of his mouth drawn up towards an ear. Thirty-eight years of soldiering. From Canada to Corsica, Valmy to Fleurus. The army was his life and always had been. He had risen through the ranks, attaining his captaincy by his bravery and willingness to risk his life for his country, for the Republic.

Legier had served under him for twenty years. He was a stockier man, powerfully built with a bull-like neck as though his head had been rammed down between his shoulders. His right ear was missing, courtesy of a piece of shrapnel, but he could hear perfectly well through the hole which remained and he made no attempt to disguise the deformity.

The main door which led into the prison itself was unguarded and the two cavalrymen exchanged disdainful glances as they approached it. Deschamps banged twice on the wood. To his surprise it swung open.

He stepped inside and saw a man slumped on the cold stone floor, musket propped against his shoulder, head flopping forward.

He grunted and looked up, trying to scramble to his feet while attempting to blink the sleep from his eyes. Gripping the musket, he lowered it so that the barrel was pointing at Deschamps.

Legier stepped forward, hand falling to the hilt of his sword but the officer waved him back, his gaze locked on to the solitary guard. 'Who are you?' the guard asked, regaining his wits.

'I want to see the Governor of the prison,'

Deschamps said flatly, unconcerned by the Charleville musket pointing at his chest.

'I need identification,' the guard said defiantly. 'The Governor is a busy man. He will not see just anyone.'

Deschamps ran appraising eyes over him. The guard was in his early twenties, dressed in the white jacket of an infantryman with a bicorn hat perched precariously on his head and short trousers holed and threadbare. He wore a pair of gaiters but no boots beneath.

'How old are you?' Deschamps asked.

The youth looked puzzled, as if the question was somehow beyond his powers of reasoning.

'Answer me, boy,' snapped Deschamps. 'You look like a child. How many more children are pretending to be soldiers in this place?'

'Answer,' Legier added menacingly.

'Sixteen,' he said falteringly. 'I am sixteen.'

'Well then, boy soldier,' Deschamps said quietly. 'Do your job. Fetch the Governor now. I have business here.'

The young man looked at each of the dragoons in turn, at the stern expressions, the scars, the uniforms. Then he turned and sprinted up the corridor.

Felix Marcognet was a tall, thin man with sad eyes and a pinched expression. His eyes darted nervously back and forth between the two dragoons, both of whom had declined his offer to sit. Marcognet himself wiped a hand over his balding pate and looked once more at the piece of paper which Deschamps had given him.

The name on the bottom of the paper, signed in bold

strokes, was that of 'Paul Barras'. Barras was one of the Directory of Seven, one of the most powerful men, not just in Paris but the whole of France.

'We need men,' said Deschamps. 'France needs men.'

'I can't help you,' Marcognet told him.

Deschamps fixed him in a withering stare.

'I'm not a well man, I have trouble breathing,' the Prison Governor pleaded. 'And I can't spare any of my guards, I—'

'It's not you *or* your guards that I want,' Deschamps said with irritation. 'You have over six hundred men in this prison. Most of them are fit enough to fight.'

'But they're criminals, scum,' Marcognet protested.

'So are most of the army.'

'I can't let you take them all.'

'I don't want them *all*.'

'I have a job to do here. I have responsibilities!'

'To whom?' Deschamps enquired. 'Your responsibilities are to France. You're a turnkey. Nothing more. You have something I need and I mean to have it.'

Marcognet swallowed hard, his gaze again flickering back and forth between the two uniformed men. Legier was tapping gently with his index finger on the hilt of his sabre.

'You won't find much here,' the Governor said.

'I'll be the judge of that,' Deschamps said. 'In case it has escaped your notice, we are at war. We need all the men we can get. Let their quality as men be of concern to me.'

'There is no quality in them,' Marcognet said scathingly. 'I have already told you what they are.'

'And I'm sure your opinion is unquestionable,' Deschamps sneered. 'Nevertheless, I want to see a full list of names of every man in this prison and I want it now.'

Deschamps paused at each door and peered indifferently through the grille at the occupant of the cell; he squinted to make out the human shape in the gloom within. With the arrival of the dawn the task was made a little easier – the cold grey light of a new morning illuminated slightly the interior of the cells and the wretches who occupied them.

Deschamps looked in at each prisoner while Marcognet read the name from a sheaf of papers and Legier put either a cross or a tick next to the name using a quill pen and ink.

'Do you treat them all as badly?' Deschamps demanded, peering in at one man who was doubled up in the middle of the cell coughing badly and clutching at his chest. He hawked loudly and spat some blood-tinged mucus from his mouth.

'They're criminals,' said Marcognet.

'They're *men*.'

'Look, Captain, I don't think you realise what running a prison entails,' Marcognet said officiously. 'It takes organisation. It takes certain skills which you are not aware of.'

'Such as?' Deschamps slid the wooden slat on the grille shut and passed along to the next cell.

'There are the prisoners to be attended to, the guards who watch them have to be kept in line,' Marcognet said. 'It is a very responsible job.'

'And how did *you* come by such a responsible job?' Deschamps chided.

The Governor coughed theatrically but didn't speak.

'Well?' the dragoon persisted.

'I have a nephew in the Directory,' Marcognet said finally, lowering his voice.

Deschamps looked at Legier who eyed the Governor with disdain and scratched at the hole where his ear had once been.

'Your brother was wounded during the storming of the Bastille, wasn't he, Legier?' Deschamps said.

'Yes, sir, he was,' Legier replied. 'Blinded in one eye when a powder keg blew up.'

'Do you know what was done to the Governor of the Bastille?' Deschamps asked, glancing at Marcognet who shook his head. 'De Launay was his name. The crowd asked him to hand over his gunpowder. He refused. He ordered his men to fire on the crowd. They killed nearly a hundred before the prison was stormed. They cut off De Launay's head with a butcher's knife.'

'What has that got to do with me?' Marcognet questioned.

'Nothing,' Deschamps said, sliding back a wooden partition to peer in at the next prisoner. 'As you say, it is a responsible job. Men in authority are not always the most popular of men and the public are fickle.'

Marcognet swallowed hard.

'Who is this?' Deschamps said, looking at the prisoner.

The Governor consulted the list. 'Roussard,' he said. 'A forger.'

'Open it up,' Deschamps said, nodding towards the door.

Marcognet put a large key from the ring he held into the lock and pushed open the door.

'On your feet,' he snapped and the occupant of the cell did as he was ordered, nodding almost politely at the newcomers.

'Leave us,' said Deschamps, looking at the Governor dismissively.

Legier stepped in front of the closed door as the tall, thin man retreated from the room muttering under his breath.

'Do you want to die in prison, forger?'

'I don't want to die at all,' Roussard said, a thin smile on his lips.

'Everyone dies, it's just a matter of when or how.'

'Perhaps. Why does it bother *you* where I die?'

'I can make sure it isn't in *here*,' Deschamps told him.

'How?'

'France needs fighting men. Better a death with honour, wouldn't you agree?'

'So you're offering me a choice between having my head cut off by the guillotine or being shot by some Englishmen, Prussians, Austrians or Italians? It isn't much of a choice.'

'You're not in a position to bargain.'

Roussard nodded, still smiling.

The two dragoons turned to leave.

'Captain,' Roussard called. 'If you need money to buy horses, I can help you. My francs are a work of art.'

The cell door slammed shut.

'I am a lover, not a fighter,' said Giresse, smiling.

'You're a horse thief,' Marcognet interrupted. 'That's why you're in *here*.'

'A horse thief, in the middle of Paris?' Deschamps said, looking surprised.

'I took some horses from the Tuileries stables,' Giresse replied.

'How many?' Deschamps asked.

'Just two,' said Giresse. 'I was going to sell the meat. Perhaps even give some to my ladies.' He smiled again.

'There will be plenty of women for you when you join the army.'

'I don't need a uniform to attract them,' said Giresse. 'It's knowing how to treat them that matters. Women are like flowers, delicate and fragrant. They need to be nurtured, cared for. I have a gift for tending those delicate blooms. The young ones need a little work to bring out their radiance, the older ones require more perseverance to make them blossom. But all the effort is worth it.'

'You should have been a poet,' Deschamps said.

'When *I'm* with a woman, it *is* poetry.'

Marcognet locked the cell door and hurried along the corridor to keep up with the two soldiers who were moving along to the next cells, studying the men within and whispering amongst themselves as they studied the occupants. Marcognet didn't like the newcomers. They were too brash, too sure of themselves. They undermined his authority. They didn't treat him with the respect he deserved. Particularly the officer. Marcognet wondered if he should speak to his nephew in the Directory about this surly military man.

'This cell.' Deschamps motioned towards the door. 'Open it up.'

Marcognet hesitated, exhaling wearily.

'Forgers, thieves, heretics, horse thieves,' he muttered as if he was reciting some kind of litany. 'What kind of army are you trying to build?'

'Once these men are in uniform, I don't care about their pasts. Besides, France cannot afford to be choosy about who wears her colours. We need men. I was sent to Paris to get men. It doesn't matter what *kind* of men. General Jourdan would accept a regiment of cripples at the moment. You saw Barras's signature on my order. I'm here because the Directory wants me to be. Surely *you* are not going to interfere with Directory business?'

Deschamps held him in an unblinking gaze, then watched as he unlocked the cell.

'Moreau,' he announced. 'A religious maniac.'

The man in the cell was kneeling, facing the barred window. Deschamps realised that he was praying.

Legier took a step towards the man but the officer held up a hand to halt him.

Moreau was a large man with immense hands. Pressed together in prayer, they looked like two hamhocks joined.

'Praying for a way out?' said Marcognet with scorn.

Moreau ignored him, his head still bowed. Finally he crossed himself then rose to his full height, which Deschamps guessed to be around six foot. He regarded the intruders warily.

'What were you praying for?' Deschamps asked.

'Forgiveness,' Moreau said. 'Not for myself. For the rest of mankind.'

'Are you the only one without sin then?' Deschamps queried.

'No one is without sin. But some carry a heavier burden than others. Some need God's forgiveness more than others.'

'Such as who?'

'Men like you for one,' Moreau said reproachfully. 'Soldiers. You kill every day. You take lives which you have no right to take. Only God has the right to decide when a man's time is up.'

'Do you think God cares about France and her people?'

'God cares about everyone.'

'Then why does he let them die in wars?'

'Men make wars, not God.'

'Men do God's will.'

'Do *you* believe in Him?'

'I've been a soldier too long to think that any God would allow some of the things that I've seen,' Deschamps declared. 'And yet I've heard so many men call on Him during those years. Some of them He's ignored. Do you think He's ignored *you*?'

Moreau looked puzzled.

'Leaving you to rot in a stinking hole like this? If he heard your prayers wouldn't he get you out?'

'I don't care about myself. I follow God's will. If it is His will that I be in here then I accept that, but God didn't put the property of the Church at the disposal of the nation. The Assembly did, five years ago.'

'And you didn't agree with that?'

'Church property is God's property,' Moreau rasped. 'No man has a right to take it.'

'You should have been a cleric,' said Deschamps.

Moreau eyed the officer silently.

'Would you fight for France?' Deschamps asked.

'Would you kill her enemies? The same enemies who would destroy your countrymen?'

'"Whosoever destroyeth my flock, I shall so destroy",' Moreau declared.

Deschamps smiled.

'He's insane,' said Marcognet, slamming the cell door on Moreau.

Deschamps peered back through the grille at the big man who had once again dropped to his knees, his huge hands clasped together beneath his chin.

'Why?' the officer asked. 'Because he believes in God?' He glanced at the Governor indifferently. 'What is the official Directory instruction concerning God? Does He exist or doesn't He? Has your nephew told you?'

Marcognet didn't like the note of sarcasm in the officer's voice and glared menacingly at Deschamps, but the gesture went unnoticed by the soldier.

Deschamps and Legier were peering into another cell.

'Rostov,' said Marcognet, seeing the man. 'A Russian. He was arrested as a political undesirable. Foreigners aren't popular here, Captain. You should know that, you spend most of your days killing them.' Marcognet managed a smug smile.

'I kill the enemy,' Deschamps told him. 'The enemies of France.'

'Not all enemies wear a uniform,' Marcognet added.

They passed to the next cell and the Governor slid back the grille.

'Delacor,' he said. 'The rapist. One of the most vicious, dangerous pieces of scum in this prison.'

'Sounds like perfect material for a corporal,' said Deschamps and both he and Legier laughed.

From inside his cell, Delacor heard the sound and looked up. He saw three sets of eyes gazing in at him. He didn't move. He merely sat in the centre of the cell, twirling a piece of straw between his thumb and index finger.

Deschamps looked into those eyes. Deep-set and black as night, they glared back at him from beneath a heavy brow with bushy eyebrows, which made it difficult to see exactly where he was looking. He could almost feel the resentment burning behind them.

'If you take him, Captain,' said Marcognet, 'he'll put a sword in your back the first chance he gets.'

'We'll see,' Deschamps murmured and passed on to the next cell.

And the next.

'Bonet, the schoolmaster,' Marcognet said. 'He refused to teach his pupils what he was told to teach them. He insisted on telling them that history was important *before* those stinking Bourbons were overthrown.'

'History didn't die with Louis the Sixteenth,' Deschamps reminded him. He pointed to one of the scars on his face. '*That's* history,' he snapped. 'Did I imagine *that*?'

'The Directory—'

Deschamps cut him short. 'Is five men. Men,' he hissed. 'They make rules. They can't change history, or its teaching.'

'To hear you speak, Captain,' Marcognet said ominously, 'one would reckon you didn't think too highly of our government.'

'You talk to me of criminals, turnkey,' the dragoon said with scorn. 'These men you keep in here are saints compared to most politicians. Show me a thief or a politician and I'll take the thief every time. At least his motives are honest. He steals because he has no food or money. He steals to feed himself or his family.'

'You want thieves?' said Marcognet defiantly. 'Here's one for you.' He slid back the grille on the next cell.

The man inside looked around at the prying eyes.

'Alain Lausard,' said Marcognet. 'Thief.'

CHAPTER 2

Lausard had heard the footsteps approaching his cell, heard the hushed, almost conspiratorial voices in the corridor beyond and now he heard the hinges of the door squeal as Marcognet opened up the cell.

Lausard looked on in mild bewilderment as the two dragoons entered the small space. Their swords bumped against their highly polished boots and the few early-morning rays of sun that penetrated the barred window bounced off the brass of their helmets.

He studied the features of the officer. The scars and the wrinkles. The hole where the sergeant's right ear used to be. They were both in their fifties, Lausard guessed, but it was difficult to be specific and at that moment it didn't matter to him. What intrigued him was why they were here in his cell at the crack of dawn.

'What did you steal?' Deschamps asked. 'What was so precious that it brought you to this place?'

Lausard met the man's gaze but didn't answer.

'The Captain asked you what you stole,' Marcognet snapped, taking a step towards the prisoner. 'Answer him, you filth.'

Lausard stood his ground, his blue eyes fixed on the Governor who finally took a step back.

'I stole bread,' Lausard said, his words directed at Deschamps but his piercing gaze still pinning Marcognet like an insect to a board. 'If it is so important to you, it was from a shop close to Notre-Dame. How much more do you want to know?'

'And you'd have died for that?' Deschamps said. 'For a few crumbs you risked your life?'

'I'd have died *without* it,' Lausard told him. 'Hunger kills as surely as the guillotine. It just takes longer.' He finally turned his attention to the officer. 'What might be crumbs to you are life or death to many people on the streets of Paris.'

'How long have you been a thief?' Deschamps asked.

'Does that matter to you?' Lausard said.

'Not to me, no,' Deschamps confessed. 'I was just thinking that you can't have been a very good thief to have been caught. How did you survive out there?' The officer gestured towards the window.

'A man learns to adapt to his surroundings. I'd been stealing for two years. My luck ran out. Just like it has for many people in this city, or this country.'

'That sounds like sedition,' Marcognet snapped.

'So what if it does?' Lausard challenged. 'I'm to be executed anyway. Thief or traitor. What difference does it make? Why should I worry about speaking my mind now, of all times? There's nothing more you can do to me anyway.'

'You insolent bastard,' hissed Marcognet, taking another step towards Lausard.

This time the younger man moved forward a pace, fists clenched. 'Thief, traitor or murderer,' he growled.

'The choice is yours. The outcome is the same.'

Marcognet stepped backwards.

'Leave us,' said Deschamps, glancing at Marcognet.

'He's a madman,' Marcognet said dismissively.

'I don't think you need to worry about us,' Deschamps assured him, tapping the hilt of his sabre.

'I'm going to be there watching the day they take your head,' Marcognet said as he stepped out of the cell.

'Perhaps I should have let you kill him,' Deschamps said. 'You wanted to, didn't you?'

'Him and all his kind. Overfed, pampered, *pekinese*. He doesn't have to worry about starving. He sits on his worthless arse because of some relative in the Directory.'

'How do you know that?'

'Word gets around in places like this but I wouldn't expect you to know that.'

'I've been in worse places than this. Have you ever been on a battlefield?'

Lausard shook his head. 'At least there you're free to die as you wish,' he said. 'There's honour in dying while fighting. There's no honour in dying on the guillotine.'

'Is dying with honour important to you?' Deschamps asked.

'It used to be. When I had something worth living for. When I knew the meaning of honour. I'm not so sure I do any more.'

'I can give you that chance again. The chance to die with honour.'

'Why are you here?'

'France needs men. France is bleeding to death.'

'France cut her own wrists. Fighting on three fronts

against nations more powerful. And what do you have for an army?'

'The truth? A collection of maniacs, fanatics and conscripts commanded by incompetents for the most part. And if that sounds like treason then perhaps it is but it's also true.' Deschamps scratched at one scarred cheek. 'France has less than sixty thousand cavalry. In some places there are ten horses to every two hundred men. Why do you think we have so many dragoons? Men have to be able to fight on foot as well as horse-back because there aren't usually enough horses for them to fight on.'

'Why are you telling me this?'

'Because I know men and I know something about you already,' Deschamps offered. 'You're no thief.'

'Then why am I in here? I was caught stealing. That makes me a thief, doesn't it?'

'Some men pray,' said Deschamps. 'It doesn't make them priests.' He sucked in a weary breath. 'Prisons all over the country are being emptied. Men like myself and Sergeant Legier, men who should be on a battlefield somewhere, have been reduced to errand boys. We run the errands of the Directory and the latest errand is to collect men. Then we have to turn them into soldiers, or at least something that passes for soldiers. We have to teach men who've never held a musket in their lives how to load and fire a Charleville, how to charge with a bayonet or swing a sabre. We have to teach men who've never saddled a horse how to ride, men who've never marched how to drill.'

'Why you?' Lausard questioned.

'Because I care about France. I want to see her great again. I have no interest in politics. This government uses its commanders like toys. Twenty-four generals have already been executed by this government. I don't fight for them, I fight for France.'

'What kind of troops do you need?'

'Infantry, cavalry, artillery. What difference does it make? I need horsemen. Can you ride?'

'As well as any of your dragoons,' said Lausard.

Deschamps smiled. 'You recognise the uniform?'

'And your rank.'

'You don't belong here.'

'Why not? I'm a thief.'

'There is more to you than that,' Deschamps said. 'Tell me the truth. Who *are* you?'

'I am nothing more than what you see. No different from any other man inside this prison. A common criminal. No more. No less. Do not bestow upon me qualities I do not have.'

'Are you so lacking in qualities?'

'Lacking perhaps in virtues. Unless hatred is a virtue.'

'You're young to have so much hatred inside you,' Deschamps said. He removed his helmet, cradling the brass head-dress beneath one arm. The long horsehair mane stirred gently as he walked slowly back and forth across the cell. 'How old are you?'

'Twenty-six,' Lausard answered, 'or three, if you follow our revolutionary calendar.'

Deschamps chuckled and glanced at Legier who managed a lean grin. The sergeant's gaze had not shifted from Lausard during their time inside his cell. It was as if he was trying to remember every detail of the younger man's features and mannerisms.

'Are you a Republican?' Deschamps enquired.

'I have no allegiance to anyone,' Lausard said without much interest.

'What about your family?'

'I have no family,' said Lausard, 'not any more. They were executed. All of them. My father, my mother, my brother and sister. Enemies of the state they called them.'

'Aristocrats? Was that their crime?'

'Girondins. I have Robespierre to thank for their deaths.'

'And how did you escape?' Deschamps asked.

Lausard exhaled wearily.

'I ran,' he said, a note of disgust in his voice. 'I returned to our home that day and they had been taken, so I ran. I was a coward. Not really the type of man you want for your army, Captain. I did nothing to save them. I hid in the gutters of Paris like some snivelling rat. I stole, I lied, I cheated. Anything to stay alive.'

'Most men would have done the same. The instinct for self-preservation is one of the strongest known to mankind. You did nothing wrong.'

'I did nothing at *all*,' Lausard hissed. 'I watched my family die. You say self-preservation is the strongest instinct, I say it is guilt. It's guilt that eats away at me. It gnaws at me like a disease. It consumes me and it will until I die, until I can be with my family again.'

'In heaven?' Deschamps said, raising an eyebrow.

'I gave up believing in God years ago, Captain.'

'Something else we have in common. Some of your companions inside this prison might think differently. There are some good Catholics in here.'

'The men in here aren't my companions,' Lausard corrected. 'I have nothing in common with them. If

they knew my background most of them would probably carry me to the guillotine themselves. And yet I am
lower than they are; at least some of them still have
pride in themselves.'

'Thieves, rapists, murderers. What do they know of
pride?' Deschamps asked.

'How many of them stood by while their family was
butchered?' Lausard challenged.

'Self-pity doesn't become you. What happened is in
the past – you must learn to live with it. It wasn't your
fault. Do you think that I spend time thinking about the
men I've killed over the years.'

'They were enemies. Soldiers who would have killed
you if they'd had the chance. There's no shame in what
you did.'

'Because a man wears a different uniform it doesn't
stop him being a man. Those I killed had wives and
families.'

'They were soldiers, they knew that death always
walked close to them.'

'How close does death stand to you?'

'Not close enough,' Lausard muttered.

'Is death the only way to cleanse this guilt?'

Lausard didn't answer.

Legier took a step towards the younger man but
Deschamps raised a hand to wave him back.

'I can promise you nothing but hardship in the
army,' he said. 'And perhaps a chance to regain some
self-respect.'

'Am I supposed to be grateful for that?'

'You have no choice anyway. I came to take every
able-bodied man from this prison, whether they want
to go or not.' He slipped the brass helmet back on his

head and turned towards the door. 'By the way,' he said, 'where did you learn to ride?'

'The Carabinier School at Chinon,' Lausard said. 'I was there for seven years.'

'You missed your vocation, my friend,' Deschamps told him as the door was opened. 'Perhaps this is your chance to try again.'

Lausard watched as the door slammed shut behind the two dragoons. He heard their footsteps echoing away up the corridor.

CHAPTER 3

The crowd had been gathering for more than thirty minutes. A steady trickle at first which grew into a torrent and now, finally, into a tidal wave.

Those who could read had scanned the proclamation nailed to the walls and word had spread rapidly. Indignation had spread through the masses, growing steadily into anger and then into an inferno of rage.

The Constitution of the Year III, posted all over Paris on that chilly October morning, declared that the Directory had given itself total power.

'They're hypocrites!' someone screamed from the crowd. 'How dare they try to rule us!'

'They sit in the Tuileries now just like the Bourbons before them,' another voice added. 'We removed one set of leeches and now we have more to take their place.'

Ripples of anger spread through this sea of people at great speed.

'We don't have to take this,' another voice intoned. '*We* are the power of Paris, we are the heart of France, not these bastards who would rule us!'

The man stepped forward, ripped the proclamation from the wall and tore it in half, tossing the pieces into the air.

The action was met by a huge cheer and the man was lifted on to the shoulders of two men standing close by. 'They cannot rule us!' he shouted as heads turned to face him. 'No one can rule us!'

An enormous cheer greeted this exclamation.

The man smiled triumphantly.

His name was Auger. A small man with a bull neck and a barrel chest, barefoot like so many of his companions.

'Will you help us?' he bellowed, pointing a finger at a red-coated National Guardsman.

A number of troops had gathered to see the proclamation, their tall bearskins nodding in the light breeze, muskets clutched to their chests.

The first man hesitated then, as the roar of the crowd heightened, he seemed to become intoxicated by the tide of emotion and he nodded, pulled off his bearskin and hoisted it aloft on the point of his bayonet.

'And you?' roared Auger to one of the other soldiers.

He mimicked his companion and, within moments, the soldiers were all waving their headgear in the air like bizarre trophies.

The baying of the crowd grew louder, becoming deafening.

'Who do these bastards in the Directory think they are?' Auger shouted. 'Have they helped to overthrow the Bourbons? Do they suffer as we suffer?'

'NO!' the crowd roared back as one.

'They have made themselves kings by their own hand,' Auger shouted again. 'Can't they remember what happened to the last king?'

More cheers of agreement and appreciation.

Auger was carried through the crowd by the two men, shouting his comments, seeing many faces follow his progress, hearing so many voices echo his anger.

'We must do something,' someone else added. 'We must teach them a lesson as we taught the fat Bourbons. Let *them* feel our anger too.'

Five or six of the National Guardsmen were stalking along behind Auger now, hands slapping appreciatively at their backs, some touching their muskets briefly, feeling the wood and steel.

'*We* have the power, not the Directory!' Auger bellowed. 'Let us show them that power!'

'There are only five thousand regular troops in Paris,' one of the guardsmen shouted. 'We outnumber them four to one if we unite.'

'Unite against this new tyranny,' added another voice, now almost drowned out by the fervent rantings of the crowd. 'Fight.'

'Yes!' another bellowed. 'Fight!'

'Fight,' Auger echoed and a huge explosion of sound erupted from the crowd. 'We will throw these bastards out of power. Kick them into the Seine!'

Every comment was met by a deafening chorus of approval.

'We march on the Tuileries,' Auger roared.

The crowd screamed back its agreement.

'Nothing will stop us. Paris is ours.'

Fists were clenched and raised in salute.

'To the Tuileries!' Auger shouted once more. 'Arm yourselves!'

Napoleon Bonaparte stopped beside one of the eight-pounder cannon and slapped his hand on the bronze barrel. The twenty-six-year-old brigadier-general ran his fingers over the metal lovingly, watched by one of the twelve-man crew who stood in readiness beside the piece.

There were forty cannon arranged across the Rue St Honoré and the thoroughfares immediately adjacent. Bonaparte had demanded them brought from the artillery park at Sablons and that task had been completed by Captain Murat, who now sat astride his magnificent grey horse watching the small man wandering slowly up and down, eyes flicking back and forth. More than once he looked at his watch but, as Murat watched, there seemed to be no urgency about his movements and even as Bonaparte straightened his hat, it seemed to be with slow, deliberate movements.

Up and down the street orders were still being shouted and one of the eight-pounders was being manoeuvred using its hand-spike, the gunners sweating profusely despite the chill in the early-morning air.

Behind the guns were lines of blue-uniformed infantry, muskets sloped, bayonets bristling, sunlight winking wickedly on the points.

Bonaparte moved behind one of the guns and ducked low, checking the barrel trajectory. Like all cannon, this was controlled by a screw mechanism called a cascabel and on top of the smooth-bore barrel was a vent. It was here that one of the gunners would apply the portfire and ignite the powder inside the barrel to send the projectile hurtling towards the target.

In this case it was canister shot.

Canister shot consisted of a tin case which ruptured upon leaving the barrel, transforming the cannon into a massive shotgun as it released up to eighty one-ounce balls which had been packed tightly within. Heavy case was also used, a more lethal version which could send up to forty three-ounce metal balls to its target at a speed in excess of 450 feet per second.

Bonaparte left the gun and wandered across towards Murat who swung himself out of the saddle as his commander-in-chief approached.

'They think we won't fire on them,' Bonaparte said, his accent harsh, still carrying the strong inflection of his Corsican homeland.

'We could try reasoning with them, sir,' Murat offered.

'Barras didn't send me here to reason with them. He sent me to stop them and that's what I intend to do. This isn't a demonstration, Murat, this is a *coup d'état*. I have heard reports that there are more than twenty thousand rising against the Directory. They must be stopped.'

'I understand that, sir,' said the cavalryman. 'But—'

Bonaparte cut him short. 'You will obey my orders when I give them?'

'Of course, sir.'

Bonaparte nodded and turned away from the other man, who watched as the Corsican once more took up position behind one of the eight-pounders.

The guns were aimed at the Church of St Roch and, already, Bonaparte could see people spilling from the building on to its steps. Most of them seemed to be civilians but, amongst them, he saw the red uniforms of the National Guard, even some white-uniformed men. For a moment the Corsican wondered if they were regular army but closer inspection revealed that they were more than likely civilians dressed in stolen tunics. Muskets were brandished in the air. He saw knives, swords, pitchforks, axes and even what looked like a long spear. The noise grew more intense as more figures tumbled out of the church into the street, most of them forming an unruly mass on and around its steps.

A stone was thrown by one of the mob. It struck the cobbles some way in front of them, skidding off the road.

'Reason with them?' Bonaparte called to Murat who looked on impassively.

The sight of the guns seemed to provoke even greater anger amongst the crowd, and they began to form up in ragged lines, as yet more of them spilled from the church. The shouts of anger escalated, and weapons were brandished more openly.

Bonaparte guessed that the closest of the crowd was little more than a hundred yards away. If they decided to rush the guns it would take them less than twenty seconds but then again, he reasoned, to rush the guns would be suicidal.

Another stone came hurtling towards the waiting artillery.

Then another.

A third struck a spongeman on the temple and he fell heavily on the cobbles, blood pouring from a nasty cut just below his hairline. Two colleagues ran to his aid, one pressing a balled-up piece of cloth to the wound.

A command was bellowed and the infantry ordered arms. 'Stand ready!' an officer roared.

Murat estimated that the crowd had already swollen to nearly a thousand. Men and women of all ages were milling around now less than one hundred yards from the mouths of the cannon, shouting angrily, gesturing defiantly at the uniformed troops who barred the way to their objective.

Bonaparte had drawn up his troops to isolate the Tuileries, where he knew the crowd to be heading. All roads leading to the Palace had been closed off, guarded by cannon, troops or both.

The mob seemed unperturbed by the presence of these regular soldiers, presumably because it outnumbered them four to one, and it seemed to the Corsican as though the mob was multiplying before his eyes, ebbing back and forth like some human sea, closing the distance between themselves and the gaping mouths of the eight-pounders by the second. They were about ninety yards away now.

'Portfires, ready,' Bonaparte said quietly to an officer beside him and the order echoed around the Rue St Honoré.

Ventsmen working at the guns hurriedly inserted a 'quick match' into the vent. This piece of cotton soaked in saltpetre and spirits of wine would then be ignited, when ordered, with the portfire, a slow-burning match which comprised a tightly wound cylinder of blue paper soaked in sugar of lead and water, which would burn slowly for up to three hours.

At every gun the portfires burned, the glow like angry fireflies.

'Ready,' officers bellowed, forced to raise their voices

to maximum volume to make themselves heard above the frenzied shouts of the still growing mob.

It seemed as if the vast mass was reproducing within itself, churning out more and more people until the entire thoroughfare was choked with them.

Another hail of stones came flying over but most of the artillerymen stood still, awaiting their moment.

Bonaparte, sheltering behind the four-wheeled caisson of one gun, could almost make out the features of the leading members of the crowd now.

One was a woman, her face contorted with rage, brandishing a meat cleaver in one pudgy hand, holding her skirt up with the other as she advanced towards the guns.

'Traitors!' a voice from the crowd roared and the cry quickly spread.

The mob was advancing steadily towards the guns. It seemed to show no fear. Many of the uniformed men within had joined the front line, and one spat disdainfully in the direction of the eight-pounders.

Another stone was hurled by a youth in his teens. Barefoot and wearing just a worn shirt and threadbare trousers, he looked briefly at the faces of those around him as if for reassurance as he saw how close he was to the waiting cannon.

Next to the youth was a man in his mid-twenties who was holding a pitchfork, the gleaming points aimed at the waiting troops. He wore a bicorn hat but the cockade was missing. In its place he had stuck a feather. He too was barefoot.

Murat looked at the mob then across at Bonaparte, who was still watching calmly.

Suddenly, with less than fifty yards to advance, the

mob rushed forward. As if an order had been given, the deliberate, measured approach became a frenzied dash, the screams and howls of anger rising in volume as they hurtled towards the guns.

'Fire!' shouted Bonaparte and the order was echoed all around the street.

The cannon opened up.

A deafening roar reverberated as the eight-pounders fired, the barrels flaming, thick black clouds of smoke belching out. As they were fired, the guns shot backwards, carried by the savage recoil of so much power. They trundled back a full seven feet.

The cannon which had so far held their fire now let forth with another thunderous barrage.

Everything was momentarily drowned out by the explosions and, for precious seconds, not even the screams of those in the line of fire were audible beneath the massive detonations.

Case shot cut into the crowd, scything it down. Some were lifted off their feet by the impact of the heavy iron balls. In places, those closest to the muzzles were simply blown to pieces by the ferocity of the discharge.

And now, as the roar began to die away, Bonaparte and the others heard the moans of agony from the wounded. Still the smoke hung over the street but as it began to drift slightly, the extent of the carnage was unveiled.

Bodies carpeted the street, in places piled two and three deep, dead lying on top of wounded.

'Reload,' Bonaparte said and the command echoed around the road that had become a slaughterhouse.

Barrels were swabbed out to extinguish any smouldering powder from the previous shot, preventing premature firing. The ventsmen, their thumbs protected by a leather stall, pressed fingers to the vents to stop the current of air from causing blow-back at the sponge-men. Then the loaders pushed fresh canisters into the hot barrels, stepping back as they were rammed into place with the opposite ends of the double-headed sponges. Another quick match was inserted. The gunners waited.

The youth who had thrown the stone was lying close to one of the eight-pounders, most of his face blasted away by a lump of metal. A wounded man was crawling across him, trying to drag himself away on what was left of his arms.

A National Guardsman was trying to scream but, with most of his bottom jaw missing, he could only manage a faint gurgle as he swallowed his own blood.

Many of the crowd had fled at the first fusillade, shocked and terrified by its ferocity. Those who remained were pulling back towards the church, some dragging wounded companions with them, others running as quickly as they could in the opposite direction.

Bonaparte watched as one man stopped long enough to pull a pair of shoes from the feet of a corpse before he too disappeared from sight down one of the side streets.

'You wanted me to reason with them, Murat,' said Bonaparte, running a hand through his hair. 'These cannon spoke to them in the only language they understand.' Again he patted one of the barrels.

In front of him, the wounded continued to scream for help.

CHAPTER 4

Lausard glanced around at the ragged lines of men formed up in the main courtyard of the Conciergerie. He guessed there were about one hundred and fifty, perhaps more.

'What the hell is going on?' Rocheteau whispered, shivering slightly in the breeze.

'We're going to be soldiers, boy,' said an older man with a huge moustache, his hair almost white.

'Shut up,' bellowed Sergeant Legier. 'No talking.'

The sergeant paced up and down before the prisoners. Captain Deschamps stood with Marcognet and, on either side of them, uniformed guards held their muskets at the ready, aimed at the prisoners.

Lausard heard the sound of horses' hooves on the cobbles and turned to see a dozen dragoons entering the courtyard from outside the prison. They were tall, powerfully built men with brass head-dresses nodding as they rode, horsehair manes flowing out behind them and carbines bumping against their saddles. Their mounts were brought to a halt behind their captain who swung himself into the saddle, lifting himself into view of the watching prisoners.

'Very pretty,' murmured Delacor, regarding the green uniforms indifferently.

The man standing next to him, a huge man with an enormous belly and thinning hair, shuffled nervously from one foot to the other. 'I can't ride a horse,' he said nervously.

'I wouldn't worry about it,' Delacor told him. 'You'll probably be dead before you get the chance.'

Joubert clasped his hands together, shuffling his fingers like fleshy playing cards.

'You look like you could *eat* a horse, never mind ride it,' Delacor observed.

'At the moment,' the big man said, his stomach rumbling loudly, 'I *could*.' He rubbed his huge gut. 'I can't remember the last time I had a decent meal.'

'You think you're the only one, fat man?' Delacor snapped. 'You've got enough blubber there to exist on for another six months.'

'Shut up!' roared Legier and his voice echoed around the courtyard.

The prisoners' attention was drawn towards the line of dragoons facing them, as the officer on the bay addressed them. 'You are men of France,' he called. 'You are her sons. You are no longer prisoners of the State. From now on you belong to the army. You will do as you are ordered. What you did before is not important. *Who* you were before is not important. You have been given another chance. A chance to regain some honour. A chance to give your lives for France.'

'That's very kind of him,' whispered Rocheteau under his breath.

Lausard never took his eyes from the dragoon captain.

'I can promise you nothing but hunger, hardship and pain,' Deschamps continued. 'But you will be free men again. Look upon that as a gift and look upon your chance to fight for France as a duty. One which you should cherish.'

Lausard lowered his gaze and swallowed hard.

Deschamps nodded to Legier, who spurred his mount forward, the animal trotting towards the main gate of the prison. The other dragoons formed up in lines of six on each side of the prisoners.

'Forward!' shouted Legier and the whole group moved forward, some of the men attempting to march, others walking as briskly as they could, some merely shuffling along.

Deschamps watched the entire ill-disciplined unit moving towards the gate and patted his horse's neck.

'Good luck, Captain,' said Marcognet, smiling.

'Be thankful I didn't take you too,' the officer snapped and rode towards the head of the group to join Legier.

Beyond the gates the prisoners saw not only more dragoons but infantry too, all crammed into the street with such density it looked impossible for them to move. There were civilians too, standing on the road-side watching the activity. A woman lifted her small child up towards one of the waiting dragoons, watching as the trooper gently stroked the child's face with a gloved hand.

'Where do you think they're taking us?' Rocheteau asked, glancing at the emotionless faces of the infantry flanking them. He almost stumbled trying to avoid stepping in a crater.

Roussard wasn't quite so lucky and he cursed as he slipped.

A hand shot out to steady him.

'Thank you,' Roussard said to the man walking next to him, who nodded and smiled, patting him on the back.

Roussard looked at his companion and noticed that the man was totally bald, but his shiny pate wasn't a legacy of old age; his face, red-cheeked and round, was that of a young man, perhaps in his early thirties. He had the bluest eyes Roussard had ever seen but they were virtually hidden by heavy eyelids and an almost protuberant forehead. The man's head had been shaved so closely that not even a hint of stubble remained. It looked as smooth as a cannon ball.

'What is your name?' Roussard asked him.

'Carbonne,' the man told him, wiping one large hand over his bald dome.

Roussard was about to say something when he felt a hand grab at the back of his neck.

'Shut up, scum,' the infantry corporal bellowed in his ear, almost throwing him to the ground. He glared at Carbonne. 'You too.'

The men marched on in silence.

The popping of musket fire seemed to drift on the breeze.

It was hard to tell from how far away it came. A mile, perhaps more.

The thunder of cannon sounded much closer.

Lausard and Rocheteau glanced at each other but neither spoke.

'Keep moving,' one of the NCOs roared and the sound of hundreds of marching feet mingled with that of horses' hooves, the jingling of harnesses and the occasional snorts of the dragoons' mounts.

Once more they heard the distant crackle of sporadic musket fire.

A moment or two of silence then the roar of cannon again.

'Perhaps the Austrians are in Paris already,' Rocheteau said quietly.

Lausard glanced over his shoulder, back at the rows of colourless faces.

Somewhere in the distance he saw smoke rising. A single black plume of it pushing its way up amongst the clouds. Very soon it was joined by another.

No one knew how far they had walked. No one knew exactly how far outside Paris they were. All they knew was that they were cold, hungry and exhausted.

The journey from the prison, which had begun in bright morning sunlight, was ending in the blood-red wash of sunset. The sun itself was a massive burnished orb slipping slowly below the horizon, its dying light turning the sky the colour of bloodstained bronze. Birds returning to their nests were black arrowheads against the crimson backdrop.

The prisoners had been ordered to halt at the foot of a low ridge which was densely wooded. A stream wound through it and the dragoons were watering their horses at the point where it left the confines of the trees. A farmhouse, about a mile to the north, was just visible in the fading light. A thin column of smoke rose from its chimney, like the plumes Lausard had seen earlier in the day as they had left Paris.

The outskirts of the capital were behind them. For

the last two miles they'd trekked along a road barely wide enough to accommodate themselves and the accompanying troops.

The infantry stood or sat cleaning their muskets, using rags taken from their packs. Several dragoons polished their saddles and harnesses.

Lausard noticed Deschamps walking across the uneven ground, clutching a pipe in one hand, puffing slowly on it, with two other officers accompanying him.

A farrier was busy removing a stone from the shoe of a horse, working away expertly while its rider stood by watching and chatting to a companion. One of them had his green cloak slung around his shoulders to ward off the cold wind which the night was bringing. From the nearby woods, birdsong signalled the end of the day and branches rustled gently in the growing breeze.

A group of infantrymen returned from the wood carrying branches. Lausard watched as they used gunpowder from a cartridge to start a fire, feeding pieces of twig in as the blaze became brighter, flames licking hungrily towards the darkening sky.

'It's all right for those bastards,' snapped Delacor. 'What about us? We'll freeze to death.'

'And starve,' Joubert added, rubbing his huge belly.

'Not you, fat man,' Delacor said irritably. 'Perhaps the rest of us should be careful you don't eat *us*.'

A chorus of guffaws greeted the remark from those closest.

'Leave him alone,' said Giresse. 'He's not the only one who's hungry.'

Delacor shot him an angry glance.

'I'd love to be in my father's baker's shop now,'

another man chipped in. 'I can almost smell the freshly baked bread.'

'Stop this torture,' Giresse said, chuckling. 'Who are you anyway?'

'My name is Charvet.' He extended a hand, which Giresse shook firmly.

'What did they lock *you* up for?' Joubert asked.

'Illegal gambling,' Charvet said. 'I was a boxer. A friend of mine used to organise the fights in an abandoned church.'

'Were you any good?' Giresse enquired.

'I never lost a fight,' Charvet told him, raising his fists as if to throw a punch.

'God will punish you,' Moreau said, with an air of finality. 'Fighting in a church. Defiling God's house with violence. You're a disgrace.'

'A friend of the Almighty, that's all we need,' said Rocheteau. 'If you're on intimate terms, couldn't you ask him for a fire and some food?'

'Blasphemy won't help you,' Moreau said.

Some of the other men chuckled.

'I'll tell you what's blasphemy,' Joubert interjected. 'Us not being given any food, that's what.'

'There is such a thing as sustenance for the soul,' Moreau said.

'To hell with that,' Joubert snapped. 'I need sustenance for my stomach.'

There was more laughter.

Rocheteau grunted, his laughter cut short as he felt a boot driven into his back.

He spun round to see a dragoon standing over him, a large moustache bristling beneath his hooked nose. He smoothed a hand over his sergeant's stripes and looked disdainfully at the group of prisoners.

'You, you and you,' he said, jabbing fingers towards Rocheteau, Lausard and Carbonne. 'Get some wood from there.' He hooked a thumb in the direction of the trees. 'Build a fire. I don't want you bastards dying on me in the night. Go.'

The three men got to their feet and trudged towards the woods, the sergeant close behind them.

'My name is Delpierre,' he said. 'Remember that.'

'How could we forget?' hissed Rocheteau under his breath.

He heard the hiss of the sabre being drawn from its scabbard, then he felt the point pressed against the back of his neck, hard enough to draw blood.

'You keep your mouth shut, convict,' Delpierre snapped. 'You don't speak unless I tell you to. If I hear you open your mouth again without permission, I'll gut you like a chicken. Understand?'

'Yes,' said Rocheteau through clenched teeth.

'Yes, *Sergeant*,' the dragoon corrected him.

'Yes, *Sergeant*,' Rocheteau echoed, waiting for the sword to be lowered. Still he felt the cold steel against the nape of his neck and Lausard turned his gaze towards Delpierre. The sergeant's face was deeply pitted, a legacy of smallpox. His eyes were deep-set, almost pig-like.

'What are you looking at?' he snapped at Lausard, finally withdrawing the sabre, running it back into its sheath. 'Pick up some wood and get a move on.'

Lausard and the others started to pick up some fallen branches from the floor of the wood. Carbonne heaved several large lumps of timber up on to his broad shoulders, his muscles bulging beneath the weight.

Rocheteau picked up some more of the drier lumber and held it before him.

'Come on,' snapped Delpierre. 'Hurry, we haven't got all night. You've got a long march ahead of you tomorrow.' He smiled crookedly. 'By the time I've finished with you, you bastards will wish you were still in that prison.'

The men headed back towards their waiting companions, picking their way through the undergrowth with care now. Darkness had descended but for a tiny remnant of blood-red sky, a crimson slash across the black curtain of the night.

Lausard moved sure-footedly through the wood, clutching his bundle of kindling.

Not so Rocheteau. He stumbled over a fallen branch and went headlong, scattering the collected timber before him.

'Pick it up, you scum,' hissed Delpierre taking a stride towards him.

He drove one boot into Rocheteau's side and the thief rolled over, ready to spring up at his tormentor, but Lausard shot out a hand and gripped his shirt.

'Leave it,' he whispered under his breath.

Delpierre looked at Lausard, then at Rocheteau. The thief was still crouched down as if ready to spring.

'Whenever you like, scum,' said Delpierre, grinning.

Lausard kept a firm grip on his companion's shirt.

'What's your name?' Delpierre asked, kicking a piece of wood towards Rocheteau.

'My name is Rocheteau.'

'And you?' He nodded in Lausard's direction.

'Lausard.'

'I'll remember that,' the dragoon said. 'We're going to get to know each other very well during the next few weeks. Now move it.'

He walked away, leaving Rocheteau to gather up the dropped wood.

'I'm going to kill him,' the thief hissed. 'I swear to God I'm going to kill that bastard.'

'Not yet,' Lausard said quietly. 'The time will come.'

'Where do you think they're taking us?'

Lausard gazed into the flames of the fire, watching the yellow tongues leaping and dancing, encouraged by the breeze.

He heard the words and lifted his gaze to see Charvet looking expectantly at the other men huddled by the meagre source of heat. It had been he who had asked the question.

All over the slope men were gathered in groups around camp fires. Prisoners and troops alike. Some were sleeping, others talking in hushed tones. Some of the troops chewed on biscuits, others drank from bottles of wine which they'd taken from their packs.

Two dragoons passed by at a walk, the harnesses of their mounts jingling in the still night air. Several infantrymen stood sentinel near to the woods, muskets sloped, their faces turned towards the prisoners. One or two tents had been set up towards the foot of the slope – for officers, Lausard presumed.

'I said, where do you think—' Charvet began.

'We heard what you said,' Delacor snapped. 'How the hell do we know where they're taking us? It's outside that stinking prison, that's all I care about.'

'How many do you think they took?' Carbonne

wondered, looking around at the smattering of camp fires and huddles of men.

'A hundred and fifty or more,' Rocheteau mused. 'Who knows?'

'Why us?' Charvet persisted.

'They're desperate for men,' Lausard said. 'Conscription didn't work. They're frightened of being overrun.'

'They're not the only ones,' Roussard added.

'The army's in a mess, the country's in a mess,' Lausard offered. 'It must be if they want men like us to help them.'

'I'm proud to fight for my country,' said a huge man seated opposite Lausard. He was well over six feet tall, powerfully built, but when he spoke his words were faltering, as if he had trouble pronouncing them.

'It was your country that locked you up, you half-wit,' Delacor snapped.

'Why were you in prison?' Lausard asked.

'They said I stole food,' the big man replied. 'But I was hungry.'

'You and half of Paris,' Giresse added.

'What's your name?'

'Tabor,' the big man replied.

'He's an idiot,' Delacor said dismissively.

'Perhaps he thinks the same about you,' Lausard chided.

The other men laughed but Delacor sat forward, leaning towards Lausard.

'You'd best be careful how you talk to me,' the rapist hissed.

'If you're trying to frighten me, don't waste your breath,' Lausard dismissed him.

'I won't frighten you, I'll kill you,' Delacor threatened.

'You're welcome to try,' Lausard said softly.

The two men locked stares for a moment longer, the firelight flickering in their glaring eyes, then Delacor sat back.

A long silence followed, finally broken by Charvet. 'So where do you think they're taking us?' he tried again.

'There's a training depot at St Germain,' Lausard said. 'It's my guess they're taking us there.'

'What makes you such an expert?' Delacor demanded.

'Trust me,' Lausard said.

'I don't trust anybody.'

'We're better off out of Paris after what happened this morning,' Carbonne suggested. 'I overheard a couple of the dragoons talking earlier. They said the mob had tried to attack the Tuileries. The army fired on them. They said over two hundred had been killed, twice that wounded.'

'Murdering bastards,' Delacor sneered.

'What choice did they have?' Lausard offered. 'If they were being attacked they had to retaliate.'

'The army will end up ruling this country,' Giresse opined.

'Then it's just as well we're going to be a part of it, isn't it?' Rocheteau said, chuckling, and the other men joined him.

Delacor merely glared at the thief.

'There'll be a price to pay,' Moreau interjected. 'God will punish us all for this.'

'I don't think God has got anything to do with what's going on at the moment,' said Lausard.

'He has abandoned us,' Moreau said wearily. 'And who can blame Him?'

'I never asked for His help in the first place,' Delacor rasped.

'You'll call on Him at some time, every man does,' Moreau persisted.

'Does He listen?' Lausard asked. 'Does He *ever* listen.'

'He hears everything.'

'Do you think He'd hear me if I asked Him for some food?' Joubert enquired.

The other men laughed, moving closer to the fire as the leaping flames gradually became flickering whisps. Rocheteau fed more wood to the pyre, waiting for the heat to spring up once again.

'You'd be surprised how long the human body can go without food,' Bonet said. 'I know, I was a schoolmaster before they arrested me.'

'Why would they want to arrest a schoolmaster?' Rocheteau asked.

'The Directory didn't want any history taught that involved the Bourbons,' Bonet said. 'I thought my pupils had a right to know what went on before Louis the Sixteenth died. History is important. It teaches us about ourselves.'

'Very interesting,' Delacor yawned, then he looked over at Carbonne. 'What's your story?'

The bald man swallowed hard. 'I was an executioner. I worked with Sanson for two years. Then, one morning, they brought a man to the guillotine. I was going to pull the lever until I realised it was my brother. I couldn't do it. I was arrested on the spot. My brother still died though.' He lowered his voice.

'You should have died with him, you bloody butcher,' said Delacor.

Carbonne shrugged.

'None of us knows *your* crime,' Lausard said, turning to face Delacor. 'Why so shy? Share it with us.'

'Go to hell!'

'In time,' Lausard countered. 'What was your crime?'

'I committed no crime,' Delacor said, feeling the eyes of the other men upon him. 'The woman was as much to blame, she encouraged me, the bitch. She—'

Lausard cut him short. 'A rapist.'

Delacor's eyes narrowed as he looked at the younger man with an expression of fury

Rocheteau hawked and spat in Delacor's direction.

Moreau crossed himself.

Roussard shook his head slowly.

Giresse held a hand before his face as if he had just smelled something rank.

'What gives any of *you* the right to judge *me*?' Delacor challenged angrily. 'We're all criminals. You're no better than me.'

All eyes were upon him but no one spoke.

The hillside was becoming darker as the fires burned out. More wood was fed into them but they remained little more than small patches of glowing embers. More and more men settled down on the cold ground to try to sleep as best they could. The whinnying of tethered horses could be heard every now and then through the stillness, along with the occasional barked commands of an NCO.

Lausard lay back, hands clasped behind his head, his gaze directed towards the stars dotting the firmament. It looked as if someone had fired crystal grapeshot at a black velvet blanket. Around him he could hear some of the men snoring but sleep continued to elude him.

When he inhaled, a peculiar cocktail of smells filled his nostrils. The acrid smell of burning wood, sweat from so many unwashed bodies, horse droppings, gun oil, smoke and the scent of grass.

When he sat up he could smell fresh air. It was the smell of freedom. Preferable to the rancid stench of his prison cell. And again Lausard felt a kind of crushing weight on his shoulders. It was as if he had been spared a second time. First he had escaped the clutches of the Jacobins and cheated the guillotine and now the army had saved him from that killing machine. Unlike his family. For fleeting seconds the images of their faces flashed into his mind and he blinked hard to drive the vision away.

He looked across at Moreau, who was sleeping with his face turned towards the fire. No doubt he would have said that God had saved Lausard, but the younger man did not believe in the existence of such a divine entity, let alone in His intervention.

Slowly he regarded the other men around him, men who had been strangers to him hours earlier. Now he knew their names and how they had come to be incarcerated. These men with whom he would share the remainder of his days. Thieves, gamblers, rapists, forgers. All kinds of criminal. And among them were a schoolmaster, an executioner, a near idiot and a Russian. If God did exist, Lausard mused, then He certainly had a sense of humour. These were the men who were going to help defend France. Men as worthless as Lausard himself.

He lay down again and tried to sleep, but again images of his family filled his mind. This time, however, he didn't chase them away; he allowed them to fill his head, allowed himself to feel the pain they brought.

It was a long time before he slept.

CHAPTER 5

As Lausard sat on the frozen hillside he was aware of two things: the cold which dug its invisible nails into him, raising the hairs on his arms, and a growing discord of shouts and curses.

The sun was struggling into a watery sky, spreading a dull dawn across the land. A single plume of smoke rose mournfully from the embers of the fire that the men had huddled around so gratefully the night before.

Rocheteau rolled over and pushed his hands close to the pile of blackened wood, hoping to draw some last vestiges of warmth from it.

Joubert rubbed his huge stomach which rumbled protestingly.

Giresse stretched and yawned.

Moreau crossed himself.

Lausard heard the sounds of a bugle close by. The dragoon trumpeter was blowing the insistent notes designed to wake the sleeping men.

The infantry had already formed up into line; three dragoons rode past, one of their horses shaking its head wildly, its rider forced to tug hard on the reins to keep the animal under control.

The tents at the bottom of the slope were still in place and, from his vantage point, Lausard could just make out the figure of Deschamps puffing on a pipe, still dressed in a shirt and breeches, a forage cap perched jauntily on his head. He was talking to three other men, gesturing up the slope towards the troops and prisoners.

Lausard was still watching the officer when he felt the shove in the back that almost caused him to over-balance.

'Come on, you bastards,' shouted Delpierre, holding Lausard's gaze as the younger man glared at him momentarily. 'On your feet, there's something I want you to see.'

He swung a boot at Delacor who was still struggling to his feet.

The other men scrambled upright, some rubbing their hands together in a futile attempt to generate some warmth in bodies chilled by a heavy frost.

Other NCOs, cavalry and infantry were moving amongst the prisoners, rousing them with similarly brutal methods. Sergeant Legier prodded men with the point of his sabre while an infantry corporal kicked others to force them to their feet.

The troops looked on impassively. Dragoons, already mounted, sat astride their mounts forming a green-coated barrier across the entrance to the woods. The early-morning sunlight twinkled on the brass casques of their helmets.

As Lausard watched, several of them moved their horses to one side and, from the resultant gap,

Delpierre appeared, pushing three men before him.

When one stumbled and fell, the sergeant drove a boot into his side then dragged him to his feet.

'What's going on?' murmured Charvet, watching the tableau before them.

No one answered. Lausard in particular was more concerned by the sight of twelve infantrymen moving into the centre of a clearing, muskets sloped. They formed into two lines, one kneeling ahead of the other, and he watched as they loaded their weapons. The manoeuvre was carried out with drill-book precision. First, each man took a cartridge from his tin-lined cartouche and bit the end off the greased paper tube. Holding the ball in his mouth he drew the hammer back one notch, opened the priming pan and poured a small amount of powder into it. The remaining powder he then poured down the barrel. The infantrymen spat the balls down the barrels, ramming the cartridge paper after it to form a wad, to hold the lead ball in place. The ramrods were replaced in their channels beneath the barrels and the Charlevilles were lifted, with mechanical precision, to blue-coated shoulders.

Delpierre strode in front of the twelve men, dragging one of the prisoners with him. The other two were pushed into position alongside him by a dragoon officer who barely looked old enough to shave.

'These men tried to escape last night,' Delpierre shouted, glancing around at the other watching prisoners. 'They are cowards. They were given the chance to fight for their country and they chose to run instead.'

Rocheteau looked anxiously at Lausard but he was staring intently at the stricken figures before him, at the twelve muskets pointing in their direction.

One of the three fugitives had dropped to his knees. Delpierre grabbed him by the collar and hauled him to his feet.

'This is *not* the kind of man that France wants,' Delpierre continued. 'When you were in prison you belonged to the State, now you belong to *us*. If you break *our* rules you pay *our* price. These men are deserters. The price *they* must pay is death.'

The man Delpierre was holding suddenly pulled away, pushing the restraining arm aside, and stood defiantly before the levelled muskets.

Delpierre met his gaze for a moment then walked away, nodding in the direction of the infantry sergeant who was standing beside the firing squad.

'Ready,' the man shouted and twelve hammers were drawn back.

Lausard gritted his teeth, the knot of muscles at the side of his jaw pulsing angrily.

Delpierre looked across and the two men locked stares. Lausard was sure he could see a faint smile flickering on the sergeant's lips.

'Fire!' roared the infantry sergeant.

The stillness of the morning was filled with the deafening retort of twelve muskets; a cloud of black smoke belched from the barrels, drifting across the slope. When the sulphurous fog cleared, two of the three men lay on the frosty ground.

Lausard could see several crimson smudges on the shirt of one. The second man was still twitching slightly. Two musket balls had hit him in the stomach, a third had shattered his left arm at the elbow.

The third man remained on his feet, untouched by the fusillade. He stood motionless, his eyes bulging wide, his body quivering slightly, gaze fixed on the firing squad which was in the process of reloading.

'Wait!' ordered Delpierre, striding towards the man.

The sergeant first inspected the bodies of the other two prisoners, prodding each with the toe of one boot. The second man groaned softly, his eyes flickering. He looked up imploringly at the dragoon, blood spilling over his lips, his one good hand now clutching at the ragged wounds in his belly, as if to hold the blood in.

Delpierre drew his sabre, pressed it against the man's throat then drove it forward, puncturing the ground beneath as he skewered the dying man's neck. He quickly pulled the sabre free and wiped the stained blade on the shirt of the prisoner, then turned to face the last of the trio.

Even from such close range, the Charleville musket was notoriously inaccurate and Delpierre wasn't entirely surprised to see that one of the men was unscathed.

'You have either God or the Devil on your side,' he said, grabbing the man by the collar. 'You might be useful.' He shoved the terrified prisoner towards Lausard and his watching companions. The man fell at Lausard's feet, gratefully accepting the helping hand he was offered. His skin was milk-white, his body quivering madly and Lausard could smell the stench of urine as he stood close to him. There was a dark stain on the front of his trousers.

'That is how any attempt to escape will be dealt with,' Delpierre said, motioning towards the two bodies.

Moreau crossed himself.

'You belong to the army now,' Delpierre continued.

'These men were given another chance and they threw it away. The rest of you look closely at them. If any of you were thinking of trying to escape, then forget about it.'

'Why did you run?' Lausard whispered to the surviving prisoner.

'Why do you think?' the man hissed. 'We're all going to die in battle anyway, if we get that far.'

'What's your name?' Lausard asked him.

'Sonnier,' he said, wiping perspiration from his face.

Delpierre was still stalking back and forth in front of the two dead bodies, his narrowed eyes scanning the rows of blank faces before him.

'If any man disobeys he will be flogged,' he shouted. 'If any man tries to run he will be executed. Keep this in your minds.' He turned and looked down at the two corpses. 'They'll be left to rot where they are. Food for scavengers. It's all they're fit for.' He wandered back up the slope to where his horse was waiting. Lausard watched as he swung himself into the saddle.

'It serves them right,' muttered Delacor. 'They shouldn't have run.'

'Do you blame them?' snapped Roussard.

'I blame them for getting caught,' Delacor said disdainfully.

'How the hell can they be deserters when they're not in uniform yet?' Rocheteau argued.

'You heard what he said,' Lausard murmured, nodding towards Delpierre who rode past close to them. 'We belong to the army now.'

'They own us,' Joubert added.

'Nobody owns *me*,' Rocheteau hissed. 'I carry no one's brand.'

'You might be carrying the mark of the lash if you don't do as they tell you,' Joubert offered.

Rocheteau spat indignantly.

'They want us to be soldiers,' said Lausard. 'Let's play their game.'

'This is no game,' Sonnier groaned. 'We'll all be killed.'

'It'll be God's will,' Moreau said.

'God has nothing to do with this,' Lausard snapped. 'And if He's got any sense, He'll keep his nose out of it. If there ever *was* a God He gave up caring a long time ago. We're on our own now. We can live or we can die.' He glanced behind him at the two corpses lying motionless on the slope.

In the sky above, several crows were already circling.

CHAPTER 6

Paul Barras ran his finger around the rim of the glass with a slight smile creasing his face. In his fortieth year, Barras, like his two companions in the room, enjoyed an almost unrivalled power in the turmoil that was revolutionary France. A member of the newly self-appointed Directory, he had amassed considerable personal wealth and used it on the one real vice he had. Women. The power was wonderful, the wealth glorious, but the unbridled affections of so many women seemed like a drug to Barras; the latest in a growing retinue had made him the talk and the envy both of his colleagues in the Directory and of those who moved in high circles. It was her face which Barras pictured in his mind now as he sat at the large table in one of the smaller state rooms of the Tuileries. Joséphine de Beauharnais. The name seemed musical to him as he thought of it, thought of her. The stunning Creole had spent her earliest years in the French West Indies before marrying Vicomte Alexandre de Beauharnais fourteen years ago. He had gone to the guillotine the previous year.

Barras and she had become lovers within a month of the execution. He sipped at his wine, wiping his mouth with the back of his hand, wiping the wistful smile away too. He got to his feet and crossed to one of the huge windows looking out over the rear gardens of the palace. There were several soldiers in sight, dressed in their familiar blue jackets and white *culottes*.

'Don't you find this all a little ironic?' said Barras, still gazing out over the gardens.

The other two men in the room looked at him in bewilderment.

'We run the country from the home of the man we helped to destroy,' Barras continued. 'Once this building belonged to the Bourbons, now it belongs to us.'

'The *country* used to belong to the Bourbons,' said Tallien. 'Now *that* belongs to us too.'

'Such power,' Barras mused, returning to the table.

'*We* didn't destroy the monarchy,' Gohier offered. 'The people did.'

'We *are* the people,' Barras reminded him. 'I for one would be proud to think that I'd been responsible in some way for removing that tyrant.' He swallowed what was left in his glass then refilled it from the container on the table.

'If we are the people, then why did the people try to destroy us?' Tallien asked. 'If they'd reached us they would have killed us. If that *coup* had been successful we'd all have been sneezing into the basket just like the King and his family did.'

'It wasn't a popular rising,' Barras said dismissively.

'It was twenty thousand people, Barras,' Tallien protested. 'How popular does it have to be for you to recognise that we are not liked?'

'Men in power never are, but decisions have to be made and we are the men who make those decisions for the betterment of France *and* her people.'

'The same people who tried to destroy us?' Tallien murmured sardonically.

'The Paris mob is no longer a force,' Barras said. 'What happened the other day has broken them.'

'You sound very sure of that,' Gohier said.

'Over two hundred of them were killed, more than twice that number wounded,' Barras said, a note of pride in his voice. 'They realise now that we are not afraid to use the army against them if necessary.'

'Did you instruct Bonaparte to fire on them?' Gohier asked.

'I ordered him to do his duty,' Barras said. 'I ordered him to protect us.' He jabbed a finger at his companions. 'He's a soldier. He acted as he saw fit.'

'Why did you choose Bonaparte?' Tallien enquired.

'He's a very able man,' Barras replied. 'He proved that at Toulon two years ago. I doubt that siege would ever have been broken without him. You should be grateful to him, Tallien.'

'I *am* grateful but I'm not sure I trust him. After all, he isn't French, is he?'

'He's Corsican,' Barras said and laughed. 'Has his loyalty ever been in doubt?'

'He was a friend of Robespierre, he was arrested,' Gohier offered.

'He was held for two weeks and he wasn't a *friend* of Robespierre's, he was under the patronage of that dictator's brother.' Barras began walking around the table. 'He's a very gifted man, a very intelligent soldier.'

'Does such a thing exist?' snorted Tallien.

'Whoever controls the army, controls the city,' Gohier said. 'If Bonaparte is as intelligent as you say, don't you think that might have occurred to him?'

'His loyalty is not in question,' Barras insisted. 'How many times do I have to say it? It is only because of him that we are here now. I cannot understand your concern. If anything does happen then we simply remove him.'

'It might not be that easy,' Gohier protested. 'If he has the army in his control—'

Barras interjected. 'So if *we* control Bonaparte then we also control the army. There isn't a more able man available.'

'Dugommier. Massena,' Gohier suggested. 'They're both very able men.'

'Bonaparte may be too young,' Tallien said.

'Is his youth cause to doubt his abilities?' Barras queried. 'Massena is the same age and yet you would not hesitate to suggest him. Serurier is a very competent soldier but I feel he is too old.'

'What of Cafferelli?' Tallien said.

'He is an engineer,' Barras countered. 'Commanding troops in the field is not his forte. Why are you all so resistant to Bonaparte? Perhaps we should be discussing how best to thank him for saving our lives and our positions instead of questioning his skills as a soldier.'

There was a long silence, finally broken by Tallien.

'You're right, Barras,' he said, sighing. 'Bonaparte should be rewarded in some way. What had you in mind?'

Barras smiled.

CHAPTER 7

Lausard couldn't be sure how many men were drawn up in the three ragged lines that stretched across the compound. He guessed around a hundred and fifty, perhaps more. He glanced furtively back and forth, his steely gaze moving from man to man.

The compound itself was surrounded by a low stone wall and tall trees. Behind the men was a number of buildings. Stables, an armoury, a commissary, an infirmary and what he could only assume were barracks. There were several water-troughs on the main parade ground and also three eight-pounder cannon, barrels pointed towards the men but unmanned. A tricolour flew proudly from the pole near the barracks, fluttering in the breeze.

The floor of the compound was partly cobbled, partly dark earth, the latter marked by the passage of many hooves and also liberal amounts of droppings. The odour mingled with the pungent smell of perspiration and unwashed bodies, one of which belonged to Lausard himself. He saw one of the men in the line ahead of him scratching a flea bite at the back of his neck. Lausard began scratching his own armpit.

As they'd entered the training camp he'd seen Captain Deschamps and two other officers ride off and now the highest-ranking men left on the parade ground were NCOs, Delpierre and Legier among them. Both of the dragoons were still mounted, Delpierre walking his horse slowly up and down the waiting lines of men.

The infantry had dispersed too. The green-jacketed dragoons were the only sentinels who kept a watch on the prisoners now. They sat, statue-like on immobile horses, watching the unwashed horde and waiting for orders. One was gently patting the neck of his mount. Two held their carbines across their chests. The weapons were identical to the Charleville muskets carried by the infantry, apart from the fact that they were thirty-seven inches long instead of the usual fifty. Like the .70 calibre infantry weapon they could also be fitted with a fifteen-inch bayonet for hand-to-hand fighting.

There were three water pumps within sight and Lausard could see several men in stable dress filling buckets with water, lining them up as neatly as chesspieces. The men were talking quietly amongst themselves, the odd laugh punctuating the conversation.

'Take a good look around you,' Delpierre shouted, his voice reverberating around the compound. 'This will be your home for the next few weeks. You may grow to love it, you may grow to hate it. That isn't important. What you *will* do is learn. You will obey when you are given an order, you will carry out that order to the letter.' The sergeant guided his horse back and forth, only now he was joined by Legier too, the men riding up and down in opposite directions, passing each other every so often.

'You will train here,' Legier shouted. 'You will become soldiers here. It is our duty to turn you into soldiers. What you were before is not important. Your life before is not important. When you pull on the uniforms you are given you will become men again. Until then you are nothing. You are clay to be moulded.'

'Moulded by *us*,' Delpierre added. 'You smell, you must be cleaned up.' He glanced across at the men working the water pumps. They were still lining up buckets of water. Delpierre rose in his stirrups and looked at the lines of prisoners. 'Strip off,' he bellowed. 'Take off those filthy tatters.'

The men hesitated.

'Now!' Delpierre roared.

Lausard pulled his shirt open, began tugging it off.

Rocheteau did likewise.

Men all along the lines began disrobing, shivering in the chill breeze.

Charvet tugged off his filthy shirt and tossed it aside, almost hitting Carbonne with it. The bald man frowned, pulling off his own dirty trousers, standing naked like so many of the other men in front and behind him. Within a matter of minutes, every prisoner stood naked, shivering in the breeze. A number in the front line clasped their hands across their groins.

'Forget your modesty,' Delpierre said mockingly.

Almost involuntarily, Moreau glanced down at Giresse who was standing beside him with his arms folded, proudly displaying his manhood.

'There are women who would kill for what you now see,' Giresse bragged.

Moreau looked away in disgust.

'I want all those uniforms gathered up now,' Delpierre shouted. 'You, you and you.' He pointed towards three men in the front rank. 'Pile them up.'

The men scuttled around, gathering the filthy rags, hurling them into one large untidy pile.

'You two, help them,' the sergeant said to some more of those waiting patiently in the cold.

The mound of discarded clothes began to grow until it was as tall as a man.

Lausard looked first at the clothes, then at the sergeant who was smiling to himself.

'In groups of five,' he roared. 'Over to the water pumps. Get cleaned up. Move it.'

The first group of men did as they were ordered and were met by a stinging deluge of freezing water, hurled by the five dragoons in fatigues.

Five more followed them. And so it went on.

Joubert spat out some water, shaking uncontrollably from the chill.

Rocheteau ran a hand through his hair, brushing the sodden strands from his face.

Lausard wiped his hands across his cheeks and chest, glad to be cleansed of the filth which clung to him like a second skin but not so happy about the way it was being removed. The cold was almost unbearable.

'What the hell are they doing with our clothes?' Delacor said, grabbing Lausard by the arm.

The prisoners looked on as two dragoons poured pitch over the cloth, ladling it from a large barrel close by. At a signal from Delpierre, the entire bundle was ignited using a small tinderbox. The flame danced and flickered in the breeze then seemed to gain strength.

There was a loud *whump* as the pitch went up, the fire spreading quickly, devouring the soaked clothes. Flames began to spring further up the mound and soon a pall of thick smoke was rising into the air.

Delacor stood watching incredulously until a bucket full of cold water struck him, shocking him back to reality. He glared at the man who'd thrown it but the dragoon merely smiled back.

On the other side of the compound several tables were set up and Lausard could see men standing behind them, stacks of clothing laid out before them. As they were directed towards these tables he saw that the clothes were predominantly blue and white. The familiar blue jackets of the infantry, but many of the tunics were white. Each man was given one bundle of clothes containing a jacket, a pair of trousers, wooden shoes and a belt.

'Put those on,' shouted Delpierre. 'You'll be given the uniforms of cavalry when you're fit to wear them.'

Lausard pulled on the blue jacket, noticing that there was a large hole in one shoulder, the edges singed.

'You'd better hope you're luckier than the man who wore it before you,' said Delpierre, looking down at him.

'I can't get this on,' grumbled Joubert, trying vainly to make the two sides of a white tunic meet across his massive belly.

Roussard was having the opposite problem. The sleeves of his jacket were about six inches too long. His trousers too were like concertinas around his ankles.

'This is a Prussian jacket,' said Bonet, slipping his navy-blue tunic on.

'Who cares where it came from?' Lausard said, fastening his brass buttons.

Tabor fastened the belt around his waist, hoisting his trousers further up, his huge hands fumbling with the material.

'Cavalry,' said Rostov dismissively. 'I've never ridden a horse in my life. How are they supposed to turn us into cavalry?'

Lausard didn't answer, he was gazing around at the other men, all now dressed or dressing in the cast-off infantry uniforms.

'Keep them clean,' Delpierre ordered. 'Others who follow you will have to make use of them.'

Rocheteau sniffed at the armpit of his jacket.

'Whoever had this one didn't bother,' he grunted. 'Why should I?'

'Where did they get them?' Joubert asked.

'The dead,' Lausard said flatly. 'Ours and the allies.'

'Wearing dead men's clothes is bad luck,' Sonnier argued.

'You're lucky someone's not wearing *yours*,' Rocheteau sniggered. 'You complain about bad luck after surviving a firing squad. You must be the luckiest man on earth.'

A number of the men chuckled.

'God decided it wasn't your time,' Moreau said.

'He's got the inaccuracy of the firing squad to thank,' Rocheteau countered. 'Not God.'

More laughter.

'Shut up,' bellowed Delpierre.

'I *said* I was going to kill that bastard,' Rocheteau muttered under his breath. 'And I will.' He shot the sergeant a malevolent glance.

'I wonder when they'll give us weapons,' Roussard mused.

'When they're sure we won't use them to escape, probably,' Lausard said. 'They *daren't* trust us yet.'

'*I'm* not running away again,' Sonnier asserted.

Bonet succeeded in fastening the buttons of the Prussian tunic he'd been given. He smoothed one sleeve, removing a piece of dried mud from the cuff.

'This looks like better quality material,' he said, touching the shoulder of Carbonne's tunic. 'Ours are thinner.'

'Too thin to stop a musket ball,' Lausard interjected, pushing a finger into the hole in his jacket's shoulder.

'Or a sabre cut,' Charvet observed, indicating a slash in the breast of his own jacket which had been hastily stitched. There was still dried blood on the white tunic.

'So many ways to die,' muttered Roussard.

Lausard didn't answer, his gaze was firmly fixed on the pile of burning clothes on the other side of the compound. The plume of thick black smoke was still rising higher, up towards the darkening sky.

A huge metal cauldron containing boiled meat and vegetables had been set up at one end of the barrack room and the smell of food was both welcome and much appreciated. The cook, a huge man with a massive moustache, ladled the broth into the metal plates each man held up, while an assistant broke off pieces of bread and passed it to them. Most ate the bread as soon as it was given to them, others dropped it into the broth.

'I wonder what it is?' Rostov asked, peering ahead of him, past the line of waiting, hungry men.

'Who cares?' Joubert grunted. 'It's food, that's all that matters. I was beginning to think I was going to die of hunger.' He inhaled deeply, savouring the rich aroma of the broth.

'Some kind of blessing should be said before we eat,' Moreau said. 'We should give thanks to God for this food.'

'We should give thanks to whoever cooked it,' Rocheteau chuckled and the other men joined in the chorus of laughter.

'I'm not thanking anyone until I've tasted it,' Lausard said, grinning.

Rocheteau patted him on the shoulder and smiled.

The barrack room itself was about fifty feet long, half that in width. Blankets were laid out on the stone floor at regular intervals. No beds. But at least the men would be spending this and many more nights under cover. They comforted themselves with that thought. Food and shelter was all they asked.

'It's still like being in prison,' Delacor said irritably. 'But at least in there they left us alone, they didn't bother us.'

'No,' Lausard mused. 'They wouldn't have bothered you until the morning they came to take you to the guillotine.'

'I'd have escaped.'

'So escape from here,' Lausard challenged. 'You hate it so much. Get out. Or are you afraid of what they'll do when they catch you?'

'I'm not afraid of anyone,' Delacor snarled, pushing closer to Lausard. 'What makes you so happy here anyway?'

'I'd rather die like a soldier than a rat in a cage.

Deschamps was right, at least there's some honour in that.'

'To hell with honour,' snapped Delacor. 'And to hell with the army.'

'If you run, they'll catch you,' Sonnier interjected. 'I *know*.'

'You got caught because you're stupid,' Delacor scathingly told him.

'Just shut up,' snapped Carbonne. 'Both of you. Haven't we got enough to concern us without bickering all the time?'

Delacor opened his mouth to say something but Lausard raised a hand to silence him. 'He's right,' he said. 'We have to stick together. We're all in this now, one way or the other. They've given us a way out. We should use it.'

'They've given us a way straight into a coffin,' Roussard offered and smiled thinly.

Lausard held out his metal plate, watching as the cook ladled meat and vegetables into it. The broth was thin and watery, the meat and the other ingredients cooked so long that the colour had been boiled from them. But that wasn't important now. All that mattered to Lausard and to everyone else was to quell the raging hunger gnawing away inside their bellies.

When each of them had received his share, they gathered together in a group. Strangers thrust together, linked only by the fact that they had been criminals and that they were now to be soldiers. Men from different backgrounds, and in some cases, different countries. Rostov wasn't the only foreigner in the unit. He'd heard that there was an Austrian, even an Irishman, somewhere amongst the other men. The others were from every region of France but predominantly from Paris and its outlying regions. Men who had enjoyed completely different upbringings, who had been forced to scratch a living as thieves or forgers or horse thieves. Every kind of criminal, every manner of man was present in the barracks.

'What will they do with us?' Charvet wondered. 'Turn us into infantry, cavalry or artillerymen?'

'This was a cavalry training depot,' said Lausard, munching on bread. 'My guess is they'll use us as horsemen.'

'I can't ride a horse,' Tabor said, looking around him anxiously.

Bonet patted his arm reassuringly.

'That's why we're here, you half-wit,' snapped Delacor. 'So they can teach us.' Then he turned to face Lausard. 'Anyway, what makes you such an expert? How do you know this used to be a cavalry training depot?'

'I spoke to Deschamps back at the prison,' Lausard said, dipping his bread into the thin broth. 'He said that the army was short of cavalry. That's why they need us as horsemen.'

'They'll have trouble finding a horse big enough for you, fat man,' said Giresse, smiling, prodding Joubert in the side.

The big man didn't answer, he just continued eating, a satisfied grin on his face.

'They'll have trouble finding horses for any of us,' Bonet interjected. 'I heard that the cavalry are using animals captured from the Austrians.'

'A horse is a horse, who cares where it comes from?' said Rocheteau.

'That's not strictly true,' Bonet said, dropping bread into his broth. 'German horses are larger than most French mounts. Spanish ponies are smaller and quicker and—'

Rocheteau interrupted, holding up his hand. 'All right, schoolmaster, I get the idea.'

Joubert drained what was left on his metal plate by lifting it to his mouth, then licking it to ensure he didn't waste any of the precious fluid. He looked longingly at Rostov who was still sipping at his broth, but the Russian merely met his gaze and shook his head gently.

'That wasn't enough,' said the fat man. 'How can they expect a man to survive on such meagre rations?'

'We all survived on *less* than this when we lived in Paris,' said Rocheteau, mopping his plate with a piece of bread.

Some of the other men nodded approvingly.

'Do you think those bastards in the Directory ever went hungry?' Carbonne asked.

'That's no way to talk about our government,' Bonet said, smiling.

'What are you going to do?' Carbonne challenged good naturedly. 'Report me?'

'I shall report you to Paul Barras personally,' Bonet replied.

The other men laughed.

'Now there's a man who *should* have sneezed into the basket,' Carbonne said and chuckled. 'I'd have done a good job on him.'

'We'd all have queued up to pull the lever,' Rocheteau added.

'That would have been *my* privilege,' Carbonne reminded him.

'He'll get his come-uppance,' Bonet murmured. 'All of them will.'

'From who?' Giresse asked.

'The army,' Lausard interjected. 'You mark my words. In two years, this army will be the power in France.'

'And we'll be a part of it,' Rocheteau said, a thin smile creeping across his face. 'We soldiers.' He got to his feet and saluted, and the gesture was met by a great cheer.

Other men in the barrack room turned to see what the noise was about, then returned to their food or settled down for the night to try to sleep. The candles which lit the room were burning down and night was throwing a dark blanket across the land.

Lausard looked at his companions in their makeshift uniforms then he gently stroked the sleeve of his own threadbare tunic.

'Soldiers,' he said quietly, then smiled.

CHAPTER 8

The men had been divided into groups of between fifteen and twenty and they now stood beneath the weak sun of a chill morning, each group assigned to a different NCO. The dragoons were dressed in short, green single-breasted jackets with no facing colours and wore breeches reinforced with leather over their boots. Sergeant Legier, who was instructing Lausard's group, wore his forage cap too.

Somewhere behind him, Lausard could hear Delpierre's voice bellowing instructions at his own gathering of men. He had also seen Captain Deschamps strolling unhurriedly across the parade ground, puffing on his pipe, apparently unconcerned at the activity all around him. A small detachment of dragoons in full dress had ridden out of the training depot less than ten minutes earlier but Lausard, like his companions, had no idea where they were going. Fewer still cared.

The young man's thoughts were interrupted by a loud metallic hiss as Legier drew his sabre from its scabbard.

'Take a good look at it, boys,' he said, his voice low.

He turned the three-foot-long blade slowly in his hand, the sun winking off the cutting edge. The polished steel blade curved all the way to a tapered point.

'This will be your friend,' Legier continued, holding the weapon at shoulder height, tilting the point towards Delacor who took an involuntary step backwards. 'You'll learn to use a carbine and pistols too, but the sword is the most important weapon you'll carry. Treat it well, learn how to use it.' He stepped towards Roussard, the blade still levelled.

'Do you want to kill me already, Sergeant?' Roussard said.

Legier managed a slight smile but it vanished like fog in a high wind. He looked at the men as he spoke, twisting the weapon in the air, allowing them to see every angle and edge of the instrument.

'There are two methods of striking an enemy,' Legier began. 'The thrust.' He drove the weapon forward, to within inches of Lausard who never took his eyes off the sergeant. 'And the cut.' He lifted the weapon high and brought it down, the blade slicing the air. 'The sword is always held in the right hand. The cut is made from right to left. The backhand cut from left to right. Everyone has their own opinion about which is the more effective. The thrust allows greater reach and the wounds caused by a thrust are more likely to be mortal. A man can survive slash wounds. Believe me.' He touched the empty hole where his ear used to be. 'It is the *point* that kills,' Legier continued. 'Thrust as often as you can. You will defeat all those you touch.' He took a couple of steps back. 'The thrust is delivered by keeping the thumb against the hilt, facing *down*. When cutting, aim for the neck or shoulder. Most men will duck if they see the blow coming, so a cut to the neck may strike the face. Aim higher and you will miss your enemy completely. Strike downward if you can.' He demonstrated once more. 'The sword will penetrate more deeply.'

The men looked on, mesmerised. Only Lausard watched with something approaching real enthusiasm.

'There are tricks too,' Legier continued. He turned the sword so that he still held the blade at shoulder height but the flat of it was horizontal. 'When thrusting into the ribs, hold the sword like this. The blade will enter cleanly *between* the ribs. Its entry will be clean and it can be withdrawn more quickly so that another blow can be struck. I've seen men break their wrists accidentally striking bone. Keep the blade flat. Don't twist it or it'll stick inside your opponent. If he falls from his horse he may even take your weapon with him. Strike quickly and pull free quickly, you will create a sawing effect. If you *do* strike bone, the steel will break it.' He patted the side of the weapon. 'As long as it is held like this.'

Roussard swallowed hard.

'What about infantry?' Tabor asked. 'How do we fight them?'

Legier took a step forward, pressing the point of the sword against the big man's chest.

'Don't speak,' the sergeant said quietly. 'Your job is to listen, *not* ask questions. Do you understand?'

Tabor nodded, glancing down at the sword tip. It didn't seem to bother him. In fact, as Lausard watched, the big man reached out and gently touched the tip.

'It's sharp,' he said, smiling at Legier then at the other men.

Bonet shot out a hand and pulled him back.

'Half-wit,' Delacor murmured under his breath.

'You fight infantry with care,' Legier said, a slight grin hovering momentarily on his lips. 'If attacked by cavalry they will form squares. The trick is to catch them in open order, preferably on open ground where they can't use cover. If you do catch them that way then ride them down. Your horses will try to avoid stepping on men if they can. The Russians, in particular, know this and use it. If their infantry cannot form squares in time they will allow you to ride over them. It is their only protection. Otherwise, strike down at them using the slash I spoke of earlier. Backhand is more effective.' He twisted the sword in his grip. 'You may come up against armoured cavalry too. The Austrian cuirassiers wear a breastplate which deflects most sword swings. Ride past them and strike at their backs. They have no back plate, no protection.'

'What is your group like, Sergeant?'

The men turned as they heard a new voice.

Lausard saw Delpierre striding towards them.

'They will learn,' Legier told him. 'And yours?'

'Cannon fodder,' he said and smirked, picking at one of the scabs on his chin.

He stood next to Legier, his eyes scanning the watching men. 'You have no cavalry uniforms because you do not deserve them yet,' he said. 'Nor do you have any horses. Or weapons.'

'How do you expect us to fight then?' Sonnier asked defiantly.

'The coward has a question,' Delpierre said and chuckled. 'Why do *you* want to know about fighting? You tried to run away.' He took a step towards Sonnier.

'If you want to fight, then fight me. Now.' He drew his sword and hurled it towards Sonnier who took a step back, looking at the blade as it struck the ground at his feet. 'Pick it up,' Delpierre told him.

Sonnier looked at the sword then at the sergeant.

'Pick it up,' Delpierre roared. 'Come on, what are you waiting for? Come on, coward. Pick it up, you spineless, snivelling scum.'

'Pick it up,' hissed Delacor.

'Go on,' Rocheteau urged under his breath. 'Run him through.'

'Cut the bastard,' Carbonne added.

Still Sonnier stood motionless, his gaze flicking back and forth from Delpierre to the sword which lay at his feet.

'Pick it up,' the sergeant shouted again. 'You gutless bastard.'

Lausard stepped in front of Sonnier, lifted the sword by its hilt then turned it in his hand and offered it to Delpierre.

'So, *you* want to fight, do you? You want to protect that coward.'

'I am returning your sword, Sergeant,' Lausard said evenly, his gaze never faltering.

'*You* fight me,' Delpierre hissed. 'Show me what you've learned.'

Delpierre suddenly grabbed the sword by its hilt, pulling it from Lausard's grip, slicing the cutting edge across the palm of his hand. The sharpened metal laid the flesh open and Lausard gasped in pain and anger as he saw blood spurt from the cut.

'Come on,' Delpierre said, grinning. 'I've spilled *your* blood. Now spill mine.'

The knot of muscles at the side of Lausard's jaw pulsed angrily, his steely gaze locked on Delpierre as if magnetised. He could feel his left hand burning and there was blood dripping from the cut.

'I promise not to hurt you,' Delpierre said mockingly.

Lausard heard the hiss as another sabre was drawn and he looked up to see Legier pulling his own blade free of the scabbard. He tossed it towards Lausard who caught it with his right hand.

Legier nodded slowly.

'A contest perhaps?' mocked Delpierre, taking a step towards Lausard who stood his ground, swaying slightly back and forth, his eyes never leaving his foe.

Delpierre swung his sword in a downward arc, the blade slicing air as it sped towards Lausard's left shoulder.

Nimbly Lausard ducked the stroke and thrust forward with his own sword, the point aimed at Delpierre's chest.

Delpierre recovered and knocked the blade away with a backhand stroke. The sound of metal on metal rang around the training ground.

Legier walked slowly around the two men, pushing the others back a few paces, watching as Lausard parried one of Delpierre's thrusts.

'Give them room,' Legier said, as fascinated by the contest as the other watchers.

Delpierre struck again, aiming for Lausard's head.

Lausard jerked back then jabbed his sword forward, catching Delpierre in the upper left shoulder. Not hard enough to puncture flesh but strongly enough to rip the material of his jacket.

Delpierre glared at him and swung his sword with even greater ferocity.

Lausard blocked the slash, ducked and drove a fist into Delpierre's stomach, then he jumped to one side and, with the point of the sword, slit open the lobe of the sergeant's right ear.

Delpierre roared in pain and rage and began hacking frenziedly at his opponent.

Lausard parried or dodged each murderous swipe of the sword, the clash of steel now filling the air.

Delpierre struck at Lausard's head, both hands gripping the sword.

Lausard felt the blade part air inches from his cheek but he edged sideways and struck Delpierre across the side with the sharpened edge of the sword, tearing his jacket again. Then he struck for the left shoulder, feinted to the right then carved a button from Delpierre's tunic.

The sergeant was raging now, hurling himself at Lausard, swinging his sword with the ferocity of a man possessed.

Lausard blocked the savage lunge and swung his foot across in front of his attacker.

Delpierre went sprawling, landing heavily on the ground and, as he rolled over, Lausard advanced towards him and thrust the point of the blade to within an inch of his throat.

Lausard was breathing heavily, perspiration running from his forehead, trickling down his cheek.

Delpierre tried to sit up but the point of the blade prevented him from raising his head more than an inch. 'I'll kill you,' he hissed, his eyes bulging madly.

'You just tried,' Lausard said quietly. '*Sergeant.*'

He increased the pressure on the sword, the tip breaking the skin, opening a tiny cut beneath Delpierre's chin. Stepping back, he glanced across at Legier then threw the sword, hilt first, back at him. The sergeant caught it, watching as Lausard turned his back on his defeated opponent.

Delpierre suddenly leaped to his feet, snatched up his sword and aimed for Lausard's unprotected back.

All Lausard heard was the arc of the steel as it moved in the air with incredible power towards him. He never had a chance to move.

There was a loud clang of steel on steel and he spun round to see that Legier had blocked the murderous downward cut.

'It's over,' Legier said to his companion.

Lausard looked at the two NCOs, watching as Delpierre sheathed his sword.

'This isn't over,' Delpierre snarled, pointing at Lausard. 'This is the beginning.'

'You should have killed him,' Rocheteau said, watching as Delpierre stalked away towards another group of men.

Lausard and Legier looked at each other for a moment but no flicker of emotion passed between them. Then Lausard nodded almost imperceptibly.

'Get back in line,' Legier ordered.

From the other side of the training ground, puffing contentedly on his pipe, Captain Deschamps watched.

CHAPTER 9

As the days stretched one into another, each becoming indistinguishable from the next, Lausard became aware that his life was beginning to take on something approaching order. There was a monotonous regularity to his existence in the army but it was preferable to the crushing feeling of worthlessness he'd been so accustomed to during his years in Paris. The nightmares still came, perhaps with slightly less regularity, but the pain was still there. Only now its severity was lessened somewhat as he channelled his feelings of uselessness into his training, concentrating every fibre on the task at hand. Only in the stillness of the night, when sleep still eluded him, did he find all the old familiar pain returning. In the darkness, alone in the barracks, his mind flooded with images of the slaughter of his family and, try as he might, he couldn't shake their possession of his waking thoughts.

No one mentioned the fight with Delpierre. No one asked him how he had learned to handle a sword so adeptly. No one seemed puzzled by his proficiency with the weapon and yet his comrades knew that to fight the way he had would have required training of the highest order. Instead they contented themselves with knowing that, among them, was a man they could trust and admire; a man who seemed as skilled as those who taught them. But Lausard wondered what their reactions would be if they knew he had learned his skills at a place many of them would see as a bastion of the class they had despised and helped to destroy. Only those with money, or their families at least, had been able to attend the Carabinier School at Chinon as he had. If his companions knew, would their admiration and respect turn to mistrust and hatred? Would they call for *his* head as they had called for the heads of so many like him?

As he stood on the parade ground glancing at his comrades, it didn't seem to matter either to him or to them. In their ignorance was his safety.

Most had adapted well to their present surroundings and to the new demands being made on them daily. They had been given wooden swords with which to practise the moves taught to them by Legier and the other NCOs. These they carried sloped, over their shoulders as they drilled, learning to march. As dragoons they would be expected to fight both on foot and on horseback.

Lausard found the entire concept a little absurd as, so far, none of them had seen so much as a musket ball, let alone the pistols, carbines and sabres they must learn to fight with. Every day they were told that the weapons would be arriving soon but from where no one seemed quite sure. It was getting to the stage where Lausard was beginning to think that he and his comrades would walk into their first battle wielding wooden swords and carbines, forced to stroll across the killing fields because they also had no horses.

Every piece of equipment, every mount, every uniform seemed to be second-hand and the greater proportion had been acquired from enemy forces currently engaged in Italy, Belgium and Prussia. Lausard could only guess at the state of the French forces fighting those enemies, but if they were suffering shortages as acutely as he and his companions then it seemed only a matter of time before the army and then the whole of revolutionary France collapsed.

Food was another commodity in short supply. Even the regular troops at the training depot sent out foragers on a daily basis to scour the land for provisions. Lausard and his men had been reduced to a diet consisting of biscuits and potatoes, the latter boiled in huge vats until they dissolved into a thick soup which the men were often forced to eat cold the following day. Drinking water too was at a premium and Lausard couldn't remember the last time he had bathed. The parade ground was full of reeking, hungry men all arranged in lines straighter than any sergeant had a right to expect. The smell of unwashed bodies was strong in the air.

Lausard could feel a flea crawling across his neck but he resisted the temptation to squash it. His eyes were fixed ahead of him, towards two dozen or more wooden objects which resembled barrels but were smoother, longer and narrower.

'These are your horses,' Sergeant Legier called, chuckling, gesturing towards the wooden objects. 'You will learn to mount and dismount on these.'

'Wooden swords, wooden guns, wooden horses,'

muttered Rocheteau. 'Our enemies will only need tinder boxes to defeat us.'

'We should be carpenters,' Giresse added. 'Not soldiers. I was a horse thief but I never stole anything like *that*.' He nodded towards the fake mounts.

'I hear the government pays four hundred francs for every horse captured,' Rocheteau whispered. 'Perhaps we should all become horse thieves. We'd be rich men.'

'You will all take your turns here,' shouted Legier, pointing at the wooden objects.

The unit was broken up into smaller groups, most of them taken away by other NCOs to drill while they awaited their turn at the wooden horses. Lausard could hear orders being shouted from all over the parade ground. He and Rocheteau were among the first called forward to the fake mounts.

'Stand beside the horse,' said Legier. 'Grip his bridle with your right hand, place your right foot in the stirrup and swing your left leg over the saddle.'

'There is no saddle, Sergeant,' Tabor said.

'There's no horse either, is there, boy?' snapped the sergeant. 'Use your imagination.'

'Just like climbing on top of a woman,' Delacor mused.

'You don't *climb* on women, you animal,' Giresse said reproachfully. 'You *ease* yourself on to them.'

'Mount up,' roared Legier, stepping back to watch his wards as they struggled to throw themselves on the wooden horses.

Lausard managed it effortlessly.

Bonet, too, accomplished the task with relative ease. As did Roussard, Carbonne and Rostov.

Joubert hoisted himself up, toppled over and

promptly fell to the ground on the other side of the object.

Charvet tried to grip the fake mount but could find no hand-hold and began swaying uncertainly.

'Use your knees,' Legier roared.

Charvet tried but failed. He fell forward.

Rocheteau swung his leg over but couldn't straighten up. With a grunt he finally fell to the ground.

'Grip with your knees,' shouted Legier again. 'Grip tightly.'

He watched those who had failed to mount struggling then shouted at those already sitting upright to dismount.

They did so with relative ease.

'Mount,' he shouted.

Again they tried. More succeeding this time.

'Dismount.'

The manoeuvre was repeated.

'Mount.'

Joubert hauled his mountainous frame upright for all of two seconds this time.

'Dismount.'

The order was becoming a litany.

Nearly every man was in position after fifteen minutes. After thirty, the orders were still being shouted with monotonous regularity.

Sonnier felt pain around his groin, his buttocks and the insides of his thighs. Some of the other men were also feeling the strain of constant friction against their inner thighs and knees.

The orders continued.

They clambered up with more precision but less speed.

Moreau saw blood soaking through his trousers at the knees, the flesh rubbed raw by the wood. Sonnier too was bleeding, crimson fluid trickling down his calves.

'Mount.'

It was all he could do to swing his bloodied leg over the fake mount.

Lausard felt the pain too and saw the flesh had been stripped from his thighs.

'Dismount.'

Rocheteau almost collapsed.

And it continued.

The men were drenched with perspiration, their tunics soaked through, hair matted to their faces. The unbearable friction was now causing intense pain with each movement, and the blood from many of them was now soaking into the wood itself.

Joubert could barely suck in the breath needed for the effort.

'Come on!' roared Legier. 'What will you be like on *real* horses? They kick, they bite, they panic. You must keep a firm grip on them. You must master them, you must pamper them, you must love them. They will carry you through battle. They could save your lives.'

Roussard toppled from the fake mount and hit the ground hard.

'Get up!' bellowed Legier, crossing towards him, glaring down at him.

Roussard struggled to his knees then dropped forward on to all fours, panting like a dog. Finally, with almost superhuman effort, he stood upright.

'Now mount up,' Legier ordered.

Roussard managed it at the second attempt and sat

astride the wooden object, eyes screwed up tight against the pain.

Lausard readjusted his position slightly, wincing at the discomfort, glancing down at the fresh spot of blood now smearing the thin material of his trousers. He wondered how much longer this was going to continue.

Thirty minutes later he was still wondering.

'They're trying to kill us,' groaned Sonnier, looking down at his bloodied legs.

'If any infection sets in you're done for,' Bonet added. 'That lot will turn gangrenous in days.' He nodded towards Sonnier's legs.

'Thanks for the information, schoolmaster,' Rocheteau grumbled, rolling on to his stomach on the straw mattress. 'I really needed to know that.'

'I just want to know what these bastards are playing at,' Delacor said. 'They want us for their army and yet, like Sonnier says, it's like they're trying to kill us before we even reach a battlefield.'

'If they didn't train us we'd be dead within seconds of reaching that battlefield,' Lausard told him.

'You call this training? This isn't training, this is torture.'

'It'll get better,' Lausard said, pulling free a piece of material that was stuck to some dried blood on his knee. He winced, noticing that the abrasions were still weeping.

'How can you be so sure?' Delacor demanded.

'Because it can't get any worse,' Lausard said flatly. 'They want us to get to the stage where we *want* to fight. Where being under fire is *better* than drilling and marching and climbing wooden horses. That's how this army works.'

'You seemed pretty sure of yourself today, schoolmaster,' said Charvet. 'Where did you learn to ride?'

'My father had a farm. I grew up with horses.'

'What happened to your family?'

'Both my parents died of smallpox. I haven't seen my brother since 'eighty-six. He's probably dead too for all I know.' Bonet spoke quietly.

'He might be in the army like you,' Rocheteau chuckled.

Some of the other men laughed too.

'My brother joined the army,' Tabor said, inspecting his bloodied legs.

'You mean there's another one like you?' Delacor said disdainfully. 'A whole family of half-wits.'

'He was killed at Fleurus,' Tabor said. 'My mother told me. They sent his shoes back to her. Why would they do that?'

'So she could remember him,' Bonet said softly, tapping the big man on the shoulder.

'What about your parents, Alain?' Rocheteau said, looking at Lausard. 'Are they still alive?'

Lausard shook his head. He had no lie ready. He didn't speak. He didn't tell the truth. That his father had been a wealthy man branded as an enemy of the State by Robespierre and his bloodthirsty allies. He didn't speak of the executions. Of the murder of his family by men like those who now regarded him as a comrade. It was simpler to remain silent.

The candles in the barrack room were burning low and, outside, night was tightening its grip. Lausard knew that with the blackness would come the dreams.

The same dream he knew so well. And dreaded.

The conversation inside the barrack room gradually dwindled to a few whispers. Moreau said a prayer before lying down on his filthy mattress. Very soon the first snores began to fill the room. Those who could sleep through the pain and discomfort did so. Others, like Lausard, lay awake in the blackness, some craving sleep, others denied it by pain. Lausard fought it until, finally, he succumbed.

CHAPTER 10

Napoleon Bonaparte ran a hand through his hair and eyed the men who sat opposite him, aware of their appraising glances. He knew one or two of them well, Paul Barras in particular, but he felt neither confidence nor trust in these men. They were not soldiers, and Bonaparte found it hard to trust those who had not worn the uniform of his country.

'I thought you would have been more impressed with your appointment, *General* Bonaparte,' said Barras, smiling. 'For a man of your age, it is a huge responsibility. I do not know any other twenty-six-year-old General of Brigade.'

'You hide your gratitude very well,' Tallien echoed.

Bonaparte shifted in his seat and gazed at each man in turn. 'Is gratitude what you expected from me?' he asked. 'I was doing my job as a soldier, nothing more. A job, gentlemen, I might add, that ensures *you* sit where you sit now.' He took a sip of his wine.

'We appreciate that,' Barras said.

'Then perhaps it is you who should be grateful,' Bonaparte said. 'Not I.'

'Are you not happy with your position then?' Gohier asked.

'Of course,' the Corsican replied. 'I seek advancement just as any soldier should, just as any *man* should. A man should never be satisfied with his lot in life. There should always be more goals to strive for.'

'And what do you imply *we* should strive for?' It was Gohier who had spoken.

'I imply nothing,' Bonaparte said flatly.

'The Paris mob is defeated,' Barras said. 'You saw to that. They are no longer the force they were. Every citizen has been ordered to surrender his weapons to the government, to us. The city is in our power once more, as is the rest of the country.'

'Then it is time you looked beyond France,' Bonaparte told them.

'And where did you have in mind?' Tallien enquired.

'Italy. The Italian campaign is faltering. The army of Italy is a shambles. Every day the Austrians and Piedmontese take advantage of our position there. We will soon be driven out completely.'

'The men in command of the armies there are very able men,' Gohier protested.

'They are too old, too slow in their thinking,' Bonaparte countered. 'Massena is a good general. He won at Loano but the victory was not followed up. Schérer did not exploit it.'

'It is easy to conduct a war from the safety of the War Office, General Bonaparte,' Tallien said. 'We appointed men we felt were equal to the task.'

'Then why has there been no progress in Italy?' the Corsican demanded. 'The campaign being fought is one of defence, not attack. No war was ever won by defending. Battles are won by attacking, campaigns are fought on the offensive. Your men in Italy don't seem to realise this.'

'We are under-strength,' Gohier protested. 'The army is without food, clothes, weapons. We force our men to ravage the land because we cannot provide them with adequate supplies. The army in Italy is an army of scarecrows, General Bonaparte.'

'Commanded by farmers,' grunted the younger man with scorn.

'Your ignorance is matched by your arrogance,' snapped Tallien.

'It is neither,' Bonaparte said challengingly.

'You show no respect for your elders,' Tallien said. 'For officers who were in uniform while you were at your mother's breast. Some of these men have been in the service of France for over thirty years.'

'It shows,' snapped Bonaparte. 'They're still using methods from thirty years ago. They belong to a different time. There is a place for them, but not at the head of an army.'

'And where would you have them placed, *General* Bonaparte?' Gohier said irritably.

'As you say, they are able soldiers,' Bonaparte offered. 'What they need is an able leader. Someone who is not afraid to take risks. The men who command the army in Italy are too cautious.'

'They don't have the luxury of recklessness,' Tallien snapped. 'We cannot afford to lose men in wild undertakings. The army doesn't have the men to lose.'

'I said nothing of recklessness. There is a difference between boldness and stupidity. I don't ask for recklessness. I don't want stupidity. I want what you all want, what the entire country wants. I want victory for France.'

'Surely we would all agree with General Bonaparte on that,' Barras interjected.

'So you prescribe the same cures as he does?' snapped Letourneur.

'I agree with him that a certain boldness is called for,' Barras countered. 'Perhaps a boldness which comes with youth.'

There was a momentary silence in the room broken by Tallien. 'So, how do you see the situation, General?'

'We have thirty-eight thousand men hemmed in along the Ligurian plain. Held there by the Austrians and the Piedmontese. The Bay of Genoa is controlled by the British Navy. Our men need to break out. Turn defence into attack, push the Austrians back. If the army is forced to remain where it is for many more months it will starve to death. Hunger will do the Austrians' job for them.'

'Still easy to say sitting here,' Tallien said.

'Easy because it is true. If the men commanding the army of Italy do not act soon then everything will be lost and, if the Austrians defeat us, who is to stop them invading France itself? Remove the men who command. You need a new sword.' Bonaparte's eyes were blazing.

Again silence descended, this time broken by Barras. 'Would you be that sword?'

'The troops need someone they can believe in.'

'And you know of such a man?' Tallien said slowly, the words emerging more as a statement than a question.

Bonaparte nodded.

CHAPTER 11

'Horses,' murmured Tabor, almost mesmerised by the sight before him.

'Well spotted,' Delacor added, his eyes narrowing as he allowed his gaze to drift along the lines of mounts facing him and his companions on the parade ground.

Lausard too watched as more than one hundred horses were driven into untidy lines by more than a dozen dragoons, some wearing stable dress, the others resplendent in their full dress uniforms. Major Deschamps rode back and forth across the parade ground, his own bay neighing excitedly, its head tossing up and down.

There were animals of every size and colour. Small ponies, larger horses, even what looked like farm horses. Bays, piebalds, blacks, greys. Lausard even spotted a white animal among them. All were unsaddled but each one had been fitted with a bridle and reins. He saw a number rear up in confusion and hoped that he didn't get one of the friskier animals for his own mount. Not all of them were shod and a number were from the Camargue – fast, compact ponies shod only on the front hooves. The air was filled with the smell of horses and droppings.

Green saddle blankets had been set up in lines and each man was directed to take up position behind one. On top of each one was a saddle, some worn, some holed. There were stirrups missing from some, the irons bent and twisted in places.

'I wonder which enemy these came from,' said Bonet, inspecting his saddle. There was a dark stain just below the pommel which he was sure was blood. He shuddered involuntarily.

'Listen to me!' a familiar voice bellowed across the training ground and Lausard looked up to see Delpierre trotting back and forth on his horse. 'Today you become cavalry. You learn how to saddle horses, how to ride horses, how to manoeuvre horses. You obey orders, you make your horse obey *you*.'

Rocheteau glanced at Lausard but said nothing. His expression spoke volumes. Lausard managed to suppress a grin.

'Your training is nearly over,' Delpierre continued. 'You came here worthless, you will leave as soldiers, but you will only leave if you learn. In three days you must be able to fight on horseback, fight the way you've been taught. You will be given weapons, uniforms, but not until *we* think you are ready and you must be ready in three days.'

He wheeled his horse and rode back down the line of waiting men, past the horses that looked as nervous as their would-be riders. Delpierre slowed down as he reached Lausard, peering at the younger man from under his brass helmet.

'You will all be given help,' he said. 'But you are

responsible for your horse, for yourselves. I will be watching for any mistakes and I will punish them.' He glared at Lausard. 'It is also your duty to take care of your kit. Each man must carry with him one pair of trousers, two shirts, gaiters, stockings, boot cuffs, forage cap, stable jacket, needles, thread, scissors, awl, brush, wax, blanco, shoe buckles, curry-comb, powder bag, sponge, razor, two handkerchiefs and a nightcap.'

'Where the hell are we supposed to put all those?' Rocheteau murmured.

'It took them over a week to find us horses,' Lausard whispered, 'I doubt if they'll find us that lot too. I'm surprised they've even got weapons for us.'

'I won't believe it until I see it,' Rocheteau replied, nudging his saddle with the toe of his shoe.

'You'll never find a horse big enough to carry you, fat man,' Delacor said, elbowing Joubert.

'There's some good animals there,' Giresse said, running his gaze over the horses.

'How do *you* know?' Roussard said.

'I did used to steal them,' Giresse reminded him.

'What if I fall off?' Tabor murmured.

'You'll be fine,' Bonet reassured him.

'Pick up your saddles!' roared Delpierre.

The men on the parade ground did so with varying degrees of enthusiasm.

'Christ,' grunted Charvet. 'That's heavy.' He almost stumbled as he struggled to lift the saddle, cloth and portmanteau.

'Don't take the Lord's name in vain,' Moreau said reproachfully.

'I wish the Lord would give me a hand with this blasted saddle,' Charvet continued.

The men stood waiting, saddles held firmly.

'Select a mount and saddle up,' Delpierre shouted.

Most of the dragoons had formed a line close to the horses and were watching with amusement as the men struggled forward clutching their saddles. They pointed at those men who seemed to be having the most difficulty.

Delpierre walked his horse back and forth, eyeing the stragglers with something less than understanding.

One man threw his saddle on to the back of a grey horse which promptly reared up, threw the saddle clear and bolted.

The man grabbed for the bridle, missed and crashed to the ground.

Sonnier lifted the saddle carefully and slid it on to his animal's back, patting the hindquarters as he did so. Then without thinking, in his haste to mount, he placed one foot in the stirrup and prepared to swing himself over. Without the girth strap being fastened, the saddle, and Sonnier with it, crashed to the ground. His horse tossed its head, as if it too was mocking him.

Lausard fastened the necessary buckles on the saddle straps and tugged at the saddle to ensure it was secure, then he placed his left foot in the stirrup and lifted himself into the saddle. The horse bucked but he tugged hard on the reins, bringing the great black animal under control immediately, using one hand to pat its neck.

Giresse was also safely mounted, as were Bonet and several of the others. All across the parade ground men were beginning to haul themselves into their saddles. A number were still struggling, half-a-dozen were scurrying around trying to catch their mounts while NCOs bellowed at them.

Lausard sat straight in the saddle, his gaze meeting Delpierre's. The sergeant rode past him then turned his horse and headed back towards Lausard. He was less than ten yards away when a horse nearby suddenly reared up on its hind legs, hurling its rider to the ground. The man landed with a sickening thud, looking up in horror as the horse lost its footing and fell on top of him. The sound of breaking bone was audible even above the combined noise of neighing animals and yelling NCOs. The horse scrambled to its feet leaving the man clutching at one leg and shouting in pain.

Two dragoons dragged him away, one of them catching the bridle of the horse as it attempted to bolt.

Moreau felt his own mount bucking under him and he gripped the reins tightly and pressed his knees into the creature, feeling the power beneath him. But the animal would not be calmed and grew more agitated.

Lausard saw that the horse was about to unseat its rider and urged his own mount across. He grabbed at the muzzle of Moreau's horse but the grey snapped at him with yellowed teeth. Lausard took the bit and pulled hard, relieved to see the horse was steadying.

Moreau loosened his grip on the reins and the animal began to calm down. It kicked out with one hind leg then stood still. Moreau looked at Lausard and nodded almost imperceptibly.

'Quite the expert, aren't you?'

Lausard turned in the saddle as he heard the voice of Delpierre behind him.

'You can use a sword, you know how to ride . . . I wonder if you can shoot a carbine from the saddle too? I bet you can.' His smile was crooked. 'You will be a useful member of this regiment, if you live. A man like you should take his place in the front line for any battle. I will see that you do.' The two men locked stares for a moment then Delpierre rode off to shout instructions at two men who had managed to fasten their saddles on but could not manage to mount.

Rocheteau flicked his reins and was almost surprised when his mount walked slowly across to Lausard. He patted the chestnut thankfully.

'What was that bastard on about?' he asked.

'Nothing important.'

'He's a dangerous man, Alain. The sooner I kill him the better.'

'Once we get into battle the Austrians will do it for you.'

'I want to do it.'

Lausard smiled. 'You and most of the regiment.'

Joubert rode up to join them, his horse already lathered. The big man himself was sweating profusely, gripping the reins so tightly that his knuckles were white.

'I don't know who's more worried,' Lausard said, grinning. 'You or the horse.'

'It's taking the weight well,' Rocheteau added, nodding towards the huge black mare which Joubert was seated on.

'This isn't natural,' Joubert protested, grunting as the horse reared slightly beneath him. 'I should have joined the infantry.' Again it seemed as if the horse would throw him but his sheer bulk appeared to keep him there.

Rocheteau's horse also bucked and he was forced to dig in his knees to prevent himself falling.

'I think I know what you mean, fat man,' he said, clinging on.

Lausard saw that nearly all of the men were mounted now, some assuredly, others decidedly not. There were one or two stray horses galloping around the parade ground; a dragoon sped after one, clutching at the bridle to slow down the frightened animal.

Deschamps and two other officers had ridden on to the parade ground, the captain still puffing at his pipe. He looked over the ragged array of men and shook his head, more in amusement than disdain, and rode towards the gates of the compound with his adjutants in close attendance. Lausard watched him go.

'Wheel, right,' roared Sergeant Legier to the struggling horsemen and as many as possible tried to complete the manoeuvre. It met with mixed success. A number of men fell from their horses, several were thrown. Lausard saw one man trying to avoid the thrashing hooves of his mount, his scream echoing through the morning air when the horse stepped on his left hand, shattering it.

Delacor felt himself slipping to one side and gripped his horse's mane to prevent himself falling, but the pain this caused the animal made it buck more wildly. Delacor's right foot came clear of the stirrup and he was sent hurtling from the saddle. He landed with a thump, rolling over, trying to suck in air, clutching at his side in pain.

He struggled to his feet, grabbed his bridle and remounted, slapping the horse hard across the neck. It promptly threw him again.

'They respond better to kindness,' Lausard advised, watching as Delacor struggled painfully to his feet.

'I don't need your advice,' he grunted, snatching at the reins once more.

The horse reared up and he toppled backwards to avoid its flashing hooves.

'Sure?' Lausard sneered and turned his horse.

'Leave him,' said Rostov, joining Lausard. 'He'll learn.'

'He'll have to,' Lausard added.

The entire untidy column was moving away from the parade ground, stragglers bringing up the rear, men cursing their horses, their saddles, their NCOs and anything else that came to mind. As the pace of the unit picked up from a walk to a trot Lausard couldn't suppress a smile. It felt good to be riding again. He felt strong and in control, almost at one with his horse, and the great black beast cavorted beneath him as if it too felt the rider's elation. He could smell the animal's sweat and his own too as he urged it on to a canter, his companions forced to do likewise. The column picked up speed.

Some more men toppled from their saddles and landed heavily on the ground as Legier and Delpierre took the column on a circuit of the parade ground, looking behind them to see the progress of their wards. Some of the dragoons joined in on either side of the column, offering either encouragement or sarcasm depending on their mood.

Lausard saw that Rocheteau had settled more comfortably into the saddle. Bonet was also moving effortlessly with his horse, and Rostov too. Even Joubert was managing to keep up although the effort seemed to be wringing yet more perspiration from his huge body.

Giresse brought his horse up alongside Lausard, smiling broadly as he rode.

'Four hundred francs for each of these mounts,' he said. 'I could retire on what's on this parade ground.'

'Remember, you control the horse, he doesn't control *you*!' Delpierre's voice boomed out over the parade ground, audible even above the sound of so many hooves and the endless chorus of shouts, grunts and curses.

'All changes of movement and formation are carried out at the trot or the gallop,' Delpierre continued, riding around as if oblivious to whatever mishaps may be befalling the men following him. 'The walk is one hundred and twenty paces a minute. The trot is two hundred and forty paces a minute. The gallop is four hundred and eighty and the charge is six hundred. Remember that and when the orders are given, obey and make your horse obey.'

'What the hell does he think we're trying to do?' said Rocheteau, gripping his reins tightly.

The ragged column continued to move falteringly around the parade ground.

CHAPTER 12

The candle was burning low, casting long shadows over the desk. Bonaparte looked up briefly and gazed around the darkened room, peering into the blackness as if seeking something, or somewhere, beyond that gloom. Perhaps Italy? He smiled, amused at his own ponderings, then he dipped the quill back into the pot of ink and continued writing.

He'd been working for more than four hours now, stopping only for some wine and cold chicken and most of that still lay untouched on one corner of the desk. He looked up again, watching the flickering yellow flame as it danced in the breeze, smoke drifting from its tip. The desk was strewn with papers and maps, an organised chaos which he knew no one but he would be able to decipher. Every letter, map and piece of paper was clear to him. He began writing again, the scratching of quill on paper the only sound in the stillness.

His new position had brought not just advancement, an increase in pay, power and responsibility; it had also brought with it a plethora of administrative work.

Something Bonaparte had mixed feelings about. He was, after all, a soldier and a soldier's place was in the field, not in an office. He was a general now and his place was to lead men. To command men. To plan and scheme and use the army in a more constructive way than it had been used so far. He sat back in his chair and exhaled wearily. The men in command didn't have his ideas, his daring or his youth. The army needed that. France needed that, but he found himself in an office still distant from the theatres of war he longed to be a part of. He rolled the quill gently between his thumb and forefinger and continued to gaze into the thick shadows.

A knock on the door startled him from his musings.

'Come in,' he called, the quill still poised between his fingers.

The soldier who stepped inside the room saluted smartly and stood to attention.

'What is it, Sergeant?'

'There is someone to see you, sir,' the sergeant informed him.

'Is it important?'

The sergeant looked bemused for a second.

'Bring them in,' Bonaparte ordered and glanced down at the piece of paper before him, waiting as he heard the sound of hushed voices and footsteps in the corridor outside. Only when he heard the sergeant's voice again did he look up.

'Your visitor, sir.'

Bonaparte looked at the newcomer, a flicker of surprise crossing his face.

The boy facing him was in his early teens. A tall youth dressed in a dark blue jacket and white breeches.

He removed the bicorn hat he'd been wearing as Bonaparte ran appraising eyes over him. Then, as Bonaparte watched, the boy saluted. Sharply, smartly and correctly.

Bonaparte nodded towards the sergeant who took a step back, closed the door and left the boy alone with the general.

'I'm sorry to disturb you, General Bonaparte.'

'You know me?'

'All of Paris knows you, sir,' the boy said.

'But I do not know *you*.'

'My name is Eugène de Beauharnais, sir. You knew my father.'

Bonaparte nodded slowly. 'I knew *of* him,' he said. 'He was President of the Constituent Assembly at one time, wasn't he?'

'And Commander of the Army of the Rhine, sir. His name was—'

'Alexandre de Beauharnais. He was executed last year.'

'He was murdered by Robespierre, sir,' the boy announced defiantly.

'Executed by the State.'

'We quibble over terms, sir. It was political murder.'

'There have been lots of deaths in France in the last few years, whether they were murders or executions depends upon your political viewpoint.'

'Robespierre ordered the execution of my father, supposedly because of his military failings. He ordered my mother imprisoned too. She would have been executed if Robespierre hadn't been overthrown.'

'What happened to her dossier? All political prisoners have dossiers on them drawn up.'

'It was stolen, sir. Stolen and disposed of.'

'By whom?'

'I don't know who stole it but it was disposed of by Delperch de la Bussière, the actor. He ate it.'

'Ate it?' Bonaparte said incredulously, a slight grin flickering on his lips.

'He performed the feat for many people, he saved many lives that way,' Eugène continued. 'It was the only way to save my mother, sir.'

Bonaparte put down the quill, reached for his wine glass and sipped at the claret.

'So what has the death of your father to do with me?' he asked. 'I had no part in it.'

'I know that, sir, I didn't mean to imply that you did, but you have my father's sword.'

'*I* have his sword?' Bonaparte said in bewilderment.

'The Directory decreed that the citizens of Paris were to give up all weapons. My father's sword was taken. I'm sure you'll agree, sir, that a sword is no use to a dead man.'

'Quite so. How may I help you?'

'I wish my father's sword returned, sir. For myself and for my mother. We wish to honour his memory.'

'An admirable sentiment. Was it your mother who sent you here to beg for your father's sword?'

'I haven't come to beg, sir,' Eugène said defiantly. 'I came to *ask you* as a soldier. I thought you would understand, a general faced by the *son* of a general. I realise that you know the meaning of honour. My father too was an honourable man. Neither I nor my mother wants his memory trodden into the dirt, even if some do.'

'And what is your mother's name?'

'Joséphine de Beauharnais.'

'How old are you, boy?'

'Fourteen, sir. I hope you will forgive the intrusion of a child.'

Bonaparte got to his feet, walked around the desk and stood close to the boy. He extended one hand and placed it on the boy's shoulder.

'Your father was a soldier and, very obviously, his blood runs through your veins,' he said. 'You will have his sword.'

The boy dropped to one knee, took Bonaparte's hand and kissed it. The general felt tears against his flesh and heard the boy's muted whimperings.

'Stand up,' he said softly, helping the boy to his feet.

He tilted the boy's chin upward and wiped the tears away with his fingers. 'Your mother should be proud of you,' he said, smiling.

'Thank you, sir.' Eugène drew himself up to attention again.

'Have you other family?'

'A sister, Hortense.'

Bonaparte nodded. 'Go back to your family now,' he said. 'Come to me again and I will present you with your father's sword.'

Eugène saluted then bowed before leaving, closing the door quietly behind him. As Bonaparte sat back down behind his desk he heard the boy's footsteps echoing away down the corridor.

The candle had all but burned out. Bonaparte picked up the quill and again turned it slowly between thumb and forefinger. The word was that Joséphine de Beauharnais was the mistress of Paul Barras. Supposedly she had been the mistress of at least two other members of the Directory. What charms this woman must have.

He smiled and consulted his pocket watch, then dipped the quill in the ink and resumed writing.

CHAPTER 13

Lausard awoke with a start when he felt the hand on his shoulder. He sat up, blinking myopically in the gloom of the barrack room. He saw Rocheteau crouching beside him and realised that his had been the hand that had disturbed him.

Alongside the thief was Giresse. As far as Lausard could see, the other men were asleep, a chorus of grunts and snores filling the room.

'What's wrong?' Lausard asked.

'We've had an idea,' Rocheteau told him, hooking a thumb in the direction of Giresse. 'Joubert's right. The food they've been giving us isn't fit for pigs. I say we go and get some that's more suited to our tastes. There's a farm about a mile from here. Where there's a farm there's food.'

Lausard nodded and scrambled nimbly but quietly to his feet.

The three men made their way quickly through the barrack room, passing others who slept as soundly as they could on straw pallets. A huge man with a thick moustache lay nearest the door, his snores rattling throughout the building. As the three men passed him he grunted, rubbed his nose then rolled on to his side. The man beside him also stirred and Lausard paused for a moment, looking down at him, waiting for him to open his eyes. He didn't.

There were no sentries at the doors of the barrack room. Peering out, the three men could see across the parade ground towards the main gates. Either side of the gates two dismounted dragoons stood at attention. Two more walked their horses across the parade ground and disappeared around a corner towards the stables.

'We can get out the back way,' Rocheteau said with assurance and slipped out first.

Thick banks of cloud covered the moon and provided the three men with enough shadows to cover them. They moved swiftly through the gloom, ducking low, running between two barracks towards the rear wall of the compound.

When they reached it, Rocheteau stopped, clasped his fingers together and offered a leg-up to his companions. Lausard accepted the offer first, hauling himself up and on to the top of the wall. He looked out as far as he could into the countryside but saw nothing. There was a dirt track running around the perimeter of the compound and he could smell fresh horse droppings in the air. Dragoons obviously patrolled this outer area too; when they might return the three men could only guess.

'Hurry,' Lausard urged, dropping down on the other side of the wall, watching as his two companions scrambled over after him.

As Rocheteau hit the ground he hissed in pain.

'My ankle,' he grunted, shaking his foot, checking that he'd done no damage. 'I landed heavily.'

'Shut up,' Lausard snapped, holding up a hand for silence.

All three of them heard it in the stillness of the night. The unmistakable jingle of bridles. There were horses close by.

They bolted for a small copse of trees on the other side of the dirt track, ducking down amongst the thick underbrush.

A moment later two dragoons trotted past, the men chatting and laughing.

They disappeared into the night, the sounds of their harnesses dying away.

'All right,' Lausard said, and the three men turned and sprinted away from the compound, only slowing down when they found themselves in even deeper woodland. Satisfied that they were well clear of detection, they slowed down to a walk, Rocheteau sucking in deep breaths and banging his chest.

'I hope you're right about this farm,' Lausard said. 'Don't you think the others might have found it by now? Delpierre's probably had it scraped clean weeks ago.'

'I bet that bastard's not starving like we are,' said Rocheteau, pushing some low branches aside.

'If they catch us,' Giresse offered, 'they'll think we're deserting.'

'Deserting to what?' Lausard grunted, 'a life back on the streets of Paris, thieving for a living, scraping around for scraps that even a dog wouldn't touch.'

'There's nothing wrong with thieving,' Rocheteau said reproachfully.

The other two men laughed.

'Anyway, what's foraging if it's not thieving?' Rocheteau asked. 'Soldiers take from the land and it's called foraging. I take from other people and it's called thieving.'

'How long did it take you to work that one out?' Lausard smiled.

'He's got a point,' added Giresse, chuckling.

'The whole army's full of thieves,' Rocheteau continued. 'And I'm not just talking about stealing food.'

The other two looked puzzled.

'Officers steal,' Rocheteau clarified. 'Have you ever seen a poor one? They steal land, they steal gold.'

'It comes with the position,' Lausard explained. 'They call it the spoils of war.'

'I'm not interested in gold or land,' Giresse said.

'We *know* what *you're* interested in,' Rocheteau said and grinned, gesturing with his hands to illustrate the shape of a woman's body.

All three of them laughed, the sound abruptly shut off as they drew closer to the edge of the wood. The first of the outer buildings of the farm was less than fifty yards away and they could hear movement. Lausard was the first to spot something moving in the gloom and he jabbed a finger in that direction.

'Pigs,' he whispered.

'Pork,' Rocheteau echoed.

They advanced stealthily across the open space between the woods and a low fence which formed the perimeter of the farm. But as they drew nearer several of the pigs began snorting and squealing and, before any of the men could react, they had bolted, scurrying off around a corner.

Lausard led the chase, vaulting the fence and pursuing the fleeing pigs, his companions close behind him.
The pigs ran into the yard and Lausard glanced around
quickly, seeing a number of other outbuildings and a
farmhouse. No lights burned in the windows.

Hearing a squeal behind him he saw that Giresse
had caught one of the pigs and was trying to hold it by
the head while it attempted to struggle free. Rocheteau
ran across to help him, holding a rock the size of his
fist. He brought it down with stunning force on the
pig's skull and the animal dropped immediately.

Lausard left his companions to their triumph and
headed towards the farmhouse, noticing that the windows were open, one hanging uselessly from its hinges.
The place looked deserted and gave off an air of
neglect. A dead dog lay close to the front door. Several
lumps of wood were strewn across the path leading to
the front door, obviously cut as fuel days or even weeks
earlier. Lausard, suddenly feeling exposed without any
weapons, knelt and picked up one of the heavy pieces,
hefting it before him like a club. He pushed against the
front door and found that it resisted.

'Alain, come on, we've got what we need,' called
Rocheteau, holding up the dead pig as if it were some
kind of trophy. But Lausard ignored him, pushing
harder against the front door which finally swung
open. He stepped inside, struck by the smell of damp.

The room was small, devoid of everything except
one battered wooden chair. Beyond was what had
clearly been the kitchen, pots and pans strewn over the
stone floor. A rat scurried across the floor, its claws
clicking on the slabs. Lausard watched as it ran over a
metal ring in the floor, rusted and neglected like the rest

of the house, and Lausard wondered if it might lead down to a cellar. He knelt down to open it.

'What are you doing?'

Lausard didn't turn when he heard Rocheteau's voice, instead he concentrated on pulling at the rusty metal ring.

'I doubt if there's a wine cellar down there,' Giresse said, ambling into the house, peering round to see if there was anything worth taking.

Lausard pulled the cellar hatch open. An over-whelming odour of decay rose up from the hole.

'There's nothing down there you'd want.'

All three men spun round as they heard the voice behind them.

Standing in the doorway was a small figure, no more than five feet tall, holding a gun which was aimed at the men. Lausard could see from the massive, yawning mouth and short barrel that the weapon was a blunderbuss; the figure brandishing it was a boy in his early teens.

'Why can't you leave us alone?' he said.

'Be careful with that, boy,' said Rocheteau, taking a step forward, a finger pointed towards the blunderbuss.

'What's in the cellar?' Lausard asked.

The boy swallowed hard. 'My family,' he said, his voice cracking. 'My father, mother and two sisters. My mother and sisters were raped and then killed. My father was shot trying to save them.'

'Who did it?' Lausard prompted.

'Soldiers,' the boy said. 'Soldiers like you.'

'Were they wearing these uniforms?' Lausard pulled at his white jacket with one hand.

'Some were. Others wore red, some had no uniforms at all. They came here a week ago. They robbed us. I hid in one of the barns. I've been there ever since. I came back in only to hide my family's bodies. I didn't know where to go or what to do. That's why I stayed here.'

'White uniforms, red uniforms,' Giresse mused. 'Deserters?'

Lausard nodded. 'We're not here to hurt you,' he reassured the boy. 'And the men who killed your family weren't soldiers. We *are*. Let us help you.'

'How?' the boy said.

'Come with us.'

Rocheteau shot his companion a wary glance. 'Are you insane? What the hell are we going to do with him? Eat him too?'

'We can't leave him here,' Lausard said, his eyes still on the boy. 'How old are you, son?'

'Thirteen.'

'Alain, we came here looking for food, not for orphans,' Rocheteau said.

'There's nothing here for you, boy,' Lausard said, one eye still on the barrel of the blunderbuss. 'Come with us. We'll help you.'

'The same way you were helping yourselves to whatever you could find here?' the boy said defiantly. 'The men who killed my family stole too. I saw you kill the pig. What else are you going to take?' Tears began to form in his eyes. 'You won't be able to have my mother's wedding ring because the others took that. They cut off her finger when they couldn't get the ring off by pulling.'

'We just wanted food,' Rocheteau said.

'We're hungry,' Giresse echoed.

'Come with us,' Lausard persisted. 'Join us.'

'We're supposed to be cavalry,' Rocheteau reminded his colleague. 'We don't have drummer-boys.'

'We have trumpeters though, don't we?' Lausard said. 'He can learn. We've learned to ride and to handle weapons. Why can't *he* learn too?'

'And what's Delpierre going to say?' Giresse enquired.

'Who cares?' Lausard said. Then, to the young lad: 'What's your name, boy?'

'Gaston.'

'I lost my family too,' Lausard told him. 'I know how you feel. I had no one to turn to, but we will help you. I swear it.' He took a couple of paces forward, hand outstretched.

The boy lifted the blunderbuss.

'Give it to me, Gaston.'

The boy's finger touched the trigger.

'Let us help you,' Lausard persisted.

He was close enough now to see tears coursing down the boy's cheeks.

Rocheteau and Giresse also took a step forward, their eyes fixed on the wavering barrel of the weapon.

'Gaston,' Lausard whispered.

The boy sniffed and allowed Lausard to pull the blunderbuss from his grasp. As he let go he felt a strong arm envelope him and he pressed his face against Lausard's chest, sobbing quietly.

'One pig, one boy,' said Giresse, smiling wanly.

'A trumpeter,' Rocheteau added.

'Another mouth to feed,' Giresse said and sighed.

Lausard ruffled the boy's hair and smiled down at him.

'Another soldier,' he whispered.

The boy stood beside the entrance to the cellar, head bowed and, watched by the three men, he whispered a prayer before shutting the trapdoor. It was like closing a tomb.

Lausard watched him, finally sliding his arm around the boy's shoulders and guiding him out of the farm-house.

Rocheteau and Giresse followed, the former carrying the dead pig.

'And how do you propose to cook that when we get back?' asked Giresse glancing at the limp carcass.

'You let me worry about that,' Rocheteau told him. 'We'll be dining on pork for the next couple of days and no one will be complaining then, will they?'

'The men who killed your family,' Giresse said to the boy, 'what else did they take?'

'They took most of the animals, even the horses,' Gaston told him. 'They killed the chickens first and ate them.'

'How many of these men were there?' Lausard asked.

'Six,' the boy said. 'They smelled bad.'

Lausard smiled. 'A bit like us, eh?'

The boy wrinkled his nose and nodded.

'They could have been regulars,' Rocheteau suggested. 'I hear that men are deserting by the *regiment* in some places.'

'I thought the Army of the Interior was meant to deal with them,' Giresse said.

'They are,' Lausard said. 'We're fighting on three fronts and yet twenty thousand men are tied up within the borders of France chasing deserters, shooting Royalists and trying to find new recruits. It's a waste of troops.'

The trio of men and the boy made their way back through the woods, picking their way over fallen branches. Rocheteau stumbled once and went sprawling, dropping the dead pig.

Giresse looked on, laughing.

'Shut up and help me up,' Rocheteau snapped, accepting the helping hand which his colleague extended. The thief snatched up the dead pig once again and threw it across his shoulder as if he was carrying a piece of baggage.

The copse ahead of them masked the road so the men slowed down, knowing they were close to the compound once more. The moon was still hidden behind thick, scudding banks of cloud so they were well covered by the gloom but, nevertheless, they approached with caution.

Lausard was the first to set foot on the dirt track which ran around the perimeter wall. He looked to his left and right then waved the others forward.

'Stop!'

The shout echoed through the stillness of the night and, suddenly, the air seemed to fill with the sound of pounding hooves.

Six dragoons galloped into sight, three from each side. It was as if the horsemen had emerged from the very darkness itself. As they reined in their mounts, Lausard saw that two of them had their carbines pressed to their shoulders, aimed at him and his companions. One of the others had his sword drawn.

Something familiar struck him about one of the men. He was sucking on a pipe.

Captain Deschamps walked his horse towards them. 'What are you doing out of the compound?'

'Foraging, sir,' Lausard said, pointing towards the pig which Rocheteau held up proudly.

'And the boy?' Deschamps continued.

'We found him in a farmhouse back there,' Lausard replied. 'He wants to join us.'

Deschamps puffed on his pipe for a moment, eyeing the three men and the boy. Then spat out a piece of tobacco.

'Lausard, I want to see you in my quarters in ten minutes,' the captain said finally. He pulled on his reins and began to wheel his horse.

'What about the pig, sir?' Rocheteau volunteered.

'Give half to these men,' Deschamps said, nodding towards the dragoons. 'You are all in the same regiment. You share your provisions.'

Rocheteau opened his mouth to protest but Lausard shot him a warning glance.

'Ten minutes, Lausard,' said Deschamps. 'The boy can stay.'

'I thought as a trumpeter, sir,' Lausard offered.

'Can you ride, boy?'

Gaston nodded.

Deschamps looked carefully at the teenager.

Gaston met the officer's gaze, noticing the slightest flicker of a smile on his lips.

Deschamps rode off accompanied by two of the dragoons.

Of the three that remained, one, a large man with a thick moustache, slid off his horse and advanced towards the waiting men.

'Half, the Captain said,' the dragoon reminded

Rocheteau, pointing at the pig. 'Come on, put it down.'

Rocheteau reluctantly dropped the dead pig in front of him then looked up as he heard the hiss of steel. The dragoon had drawn his sword. He prodded the carcass with the point.

'It's dead,' Rocheteau grunted. 'You're safe.'

'Funny man,' said the dragoon with irritation.

'Ten francs says you can't split it with one stroke,' Lausard challenged.

'You haven't got the ten francs to bet with,' the dragoon said mockingly.

'All right,' Lausard continued, 'if you split the pig with one stroke you keep it all. If *I* split it with one stroke, *we* keep it all.'

'Go on, Charnier,' one of the other horsemen coaxed. 'Do it.'

'You're on.' The dragoon stepped forward, aiming the blade and raising the sharpened steel.

He brought the sword down with incredible power but the blade smashed into the pig's spine, sheared off and merely sliced a large chunk from the hide.

Lausard held out his hand for the sword which Charnier passed to him, watching as the young man raised the blade, paused a second then brought it down with stunning ferocity.

The blade struck across the spine splitting the pig cleanly in two.

'No one said which *direction* it had to be cut,' Lausard said smugly, tossing the sabre back to Charnier.

The dragoon looked at him angrily for a moment then his face creased into a smile. Behind him, his companions were laughing too. Charnier slapped him on the shoulder.

'Come on,' he said. 'We'll take you to Deschamps's quarters.'

The room was humble. As he looked around Deschamps's quarters, Lausard took in its contents: a desk, two chairs, a wooden bed with a mattress very similar to the one he and his colleagues slept on and, in one corner, a tin bath. Perhaps the only concession to luxury. The small dwelling place was lit by the dull orange glow of four candles.

'Sit down, Lausard,' Deschamps said, nodding towards the other chair, watching as Lausard did so.

'I trust you solved the problem with the pig?' the captain said and smiled.

'I can explain that, sir . . .' Lausard began.

'I didn't ask you to explain it, Lausard. The entire French army has survived over the years by its foraging skills. Now we move too quickly to be fed by a supply train. Our men carry three days' rations at most. Did you know that Austrian troops carry nine days' rations?' He smiled again. 'The French army is not dependent on the commissary but on the land. You showed initiative. You have since you got here. You've adapted well but I thought you would.'

'Meaning what, sir?'

'Come, come, Lausard. I *know* who you are, *what* you are. You told me back in the Conciergerie. Surely your memory isn't that short.'

'You know *about* me, sir, but you don't know me.'

'I know what I've seen. You ride better than most of my men, you use a sword as well as any man I've ever seen, you handle a carbine and a pistol with ease. If I had a regiment of men like you, men with your abilities, then I would be very happy. If I had a *division* of men like you then this war would be over very soon.'

'Thank you, sir.'

'I'm merely telling you the truth, Lausard. The others have seen it too. The men alongside you respect your abilities, they look up to you.' He smiled. 'These men you despise.'

'I never said that,' Lausard corrected him. 'I don't despise them.'

'Lausard. The blood of a different class runs through your veins. Not the same blood as the men you share your life with now, not the same class. You said yourself that if they knew your background they'd probably carry you to the guillotine themselves. Your family were aristocrats. Enemies to all the men in this training depot, enemies to all the men in this army. You are their enemy, they just don't know it.'

'And do you intend to tell them, sir?'

'I told you before, I don't care about your past, I don't care what you were. All I know is that you are a fine soldier and France needs men like you. I just find it ironic that you are so highly thought of by the very men who would have called for your blood two years ago. It seems too that you have an actor's skill for hiding your true feelings. Don't try to tell me you don't find these men abhorrent. They are beneath you, Lausard, and yet, around them, you act like the gutter rats that they are.'

'Perhaps I am more comfortable in the gutter, sir,' Lausard said.

'Perhaps,' mused Deschamps, pouring himself a glass of wine from the bottle on the table. He filled another glass and pushed it towards Lausard who accepted hesitantly.

'The other day,' Deschamps said, 'why didn't you kill Sergeant Delpierre? I saw the fight. You could have killed him. Why didn't you?'

'Are you sorry I didn't, sir?'

'A question countered with a question – don't you ever give a straight answer?' He sipped his wine.

'Which answer did you want to hear, sir?'

'You could have killed him but you didn't. You showed strength of mind as well as fighting ability. You have many qualities to be admired, Lausard. Be careful they do not trip you up.'

Lausard sipped at the wine, his gaze drawn to one of the candle flames. He watched it flicker in the slight breeze.

'Did you expect me to hate these men, sir?' he asked finally.

'I could have understood your dislike of them,' Deschamps told him. 'After all, you have more in common with our enemies than you do with our own soldiers. Britain, Austria and Prussia all retain monarchies. *Their* aristocracies have not been wiped out by those they formerly ruled. The Directory would have us believe that part of our mission in this war is to bring fraternity to countries ruled by monarchies.' He raised his glass in mock salute. 'We are on a mission of mercy and liberation, Lausard.'

'Excuse me if I do not join you in the toast, sir,' said the younger man.

A heavy silence descended.

Then Deschamps spoke. 'Each dragoon regiment is made up of three squadrons. Those squadrons need

NCOs. I am making you a sergeant in your squadron, Lausard. Pick two corporals to serve with you.'

Lausard looked momentarily stunned by the officer's declaration.

'This regiment leaves for Italy in two days,' Deschamps continued. 'The training is nearly over. All we can teach you we have. The next time you draw swords or fire carbines it will be at men, not straw dummies. And those men will fight back. Some of us will die, perhaps *all* of us. Who knows?'

'Who cares?' Lausard said flatly.

'Quite so, *Sergeant* Lausard.' Deschamps saluted.

Lausard rose and returned the gesture.

'You may go,' Deschamps told him, turning his back.

He heard Lausard's footsteps then the door closing behind him.

CHAPTER 14

'I should hate you,' murmured Joséphine de Beauharnais, tracing patterns across the sheets with slender fingers.

Napoleon Bonaparte handed her another glass of wine and slipped back beneath the covers with her, feeling the warmth of her nakedness beside him. He remained propped up on one elbow, staring down at her, intoxicated by her beauty, marvelling at the perfection of her features and the dusky hue of her skin, so rich against the perfectly white sheets. Her shiny black hair was spread across the pillow and he continued to gaze at her as she turned the glass between her fingers, eyes closed momentarily.

Gently, Bonaparte drew back the sheet, pulling it down to reveal the smooth swell of her breasts and the flatness of her stomach with the tiny triangle of dark hair at its base. Eyes still closed, she smiled, aware of his appraising look. She drew one long, slender leg up and nudged him with her knee.

As if he were wrapping some priceless artifact, after

first pulling down the sheets he then replaced them, hiding her exquisite body from view for the time being.

'Why should you hate me?' he said.

'You had my husband executed,' she said, touching his cheek with her hand, brushing his skin lightly.

'I had nothing to do with your husband's death.'

'The men you represent did.'

'They were politicians. I am a soldier.'

'So was my husband.'

He traced the outline of her lower lip with his finger.

'You fight for the politicians who had him executed,' Joséphine whispered, flicking her tongue out to lick the roving digit.

'I fight for France,' he said softly.

'You're a soldier in their pay.'

'Then feel free to hate me, but if you do then you have a strange way of showing it.'

Joséphine smiled. 'My son called you an honourable man.'

'He's a fine boy. A credit to you and your husband.'

'But was he right? Are you an honourable man? I know you are many things. Powerful, ambitious and influential.'

'Is that why you are here? Paul Barras had those qualities – is that why you were his too?'

'I was never his,' she snapped.

'You were his mistress. What would he say if he could see you now?'

'I don't care what he would say. What could he do to me? Or to you? You are the one with the power now.' She leaned forward and kissed him. Bonaparte felt her slide closer to him, her lean body pressing against him.

He enveloped her in his arms, gripping her to him. His hand looked almost iridescent against the tan of her skin. She was like some glorious living carving, hewn from the most supple bough. A monument to the genius of a master. And she was his.

'Why did you come to me in the beginning?' he asked when they finally broke their embrace.

'I wanted to thank you for returning my husband's sword. It meant so much, especially to my son. He wept when he held it. Perhaps he wept for the memory of his father and so many others like him.'

'He told me how you escaped the guillotine.'

'My family had been rich. To Robespierre I was an enemy, just like my husband. I was lucky to escape with my life.'

'And now you have that life, what do you intend to do with it? Would you share it? With me?'

She laughed and the sound was almost musical to Bonaparte's ears. He gazed at her with ill-disguised awe.

'I leave for Italy . . .'

She put a finger to his lips to silence him.

'Don't talk to me of war,' she said softly. 'I do not wish to know of it.'

'Of what shall I speak then?'

'Of love.'

Again that musical laugh. Again she kissed him.

'I know more of war than love,' he said, with a hint of sadness in his voice.

'Soldiers need to love,' Joséphine said.

'Love is a dangerous thing.' He gazed into her eyes and felt as if he were drowning there; but, mesmerised, he didn't attempt to fight the feeling. If this was love then he surrendered to it, allowed himself to be enveloped by it.

Joséphine saw that look in his eyes and she smiled. It was a smile of triumph.

CHAPTER 15

There were two bodies in the road. One was naked, the other retained some semblance of dignity, its trousers still intact.

Captain Deschamps held up a hand to halt the column and turned to Lausard who was in the front line of the cavalry detachment. He nodded towards the corpses and Lausard rode ahead, joined by Rostov who was having trouble controlling his horse; the animal, like most of the men in the unit, was troubled by the intense heat. A lesser horseman than the Russian might well have been forced to abandon the creature but Rostov was as good a rider as anyone in the regiment and, as he and Lausard trotted their horses along the dusty road, the chestnut pony he rode gradually calmed down.

The heat was almost intolerable. In a cloudless sky the sun had risen to its zenith and burned there like a massive blazing cannon ball. Despite the fact that they were on the coast road from Nice to Savona, currently eight miles south of Albenga, no sea breeze had blessed their passage. Nothing had eased the tortuous journey and the murderous heat. Italy in April was as hot and dry as any desert, the men had discovered. Their uniforms did little to help their situation. Their thick, green woollen jackets were buttoned to the neck and the brass helmets grew hot under the burning sun. Most men had removed their usual thick leather gauntlets but most officers retained them.

Inside his own bleached leather breeches, Lausard could feel the sweat running down his legs and he was sure it was puddling in his boots. He glanced across at his companion and noticed how red Rostov's skin was; he'd caught the sun, his fair skin exposed for too long to the searing rays. Flesh was already peeling from his nose and chin. But the Russian ignored the heat as best he could, despite the rivulets of sweat pouring down the side of his face. Every now and then he would wipe the stinging, salty droplets from his eyes with his fingers.

Dust rose in small clouds every time the horses put a hoof on the road, something else which exacerbated the raging thirst suffered by men and horses alike. Lausard had about half a canteen of water left but he was saving it for as long as he could. Rostov had drunk the last of his earlier that morning, allowing his horse to lick some of the precious liquid from his cupped hand. As they rode, the animal's tongue lolled thickly from one corner of its foaming mouth.

Lausard's mount, a powerful black animal, was sweating profusely. Forced to contend with not only the heat but also the weight of its rider and his equipment, it was lathered across much of its front and hindquarters. The horse bucked once, as if anxious to be rid of both but Lausard tugged on the reins to subdue it, bringing it to a halt as he and Rostov reached the bodies.

The Russian dismounted and prodded the naked body with the toe of one boot, flipping the man over on to his back.

'Jesus,' he grunted, looking down at the corpse, waving a hand in front of him as the nauseating stench of decay attacked his nostrils.

There was a wound in the left side of the man's stomach and it was still choked with congealed blood, but what caused the Russian to recoil was the cut that had clearly killed the man. His throat had been slit from ear to ear, the wound gaping open like the gills of a fish.

He checked the other body and saw that it too had had its throat cut.

'They've been dead a couple of days,' Lausard said, gazing down at the corpses. The heat had accelerated their putrefaction.

Rostov swung himself back on to his horse while Lausard signalled Deschamps to bring the column on. The unit moved forward at a walk.

'Do you think they're our men?' asked Joubert, looking towards the tableau ahead.

'This far south, they must be,' Giresse said.

'Deserters probably,' Charvet added. 'Probably died of thirst.'

'Like hell,' Delacor said scornfully. 'The "Barbets" got them I'll bet.'

'What are "Barbets"?' Joubert asked.

'Local guerrilla fighters,' Delacor explained. 'You never hear or see them until they slit your throat.' He looked at Joubert and drew a hand swiftly across his own neck. 'Keep your eyes peeled, fat man.'

The head of the column drew level with the dead

bodies and many men glanced at the corpses with a combination of revulsion and morbid curiosity. Some looked on with relief. At least it wasn't *them* lying there.

Deschamps detailed two men to bury the bodies, telling them to rejoin the column as quickly as they could.

'Rather them than me,' Delacor offered, watching as the dragoons pulled the bodies to one side of the road. 'If those murdering bastards come back there'll be four graves there, not two.'

'Why don't they come out in the open and fight like men?' Tabor said.

'They're too clever for that, you half-wit,' snapped Delacor. 'They operate in small groups, keep to the hills and the woods, and pick their moment.' He looked around. 'They could be watching us right now.'

The ground to their left sloped upwards sharply about two hundred yards beyond, the hillside rising steeply. Outcrops of trees clung to the inclines as if gripping on with their roots. Elsewhere rocks stuck out from the slopes, baked hot by the scorching sun.

Gaston looked around and felt a shiver run up the back of his neck despite the heat. He was wearing the scarlet jacket of a trumpeter which was a couple of sizes too big for him, as was his helmet which he had to push back constantly because it kept slipping down over his eyes. His breeches were also too big and he'd been forced to pad them out around the backside with balled-up pieces of material ripped from an old shirt Lausard had given him. But this did have its advantages. He didn't feel as saddle-sore as some of the men who rode with him. Many a trooper shifted uncomfortably in his saddle, aware all too readily of the blisters that had formed on the insides of his thighs and on his buttocks.

Up ahead, the road turned sharply to the right and the column reduced speed as the hills rose to obscure their view of what lay around the bend.

Roussard was conscious of the sword bumping against his boot as he rode. He wondered how long it would be before he had to use it. As the column slowed down he glanced across at Moreau who was aware of his gaze. He tried to smile reassuringly but the gesture failed, coming across more as a crooked smirk. Moreau crossed himself

'Take two men and ride ahead,' Deschamps said to Lausard. 'See if you can link up with the scouts you sent out earlier. We'll continue along this road.'

Lausard saluted, motioned to Rostov and Giresse and the three of them rode off down the road, great clouds of choking dust rising into the baking air behind them. Deschamps watched them go, disappearing around the bend in the road which wound through the hills and rocks like a parched tongue. Within minutes they were out of sight.

The column kept moving.

'Can't we find some water somewhere?' asked Giresse. 'I don't know who's going to drop first, me or my horse.' He patted the animal's lathered neck.

'Hopefully Rocheteau and the others will have found food *and* water,' Rostov said.

'There won't be much food around here,' Lausard responded, with an air of certainty. 'A combination of the locals and our men foraging . . .' He allowed the sentence to trail off, shrugging his shoulders.

'Where's the nearest village?' Rostov asked, wiping sweat from his face.

'A mile up ahead,' Lausard said, pointing to a range of low hills. 'My guess is that's where Rocheteau and the others are.'

'Talk of the Devil,' murmured Giresse and nodded in the direction of a lone figure on the crest of the ridge.

From the uniform and the horsehair mane which flew out behind the speeding rider the men could tell that the newcomer was a dragoon. He was riding hard, hunched low over his saddle.

'It's Bonet,' Lausard said under his breath, squinting to make out the features of the speeding horseman.

The ex-schoolmaster reined in his horse, pulling so hard on the leather that the animal reared up for a second.

'What's the hurry, schoolmaster?' Giresse said, smiling, but the smile faded as he saw the look of concern on his companion's face.

'The village is occupied,' Bonet said breathlessly.

'Austrians or Piedmontese?' Lausard asked.

'Frenchmen. Deserters,' Bonet said. 'They've got Rocheteau and Carbonne.'

'What do you mean got *them*?' Lausard prompted. 'Are they dead?'

Bonet could hardly suck in the breath to speak. He swallowed as best he could with a parched throat.

'We found the village,' he said. 'It looked deserted. There was food there, water too. Rice, some bread. We were loading up for ourselves when they appeared from some of the houses. We didn't have time to get back to our horses.'

'How did *you* get out?' Lausard queried.

'I ran for it while Rocheteau and Carbonne held them off,' the ex-schoolmaster said, still gasping for air. His face was sheathed in sweat, the skin crimson.

'How long ago did this happen?' Lausard pressed, watching as his colleague removed his brass helmet and ran a hand through his sopping hair. 'We didn't hear any shots.'

'There was none,' Bonet explained. 'They have muskets but no powder. They attacked us with bayonets.'

'How many are there?'

'A dozen, maybe more.'

Lausard leaned forward in his saddle and gripped Bonet by the arm.

'I don't want to know how many there *might* be,' he said. 'Think. How many? Exactly.'

Bonet nodded. 'Fourteen that I saw, that I counted,' he said finally.

'All carrying muskets?' Lausard persisted.

'Six have muskets,' Bonet told him. 'One, I think he's the leader, has a sword. The others are using bayonets.'

Lausard sat back in his saddle and looked towards the top of the ridge.

'Do we go back for the rest of the column?' Giresse asked.

Lausard shook his head. 'Is there any cover on the reverse slope?' he asked Bonet. 'Could we reach the village without them seeing us?'

'On foot, yes,' Bonet proclaimed. 'But if you go in, they'll kill us. They'll certainly kill Rocheteau and Carbonne. We couldn't reach them in time.'

'How many are guarding them?' Lausard demanded.

'Just two.'

'Four against fourteen, Alain,' said Giresse, falter-ingly.

'Are you a gambling man, Rostov?' Lausard asked.

'Those odds sound fine to me,' the Russian said and grinned.

'If there were fourteen *women* in that village you'd be in there quickly enough,' Lausard said to Giresse.

'That's true,' he said, chuckling nervously.

'Come on,' said Lausard and urged his horse on to a walk.

'Alain, they're Frenchmen,' said Bonet. 'You're going to kill Frenchmen?'

'Do you think they'd have had second thoughts about killing you?' Lausard pulled one of the pistols from its holster on his saddle and loaded it, replacing it carefully as the others looked on.

'They're soldiers like us,' Bonet protested.

'They're not like *us*,' Lausard snapped. 'And if you were down there, Bonet, would you expect Rocheteau or Carbonne to come back for *you*?'

There was a heavy silence, broken only by the low panting and occasional whinnying of the horses.

Bonet finally nodded.

'Come on,' said Lausard.

The tiny collection of dwellings which Lausard sur-veyed from the cover of thick bushes barely merited the description of village but, nevertheless, the huddle of buildings was called Villa Borghese. Or so a sign proudly displayed in what passed for the village square proclaimed. The square also had a well, but from where he was Lausard could see that the bucket was gone and the cranking handle rusty from lack of use. The well, like the village itself, had dried up long ago. Those who once called it home had left, either having fled or been driven out by any one of three armies currently in the area.

However, it was not empty now and Lausard carefully scrutinised those who inhabited its tiny square. He could see ten men, all dressed in blue jackets. Infantry. Another had removed his thick tunic. They were, without exception, shoeless and filthy. Their knapsacks bulged with whatever food they'd been able to collect and also with bounty they'd secured on their trek through Italy. Though most of it, he guessed, had been acquired since they fled from their regiment.

One of the men was busily wrapping pieces of cloth around his feet and Lausard could see that there was blood soaking through the makeshift bandages. Another had his arm in a sling. A third sported a bandage which covered most of the left side of his face and head.

Three, Lausard mused, who shouldn't offer too much resistance. But where were the rest? Bonet had said there were fourteen of them. Lausard counted again. He saw only ten.

Another, a tall man with a huge thick moustache, emerged from one of the tiny houses, a sword gripped in his fist.

The leader, according to Bonet. He looked fitter and sturdier than his colleagues and, despite the ragged uniform which he wore, the man seemed to exude an air of authority. As well as the bulging knapsack slung around his back he also carried several small leather pouches which hung from his belt. Lausard guessed that these contained more plunder.

Only one of the men was actually carrying his musket. The other Charlevilles were propped up against the side of the wall, bayonets glistening in the sunlight.

'Where are Rocheteau and Carbonne?' Lausard whispered.

Bonet pointed towards the house from which the tall man had emerged.

'So, there are three more of them in there,' Lausard mused.

He and Bonet were no more than twenty yards from the house, well hidden by thickly planted trees and tall hedges. Giresse and Rostov should now be around the other side of the house. The horses had been tethered about a hundred yards back in the trees, out of earshot. Each of the men carried his carbine, one of his pistols and his sword. The two horses which belonged to Rocheteau and Carbonne were tethered outside one of Villa Borghese's tiny dwellings with a young lad no older than fourteen watching them. Lausard looked at his companion and Bonet met his gaze and nodded.

They sprang to their feet as one.

Both ran towards the square, bursting from the cover of the trees.

The blue-clad infantry seemed stunned by the sudden intrusion. Two of them raised their hands in surrender immediately.

Bonet paused, swung the carbine up to his shoulder and fired.

The .70 lead ball struck one of the men in the shoulder, shattered his collar-bone and ploughed on deep into his back. Blood spurted from the wound and the man screamed, dropping to his knees, clutching at the wound.

Lausard came upon his first two opponents and used his pistol against the first, sticking the barrel against the man's face and firing. The man fell backwards as Lausard pulled his sword free of its scabbard and aimed a mighty backhand slash at the other deserter, who instinctively raised his hand to protect his face. The razor-sharp steel sliced effortlessly through the hand, between thumb and forefinger, sending blood spraying into the air. The man shrieked and turned to run but Lausard drove the sword into his stomach, feeling the muscles tighten around the blade as he first punched it in then ripped it free. The man fell at his feet.

Of the remaining deserters, six immediately ran for the trees, anxious to escape these maniacs who were attacking them. One ran straight into Rostov who was scurrying into the square from the opposite direction.

The Russian cut his foe across the face with his sword, slicing away one eyebrow and most of the forehead around it, but the man kept running.

Three men emerged from the house and hurtled after their fleeing colleagues.

Giresse aimed his carbine at one but, seeing the man was already more interested in escaping than fighting, he lowered the weapon and advanced towards the tethered horses. The young lad holding them was weeping uncontrollably, transfixed by what had happened.

'Run,' snarled Giresse and the boy did, a dark stain spreading across his groin.

The man with the moustache stood his ground, lifting his sword to confront Lausard, who met his furious gaze.

'Go while you can,' Lausard said forcefully.

The man looked at him then at the other dragoons who were closing in around him. He lowered the sword slightly and reached for one of the pouches fastened to his belt.

'Just go,' Lausard told him. 'I don't want your money.'

'I do,' Giresse interjected, holding out his hand for the pouch.

The man tossed it to him, dropped the sword and ran, disappearing into the woods.

Rostov walked into the house where Bonet had said that Rocheteau and Carbonne were being held. He emerged a moment later with his two colleagues, both of whom had been stripped of their boots and buttons.

Lausard laughed as he saw them.

Bonet meanwhile was staring down at the man he'd shot, inspecting the wound, noticing, with revulsion, that part of the collar-bone was sticking through the flesh. The injured man's face was the colour of rancid butter and he looked imploringly at Bonet for help.

The ex-schoolmaster felt his stomach contract as he continued to gape at the wound in the deserter's shoulder. 'What can we do for him?' Bonet asked, his own face now pale.

'Do for him?' Rocheteau shouted angrily, and he snatched the carbine from Bonet and slammed it into the face of the wounded man with incredible force, smashing his nose, splitting his lips and forehead.

'Stop it!' shrieked Bonet, trying to step between Rocheteau and the injured man but Carbonne pulled him aside, watching as Rocheteau struck again, the next blow cracking the man's skull. The third finished him off.

Rocheteau spat on the body and handed the carbine back to Bonet, who was staring in horror at the body. He turned away and vomited until there was nothing left in his stomach.

'They would have killed us,' Carbonne said, crossing to his horse. He found his own boots stuffed untidily inside his portmanteau. 'They're lucky *I* didn't get my hands on them.'

'We just killed three of our own countrymen,' blurted Bonet. 'Don't you understand that? They weren't Austrians or Russians or Prussians. They were French. Like us.'

'If you feel so strongly about it,' Rocheteau snapped, 'you stay behind and bury them.' He knelt beside one of the bodies and went swiftly through the pockets, pulling out the contents of the knapsack. The search didn't yield much apart from a small bottle of wine and some stale biscuits but it was better than nothing.

'There's rice and bread in one of the houses,' Carbonne said.

'Enough for all of us?' Lausard asked.

'*Some* of us,' Carbonne said.

'How can you talk about food after what we've done?' Bonet said.

'We'll do much worse before this war is over,' Lausard warned him.

'Will it make you feel better if they're buried?' Rocheteau snapped, grabbing the heels of the nearest corpse. 'Right, schoolmaster, I'll lay them to rest.'

He dragged the body to the edge of the well, sat it on the side for a second then pushed it in. There was a second's silence then a loud thump. 'Happier now?'

The other men laughed.

Bonet shook his head in despair.

'Load up and let's get out of here,' Lausard said.

'Have we turned into savages?' Bonet asked imploringly.

'Do you think you weren't before,' snapped Lausard.

Flies were already beginning to buzz around the puddles of blood in the square.

CHAPTER 16

The two men who waited inside General Bonaparte's tent could not have been more different. Diametrically opposed in every aspect ranging from age to social background, they were drawn together by the fact that both were divisional commanders in the Army of Italy. They had nothing more in common. Their only bond was the army.

Jean Mathieu Philibert Serurier was in his fifty-third year. He was a tall gloomy man with a scar on his lip acquired during his thirty-four years service with the old Royal Army before the overthrow of the Bourbons. He had an aristocratic air about him which seemed totally out of place within the new citizen army. He walked agitatedly back and forth before the desk inside the tent, which was strewn with maps and documents. Serurier seemed less interested in those than in the time, as he continually consulted a pocket watch retrieved from his uniform.

His companion inside the tent noticed this constant clock watching and felt compelled to check his own time-piece, wondering what his colleague found so fascinating about the slow advance of the hands around the ornate face of the watch.

Pierre François Charles Augereau was thirty-eight years old, a product of the Paris gutters, like many of the men who served beneath him. He rejoiced in his nickname 'child of the people'; clung to it as if it were some medal of great importance to him, bestowed with affection by his troops. He was even taller than Serurier and, combined with a huge hooked nose, this made him difficult to ignore.

'Staring at that watch isn't going to make the time go any quicker,' he told his companion. 'Leave the bastard thing alone.'

Serurier glanced at him with ill-disguised contempt.

'It's a good job that your abilities as a soldier out-weigh your shortcomings as a gentleman,' said the older officer, making no attempt to conceal the distaste in his tone.

Augereau hawked loudly and spat on the floor.

'That's what I think of gentlemen,' he said. 'Gentlemen have no place in this army. This war is fought by ordinary men.'

'But we are not ordinary men who command them,' Serurier said. 'At least some of us aren't.'

'We are all the same under these uniforms,' the younger man said. 'We all bleed when we're cut. We all go hungry when we don't eat. We all ride the same way. Horses *and* women.'

'You really are quite appalling,' Serurier snapped, glancing again at his watch.

'Why are you so interested in the time?' Augereau asked.

'I wondered where our new commander was.' Again

there was disdain in his voice. 'My God, he looks more like a mathematician than a general and I suspect he is only a general because of Barras.'

'A political soldier, you think? Well, he's riding Barras's old mistress too. Seems Bonaparte got more than his rank from the Directory.' Augereau cracked out laughing but was not joined by his companion.

He was still laughing when the flap of the tent opened and a third man joined them.

'Massena,' Augereau said, still chuckling. 'You're late. If you don't believe me, consult Serurier's watch. It's all he's been doing for the past ten minutes.'

André Massena was a thin, dark man with pinched features. He was the same age as Augereau but looked younger. His dark blue jacket with its gold epaulettes and embroidery was immaculately pressed and clean. He looked as if he'd just left a tailor's shop, not ridden miles across parched, dry countryside. There was barely a trace of perspiration on him. He had served at Toulon with Bonaparte three years earlier and knew the abilities of his new commander.

'So, Massena,' Augereau continued, 'what do you think of General Bonaparte? Serurier here thinks he comes to us only because of Paul Barras and the Directory.'

'I didn't say that,' Serurier protested.

'And he has Barras's mistress too,' Augereau continued.

'Then he is a lucky man,' Massena said. 'She is a rare beauty.'

Augereau laughed again. 'You would ride her yourself, given the chance,' he joked.

Again Serurier looked on with contempt.

When the flap of the tent opened a second time all three men drew themselves to attention to greet the newcomer.

Bonaparte nodded a greeting to them and took up a position behind his desk. He ran his hands over the largest of the maps there, sweeping others to the ground.

'Italy,' he said, pointing at the map. 'It should be our triumph, it is becoming our graveyard. The Army of Italy was raised four years ago and it numbered one hundred and six thousand men. Now, it is disintegrating. Casualties, sickness and desertion have reduced it to sixty-three thousand. Of that number, less than thirty-eight thousand are effective. Of those, many have no shoes, no muskets, no bayonets, no powder. There isn't enough food to go around. The infantry fights in rags, the cavalry rides horses that have been on half rations for a year and, as I speak, we have less than sixty field guns working.' He sucked in a deep breath. 'Royalist agents are at work within the ranks, poisoning the minds of those who will listen to them. The Third Battalion of the Two Hundred and Ninth mutinied at Nice. Even your division, Serurier, defied orders. There is talk of mutiny every day and every soldier in the army is starving. And yet, with these men – men who cannot remember the last time they ate a good meal, had efficient equipment or received any pay – with men such as these we are expected to win this war.' A slight smile flickered on his lips. 'And I tell you, gentlemen, we will.'

'How, General, do you propose to win this victory?' Serurier asked. 'Or perhaps miracle would be a more apt word.'

'The army needs money,' Bonaparte said. 'The men need food but, above all, they need a victory.'

'I agree, sir,' said Serurier condescendingly. 'But that victory will be harder to gain with troops in the condition you described. It is a vicious circle. They need a victory and yet they will not fight well because they haven't the equipment or the supplies needed to gain one.'

'Massena here won at Loano with just such men,' Bonaparte corrected him. 'They will fight, trust me, I know these men. They are men like us.'

'Not like Serurier,' Augereau said scornfully. 'His men obey him because he is a tyrant.'

'I don't care what methods my generals use to command their men,' Bonaparte said. 'All that matters is that they obey.'

'You expect them to fight for no food *and* no pay?' Augereau challenged.

'The Directory entrusted me with some money,' Bonaparte said. 'I have already instructed my chief commissary to organise a small issue of pay. Loans have been secured from some of the merchants in Genoa and a captured privateer has been sold for fifty thousand francs.'

'You should get them to investigate those damned contractors too,' said Augereau. 'They've made fortunes for themselves by giving our men short rations.'

'It is all in hand,' Bonaparte reassured him. 'The rest of it is up to us. To *lead* these men to victory.'

'And what is your plan, sir?' Serurier asked.

'The mountains between Nice and Genoa can be crossed by six different passes and valleys,' Bonaparte said, indicating the area on the map. 'The fighting in this campaign will centre on control of those because, once through them, we are in Piedmont. Once their forces are destroyed we can concentrate on defeating the Austrians.' The other men drew closer to the map, listening to Bonaparte's excited voice, riveted by his passion. 'The Col di Tende, here, leads into the very heart of Piedmont. It is guarded by the fortress of Cuneo. Also leading into Piedmont is the second crossing point. Here, the valley of the River Tanaro. The Col di Cadibona offers us a way into Piedmont through Ceva or into Lombardy by the branches of the River Bormida. The Col di Giovo is more difficult to move through but we must still find a way. Finally, here, the Turchino pass and here, the Bochetta pass.' He stepped back slightly. 'Once these mountains are conquered, Lombardy is ours. No more barren hillsides and scorched plains, gentlemen, just the richness of Lombardy and Piedmont. Our men can live off the land without difficulty. We can replenish, recuperate and regain our strength before we push the Austrians out of Italy.'

'Do we know the opposition's strength?' Massena asked, his eyes still focused on the map.

'Somewhere around fifty-two thousand Austrians and Piedmontese.'

'And we are thirty-seven thousand,' Massena murmured.

'But our forces are concentrated. The Austrians and Piedmontese are thinly spread and, what is more, they do not trust each other. We will be up against armies who are not united and the weak point is here.' Bonaparte pointed to a place on the map. 'Carcare. Once we take that town we turn and defeat Colli and his Piedmontese. He will be cut off from his allies.'

'Where is the best place to cross?' The question came from Augereau.

'The Col di Cadibona,' Bonaparte told him. 'It is closer to Carcare and it also offers good ground for moving artillery. It means we can move quickly, before the enemy can concentrate its forces. Massena, your division will move to join Augereau's troops. You will attack through San Giacomo, joining to assault Carcare. In two days we should be able to concentrate twenty-four thousand men there.'

No one spoke.

The silence was finally broken by Serurier. 'A bold plan,' he said without enthusiasm.

'A *good* plan,' Augereau said and smiled.

'If it works,' Massena added.

'It *will* work,' Bonaparte assured them, total conviction in his voice.

CHAPTER 17

'Here,' called Rocheteau, emerging from the trees. 'Skin those.' He hurled two rabbits towards the camp fire, grinning as they landed with a thud at the feet of Joubert. The big man looked at them hungrily, as if prepared to devour them as they were. He rubbed his voluminous belly with one pudgy hand, listening to it rumble.

The other men also looked on longingly, watching as Bonet reached for one of the rabbits and slit the skin with the tip of his bayonet.

Lausard was surprised to see Gaston snatch up the other dead animal and proceed to do the same.

'Farm boy,' Giresse said smiling.

'Where did you find them?' Lausard enquired, watching as Rocheteau knelt beside the fire, warming his hands.

'The woods are swarming with them,' the corporal said. 'You just have to be quick enough.' He nudged Joubert in the side. 'You wouldn't have been much help to us, fat man.'

'He could have rolled on them,' Roussard offered.

The other men laughed.

A large tin pot was suspended over the fire, half filled with water. Rostov had taken it from one of the houses in Villa Borghese. The implement had been dangling from his saddle, attached by a piece of leather. The water had come from a small stream at the bottom of the ridge the men were now camped on. Fires had been lit all over the ridge, smoke rising into a sky the colour of burnished gold. However, despite the passing of the sun, the night was still humid. Mosquitoes hovered around, seeking any uncovered flesh. Delacor swatted one of the insects as it bit into his neck. He wiped the squashed remains on the grass.

The horses had been watered at the stream before any of the men had been allowed to set up camp. They were now tethered in long rows, watched by sentries. Dragoons ambled up and down with carbines sloped, some looking longingly up the ridge towards their companions, eagerly awaiting the time when they would be relieved, when they could eat and rest.

Sonnier was one of those who gazed at the array of comforting fires and trudged obediently back and forth, turning to look every so often when he heard a horse whinny or scuff the ground.

Sentries guarded the approaches to the wood as well. Like the men near the stream, they also carried their carbines sloped, the fifteen-inch bayonets fixed and twinkling in the light of so many fires. Like many men in their position in the French army, they had their weapons loaded with 'running ball', where the only charge of gunpowder was in the priming pan. It saved on powder which was, like most things on the campaign, at a premium.

Bonet and Gaston finished skinning and gutting the rabbits and set about cutting them into pieces which they then dropped into the boiling water suspended over the fire. Carbonne had found a few wild potatoes in the woods and he dropped those in alongside the rabbit pieces, not bothering to remove the dirt first. The entire potful of food began to turn a shade of brown but the men didn't care what it looked like, only that they were going to eat. Rice was also added and they gathered around eagerly awaiting their feast. None of them knew how long it would be before they ate again.

Most of the other units in the regiment weren't so lucky. They were forced to make do with biscuits. A fight had almost broken out between Charnier and a rival dragoon over who had claim on a dead dog they'd found at the roadside earlier that evening, but Charnier had taken it and the creature was now being turned on a makeshift spit over the fire, which he and his men had made.

Lausard sat gazing down the slope at the tents which had been erected for Deschamps and the other officers. He could see the captain strolling in and out of his tent, dressed only in a shirt and breeches. Lausard wondered if the officer was as anxious to see action as *he* was. Time seemed to have lost its meaning. The days had become a blur of marches beneath the blistering sun over roads sometimes barely wide enough to accommodate three horses moving abreast, most of them rutted, parched causeways. Hills crowded in on the roads in most places as if threatening to crush them out of existence and the thick growths of trees made the men nervous, wondering if their movements were being watched by the local guerrillas. Lausard didn't doubt for one second that they were.

They'd already lost over a dozen horses, made lame by the terrain. The only consolation was that the animals, once shot, had been cut up for food. That feeling of consolation wasn't shared by their riders, however, who trudged along on foot, finding it difficult to keep up and generally slowing the column as it advanced further towards the fighting which everyone knew would come soon.

They had passed regiments of infantry without shoes. Some without muskets, and stories had filtered through to them about battles already fought, of how the Austrians and Piedmontese were better equipped and fed, of how the hostility of the locals that remained made passing through every village that bit harder. In places, food had been burned to prevent the advancing French from making use of it and, in one village, two dozen oxen had been poisoned rather than let them fall into the hands of the invaders. A number of men in the regiment were sick too. Lausard thought it was mainly lack of food and bad water but rumours were circulating of a typhus epidemic. Everyone was on edge. Lausard thought that the chance of combat might be a good thing if only to relieve the worries of day-to-day campaigning. When faced with some of the problems they encountered, the prospect of battle didn't seem so terrifying after all. Combat, he mused, should go a long way to making the men forget the saddle-sores and the constant gnawing in their bellies.

But when would that battle come? He ran a hand through his hair and exhaled deeply.

'Alain.'

He turned at the sound of his name to see Rocheteau holding a metal plate towards him. A couple of pieces of rabbit meat were floating in brown gravy with some potatoes and rice. Lausard pulled a spoon from one of his pockets, blew the dust from it and began eating.

'We'd better save some for Sonnier,' said Giresse, 'for when he comes back from sentry duty.'

'To hell with him,' Delacor snapped. 'All the more for us.'

Lausard glared at the man then nodded to Giresse. 'Save him some,' he said quietly.

'This might be the last meal we eat for a while,' Charvet observed.

'It might be the last meal we *ever* eat,' Joubert added, gravy dripping from his chin as he stuffed the food into his mouth.

'With God's help we'll all get through it,' Moreau added.

'Do you honestly think God gives a damn about us or anyone else in this stinking army?' Delacor sneered.

'God cares about everyone,' Moreau continued. 'Even *you*.'

The other men laughed.

Delacor didn't see the joke.

'Well, I don't need *His* help,' he said irritably.

'When you run up against the Austrians you might change your mind,' Tabor added.

'Shut up, you half-wit, I don't need *your* opinion.'

'Stop squabbling amongst yourselves,' Bonet said. 'We're not here to fight each other.'

As he spoke he looked across at Lausard.

'If you're referring to those deserters, Bonet,' said

Lausard without looking up from his food, 'you know my opinion. They would have killed *us*.'

'Yes, they would,' Rocheteau added.

'What happened?' Roussard pressed.

'It isn't important,' Lausard replied. 'Forget about it. It's in the past and the past doesn't matter.'

Lausard tried to convince himself that was true. He'd been trying to, ever since the death of his family, but he knew that the past *did* matter. It did to him. It ate away at him like some canker and he knew it would continue to do so as long as he lived. As long as he walked, his guilt would walk with him like an extra shadow.

The sky was darkening rapidly now, bringing with it a chill but welcome westerly breeze, which ruffled the men's hair and caused them to draw nearer the fire. Some were already lying down on their blankets, saddles used as makeshift pillows. Rocheteau was busy sewing a button back on his tunic. Rostov took the now empty tin pot from the bayonet which held it above the fire and made his way down to the stream to wash it out in the cool water. All the men would fill their canteens from the stream in the morning before leaving. Most had drained the contents already as soon as the order had been given to make camp, urged on by their uncontrollable thirsts. The dust had stuck in their throats and noses until it seemed that it would suffocate them.

As Rostov washed the pot he heard the dull clank of a hammer and looked across to see that the regimental farrier and two of his assistants were shoeing a large bay. They wore the appropriate insignia on their sleeves; suitably enough, a silver horseshoe. The animal seemed unconcerned by the running repairs being performed on it and stood obediently as the farrier first removed the old shoe then replaced it with another, which he'd taken from a dead horse earlier in the day, pounding it into shape as best he could on a flat rock by the edge of the stream.

As Rostov made his way back up the slope he saw Charnier and his companions finishing off what was left of the dog they had cooked. One of the men was sucking contentedly on a pipe despite the fact that it had no tobacco in it.

Heading down the slope towards him was Lausard.

'Charvet and Roussard are taking first watch,' Lausard informed him. 'You try to get some sleep, you and Moreau can take the next one.'

'What about you?' Rostov asked. 'When will you sleep?'

Lausard smiled.

'I don't sleep too well,' he said. 'I haven't for a while now.'

'Nervous?'

'Bad dreams.'

Lausard patted his colleague on the shoulder then continued on down the slope alone, his cape now slung around his shoulders to protect him from the increasingly chilly wind. The material flapped in the breeze like the wings of a gigantic bat and, as he walked, his sword bumped against his boot.

Reaching the bottom of the ridge he found Sonnier still walking obediently up and down in front of the horses.

'There's food back there for you,' Lausard told him. 'Tabor's on his way down to relieve you.'

'Good, I'm starving.'

'You and half the army.'

Sonnier watched as Lausard walked off along the floor of the valley, following the gently flowing stream, walking as close to its edge as he could without losing his footing on the powdery dirt. Every now and then he kicked loose stones into the stream, watching the small geysers of water rise and the ripples spread.

The smell of horse droppings was strong in the air, carried on the breeze, but far from recoiling, Lausard inhaled deeply, savouring the odour which was mixed with the smell of grass and earth. It was the smell of freedom. A glorious aroma compared to the fetid stench he'd had to live with in his prison cell or the rank mephitis of the Paris gutters which had clogged his nostrils for so long before that.

He made his way back up the slope, skirting dying camp fires, drawing one or two glances from men who could not sleep. He wondered what *their* reasons for wakefulness were. Fear? Excitement? Foreboding?

He walked along the very outskirts of the camp, passing sentries every twenty yards, exchanging nods with them. Drawing nearer to the top of the ridge the trees grew so thickly and the darkness seemed so dense as to be palpable. He could barely see the dragoons who stood sentinel close to the trees. In fact, he was barely three feet away when he realised that the man ahead of him was busy urinating into a bush, his carbine propped against the tree beside him.

Moving quickly but stealthily, Lausard went over to the man who was sighing contentedly as he emptied his bladder. Then, with one swift movement, Lausard drew his pistol and pressed it to the back of the sentry's head.

He clicked back the hammer and the man raised both hands, his breeches still gaping.

It was all Lausard could do to suppress a grin. 'You're supposed to be keeping watch, not watering the land.' He removed the pistol and pushed the hammer back down.

'Sorry, Sergeant,' said the man who still had his breeches open.

'Delpierre would have had you shot if *he'd* caught you.'

The man saluted. 'I know, Sergeant,' he jabbered. 'It won't happen again, Sergeant.'

Lausard nodded. 'Trooper,' he said, again trying to keep a straight face, 'you should fasten your breeches now.'

The man did so hurriedly as Lausard walked on, heading for the next outpost.

Two sentries up ahead stood motionless, both seeming as if they were a part of the night; dark shapes which had detached themselves from the blackness and become tangible. Neither turned as he approached, despite the fact that his sword clanked against his boot as he drew nearer.

'Asleep on duty?' Lausard murmured to himself.

He reached out and grabbed the first man's shoulder. The dragoon toppled backwards, falling flat on his back at Lausard's feet. His throat had been cut from ear to ear. Blood was still draining from the riven veins and arteries.

Lausard looked across at the other soldier, realising now that his body leaned against the tree close by.

A knife had been used on him too. Driven skilfully, with great power and precision, into the base of his skull. His eyes were open and staring wide, bulging like a fish on a hot skillet. Thin trickles of crimson ran from his nose and ears.

Lausard spun round, pulling his sword free with one hand, his pistol with the other, while preparing to shout a warning to the other sentries, to rouse the regiment from its slumber.

It was then that he heard the first gunshot.

CHAPTER 18

The bang sounded like a thundercrack in the stillness of the night. The crack reverberated around the valley, followed all too soon by another. Then another.

Lausard turned in the direction of the sounds and realised they were coming from the bottom of the slope. He heard shouts now, not just from the base of the ridge but also closer by. Men, roused from their slumbers by the noise, were staggering to their feet, some reaching for weapons, others trying to regain their wits, to shake the sleep from their minds.

There were more gunshots. Then the whinnying and screams of horses. A carbine was fired, the muzzle and pan flash briefly illuminating the firer.

The light from the camp fires was dim, barely strong enough for Lausard to see the base of the slope but he hurtled towards it nonetheless.

The horses were restless now, many hooves pounding the ground. Their cries grew louder, their anxiety increased. Dark shapes moved amongst them and Lausard knew they were not dragoons.

One of the shapes raised a pistol and placed it

against the head of a grey horse. There was a loud bang and then the animal crashed to the ground taking two other horses with it as it fell. Now the animals became almost frantic. Steel glinted brightly in the gloom.

More dragoons were charging down the slope now and he saw Sergeant Legier, sword drawn, running past him. Other men ran to the aid of the horses, some stumbling in the darkness. Lausard saw one man go sprawling headlong as he tripped over a rock, his carbine falling from his grasp.

Then he saw the dark shapes among the horses again.

He rushed towards one, forcing his way through the lines of terrified animals. Clouds of dust were being raised by the churning hooves, further limiting his vision.

When no more than three feet away, the man turned to see Lausard; in the gloom the dragoon could just make out the face of his opponent – bearded, his hair long and dirty, his eyes wide and almost frenzied. He cursed at Lausard in Italian and aimed a pistol but he was too slow. Lausard drove the point of his sword forward, hurling all his weight behind the thrust. The blade punctured the man's chest just below the sternum and erupted from his back. Lausard pulled him on to the steel, twisted it once then pulled it free, striking at his dying enemy with a powerful backhand slash that almost severed the man's right arm at the shoulder. He dropped to his knees and Lausard drove the blade through his throat, ignoring the blood that jetted on to his breeches.

'Sergeant.'

The shout made him turn and he spun round in time

to see another of the guerrillas racing towards him.

Lausard ducked down, drove his shoulder into the man's chest and knocked him on to his back, stepping forward and driving his sword into the guerrilla's belly and chest.

'They're after the horses!' Lausard shouted as another shot exploded close by him and he saw Sonnier with a carbine and a cloud of smoke surrounding him.

The panic spreading through the horses was so great by now that Lausard feared a stampede. Many of the horses were rearing up, anxious to escape their attackers. One struck out with its hind legs, catching a dragoon in the face, the impact shattering a cheekbone and his nose. He dropped to his knees, his face a bloody ruin.

Elsewhere, men were grabbing animals, trying to calm them, but the guerrillas continued to run among them, firing into the air, sometimes into the mass of horses. Those without guns slashed with knives at the helpless animals.

Lausard could not tell how many guerrillas there were; the darkness hid them too effectively. But whatever their number they seemed to be succeeding in their mission. He saw another horse go down, hamstrung with two slashes of a knife. Two of the dark figures ran from the camp, scampering over the rocky terrain towards some trees on the other side of the stream.

'Sonnier!' Lausard shouted. 'Come on.' And he was scrambling for a horse, gripping its mane to haul himself on to the animal's bare back, hurtling after the fleeing guerrillas. Sonnier pulled another cartridge from his cartouche, bit off the ball, held it in his mouth while pouring powder down the barrel, then spat the ball after it, rammed wadding down and replaced the rod, all with a speed which surprised him. Then, gripping the carbine in one hand, he too hauled himself on to a horse and rode after Lausard and the fleeing 'Barbets'.

Lausard knew he had to catch the running men before they reached the relative safety of the woods and he could see that his horse was gaining on the fugitives. The animal splashed through the stream, almost stumbled, but then went on, closing the gap on the fleeing men. Lausard raised his sword and drew alongside the closer of the two men, swinging his sabre down with great power, catching the man across the shoulders, a blow which sent him flying. He hit the ground and rolled over moaning in agony, his cries rising to screams of terror as Sonnier rode over him, the horse trampling the body beneath its hooves.

The second Barbet had almost reached the woods. He turned and fired his pistol at Lausard, who actually heard the ball whistle past his ear. Then the horse slammed into the guerrilla, knocking him to the ground. He hit the ground hard but, despite being dazed, tried to clamber to his feet. Lausard leaped from the animal's back and hurled himself at the disorientated man, driving the pommel of his sword into his face. The man dropped to his knees and Lausard kicked him hard in the stomach. He went down, curled into a foetal position.

Sonnier approached seconds later.

'Watch him,' ordered Lausard.

Sonnier raised his carbine to his shoulder and aimed it at the fallen fugitive.

Lausard went back to the first man, prodding the body with the toe of his boot. He was still alive but for how much longer Lausard could only guess. What his sabre cut had started, the hooves of Sonnier's horse had all but finished. Blood was running freely from his mouth and nose, and he was clutching his stomach. Lausard guessed that the hooves must have caused some internal damage. The man would be no use to them.

Lausard ran his sword through the guerrilla's throat.

He went back towards the other guerrilla, who was still lying on the ground with Sonnier's carbine pointed at him. Lausard hauled him to his feet, aware now that the gunshots and sounds of panic from the camp had died away. Even the horses had quietened down, their exhortations now limited to the odd whinny. He could hear many voices.

The Barbets had obviously fled, disappearing back into the night like spectres. All except the one he now had a firm grip on. Lausard heard more horses coming towards him and he saw Deschamps, an officer he recognised as Lieutenant Royere and two troopers riding closer. Deschamps and Royere dismounted and approached Lausard and his captive.

'They killed six horses,' Deschamps told him. 'Four more will have to be destroyed.'

He regarded the captured guerrilla angrily.

'Ask him where he's from,' he instructed Royere, who did so in faultless Italian. 'Which village?'

The man muttered something under his breath then spat on the ground in front of Royere.

The lieutenant didn't react but simply repeated the question.

The guerrilla rasped a few words at him, leering into the Frenchman's face. Lausard took a step forward as if to restrain him but the officer merely held up a hand as if to dismiss the gesture.

'He said he hopes we all rot in hell,' Royere said, not taking his eyes from the prisoner.

'Ask him if he's seen any Austrians,' Deschamps instructed.

Royere repeated the question in Italian.

The man merely smiled.

He said something and, again, Royere's expression did not change.

'He won't cooperate, sir,' the lieutenant said.

Deschamps nodded and, with one fluid movement, Royere pulled his pistol free, pressed it to the man's temple and fired. From such close range, the guerrilla's entire face was blackened by the pistol's discharge, one portion of his skull staved in by the ball as surely as if he'd been hit with a red-hot hammer. The body rolled over and ended up face down in the stream.

'Post extra sentries,' said Deschamps. 'We move out at dawn.'

CHAPTER 19

Bonaparte saw the cloud of dust before he saw the horseman.

He rose slowly from his seat and placed one hand over his eyes to shield them from the sun, squinting into the distance to try to pick out the image hidden beneath the dense clouds of dust.

Beside him, Colonel Joachim Murat reached for his telescope, extended it and watched through the eye-piece.

The rider was dressed in a dark blue dolman jacket and matching breeches. A red cloth 'wing' flapped behind him as he rode, wrapped around his conical mirliton cap.

'Hussar,' said Murat quietly, handing the glass to Bonaparte, who fixed the rider in the single eye of the telescope.

As the hussar drew nearer, those infantry who were resting close by the road lifted their headgear into the air and cheered the speeding horseman as he swept past them. His horse was badly lathered, its tongue lolling from one side of its mouth.

The rider rode on through other troops, past a unit of horse artillery who were trying to manoeuvre a four-pounder into position on its limber, struggling to secure the cannon. The men were sweating profusely beneath the burning sun.

Bonaparte handed the telescope back to Murat as he saw the hussar heading up the hill towards his position. He could now see the man clearly. He was young, barely out of his teens, his hair long and plaited as was the manner of the hussars. He had the beginnings of a moustache but certainly nothing to compete with some of the massive growths sported by these most flamboyant of cavalrymen. Some of the younger troopers, unable to grow a sufficiently impressive moustache, had been known to blacken their top lips with burned cork until the sought-after facial hair appeared. As he rode, his black leather sabretache flapped behind him and Bonaparte could hear the harness jingling madly as he closed to within a few yards, tugging hard on the reins to halt his mount.

The hussar leaped from the saddle and almost overbalanced, such was his eagerness to reach Bonaparte. His jacket was soaked with sweat, great dark rings of it fanning out from beneath both arms and soaking through the back of his dolman. He wiped sweat from his eyes and saluted.

Bonaparte returned the gesture.

'I have news from General Massena, sir,' said the trooper breathlessly and he fumbled inside his jacket for a piece of paper, which he presented to Bonaparte.

Bonaparte read it swiftly, the expression on his face darkening.

'The Austrians have attacked at Voltri,' he said, not

taking his eyes from the paper. 'Two columns attacked Cervoni's brigade.'

'What damage?' Murat asked.

'It doesn't say what casualties he sustained, only that he managed to organise a retreat,' Bonaparte said, handing the piece of paper to his companion.

The hussar was still standing to attention before the general, still sucking in great lungfuls of air, sweat pouring from his face.

'Did you come from Voltri?' Bonaparte asked him.

'Yes, sir,' the exhausted horseman answered and, for the first time, Bonaparte noticed that there was blood on the man's uniform, some splashed on his left arm and breeches.

'Are you wounded?' the general enquired, pointing at the blood.

'That's not my blood, sir,' he answered, again sucking in a deep breath. 'Sir, General Massena requests orders immediately. He thinks he should move his troops to block the attack on Voltri.'

'No!' snapped Bonaparte. He looked towards Murat. 'The Austrians have shown their hand too soon. They have revealed their position.' He looked at the hussar. 'I need you to ride back to General Massena now. Can you do that?'

'If you will oblige me with a fresh horse, sir, I will go immediately.'

Bonaparte smiled, watching as the hussar pulled his saddle, complete with its sheepskin shabrack, from his exhausted animal and hurriedly flung it over the back of a small chestnut horse which had been brought over by Murat.

In a matter of moments the hussar was ready. He

swung himself into the saddle, took the order from Bonaparte and rode off.

'The Austrians thought they would take me by surprise,' Bonaparte said, watching the hussar galloping back down the slope and on to the road. 'They will see what a surprise I have for them.'

The road on which Lausard and his companions travelled seemed to be the only one in Italy capable of accepting the passage of troops and equipment. At least that was the way it felt to Lausard when he saw the number of men clogging it. During their march they had passed all kinds of infantry, most of them in the same ragged state they always appeared to be in. Some at least had shoes, a few even wore gaiters too, but the majority were barefoot as usual. One man, in a pair of cavalry boots which were clearly too small for him, walked as though each step were painful but, Lausard guessed, his feet were probably so swollen by now, it was impossible to remove the boots anyway. Other men had simply wrapped pieces of cloth around their feet. Some carried their jackets over their shoulders or slung atop their packs but this did little to alleviate their suffering beneath the sun which was still burning ferociously in a clear azure sky. Others merely trudged on, sweat pouring from them, some with muskets sloped, others dragging them by their straps. Those who *had* weapons were among the lucky ones. Whether those weapons had powder, ball or flint, Lausard didn't know. They had heard a rumour earlier in the day that the thousand men of Augereau's division had no firearms at all. Lausard himself, like most of the men in his regiment, carried twenty-five rounds, although Rostov and Joubert had traded some cartridges for biscuits with an infantry unit they'd passed not too far back.

However, for the most part, the woefully equipped foot soldiers moved with a speed and purpose that their commanders had little right to expect. They had suffered badly during the last year or so, desperately short of food and supplies, driven more by their hunger and desire to plunder than any revolutionary ideals. They didn't care for the politics of the war. Ethics and morality were for those 'pekinese' back in Paris; these men wanted nothing more than a good meal and the chance to gather some riches for themselves. If they had to fight battles to get those things, then so be it.

Lausard guided his horse carefully past three foot soldiers who were marching close to the roadside, aware of their glances up at him.

'New boys,' said one of the infantry, chuckling. 'Look at their uniforms. Not even a dust mark.'

'You'll have more than dust marks when we run into the Austrians,' quipped another.

'They're pretty, but not as pretty as the hussars,' said another infantryman, a large man with a thick growth of beard.

'The hussars,' snorted another. 'Those peacock bastards.'

A chorus of laughter rippled through those troops within earshot.

'Have you any spare powder?' one of the infantrymen asked Delacor, pulling at the cavalryman's stirrup.

'What are you offering in exchange?' Delacor asked.

'I haven't got much but—'

'Then I've got no powder,' Delacor snapped, pulling his foot away.

The infantryman overbalanced and almost fell as he stepped back, avoiding Delacor's horse which bumped him.

One of the other foot soldiers slapped the beast's flank and it reared up suddenly. Delacor was fortunate to remain in the saddle as the bay rose on to its hind legs. He gripped the bridle and managed to bring the animal under control but its sudden movement startled a handful of other horses close by.

'You bloody fool!' snapped Carbonne at the infantryman, who merely spat in his direction.

'He started it,' snarled one of the other foot soldiers, pointing at Delacor. 'You bastards are all the same. You think you're better than us. Well, you'll find out when you get into battle, it's not so easy to hide when you're on a horse.'

'Is that what you do during a battle then?' asked Lausard. 'Hide?'

The cavalrymen nearby laughed.

'You think you're a funny man,' the infantryman said. 'See if you're still laughing when you've got an Austrian bayonet up your arse.'

It was the foot soldiers turn to laugh.

'You let us do the dirty work then you ride in and take the glory,' the infantryman said scornfully. 'All of you bastards are the same.'

'Not all of us,' Lausard told him and guided his horse back towards the head of the column.

Ahead, blocking the road was an artillery train made up of four eight-pounder guns, their limbers and two caissons. A wheel had come off one of the ammunition carts and five blue-coated gunners were trying desperately to fix it while a sergeant bellowed at them. The barrels of the cannon sparkled in the sunlight.

Lausard watched as Deschamps and Royere took their horses past the stranded caisson, finding enough room to bypass it on the narrow road. Lausard waited a moment then spurred his own mount on, followed by Rocheteau and Giresse. The remainder of the men did likewise and soon the entire regiment was slipping past the cursing gunners who were still struggling manfully with the wheel. Lausard guessed that it would be another hour or more of struggling along this cramped, overcrowded road before the order to halt would finally be given.

They set up camp on a gentle slope overlooking a valley dense with trees. Several small streams snaked along the valley floor. The slope opposite was also thickly wooded. Beyond it, they all knew, the Austrians waited.

Lausard stood gazing at the far slope, squinting in the dying rays of the sun, one hand cupped over his eyes as he peered towards the opposite ridge. He could see figures moving there.

'Are they getting ready for us?'

The voice startled him and he looked around to see that Rocheteau had joined him and was also gazing in the direction of the figures on the distant ridge. He drew a telescope from his tunic pocket, pulled it to its furthest extension and began looking through it.

'Where did you get that?' Lausard asked.

'I took it off one of those deserters back at Villa Borghese.' Rocheteau said, passing him the instrument.

The troops moving about on the opposite ridge were, without any doubt, Austrians; their white jackets and breeches marked them out as such. But those in white jackets seemed to be outnumbered by those in brown.

'Artillery,' murmured Lausard, his observation confirmed when he saw six limbers being dragged into place by teams of horses, these guns in turn being man-handled into position by the brown-coated troops, the barrels facing the French position. Half-a-dozen six-pounders were arrayed along the ridge.

'They're not going to make it easy for us, are they?' Rocheteau mused, watching the guns.

'We're all going to be killed.' Joubert had joined them.

'Thank you for that cheerful thought, fat man,' Rocheteau said.

Lausard handed the telescope back to his companion, his attention caught by something much closer than the Austrians. Along the floor of the valley, two French demi-brigades were setting up camp and Lausard could hear their officers and NCOs shouting orders.

'There will be a battle tomorrow, won't there?' Joubert asked warily.

Lausard nodded.

'Our first battle,' Rocheteau echoed, his voice a little more solemn than usual. 'It makes you wish we were back in Paris, doesn't it, Alain?'

'No,' said Lausard, 'at least here we're free.'

'I didn't mean in prison, I meant—'

'I know what you meant. And I'd still rather be here than living like a rat in a sewer. We weren't free when we lived on the streets, we were just a different kind of prisoner.'

Rocheteau looked at him in bewilderment for a second then patted his shoulder. 'Perhaps you're right.'

'Charvet and Tabor are collecting wood for a fire,' said Rostov, coming up alongside. Then his attention was also drawn to the activity on the opposite ridge. More guns had been dragged into place, all barrels pointing towards the French. A number of camp fires had sprung up on the slope too as the Austrians tried to make themselves more comfortable.

'Do you think they're as scared as we are?' Joubert asked.

'Everyone's scared,' said Rostov. 'If they've got any sense. No man wants to die.'

Lausard didn't answer, he merely continued gazing at the Austrians. Below him, more infantry had arrived and were setting up camp. He estimated that there were close to fifteen hundred of them, perhaps more.

'I hope Bonaparte knows what he's doing,' Rocheteau said under his breath.

'Do you doubt our General?' Lausard asked and smiled.

'Ask me this time tomorrow.'

The sun sank a little lower in the sky, the heavens began to turn the colour of blood.

'"Soldiers. You are hungry and naked; the government owes you much but can give you nothing. The patience and courage which you have displayed among these rocks are admirable; but they bring you no glory. Not a glimmer falls upon you. I will lead you into the most fertile plains on earth. Rich provinces, opulent towns, all shall be at your disposal; there you will find honour, glory and riches. Soldiers of Italy, will you be lacking in courage or endurance?"'

Lausard watched and listened as the proclamation was read out by the aide-de-camp. The man was dressed in a dark blue hussar uniform with a red pelisse slung around his shoulders. The golden braid both on his dolman and pelisse seemed to gleam in the light of the setting sun, as though strips of precious metal had been stitched to the material. His uniform was undirtied by the dust of the roads, his boots sparkling; even his spurs glinted.

Lausard looked down at his own boots. They were two-toned where the dust and grime clung so thickly to them. Even his jacket carried a thin sheen of dust, making it look grey instead of green. He patted the sleeves to remove the choking particles.

All around stood the men of his regiment; they had been joined by infantrymen, sappers, artillerymen, even the farriers were present. These men cheered every so often and the aide paused, smiling sometimes at the raucous reaction garnered by the proclamation, but he continued reading, perched high on an artillery caisson.

'"You will fight a battle tomorrow which will open up the gates of Piedmont,"' the aide continued. '"I will lead you through those gates and on to glory and riches. I will be with you tomorrow, every one of you, at your side as you fight and together we will win a glorious victory. Your General, Napoleon Bonaparte."'

A huge cheer greeted the end of the reading and the aide looked around at the sea of faces as if he personally was enjoying the adulation, then he stepped down from the ammunition wagon and climbed on to his horse.

'Vive Bonaparte!' someone shouted and the cry was taken up by others.

Lausard looked on in silence, watching as some of his companions joined in the cheering.

Charvet even lifted his brass helmet up on the end of his sword and raised it into the air.

Gaston looked on with bewilderment, pushing his helmet back on his head.

'He's going to get us all killed,' grunted Delacor. 'Why cheer him?'

'It's thanks to Bonaparte that you've still got your head,' Bonet told him. 'If the army hadn't needed men, we'd still be in prison now.'

'*He'd* have had your head,' said Rocheteau, pointing at Carbonne and grinning.

The bald man didn't seem to be listening. Like Charvet he had lifted his helmet high into the air on the tip of his sword and was cheering wildly. The former executioner was shouting Bonaparte's name at the top of his voice.

Tabor began clapping but he wasn't really sure why. He was grinning maniacally, his huge hands slapping together excitedly.

Through a crowd of troopers, Lausard saw Sergeant Delpierre heading down the slope. He was chewing on a piece of tobacco.

Lausard took a step across towards him, forcing the older man almost to collide with him.

'Not joining in the celebrations?' Lausard said, staring at the other sergeant.

'I don't need to jump about like some girl,' Delpierre hissed. 'I *know* we'll win. You just make sure you do as you're told.'

'You have no authority over me,' Lausard snapped. 'We're of equal rank now, remember?'

'There'll be nowhere to hide tomorrow. Not for you or any of your scum.'

'I won't be hiding and neither will they. Where will you be, Delpierre?'

As Delpierre leaned close to him Lausard could smell the tobacco on his breath.

'I'll be right beside *you*, Lausard. If you feel steel in your back,' he snapped, 'you'd better check if it's Austrian or not.'

Lausard's eyes narrowed, but he held his tongue.

The two men glared at each other for a moment longer then Delpierre disappeared into the still cheering crowd.

'What did that bastard want?' asked Rocheteau.

'Nothing important.'

The cheering of Bonaparte's name was still going on. It had grown to almost deafening proportions by now but Lausard seemed unmoved by the show of adulation. He made his way slowly back up the slope.

Despite the fact that the slopes and the valley floor were seething with men, Lausard might as well have been alone. He glanced at faces as he passed, looking indifferently at them, sometimes even at men from his own regiment.

The sky had darkened and the glow of camp fires lit the ridges on both sides of the valley. In the middle, where the stream criss-crossed, the tree-filled floor was a black void. Lausard thought that it resembled an enormous open grave. He suspected that, the following day, that was precisely what it would become.

CHAPTER 20

Lausard couldn't remember the last time he'd watched the sun rise. He began to wonder if he would ever again see it perform its unstoppable climb into the heavens, spreading light, banishing the night and ushering in a day of warmth and beauty. A sunrise, he mused, like a sunset, should be watched with a lover. He should be lying with a beautiful woman now, her head on his chest, his hand stroking her hair. Together they should be watching the beginning of a new day and savouring the joys it might bring.

He blinked hard, trying to shake himself from his musings. Rather than watching this sunrise with a lover he was watching it from the saddle of his horse, the smell of sweat and horses strong in his nostrils, and the day that was breaking held the promise not of joy and beauty but of pain and suffering.

He looked along the line of dragoons. He and his men had been mounted for over twenty minutes and the entire routine had been conducted in an eerie silence, broken only by the jingling of harnesses and the occasional whinny of a horse. The animals were also nervous and troopers tried to reassure them; troopers who themselves were feeling anything ranging from apprehension to pure terror, men who had never fought a battle in their lives and many shuddered to think this could be their first and last experience of one.

The regiment was drawn up in lines because of the slope. Once the order to advance was given, that linear formation would be transformed into a column, Lausard thought, although, looking at the terrain they would be forced to cross, an open-order advance might be more advisable.

Below them, already on the valley floor, the infantry waited in line, standards still lowered, drums still silent. Those in possession of bayonets already had them fitted. As with the cavalry, a curious, almost reverential silence lay over them like a blanket.

On the lower reaches of the slopes there was a little more activity. Six eight-pounder guns had been placed in position the previous evening and now Lausard watched as their corporals made last-minute adjustments to the screw-elevators at the sealed ends of the barrels. The effective range of an eight-pounder firing roundshot was about fifteen hundred yards. As the battle wore on, Lausard had no doubt that these guns would be moved closer to the Austrian positions.

Captain Deschamps was walking his horse back and forth before the waiting dragoons, Lieutenant Royere close behind him, the younger officer glancing across the valley every few seconds.

The sky was a beautiful shade of orange now, white clouds scudding across it, pushed by the light breeze which had risen with the sun.

'What the hell are they waiting for?' whispered Roussard from the rank behind.

Lausard glanced around at him and shrugged.

'What is this place called?' Tabor asked.

'Why?' snapped Delacor. 'Do you want to know where you're going to die?'

'It's beautiful,' Tabor continued, 'very beautiful. It reminds me of my home.'

'Shut up, you half-wit!' Delacor berated. 'We've got other things to think about now.'

Tabor seemed mesmerised by the sky and the slowly rising sun. 'So beautiful,' he repeated quietly.

Moreau calmed his horse as it pawed the ground with one hoof. He patted its neck then crossed himself.

Giresse scratched thoughtfully at his unshaven chin and gazed out over the valley. 'Tabor's right,' he said, 'it *is* beautiful.'

'There's a town over that opposite ridge called Montenotte,' Bonet informed them.

'Keep the noise down,' shouted an all-too-familiar voice from further along the line and Lausard glanced along to see Delpierre pointing at a couple of troopers close by him. Further along Sergeant Legier was gently patting his mount's neck.

'How much longer do we have to wait?' Roussard whispered, perspiration beading his forehead.

Lausard saw Deschamps and Royere train their telescopes on the far ridge but it was somewhere off to the west that his attention was drawn towards. A sound like distant thunder suddenly rolled across the landscape. It was followed by another rumble, then another.

A number of horses whinnied excitedly, their riders gripping the bridles tightly.

Moreau crossed himself again.

Rocheteau slipped his telescope from his jacket and peered through it at the opposite ridge.

'Nothing moving,' he said quietly then handed the glass to Lausard, who could see the Austrian gunners standing statue-like beside their cannons.

More rumbling came from the west. Lausard turned in his saddle and tried to see something in the direction of the sound but it was useless. Hills rose all around them.

He handed the telescope back to Rocheteau.

Down below there were shouts from the infantry officers and movement beneath the tricolours waving in the gentle breeze.

'I think the wait is over,' he murmured.

The roar as the French eight-pounders opened up was deafening. All six pieces opened up simultaneously, a great spout of fire erupting from each barrel as it hurled its projectile towards the enemy. Huge clouds of thick black and grey smoke suddenly spread across the ridge. The sound reverberated around the valley, ringing in the ears of man and horse alike.

A number of the animals reacted violently, rearing up and bucking wildly and at least eight men were thrown from their saddles. Lausard saw two more horses bolt from the line, their riders desperately trying to rein them in. NCOs roared orders and rebukes, trying to make themselves heard as the second salvo of cannon fire was unleashed.

Lausard himself gripped the reins as tightly as he could, his own horse unnerved by the thunderous explosions. The smoke covering the ridge was now thick and noxious like black man-made fog. The stench of sulphur was strong in the air.

The eight-man crews struggled to push the guns back into position after each round had been fired. The eight-pounder, weighing over a thousand pounds, was capable of moving backwards anything up to twelve feet after each discharge. The blue-coated crews manoeuvred the pieces back into their original positions and waited for the corporal to sight it, while the spongeman furiously cleaned the inside of the barrel with a damp swab. Lausard saw pieces of burning ember falling to the ground around the gun and he watched as another artilleryman hurriedly stamped on the dry grass which threatened to ignite like a tinder box.

Rocheteau's horse reared wildly in the noise and he was lucky to remain in the saddle as it kicked out its forelegs, but he held on and managed to calm the beast.

Gaston was gripping his reins tightly, pulling on them, trying to whisper encouragement to his mount, aware of how hard his own heart was thudding against his ribs.

A number of dismounted dragoons were chasing after their fleeing mounts. One soldier grabbed at the reins and managed to regain control of his animal but another trooper wasn't so lucky and was forced to chase his mount towards the valley floor. Both man and horse disappeared from sight in the thick smoke.

All down the line the process of reloading continued, and fresh balls were shoved into the barrels of the guns. Expert gunners could expect to fire two rounds a minute, sometimes three, depending on the size of the piece and the ammunition they were firing. But, because of the immense recoil and the need to re-sight the gun after each shot, the process was slower than anyone would have liked. It was strength-sapping, back-breaking work, all performed inside a shroud of reeking smoke which stung the eyes and parched the throat.

From the valley floor there was a new sound – the staccato rattle of drums. Through the drifting smoke Lausard saw that the infantry were beginning to advance. The tricolours were raised high and, even from such a distance, he heard shouts of '*Vive la République*'. This was met by a loud cheer. The cheering, the drumming and the shouts of officers all rose into one mighty crescendo of sound. It was eclipsed seconds later as the cannon opened fire once more.

Again horses panicked and their riders tried to calm them. More smoke rolled across the ridge, joining the fog which already hovered there, pushed like low-lying cloud by the breeze sweeping across the valley.

Throughout each eruption, Bonet's horse stood motionless, only tossing its head once or twice. He looked on in amazement as the animal calmly bent its head and began nibbling at the dry grass on the slope.

'I wish *I* felt that calm,' said Giresse, indicating the animal. He swallowed hard and managed a small smile.

Bonet nodded in agreement but couldn't return the smile.

Sonnier screwed up his eyes as a bank of smoke drifted over him, millions of tiny cinders floating in it, some sticking to his face. His horse was pawing the ground impatiently and then it emptied its bowels noisily. A number of animals had done the same and the stench of gunpowder now mingled with the stench of excrement and urine.

Lausard could smell his own sweat, some of which

he tried to reassure himself was from the heat of the day. The sun had now risen to a much higher point in the clear sky. Its light twinkled on the bayonets of the advancing infantry, at least those that Lausard could see through the stinking fog produced by the guns. So dense was the black and grey haze that it was impossible to see the far end of the line. Visibility was down to about one hundred yards unless the smoke was dispersed momentarily by a breeze and, always, there was that choking stench.

Rocheteau hawked and spat in an attempt to clear the smell and the cinders from his nose and mouth.

Roussard was coughing uncontrollably, waving one hand in front of his face as the black smog closed around him.

'What the hell is going on?' he said.

'A battle, you bloody idiot,' said Rocheteau. 'What do you think?'

Most of the horses were calming down now, growing a little more accustomed to the massive blasts which came from the cannons in front of them. Lausard reasoned that those animals which remained most unaffected were remounts that had taken part in battles prior to their capture by the French. His own horse seemed to have overcome its initial shock and was now grazing. Like its rider it waited.

The opposite ridge was hidden from view for the most part by the smoke from the French guns but Lausard and the others began to wonder how long it would be before the Austrians started firing back. Lausard felt a shiver run up the back of his neck. He saw, through a break in the smoke screen, Deschamps and Royere walking their horses across the ridge past the front of the regiment. Deschamps was pointing at something in the distance that Lausard couldn't see. The two officers both looked through their telescopes then were hidden as more smoke enveloped them.

In the valley the infantry were approaching the first of the small streams which criss-crossed the valley floor, wading through the knee-high water with ease, splashing almost gleefully in the cool liquid before moving up a gentle slope towards some trees. Officers ran before them, urging them on, and the drums continued to rattle.

Ahead of the main body of men the voltigeurs raced, a body of sharpshooters who would try to pick off enemy gunners and officers once they were close enough.

The infantry had already manoeuvred into columns and they continued their steady advance, urged on by officers and NCOs and the constant shouts of encouragement which they themselves bellowed as if to reassure themselves and their comrades.

'Advance.'

Lausard heard the order, saw Deschamps standing in his stirrups to signal the movement and, as one, the dragoons began to move forward down the slope. Like everyone else, Lausard felt his heart begin to beat that little bit faster.

Bonet's heart was thudding so hard against his ribs he feared it would burst.

Moreau crossed himself.

'So this is it,' Rocheteau said, swallowing hard.

Lausard didn't answer, his eyes were fixed ahead. He and his comrades rode past the sweating artillerymen who were busily reloading their pieces.

'Good luck!' called a corporal, his face drenched, his skin blackened by powder. 'Give them hell.'

'We're going to die, aren't we?' Roussard said, his voice shaky, his breath coming in gasps.

Lausard didn't look at him, he simply shook his head almost imperceptibly and murmured, 'Some of us.'

He saw Deschamps and Royere ahead of him, their horses walking, apparently unconcerned.

Beside him Rocheteau was clutching his horse's reins tightly and gazing ahead.

Gaston looked around him at the pale faces of his companions, some of their expressions showing naked fear.

Rostov's features looked as if they were set in stone. The Russian sat upright in his saddle, sword bumping against his boot.

Lausard guessed that there was something like a thousand yards between the two ridges and he looked up towards the waiting enemy gunners, who were now swarming around their guns like flies round rotten fruit.

Up ahead, the infantry were quickening their pace, the drums beating with an ever-increasing tempo. It seemed to match the beating of Lausard's heart.

High above, the sky was clear, the last of the cloud having been burned away by the sun. It was going to be a beautiful day.

The Austrian guns opened up.

CHAPTER 21

A series of dull thuds followed by distant puffs of smoke was how the opening Austrian volley looked to Lausard as he guided his somewhat skittish horse across the stream. The enemy guns were still out of range as far as he could tell. Nevertheless, the very sight of them finally being brought into action was enough to send shivers up and down many spines, not least that of Roussard who watched the Austrian gun crews realigning their cannon. To him they seemed to be moving twice as quickly as the French gunners and, indeed, a moment later, another volley of roundshot came into the valley.

A few hundred yards ahead the infantry continued to advance, covered by the hordes of voltigeurs who as yet had not fired a shot. They darted back and forth, seeking cover behind rocks and trees, even ditches in the ground.

Lausard could still hear the beating of the drums and the shouts of the officers, even above the jingling of so many harnesses. To his left and right he saw that the line was breaking up in places as dragoons forced their mounts over the increasingly uneven terrain.

They were roughly halfway across the valley by now and – in addition to the cannon ahead of them – they could still hear the occasional rumbles off to the west as General La Harpe's men attacked the Austrians from the other side, their advance having started a little earlier.

Up ahead the infantry were coming into range.

Three roundshot struck the ground ahead of the leading line of foot soldiers. The first buried itself in the hard earth, the second hit a rock, shattered it, then rolled harmlessly into a ditch, but the third ploughed into the men with terrible results.

The men hit seemed to disintegrate, their bodies squashed; blood sprayed in all directions, spattering those nearby and slowing many men in their tracks, but the drums seemed to beat only louder, the officers to exhort more vociferously. The advance continued as more of the deadly balls began to find their mark.

Another struck the ground and ricocheted up again taking out three men.

A spent ball rolled towards the advancing cavalry, the iron covered in blood.

Lausard looked down at it, knowing that they themselves were in range now.

Fifty feet ahead there was an explosion and several men were catapulted into the air by the impact, their screams of agony audible above all other sound. Lausard realised that the Austrian gunners were firing shells as well as roundshot. The fuse on them was usually timed to burn for five seconds but sometimes they would explode in mid air, sometimes they would roll around on the ground for a while before detonating. However they worked, they were lethal.

Lausard looked again to his right and left. He saw Moreau cross himself and glance briefly towards the sky which was as clear as he'd ever seen it. A deep azure blue.

A roundshot struck a small tree less than twenty feet to the right, the metal ball smashing the trunk and bringing the tree down. It crashed to earth and a number of horses nearby reared up in fear.

'They're getting closer,' hissed Giresse, gripping his reins ever more tightly. A cloud of thick smoke from the explosion enveloped them and Lausard found that he had to guide his horse slightly to the left to prevent it stepping on the torn and bloodied corpse of an infantryman.

'Jesus Christ!' murmured Sonnier, gaping at what little was left of the soldier. He felt his stomach contract and looked away, the smell of gunpowder now strong in his nostrils as the smoke continued to drift across the valley floor.

'Where is your God now?' Delacor shouted at Moreau, pointing at the dead infantryman.

Moreau was about to answer when a roundshot struck the ground ahead of the advancing dragoons. It spun up and slammed into his horse. The animal let out a squeal of pain and fell in an untidy heap, both its front legs shattered by the impact. Moreau was thrown from the saddle as the animal went down and as he rolled over he felt its warm blood splash his face and neck.

The dying animal crashed into Delacor's mount, bringing it down too. Delacor hit the ground hard and rolled over groaning, clutching at his side, trying to scramble to his feet to avoid the oncoming hooves of his companions' horses. His own horse was up in seconds, leaping to its feet, bucking wildly and Delacor shot out a hand to grab its bridle.

To the right a shell landed and exploded with a deafening bang. Three dragoons were blasted from their saddles by the detonation, two horses went down, one dead before it hit the ground, its head almost severed by a lump of iron. Thick blood, of both animal and man, sprayed into the air and Lausard saw one of the dragoons lying on his back, stomach ripped open, screaming, but any sound was lost in the noise all around.

More thick black smoke drifted across the valley floor.

Moreau grabbed at the reins of a riderless horse as it passed and he managed, more by luck than judgement, to halt the frightened animal. He quickly swung himself into the saddle and looked across to see that Delacor had already remounted. The two of them rejoined the advancing regiment, aware now of the popping and cracking of musket fire both from their own voltigeurs up ahead and also from some Austrian infantry on the ridge.

Lausard guessed there were about seven or eight hundred yards between them and the enemy now.

The infantry drummers quickened the pace of their tattoo, shouts became more frenzied and the cry suddenly went up '*En avant*'.

The infantry charged.

'Hold!' roared Deschamps, galloping across the front of his anxious horsemen. His sword was already unsheathed. Lieutenant Royere galloped after him, his attention fixed on the ridge and on the attacking infantry.

The Austrian gunners redoubled their efforts as the French swept closer and began to load their cannon with case shot. The canisters full of metal balls waited like gigantic shotguns as the infantry charged closer, still protected by the constant harassing fire of their own sharpshooters.

The dragoons came to a halt in two ragged lines.

'What the hell are we waiting for?' Rocheteau called, watching as the infantry began to charge up the slope, the incline slowing their hectic advance slightly. Tricolours waved proudly in the breeze. A number of the infantry had raised their bicorn hats up on the tips of their bayonets.

'Let the Austrians use up their ammunition on those fools,' said Delacor, nodding towards the infantry who were now less than one hundred yards from the waiting cannon.

Lausard watched intently as the waves of blue-clad troops rushed towards the Austrians. The beating of the drums had ceased, lost now beneath the cacophony of shouts and cries, some of fear because the infantry were less than fifty yards from the mouths of the cannon and they knew what the gunners were waiting for.

The six-pounders opened up with a deafening roar, spewing their lethal loads of case shot at the infantry who were struck at point-blank range. Dozens went down in the hail of metal, and those who didn't fall were splattered with the blood of fallen comrades. A tricolour fell from the hands of its bearer, the man having lost most of his face and the left side of his head. More willing hands snatched it up and carried it forward over ground now stained with the life fluid of dead and dying.

As if angered by the loss of so many of their companions, the blue-clad infantry threw themselves on the Austrian guns, using their bayonets on those gunners who had not turned and fled.

The first Austrian infantry column moved up to the crest of the ridge to meet the frenzied attack of the French, and Lausard watched as it moved ponderously into line in an attempt to fire. But the men in white tunics were shaken by the ferocity of the French attack; with musket fire peppering their own lines from the dozens of sharpshooters still swarming over the ridge, they couldn't unleash a complete volley. There was a series of loud bangs as several units managed to discharge their muskets into the French but it seemed to have little effect and now the French themselves were forming lines and firing back volleys.

The dragoons, from their position at the base of the ridge, sat in virtual silence watching as the foot soldiers battled. Moreau wiped blood from the pommel of the horse he'd acquired.

Gaston thought how alike were the colour of the blood and the hue of his own jacket. He shuddered involuntarily.

Other officers had joined Deschamps and Royere to look at the unfolding action through telescopes. Deschamps was motioning towards a depression in the ridge off to the right, beyond the extent of the Austrian line.

Rocheteau also saw the gaggle of officers and said: 'Do you think they'll send us?' He struggled to keep his frightened horse calm.

Before Lausard could answer there was a rumbling from behind them and the men turned to see three of the eight-pounders being hauled towards the Austrian ridge on their limbers, the horses straining under the effort of pulling. Artillerymen ran alongside, urging the animals on, occasionally helping to manoeuvre the cannon over particularly awkward stretches of ground.

The guns passed and continued up the slope to where the Austrian and French infantry were still facing each other, still firing into each other's massed ranks but Lausard could see that the white-coated Austrians were giving ground, falling back towards another steeper ridge about five hundred yards behind their first position. Smoke was lying thickly over the battlefield now, twisting and swirling around the fighting men.

'This waiting is driving me insane,' said Delacor.

'You're already insane,' Bonet retorted.

'Shut up, schoolmaster.'

'I'd rather be sitting here than stuck in the middle of that lot,' said Roussard, nodding towards the battle on the ridge.

'Why don't they get it over with?' Rocheteau wanted to know. 'Let's go now.'

Lausard shook his head. 'Soon,' he whispered under his breath, eyes still riveted to the infantry duel.

The eight-pounders had unlimbered by now and as he watched they fired a withering salvo into the tightly packed Austrian ranks, turning many of the white tunics red.

The column wavered then began to split.

It was becoming difficult to see what was going on, so great was the thickness of smoke. The dragoons were aware only of reeking black and grey clouds, the rattle of musket fire and the occasional roar of a cannon.

Deschamps emerged from a bank of smoke no more than ten feet from Lausard and he heard him roar the order for the dragoons to advance but, once more, it was a leisurely walk not a charge. Lausard felt cheated as he led his horse forward towards the fighting. He wanted Deschamps to give the order; he wanted to be sent at the Austrians riding at full tilt. It seemed it was not to be.

They advanced up the slope, many of them unable to prevent their horses stepping on the bodies of the dead and wounded.

An infantryman with one arm blown off below the elbow covered his head with his remaining hand as the horses passed. Another was sitting gazing down at a hole in his stomach. One of his hands was clutched to the wound while the other hand held that of a man who seemed to be little more than a mass of crimson from head to foot. As the soldier lay on the grass, his life blood seeping from him, he nodded at Lausard as he passed and the sergeant respectfully returned the gesture.

Parts of the parched hillside had been burned black, the dry grass which grew there so sparsely having been incinerated by fallen used cartridges. The smell of burned wood mingled with the coppery odour of blood, the stench of both human and animal excrement and the ever-present choking stink of gunpowder.

As the dragoons moved further up the ridge the smoke became thicker and the noise almost intolerable. Horses became more nervous. One reared, threw its rider and fell backwards, crashing into three more troopers behind.

Lausard heard horses' hooves away to his left but he could barely see where Royere was taking two squadrons of dragoons, leading them away at a canter. He and his companions continued to advance at a walk, through another curtain of fumes which nearly blinded them.

They passed an Austrian six-pounder which had been overturned by the French infantry.

To his right, one of the eight-pounder crews was limbering up again, attaching the cannon to the wooden wagon which transported it. Lausard thought that the horses which pulled it barely looked up to the task, the drivers perched precariously on their skinny backs. Most of the crew drivers were civilian contractors, even more reluctant to be on a battlefield than many of the troops who now surrounded him.

More bodies littered the top of the ridge and in many places the ground was slicked with blood. Screams of the wounded were inaudible over the crash of battle and those not shrieking in pain were crawling from body to body, desperately trying to find water in an unused canteen.

A breeze suddenly swept a particularly thick bank of smoke away and Lausard saw Austrian troops no more than five hundred yards away. And they had broken. The centre and left of the line still seemed to be holding firm but many of the white-coated troops were fleeing.

He felt a sudden surge of adrenaline pump through his body. The hair at the nape of his neck stiffened and he drew in a deep breath.

'Draw swords!' roared Deschamps, rising in his saddle.

The sound of hundreds of sabres being pulled from

their scabbards reminded Lausard of the hissing of a thousand snakes.

'At last,' he murmured, glancing at Rocheteau who looked back at him blankly, his own face already stained with powder and greasy with sweat.

'Advance by squadron,' shouted Deschamps. 'Trumpeters, sound the charge.'

Gaston, like the other seven trumpeters, did as he was ordered and the ring of the notes began to fill the air, rising above the shouts, screams, gunshots and jingling harnesses.

The dragoons moved off at a trot, their speed building gradually to a canter. This was what Lausard had dreamed of, what he had sought.

The canter increased to a gallop over the last two hundred yards, the sound of thundering hooves the only sound anyone seemed to be aware of. Swords glinted in the sunlight which also struck their brass helmets. As if caught up in the excitement of the charge the horses whinnied, eyes rolling in their sockets.

The Austrians had neither time nor opportunity to form squares to protect themselves from the sudden attack.

The front line of dragoons crashed into them and rode them down.

Lausard struck to his left and shaved off the ear of an infantryman.

He struck again, using all his strength to cut down through the shako of an Austrian, a blow which cut the headgear cleanly in two before ploughing into the top of the man's skull.

Other fleeing troops were trampled to death by the churning hooves of the French horses.

Rostov drove his sword down, skewering an officer through the cheek.

Delacor slashed at a running man's back and caught him across the nape of the neck, the blow causing him to stagger in front of his attacker. What the sword cut had begun, the hooves finished.

One or two Austrians turned and tried to protect themselves but it was futile. The sheer bulk of the horses was too much for them and those not cut down by swords were buffeted and crushed.

A corporal drove his bayonet at Charvet in a desperate attempt to defend himself but Charvet knocked the weapon to one side and slashed the man across the face.

Even Lausard's horse was snapping and biting at the Austrians as they ran, and Lausard cut down two more of the white-coated troops.

They rode over a small ridge, urged on by Deschamps but barely needing any encouragement. It was as if Lausard's frenzy had infected all the men around him.

A ripple of bangs sounded as a line of Austrian troops opened fire.

A number of horses were hit.

One close to Lausard went down, somersaulted and threw its rider from the saddle. Another fell sideways, crashing into those following, causing more to stumble and fall, many unseating their riders.

Roussard guided his horse over a tangle of struggling men and horses, urging the animal to leap the mêlée, which it did, landing surefootedly and charging on.

Rocheteau heard a loud clang and realised that one

of the musket balls had struck his helmet just above the crown. Allowing himself a brief sigh of relief, he rode on towards the line of Austrians, who were trying to reload. Only a handful managed it before the dragoons crashed into them. The volley they unleashed did little damage but Lausard saw more horses fall and, to his right, a dragoon was struck in the eye by one of the balls. He toppled backwards out of the saddle. Another clutched at his chest, his horse careering across the front of the charging dragoons, its dying rider still upright in the saddle.

The last few Austrians were ridden down, their screams lost beneath the thundering of hooves, a sound which was now mingling with the roar of cannon and the shouts of charging infantry.

'They're running!' bellowed Lausard, striking at another opponent.

The Austrians had broken.

All over the ridge and beyond, white-uniformed troops were fleeing for their lives, most of them throwing away their muskets. Some tried to surrender but many were just ridden down or sabred. An officer tried one final futile stand and swung his sword at Lausard who slashed at the man, severing his hand at the wrist. The officer screamed as his hand went spinning into the air, still gripping his sword. Blood spouted from the stump as he turned to meet a thrust from Joubert, who was almost pulled from his saddle as his sword remained firmly embedded in his foe. The officer dropped to his knees, hunched over as if in prayer, the sword still stuck through him.

Deschamps, his face and jacket spattered with blood, shouted for the trumpeters to sound the recall, and

Gaston and the others began to blow furiously.

The charge began to falter as horses slowed down, reined in by their riders who felt an exhilaration unlike anything they'd ever felt before. Lausard was breathing heavily, from the exertion but also from excitement. His face was sheathed in sweat and blood, his breeches and saddle also spattered with gore. His horse had been cut across the hindquarters by a bayonet but the wound wasn't deep and the animal seemed untroubled by the gash.

Carbonne wiped blood from his eyes and realised that a musket ball had grazed his forehead.

Bonet was nursing a bruised knuckle where a spent ball had struck him on the hand but otherwise he was uninjured.

Royere galloped out of a smoke-bank looking at the dragoons, trying to appraise the damage. He saw Lausard and nodded, a thin smile hovering on his lips. Lausard returned the gesture and noticed that the officer was bleeding from a wound in his shoulder.

'Are you all right, sir?'

'It went straight through.' Royere touched the wound tentatively with a gloved hand. When he brought the hand away his fingers were slick with blood.

'Get that wound seen to,' Deschamps instructed him.

Royere nodded. 'The Austrians are falling back, sir,' he said, smiling.

Deschamps didn't answer. He nodded curtly, then turned to Sergeant Legier who had also ridden up, his own sword bloody, his horse limping slightly from a cut on its left forelock.

'Take number two squadron and follow them,'

Deschamps told Legier. 'I want them watched, not engaged. Send back reports every hour.'

Legier saluted and wheeled his horse away.

Only now did Royere finally slip forward slightly in his saddle and Lausard shot out a hand to support him.

'See that the Lieutenant gets that wound attended to, Sergeant Lausard,' Deschamps told him. 'I want every trooper ready to move out in six hours.'

'Those thieving bastards,' said Rocheteau, glaring at the infantry who were busily robbing the dead Austrians. 'Look at them.'

'Yes,' snapped Giresse. 'They will take everything.'

'There'll be nothing left for us,' Rocheteau said smiling. Both men dismounted, the corporal running towards a dead officer who was lying close by. He flipped the body over and began pulling the buttons free.

Giresse was going through the pack of a dead private, delighted when he found half a bottle of wine inside.

Other troopers were dismounting now, eager not to miss out on the bounty.

Lausard looked around him at the scavenging dragoons, leading Royere's horse with his free hand.

'Once a thief always a thief, eh, Lausard?' said the officer, smiling weakly. 'I think they've earned it, don't you?'

Lausard didn't answer.

The dead Austrian was in his early forties. A distinguished-looking man with a thick moustache and sideboards flecked with grey. His face was relatively unmarked, the wound which had killed him having been received to the back of his skull. In fact, both his eyes were still open and Delacor paused to peer into those lifeless pools as if fearing that the man was still watching him. He waited a moment as if mesmerised by the staring eyes then, gently, he reached forward and closed the lids. He moved away from the body, scuttling across to another Austrian who'd been killed by a musket ball which had struck him in the chest. Delacor swiftly and expertly went through his pockets and pack, coming up with some tobacco, a pair of socks and a piece of cheese wrapped in muslin. He took a bite before stuffing it into his own pack.

Several dragoons were shepherding some Austrian prisoners towards the French ridge, which was all but deserted now. The prisoners had been stripped of everything except their breeches and shirts and they trudged along, some with their hands behind their heads, some walking sullenly, others supporting injured comrades.

Lausard watched the dismal little procession from his saddle then allowed his gaze to drift once again over the ridge and the valley. The dead of both sides were being collected together by some infantrymen, who were dragging the corpses towards a series of large holes that had been dug in the rock-hard earth. Lausard guessed that none of the mass graves was deeper than about two or three feet, barely sufficient to cover the corpses and sure to attract scavengers. Every corpse was naked, clothes, equipment and personal effects having been taken by the burial parties. The clothes and weapons had been piled high into two wagons drawn by some scrawny-looking mules. General Augereau's division of a thousand men, who had no firearms, had been forced to advance anyway and the captured enemy muskets were to be distributed amongst them.

A French artillery crew was busily limbering up an Austrian six-pounder in preparation for it to be hauled away. A shortage of horses for the campaign had ensured that not only were the bulk of the cavalry understrength but also the artillery lacked horses. Lausard was beginning to wonder if there was anything which the Army of Italy was *not* lacking. And yet, despite these shortcomings, they had won their first victory under Bonaparte and, again, Lausard found a certain irony in his situation. He, the son of an aristocratic family forced to hide in the gutters of Paris, driven to fight and live alongside men he would normally have shunned, was fighting in an army commanded by a Corsican peasant who was forced to prove himself to older and so-to-say socially superior officers, many of whom resented both his youth and his lack of social skills.

He walked his horse slowly across the ridge, guiding it past one of the mass graves, through dry, burned grass, avoiding bodies where he could. The ground was spattered with blood, which had dried so quickly beneath the scorching sun that even the flies had enjoyed only a brief feast. They swarmed over the bodies of the dead, of course, but those too were hauled away as swiftly as possible.

The smoke had cleared but the air still smelled of spent cartridges. The slope was littered with musket balls and roundshot, pieces of blackened wadding and burned paper from so many cartridges. In the clear sky overhead a number of crows circled, waiting to descend on the dead when the opportunity presented itself.

The sun glinted off something golden in the dry grass ahead and Lausard dismounted to see what it was, surprised that anything of value had been left behind by his scavenging comrades. What he found fitted into the palm of his hand. At first he thought it was a watch but as he flipped it open he realised that it was a locket. An inscription in the lid read:

To My Dearest Karl With Love From Madelaine.

He inspected the tiny painting of a young woman, her features as delicate as porcelain, then he snapped the locket shut and slipped it into his pocket, wondering where the owner was now. Had he fled with the other Austrian troops? Was he lying wounded somewhere or had his body already been pushed into one of the mass graves? Lausard swung himself back into the saddle, his gaze scanning the ridge and beyond.

In the distance he could hear the occasional popping of musket fire but, other than that, the battlefield and its surrounding area was relatively quiet.

He saw Gaston and Rostov approaching, also walking their horses slowly across the scorched ridge. The young boy was wiping his head with the sleeve of his tunic, his brass helmet held beneath the other arm. He was gazing around at the activity, occasionally looking intently at one of the dead. Rostov seemed unmoved by it all, hardly blinking as two drummer boys helped a French infantryman, his right foot shattered, down the slope towards the temporary field hospital. There, a group of surgeons and their assistants did their best for the injured of both sides, although the remedies were at best rudimentary and at worst as lethal as the wounds themselves.

'Not joining the scavengers?' Lausard asked, pointing at the French troops still busily searching the pockets and packs of the dead.

'I took some bread from one of them,' the Russian told him. 'We shared it.' He nodded towards Gaston.

Lausard reached into his pocket and pulled out the locket, allowing the Russian to inspect it.

'She's a good-looking woman,' he said admiringly. 'I wonder who'll be keeping her company from now on?' He tossed the locket back to Lausard.

'How many do you think died here today?' Gaston asked.

Lausard could only shrug. 'Does it matter?'

'I was curious,' Gaston told him.

'Death makes men curious,' Lausard said. 'It makes us realise our own mortality.'

'Our first battle, our first victory,' Rostov said, a note of pride in his voice.

Lausard nodded. 'It certainly won't be our last,' he said quietly.

'You don't sound too disappointed, Alain,' Rostov observed.

Lausard shook his head almost imperceptibly.

CHAPTER 22

General Bonaparte raised his wine glass, a smile on his thin features.

'Hannibal crossed the Alps,' he said, looking around at his officers. 'We have outflanked them.' A chorus of approving murmurs and laughs greeted the remark and the other men drank their wine, enjoying the occasion, celebrating the toast with their commander.

'In fifteen days we have brought Piedmont to its knees,' the general continued. 'We have won battles at Montenotte, Millesimo, Dego and Mondovi. We have taken twenty-one colours, fifty-five pieces of artillery, captured fifteen thousand and killed or wounded ten thousand. All for the cost of six thousand of our own casualties. I tell you, gentlemen, we are only at the beginning.' He took another sip of wine. 'I have already written to the Directory asking for another ten thousand reinforcements. We will need them to complete our task.'

'You expect help from those bastards?' Augereau snapped at his commander.

'*They* are our government,' Bonaparte reminded him.

'They care nothing for us. They are as corrupt as the Bourbons were. They know nothing of what happens here.'

'They know what I tell them,' Bonaparte said. 'They know what I allow them to know.'

A ripple of laughter travelled around the men.

'Do they know that La Harpe's men mutinied?' Serurier asked, not looking at his commander.

'That was an unfortunate incident but one which could not have been avoided,' Bonaparte said dismissively. 'The problem has been rectified now.'

'They mutinied because they were not allowed to share in the looting of Mondovi,' the older man sneered. 'They behaved like common thieves, not soldiers.'

'Most of the army consists of thieves,' Massena offered. 'That includes officers too.'

There was more laughter.

Serurier did not join in. He shook his head wearily.

'The French army exists by foraging, you know that,' Bonaparte reminded him.

'And by stealing?'

'They haven't been paid for so long they've forgotten what sous look like,' Massena interjected.

'They're entitled to share in our victory by whatever means,' Bonaparte continued. 'They obey orders, they carry out my wishes. That is all I ask of *any* man.' He fixed Serurier in an unblinking stare. 'Loyalty.'

'So we buy their loyalty by letting them ravage the countryside?' Serurier snapped.

'We already have their loyalty, we don't *buy* that with bounty, we *instil* it with victory.'

'And where will our next victory come?' Augereau

wanted to know. 'We've beaten the Piedmontese, we've even beaten the Alps. How do we beat the river? That bastard could destroy us, even if the Austrians can't.'

'The Po is a fast-flowing river,' Massena added. 'It would be difficult enough to cross even without Beaulieu and his Austrians so close. We have no bridging train. We will have to cross at one of the established points and they are all guarded and fortified.'

'So, how the hell do we get over this river?' Augereau persisted, filling his glass again and looking down at the map spread out on the table before them.

'Not only must we cross it,' Bonaparte said, 'we must force Beaulieu to fight, to commit his forces, but he seems more intent on running.'

'The north bank is a stronger position,' Massena observed. 'He wants to meet us there.'

'So, where do we cross?' Augereau asked.

'There are three places,' Bonaparte informed him, turning his attention to the map. 'Here, at Valenza, is the closest. But it is also the most dangerous because it is nearest to the main Austrian force. We could move quickly but we run the risk of being attacked while we're crossing.'

'If the Austrians catch us strung out, crossing those bridges, they'll destroy us,' said Augereau.

Bonaparte ignored the other man's comment and pointed at another spot on the map. 'Or we could cross here, south of Pavia,' he said. 'If we do that, it puts us *behind* Beaulieu. We will disrupt his lines of communication but, again, the problem is that the main Austrian force is very close. I suggest we cross here, at Piacenza.'

'But that's fifty miles away,' Serurier said incredulously.

'And the Po is at its deepest and widest there,' added Augereau.

'It looks the most hazardous of all crossing points,' Massena offered.

Bonaparte smiled. 'If we cross there,' he said, 'we cross as close as possible to Milan itself and we also turn the three lines of defence which Beaulieu has prepared along the Agogna, the Terdoppio and the Ticino. Pavia will be turned and if Beaulieu chooses to defend it we will be between him and his supply depots.' He stood back smugly, eyes flicking across the faces of his companions.

'It's dangerous,' Augereau countered.

'Wherever we cross is dangerous.'

'But it's fifty miles away,' Serurier said.

'Speed and surprise will be our allies. The risks are worthwhile,' Bonaparte proclaimed. 'At worst we might force Beaulieu to retreat piecemeal which will make him easier to destroy. At best, we will catch his entire force and *make* him stand and fight.'

'I still think it's risky,' Serurier reiterated wearily.

'It is, but you and Massena will help deflect interest from our main force by distracting the Austrians into thinking you and your men are crossing at Valenza,' Bonaparte told him. 'We need that diversion.' He looked around at his officers. 'Have faith, gentlemen. Victory awaits us.'

CHAPTER 23

The explosion brought down three horses and sent several more dashing madly to one side where they collided with other riders.

Lausard felt himself thrown through the air. He hit the ground with a thud and rolled over, desperate to avoid his falling horse which whinnied in fear then scrambled back to its feet. It reared but did not run.

Lausard hauled himself to his feet, caught the reins of the terrified animal and steadied it, glancing around him briefly at the damage the Austrian shell had caused.

One of the trio of horses brought down was lying motionless and even a quick inspection revealed that it was dead, blood spouting from a wound in its neck. The other two were back on their feet, one bleeding from a gash on its flank, the other limping slightly, a piece of flying steel having cracked its left front hoof. The riders were relatively unscathed: one was clutching his forearm, cursing the pain and the blood which stained his green tunic; the second had lost his brass helmet and was staggering around looking for it; while

the third had sustained nothing more than a split lip
when he'd hit the ground.

Lausard remounted, watched by Rocheteau, who
seemed reassured by the nod the sergeant gave him.

Another blast erupted about twenty yards to their
left and the dragoons saw several infantrymen drop.

The Austrian cannon on the north bank of the Adda
River were keeping up a steady fire with both shell and
roundshot, their fire concentrated on the bridge across
the river which linked the two parts of the town of
Lodi. It was the only crossing point and would have to
be stormed if the French were to progress. Through a
rolling fog of smoke, Lausard counted six guns at the
far end of the bridge itself and another three on either
side, designed to catch any charging French troops in a
withering enfilade fire when they chose to attack.

The French artillery fired back and Tabor watched as
a four-pounder was loaded, fired and then thrown
backwards with the recoil, its shell hurled towards the
Austrians on the far bank. He saw the speeding black
object strike its target and there was a massive explosion as an enemy artillery caisson blew up, a mushroom
cloud of black and red smoke rising into the air.

A great cheer accompanied the blast and many of the
infantry shouted words of encouragement as they
waited their turn to assault the bridge. Flags, some
shredded by fire, were held proudly aloft in the smoke-
darkened air.

'It looks like Bonaparte did a good job,' said
Rocheteau as another salvo of roundshot exploded
from the French guns, all of the shots striking targets on
the far bank. Austrian troops went down and the cheering of the French grew in volume.

'I wouldn't want to be the first one on to that bridge,' said Joubert, eyeing the formidable array of firepower which the Austrians had amassed.

'I'd rather swim the river,' Roussard added.

'At this rate we might have to,' Lausard said, his voice drowned out by another explosion nearby.

Lumps of earth and a cloud of dust came out of the sky to envelope the dragoons.

Gaston was almost knocked from his horse by a large piece of rock which banged against his helmet with an audible clang.

Rochereau shot out a hand to support the boy who swayed uncertainly in his saddle for a moment before steadying himself.

Lieutenant Royere, his wounded shoulder bandaged, rode past. His voice was barely audible above the roar of cannon but he was signalling for the dragoons to follow him and the men at the front of the column duly did so, galloping across the path of the waiting infantry. Others looked with trepidation towards the bridge, knowing that they would soon be ordered to charge its bristling defences. They had driven the Austrians out of Lodi with relative ease earlier in the morning but the bridge presented a different obstacle altogether. Many felt a twinge of fear at the thought of charging across it into such furious fire.

'They'll be slaughtered,' Roussard remarked as the dragoons rode by.

'God help them,' echoed Bonet.

'If God's got any sense, He'll be far away from here,' Rostov said.

'He is here with us,' Moreau rebuked, 'He is always with us.'

'Then I wish He'd tell us what's going on,' Giresse said. 'Where are we going? If the bridge is the only way across that river why the hell are we riding away from it?'

'There must be fords up and down it somewhere,' Lausard called, glancing across the fast-flowing water. He caught sight of more Austrian troops arrayed on the opposite bank but then they began to disappear from view among the trees along the riverside. The steeples of two or three churches strained above the tree-tops but the houses of Lodi were effectively hidden behind the green. Smoke rose into the air though, drifting up into the blue sky from buildings which had been set ablaze by the continuing bombardment. Pulling clear of the main hub of the battle, the dragoons found themselves surrounded on both sides by heavily leafed trees. Occasionally there would be a break in the screen and the river would come into view once more but, otherwise, the sounds of fighting began to recede.

Lausard saw men moving in the trees up ahead. Blue- or red-jacketed troops. There was a number of horses too, some tethered, others standing obediently, chewing at the short grass on the bank.

'Hussars,' said Rocheteau, catching a better view. One of their officers was sitting by the roadside chewing contentedly on a piece of stale bread. He nodded perfunctorily towards Royere who reined in his horse, waving a hand to slow the following dragoons.

'We're looking for a ford,' Royere announced.

'What do you think we're doing?' the hussar officer asked, grinning. 'Picking daisies? There's no way across this damned river other than the bridge.'

'There has to be a shallower crossing point some-where,' Royere insisted.

'Bonaparte's sent men in both directions to find one but it's a waste of time,' the hussar continued, chewing the last of his bread. 'Still, it keeps us out of the Austrian fire, doesn't it?'

Royere shook his head irritably and prepared to lead the waiting dragoons on.

'You'll find nothing further up the bank,' the hussar insisted.

'How far up have you checked?' Royere demanded.

The hussar shrugged. 'Far enough. Why not wait? Let the infantry take the bridge, we can cross in peace.' He laughed.

Royere didn't share the joke; he waved his hand for the dragoons to follow him and they galloped off along the riverside road, leaving the hussars behind.

'Perhaps he was right,' offered Rocheteau, glancing back at the hussar officer. 'Perhaps there is no ford.'

Lausard looked at his companion briefly. 'Then we might have to charge the bridge.'

Rocheteau held his sergeant's gaze for a second and found the steely look in his eyes almost unnerving.

They were approaching a bend in the road where the trees were not so dense, giving a clearer view of the river. Behind them, the sound of musket fire seemed to have intensified and Lausard guessed that the French infantry had begun its assault on the bridge. Smoke was still rising in clouds above the town, part of which had caught fire under the shelling.

Royere suddenly reined in his horse and waved a hand to halt the column.

Lausard watched as the officer pulled out a telescope and scanned the far bank.

The trees on the other side were also more sparse and, clearly visible amongst them, even without the benefit of a telescope, was a number of cavalrymen, some of whom were formed up into lines facing the river.

Royere surveyed the Austrian troops, trying to pick out exactly which type of men he was facing. Most carried carbines and their grey uniforms marked them out as mounted hussars.

'That must be the ford,' said Lausard, pointing towards the enemy cavalry.

'How do you know?' Delacor asked him.

'Why else would the Austrians be guarding that part of the bank?'

Royere walked his horse towards the edge of the river and rose in his saddle. There was a crack from the far bank and a musket ball dropped harmlessly into the water about ten feet to his right.

'We're going across,' he shouted to the waiting dragoons. 'Draw swords.'

The air was filled with the familiar metallic hiss of fifty swords being drawn and the dragoons formed up into two lines behind the lieutenant.

'Charnier,' he snapped at one of the men closest to him. 'Ride back to Lodi and bring the rest of the regiment. Tell Captain Deschamps we need reinforcements now.'

The trooper nodded and galloped off.

'Why the hell don't we just wait for the others?' Roussard queried, peering across the river at the hussars, a number of whom had now dismounted and were taking up firing positions behind trees and bushes on the far bank. The rest were forming up into lines.

'Because the Austrians will be calling for reinforcements too,' Bonet told him. 'By the time the others reach us we could be facing twice that number.'

'We don't know how many there are now,' Sonnier protested.

'Forward!' ordered Royere and the dragoons advanced down the river bank at a walk, the officer's horse leading the way into the shallows, water splashing up around its hooves.

Lausard gripped his reins tightly as their horses entered deeper water which rose past the animals' forelocks to their hindquarters. Some whinnied fearfully as the water lapped around them and many of the men felt the river pouring into their boots. Water was splashing up all around them and now small geysers began to shoot up as more musket fire was directed at them by the Austrians. A ball whizzed past Rocheteau's ear and struck the helmet of the man behind him, spinning away harmlessly.

The depth of the water was slowing the advance of the dragoons and Lausard urged his mount on, realising that they were now halfway across; the water level would begin to drop again at any moment but the journey seemed to be taking an eternity. To his left a dragoon was struck in the face by a musket ball. He screamed and toppled from the saddle, his horse trying to rear up as the body fell with a loud splash, blood staining the water nearby.

A horse was struck in the neck and fell forward, pitching its rider into the water. He surfaced spluttering for air.

The water smelled rank, its odour mingling with a stench of sweat and a gradually more pervasive odour of gunpowder.

Downriver Lausard noticed that the bridge was being attacked, blue-clad French infantry swarming across it into ferocious fire. To him that did not seem as important as the realisation that the water was becoming more shallow again. The dragoons and their horses were beginning to rise up out of the water, the animals gaining a firmer footing.

A salvo of musket fire swept them and two more men were unhorsed.

'Jesus!' hissed Rocheteau, his gaze fixed on the far bank. 'They'll pick us all off before we reach them.'

Royere was urging his mount on, up into the shallows.

He waved his sword high above his head.

'Charge!' he bellowed.

The dragoons did as they were ordered, battling against the flowing water and also against the incline of the bank and driving their horses on towards the Austrians. The hussars moved forward at a canter, swords drawn, intent on meeting the French before they could clear the river.

The enemy cavalry came down the opposite slope led by a huge officer on a black horse, who headed straight for Royere.

Gaston pressed the bugle to his lips and blasted out the notes which signalled the charge and the dragoons flung themselves forward as best they could.

Royere met the Austrian officer, blocking his downward stroke and slashing at his face, carving a huge gash in his opponent's cheek, but the huge man scarcely

seemed to notice and struck at the lieutenant once
again, this time with such power that he almost
knocked Royere from his horse. The animal reared and
a thrust aimed at Royere caught it in the shoulder.
Blood jetted from the wound and the horse whinnied in
pain, toppling to one side, flinging the lieutenant from
the saddle. He dragged himself to his feet, confused,
turning in time to see the Austrian's sabre flash above
his head. He had no chance to raise his own weapon in
defence. He waited for the cut that would kill him.

There was a loud bang and the officer toppled from
his horse trailing blood in the air behind him.

Royere, waist-deep in water, spun round and saw
that Lausard had shot the man from point-blank range
with one of his pistols, the weapon still smoking in his
fist. He re-holstered it and extended the same hand to
Royere who nodded and allowed himself to be pulled
upright.

Rocheteau grabbed the reins of the dead Austrian's
horse and Royere swung himself into the saddle. He
looked both at Lausard then at Rocheteau but no
words were exchanged. There was no time.

A second line of mounted hussars crashed into the
dragoons now fighting their way through shallower
water. The horses dug their rear hooves into the mud
and headed for the bank.

Carbonne drove his sword deep into the chest of an
attacker, hearing a crack as the steel smashed bone and
grated against a rib before he tugged it free.

Delacor, meanwhile, ducked beneath a sword swipe
and used his elbow to fend off the Austrian, slamming
the point of it into the man's face. As his injured foe
wavered in the saddle, Delacor stabbed him in the

stomach and shoulder, smiling as the body toppled into the water.

The horses too seemed gripped by the savagery of the moment and they snapped and bit at each other and more often than not, at other riders as the two sets of cavalrymen clashed in the shallows where the water was already turning red beneath the churning hooves. The air was filled with the clanging of steel on steel and, to Bonet, it sounded as if dozens of blacksmiths were at work.

Charvet hissed in pain as a sword cut opened his arm from elbow to wrist, blood spurting from the wound. As the Austrian struck at him again he seized the man's arm with his free hand and yanked so hard that he pulled the man from his saddle. The hussar fell into the water, rising quickly to avoid the hooves of the horses. Charvet kicked out at him, his boot catching the man in the face. As he reeled from the impact, the Frenchman caught him across the shoulder with a devastating backhand slash.

Despite their own comrades now being in the line of fire, the dismounted hussars on the bank kept up their fusillade and several more dragoons went down, killed or wounded. But now, by sheer savage determination, the dragoons were beginning to force their opponents back, to reach the dry ground of the bank where their horses could get a firm foothold. The desperation in their fighting seemed to take the hussars by surprise and a number wheeled their mounts and galloped away.

Lausard and Rocheteau, alongside Royere, led the green-coated dragoons up the bank. Lausard, his face spattered with blood, struck down two Austrians, riding over one with his horse, his eyes scanning the bank for more enemies.

Sonnier pulled his carbine free and shot down one of the hussars, smiling as he saw the man clutching at his chest. Before he could reload, Sonnier was faced with another man and he swung the carbine like a club, smashing the butt into the Austrian's face.

Those hussars on foot suddenly ran for their tethered mounts and Lausard wondered why. Although the dragoons had reached the bank, they were still out-numbered, their horses exhausted.

'Look!' shouted Giresse and Lausard turned to see the remainder of the regiment, led by Deschamps, pour-ing into the river, churning across it. On either flank, hussars supported the attack.

Seeing the oncoming green mass Lausard managed a smile.

A number of the hussars were throwing away their weapons and raising their hands in surrender. Those who could were fleeing, some leaving their horses behind as they ran for sanctuary in the trees.

A cheer went up from the dragoons, but Lausard's attention was now concentrated on the fleeing hussars who were heading back in the direction of Lodi. He glanced downriver towards the town, which was shrouded in smoke now, the bridge a mass of blue-jacketed troops. He could see tricolours waving on the bridge, he could even see one or two on the northern bank.

'Victory?' said Giresse breathlessly, also seeing the French infantry swarming across the bridge.

Lausard looked back at the fleeing hussars then at the blazing inferno that was Lodi, flames licking towards the sky. He could feel the blood drying on his face but he made no attempt to wipe it away. It was dripping from his sabre too and he held the weapon aloft in triumph, his gesture suddenly copied by a dozen of his comrades. The sound of cheering began to grow louder.

CHAPTER 24

'They call him "The Little Corporal",' said Paul Barras, his voice heavy with scorn. 'The whole army loves him. *He* controls them, not us.'

'Did we ever?' Tallien asked. 'What's the harm in an army cherishing its commander? They will fight more vigorously for one they respect than one they despise.'

'And if that commander's aspirations are not just military but political, then he becomes twice as deadly,' Barras retorted. 'Bonaparte is as interested in the politics of this war as he is in the soldiery.'

'You sound as if you fear him, Barras,' Gohier said, polishing his spectacles with a small handkerchief.

'Perhaps we should *all* fear him a little. It may well prolong our careers, perhaps even our lives.'

'You overreact,' Letourneur said.

'Do I? Perhaps I know him better than you.'

'You were the one who was singing his praises until he stole your mistress,' Letourneur chided. 'Perhaps your dislike of Bonaparte stems from his personal achievements rather than any danger he may present as a political adversary.'

A heavy silence fell over the room, broken by Barras who glared at his companion. 'Bonaparte didn't steal my mistress,' he hissed. 'Our affair was over anyway. I had no further use for her.'

'As you say,' Letourneur murmured. 'The fact remains that, six months ago, when you recommended we give Bonaparte command of the Army of Italy, *you* were one of his leading supporters. Now you would see him deprived of that command because of a personal matter between the two of you.'

'I care nothing for Bonaparte in this matter,' Barras lied. 'My concern is for France and I fear for her with this Corsican in charge of our army. We tried to limit his power, we tried to split his command with Kellermann but he protested so we backed down. He has resisted *all* attempts to limit his control over the Army of Italy and we have *allowed* him to resist.'

'What choice do we have?' Tallien said. 'Before he took over the army was a shambles, the war was being lost. He has transformed those men with nothing but his personality and his skill as a leader, and you seek to restrain him.'

'For the good of France,' Barras said.

Tallien waved the suggestion away. 'The economy of France was collapsing,' he continued, 'the amount of plunder arriving daily from Italy, from Bonaparte, is what keeps this country on its feet. We need his victories for the financial gain they bring us and they give the people something to celebrate too. Conquests *outside* France make her people forget some of the hardships they endure. I say good luck to our "little corporal".'

'Why is he called by that name?' Gohier enquired.

'At Lodi he personally sighted some of the cannon during the battle,' Barras said haughtily. 'A task usually reserved for an artillery corporal.' Again there was scorn in his voice.

'His list of victories is impressive,' Tallien said.

'He has still failed to take Mantua,' said Barras. 'That fortress is the key to this campaign. Until it falls Bonaparte has achieved nothing.'

'So now you are a tactician as well?' Tallien challenged. 'How can you be so dismissive of what he has done? The summer is almost over and he has been triumphant in his battles; he has taken Milan, he has bled Italy to finance France and he has ensured that Spain has become our ally against the British. What more can he do?'

Barras had no answer. He sat back in his seat, clasping his hands before him as if in prayer.

'So, what arguments can you offer now?' Tallien continued. 'Do you still want to see Bonaparte replaced as head of the Army of Italy? Do you think Kellermann could do a better job?' He glanced around at his colleagues. 'Do any of you?'

The question was met by a chorus of grunts and headshaking.

'I still say that the Austrians were not *driven* out of Lombardy, they were *frightened* out,' Barras urged.

'They are out, that is all that matters,' Gohier said.

'In time we will all grow rich with Bonaparte's help,' Letourneur said, smiling. 'Why distrust him so?'

'At the moment he is harmless because he is five hundred miles away,' Barras argued, 'but mark my words, when he returns, *if* he does, then we may all do

well to reserve a little mistrust for him and for his army
because that is what it is. *His* army. We may have more
to fear from Bonaparte, in the long run, than the
Austrians.'

CHAPTER 25

Delacor reached out a hand, grabbed a fistful of grapes from the vine and squeezed them above his mouth, savouring the sweet juice that flowed from them. All around him other men were doing the same, slaking their thirsts with the liquid from the overripe grapes. Some had already begun to wither on the vines, unharvested and untended. Other bunches were fat and swollen with sweet fluid and the dragoons accepted the prize eagerly.

For the last twenty minutes they had been riding through countryside rich in provisions. Through rice fields, olive groves and vineyards, all but a few abandoned by their former owners whose tiled farmhouses stood empty. Many had been looted but the haul of valuables from these humble dwellings was nothing compared to the hoard of food which could be gathered, and the troops had collected as much as they could carry. What could not be stuffed into packs and portmanteaus had been eaten during the journey. They swept through the farms like locusts, stripping everything from the trees and vines.

Lausard chewed on a handful of grapes and looked up the road ahead to where Colonel Lannes and his aides were riding. Lannes was a tall, powerfully built man, a great friend of Bonaparte's and also the same age. Lausard could pick him out easily with his blue uniform and its sparkling gold epaulettes. Most of the army admired Lannes for his bravery. He had been the first man across the Po River and he'd sustained numerous wounds during the campaign so far. The troops respected and liked him. He also had a streak of ruthlessness about him which made him perfect for their present task.

'It's about time someone taught these Italian bastards a lesson,' Delacor opined, wiping juice from his mouth with the back of his hand. 'None of them are to be trusted. I mean to say, we liberate them and what do they do? Stab us in the back.'

'This isn't the first time they've revolted either,' Charvet offered. 'I heard that the garrison at Pavia actually surrendered.'

'Gutless bastards,' snapped Delacor.

'Bonaparte had the officer in charge shot,' Charvet continued.

'So what the hell are we supposed to do here?' Rocheteau said.

'Teach these Italians a lesson,' Delacor rasped.

'We're making war on women and children,' Bonet protested. 'They're innocent.'

'There are no innocents in war,' Lausard said, still chewing on some grapes. He spat out a couple of pips and pulled another handful from the vine closest to him.

'Our fight is with the Austrians,' Bonet persisted.

'These Italians have brought this upon themselves,' Rocheteau sneered.

'Yes, they should have kept out of our affairs,' Delacor echoed.

'We are not liberators to *them*, we are invaders, as unwelcome as the Austrians,' Bonet protested. 'What do you expect them to do?'

'It isn't just a matter of killing innocents,' said Giresse. 'How can we subdue the Austrians when we can't even control those people we've conquered.'

'Conquered?' Bonet said incredulously. 'In one breath we call ourselves liberators, in the next conquerors. What *are* we?'

'Soldiers,' Lausard said. 'Which is why we do our duty. Why we do as we are ordered and if that order is to burn a village then we do it. If that order is to charge an enemy position then we do it, and if that order is to kill women and children we do that too.'

'It isn't right,' Bonet said.

'Since when has war been right?' Lausard replied. 'But we are a part of it, schoolmaster, and we are here to obey orders, no matter what we think of them.'

'Maybe you should have stayed in Paris and kept your date with the guillotine,' said Rocheteau. 'At least you couldn't have moaned then.'

'*He* would,' Carbonne offered and the men around him chuckled. 'That's what you're best at, isn't it, schoolmaster? Complaining.'

'I was making an observation,' Bonet hissed. 'Just because we have to carry out orders doesn't mean we have to *like* them. My God, some of you actually sound as if you're looking forward to this.'

'And why shouldn't we?' said Delacor. 'Have you

forgotten what the "Barbets" did to us when we first came here?'

'These people we come to slaughter aren't guerrillas,' Bonet countered. 'They're innocent—'

'Oh, shut up!' Rocheteau advised, 'or you might find that the Italians aren't the only ones getting shot.'

There was more laughter among the men.

'You're worse than His Holiness there.' Rocheteau indicated Moreau with his finger. 'I suppose you disagree with all this too, do you, Moreau?'

'If it is God's will then I go along with it,' Moreau answered, crossing himself.

'You see, even the Almighty is against you,' Rocheteau said, turning his gaze back on Bonet.

Lausard said, 'God has nothing to do with this. He stopped caring about this army a long time ago.'

'God *is* with us,' Moreau objected. 'He *has* been from the beginning and He is now.'

'Well,' Rocheteau mused, 'I'd like a word with Him. I think my horse is going lame, I want to know if He can fix it.'

This was met with more howls of laughter.

'I hope He has patience with your blasphemy,' Moreau rebuked him.

'How can you still believe in a God after some of the things you've seen during this campaign?' Lausard asked.

'God is not to blame for this war or for the men who've died in it,' Moreau explained.

'Tell that to their families,' Bonet sneered.

'Most of them probably haven't even got families,' Lausard said. 'They're like us. They've got no one. Nobody's going to miss us if we die. Whether we'd have died back in Paris or here on some Italian hillside, we won't be missed.'

Giresse said, 'You speak for yourself. I can think of a couple of dozen women who'd be heartbroken if anything happened to me.'

Again there was laughter and even Lausard managed a smile.

'I'm surprised we haven't all died of hunger by now,' said Joubert.

'You know, you and Bonet make a good pair, fat man,' Rocheteau told the big man. 'Neither of you ever stops complaining. You about your belly and him about the rights and wrongs of this stinking war.'

'Why don't you *all* shut up,' Rostov interjected. 'You French, you're like a bunch of chickens, squawk, squawk, squawk.'

'And I suppose Russians never complain?' Joubert countered.

'No, we don't. We face each task as it comes and we get on with it. That is the nature of my people.'

'If you loved your people so much what were you doing in France?' Carbonne pointed out. 'That was why you were arrested, wasn't it, for being a foreigner?'

'My country is harsh,' the Russian told him. 'The climate, the land, the rich. Those who have plenty care nothing for the rest.'

'That was like those Bourbons,' Rocheteau said. 'And all the other rich bastards back in France. They weren't so powerful when they were walking to meet the guillotine though, were they?'

There was more laughter but Lausard didn't join in.

'I say all the rich in every country should be hung from the lamp-posts,' was Delacor's offering.

There were some cheers of agreement.

Lausard gazed blankly at Delacor, who was slightly puzzled by the darkness in the sergeant's expression.

'Then you'll have to hang most of the officers in the army,' Bonet interjected. 'They're all becoming rich from plundering Italian cities.'

'That's different,' Delacor said.

'How?' Lausard asked. 'Isn't one rich man the same as the next? Shouldn't they all be judged as harshly? There are no good rich men, are there, Delacor? Just as there are no innocents in this war. Everyone gets the same treatment.'

It was Rocheteau's turn to eye Lausard with something akin to bewilderment but, before he could question his friend's vehemence, the column was called to a halt and told to form up in lines at the base of a gentle slope. On the crest of the ridge, Lannes and his aides were sheltered by a clump of poplars, their attention drawn to whatever lay in the shallow valley beyond. After a moment or two of wild gesticulation from a number of the blue-clad officers, Lausard saw them, led by Lannes himself, riding back towards the waiting dragoons. The small group came to a halt ten yards from the leading cavalrymen and Lannes rose in his stirrups, waving his bicorn in his hand to attract their attention.

'Soldiers of France,' he began. 'Over that crest lies the village of St Vicini. It has risen against us, against General Bonaparte, against France. Its people have ignored our kindness, they have shown the kind of treachery which cannot be tolerated. They have murdered our soldiers, just as the people of Tortona, Pozzolo and Arquarta have risen and murdered our

men. This cannot be allowed.' Lannes looked from face
to face as if scrutinising each of the waiting dragoons.
'Where these towns and villages rise, others will follow.
If they see that we do not react to this treachery they
will think us weak. They will side with our enemies to
try to defeat us but we have fought too hard for that,
you have fought too bravely to be betrayed by such as
these.' He waved a hand towards the crest of the ridge.
'The village is yours. Everything it contains is yours.
Destroy it and those who dwell within it. Destroy the
traitors who would stab you in the back. Take from
them what you will. They must become an example.
The rest of this country must learn the folly of resisting
the French Republic.' He drew his sword and waved it
above his head, his features set in stern lines. '*Vive
Bonaparte! Vive la République!*'

The dragoons moved forward.

The dead woman was in her early twenties.

Lausard wondered if she might even be a little
younger but it was difficult to tell. The sabre cut that
had killed her had laid open one cheek to the bone,
shattered her jawbone and spilled several of her teeth
on to the cobbled street.

He rode slowly past the corpse, shielding his eyes
momentarily from a fierce eruption of flames spewing
from one of the many burning houses. The heat from
the fire combined with the scorching sun and the exertions of the past thirty minutes had caused Lausard to
sweat heavily and he felt droplets of the salty fluid
trickling down his cheeks and neck.

The entire village of St Vicini was ablaze, even the
tiny church which dominated the central square was

burning from door to spire. Two dozen bodies were piled unceremoniously in front of it. All of them men, all of them shot on the orders of Lannes. Blood had spread out around them in a wide pool, now slowly congealing. Elsewhere, bodies had fallen where they'd been hit; men, women and children shot, sabred or simply ridden down by the dragoons who had swept through their village like vengeful demons.

Two of the green-clad troops galloped past, blood still smeared on their swords, one of them carrying a small sack of rice he'd taken from one of the houses before incinerating it. It was a meagre bounty and the entire village had yielded little in the way of spoils. Some food, the odd piece of jewellery and that was all. But the object of St Vicini's destruction hadn't been gain. The village had been a sacrifice, an example.

Lausard wondered if the gesture would have the desired effect. He guided his horse down the street, the animal lifting its hooves to avoid stepping on the body of an old man who'd been stabbed in the chest and back. Slumped in the doorway of the house behind him was a younger man, his body half-devoured by the flames consuming the building.

Lausard took off his helmet and ran a hand through his hair.

'Another glorious victory for the Republic.'

He heard the weary voice and turned to see Bonet had joined him. The ex-schoolmaster was perspiring profusely too, his horse heavily lathered.

'It had to be done,' Lausard told him.

'Do you honestly believe that, Alain?'

'I believe that these towns and villages that have

risen against us are of strategic importance and that they must not be allowed to stop us winning this war. Is that enough for you?'

'Is that your justification for this butchery?'

'I don't *need* to justify it,' Lausard responded angrily. 'We did as we were ordered. It's as simple as that and we'll do it again and again and again if we have to. Because we have no choice.'

'Because we're soldiers?' Bonet chided.

'Yes, and if that is the only way this war can be won then so be it.'

'Slaughtering women and children isn't going to bring us victory. Where's the glory in that?'

Lausard laughed scornfully. 'In case you'd forgotten, none of us is a part of this army because we wanted glory. We're here because there's nowhere else for us to go. We're here because we chose to take our chances here rather than die like sewer rats in some filthy prison. Or perhaps you'd prefer to be back there.'

'Don't tell me you agree with this slaughter because I won't believe you.'

Lausard didn't speak. He fixed the schoolmaster in an unblinking stare and carefully replaced his brass helmet.

'Don't expect me to pity them, Bonet,' he said finally, glancing towards the burning church and the pile of corpses which lay before it. 'There's no room for pity in war.'

'Nor compassion?' Bonet said softly.

Lausard shook his head.

Rocheteau and Delacor brought their horses trotting up the street, a barking dog following them. It seemed to be the only inhabitant of St Vicini left alive and it darted back and forth behind and between the horses' legs as the dragoons guided their mounts towards their companions. Delacor shouted at the dog but it refused to leave them.

'Easy pickings,' said Delacor smiling, looking around at the blazing village.

Bonet threw him a disgusted glance.

'What's wrong with you, schoolmaster?' Delacor teased. 'Not got the stomach for it?'

'Not for *this*,' Bonet grunted.

'What about *this*?' said Delacor, reaching round to his portmanteau. He pulled a golden candlestick from it and held it before him like a trophy. 'I took it from the church.'

'And I got the other one,' Rocheteau echoed, holding up another candlestick.

Bonet was unimpressed.

'This'll be worth five loaves of bread,' Delacor chided. 'Don't expect me to share any of it with you, schoolmaster.'

'I wouldn't want it,' said Bonet and wheeled his horse, guiding it up the street to where a number of the dragoons had already formed a ragged column.

'What's the matter with him?' said Rocheteau. 'He's more pious than Moreau and that's saying something.'

'He's had an attack of conscience,' Lausard said dismissively. 'He doesn't think we should be killing women and children.'

'Do you?' Rocheteau asked.

'I don't know what to think,' Lausard said. 'Perhaps it's best not to. I don't know if what we're doing is right or wrong; I don't even *care*. Besides, since when have right and wrong mattered?'

Rocheteau pushed the candlestick back into his port-manteau. 'Did you get anything for yourself?'

'Nothing worth taking from here,' Lausard said, sur-veying the carnage. Large cinders were floating up into the bright sky, carried on the updraught created by so many fires. The roof of one of the small houses col-lapsed, sending up a shower of sparks. Lausard's horse reared at the sight but he steadied it. The dog continued to dash around the horses, barking wildly until it finally dashed off up the street towards the other dragoons. Delacor raced after it, yelling angrily at the animal.

'He raped one of the women before he killed her,' Rocheteau told Lausard. 'Giresse saw him, he told me.'

'That's what he was in prison for, wasn't it?' Lausard said, unmoved. 'Men like him don't change.'

'What about us, Alain? Have *we* changed?'

'We know how to kill now. That's all that's different about us. Men don't change and we're the same as any man.'

'We're better than Delacor. We're not rapists.'

'Thieves, murderers, rapists. What's the difference?'

Lausard rode slowly up the street, the heat from the burning buildings searing him from both sides. Moreau rode past him, also sweating from the effect of the roar-ing flames.

'They're like the fires of hell,' he said. 'And they're waiting for us all.'

'Let them wait,' Lausard whispered under his breath.

The stench was appalling but Bonaparte barely seemed to notice it. The air reeked with a foul combination of blood, sweat, urine, infection and vomit. He didn't recoil but the smell inside the field hospital at Albaredo caused his companion, Captain Jean Baptiste Bessieres, to wrinkle his nose visibly. Bonaparte suppressed a grin and leaned closer to his companion.

'For the son of a surgeon, my friend, you have a strong dislike of hospitals,' he said and chuckled.

Bessieres ignored the comment and scanned the rows of wounded who filled the building.

'As a soldier I have a strong dislike of death,' he said finally. 'This is a place of death, not healing.'

'These men were wounded fighting for France, do you expect me to abandon them? Those who recover will fight on once again. God knows, we can afford to lose no more men.'

'I don't expect you to abandon them, sir,' Bessieres said indignantly. 'I wish there was more that could be *done* for the poor wretches. Perhaps if the government hadn't abolished medical schools then there'd be more doctors to cope.'

'Larrey and Desgenettes do their best,' Bonaparte said, waving away one of his aides who attempted to accompany him to the nearest patient. 'They are even more acutely aware of the problem than we are.'

The man lying closest was opening and closing his mouth slowly and soundlessly like a stranded fish. His head was heavily bandaged from the scalp to the nose. Blood had soaked through the filthy bandages in several places. Bonaparte reached out and took the man's hand, squeezing it.

'Can you hear me?' he said quietly.

'Doctor?' the man croaked, his throat dry and parched from lack of water.

'No, it is not the doctor. It is your general. I am Bonaparte. At which battle were you wounded?'

'Lonato, sir,' the man told him. 'I would have given my life for you, my General; instead I gave my eyes.'

Bonaparte patted the man's hand and moved to the next patient, who was lying motionless on his straw pallet. His face was the colour of rotten cheese and thick saliva was dribbling from his lips. He didn't respond when Bonaparte spoke to him. Bessieres reached out a hand and pressed it to the man's throat, feeling for a pulse. He detected one but it was incredibly weak.

'He needs a priest, not a doctor,' said the captain softly.

Orderlies in ragged blue uniforms were tending to the men in the hospital as best they could and Bonaparte saw a tall man with black hair and a thick moustache moving swiftly from patient to patient but he could do little more than inspect their wounds. Finally he noticed Bonaparte and scuttled across to him, two orderlies in pursuit.

'I don't want to interrupt your work, Doctor,' Bonaparte said. 'Please continue.'

'I was not told of your visit, sir,' the doctor said apologetically.

'Just go about your business, please,' Bonaparte urged. 'We will follow.'

The doctor moved to the next man and began unbandaging his upper arm, finally revealing a mottled greyish-pink area of flesh surrounding a deep wound. Pus had formed yellowish nodules in many places around the wound and the smell was foul.

'Gangrene is beginning to set in,' said the doctor. 'We probed for the ball but it was too deep. I left it in, I thought it might work itself free but . . .' He shook his head in despair.

The injured man saluted with his good arm and Bonaparte returned the gesture with a smile.

'Where did this happen?' he asked.

'On the bridge at Lodi, sir,' the man informed him. 'I was in the charge that kicked the Austrians off.' He smiled, revealing a set of discoloured teeth.

'I'll have to amputate the arm,' the doctor said. 'Before the poison spreads.'

The patient ignored the comment, his face still beaming as he looked at Bonaparte, who was already moving to the next wounded soldier.

The next man was wearing a shirt and cavalry breeches. His right leg had been amputated below the knee, both his hands were heavily bandaged and there was a nasty cut across his forehead.

'A roundshot killed his horse at Borghetto,' said the doctor. 'The same one that took off his leg. He was ridden over by several other men. He'll probably lose his hands too.'

The cavalryman tried to salute but the movement was impossible. Bonaparte patted his shoulder then followed the doctor to the next bed.

'Fever,' the doctor said. 'More than half the men in here are suffering with it. Field hospitals up and down the country have more men out of action through sickness than with wounds. And there isn't a thing we can do to help them,' the doctor added. 'Those who are strong enough usually survive but the weaker ones have no chance. Without fresh water and enough food these men have less chance of survival.'

'Another victory will be all the nourishment they need,' Bonaparte said.

'I hope you're right, sir,' the doctor said quietly.

The next man had sustained several wounds but he looked strong enough and tried to rise to salute as Bonaparte drew nearer. The general shook his head and helped lay the man down again, looking over the mass of bandages covering him.

'You look like a brave man,' Bonaparte said, smiling.

'Those Austrian bastards won't kill me easily, sir,' the soldier replied. 'They sabred me at Mondovi.' He pointed to his bandaged head. 'Shot me at Lodi.' He indicated his shoulder. 'And two of them stabbed me with bayonets at Lonato.' He gently touched his thigh and calf. 'But they couldn't kill me.'

'Good man,' Bonaparte encouraged.

'I want to get back into action again,' the soldier informed him proudly. 'I want to fight for *you*.'

'Which unit are you with?' Bonaparte enquired.

'The Eighty-first Demi-Brigade, sir.'

'Will he survive?' Bessieres said to the doctor, his voice a whisper.

The medical man nodded.

'Do you have a family back in France?' Bonaparte asked the man.

'I have a wife and two sons, sir. When they are old enough they will fight for you too. We would all fight and die for you, General.'

Bonaparte smiled and moved on.

He passed two men being tended by orderlies. One was vomiting dark fluid into a metal bowl, some of it spilling on to the stone floor. The other was being held down while a wound in his upper thigh was re-bandaged. His eyes were rolling wildly in their sockets, his lips fluttering.

'He has fever as well as the wound,' the doctor muttered.

'Haven't you seen enough, sir?' Bessieres asked.

Bonaparte fixed him in a stare for a moment then followed the doctor towards the next man. An infantry-man with a stomach wound. Then the next. An artillery sergeant paralysed by a piece of metal that had shattered part of his lower spine.

Men with fever. Men with dysentery. Men slowly bleeding to death internally. Men without limbs. Men with no eyes. The parade of misery continued.

'We will win,' Bonaparte said, finally turning back towards the main doors of the hospital. 'We will beat the Austrians *and* whatever nature sends against us. Malaria, smallpox or your Walcheren fever will not stop us. Caesar and Alexander faced the same problems but they conquered despite them. So will we.'

'Alexander died of fever, sir,' Bessieres reminded him.

'In Babylon,' Bonaparte mused. 'Not in Northern Italy. Do you not feel it, Bessieres? Destiny. I *know* we will win as surely as if God Himself had told me.' He turned and headed out of the hospital.

The cries of the sick and wounded echoed behind him.

CHAPTER 26

The breath of both men and horses clouded in the chilly early-morning air. The sun was a watery circlet in a washed-out sky and the feeble rays it emitted twinkled dully on the blanket of light frost covering the ground. A narrow stream ran parallel to the cavalry's route and Lausard noticed that parts of it were frozen. Elsewhere the clear water bubbled up through rents in the ice and the men had already stopped to fill their canteens.

Lausard shivered slightly as he rode. The weather had turned decidedly colder during the last two days and he thought back to the beginning of the campaign when they had all ridden across Italy in scorching heat, complaining about the stifling temperatures. Now, halfway through November, there wasn't a man amongst them who wouldn't have traded these chill mornings and cloudy days for just one of the searing April afternoons. Like the other ten men with him, Captain Deschamps included, Lausard wore his cloak and he was glad of it. The garment, like the rest of his equipment, was showing signs of the rigours of eight

months' campaigning. His boots had a hole in one sole.
His breeches were worn at the knees and his tunic had
been repaired more times than he cared to remember.
He'd lost a gauntlet at Arcola a week earlier, the glove
mislaid in one of the dykes which surrounded the town.
The horse he'd been riding had been hit by an Austrian
bullet and as it went down, it had catapulted him into
the stagnant water of a swampy tributary of the River
Alpone. Many others had followed him but not all had
been as fortunate. The three-day battle had cost the
lives of at least fifty of the dragoon regiment and many
more had been wounded. He had heard that the army
itself had sustained over four thousand casualties and
Bonaparte himself had only been saved from death by
the intervention of two mounted guides who had swept
him from the bridge into a quagmire below.

Since then the fighting had petered out into a series
of clashes between foragers or scouts, never more than
a hundred men at a time. Indeed, since the battle, the
whole of the cavalry had been used mainly for reconnaissance as Bonaparte sought to find his foe and bring
him to one final, conclusive battle. The days had passed
but the French cavalry patrols had made no contact.

Food was still scarce and patrols usually combined
their searches for the Austrians with hunts for sustenance. The patrol on this chilly morning was doing the
same.

'What time is it?' Lausard asked Rocheteau who
rode alongside him.

The corporal pulled a gold pocket watch from his
tunic and flipped it open. He'd taken it from an
Austrian officer at Arcola, along with a ring from the
man's little finger. Unable to loosen the gold band,

Rocheteau had simply cut the digit free with a knife then pocketed it.

'It's just after seven,' he told his colleague, slipping the watch back inside his tunic. Like Lausard, Rocheteau had lost a horse at Arcola. The unfortunate beast had slipped on one of the muddy banks of the River Adige and broken a foreleg. Rocheteau had had to shoot it. The animal had then been cut up and the meat eaten by the men. Waste was something the Army of Italy could not afford.

'I should be in bed with my woman at this time of the morning,' Giresse complained.

'Which woman?' asked Lausard.

'*Any* woman,' Giresse said and chuckled.

'Do you ever think about anything other than women?' Rocheteau asked him.

'Yes, I think about food and wine and a warm fire and a soft bed and I think about women again. Didn't you have a woman, Rocheteau?'

'I was married for a time,' the corporal announced.

Both Lausard and Giresse looked at him incredulously.

'She was a fine-looking woman too,' Rocheteau continued, 'but she caught a fever back in 'eighty-five and died. I missed her. I didn't get much for her clothes when I sold them either,' he added with disgust. 'Barely enough to pay for her burial. She was a good woman though and a damned fine pickpocket.'

The other men laughed.

'It sounds like a match made in heaven,' Lausard said, grinning.

'I taught her everything I knew, all the tricks of my trade,' Rocheteau proclaimed proudly.

'Your trade was thieving,' Giresse reminded him.

'At least I only stole watches and money and food, not horses like you,' Rocheteau said indignantly.

'What about you, Alain?' Giresse asked. 'Tell us about the women in your life, the ones you left behind.'

'There was no one special,' he said flatly. 'There *were* women but none that I loved, none I would have married like Rocheteau here.'

How could he tell them about the women he'd known? How could he tell them of the grand parties and balls his parents organised, of the cultured, sophisticated and beautiful women who had attended – women he had seduced so easily. Most of them had probably met their deaths beneath the blade of the guillotine by now. Just like his family. They were either dead or they had fled the country along with the rest of the rich and the privileged. How could he tell these two men about a world they could never hope to understand, a world they had helped destroy?

'I wanted my freedom,' he said, forcing a smile. 'I didn't want to be tied to one woman all my life.'

'Quite right,' Giresse said with a chuckle. 'Why pick one apple when you have an entire basket before you?'

'I knew a woman once,' Tabor interjected, his words slow, almost slurred.

'And who was she, my friend?' Lausard asked, looking at the big man.

'She was a friend of my sister,' he said, smiling at the recollection. 'I can't remember her name,' he added.

'And did you become close?' Giresse wanted to know, grinning.

'She taught me how to dance,' said Tabor. 'My mother would sing and I would dance.'

'You don't look very graceful,' Rocheteau offered.

'My mother said I was a good dancer,' Tabor said, his voice now lower, his tone softening. 'I miss her but I suppose we all have people we miss, don't we?'

Lausard didn't answer, he merely directed his gaze ahead, as if that simple action would wipe away his own memories. Images of his family hovered inside his head but he struggled to push them away.

A shout from one of the leading dragoons helped him complete the task. He looked across to where the trooper was waiting on his horse, gesturing through a copse of trees towards a small group of buildings – a barn, a house and a pigsty. The other dragoons reined in, two of them dismounting and pulling carbines from their saddles.

'We can ride through those trees,' Rocheteau said. 'There's enough room for the horses.'

To prove his point he guided his mount into the small wood, the animal nuzzling at a frost-covered branch as it passed.

'Watch the road,' Deschamps told the two dismounted troopers, then the captain followed Rocheteau and the others into the wood, discovering, like his troopers, that the trees had not been very densely planted. The mounted men moved through them with ease, the hooves disturbing piles of fallen leaves.

A bird rose suddenly into the air, disturbed by the intruders. It went up into the morning sky, squawking loudly, and Lausard gripped his horse's bridle tightly to prevent it rearing at the sudden outburst.

Up ahead, something moved.

The men clearly saw the first of two figures wander

into view. Both hussars. Both dismounted. They were dressed in dark blue pelisses and grey overalls and were chatting happily, apparently unaware that the dragoons were less than one hundred yards from them.

'Austrians,' said Deschamps. 'I wonder how many there are?'

Another trooper came into view, mounted on a small bay and he paused to speak to his two dismounted companions.

'I think it's just a patrol,' said Lausard, noticing two more of the enemy cavalrymen.

'They're probably looking for food, like us,' Giresse added quietly, his gaze never leaving the Austrians.

'If this is an advance patrol then the main body must be close,' Deschamps mused. 'We'd better report this.'

He wheeled his horse slowly and silently and began heading back through the wood.

The gunshots sounded like thundercracks in the stillness of the morning.

The sudden noise caused the horse to Lausard's right to rear up, snorting loudly. The dragoon riding it was unable to control it and, spinning round, the horse clattered into a tree, knocking several of the lower branches down and churning up the ground with its hooves.

The Austrian hussars turned towards the sound of the commotion and Lausard saw one of them point, then heard him shouting something.

Then there were more shots and the dragoons realised that they were coming from behind them, in the direction of the road.

Rocheteau pulled his carbine free as he saw three hussars galloping towards the wood. He took aim and shot one of them in the chest, the heavy lead ball toppling the man from the saddle.

The other two kept coming, although Lausard did notice that one had slowed his pace, wondering exactly how many adversaries were hidden by the wood. But the dragoons had already turned and were heading back through the trees towards the road where the sound of firing had ceased.

Lausard and Rocheteau burst from the copse to be confronted by a dozen hussars. Glancing quickly to his right Lausard saw that one of the dragoons was lying face down on the road, his horse having bolted, the second man was on his knees, clutching at a wound in his chest. A sabre cut had opened his throat and blood was spilling down the front of his tunic. But this tableau had barely registered with Lausard before the hussar closest to him attacked, aiming his sabre at the Frenchman's head. Lausard ducked sideways, feeling the air part close to his left ear. Pulling one of his pistols free, he jammed it against the stomach of his attacker and fired. The retort was muffled by such close contact and both men were enveloped by a small cloud of black smoke as the hussar toppled from his saddle and fell heavily.

Rocheteau dragged his sword free and drove it at his nearest opponent, spearing the man through the top of the right arm then again in the face. The hussar's horse reared wildly, dumping its rider from the saddle.

More of the dragoons were emerging from the wood but Lausard realised that the road seemed to be a mass of men on sleek ponies in dark-blue uniforms. There were at least thirty Austrian cavalry, all eager to attack the emerging French.

Deschamps saw their numbers and had no doubt of what to do.

'Retreat!' he roared and the men wheeled their horses and put spurs to them, hurtling back down the road with a number of hussars in pursuit. The thunder of churning hooves filled the early-morning air and Lausard heard the crack of a carbine from behind him, ducking involuntarily as the ball whizzed past him.

He risked a glance over his shoulder to see how close the pursuing Austrians were, and saw several of the blue-clad horsemen no more than ten yards behind, sabres waving wildly in the air. Their horses looked fresher but, he thought, not as powerful as those of the dragoons. If the chase went on much longer then the dragoons should be able to outdistance them. However, none of the Austrians was showing any sign of giving up the chase.

There was another shot and Lausard heard the sound of a horse neighing in pain; he looked across to see that Deschamps's mount had been struck in the hindquarters by a bullet. The animal was faltering, blood pumping from the wound. Deschamps urged it on but the injury was beginning to slow it down.

Lausard leaned across and caught the bridle, nodding towards a sharp incline which led down to a stream. Deschamps understood and guided his mount in that direction, Lausard and Rocheteau riding with him.

Several hussars also darted off the road to pursue this quarry. Lausard counted six of them. The remainder continued to chase the other fleeing dragoons.

There was a hedge at the top of the incline formed by some small bushes. Lausard rode his horse straight through the barrier but Deschamps's wounded mount tried to jump it. The animal cleared the obstacle but lost its footing on the other side and pitched forward, spilling Deschamps from the saddle and rolling over him.

The full weight of the fallen beast crushed the captain's left leg and he screamed as he felt several bones snap. The horse tried to scramble to its feet and almost trampled him in the process, but he covered his head with both hands and waited for the stricken animal to move clear. When he tried to rise it felt as if someone had set fire to his leg. Searing pain spread from his calf to his thigh and he fell down again, aware of the ground vibrating as the Austrian hussars drew nearer.

Lausard and Rocheteau had both turned their mounts to meet the onrushing light cavalry. Lausard drew his other pistol and shot the leading horse in the head. It dropped like a stone, its rider flung from the saddle; two animals immediately behind it crashed into the carcass and also fell.

With three of the hussars unhorsed, Lausard and Rocheteau drove their own mounts forward.

Rocheteau stabbed the first man in the chest then swung his sword in a devastating backhand swipe which sent the hussar crashing to the ground.

Lausard parried a sabre cut and drove his fist into the face of his attacker. As the dazed hussar reeled in the saddle, Lausard's sword was driven into his stomach and chest. The horse bolted, the dying rider still hunched over his saddle.

The hussar still mounted wheeled his horse and rode off. The remaining three were trying to swing themselves back on to horses but Lausard cut one down as he tried to grab the horse's bridle.

Rocheteau simply rode his horse into another, knocking him to the ground, allowing the animal to trample on the fallen Austrian who lay still on the frozen earth. The riderless horses bolted and the one hussar who was still alive raised his arms in surrender.

Lausard looked at the man and for a second thought about cutting him down, but then he lowered his sword, his breath coming in gasps from the exertion of the fight.

'Watch him,' he said to Rocheteau then dismounted himself and scuttled back over the incline to Deschamps, who was lying on his back, his face crumpled in pain, his left leg bloodied. He could see something white and gleaming poking through the material of his breeches and realised that it was a portion of splintered bone.

'You should have left me,' the officer croaked. 'When the surgeon sees this, he'll have my leg.'

'Can you stand if I help you?' Lausard asked, offering himself as support for the injured officer, virtually carrying him back towards the crest where Rocheteau was holding the remaining hussar at pistol point. The Austrian was in his early twenties and his face was ashen. There was a small cut on his forehead from his fall and his uniform was stained with mud. Rocheteau had already taken his weapons.

'I ought to shoot you here and now, you bastard,' Rocheteau snapped.

'No, please,' said the hussar, looking to Lausard as if expecting help.

'Give me one reason why I shouldn't?' Rocheteau said.

'Gold,' the cavalryman said. 'Lots of it.'

Rocheteau looked at Lausard.

'I can tell you where it is,' the hussar blurted out.

'That's not important now,' Lausard said, helping Deschamps towards his horse. The captain's own mount could barely walk now, weak from loss of blood and its crashing fall.

'I can't ride like this,' Deschamps said, nodding to his shattered leg. He stood on one leg leaning on Lausard's shoulder.

Lausard left him hanging on to his wounded horse while he mounted his own. Then he reached down, offering the captain his arm.

'Pull yourself up, sir,' he said, steadying the horse while Deschamps hauled himself up by the strength of his arms alone.

'Jesus!' gasped Deschamps, the effort bringing fresh pain, but he fastened his arms around Lausard's waist and clung on.

'What about him?' Rocheteau said, indicating the hussar.

'He's ridden long enough,' said Lausard. 'Let's see how well he runs.'

'You try to escape and I'll put a ball through your skull,' Rocheteau said. 'What about the others, Alain?'

'We'll worry about them when we get back to camp,' said Lausard. 'Come on.'

They set off at a trot, the hussar running alongside Rocheteau's horse. 'I could ride with you,' he suggested.

'Shut up and save your breath,' Rocheteau hissed. 'You're going to need it. And if you're lying about this gold I'll personally cut your throat. Now keep running.'

CHAPTER 27

'I swear to God it's getting colder,' said Rocheteau, pulling his cloak more tightly around him and staring into the flames of the camp fire. 'Mind you, I don't suppose that bothers you, does it, Rostov? I mean, you Russians, you're used to the cold, aren't you?'

'It isn't cold all year round in Russia, you idiot,' Rostov said, grinning. 'We do have summers too you know.'

'How do you know when it's summer? Do you get only one inch of snow instead of six?'

The men around the fire laughed.

'We're cold because we haven't had enough to eat,' said Joubert forlornly, cupping his much-reduced waist. 'I haven't eaten for four days.'

'You liar, fat man,' said Delacor. 'We all ate yesterday.'

'I wouldn't call a piece of rabbit a *meal*,' Joubert complained.

'We should be thankful for whatever we get,' Moreau said. 'We should thank God for it.'

'Do we thank Him for frostbite too?' Delacor rubbed his hands and held them closer to the fire. 'I bet the Austrians aren't suffering like this.'

'Everybody's suffering,' Bonet said. 'Us *and* them.'

'Well, I care about myself, not the stinking Austrians and *I'm* cold,' Delacor hissed.

'No sign of them for four days,' Rocheteau mused. 'Not so much as a horse apple.' He chuckled. 'Perhaps they've all gone home.'

'Good,' Roussard said. 'Then we can go home too.'

'To what?' Rocheteau asked.

'If the Austrians go home then this war will be over,' Roussard continued. 'Isn't that what we all want?'

'I think they've got something in store for us,' Giresse mused. 'There's a battle coming, you mark my words.'

'Did anyone get anything out of the prisoners you took?' Giresse said. 'They must know where the main Austrian force is.'

'The one I took was too frightened to say much,' Rocheteau said. 'I don't know about the others.' He had wondered whether to mention the gold that the Austrian had spoken of but thought better of it. If it did exist and they found it, Rocheteau didn't plan on sharing too much of it with his companions. Not if he could help it.

'I wonder how Captain Deschamps is?' Tabor said.

'They'll have had his leg off by now,' Delacor stated flatly. He held up a piece of wood, ready to toss it on the fire. 'Perhaps we ought to save this for him. He might need it.'

Some of the men laughed.

'What for?' Tabor said blankly.

'For a wooden leg, you half-wit,' Delacor sighed, then threw the stick on the fire.

Around them, a dozen other fires burned in the darkness.

The hills which rose on three sides of the encamped dragoons did little to lessen the effect of the freezing wind sweeping across the night-shrouded land. As Lausard walked through the camp he passed many men trying to sleep, huddled around fires, wrapped in their cloaks and saddle blankets, some with their heads resting on their saddles.

Sentries, shivering in the chill of the night, walked ceaselessly back and forth, patrolling the perimeter of the camp, while others guarded the horses. Two farriers were busy shoeing some captured Austrian ponies. A number of dragoons were cleaning their weapons. Some were smoking. Others, like himself, were strolling around the camp, unable to sleep, either because of the cold or through restlessness. This was the case with Lausard. He walked past a corporal who was snoring loudly, oblivious to the cold and the chatter of his companions. How Lausard envied him. What he wouldn't give for one peaceful, uninterrupted night of slumber, untainted by dreams.

'So, I'm not the only one who can't sleep.'

The voice startled him and he spun round to see Lieutenant Royere striding towards him, his cloak flapping.

'I hate the cold weather,' Royere said. 'I always have. I suppose that's what comes of being brought up in Navarre. I don't ever remember seeing snow when I was a child.'

'Whereabouts in Navarre?' Lausard asked him.

'A village about ten miles from Biarritz. My father was a miller.'

'Why did you join the army?'

'Patriotic zeal,' said Royere, laughing. 'That's the answer most officers in this army would give you, isn't it?'

Lausard regarded him quizzically.

'There isn't a man in this army who could tell you what he's fighting for now, Lausard,' the lieutenant said wearily. 'It isn't patriotism and it's certainly nothing to do with politics. Perhaps at the beginning there was a handful of men who actually believed that the object of this war was to spread the Republican doctrine but no one can even remember what *that* is any more.'

The two men began walking slowly, Royere glancing up at the velvet sky and watery moon.

'This war was supposed to be one of liberation,' Royere said. 'Our armies were going to march across Europe freeing the masses from the yoke of Royalist tyranny.' He laughed again but it had a bitter, hollow sound. 'It's a war of conquest, like all wars. There's no gallant motive behind our struggle.'

'You sound disappointed, Lieutenant.'

'Perhaps I am. There's a little bit of the idealist still left in me but I'm sure the years and the battles will grind it away.' He exhaled deeply. 'But what about you, Lausard? What do you think of this war?'

'I'm a soldier, Lieutenant. I'm not supposed to think, just obey orders.'

Royere smiled. 'Come on then,' he said. 'I've bared my soul to you. Tell me something about yourself. Where are you from?'

'Is it important?'

'I'm curious. I think I have the right to know something about the man who saved my life.'

Lausard shrugged.

'You seem to be making a habit of saving men's lives, Lausard,' Royere observed. 'You saved mine at Lodi and then you saved the life of Captain Deschamps.'

'I did what anyone in that position would have done,' Lausard said.

'Not every man would have displayed such courage. You underestimate yourself.'

'Men with little to live for usually possess more courage. If a man sees no worth in life, then death holds no fear. It is easy to be brave when dying is easier then living.'

'And you have nothing worth living for?'

'I have no family, no friends. All I own is this uniform and that was given to me by the State.'

'But you must have had someone before you joined the army? A family, a wife perhaps?'

'There is no one. If I die there will be no one to mourn for me and that is how I want it. I live day to day, hour to hour, like the other men in the army. If I hadn't joined I'd be dead by now. Executed. You seem to forget, Lieutenant, I was a thief.'

'Well, what you *were* is not important any longer,' Royere told him. 'It is what you *are* that matters.' He extended his right hand. 'For my life.'

Lausard shook the offered hand.

'I thank you,' said Royere with genuine warmth.

The two men continued walking slowly.

'You still haven't told me where you're from,' Royere reminded him.

'South of Paris, my family had a house and . . .' he allowed the sentence to trail off.

'I thought you had no family.'

'I haven't any longer, they're dead.'

'I'm sorry.'

'So am I.'

'What was it? An illness? An accident?'

'A mistake,' Lausard said, and smiled at the puzzled look on the officer's face.

Before either of them could say any more a shout filled the night and both of them spun round towards its source.

'Horsemen approaching,' a sentry called.

Royere and Lausard scurried across towards the man who had called out and, quite clearly, they could see two mounted men making their way to the camp.

'If they were Austrians I think there'd be more of them,' Lausard said quietly, squinting through the gloom to make out the men's uniforms.

'They're wearing dragoon uniforms,' Royere said, noticing the swirling horsehair manes on their helmets.

The horsemen were no more than twenty yards away and Royere, Lausard and the sentry moved towards them, the sentry raising his carbine. Lausard touched the hilt of his sword.

'Identify yourself,' Royere called.

The horsemen slowed virtually to a halt, while the sentry kept his carbine aimed at the first of them.

'Who are you?'

The leading man removed his helmet to reveal a youthful face, short-cropped hair and cheeks which had not long felt the caress of a razor. His companion was a little older.

'Who's in charge here?' the younger man asked, eyeing Royere, Lausard and the sentry almost with contempt.

Lausard noticed how clean his uniform and horse furniture were compared to the men of the squadron. Gold epaulettes on his shoulders marked him out as an officer.

'I am in charge,' Royere said.

'You owe me a salute, Lieutenant,' said the younger man. 'I am Captain Joseph Cezar. I am your new squadron commander.'

Both Lausard and Royere looked puzzled for a moment, taken aback by the appearance of this new officer, then they both saluted stiffly.

'This is my adjutant, Lieutenant Marquet,' Cezar told them, motioning towards the man at his side who looked a little older. He had a thick moustache which had not been trimmed in months, swarthy skin and dark, hooded eyes.

'Have you any news of Captain Deschamps, sir?' asked Royere.

'I am an officer of dragoons, not a surgeon,' snapped Cezar. 'But if you men are an example of the rest of this squadron then Deschamps couldn't have been much of an officer.' Cezar swung himself out of the saddle and stood close to Royere and Lausard. 'Your uniforms are filthy, they are a disgrace.' He wrinkled his nose. 'And when was the last time you bathed?'

'We don't have much opportunity for bathing, sir,' Lausard said. 'We've been too busy fighting. That is why our uniforms are so dirty. However, may I compliment you on how clean yours is?'

'What is your name?' Cezar said, stepping closer to Lausard.

'Sergeant Lausard, sir.'

'The army must be very short of good men if some-one as insolent as you can make the rank of sergeant.'

'I agree, sir, but then again, it is usually officers who make such appointments, isn't it?'

'Sergeant Lausard saved Captain Deschamps's life,' Royere interjected. 'And mine too.'

'Am I supposed to be impressed by that?' Cezar snapped. 'He was only doing his duty.'

'Not *all* officers are worth saving, sir,' said Lausard, looking past the captain.

Cezar glared at him momentarily then turned his attention back to Royere.

'I want a full inspection of this squadron at five tomorrow morning. Do you understand?' he hissed.

'Yes, sir,' Royere answered.

'Every man is to be present.'

'We have some sick—'

Cezar cut him short. '*Every* man,' he shouted. 'I want no excuses. Any man not present will be pun-ished. Understood?'

Royere nodded.

'You're dismissed. You too, Lausard. I'll be keeping a special eye out for you tomorrow.'

'Thank you, sir,' said Lausard. 'I hope you won't be disappointed.'

'I'd better not be, for your sake.'

The men saluted and turned to walk away.

'Wait,' Cezar said. 'There are two more things. I understand that you took some prisoners recently.'

'Only three, sir,' Royere informed him.

'I want to speak to them,' Cezar said.

'We've already interrogated them, sir, they know

nothing of any importance. Nothing our own reconnaissance hasn't already told us.'

'I will speak to them in the morning after the inspection,' said Cezar dismissively. 'Lausard, you can show Lieutenant Marquet and myself to our quarters.'

'Your quarters, sir?' Lausard queried quietly.

'Yes, you idiot. Where are they?'

Lausard motioned around him.

'You're looking at them, sir,' he said softly. 'I hope you will be comfortable on whichever piece of open ground you choose.' He saluted and walked off, Cezar glaring at his broad back as he disappeared into the gloom.

Royere caught him up. 'It seems he's taken a strong dislike to you, Lausard.'

'I'll survive,' Lausard grunted.

'Be careful with him. He doesn't live in the same world we live in.'

'I know. He's living in *my* world now.'

The fire had burned down to little more than embers by the time Lausard returned, warming his hands over the glowing fragments, pulling at his cloak as the wind whipped by ferociously.

Most of the men of his unit were sleeping fitfully, cocooned beneath cloaks and saddle blankets. Lausard settled himself beside the fire, glancing across at Charvet who was snoring loudly enough to wake the dead. Beside him Gaston lay with his head against the man's chest, seeking the extra warmth of human contact. On the other side, the mountainous frame of Joubert at least kept some of the wind from blowing in Roussard's face. He stirred in his sleep, murmured something incomprehensible, then rolled over.

'Where the hell have you been?'

Lausard looked around to see a bleary-eyed Rocheteau looking up at him.

'Walking,' said Lausard quietly. 'Thinking.'

'About what?' Rocheteau asked. 'The only thing I can think about is trying to sleep in this bloody wind.'

'Deschamps's replacement has just arrived,' Lausard said. 'Captain Joseph Cezar.' He spoke the words with disdain. 'Our new squadron commander.'

'What's he like?'

'You'll see for yourself tomorrow morning when he reviews the unit.'

Rocheteau sat up. 'A review? Where does he think he is? In some training school?' he snorted. 'What kind of officer is he?'

'A clean one. I doubt if he's been in the field for more than a week. He knows about our prisoners. Don't ask me how. He says he wants to talk to them.'

'What if he finds out about the gold,' Rocheteau said.

'There is no gold. That Austrian told you that to save his skin.'

'You know your trouble, Alain, you've got no faith.'

'Even if the gold does exist, *we'll* never get our hands on it. The Austrians have probably got it locked up inside Mantua and God knows how long it will be before we get inside *that* place.'

'It could be part of their baggage train,' Rocheteau said hopefully.

Lausard smiled and said, 'Go back to sleep. Dream about your gold.'

'This Cezar,' Rocheteau persisted, 'what's he really

like? He doesn't sound much like old Deschamps. Not one of us, eh?'

Lausard shook his head.

'No,' he mused. 'Not one of us.'

But what, he wondered, was he now? He was an important part of this unit but he wasn't like these men he fought with, or shared his meagre rations with. They coexisted in blissful ignorance. They had welcomed him as one of their own and Lausard had embraced that. Perhaps, he reasoned, as time went on the façade would become reality. He would become like the thieves, rapists, forgers and pickpockets he shared his new life with. After all, there was nothing of his old life left.

He watched the embers dying, one last tiny yellow flame rearing up defiantly before the breeze killed it.

Lausard settled down to try to sleep but it was many hours before that merciful oblivion claimed him.

CHAPTER 28

Dawn rose grey and dirty, spreading over the land like the smoke from a thousand guns. The heavens were crowded with grey cloud which scudded and shifted uneasily, swollen and dark as bruises. Rain was in the air although the icy wind threatened to turn it to sleet. Horses and men shuddered in the early morning, many of the animals skittish and unsettled. Like the men they carried, the animals ate sparingly and rarely enjoyed enough to fill their bellies. Troopers in threadbare, torn and holed uniforms sat in lines, some calming their mounts with reassuring pats, others rubbing their own eyes to force the weariness from them. They felt stinging spots of icy rain and shivered in their cloaks. Brass helmets were covered by oilskins, designed to protect the metal against the elements. Saddle cloths, some singed by fire in battle, others torn or ripped by bullets or bayonets, flapped forlornly in the breeze. Some horses pawed the ground impatiently, others merely stood shivering, heads lowered.

Lausard patted the neck of his own horse as it

chewed at the grass. On one side of him Rocheteau sat upright, watching to the left and right, his face set in firm lines. To his left Delacor gazed ahead blankly, his cheeks flushed, his eyes heavy from lack of sleep. None of the men had enjoyed much rest the previous night. The wind which had whipped across the land all through the hours of darkness had gradually increased in severity until even the thickest garments could not keep out its stinging chill. Even Rostov, seated in line behind Lausard, was shivering. The Russian glanced to his right and saw that Sonnier was slumped forward slightly in his saddle, his eyes half-closed. The Russian dug him in the ribs and Sonnier sat bolt upright as if pricked with a sword.

'Who is this bastard anyway?' said Delacor. 'A field inspection. Who does he think he is?'

He cast a quick glance towards one end of the line where Captain Cezar, Lieutenant Marquet and Royere were moving slowly along the ranks of dragoons, the captain pausing every so often to take a closer look at one of the men or his horse.

'He's our new commander,' Lausard said quietly. 'That's who he is.'

'Where is old Deschamps?' Rocheteau asked.

'Your guess is as good as mine,' Lausard murmured, aware that the officers were drawing closer. 'But even if he's still alive, it looks as if we're stuck with this fool for the time being.'

'God help us,' Moreau added, crossing himself.

'What do you know about him, Alain?' Rocheteau whispered.

'Only what I saw last night. He's ambitious and he's keen.'

'What about the other one? His adjutant,' Rocheteau persisted.

Lausard could only shake his head. 'I don't know,' he murmured. 'Not yet.'

Cezar was less than ten feet away now, leaning forward to inspect Charvet's tunic which still bore a hole in one shoulder.

'Your tunic is damaged,' the officer snapped. 'Repair it.'

He looked at Tabor. 'That shabrack is filthy. If you keep the rest of your equipment in such a disgusting state then you can expect regular visits from me. Clean yourself up.'

Tabor saluted.

'All of you,' Cezar bellowed. 'You are a disgrace. You are dirty, your horses are badly cared for, your uniforms are fit for rags. *You* are not fit to wear them as soldiers of France.' He turned his attention to Lausard. 'Let me see your sword.'

Lausard pulled it free in one fluid movement and held the point inches from the officer's face.

Cezar looked at Lausard then at the gleaming blade, the wicked point poised close to his nose.

'*Keep* it clean,' he hissed.

Lausard slid the weapon back into its scabbard.

'All of you, remember that,' the officer called. 'Never sheath a damp or dirty sword. It will rust, the metal will rot.' He shot Lausard a final, withering glance then moved on, immediately spotting a hole in Delacor's breeches.

'How do you explain that?' he said jabbing at the rip.

'It was a bayonet cut at Arcola, sir,' Delacor announced.

'And why has it not been repaired?' Cezar demanded. 'This is a sign of ill-discipline.' He wheeled his horse and rode to within a few yards of the leading rank of dragoons. 'The officer before me was weak. He allowed lapses of discipline which I will *not* allow. I am not here to be your friend, I am here to lead you. You are here to obey *my* orders. I know about this squadron, I know about this regiment. I know some of you were criminals, taken from prisons to fight for France. Well, if your discipline doesn't improve you will be treated like criminals again.' He rode his horse slowly back and forth, his eyes never leaving the lines of green-clad troops. 'There will be inspections every morning. I will drive you hard, sometimes to breaking point, sometimes beyond. Any man who cannot adapt will be punished. I have no need of fools in this squadron. I will not tolerate indiscipline. You are scum and, until you prove otherwise, that is how you will be treated. All of you.'

Lausard caught Royere's eye and something passed, unspoken, between the two men. The lieutenant shook his head almost imperceptibly then fixed his piercing stare on the captain.

'For those of you who do not know my name, it is Captain Cezar,' the officer proclaimed. 'I attended the same military school at Brienne as General Bonaparte. I learned what he learned. I know what *he* knows. Remember that.' He turned to Royere. 'I want patrols sent out. They will ride for fifty miles north and west and report back to me every hour. The rest of the squadron will move north. Understood?'

'Yes, sir,' said Royere, preparing to leave.

'When that's done, I want to speak to the prisoners.'

*

Lausard guessed that not one of the captive Austrians was any older than twenty-five. One of them sat on a fallen tree rubbing his hands together, the other two stood, aware of the watchful eyes of their captors and the carbines which were trained on them. They looked weary more than apprehensive, cold rather than terrified. The gold braid had been stripped from their dolman jackets which hung open. Most of their equipment had also been taken. One still had his sabretache but it had been emptied of personal effects.

'Which regiment are you with?' Cezar asked one of the prisoners standing up.

He was about to answer when one of the other men stepped close to him and put a hand across his mouth.

'It would be easier for all of us if you cooperated,' the captain said, drawing his sword. 'Which regiment?' he repeated, pressing the point of the blade against the cheek of the second hussar.

The man eyed the officer warily for a moment but still didn't answer.

Cezar cut him. Blood ran from the gash on his cheek and the man yelped.

'The Eleventh,' said the third man, jumping to his feet, holding up his hands in supplication.

'Ah, some cooperation,' Cezar said and smiled.

Two Austrians stepped back slightly, the one with the cut cheek pressing his hand to the gash in an effort to stem the flow of blood.

'Where is the main Austrian army?' Cezar addressed the hussar who had spoken.

The hussar shook his head.

'Come, come, you're not in a position to lie,' Cezar insisted. 'Where is your main force? Ten miles, twenty? Thirty? Which direction? North? West?'

'I cannot tell you,' the hussar said.

'Very well,' Cezar said.

The sword flashed forward with such dizzying speed and accuracy that everyone was taken by surprise.

The blade pierced the hussar's throat just below his larynx. The body remained upright for a few seconds then fell forward.

'I will ask again,' Cezar said, stepping towards the trooper who was already cut on the cheek. 'Where is the main force of your army?'

'Sir, you can't do this,' said Royere, stepping forward. 'The rules of war state that prisoners must be cared for until their exchange can be arranged.'

'Don't tell me what I can and can't do,' snarled Cezar. 'Besides, we scarcely have enough food for our own men – do you think I'm going to waste any more supplies keeping these enemies of France alive?'

Royere stepped back and shot a helpless glance at Lausard who was gazing not at the Austrians but at Cezar.

'Is the baggage train with the main force?' the captain demanded.

Lausard looked puzzled.

Even the Austrians looked bewildered by the question.

'Where is the baggage train?' Cezar raised the sword so that it was pressed against the tip of the injured man's nose.

'What's so important about the baggage train?' Royere said.

His question was met by a withering stare from Cezar.

The Austrian swallowed hard.

'It's true, isn't it?' Cezar asked quietly. 'It's true about what's being carried?'

The wounded man didn't answer.

Cezar whipped the point of the sword across his face, splitting open a nostril. Blood burst from him and sprayed the hussar's companion, who looked frantically around at the other Frenchmen, but none of them moved. No one tried to prevent this madman from pressing the end of his sword against the Austrian's ear.

'How much gold is there?' Cezar demanded.

Lausard looked at the hussar. So, what he'd said to Rocheteau had been true?

'How much?' the captain snarled.

Still no answer.

He sliced off the Austrian's left ear.

The man shrieked and clapped a hand to the bleeding hole.

'How much gold?' Cezar persisted.

'I don't know,' the hussar said, his face now a mask of blood.

Cezar stabbed him in the stomach, pushing the blade until it exited through the hussar's back, blood dripping from the tip. He tugged it free, the dying man falling at his feet.

The third hussar took a step back, his face the colour of rancid butter.

'How much gold is being carried on the baggage train?' Cezar said evenly.

'One hundred thousand marks,' the young hussar blurted out. 'Coin.'

Lausard stroked his chin thoughtfully then glanced

at Royere who was still looking on with bewildered anger.

'And the gold is with the main baggage train?' Cezar persisted.

The hussar nodded.

'And that baggage train is with the main force?'

Again the hussar nodded.

'Which is where?'

The hussar shook his head.

Cezar raised his sword.

'Where?'

'I can't tell you,' the trooper said, his face pale.

'Very well,' said Cezar almost resignedly, then drove the sword twice into the hussar's chest, ignoring the blood which just missed his tunic. He stood over the dead hussar for a moment then wiped his blade on the dead man's dolman and slid it back into the scabbard.

Lausard watched him.

'Sir,' said Royere, stepping forward. 'I must protest strongly about your treatment of these prisoners.'

'These spies,' said Cezar.

'They were not spies, sir. They were captured several days ago in combat. They were ordinary soldiers who should have been afforded the dignity—'

Cezar stepped closer to him snarling, 'Don't preach to me about dignity, Royere. This is a war. They were enemy soldiers and I killed them. They would have done the same to me given the chance.'

'They were unarmed,' Royere snapped defiantly.

'What did you see, Lieutenant Marquet?' Cezar asked his own adjutant.

'I saw you attacked and forced to defend yourself, sir,' Marquet said, a slight grin hovering on his lips.

'And you, Lausard?' the officer asked. 'What did *you* see?'

'Nothing very impressive, sir,' Lausard said, his gaze never leaving the officer.

Cezar and Marquet turned to walk away but the captain paused a moment, turning to Royere.

'I want full reports as soon as the patrols return,' he said. 'Understood? And get these' – he nodded to the three dead Austrians – 'out of the way. Bury them, throw them over the nearest gorge. Just get rid of them.' He and his adjutant walked away.

'Murdering bastard,' hissed Royere, glancing down at the nearest of the dead Austrians.

'I wonder why he's so interested in that gold?' Lausard mused.

'If it's part of the Austrian baggage train I don't know how he thinks he's going to get hold of it anyway,' Royere said.

'I'm sure our new captain has already thought of that.'

'One hundred thousand in gold coins – how is he going to carry it, even if he manages to find it?' Royere said dismissively.

'I don't somehow think he'll be doing it alone,' Lausard murmured. 'My guess is he'll want some help.'

The two men looked silently at each other.

CHAPTER 29

Bonaparte pulled up the collar of his greatcoat and stuffed both hands into the deep pockets. As he walked he seemed to be gazing off into space, his eyes attracted by some far-off object which Bessieres himself could not see. He walked slightly behind his commander, matching the Corsican stride for stride as they moved briskly along the top of the ridge.

Below them on the road, moving slowly due to the narrowness of the thoroughfare, the massed ranks of infantry, artillery and a few cavalry flowed like a human river. Many of the men marched stiffly, their feet frozen and painful from so many days of similar marching. Others merely slouched along, muskets by their sides. The artillery drivers did their best to force some effort out of animals that were practically starving to death. But, despite their wretched condition, the French soldiers moved with purpose and an almost robotic determination.

Bonaparte paused and gazed down at them, his pinched features expressionless.

'They are starving, freezing and homesick,' he said,

'and yet, they have conquered most of Northern Italy.'

'Under your command, sir,' Bessieres added.

'And they never question it, Bessieres. They obey my every order willingly, almost blindly.'

'Because they trust you, sir. They love you. You have brought them victories they could never have dreamed of.'

'I wish Barras and those other ninnies in Paris could see them. They want peace, Bessieres. Those preening *pekinese* want an end to this war. Barras, Carnot, Tallien. All of the Directory want this conflict finished. They want peace.'

'There's nothing wrong with that, sir, is there?'

'I myself want peace. I want it for those soldiers,' he nodded towards the men below. 'I don't enjoy sending men to their deaths. I lose a son every time one of them dies.' He took off his bicorn and ran a hand through his long hair. 'But I will lose many more if it brings about a lasting peace and gain for France. The Directory see no further than the ends of their noses. They believe I triumph here for *them*. And now they want me to make peace, even if it is a peace of compromise.' He shook his head. 'If peace is to be made it is for me to make it and I will not consider that until the Austrians are beaten once and for all.'

'They will not give up while Mantua holds out,' Bessieres observed.

'I know, and I know that their only hope is to relieve it,' Bonaparte mused. 'It is the key to the door of Italy, Bessieres. Once that fortress falls, this country is ours, but it is a hindrance to me. I have ten thousand men besieging it, the same number protecting our lines of communication from it. Men I need here. As long as I am short of men I must defend, but this war, these gains, they have been made from attacking not sitting around waiting for the Austrians to attack.'

'We have nearly thirty-five thousand men on the move, sir,' Bessieres reminded him.

'And the Austrians have over forty-five thousand.'

'We've beaten them before with smaller numbers.'

'But that was while we were on the offensive. No. I must wait for the Austrians to attack. It's just a question of where that attack will come. There are three ways they can approach Mantua. They can use the Brenta valley to Vicenza, they can move down the Adige or they can move along our rear using the River Chiese. The problem is that we are thinly spread. If they attack we will need to concentrate all our forces at that one point, and quickly, otherwise all may be lost. Everything you and I and these men have fought for could be worthless. But I can do nothing until the Austrians show their hand.'

He stopped walking and stood, arms crossed, looking down into the valley where the steady stream of men, horses and equipment continued to flow past.

Bessieres looked up at the cloud-bruised sky and, as he did, he felt the first drops of rain against his skin.

Lausard didn't know the man's name. He'd seen his face on a number of occasions but he'd never bothered to ask his name. It hadn't seemed important. After all, like all the men in the squadron, he could be dead soon, why get close? But now, as he stood with the rest of the dragoons, he was curious as to the identity of this man. This man who stood naked on a small boulder, his carbine held in one hand, his sword in the other. His arms were extended on either side of him in cruciform shape and Lausard could see the muscles bulging as he struggled to hold the weapons aloft. In a soggy heap in front of him lay his uniform. His horse stood close by, Marquet holding the reins, his own gaze fixed on the rows of watching dragoons with that almost imperceptible smile playing across his thin lips.

The rain, which had begun over an hour ago as fine drizzle, was now hammering down, blasted by the chill breeze. The naked man holding the weapons was shivering almost uncontrollably. His knees buckled slightly and it looked as though he was going to fall but by a supreme effort of will he remained upright.

'If you release those weapons before I give you the order you will be flogged,' shouted Captain Cezar, who sat astride his horse gazing at the naked man. 'That goes for all of you. Commit a crime and you will be flogged. Step out of line and you will be flogged. Question my authority and you will be flogged.'

'He can't do that,' murmured Bonet. 'Punishment like that has been banned.'

'Try telling that to Cezar,' Lausard said.

'This man,' shouted the captain, pointing at the bedraggled figure before him, 'was told to keep his powder dry, to keep his sword clean. He did neither. He disobeyed. He is no use to me. He is no use to you. If the Austrians had attacked he would have been unable to fight. I do not want men like this in my squadron.'

Lausard fixed the captain in an unblinking stare.

'He's insane,' whispered Rocheteau.

Lausard didn't answer, his stare was still riveted on the officer.

With a grunt, the naked man finally lost his battle and fell forward, sprawling on the wet grass. Marquet kicked him in the ribs in an effort to revive him but the action drew only groans from the prone figure.

'Get up, you bastard!' the lieutenant shouted but the man wouldn't move.

Moreau crossed himself.

Marquet kicked the man again but he could only drag himself up on to all fours.

'You should stay in that position,' chided the lieutenant. 'You are nothing more than a dog.'

Both Marquet and Cezar laughed, watching as the man tried to drag himself upright.

He finally managed it but could stand there for only a second or two before he crashed backwards and lay still.

'Leave him there,' Cezar said. Then, turning to the watching men: 'The rest of you mount up and remember what you've seen here today. The next time it could be one of you. Or it could be worse for you. I'll see the skin taken off any of your backs if you disobey me or slip below the standards I demand.' He walked his horse slowly back and forth. 'There will be a new inspection at dawn tomorrow, before we rendezvous with the rest of the army.'

'If I had my way, Cezar would have a rendezvous with my sword,' hissed Rocheteau, hauling himself up into the saddle.

Lausard heard his companion but his attention was elsewhere. His interest was drawn towards the crest of the ridge ahead of them, his eyes fixed on the single horseman galloping towards them.

*

Bonaparte read the despatch once more then handed it to Bessieres.

'It is as you feared, sir,' said the captain, scanning the report.

'As I had *hoped*, you mean,' Bonaparte said, then turned to the horseman who had brought the news. He was a thick-set man in his early twenties, his long hair plaited at the temples and the back, a red pelisse fastened over his jacket. His horse was badly lathered but still fresh.

'Ride back immediately,' he told the hussar. 'Tell the General he must hold firm at all costs. Tell him that we will join him before nightfall.'

The rider saluted, wheeled his horse and raced off.

Bonaparte turned as he heard another horse approaching and saw Murat riding to join him.

'What news?' Murat asked.

'The enemy's plan is at last unmasked,' said Bonaparte gleefully. 'They have attacked La Corona, Joubert has been forced to withdraw to Rivoli. Another Austrian column has attacked Legnano and the main force is advancing through the Adige valley.'

'To Rivoli you say?' Murat asked.

Bonaparte nodded. 'It is there we will find our victory,' he said defiantly.

'And what if Joubert's men can't hold them until we arrive?

'They *will* hold,' Bonaparte asserted.

Murat was less impressed. 'I hope to God you're right.'

CHAPTER 30

Lausard heard the screams before he saw their source. The wagon carrying the wounded was packed to overflowing and bumped over the rough road which led towards the village of Rivoli; the constant jarring only intensified the suffering of the already agonised human cargo.

The column of dragoons parted to let the wagon through, which was followed by a second and then a third, each filled with wounded and dying men.

Beneath the light of the full moon, their faces looked like those of ghosts. Blood, which stained so many of them, appeared black in the silvery glow and Lausard could see that the dark liquid had splashed the drivers in places and, occasionally, even the horses that drew the wagons.

The procession of pain passed through the centre of the horsemen and out of sight, although the groans and shrieks seemed to hang in the air, ringing in the ears of the dragoons.

All around the men steep mountains rose up into the blackness, as if the outcrops of rock were reaching for the heavens themselves. To the east was a view across the plateau of Rivoli and also the Adige River. Above all was the huge edifice of Monte Pipolo. Lausard could see several units of infantry camped on the rocky ground close to the village of Rivoli itself and many fires burned in and around the hamlet as the foot soldiers tried vainly to arm themselves against the chilly night breezes.

The ground began to slope upwards sharply and Rocheteau had to grip his reins tightly to prevent his horse from stumbling on the rock-strewn slope. Elsewhere, other troopers were finding similar problems. Horses strained under the weight of their riders and their equipment, trying to find a foothold on the treacherous terrain.

As the cavalrymen climbed higher up, they moved past increasing numbers of infantry but these were not sitting around camp fires; many were receiving treatment from overworked doctors and their assistants who had set up a number of dressing stations on the reverse slope of the plateau. Lausard could only guess at how many had been wounded in the fighting earlier that day, but of that number it appeared that many were due to be sent back into conflict as soon as they had been patched up. The men waited obediently in lines, those who were having trouble standing supported by comrades. Their wounds were not treated, simply bandaged and then they made their way back across the plateau to rejoin their units.

The huge silver moon glinted on the surface of the Adige and beyond the river Lausard could see more camp fires. He could even see cannon. It took him only a moment to realise that they were Austrian.

Four horsemen galloped past and Rocheteau nudged Lausard as he saw the white plume on the bicorn of one of the men.

'That's Bonaparte, isn't it?' he said, pointing in the direction of the swiftly moving men.

But they had already been swallowed up by the gloom before Lausard could pick out the general. All he saw was the small geysers of dust thrown up by the horses' hooves.

A chorus of cheers from up ahead told him that Rocheteau had indeed been right. Great shouts of '*Vive Bonaparte*' echoed across the plateau and seemed to reverberate off the mountains and cliffs, which closed around the French position like granite fingers.

The ground was finally beginning to level out slightly as the dragoons reached the top of the plateau and Lausard heard the order to dismount and set up camp.

'Perhaps we'll get something to eat now,' said Joubert feeling hopeful.

'You'll be lucky,' Rocheteau snorted. 'The infantry will have scraped this place clean by now. We'll be fortunate if we can find enough wood to make a fire, let alone some food.'

'I don't know how you can think about eating when we're going to fight a battle tomorrow,' said Roussard.

'You might as well die on a full stomach,' said Rocheteau, chuckling.

'If that bastard Cezar has anything to do with it, we'll probably all be killed anyway,' Delacor sneered. 'Bloody glory boy.'

'May God have mercy on all of us,' Moreau prayed. 'Except Cezar and that lap-dog of his, Marquet,'

Delacor added. 'They'll kill more of us than the Austrians ever will.'

'You could just be right,' Lausard murmured and headed off into the darkness.

'Alain, where are you going?' Rocheteau called after him.

'For a walk in the moonlight,' Lausard said, smiling.

'That should be done with a woman,' Giresse told him.

'If I find one, I'll remember that,' Lausard called back.

The breeze whipped the horsehair mane of his helmet around his face as he walked, passing between more camp fires and more troops. Some horse artillery had set up a fire close to their four-pounder gun and they sat around smoking, casting cursory glances at the dragoon as he passed.

Two hussars were walking across the plateau too, inspecting the ground over which it was likely they would have to charge the following day. Both nodded as Lausard passed them and he returned the gesture.

Drummer boys were using their instruments as seats as they huddled around fires, warming their hands. Most of them were shoeless, as were the bulk of the infantry. Some had already settled down to sleep, heads resting on their bulging packs, some resting on their comrades. Other men lay talking quietly or smoking. Some were praying.

Some men were playing cards, using pebbles to bet with in the absence of money. Anything to pass the time, to take their minds off the coming battle, to banish, even momentarily, thoughts of their impending death.

As Lausard walked, the scabbard of his sword trailed on the rough ground and a number of heads turned to watch him pass by. An artilleryman, sitting on the trail of the gun smoking a pipe, waved to him.

'Lost your horse?' he called.

'Last time I saw him, he was with your mother,' Lausard told him and heard the other members of the crew laughing heartily.

Ahead of him, the plateau began to slope away once again and, across the valley, in the direction of the village of Caprino, he could see hundreds of flickering yellow spots. The camp fires of the Austrian army. There seemed to be five distinct camps, each belonging to a column. Spread from Lake Garda in the west, across to the Adige in the east, the enemy were encamped across a four-mile front. It reminded Lausard of thousands of candles burning in the gloom.

The terrain favoured the defenders and most of the French troops were drawn up along the horseshoe formation of the Trombalore heights. The only good roads available to the Austrians were either side of the Adige but only the western route offered the attackers a clear and direct approach to Rivoli itself by way of the gorge and village of Osteria. Another village, called San Marco, clung precipitously to the easternmost edge of the plateau, and Lausard, like his commanding general, realised that this position could be crucial to the outcome of the battle.

He stood with his arms folded, looking across the plateau at the masses of French troops and then, once more, looked out towards the myriad Austrian camp fires. Somewhere down there was the baggage train which Cezar wanted to find so badly. One hundred thousand in gold. Lausard stroked his chin thoughtfully. He knew that officers and private soldiers alike had spent time and effort pillaging Italy for riches. Stories of entire shipments of art treasures being escorted back to France had reached the men. Commanders, it seemed, were as eager to line their pockets as common soldiers. Lausard shook his head. Those same commanders who had helped to destroy the rich were now setting *themselves* up with fortunes. People said that war was insane; then so too were the men who waged it. Perhaps the whole world was insane, himself included. He gazed up at the sky, past the thrusting peaks of the mountains, at the stars shimmering against the black backdrop. They looked like distant camp fires, Lausard thought. The moon passed momentarily behind a bank of cloud and the plateau was plunged into darkness for precious seconds, but then the silver light slowly began to creep across the rocks once more, illuminating so many men waiting for the coming day. Waiting and wondering if they would see the next moon.

Lausard turned and headed back towards his unit.

'That is one of the keys to our position,' said Bonaparte, pointing towards San Marco. 'If we hold it we will divide the Austrian attack in two. The entire battle could hinge on that position. That and how quickly your men get here, Massena.'

The dark-haired general nodded.

'My men should be here in less than three hours,' he said, confidently.

'Good,' Bonaparte said. 'When they arrive you will hold the valley on the left flank. Use one brigade. The rest of your division I want as a reserve around Rivoli itself. Understood?' He turned to one of the other officers. 'Joubert, you will use one brigade to hold San Marco and the Osteria gorge. Use your other two brigades to meet the first Austrian advance against the heights.'

'How can you be sure that's where they'll attack first?' Joubert asked.

Bonaparte waved a hand towards the mass of camp fires before them.

'There must be ten or twelve thousand men there,' he said. 'They're not there for show. That is where the first attack will come. Trust me.' He pushed his telescope shut and slipped it into the pocket of his tunic. 'They are spread too thinly,' he said. 'Our opponent chooses to use a scythe, not a hammer.' He smiled to himself.

'What if they cross the river and outflank us?' Massena said.

'You and your men will make sure they do not.'

'My men are tired, General,' Joubert said. 'They have fought today and now you expect them to fight again in the morning.'

'And the morning after that and the morning after that if necessary, Joubert,' Bonaparte said. 'I want them to fight for as long as it takes to win this war and I know they will. I know *you* will.' He placed one hand on the officer's shoulder.

'My men will not fail you, General,' Joubert assured his commander.

'The total Austrian strength is around twenty-eight thousand,' Bessieres said. 'Our strength, at the moment, is ten thousand.'

'Two Frenchmen are worth four Austrians any day,' Bonaparte said, smiling. 'Our troops move quicker and that is what this battle will depend on. It will be a race against time, gentlemen. Let us hope that our watches are working.'

The men laughed.

'If we fail tomorrow then everything we have won so far in this campaign will be lost,' Bonaparte said, his voice now low, his gaze fixed on the Austrian camp fires. 'If the Austrians defeat us, drive us back, then they will be able to reinforce Mantua. If we beat them then the fortress cannot hold out. The war will be won.' He looked around at his companions. 'Now, gentlemen, I suggest you get some sleep while you can. We have pressing business in the morning.' He glanced at his pocket watch. 'And morning is not that far away.'

CHAPTER 31

The air was thick with the cloying smell of gunpowder. Great clouds of noxious smoke drifted across the plateau like choking banks of hissing fog, occasionally parted by a breeze to reveal the ebb and flow of battle below.

Messengers galloped frantically back and forth on lathered horses, clutching orders, bringing reports to Bonaparte from every part of the French position.

The sound of cannon fire was accompanied by a non-stop crackle of muskets as both sides poured fusillades relentlessly into each other. The sounds drifted up from below, carried to the top of the Rivoli plateau on the wind and the swirling banks of smoke.

Lausard's horse pawed the ground impatiently. He himself peered to right and left in an attempt to see something of the battle which he and all his comrades could hear raging. The din of fighting seemed to be coming from all around them, the most intense clashes coming from the eastern end of the French positions around San Marco and the Osteria gorge.

The Adige, which had looked like a strip of silver

the previous night beneath the moonlight, now resembled a dark-blue snake writhing amidst the rocks and mountains. From its eastern bank, Austrian artillery were shelling the French troops in and around San Marco and, every now and then, great plumes of fire would shoot skyward, sometimes blasting men in the air.

The initial Austrian advance against the Trombalore heights had been checked but bitter fighting was still going on all across the front of the French positions.

Lausard sucked in a gunpowder-tainted breath and nudged Rocheteau. 'What time is it?'

'Just after ten.'

'How much longer are they going to leave us sitting here?' Giresse asked in agitation. 'We've been in the saddle more than three hours already.'

'I don't care if they leave us here for the whole battle,' Roussard said.

'It sounds as if we're surrounded.' Carbonne looked around. 'There's gunfire coming from all directions.'

'And all we can do is sit and wait,' Giresse hissed.

Captain Cezar walked his horse past the front line of the dragoons, his interest drawn to a rider who was galloping hell for leather across the plateau towards the tent where Bonaparte had set up his headquarters.

'Something's going on,' said Giresse.

'A battle, I think,' said Lausard cryptically.

Moments later, Bonaparte, Bessieres and a dozen mounted guides followed the horseman back across the plateau, heading for the western end of the French line. The dragoons watched as they disappeared down the sharp slope, swallowed up by dense clouds of smoke.

'If only we knew what was happening,' Giresse said.

'It's probably best that we don't,' Roussard offered, trying to calm his own skittish horse.

The cannon and musket fire were growing in intensity. Again Lausard took a deep breath, again tasting gunpowder. He saw three four-pounders being limbered up, the crews sweating and straining under the effort, then the drivers leaped into position and the guns were hurried away in the direction of the gorge.

Even the mountains themselves appeared wreathed in smoke, the gunfire reverberating around them.

Lausard and the rest of the dragoons continued to wait.

'My God, they're running,' said Bessieres, seeing dozens of French infantry streaming towards them, many throwing their weapons away in panic.

'The Eighty-fifth has broken!' someone shouted and Bonaparte saw a big sergeant reeling towards him, blood pouring down his face. 'Save yourself,' the man said and dropped to his knees close to Bonaparte's horse. Fleeing men streamed past him, some of them bumping into the horses of the guides in an effort to escape the oncoming Austrians, some of whom were already forming a line preparatory to delivering a volley of fire into the backs of the running men.

The fusillade swept the French and more men crashed to the ground.

A guide close to Bonaparte fell from his horse, blood streaming from a chest wound. Another man pitched forward as his horse was hit in the neck and head by bullets.

A dozen infantrymen went down, shot in the back as they fled.

'They'll cut us off from our reinforcements,' said Bonaparte, watching the advancing Austrians with apparent calm. 'Outflank us. Massena, you must plug the gap now.'

More French infantry were sprinting over the rough ground, some even discarding their packs in an attempt to make themselves lighter as they ran. Others had paused and were trying to rally, officers bellowing at them.

Bessieres and half-a-dozen of the guides rode forward and joined fifteen infantrymen who had rallied close to an outcrop of rocks and were preparing to fire back at the Austrians. From the saddle, the mounted guides aimed their carbines and, when the order was given to fire, added their own to that of the infantry.

A number of Austrians went down but the sheer mass of men was unaffected by this minor annoyance and they now lowered their bayonets and continued to advance with well-ordered determination.

'Bring up the Eighteenth,' Bonaparte shouted, watching as Massena led three columns of men forward, drums beating and colours flying in the smoke-filled air. A battery of horse artillery galloped up alongside them. The columns of men began to spread out into lines, preparing to bring their full fire power to bear against the Austrians.

'Sir, you must take cover,' Bessieres called to Bonaparte who merely wheeled his horse and galloped back and forth across the front of the deploying Eighteenth Demi-Brigade, his bicorn held high above his head.

'Brave Eighteenth,' he shouted. 'I know you, the enemy will not stand before you.'

The men cheered.

Stragglers from the broken Eighty-fifth were still streaming past and some of the other troops spat at them as they ran but they ignored it, anxious only to be away from the battlefield.

'Cowards!' roared a corporal at the fleeing men.

Massena drew his sabre and walked his horse back and forth in front of the Demi-Brigade.

'Comrades,' he called. 'In front of you are four thousand young men belonging to the richest families in Vienna. They have come with post-horses as far as Bassano. I recommend them to you.' He smiled and pointed his sabre at the oncoming Austrians who were now less than two hundred yards away.

The men of the Eighteenth roared their approval and steadied themselves, squinting down the barrels of their muskets as the white-coated masses drew nearer, urged on by their own officers. But the ground between the two sets of troops was uneven and also littered with discarded weapons, equipment and bodies. The Austrians began to break formation slightly, unable to retain their rigid column on such terrain.

One hundred yards and they were able to see the faces of the French waiting for them, muskets primed and ready.

Fifty yards.

The crews at the trio of four-pounders awaited the order of fire.

Bonaparte, Bessieres and a number of the guides had taken shelter behind the front line of French troops. They watched intently as the Austrians came to within forty yards, their bayonets glinting.

Thirty yards.

'Fire!'

The shout seemed to fill the valley and a series of thunderous blasts followed as both the French infantry and the artillery opened up, sweeping the Austrian columns with fire and pouring canister shot from cannon into them from close range.

Huge blankets of smoke covered the field but the French fired again, unable to see their enemy but knowing where the Austrians were. They could hear screams of agony, shouts of officers. Through the fog, some of the men saw a colour fall and the sight drew another huge cheer from the infantry

The gunners on the four-pounders worked quickly to reload, preparing to fire yet more shot into the shaken enemy.

When a gust of wind finally blew some of the choking smoke aside, Bonaparte saw that dozens of Austrians were lying dead or dying on the littered ground, their white uniforms spattered with crimson. The advance had halted, the remaining troops wavering, unsure whether to move forward or not.

A volley of fire from the four-pounders seemed to make up their minds for them. The barrels flamed and canister shot erupted from the barrels, scything down dozens more of the bewildered Austrians.

Smoke again obscured Bonaparte's view but he heard Massena roar out the order to fix bayonets and the French infantry did so with mechanical precision.

'They will not stand,' Bonaparte said, squinting to see through the rolling smoke. 'They *cannot*.'

Bessieres pointed to a break in the smoke and they both saw the Austrians retreating, trying to retain as much order as possible but many were stumbling over the bodies of their fallen comrades.

Bonaparte smiled, his white horse bucking excitedly beneath him.

'They are safe with Massena,' he said, seeing the general rise in his stirrups and urge the infantry forward. 'We must see what the situation is elsewhere.'

The French infantry swept forward with a huge cheer.

The village of San Marco was on fire.

Every dwelling in it seemed to be aflame and the smoke rose like a black shroud over the Osteria gorge.

French infantry occupying the houses fled. Those unable to were burned to death inside buildings that had been transformed into funeral pyres. The stink of gunpowder began to mingle with another, sickly sweet stench – that of burning human flesh.

In the narrow streets, Austrian and French troops fought hand-to-hand amidst the raging inferno, as cannon balls from the Austrian batteries across the Adige tore into the village, sometimes killing friend and foe alike.

French artillery fired back, although most of the time they were firing blind due to the choking smoke. Their faces blackened, their throats parched by the choking fumes, they sweated over their guns, keeping up a more or less constant fire in an effort to keep the Austrian infantry back, but it seemed to be a useless effort. The French were forced back up the slopes towards the plateau of Rivoli itself and the white-coated Austrians pressed on through the blazing inferno of San Marco.

'Pull back!' shouted an officer but his words were

silenced seconds later when a roundshot took off his head. The decapitated body remained upright for a second, spouting blood into the air, then fell forward.

The wounded were left where they fell, such was the French infantry's desire to escape the burning village. In places the smoke was so thick that men couldn't see more than a foot ahead. Some had abandoned their weapons and were attempting to climb the craggy outcrops of rock which led upwards to the top of the plateau.

Lausard saw the first of these bedraggled, smoke-stained and blood-splashed figures stumble out of a bank of smoke then fall to the ground less than a hundred yards away. He was followed by another, then another, the last of them carrying a faded tricolour which was singed and blackened.

Captain Cezar saw them too and walked his horse across towards the men. Lausard saw him leaning down speaking to the dazed infantrymen.

'How much longer are we to sit here?' Lausard asked, his words directed at no one in particular.

However, they were heard by Lieutenant Marquet.

'You will sit here for as long as you are ordered,' he hissed.

'Our men are being slaughtered down in that valley,' Lausard said. 'Are we to sit and watch it?'

'Just keep your mouth shut, Lausard,' snapped Marquet. 'The Captain cannot move without orders either.'

'But will he move *with* them?' Lausard challenged.

Marquet was about to answer when several loud shouts of '*Vive Bonaparte*' echoed across the plateau and the dragoons turned to see Bonaparte riding ahead of two columns of infantry, Bessieres and a dozen mounted guides with him. Rumbling up alongside came a battery of four-pounders.

Cezar saw him too and rode back to join his regiment.

The infantry passed by, drums beating, some of them looking disdainfully at the stationary cavalry before they disappeared down the steep eastern side of the plateau, picking their way over the difficult terrain leading down into the blazing hell of San Marco and the Osteria gorge.

The four-pounders were taken to the rim of the plateau and then unlimbered. They began firing immediately, blasting the oncoming Austrians with case shot.

Suddenly, there was a fearsome explosion less than twenty yards from Lausard. The blast caused several horses to rear, one throwing its rider.

'Where the hell did that come from?' said Rocheteau, looking around anxiously.

Lausard looked up and saw several puffs of smoke coming from the north-east, from the slopes of Mount Magnone which rose above the plateau.

Another blast erupted nearby and Lausard pointed to the Austrian guns that had begun to fire down on the French. Smoke, lumps of earth and metal flew into the air only to rain down again on the men below. A lump of metal the size of a man's little finger pierced the shoulder of a horse close by and passed straight through the animal, embedding itself in the rider's thigh. The dragoon shrieked and clapped both hands to the wound as blood stained his gauntlets. Next to him another man toppled from the saddle clutching his face. Three horses went down, only one of them getting to its feet again, blood pouring down its hind leg from a wound in its flank.

Another piece of flying steel cut cleanly through the ear of Rocheteau's mount and he had to use all his skill to prevent the animal throwing him.

Lausard saw Bonaparte's white horse rear then fall, hurling its rider to the ground.

'No,' he rasped, seeing Bonaparte hit the ground hard. But he rolled over and sprang to his feet, splashed with the blood of his wounded mount. One of the aides leaped from the saddle and held the bridle of his own horse, offering it to the young general, who nodded and prepared to swing himself astride the new mount.

Men all around looked on in horror as they saw their leader wiping blood and dust from his uniform, but he rose in his stirrups and waved his hat above his head to signal he was unhurt. Deafening cheers greeted his reappearance but those cheers themselves were eclipsed a moment later by two shattering explosions. They came from just below the rim of the valley but were so enormous that the shock waves could practically be felt across the entire plateau. Two massive plumes of black and red smoke mushroomed up into the already blackened heavens.

'We've hit two powder wagons,' an artilleryman bellowed triumphantly.

Pieces of wood were still spiralling upwards, propelled by the savagery of the blasts. Lausard even saw part of a wheel spinning into the air.

Bonaparte rode to the lip of the plateau then turned and looked towards the dragoons.

'Ride them down!' he roared. 'They are lost. Drive them from the gorge.'

'Draw swords,' bellowed Cezar and the dragoons did so as one man, the three-foot lengths of steel brandished above their heads.

'At last,' said Lausard.

'A charge down the side of a mountain,' Roussard murmured. 'We haven't got a chance.'

Moreau crossed himself as the lines began to move forward, Cezar at their head. Gaston spurred his mount up alongside the officer, ready to sound the notes which would signal the charge. He could see down into the gorge now, to the bewildered Austrians and the exploded powder wagons. All around the remains of both there were dozens of bodies. Two cannon had been overturned and Gaston could see a man trapped beneath the carriage of a six-pounder, his legs pulped by the weight of the artillery piece. All around him, the crew of the gun were dead and no one else was helping to free him.

Lausard saw more horsemen to the right, their blue uniforms and shabracks marking them out as chasseurs. Their officer was carrying the curved sabre of light cavalry and he was waving it frenziedly in the air above his head, screaming instructions to his men. Lausard watched as the chasseurs hurtled over the rim of the plateau and the charge began.

'Charge!' roared Cezar and the dragoons followed, swept along by a sudden insane exhilaration. The release of so much tension was mixed with a sheer exultation of moving at speed on horses that were every bit as anxious to flex their muscles. Over it all, the trumpets sounded the charge and the green- and blue-clad horsemen rushed down the slope towards the Austrians.

Those in the front ranks had little chance.

Lausard sabred one man across the face, then cut right and slashed downwards so violently that he split a man's cranium open.

Rocheteau rode his horse into two white-clad grenadiers, one of them crushed beneath the hooves, the other knocked to one side where Giresse drove his own sword through the man's neck.

Slashing to right and left, Delacor cut down more infantrymen.

Cezar struck a sergeant so hard across the back of the neck that he almost severed his head.

Blood from their helpless foes splashed the raging horsemen and this seemed to inflame them even more.

Moreau cut down three men, one of them a boy in his teens.

Some of the Austrians turned and ran, others tried to take shelter behind rocks or near to the burning houses of San Marco. They managed to get off a volley of musket fire in an attempt to halt the charge.

A dragoon close to Lausard was hit, his horse slipping on the slope, falling and catapulting its wounded rider from the saddle. He fell shrieking beneath the hooves of his comrades who were unable to avoid him.

Two more horses went down, taking their riders with them. Those dragoons behind tried to jump the fallen animals but the steep incline made it impossible and more fell.

Lausard could see the burning inferno that was San Marco now, he could smell the burning flesh.

A French artilleryman with one arm blown off knelt and cheered as the cavalry swept past, the hooves sending clouds of dust into the air to mix with the reeking smoke. The air was practically unbreathable. It clogged the nostrils of men and horses alike, millions of tiny cinders from the burning town also stinging their eyes, but most of the men barely noticed as they were swept along, swords raised high, dripping blood, ready to be brought down whenever more enemy troops came within striking distance.

The smoke enveloped them making it almost impossible to see. They could have been charging off the edge of the world for all they knew. Insistent blasts from the trumpets were all that guided them. The vast, swiftly moving mass thundered down the slope and through the scorched, burning remains of San Marco, many of the horses whinnying in fear as flames licked from the blazing buildings. The roof of one fell in, collapsing with a huge shower of sparks, smoke and flame and it was all Lausard could do to keep control of his horse.

Another dragoon was hit in the chest and face and toppled sideways, falling from his mount into what was left of a burning house. Lausard heard his screams as he galloped past, his own voice rising to a shout of furious exultation. Smoke filled his lungs and pieces of burning debris singed his skin and his uniform but he rode on, searching through the inferno for any Austrian troops who had escaped the first mad charge. Most of the enemy soldiers had either fled or simply thrown away their weapons. Lausard saw many with their arms raised and he could hear their shouts through the din of men and horses.

'Prisoners!' they called helplessly.

A number of the dragoons ignored their pleas to surrender and Lausard saw a group of Austrians ridden or sabred down despite their desire to be taken alive.

Anything to escape the ferocity of these charging cavalry.

French infantry were spilling down the slope too, bayonets fixed, and it was they who took most of the prisoners.

Some of the cavalry rode on almost as far as the banks of the Adige but a few shots from enemy batteries on the far bank soon halted them.

Despite the speed of the charge, few of the horses seemed to be blown; they were as enthusiastic as their riders and leaped around like spring lambs, seemingly oblivious to the burning buildings and wreckage all around. Bodies were everywhere. French and Austrian. Dead and dying horses, shattered cannon and caissons, overturned wagons. An Austrian standard bearer, his left leg holed by a bullet, his face gashed open by a sword cut had crawled up against one of these wagons, the colour still gripped in his bloodied hands. Lausard galloped over to him, grabbed the standard and yanked it from his grip, lifting it into the air.

Those who saw him do it shouted in triumph, their delighted cries heard even above the continued explosions and the fire from San Marco.

Lausard rode towards Captain Cezar and thrust the standard at him. 'A present for you,' he said, his face set in hard lines, his cheeks blackened, his uniform splashed with blood.

Cezar took it then handed it to a trooper and told him to take it to the rear.

Lieutenant Royere rode past and slapped Lausard on the back. The officer's horse was limping slightly where a musket ball had grazed its hindquarters but it seemed lively enough. One corner of the lieutenant's shabrack had been shot away and there was a dent in his scabbard where another musket ball had struck the metal but the officer seemed untouched. He wiped sweat from his face with his sleeve and looked around him to see how many of the dragoons had fallen. Then Lausard lost sight of him as he disappeared into a swirling bank of smoke.

Prisoners were being escorted away now, their faces pale, their heads downcast but they seemed relieved to be out of the fighting and although they outnumbered their captors, they strode along obediently. An entire battalion of the Deutschmeister regiment had surrendered *en masse* and now trudged towards the rear escorted by the jubilant French infantry.

Lausard looked around him and saw more blue-clad infantry taking up positions in the remains of San Marco and on the ground beyond.

The Osteria gorge was firmly in French hands once more.

Bonaparte raised the telescope to his eye and squinted through it, watching the troops moving before him. His uniform was stained with sweat and mud, splashed with blood and torn on one sleeve but he himself was uninjured and he rode his horse slowly along the body-strewn length of the Trombalore heights with half-a-dozen guides and messengers in attendance.

Bessieres, his face blackened by powder and smoke, rode with him. He wiped his face with the back of his hand and inhaled, sucking down the acrid air.

All around dead and wounded men lay. An eight-pounder stood close by, its crew scattered around it, every one of them dead or dying. Even the limber horses were dead, still strapped in their harnesses.

Bonaparte kept his telescope trained on the slopes of Mount Baldo, certain now that the Austrians were retreating in disorder.

'It is the victory you wanted, General,' said Bessieres, looking through his own telescope.

Bonaparte nodded slightly.

'Take some cavalry and pursue them,' he said. 'I don't want to give them the chance to regroup.'

He pulled a pocket watch from his tunic and flipped it open.

Six minutes past five.

He swept the battlefield with his telescope once more and saw that, along the length of their line, the Austrians were falling back.

CHAPTER 32

Lausard surprised even himself with the speed that he fell asleep, exhausted by the exertions of the day. He and the remainder of the squadron had withdrawn to the village of Rivoli and had found quarters in several of the houses, competing with some infantry for the right to occupy the dwellings. Lausard couldn't remember the last time he'd slept with a roof over his head and, what was more, he slept without the intrusion of dreams. Even Joubert's snoring didn't wake him.

What did rouse him from his slumber was a sharp kick.

He woke suddenly and spun round, immediately alert, one hand reaching for the pistol he kept close to him. He thrust the barrel in the direction of the intruder and saw Lieutenant Marquet standing over him. Lausard kept the pistol aimed at the officer for a few moments, his eyes narrowing and, briefly, he saw the uncertainty in Marquet's expression. As if he was unsure whether or not Lausard was going to pull the trigger. Lausard finally replaced the weapon.

'Captain Cezar wants to see you,' said Marquet. 'Now.'

Rocheteau had also woken and he turned over and looked contemptuously at the officer.

Lausard got to his feet and watched as Marquet left the room.

'Alain,' said Rocheteau. 'Be careful of that bloody butcher.'

Lausard nodded then followed the lieutenant out into the street.

'You fought well this afternoon,' Marquet said, 'You are a good horseman.'

Lausard didn't answer.

The men crossed the main square of the village and headed towards what had once been an inn. Several horses were tethered outside, one of them urinating gushingly as the two men passed. Lausard grinned as the steaming liquid splashed on to Marquet's boots.

The rooms downstairs were occupied by dragoons, also sleeping. But Marquet ushered Lausard upstairs where, as he climbed the stairs, he could see the dull yellow light of a candle burning in one of the upper-storey rooms. Marquet knocked on the door and walked in.

Inside the room there was a bed and a small fire had been lit in the grate. Elsewhere, only the candlelight illuminated the occupants of the room. Seated on a chair close to the window was Sergeant Delpierre. The bed was occupied by Captain Cezar who was wearing just his shirt and breeches. He was sipping from a glass of brandy.

'It's good brandy,' he said, raising the glass. 'I

liberated it from the cellar.' The officer grinned.

Lausard didn't even smile; rather he drew himself to attention and saluted.

'Is that why I was brought here in the middle of the night, sir, to discuss the merits of Italian brandy?'

'No, it wasn't, you insolent bastard,' Cezar snapped. 'Now sit down.' He motioned towards a chair close to Delpierre.

'I'd rather stand, sir,' Lausard insisted.

'Sit down!' Cezar barked and watched as the sergeant did as he was ordered, removing his helmet in the process.

'You know Sergeant Delpierre,' Cezar said.

The two NCOs merely glared at each other.

'You don't need *him*, sir,' Delpierre hissed. 'Or any of those scum like him. They're prisoners you know, convicts . . .'

'I know what they are. Shut up. I even know a little about Sergeant Lausard here.' The officer swung himself upright and padded across to the window, looking out over the square.

Lausard stiffened slightly wondering just how much the officer *did* know. He couldn't know of his background, he reasoned. But if he did and he spoke of it with Delpierre in the room then word would spread. He would become an outcast amongst men who called themselves his comrades. Nevertheless, his concern did not show in his expression.

'I know that he is a good fighter,' said Cezar. 'The kind of man I need for this mission.'

'What mission?' Lausard said.

The officer took another sip of brandy.

'You heard me speak of the Austrian gold,' he said.

'You were there when those Austrian prisoners told me about it.'

'I was there when you murdered three prisoners of war, sir.'

'You heard them speak of the gold?'

'They could have been lying. What makes you so sure it even exists?'

'I've been aware of its existence for over a month,' Cezar said. 'Those Austrians merely confirmed it. I spoke to some of the men captured today and they mentioned it too.'

'What has this got to do with me?' Lausard said.

'You are going to help me retrieve it,' Cezar told him.

'Why should I?'

'Because I'm giving you an order. Disobey and I'll have you shot.'

'Then do it, sir,' Lausard challenged.

'Don't you want to end this war a rich man, Lausard? I am giving you that opportunity,' Cezar said. 'Men have made fortunes already from this war. Every day thousands of francs' worth of art and gold head back to France. I don't intend to leave this country with less than I came in. Sergeant Delpierre is more than willing to help.'

'He would be, he'd sell his own mother for ten francs.'

'The money on that Austrian baggage train is to finance this war,' Cezar said. 'It is to finance troops and equipment to be used *against* France. If you refuse to help me capture it I will have you charged and tried for treason.'

Lausard's expression revealed nothing, his face cast

in deep shadow by the candlelight, but there was a fire burning in his eyes – a fire of anger.

Delpierre looked on with a twisted grin.

'The Austrians are beaten, they are running,' Lausard said. 'But they still outnumber us, unless you're planning to take the entire army with you to steal their gold.'

'Ten men,' Cezar told him. 'Myself, Delpierre, Lieutenant Marquet, you and six of your men. That is all it will take. A small unit will have more chance of success.'

'You're insane,' Lausard said. 'Ten men against an entire army? What chance will we have? You won't have any use for gold. All you'll need is a hole in the ground.'

'*Not* an army,' Cezar snapped. 'A disorganised rabble. Beaten men who want nothing more than to escape, to get back to their homes and families.'

'How do you know where the baggage train is?'

'Intelligence reports say that it is thirty miles north of here.'

'Thirty miles behind enemy lines and we're just going to ride in and take it?' He shook his head. 'How can you threaten me with a firing squad when all you're promising me is suicide?' He chuckled.

Cezar nodded towards Marquet who disappeared momentarily into the next room. He reappeared a second later and threw something in Lausard's direction. It landed with a thud at his feet and he looked down at it.

A white tunic, breeches, gaiters, shoes and a battered shako were held together in an untidy package by a piece of rope.

'An Austrian uniform,' said Lausard.

'And there are nine more like it in the next room,' Cezar informed him. 'Taken from prisoners tonight. We locate the baggage train, ride in dressed as Austrians and take it, then we ride out again.'

'Just like that?'

'Select six of your best men and report back here before dawn. Now get out. You too, Delpierre.'

Lausard replaced his helmet and saluted, pausing for a moment.

'There are over a hundred thousand marks in gold in that baggage train. Are you going to take all of it for yourself?'

'There will be one thousand marks for each man who returns,' Cezar told him.

Lausard nodded then saluted again and left, closely followed by Delpierre.

Cezar heard their footsteps echoing away down the stairs and looked at Marquet.

'One thousand marks for each man who returns,' he repeated.

Both men began to laugh.

CHAPTER 33

The sentries standing sentinel at the ford across the Adige near Ceradino watched in silence as a single line of dragoons crossed the freezing water. One of the men counted ten of them. He even nodded a greeting as they passed but none of the men acknowledged the gesture; they seemed too intent on controlling their horses who shook themselves free of water on emerging from the river. The sentries watched as the small column headed off up the valley at a canter, disappearing into the early-morning gloom. Dawn was still over an hour away and the horsemen were soon out of sight.

The valley floor was strewn with discarded weapons and spent musket balls. An artillery caisson lay on one side of the narrow road, two of its wheels blown off. Its contents had been spilled on to the rocky ground and Lausard noticed absently that a dead dog was lying among the spilled roundshot. In addition to weapons, there were also discarded packs and even a few items of clothing. Shakos, jackets and a few dozen overcoats were strewn across the valley floor – evidence of the speed of the Austrian retreat.

A dead horse lay near the road, stripped of its shabrack. When the light came, Rocheteau reasoned, crows would swoop down to feast.

Behind him Sonnier, Carbonne, Charvet, Giresse and Moreau rode, while up ahead, past Lausard, he could see Delpierre, Marquet and Cezar.

Rocheteau urged a little more speed from his mount and drew up alongside Lausard, who barely seemed to notice him.

'Did he really say a thousand for all of us?' Rocheteau asked.

Lausard nodded.

'That's ten thousand he'll have to give away then,' Rocheteau said and grinned.

'It still leaves the bastard ninety thousand to himself, doesn't it?' Lausard observed. 'He thinks he's being generous.'

'Do you trust him?'

'I don't trust *anyone*.'

'I wonder why he wanted that bastard Delpierre with him?' Rocheteau mused. 'What's that pig going to do with a thousand marks in gold?'

'We've got to get our hands on it first,' Lausard reminded him. 'The Austrians aren't just going to sit back and let us carry it away.' His horse snorted as if in agreement, its breath clouding in the freezing air.

Lausard glanced up at the sky and saw that dawn was trying to force its way across the heavens, straining over the peaks of the mountains surrounding the men ominously like the walls of a huge tomb. The sky remained the colour of wet granite and clouds bulged menacingly with the threat of rain or even snow. It was certainly cold enough, the ground bone hard with frost.

The route they were following sloped up sharply and one or two of the horses found it difficult to keep their footing on the slippery, unforgiving terrain, but their riders urged them on towards the crest of the next ridge. Leafless trees waved skeletal branches at them, coaxed by the breeze which seemed to dart down every rift in the land.

Every few hundred yards they passed discarded weapons, abandoned cannon, dead horses and sometimes men. Bodies were twisted into unearthly positions by a combination of rigor mortis and the biting cold, and Lausard guessed that the freezing temperatures had probably claimed many lives during the night. That combined with a lack of medical care had probably killed as many of the enemy troops as the French had the day before. One corpse was sitting upright, eyes still wide open, the skin already beginning to darken. The dead Austrian toppled over as the horses passed close by, his feet now pointing towards the sky. Near him two other bodies were also frozen solid, hands outstretched as if soliciting help.

Up ahead, Cezar turned his horse and set off up a particularly steep incline, followed by the other men. Lausard glanced up the slope to see a church perched about halfway up looking strangely incongruous with no other buildings anywhere near it and none, as far as he knew, within five miles in any direction. Whoever had built this place had enjoyed solitude, he decided. There was a barely discernible dirt track leading to the church and it was up this that the dragoons spurred their mounts, Cezar slowing his pace slightly as he drew nearer the building.

There was a wagon outside, one wheel missing

from the back, the horses gone. When closer, Lausard saw another wagon and, as he rode his horse around it, he saw that there were four dead Austrians in the back. All had been stripped of their uniforms and equipment, their naked bodies mottled with the cold, the blood from their death wounds now congealed black.

The silence was overpowering, broken only by the jingling of harnesses as the dragoons brought their horses to a halt outside the church.

Moreau looked up at the short steeple and muttered a prayer.

Cezar swung himself out of the saddle, followed by Marquet, and pulled his sabre free of the scabbard. He approached the church door, signalling for the other men to cover him.

Sonnier pulled his carbine from the boot on his saddle and swung it up to his shoulder, moving the barrel from steeple to door, alert for any movement.

Lausard, armed with both a pistol and a sword, drew up close to Cezar. Rocheteau eased back the hammer of his pistol, ears and eyes alert.

It was Carbonne who heard the sounds first.

The former executioner whistled gently through his teeth then tapped one ear, an indication for his colleagues to listen.

At first they heard nothing but the whining of the wind over the freezing hillside, then Lausard also heard something. A low, barely audible moan and it was coming from inside the church.

Cezar pushed the door and it swung open, the rusty hinges groaning.

The men looked inside.

'Jesus!' hissed Rocheteau, taking a step inside the church.

There must have been thirty or forty Austrians inside.

Lausard could see immediately that all but a handful were already dead.

'They must have left their wounded here,' he murmured, noticing that one man was lying on the altar at the far end of the church.

'Left them to die,' said Rocheteau, inspecting a man who had been shot in the stomach and arm. 'Their wounds haven't even been dressed.'

Moreau knelt beside a man who was clearly clinging to life by a monumental effort, and as the Austrian looked up at him, Moreau traced the sign of the cross on the dying man's forehead. The Austrian managed a weak smile, blood clogging his mouth, spilling over his lips. He had a bayonet wound just below the sternum.

Cezar walked without concern among the bodies, inspecting each one for any signs of life, ignoring the puddles of blood that had formed on the freezing stone floor of the church. In one corner a man was shuddering violently although he had a thick cloak wrapped around his shoulders. His eyes were bandaged, the dressing soaked with blood. He turned towards the sound of footsteps, his lips moving soundlessly. In his lap he cradled a head which had most of its left side missing and the blinded man was drenched in its blood.

He babbled something in German but Cezar turned away.

'What did he want?' Lausard enquired.

'Some water,' Cezar said. 'I don't know why, he'll be dead in an hour.'

'Charvet,' Lausard called. 'Fetch my canteen.'

'I said he'll be dead in an hour,' Cezar snapped, grabbing Lausard's arm.

'Why wait an hour?' Delpierre said and with one fluid movement drew his sword and ran it through the throat of the wounded Austrian.

Lausard glared at him.

'How dare you take a life in the house of God?' Moreau shrieked.

'It looks like God gave up caring about this lot a long time ago,' Delpierre insisted, wiping his sword on a dead Austrian's tunic.

'You would have wasted your own water on an enemy?' Cezar asked Lausard.

'There are enemies I would sooner share with than some of those I'm supposed to call comrades,' Lausard snarled, looking first at Cezar then at Delpierre.

'This isn't a mercy mission, Lausard,' Cezar reminded him. 'Why don't you stop behaving like some angel of mercy and start acting like a soldier?'

'Is it the act of a soldier to murder wounded men?' Lausard retorted angrily. 'Is it the act of a soldier to chase after personal gain when there is still a war to be fought?'

'I told you before, the gold which we are to seize would be used against France,' Cezar insisted. 'It is as much a part of our duty as fighting the enemy and you and your men will obey my orders. Fetch the uniforms from your horses.'

Lausard hesitated a moment then walked out to his horse followed by his men. From inside his portmanteau he took out a bundle which he carried back into the church.

The men changed quickly, prompted to speed by the chill as well as the desire to get away from this place of death.

'Not you,' said Cezar, pointing at Giresse. 'You stay here. Guard the horses and our equipment. You will ride with us until we reach the Austrians then return here with our horses. Once we have taken the gold we will rendezvous back here.'

'There isn't enough food for all the horses,' Giresse complained.

'Find some,' Cezar instructed.

'What about them?' Giresse wanted to know, gesturing around him at the dead Austrians.

'You want something to fill your time, don't you?' Cezar said with a chuckle. 'Bury them.'

Rocheteau smoothed his hands over the white Austrian tunic then propped the shako on his head. 'What if we're stopped?' he queried. 'They'll know we're French.'

'Just keep your mouths shut and stay close to me,' Cezar instructed, wiping a piece of fluff from the sleeve of his jacket.

Lausard fastened the gaiters around his calf then stamped his feet, pushing them more firmly into the boots.

'If he's staying here,' said Delpierre, pointing at Giresse, 'I don't think he should get a share of the gold. He's not risking his life the way we are.'

'Go to hell!' snarled Giresse. 'I have to sit here surrounded by all these bloody corpses. That makes my job worth payment.'

'He should get half of what we get then,' Delpierre persisted.

'He can have *your* share,' Rocheteau said. 'How do you know you'll be coming back alive?'

'Yes,' Carbonne echoed. 'Someone might put a bullet in you. Someone in an Austrian uniform.' He grinned and tugged at his sleeve.

'You try it and I'll kill you,' threatened Delpierre.

'If you kill him you'd better kill me too,' Moreau said menacingly.

'Shut up, all of you!' Cezar snapped.

'Captain.'

Marquet's shout made them all turn, and Lausard saw that the other officer was by the window of the church, looking down into the valley.

'Austrians,' he said.

The other men joined him at the window and squinted through the gloom.

A ragged column of white-uniformed men was making its way along the valley floor. A mixture of infantry and artillery accompanied by three blue-clad horsemen, two of whom were on one horse.

'What now?' Lausard asked.

Cezar smiled.

'We join them,' he said quietly.

Lausard counted twenty-seven Austrians in the ill-assorted group struggling along the valley floor. Two brown-uniformed artillerymen were stumbling behind the infantry, one of them still carrying the sponge used to swab out cannon barrels after every round. It seemed to be all he had in the way of a weapon. The three hussars looked similarly worse for wear, one of them seated on the back of his companion's horse, his head on the leading man's shoulder, one arm dangling uselessly at his side. Blood dripped from his frozen fingers and the sleeve of his blue jacket was heavily stained. The other man who rode a bay carried just a carbine; there was no sign of a sabre. The infantry were nearly all armed although few of them still retained their packs and most were without headgear. One had wrapped a scarf around his face to keep out the biting cold but his ears were scarlet, his eyes streaming. All the men were powder-blackened and moved with the gait of defeated, frightened individuals. A private with a huge moustache was dragging his musket along the ground, the butt scraping over the frozen terrain.

It was he who noticed Lausard and the others moving down the hill from the church and gestured to his comrades.

'Remember, just keep your mouths shut and stay close to me,' Cezar reminded them as they drew nearer.

The fugitives were without an officer so he approached the corporal who marched at the head of the lowly band.

'Have you come from Rivoli like us?' Cezar asked in perfect German.

'No,' said the man, breathlessly. 'From La Corona. The French attacked there this morning. It is over.' He carried on marching, his eyes as lifeless as those of a fish on a slab. 'This general of theirs, he is a young madman. He attacks from the right, the left and the rear. It's an intolerable way of making war.'

'We sheltered up there last night,' Cezar said, motioning towards the church but the corporal merely nodded without looking around.

'Where are you heading for?' the captain persisted.

'Home,' said the defeated corporal.

'I need to find my brother,' Cezar lied. 'He is with the baggage train.'

'It went west, to Allenta. Half a day's march from here. It is over.' He repeated the words like some kind of litany.

'West,' Cezar muttered under his breath. He raised an arm and motioned for Lausard and the others to follow.

'The French are still advancing,' said the corporal. 'It is over.'

Cezar ignored him and marched on, the other men close behind him.

Lausard cast a quick glance back at the shattered Austrians.

'And *we* did that to them?' said Rocheteau, affording himself a brief smile. 'We must be better soldiers than we thought.'

'Half a day's march,' said Cezar. 'And that gold will be ours. Come on.'

Lausard felt the first flecks of snow beginning to fall.

'To hell with this marching,' said Charvet, breathlessly. 'I wish I had my horse with me now.'

'We're supposed to be able to fight on foot as well as horseback,' said Lausard, striding along.

'Yes, get your feet up, you lazy bastard,' snapped Delpierre. 'Otherwise we'll leave you here.'

'The only one we're leaving behind is *you*,' Lausard said, pushing the other sergeant.

Delpierre shot him a warning glance but Lausard returned the stare with a look even more venomous.

Rocheteau moved closer to his colleague as if to reinforce the words.

'I said I'd kill you back at the training depot,' he told Delpierre. 'When you feel that steel in your back, Delpierre, you'll know it's mine.'

'Is that the only way you dare face me then, convict? The coward's way? From behind?' Delpierre spat on the ground close to Rocheteau who lunged forward.

Lausard shot out a hand to restrain his colleague.

'Go on,' Delpierre chided. 'Let your dog off his leash.'

'Bridge ahead!'

The shout came from Cezar and it distracted the feuding men, drawing their attention towards where the officer was pointing.

A wooden bridge spanned the Adige and offered the only crossing point for five miles in either direction. On the far bank, the men could see more Austrian troops, another motley collection of fugitives from various regiments. All with one thing on their minds. To escape the pursuing French. There were cavalry amongst them, grey-clad mounted jägers, and Lausard spotted half-a-dozen cuirassiers, their laquered black cuirasses gleaming even in the dullness of the morning. A number were walking, leading horses by the bridles and the animals looked as weary as their riders. Some had been wounded and were limping along, trying to keep up with the others. Many of the men had discarded their portmanteaus in order to lighten the load. Two jägers had even thrown away their carbines and were now equipped solely with swords. A leading cuirassier rode with his right thigh heavily bandaged, blood seeping through the dressing. An infantryman was stumbling along behind him, gripping his horse's tail. Behind them were two ammunition wagons and a pair of six-pounders was being dragged along by horses that looked ready to drop. The gunners rode on the caissons, heads down, uniforms stained and blackened.

Cezar led the French across the bridge, raising his hand to one of the cuirassiers in greeting but the man could only nod in return. None of the Austrians appeared to even notice the group of nine joining them.

'Have you any wounded?' the cuirassier with the leg wound asked, leaning over in his saddle slightly, his face pale.

'We left three men back there,' said Cezar, motioning behind him. 'We heard that some of the army were regrouping at Allenta.'

'No one is regrouping anywhere,' the cavalryman told him. 'We're not retreating, we're running.'

'Is it far to Allenta now?' Cezar persisted.

The cuirassier pointed towards an outcrop of low cliffs about a mile ahead.

'There's a pass that leads through those mountains,' he said. 'Allenta is just beyond it.'

Cezar nodded and he and the others joined the forlorn little column.

Lausard looked swiftly around at the dispirited Austrians and saw the same resigned look on all their faces. It was the face of defeat.

One of the infantry touched his arm and said something which he didn't understand.

Lausard could only shrug, wondering how many more eyes were focusing on him.

The Austrian repeated whatever he had said but Lausard merely tapped his ears and shook his head, feigning deafness.

The Austrian seemed to accept this and nodded but

then moved to Rocheteau instead and spoke the same words again.

Cezar turned and saw what was happening, aware that the continued silence of his men was beginning to arouse suspicion, even amongst troops whose spirits were so battered. Beaten they may be, stupid they were not.

Rocheteau pulled away from the insistent grip of the Austrian infantryman and eyed him menacingly, aware now that other eyes were turning towards him. The Austrian was now raising his voice, snapping angrily at Rocheteau in German.

Lausard stepped forward and pushed the man away but he was undeterred.

Cezar caught Lausard's eye, nodding slightly.

There were about fifteen Austrians. Seven of them mounted, three wounded, the others trudging along dejectedly, and a number had no weapons. The odds seemed fair.

One of the jägers spurred his horse forward to see what the fuss was between Rocheteau and the infantry-man, then he too called something to Rocheteau in German which was also ignored.

He rode close to Carbonne and said the same thing to him, meeting with a similar blank response.

'Who the hell are you?' the jäger barked and Cezar saw his hand drop to his sword.

'Now!' bellowed the captain.

Carbonne grabbed the jäger's bridle and pulled with all his strength, tipping the horse and its rider over, the cavalryman spilling from the saddle. Carbonne kicked him hard in the face and snatched up his sword.

Rocheteau pulled the musket from the hands of his

startled opponent and fired it, point-blank, into his chest.

One of the cuirassiers swung his sword at Rocheteau but he managed to parry the blow with the butt of the musket, using the weapon like a club, knocking the horseman from his saddle and then driving the bayonet into his face, watching as the man rolled away screaming, clutching the gaping gashed wound. Rocheteau took no chances and ran the bayonet into his back.

Charvet grabbed an artilleryman close to him and drove one powerful fist into his face, lifting him bodily into the air before hurling him down on to the bone-hard ground with incredible force.

Lausard grabbed the stirrup of the cuirassier officer and pulled, jerking the man from the saddle. He landed on his bandaged thigh, shouting in pain. Lausard swung himself into the saddle, the Austrian horse rearing in panic. It brought its front hooves down on the wounded officer, one of them caving in part of his forehead.

Rocheteau ripped the sabre from the hand of his dead foe and flung it to Lausard who caught it by the hilt, hefting it before him.

Delpierre pulled a pistol from one of the cuirassiers and shot an infantryman as he raised his hands in surrender.

The remaining Austrians raced back down the road as fast as they could, anxious to be away from these madmen who butchered them despite wearing the same uniform. Delpierre snatched up a musket and swung it up to his shoulder, taking aim at the fleeing men but the shot missed and Cezar knocked the barrel down.

'Let them go,' he said, looking at the carnage around the Frenchmen.

Six more bodies lay on the ground around them. The terrified Austrians had also abandoned the ammunition wagons and the six-pounders.

Apart from the horse Lausard rode, the others had bolted in terror, one of them dashing off across the wooden bridge towards the other bank of the Adige. It galloped off into the distance, reins flapping around its head.

'They'll bring reinforcements,' said Delpierre. 'We should have killed them all.'

'Reinforcements from where?' snorted Cezar. 'By the time they reach the rest of their army we'll have got the gold and be on the way back.'

Rocheteau was busily rifling the pockets of the dead men. He found little: some coins, a piece of gold chain and a letter he couldn't read so he balled it up and tossed it away. Charvet found a fork on one of the infantrymen and slipped it into his pocket. Rocheteau's only other discovery was a knife. About four inches long, double-edged and wickedly sharp. He smiled and slid it into his belt.

'This is perfect,' Cezar said, 'we'll take the gold and come back this way, we'll use this bridge to cross back to the other bank but I want to make sure no one follows us over. You two' – he pointed a finger at Moreau and Sonnier – 'take some powder from those ammunition wagons and set charges on the bridge. Both banks.'

'But how do we do that?' Sonnier said. 'We're not engineers.'

'You're supposed to be soldiers,' Cezar snapped. 'Work it out and do it. Understood?'

The two men nodded and began unloading barrels of gunpowder from the first of the wagons.

'You're leaving two more men behind?' Lausard queried. 'That means there're only seven of us going in to Allenta to get the gold.'

'The fewer of us there are the more chance we've got of getting in and out quickly,' Cezar told him.

'And more chance of getting killed,' murmured Rocheteau.

'What if more Austrians come along this road?' Lausard offered. 'We'll be trapped between them.'

'Not if we move quickly,' Cezar said, looking up at Lausard who had managed to bring the Austrian horse under control. 'Now get off that horse, Lausard.'

The two men locked stares.

'Get down!' Cezar insisted. 'I need the horse. I will ride ahead into Allenta, locate the gold then we can strike tonight.'

'Why you?' Lausard said.

'Because I'm the only one who can speak German, you idiot.'

Lausard hesitated a moment then swung himself out of the saddle. He held the reins then, as Cezar moved to take them, he let them slip from his hand. The officer glared at him. 'You are all under the command of Lieutenant Marquet for the time being.' Cezar swung himself into the saddle. 'Through the pass to Allenta. You must be there before nightfall.'

He rode off, the other men standing watching as he guided the horse along the road towards the mountains.

'I don't trust that bastard,' Rocheteau said under his breath.

Lausard didn't speak.

'Get these bodies out of the way,' Marquet shouted.

'What shall we do with them?' Carbonne asked.

'Throw them in the river, you fool,' the lieutenant hissed, watching as Sonnier grabbed one of the dead Austrians by the ankles and hauled him to the bank, pushing to propel the body towards its watery grave.

'This one isn't dead,' Carbonne said, kneeling close to one of the fallen Austrians.

'Throw him in,' ordered Marquet.

Carbonne hesitated.

'Do it, damn you!' Marquet snarled, watching as the former executioner lifted the man bodily then rolled him down the bank.

'Who cares if they're alive or dead?' Delpierre sneered, pulling a cuirassier towards the bank. 'To hell with them.' He watched as the body rolled into the water. 'What's wrong? Haven't you got the stomach for it?' He looked at Lausard and grinned.

'It's *you* I can't stomach,' said Lausard.

His companions laughed.

'You think you're clever, don't you?' Delpierre said, taking a step towards the younger man.

'Compared to you, a mule is clever. *And* more useful.'

'Funny man,' hissed Delpierre. 'I'll wipe that smile off your smug face.'

'Shut up,' Marquet snapped. 'Enough of this petty stupidity.'

'When this is over, Lausard,' Delpierre continued, 'I'm going to kill you.'

'You can try,' Lausard told him. 'Any time you can try.'

Delpierre suddenly felt something cold against the back of his neck. He turned slightly to see that

Rocheteau had the tip of the knife pressed against his skin, only a fraction more pressure required to puncture it.

'But you'd better watch your back,' Rocheteau said softly. He pulled the knife away and slid it back into his belt.

'Come on!' Marquet shouted, striding off down the road. 'We're wasting time. Move.'

The mountains towered above them, their peaks thrusting up into the sky as if threatening to puncture the clouds.

Sonnier and Moreau waited a moment, watching their colleagues trudge off towards the pass, then they began rolling barrels of powder across the bridge to the far bank. Despite the deep cold, they were soon sweating from the exertion.

'I hope to God this works,' grunted Sonnier, lifting another of the barrels from the ammunition wagon.

Moreau nodded in agreement then looked towards the pass. 'I don't know how they're going to get out of there in one piece,' he said.

Sonnier patted his shoulder. 'Come on,' he said. 'Let's get the rest of this powder unloaded. Then we can try to work out what to do with it.'

They continued with their task.

Moreau glanced across the abandoned six-pounders, his eyes lighting up.

'I've got an idea,' he said, grinning.

CHAPTER 34

The village of Allenta sheltered within the towering peaks of the mountains like a moth in a cocoon. Houses had been built not only on the floor of the ravine but also on the lower slopes. Many buildings seemed barely to cling on to the rock which rose, in several places, as sheer walls with hardly a handhold. Higher up there were ledges, some so precarious they didn't look capable of supporting the weight of a man, but others had been cut into the rock either by nature herself or by the inhabitants of the region so that the mountains could be crossed through the ravine or by way of the precipitous paths.

A number of Austrian troops were in the village, seeking warmth in the abandoned houses where they could. The streets were filled with wagons of all description, jostling for a place with artillery and cannon. Infantry and cavalry added to the congestion, some stopping in the village, others only too anxious to continue through the pass.

The inn had been taken over by meagre Austrian medical services and was being used as a dressing station. Wounded troops, those at least who could stand, queued up outside waiting their turn, shivering in the freezing wind. Elsewhere, wagons full of injured men trundled with difficulty through the already clogged streets, their forlorn cargoes moaning and shouting with each bump of the wheels.

Exhausted horses stood motionless in their harnesses, waiting for equally tired drivers to guide them through the streets and away from the place. But the tide of humanity which flowed through Allenta was moving slowly, far too slowly for those who sought sanctuary beyond the mountains. Infantry and cavalry alike had chosen the more hazardous mountain routes to speed their escape. Word had reached the village less than an hour ago that the French were no more than fifteen miles away and this rumour served only to increase the panic and fear already rife among the survivors of the Austrian army.

Cezar had heard these rumours as he wandered through the town, dressed in the uniform of his enemy. He'd even paused to eat some scraps of food with a group of infantrymen who'd arrived from La Corona that day. They had told him of the fighting and he, in turn, had lied about his own unit's involvement at the battle of Rivoli. Not for one second did he feel that they suspected he was an impostor, such were his demeanour and the quality of his German. His command of the language was virtually flawless and the men he spoke to had no reason to doubt his sincerity. Talk had inevitably turned to the baggage train – although most of the men seemed more concerned with moving on – and Cezar had been forced to suppress a smile when some had discussed the amount of gold concerned.

Now he sat on the steps of what had once been the entrance to a blacksmith's shop gazing across at the wagon which held the gold. It was being pulled by four stout grey horses which looked fresher than most of the beasts passing through. They stood obediently, heads down, waiting for their driver to urge them forward when he was ready. But of the driver there was no sign. The wagon and three other wagons which made up the rest of the baggage train were surrounded by sentries. Cezar could see the driver of the second wagon perched on his seat puffing on a pipe. Tarpaulins had been secured over all four wagons, held in place by thick rope. There were a number of bullet holes in the side of one wagon but otherwise the train and those who guarded it looked in very good condition. The men, particularly, looked more confident than their beaten comrades who passed through the village. Cezar told himself that those who guarded the gold probably hadn't fought in either of the actions of the last two days.

He got to his feet and wandered across to where he had tethered his horse, the animal flicking its head back and forth agitatedly. Patting its neck to calm it, his eyes remained fixed on the baggage train. He was still gazing at the collection of wagons when he felt a hand on his shoulder.

He spun around.

Lausard was standing behind him, his cheeks scarlet from the cold.

'Where the hell have you been?' Cezar said angrily, his heart thudding against his ribs. 'Where are the others?'

'Around,' said Lausard.

'What's that supposed to mean?' Cezar hissed. 'I told you to be here before nightfall. To be ready.'

'We *are* here and we *are* ready, Captain,' Lausard said. 'There were more Austrian troops on the road into the village. We had to avoid them. It took time.'

'Where are the rest?'

'They are in the village.'

'What about Lieutenant Marquet?'

As if in answer to the officer's question, Marquet appeared through a group of infantrymen and strode towards his commander and Lausard.

'Carbonne is waiting outside the village with horses for us all,' Lausard said.

'Did you order this?' Cezar demanded, looking angrily at his subordinate.

'Sergeant Lausard's idea seemed like a good one, Captain. I saw no reason to disagree with him,' Marquet said.

'What idea?'

'The Austrians aren't going to just let us walk out of here with that gold, are they?' Lausard offered. 'We're going to have to take it and, once we've got it, we're going to have to move fast. Like it or not, Captain, you might be in charge but the success of this whole operation relies on *my* men.'

'You insolent bastard,' Cezar snarled through gritted teeth.

'That may be,' Lausard replied, 'but if you want that gold then *you'll* do as *I* say.'

'I'll have you shot when we get back,' Cezar threatened. 'I will not stand for this.'

Two hussars riding past glanced at the trio of squabbling men but said nothing. Lausard noticed their interest and glared at Cezar. The officer turned to the horsemen and spoke some words in German and Lausard was relieved when the hussars nodded and continued on their way.

High above them, the sky was beginning to darken, the onset of dusk that much quicker due to the thick banks of dark cloud.

'Another hour,' Lausard said quietly. 'We should get off the street.'

'If this plan of yours doesn't work, Lausard, I'll kill you myself,' Cezar told him.

Unconcerned by the officer's comments, Lausard said: 'If it doesn't work, Captain, you won't have to kill me, the Austrians will do it for you.'

He turned and walked away.

Rocheteau looked at his pocket watch, squinting in the gloom as the hands crawled round.

Beside him, Charvet and Delpierre sheltered in a stable next to the inn, watching through the slits in the door, their eyes on the baggage train.

Straw had been built up in a pile at the back of the building and, at a nod from Rocheteau, Charvet scuttled over to it and began striking a flint he'd taken from a musket against the stone floor. At the third attempt sparks flew upwards and Charvet grinned, pushing more straw into the flashes of fire. The straw caught light, crackled then died. Charvet tried again, cursing under his breath.

'Come on,' urged Rocheteau.

'It's damp,' Charvet said angrily. 'The damned straw is damp.'

He struck the flint again but this time the sparks

flared. Some pieces were beginning to smoulder but there seemed to be more smoke than fire – reeking black and grey smoke that stung his eyes and stuck in his throat. Gradually flames began to lick upwards, dancing in the gloom and Charvet pushed more straw on to the growing blaze.

He nodded towards Rocheteau and Delpierre. The other two men got to their feet, pushing open the door of the stable and slipping out into the street. Charvet followed seconds later, leaving the door open, allowing the chill night air to fan the flames which were growing by the second.

Lausard saw the smoke beginning to rise into the air and he smiled. A number of horses tethered near the stable were pawing the ground, able to smell the smoke. Sentries, disturbed by the nervous horses, began looking around to find the cause of their distress.

The wagon transporting the gold was thirty or forty yards from the stable and the sentries guarding it were still unaware of the commotion. Their horses had just been fed and they remained contentedly in harness.

Lausard got to his feet, looking up and down the street, seeing that it was clear apart from some hussars who were standing around smoking and talking almost directly opposite the stable. It was one of them who first noticed flames leaping from the building, his shouts echoing around the street.

'Come on,' said Lausard, drawing a knife from his tunic. He'd taken it from an Austrian corporal earlier in the day and now he held the blade before him, gripping it tightly in one fist.

Cezar and Marquet followed him, heading towards the gold wagon.

Men were spilling into the street now from many of the houses, alerted by the cries of fire and shocked to see that the stable was ablaze. The flames leaped high in the air, illuminating everything roundabout with a hellish red glow.

Lausard ran at one of the sentries and drove the knife into his back before he could turn, twisting it, feeling warm blood on his hand. He snatched the man's musket from his grasp then let the body fall.

Cezar took out another Austrian, grabbing him by the back of the head and ramming his face against one of the wheels. The man staggered, dropped his musket and fell to the ground. Cezar snatched up the weapon and threw it to Marquet, who caught it and swung it up to his shoulder.

From the other side of the wagon, Rocheteau slid his arm around an Austrian's neck, jerked him off his feet and drove the knife into his neck at the point of his jaw and his ear, feeling it scrape bone. He too took the dead man's musket, using the bayonet to despatch the other guard who came at him.

Fire was now rising high into the air, huge sheets of flame devouring the stable, black smoke belching from the inferno. But the blaze seemed secondary to some of the Austrians who had spilled into the street. They had noticed the scuffling around the baggage train and a number of them began to move towards it, bewildered by what was happening.

'Get in!' shouted Lausard to the others, clambering into the back of the wagon while Rocheteau and Delpierre took their position on the driver's seat,

Rocheteau snapping the reins to force the horses forward.

A musket cracked and Lausard heard a ball whizz past his ear. Another struck the side of the wagon blasting a piece of wood free.

'Go!' Lausard ordered as more Austrians ran into the street, their faces illuminated by the blazing stable.

The horses reared, whinnied, then set off, urged on by Rocheteau.

An officer tried to clamber into the wagon but Cezar struck him hard in the face and he fell to the ground, screaming as the wagon passed over him.

Charvet fired his musket at three men chasing the wagon and saw one of them fall, skidding on the cobbled street.

Lausard fired off a shot from one of the captured muskets, the bullet hitting one of their pursuers in the shoulder.

'Come on!' yelled Rocheteau, snapping the reins almost frenziedly, the horses using all their strength to haul the wagon along, the wheels rumbling over the ground, the precious cargo bumping about beneath the tarpaulin.

The wagon was moving quickly now, easily outstripping the chasing foot soldiers.

The explosion was deafening.

Even the men in the wagon ducked down at the ferocity of the detonation. The stable was ripped apart by the blast, lumps of wood spinning fully fifty feet into the air, a mushroom of flame leaping skyward.

Lausard smiled with relief as he saw the pursuing Austrians reeling. 'I was wondering when that powder keg was going to go off,' he said, slapping Rocheteau on the shoulder, but the corporal was more concerned with guiding the horses along. The wagon was now careering out of Allenta at speed, its occupants forced to cling to the sides to stop themselves being thrown out.

In the blinding light of the explosion Cezar saw horsemen in the street, sabres raised above their heads. Half-a-dozen hussars were charging down the street in pursuit.

'We'll never outrun them,' Cezar shouted as Rocheteau roared encouragement to the horses, their hooves thundering on the uneven road. The wagon bumped and swayed alarmingly but Rocheteau remained hunched in the driver's seat, his face sheathed in sweat.

The hussars drew nearer. One tried a shot with his carbine but the bullet sang harmlessly through the air and smacked off a tree.

'I hope Carbonne is ready with those horses,' said Charvet, reloading the musket, tasting powder in his mouth as he bit the end off the cartridge. Crouching in the back of the speeding wagon, he rammed both ball and wadding down the barrel then swung the weapon up to his shoulder, firing at the hussars.

More by luck than judgement he hit one of their horses, the bullet catching the animal in the eye. It reared, squealing in pain, then toppled forward, pitching its rider from the saddle and tripping two of the other horses. They went down in an untidy heap but the others rode on.

'Get rid of some of the gold,' shouted Lausard, undoing the ropes which held the tarpaulin firm. 'We've got to lighten the load or they'll catch us.'

'Leave it!' roared Cezar, grabbing Lausard's wrist. 'We're not leaving any of it behind.'

'It's slowing us down,' Lausard bellowed back.

Cezar kept a firm grip on the sergeant's wrist until Lausard shook loose.

The leading hussars were only about a hundred yards from the speeding wagon by now and one fired a pistol at the vehicle.

Marquet hissed in pain as the ball clipped his ear, ripping away part of the lobe and splashing his face with blood.

The valley was narrowing, the rocks climbing precipitously on either side of the road.

'There's more of them,' shouted Charvet, spotting that about a dozen more Austrian cavalry had joined the chase and were bearing down on the wagon. 'We'll never do it.'

Lausard took his knife and, with one swift movement, cut a rope, pushing one of the boxes from the back of the wagon.

'What are you doing?' shrieked Cezar, watching in horror as the chest cracked open, spilling its precious cargo all over the ground. Gold pieces were flung up into the air by the churning hooves of the pursuing hussars; some of them slowed their mounts, looking down at the gold.

'Leave it alone,' Cezar roared, trying to wrestle the knife from Lausard's grip.

'Up ahead,' Rocheteau bellowed, finding it difficult to make himself heard above the thundering hooves of the horses.

Horses were waiting by the roadside and Carbonne stood in his stirrups signalling. Lausard knew that they were not going to have time to transfer to the waiting mounts.

'Ride!' he shouted to Carbonne, who hesitated a moment then set off with the other horses. Tied together by their bridles, they galloped along behind him.

'How far to that bridge?' Rocheteau hissed, still urging more effort from the horses pulling the wagon. Moving at such speed and hauling such a heavy cargo was causing them to tire; despite his maniacal shouts and snapping of the reins, they were beginning to slow down. 'Come on, come on!' he yelled frantically.

Carbonne guided the spare horses closer to the speeding wagon, the leading mount no more than three feet from the side of the vehicle.

'Hold them there,' Lausard called, steadying himself.

'What are you doing?' Cezar demanded, watching as Lausard crouched, his eyes fixed on the lead horse.

Lausard knew that if he mistimed his jump he would either be crushed beneath the wheels of the wagon or trampled by the hooves of the horses, but he had no choice. There was no time to think of failure.

Or death.

The wagon hit a bump and he almost overbalanced.

It was now or never.

He jumped.

For what seemed like an eternity he appeared to hang in empty air then he landed on the back of a grey horse, grabbing at its mane to pull himself upright. He snatched at the reins and immediately dug his heels into the horse, driving it fiercely.

'Come back, you stinking coward!' Delpierre

shouted after him, shaking his fist at Lausard, who was disappearing rapidly into the darkness ahead.

The wagon thundered on.

The hussars drew nearer.

CHAPTER 35

They had heard the explosion. They had watched the sky above Allenta turn red. Now Sonnier and Moreau listened to the popping musketry echoing through the stillness of the night, drawing ever nearer.

Moreau paced back and forth, looking at the bridge across the river then towards the sound of the gunfire. Sonnier was squatting beside the river bank, absently throwing small stones into the dark water. Their horses were tethered on the far bank, both animals chewing at shrivelled grass growing sparsely on the stony ground.

A keg of gunpowder had been set at each corner of the bridge, slightly below the parapet. Long dark trails of powder up to fifty yards long led from each barrel. These would serve as fuses when the time came and, from the sounds of gunfire heading their way, that time was approaching fast.

'I wonder what's happening?' Moreau mused aloud.

'They've probably all been killed by now,' Sonnier suggested, throwing a last stone into the river and getting to his feet.

'Look,' said Moreau, pointing into the gloom.

Both men squinted through the darkness and saw a solitary figure galloping towards them.

'Austrian?' Sonnier murmured.

Moreau lifted his musket to his shoulder in readiness.

'No, wait,' Sonnier said, pushing the barrel aside. Even in the dull light he could make out Lausard's features.

'Get across the bridge now!' Lausard yelled. 'Light the powder.'

'What about the others?'

'They're coming and they've got company,' Lausard said, wheeling the horse.

All three men heard the sound of thundering hooves and the wagon lurched into view, Rocheteau almost standing in the driver's platform.

'Light it!' Lausard shouted again.

Sonnier and Moreau ran across the bridge to the far bank and, for the first time, Lausard noticed that Sonnier was carrying something in his hand. Something which glowed red at the tip. It was a portfire from one of the discarded cannons. But then his attention was wrenched back to the wagon which was turning quickly – too quickly. It was carrying too much weight. It was going to topple over.

'Swing the leaders wide!' Lausard roared at Rocheteau. 'It's tipping. Rocheteau felt the wagon begin to list to one side.

Carbonne raced across the bridge ahead of the wagon, after releasing the spare horses, allowing them to run back towards the pursuing Austrians, causing at least a temporary hindrance.

One of the wagon's rear wheels was actually leaving the ground.

Charvet gripped the edge of the vehicle, convinced he was about to be sent flying. Delpierre gripped the seat more tightly, his eyes bulging in their sockets. Rocheteau tugged on the reins, trying to slow the horses to make the turn easier. He dragged hard on the leather until the muscles in his forearms bulged.

The rear wheel rose higher off the ground.

Lausard could only look on helplessly as the wagon swayed, teetering precariously. It was inches away from going now.

'No!' roared Rocheteau and hauled the two lead horses back with all his strength.

For interminable seconds the wagon lurched sideways, then it slammed back down on all four wheels and the horses were thundering across the wooden bridge, the sound reverberating through the night.

Sonnier lit one of the gunpowder trails, ran across and lit the second. A hissing sound followed and the ball of fire began to devour the streams of black powder.

Rocheteau felt another enormous jolt, the impact strong enough to send Marquet falling from the back of the wagon.

'What the hell was that?' Rocheteau hissed, then cursed as the wagon rolled backwards.

One of the rear wheels had crashed through the flimsy wooden struts of the bridge and was firmly wedged.

Rocheteau whipped up the horses but they couldn't budge the stricken vehicle.

Lausard pulled a pistol free and fired it in the

direction of the oncoming hussars, a number of whom had now dismounted and were preparing to fire their carbines at the stricken wagon.

'Push!' bellowed Cezar and the men jumped down and ran to the rear of the wagon, throwing their collective weight and strength behind it while Rocheteau urged the horses on to greater effort.

'Hurry!' shouted Sonnier. 'The powder's lit.'

He saw the trail burning up with alarming speed, each trail heading for its allotted keg, sputtering and crackling as the fire danced along it.

'Get this wagon free,' snarled Cezar, watching the sweating, straining men who were all too aware that they were going to be shot by their pursuers or blown sky high.

The black powder trails were now less than fifty feet long, the flame speeding along them.

Moreau rushed back on to the bridge to add his weight to that of the men already pushing and the wagon began to lift slightly.

Lausard leaped from his horse and ran to one of the powder kegs on his side of the river. He lifted it and pushed it towards the Austrians, watching the powder spill out behind the rolling barrel. Holding the pistol close to the stream of coarse grains he fired, the spark from the pan igniting the powder, the fireball chasing the explosive stream to its source.

The Austrians who realised what was happening had scattered, trying to escape from the rolling barrel which was spewing out its own fuse behind it. A fuse which was being devoured rapidly by the flame.

And then it caught up.

The keg exploded, a shrieking ball of red and yellow

flame which seared the eyes of those watching. It was accompanied by a concussion blast which flattened anyone within a twenty-yard radius. Men and horses were sent tumbling by the blast and even the French troops pushing at the jammed wagon chanced a glance behind them at the pall of black smoke spreading upwards into the night sky.

'Keep pushing!' roared Cezar, now aware of Lausard's presence on the bridge, of his considerable strength shoving against the wagon.

'Come on,' bellowed Sonnier, watching the trails of powder burning down rapidly towards the kegs.

Twenty feet.

The wagon began to move.

Fifteen feet.

Rocheteau shouted encouragement to both horses and men alike as he felt the wagon lurch forward.

Ten feet.

The wagon pulled free and rolled several yards. He whipped up the horses who bolted forward, dragging the vehicle across the last few feet of bridge and on to the far bank.

Sonnier had one eye on the speeding flame, the other on his companions who were now running for their lives to reach safety, oblivious to the musket balls which whizzed through the air around them, aware only that the bridge was about to be obliterated and them along with it.

Lausard was at the back of the fleeing band and he actually saw the last length of black powder burning down.

Five feet.

He pushed Carbonne ahead of him, urging him on.

Two feet.

Two Austrians had spurred their horses on to the bridge in pursuit of the Frenchmen. They reached the middle of the bridge as the twin kegs exploded simultaneously.

One end of the bridge simply vanished, obliterated by the ferocity of the blast. Lumps of wood were sent spiralling up in the air, carried on a shrieking plume of fire and smoke. The parapet was ripped apart by the explosion, the sound deafening.

Lausard hugged the ground and shouted, his bellow drowned by the ear-splitting bang and then the shrieks of men and horses as they plummeted into the water below. Debris rained down on the ground or into the water.

On the other bank the Austrians could only look on with dazed awe as the end portion of the bridge rose into the air, splitting and disintegrating to matchwood.

When Lausard finally scrambled to his feet he looked across at the other bank and saw that the hussars were gone. The bridge had tipped into the river, portions of it now being carried away by the current. Smoke drifted across the ground in a poisonous fog.

Charvet struggled to his knees, his ears still ringing.

Rocheteau shook his head and grinned, gazing at the remains of the bridge.

'Jesus,' he whispered. 'That was some firework display.'

Moreau, looking heavenward, mumbled a few words of thanks.

Charvet and Carbonne walked over to the river bank, the ground there cratered deeply in two places. Smoke was rising from the holes.

They merely looked at each other.

'I think we did a good job there,' Sonnier said and grinned, regarding the devastation with something akin to pride.

Lausard wiped his forehead with the back of his hand, leaving a black streak across his skin where the powder had stained it.

'The gold is ours, Captain,' he said to Cezar. 'Time to take it home and share it out.'

Rocheteau laughed, a whooping sound of pure joy.

Cezar looked at Lausard then at the wagon full of gold.

He said nothing.

Lausard finished buttoning his green tunic then ran a hand along one sleeve, a faint smile on his face. It felt good to be wearing his own uniform once more. The Austrian one he'd taken off lay discarded in a pile with others that his colleagues had taken off. Rocheteau, Sonnier and Charvet, on the other hand, still wore the white uniform of their enemies.

'Why the hell do we have to keep these on?' Rocheteau wanted to know.

'You've been told once,' Cezar said, adjusting his girth strap and green saddle cloth. 'We're heading back towards Rivoli now, towards our own lines but we don't know if we might run into some more Austrians. If we do then those of you dressed as dragoons will pretend to be prisoners and pass through them. If we reach our own men first then the opposite will apply.'

'So why are you riding on ahead then, Captain?' Lausard asked.

'It will be easier for one man to get through unseen,'

Cezar said. 'I can warn our troops that you're coming.'

'And you trust us with all this gold?' said Lausard.

Cezar met his baleful gaze.

'What if we decide to just run for it?' Lausard said. 'Take the gold with us.'

'You wouldn't dare,' Cezar hissed.

Delpierre looked at both men then at the gold-laden wagon and licked his lips like a starving man before a banquet.

'Is that back wheel all right?' Carbonne said, watching as Giresse and Sonnier tugged and pulled at it.

'It'll hold long enough to get us back,' Giresse told him.

Cezar swung himself into the saddle and pulled out a pocket watch.

'It shouldn't take me long to reach our lines,' he said. 'You follow on in an hour.'

Rocheteau checked his own watch and showed it to Lausard who noted the time.

'Lieutenant Marquet is in command until you reach our lines again,' Cezar continued, then he dug his knees into his mount and set off down the steep slope which led away from the church and back to the narrow road snaking along the valley floor, parallel to the Adige.

The other men watched him go.

'And what if he doesn't make it back to our lines?' said Delpierre. 'What if the Austrians stop him first?'

'There are no Austrians between here and Rivoli,' Marquet said with an air of certainty. 'None that could be a threat to us.'

'How do you know that?' Delpierre insisted.

'They're still too busy running.'

'He's got more chance alone,' Rocheteau said. 'We're the ones who are more likely to run into trouble if there *are* any Austrians about.' He looked at Lausard. 'That's right, isn't it, Alain?'

Lausard ignored him. He was walking around the wagon peering at it suspiciously.

'What are you doing?' Marquet asked.

Lausard slid the knife from his belt and moved closer to the tarpaulin covering the contents of the wagon.

'I'm going to see what else is in this thing,' he said, cutting one of the ropes with the knife, pulling it away from the canvas covering.

'Get away from there, Lausard,' the lieutenant ordered angrily.

'Don't tell me you're not curious, Lieutenant,' Lausard said, cutting a second rope.

'That property belongs to France now,' Marquet said, sliding a pistol from his belt. 'Get away from it.'

'Am I not a soldier of France?' Lausard challenged. 'If it belongs to France then surely it belongs to me.'

Marquet raised the pistol.

'I'm warning you,' he said, the gun aimed at Lausard's head.

Only then did he feel the chill brush of steel against his neck.

Out of the corner of his eye he could see that Rocheteau had a sword pressed against his flesh.

'If I was you, Lieutenant,' Rocheteau warned, 'I'd put the pistol down.'

'You raise a weapon against one of your own officers?' Marquet said.

'Absolutely,' Rocheteau breathed, pressing a little harder with the sword point.

Sonnier lifted his carbine to his shoulder and aimed it at the officer.

'You forget, Lieutenant,' he said, thumbing back the hammer. 'We're criminals. We have no respect for anyone or anything. That is what we've always been told.'

'Delpierre,' Marquet said, swallowing hard. 'Place them under arrest.'

'You stay where you are,' Charvet said, lifting his musket and prodding the bayonet in Delpierre's direction.

'Look for all I care,' Delpierre said. 'See how much gold there is. See how much richer we'll be when we get back.'

Lausard pulled the canvas away to reveal what lay beneath.

There were several bundles of cloaks, tied together with thick rope. Blankets, greatcoats and a number of small, square chests. Lausard leaned close to one and inhaled.

'Coffee,' he said approvingly.

There were other chests which he prised open. Inside these were tin cups, plates, knives, forks and spoons.

It was only as Lausard clambered further on to the wagon that he realised the whole floor of the vehicle was covered by a thick coating of gunpowder. Two barrels of the stuff were secured to the side of the wagon but one had been holed by a bullet, causing the coarse black grains to spill out into the wagon itself.

He came to the first of many, identical, wooden chests and slid his knife beneath lid and frame, prising the top off. It came away with a groan of splitting wood.

He stuffed a hand in and lifted it above his head.

The other men saw the gold coins gripped in his fist. He let them fall and they heard them chinking against other coins inside the box.

'Let's take it,' Delpierre suggested.

'And go where?' said Lausard. 'What are we going to do, desert?'

'Let's share it out and go our own way,' Delpierre insisted. 'Every man for himself. Equal shares.'

'You can't do that,' Marquet snapped, taking a step forward.

'We can do what we like,' Delpierre hissed.

'No,' Lausard said, 'the gold goes back and so do we.'

'You're mad,' Delpierre snarled. 'We won't get another chance like this, you fool.'

'We go back,' Lausard repeated, pulling the canvas back into position over the gold and fastening it with one of the heavy lengths of hemp.

'I'm pleased you've seen sense, Lausard,' Marquet said, relieved also that Rocheteau had pulled the sword away from his neck.

The sergeant jumped down from the wagon, wiping his hands on the tarpaulin in an effort to remove some of the spilled gunpowder that blackened his hands. He looked indifferently at Marquet.

'You're in charge, Lieutenant,' he said. 'Take us back.'

CHAPTER 36

'Rider coming in!'

The shout from the sentry echoed around the low valley where the advanced unit of French infantry had halted.

The sentry, a private named Caron, watched as the horseman spurred his grey mount down the sharp incline leading from the top of the valley towards the road which bisected it. He could not see the identity of the rider as yet, the uniform colour being difficult to distinguish in the early-morning mist which hung over the valley. All Caron knew was that the rider looked to be in a hurry.

Caron called to one of the other sentries and asked him if he could see the colour of the tunic on the oncoming horseman, and together the two men peered more closely at the rapidly approaching figure.

'Green,' said the other, nodding.

'Green,' echoed Caron in agreement. 'It's a dragoon. One of ours.' The rider was close enough now for the men to see the horsehair mane of his helmet trailing out behind him as he rode.

Even so, both levelled their muskets as he drew nearer.

Caron held up a hand to halt him.

Cezar pulled on his reins and his horse reared up panting, its tongue lolling from one corner of its mouth, its hide lathered.

'Where have you come from?' Caron asked, his Charleville still levelled at the dragoon.

'Where is your commander?' Cezar demanded, ignoring the question.

'I asked where you had come from, I—'

Cezar slapped angrily at his epaulettes. 'Do you know what these are, you bloody fool? I am a captain of dragoons. Do not question me like some common foot soldier. Get your commander.'

Caron and his companion looked at each other for a moment then the other man scuttled off over the lip of a depression in the ground. He returned a moment later with a huge man dressed in a torn and powder-stained blue jacket. The man was chewing on a piece of bread.

'Are you in charge of this regiment?' Cezar snapped at the big man.

'No, sir,' said the big man. 'Colonel Declerc commands the Twenty-third Demi-Brigade. I am Sergeant Bertrand of the Twenty-third's light infantry.'

'How many men have you under your command?'

'Fifty, sir,' Bertrand told him. 'We were sent ahead to act as foragers and scouts.'

'How far away is the main army?'

'About three miles to the south. May I ask which unit you are from, sir?'

'Fifth Dragoons. We have been on a scouting mission.'

'I thought all the cavalry were either with General Bonaparte or General Massena,' Bertrand said. 'That is why *we* were scouting.'

'Well you were wrong, weren't you? I need your men, Sergeant, and I need them now. Myself and my men ran into some Austrians last night and I think they are following us. We captured one of their supply wagons.'

'We heard that the Austrians were running, sir,' Bertrand insisted.

'Are you calling me a liar, Sergeant? I'll have use of your men – now get them into line and get them ready now. Do you understand?'

Bertrand hesitated, taking a last bite of his bread.

'Do it, you imbecile,' snarled Cezar. 'The longer you hesitate, the more danger my men are in.'

Bertrand nodded then spun round and sprinted off.

Rocheteau turned in his seat and looked at the contents of the wagon, a grin on his grizzled features.

'Gold, food, wine,' he mused. 'Perhaps Delpierre is right. We ought to take it for ourselves. As a reward. After all, that bastard Cezar did nearly get us all killed.'

Riding alongside the wagon, Lausard shook his head. 'We go back,' he said flatly.

On the other side of the wagon Giresse also glanced at the tarpaulin covering the gold and clucked his tongue. 'One hundred thousand in gold,' he said, shaking his head. 'We wouldn't see that much if we lived to be a hundred. What do you think Cezar's going to do with it all?'

'Just what the other officers who've been picking this country clean over the last few months have been doing,' Lausard said. 'Buy himself a house and mistress back in France.'

'With money like that he could buy any woman he wanted,' Giresse said enviously. 'He could buy a princess.'

'Royalty is in short supply in France these days in case you hadn't noticed,' Carbonne threw in from his position in the back of the wagon.

The other men laughed.

Up ahead, Lieutenant Marquet glanced back to see what was going on but he said nothing and rode on, accompanied by Delpierre. They rode twenty yards ahead of the wagon, Lausard and Giresse on either side of it, with Charvet and Sonnier bringing up the rear. Rocheteau drove the wagon while Carbonne and Moreau were nestled in the back of it. Moreau was looking intently at a small box hidden amongst the gold crates and he reached for it, surprised at how light it was.

'What do you think is in here, Alain?' He flicked at the small padlock which sealed the box.

'Have a look,' Lausard told him, slowing his horse slightly, watching as Moreau used the butt of his musket to smash the lock. He lifted the lid.

'Hardly worth it,' said Carbonne, looking in at the collection of papers, maps and documents within.

'Let me see that,' Lausard said, holding out his hand, waiting until Moreau handed him the top sheet.

He scanned it quickly. 'My God,' he whispered under his breath.

'They're probably love letters,' said Giresse, grinning.

'They're a lot more than that,' Lausard said. 'Give

them to me,' he said to Moreau, who handed him the remainder of the documents.

Lausard stuffed them into his portmanteau.

'What's so important about them, Alain?' asked Rocheteau. 'They're only maps and numbers.'

'I'll tell you when we get back.'

The early-morning sun was fighting its way up into the sky, but the mist was burning off slowly and the wagon was forced to move with care over the treacherous, stony roads. One of the wheels bumped jarringly over a rock, almost tipping Carbonne out of the wagon but he held on to the side, muttering as he saw more spilled gunpowder blacken his already filthy trousers.

Lausard looked back to where Sonnier and Charvet were riding, also leading the spare horses.

Sonnier raised a hand to signal that they were all right.

'We can't be far from our own lines now,' said Rocheteau.

'That depends how far the army advanced,' Lausard reminded him.

'Look,' Giresse said, pointing down into the valley below.

Even through the mist, they could see blue-jacketed French infantry.

Rocheteau smiled. 'Looks like we made it,' he said and grinned.

Lausard watched the swiftly moving column of troops marching along the valley floor, muskets sloped, bayonets glinting in the watery sunlight.

Cezar lowered his telescope, able now to see the wagon and riders more easily as they carefully negotiated the steep incline leading down from the hills to the valley floor and the road.

'Deploy your men across the road, Sergeant,' Cezar instructed Bertrand and the large man barked out a series of orders, forcing his men into a double line across the narrow track.

Cezar watched the wagon, a slight smile on his face. The gold. At last.

He could see Marquet riding ahead of the wagon with Delpierre at his side, with Rocheteau, still wearing a white uniform, holding the reins which guided the tired horses.

'Make ready,' Cezar shouted and watched as the infantry loaded their muskets. 'On my order, Sergeant. We have to be sure they're not Austrians.' He peered through his telescope once more, picking out Lausard's features. Set hard, his cheeks powder-stained.

The two lines of French infantry had their muskets ready waiting for a command. Some could see the white uniforms now but Bertrand also spotted some green dragoon tunics.

'There are French soldiers in the wagon, sir,' he said.

'It could be a trap,' Cezar said. 'Can't you see the Austrian uniforms too?'

Bertrand nodded slowly but his eyes were riveted on the green uniforms.

The wagon was less than two hundred yards away now and drawing closer.

'On my order,' Cezar said quietly.

'Sir, I'm sure they are all French soldiers,' Bertrand insisted.

'Then explain the Austrian uniforms. I'm telling you, it's a trap.' He drew his sword. 'Prepare to fire.'

'Sir, I can't give that order until we're sure—'

'Damn you, Sergeant!' Cezar yelled. 'Then *I'll* give it.'

'It looks like a welcoming committee,' said Carbonne, smiling as he saw the lines of blue-clad troops.

Lausard said nothing. He guided his horse on at a walk, his eyes scanning the rows of infantry.

Then he saw Cezar.

For brief, interminable seconds, it felt to Lausard as if he and the officer were looking directly into each other's eyes, despite the distance between them.

Lausard saw the officer raise his sword.

He saw the two lines of troops raise their muskets to their shoulders.

'What the hell are they doing?' Rocheteau murmured, pulling slightly on the reins to slow the wagon a little.

Ahead, Marquet and Delpierre also saw the twin rows of Charlevilles now pointing at them.

From such close range, in the stillness of the morning, Cezar's shout was clearly audible.

With a great sweeping motion of his sword he roared: 'Fire!'

CHAPTER 37

The shout reverberated around the valley and the men in and around the wagon flinched involuntarily, expecting a hail of musket balls.

Nothing happened. Neither of the lines opened fire. The valley remained silent.

Suddenly Lausard understood why Cezar had insisted that not all of them revert to their dragoon uniforms. He realised that he was staring death in the face.

The muskets wavered, some men perhaps as uncertain of the identity of those ahead of them as Bertrand.

Cezar roared the order once again.

Marquet actually looked round at Lausard, a questioning, pitiful look on his face.

Then the front rank opened fire.

The valley was filled by a rolling wall of sound as the muskets crackled, spewing smoke, wadding and lead towards the men and the wagon.

Marquet was hit in the chest and face, his horse crumpling to the ground bleeding from a dozen wounds.

A musket ball hit Delpierre in the shoulder, the impact shattering his collar bone and lifting him from his saddle as his horse reared in pain and terror. The animal itself had been hit in the side and the neck.

Rocheteau heard bullets singing past his ears. One struck his right arm and tore a hole in the material without puncturing flesh. Another grazed his cheek.

Two of the horses pulling the wagon went down in an untidy heap. A third was hit in the muzzle and began bucking wildly despite the confines of the harness.

'No!' shrieked Carbonne, hissing in pain a moment later as a musket ball struck him in the fleshy part of the side and tore its way through.

'Stop it!' screamed Moreau, riding forward.

He, like the other men, heard the order Cezar bellowed.

'Second rank. Fire.'

There was another rolling volley, more choking smoke and death came flying towards them once again, propelled by the charges from each pan.

Moreau's horse was hit.

Sonnier felt a ball strike his helmet and clang off the brass. Another hit him in the leg just below the knee, passing through his calf. A third took off his left little finger.

Lausard drew his sword and rode forward waving it in the air.

'We're French soldiers!' he roared, his face blackened by powder, his features contorted with rage.

Cezar was ordering the infantry to reload.

However, Sergeant Bertrand was pushing many of his men's guns to one side, the look of horror on his face telling Lausard that he realised a dreadful mistake had been made.

Smoke seemed to fill the valley and the choking stench of gunpowder filled the air.

'It's a trap, keep firing!' roared Cezar but, by now, Lausard had reached the infantry and he stood in his saddle to allow the men a clear sight of him and his dragoon uniform.

'*Vive Bonaparte!*' he bellowed, his sword still gripped in his fist.

Cezar saw him and his right hand fell to his pistol, ready to pull it from its holster.

'I'm sorry,' Bertrand said, gazing first at Lausard and then at the other men and horses who had been fired upon.

They were walking or riding towards the French lines.

Marquet, however, lay motionless beside his horse.

Charvet was supporting Sonnier. Rocheteau used his knife to cut the wagon traces and release the one horse that hadn't been hit by the fusillades. Blood was running down his face.

Moreau crossed to Delpierre and helped him to his feet, noticing that a piece of jagged bone was protruding through his jacket from the wound he'd received.

'Help them!' Bertrand shouted and several of his men scurried forward to aid the stricken dragoons.

Lausard and Cezar remained within feet of each other, their stares locked.

'You wanted us all dead, didn't you?' snarled Lausard.

'You'll never prove it,' Cezar said under his breath. 'It was a mistake. An understandable mistake. I saw

Austrian uniforms, I suspected an attack, I ordered these men to fire on what I thought to be enemy troops.'

'You *knew* who we were,' Lausard rasped, shifting his sword to the other hand.

Cezar's hand closed over the butt of his pistol.

'Your gold is there, Captain,' Lausard said, motioning towards the wagon, now abandoned eighty yards away. 'Don't you want it? You wanted it badly enough to kill your own men for. Why not take it?'

Lausard suddenly wheeled his horse and rode back towards the wagon, sheathing his sabre as he did

The other men turned to watch what was happening. They saw Lausard reach into the wagon and pull something free.

'You want your gold, Captain?' Lausard shouted. 'Come and get it.'

Rocheteau saw what his companion clutched in one fist. It was one of the portfires they'd taken from the Austrian cannon.

Lausard fired his pistol close to it, the flash from the pan igniting the portfire.

In a flash, Cezar realised Lausard's intentions.

He saw the lighted portfire hovering above the wagon.

Lausard dropped it, put spurs to his horse and ducked low over the saddle, hurtling back towards the French lines.

The gunpowder in the bottom of the wagon ignited immediately, the entire floor of the vehicle rapidly turning into a glowing red carpet of fire, with probing tongues of flame flickering and reaching for the barrels of gunpowder on either side of the wagon.

Cezar opened his mouth to shout something.

It was drowned by the deafening roar as the wagon exploded.

Lumps of wood, metal and flapping tails of tarpaulin were sent spiralling into the air but, propelled highest by the massive blast, was the gold. A great gleaming fountain of the precious coins rose into the air before raining down like gilt tears, spinning and bouncing all over the hard ground.

The men looked on in dumbstruck amazement at the explosion and its aftermath but then, as the first gleaming circlets began falling close to them, the infantry seemed to understand what was going on, what this precious rain really was.

The shout went up and spread along the lines until it seemed to fill the valley.

'Gold!'

The word was echoed again and again and then everything else was forgotten as the entire unit surged forward, scrabbling for handfuls of the scattered metal.

Lausard rode towards Cezar who was sitting motionless on his horse, his face drained of colour as he watched the infantry swarming over the ground, stuffing coins into their pockets and packs, some of them whooping with delight.

'Your gold, Captain,' Lausard said softly, motioning towards the scattered treasure.

The knot of muscles at the side of Cezar's jaw throbbed furiously.

'You ordered us to bring it back,' Lausard continued. 'There it is.'

Cezar was shaking with rage, the reins gripped tightly in his fists. He sat there a moment longer then wheeled his horse and rode away.

Away from the scenes of ecstatic scavenging and laughter, from the wreck of the wagon and the spilled gold.

Lausard dismounted, spotting one single gold coin close by. He looked at both sides carefully then slipped the coin into his pocket.

When he looked over at his men, Rocheteau was smiling.

'You're insane,' he told Lausard. 'We could all have been rich beyond our wildest dreams.'

'Or dead,' said Lausard, pulling the gold coin from his pocket. He flipped it towards Rocheteau who caught it in his palm and looked down at it.

'Now you're rich,' Lausard told him, grinning.

The other men began to laugh. And it was a sound so joyous they wondered how long it would be before they heard it again.

CHAPTER 38

'And you blew up a hundred thousand in gold? You must be mad,' said Delacor, shaking his head.

'You might just be right,' Lausard said, warming his hands and gazing into the leaping flames of the camp fire.

Nearby other fires burned and men huddled around them seeking what meagre warmth they could, and taking any protection from the biting wind which was whipping through the hills and valleys. A line of trees at the top of the ridge swayed and bowed dependent on the wind. Lausard looked over at them for a moment; around them sentries moved about, some occasionally stopping to chat as they patrolled. Two men were sharing a pipe, thinking they were hidden from prying eyes by some tall bushes.

'So, what now?' asked Giresse. 'The Austrians are beaten. When do we get to go home?'

'Home?' said Delacor scornfully. 'Home was a prison cell before we joined the army, wasn't it? I don't want to go back there.'

'Do you want to carry on fighting then?' Giresse persisted.

'What choice do we have?' Bonet said. 'We're soldiers now. It's our job to fight, isn't it?'

Lausard nodded. 'There's nothing back in France for any of us.'

'What about the women?' Giresse said and the other men laughed.

'There'll be plenty of women in Vienna when we reach it,' Rocheteau reassured him.

'*If we reach it*,' Roussard threw in.

'Roussard's right,' Bonet echoed. 'There aren't enough of us to advance on Vienna. The army isn't strong enough.'

'Since when did you become a military genius, schoolmaster?' Delacor snapped. 'How the hell do *you* know what's going on?'

'Just look around you,' he said, making an expansive gesture with his hand. 'This army is tired, ill-equipped and starving.'

'It's been like that ever since last summer,' Lausard reminded him.

'I agree with the part about starving,' Joubert interjected, rubbing his reduced but still prominent belly.

'Shut up, fat man,' Delacor said, slapping his colleague on the shoulder. 'I should think your horse must be grateful that you've lost some weight.'

The other men laughed.

'I heard that we're not advancing to Vienna,' Rostov offered. 'I heard a rumour that we're to pay the Pope a visit.'

'We're going to attack Rome?' Moreau said incredulously. 'That's blasphemy. God will strike us all down.'

'That old bastard has been against us ever since this war began,' Rostov said.

'He did try to raise an army against us last year,' Rocheteau reminded Moreau.

'He thinks we're all heathens,' Giresse said, smiling.

Lausard laughed and said, 'I think he might be right. Can you imagine what it would be like if the whole of Italy, including the Vatican, became a republic? A republic of thirty million with our morals and vices.' He shook his head.

'I haven't got any vices,' Charvet said innocently.

'What are vices?' Tabor wanted to know.

'Shut up, you half-wit,' Delacor snapped. 'It's not important.'

Bonet patted Tabor lightly on the shoulder. 'Whichever way we march there'll be bloodshed,' he said.

'What else do you expect in a war?' Lausard said dismissively.

Hunkered down on his haunches he continued to stare into the dancing flames of the fire.

It was Rocheteau who noticed the six men marching down the slope but he didn't know at first that they were heading for himself and his comrades. Only when he saw Lieutenant Royere leading them did he guess their target. He wondered why the five dragoons with the officer were all carrying their carbines over their shoulders.

'We've got company,' he said, nodding towards the men.

Lausard turned, saw Royere and got to his feet.

The officer extended a hand which Lausard shook warmly.

'It's good to have you back, Lausard,' the lieutenant said. 'I wish that my visit was for a different reason.'

'What's wrong, Lieutenant?' Lausard glanced at the other dragoons who flanked the officer.

'This isn't a social call, I'm afraid.'

'Is it me you want?' Lausard asked.

Royere nodded. 'I'm going to have to ask you to come with me, Sergeant,' he said almost apologetically. 'I'm placing you under arrest on the orders of Captain Cezar.'

'What's the charge?' enquired Lausard, straightening his cape.

'Deliberate destruction of Republican funds.' He shook his head. 'Believe me, my friend, I wanted no part of this.'

Lausard smiled and said, 'When is the hearing?'

'Now. Before General Bonaparte himself. I am to escort you to his tent.'

'I know the charge,' Lausard said. 'What is the penalty?'

'Death by firing squad,' Royere said. 'And I tell you now, that bastard Cezar means to see you dead.'

'Then we'd better go,' Lausard said.

'I said we should have killed the pig,' hissed Rocheteau.

Lausard stepped into line beside Royere, the other dragoons closing ranks around them. Rocheteau and the others watched as the sombre little band disappeared up the slope, moving swiftly through the maze of camp fires, past men who sometimes gave them cursory looks before returning their attention to the warmth of their own fires or to conversations with comrades. Others were trying to sleep. Those fortunate enough to have food ate it, savouring the tiniest morsel like gourmets at a banquet.

At the bottom of the slope Lausard saw a large tent, a tricolour flying high above it. Outside, a number of dismounted guides stood sentinel, others walked their horses back and forth. Three staff officers were standing close to the tent entrance smoking and talking but their conversation ended abruptly as they saw the procession of dragoons drawing closer.

Lausard recognised one of the officers as Colonel Lannes who had led them in the attack on St Vincini. Lannes watched indifferently as Lausard and his escort halted by the two guides closest to the entrance of the tent. One disappeared inside and, a second later, Lausard heard a voice call for them to enter.

He passed through the tent flap behind Royere.

Bonaparte was sitting in a chair sipping from a glass of wine, a cloak around his shoulders.

Bessieres stood close by him and, to their right, Lausard saw Captain Cezar standing at ease, one hand on the hilt of his sword.

'You are Sergeant Alain Lausard of the Fifth Dragoons?' said Bonaparte, suddenly rising to his feet as if galvanised by Lausard's appearance.

Lausard drew himself to attention and saluted.

'Yes, sir,' he said sharply.

'And you know why you're here?' Bonaparte continued.

Lausard didn't answer.

'Do you know how many muskets could have been bought with one hundred thousand in gold?' Bonaparte said, moving closer to Lausard, his eyes blazing angrily. 'Do you know how many men could have been provided with shoes? How many horses that money could have bought? How much food it would have provided? This army lacks everything except courage and belief. I have fought an entire campaign with just those qualities. Qualities which you yourself must have. Were you at Montenotte? At Arcola? At Rivoli?'

'Yes, sir,' Lausard replied flatly. 'And many more.'

'Then you have these qualities,' Bonaparte snapped. 'You know their value. You also know what it is like to fight on an empty stomach, to ride tired horses, to scavenge like a jackal in order to stay alive. If you know these things why did you not know the value of one hundred thousand in gold?'

A heavy silence descended, finally broken by Bonaparte himself.

'You disobeyed a direct order when you blew up that wagon and destroyed the gold.'

'I disobeyed no order, sir, because I had been *given* no order,' Lausard protested.

'Captain Cezar says that you were told to bring the wagon back to our lines,' said Bonaparte.

'And I did, sir. If I'd thought that money was to be used by the Republic I would not have destroyed it.'

Cezar's smug expression disappeared and he looked anxiously first at Bonaparte then at Lausard.

'That gold was for Captain Cezar's personal use,' Lausard continued. 'It was never intended for the Republic.'

'That's a lie,' hissed Cezar.

Bonaparte raised a hand to silence him. 'Can you prove this?' he asked Lausard.

'No, sir, just as Captain Cezar cannot prove that I

blew up that gold deliberately,' Lausard said with an air of finality.

'So it is Captain Cezar's word against yours, Sergeant,' Bonaparte reminded him. 'Who do you expect me to believe?'

'I trust you will believe your own judgement, sir.'

'And if that judgement is in favour of the Captain, then you will die.'

'Every man dies, sir, it's just a matter of when.'

Bonaparte smiled.

'You show no fear for a man who might shortly be facing twelve muskets, Sergeant,' Bonaparte observed. 'What can you offer in your defence?'

Lausard reached inside his cloak and pulled some papers from his tunic pocket. He handed them to Bonaparte who looked at the top sheet then motioned Bessieres to him.

Cezar looked on in bewilderment as they pored over the pieces of parchment.

'My God!' murmured Bessieres.

'I have more in my portmanteau, sir,' Lausard said.

'Where did you get them?' Bonaparte asked.

'From the wagon,' Lausard said. 'I thought that perhaps some things might be of even more value to the Republic than gold.'

Bonaparte held up one of the pieces of paper, a smile on his thin lips.

'Details of Austrian dispositions,' he said. 'Orders from and to the Aulic Council, requests for men and equipment.'

'There are unit strengths here too,' Bessieres added. 'These papers must contain the composition and position of every Austrian unit in Italy and the Tyrol.'

'We have their secrets in our hands.' Bonaparte laughed.

Bessieres joined him in the cheerful sound.

Royere grinned broadly.

Even Lausard managed a smile.

Cezar looked on furiously.

'Sergeant, bring the rest of your treasure to me as soon as possible,' Bonaparte said. Then he smiled and turned to face Cezar. 'I congratulate you too, Captain. You acted on your own initiative. It took great bravery to seize that baggage train. Your risks have paid dividends. The entire army, France herself, will benefit.' He raised one of the pieces of paper triumphantly.

Cezar forced a smile.

Lausard looked across at him.

'But such initiative must not go unrewarded,' Bonaparte continued. 'Good officers are always difficult to find. Your daring has been put to good effect here. I think the Army of the Rhine would benefit from your ideas and courage. They have more need of you now than I have. With these documents the Sergeant found we will force the Austrians to negotiate. They cannot run from us because we know where they will hide. They cannot escape us because we know where they will run. I need men like you elsewhere. You will leave for the Army of the Rhine tomorrow, Captain. Well done.'

'But, sir—' blabbered Cezar.

'I will hear no arguments,' Bonaparte said. 'No false modesty, Captain. Your skill will benefit France's other main army as it has done here.'

Lausard looked impassively at his commander, then

at Cezar. 'Congratulations, sir,' he said, unable to conceal his smile.

Cezar glared back at him.

'If you leave before dawn you should reach the Aviso in a matter of days,' Bonaparte said. 'I will send four of my guides with you.'

'You are very kind, sir,' said Cezar through clenched teeth. He was almost shaking with rage as he saluted.

Bonaparte turned to face Lausard, his expression darkening somewhat.

'Sergeant Lausard,' be began, 'while I applaud your courage, you must understand that the loss of so much gold cannot be allowed to pass without some gesture from me. There must be a punishment for destroying funds which would have been so useful to the Republic.'

It was Cezar's turn to smile.

Lausard stood at attention, his face impassive.

Bonaparte was only a foot or so from him, his eyes fixed on the dragoon.

'You will lose one month's pay for this action,' Bonaparte said quietly.

Cezar clenched his fists so tightly he felt as if his knuckles would crack. He wanted to scream that the punishment should be more severe. A flogging at least. The knot of muscles at the side of his jaw throbbed furiously.

Bonaparte eyed the sleeves of Lausard's tunic, his gaze drawn to the chevrons that signified his rank.

'You will lose your rank too, Sergeant. Although, I suspect, not for very long.'

Lausard thought he caught the hint of a smile on Bonaparte's lips, then he turned his back on the men.

'You may leave us, gentlemen,' he said.

Lausard, Royere and Cezar saluted then trooped out of the tent.

They were less than ten paces from the entrance when Cezar turned on Lausard.

'You think you've won, don't you?' he snarled furiously.

Lausard didn't answer. He simply held the officer's gaze.

'You haven't seen the last of me, Lausard, I promise you that,' Cezar insisted.

'We'll see, Captain. I hope the men under your command in the Army of the Rhine feel the same way about you as myself and my men have.'

'I should have killed you,' Cezar hissed. 'And one day I will.'

'I'll look forward to the day you *try*, Captain,' Lausard said, smiling.

He turned and walked away, accompanied by Royere.

'You lead a charmed life, my friend,' said Royere with a smile. 'One would think that God is personally protecting you.'

'God has nothing to do with it,' Lausard said. '*These* are my protection.' He tapped his forehead with one index finger then gently patted the hilt of his sword with his other hand. 'They are all I need.'

Royere looked up at the cloud-filled sky and muttered something under his breath. He felt the first drops of rain against his face.

'They say that when it rains the angels are weeping,' the officer observed.

Lausard nodded. 'Then there'll be lots more tears

shed before the end of *this* war,' he said. 'And not just by angels.'

Royere watched him as he set off down the hill back towards his unit, the darkness swallowing him up. The lieutenant looked up once again at the bloated clouds.

The rain continued to fall.

Bonaparte's Invaders

One

The ship lurched violently back and forth, then from side to side, the waves battering it with such relentless force that Alain Lausard was convinced the frigate would capsize.

It was a conviction the dragoon private had held ever since the thirty-six-gun *L'Esperance* had left Toulon harbour twenty-two days earlier. He was amazed that the vessel had not been sunk by the turbulent seas or overturned by the powerful winds that had followed the French fleet as surely as the flocks of seagulls, which even now swooped and dived overhead. They were like living clouds, constantly undulating and shifting position as they travelled above the ships, often diving to sea level to feed.

The realization of what they were feeding on brought fresh contractions to Lausard's stomach, and he gripped the side of the main deck rail and closed his eyes, trying to fight back the sickness that afflicted him.

It was a battle he could not hope to win and, finally, with a despairing, even angry groan, he leaned over and vomited once again.

Half a dozen seagulls sped down towards the water, anxious to feed on the regurgitated contents of Lausard's stomach, just as they had been doing for the entire voyage. It was a common scene in the choppy water around the ships of the French armada, and one, Lausard had no doubt, that would continue, although for how long no one knew as no one knew their ultimate destination.

He remained leaning limply over the side of the frigate for a moment longer then slowly straightened up, wiping his mouth with the back of his hand. To his right and left, in front and behind him, all he could see were sea, ships and sky. His world had been reduced to those three sights during the course of the last twenty-two days. Plus the merciless rocking of the frigate on the water, the sound of the wind in the rigging, the flapping of sails, the stench of salt air and vomit, of thousands of unwashed men crammed together throughout the fleet. The daily routine of eating what passed for rations, trying to find water that wasn't stagnant, only to bring everything up again an hour or so later. The constant bickering with the crew of the frigate; the boredom, the smells. The sheer misery of sea travel. His entire existence had been transformed into this floating purgatory that showed no sign of ending. And he knew it was the same for every one of his colleagues, for every single man aboard every ship in the entire vast fleet.

Led by the flagship *L'Orient*, on which Napoleon Bonaparte himself was sailing, the massive collection of vessels had sailed out of Toulon harbour what seemed like an eternity ago. The flagship herself had towered above them like a fortress, a vast floating citadel bristling with three tiers of forty cannon each and crewed by over a thousand men. For those who had watched from shore the sight was breathtaking. Thirteen ships of the line, some carrying anywhere between seventy-four to one hundred and ten cannon, forty-two frigates, brigs, avisos and other smaller vessels and over one hundred and thirty transports of all kinds had left the harbour. Aboard were seventeen thousand troops and as many sailors and marines, over one thousand pieces of field artillery, a hundred thousand rounds of ammunition, over five hundred vehicles and seven hundred horses.

The fleet had been further swelled by three lesser convoys from Genoa, Ajaccio and Civita Vecchia, bringing the total of men to about fifty-five thousand and the number of sail to almost four hundred. On the open sea, the armada covered four square miles. Looking around, Lausard could see no end to the massive flotilla. The world consisted of sea, ships and sky.

L'Esperance was typical of its class. Crewed by three hundred men, it boasted an impressive array of firepower. On its main deck it sported twenty-six twelve-pounder cannon, and on the quarterdeck were eight six-pounders and two carronades, while the forecastle boasted two six-pounders and two carronades. The men had marvelled at the size of these weapons and the thirty-six-pound projectiles that they fired. The ex-schoolmaster Bonet had guessed that it would take four men to carry each of the missiles when the time came to unleash them.

Bonet's curiosity had not been shared by the other men of the unit, who were by turn puzzled, indifferent or irritated by his interest in the workings of the ship. Like Lausard, they had other things on their minds – namely their destination. Although even that seemed to have taken on secondary importance as they struggled to cope with life aboard ship.

'Personally, I don't *care* where we're going,' the forger Roussard declared, clutching his stomach. 'In fact, if we're on this stinking boat much longer I doubt if any of us will survive to see land again.' He looked pitifully at Lausard then bent double over the side of the ship and retched, his stomach offering up no more.

Carbonne wiped his bald head with his forage cap and exhaled wearily. 'Where do *you* think we're going, Alain?' he asked Lausard.

'I wish I knew. It isn't England, I know that.'

'Someone said Naples,' Charvet offered, loosening another button on his thick woollen tunic, aware of the heat as well as the uncomfortable motion of the frigate.

'I heard Sicily,' Rocheteau said.

'Wherever it is, I hope there's plenty to eat.' Joubert rubbed his shrunken but still huge belly. 'I'm starving.'

'You're always starving, fat man,' Delacor snarled. 'How can you even think of food at a time like this? The last thing I need is a meal.' He tried not to think about his lurching stomach, hoping the contractions would subside.

'It must be a rich country where we're going,' Sonnier said. 'After all, Bonaparte promised we'd all have enough money to buy six acres of land each when we returned.'

'We'll be lucky if we ever see land again, never mind be lucky enough to *buy* any for ourselves,' Rostov snapped. The big Russian was sitting cross-legged on the deck, his head bowed as if in prayer. He had found that staying off his feet reduced the effects of the seasickness a little but not enough to bring him any lasting relief.

'I thought being in prison was bad,' Giresse bemoaned, 'but this is worse. The food there might not have been fit for pigs but at least we could keep it down.'

'Six acres,' Bonet sighed wistfully. 'That's a lot of land. I think I'd build my own school. I enjoyed teaching.'

'Until they locked you up for it,' Delacor reminded him.

'They locked me up for not teaching what the Directory ordered. They locked me up because I taught the truth.'

'They still locked you up. You're still a criminal like the rest of us.'

'We're not criminals any more,' Lausard corrected Delacor, 'we're soldiers.' There was a note of pride in his tone.

'Soldiers belong on land,' Rocheteau told him, still clutching his belly. 'What the hell are we doing here, anyway? We should be back in France drinking wine, eating bread and enjoying our victory.'

'*And* the women,' Giresse added.

A ripple of laughter rose from the green-clad dragoons; it had become an unfamiliar sound in the past weeks.

However, their laughter was soon stifled as a wave slammed into the side of the ship, sending some of the men toppling over like human skittles. A great spray of sea water covered the deck and the men, but it was dried almost immediately by the hot sun. Lausard looked down at his tunic and saw the wool was covered by a thin white crust of dried salt; he brushed some of it away in disgust.

As the men picked themselves up and brushed themselves down they heard laughter.

Lausard looked round to see two seamen emerging from a nearby hatch.

One was stripped to the waist and barefoot, his black hair tied back in a long ponytail. The other was dressed in a dark blue tunic and white trousers. The black bicorn he wore marked him out as being of a certain rank but there was little else to signify his seniority. Both men regarded the dragoons with ill-disguised contempt. It was a look the troops had become well acquainted with during their time on the frigate. Their presence was resented by the sailors with a vehemence that matched their own distaste at being aboard the ship.

'Still not learned to stand up?' the man in the blue jacket teased.

The dragoons knew him as Marek, a gunnery sergeant who commanded a battery on the main deck. Like most of his colleagues, he was deeply tanned, his skin rough and pitted, his hands like ham hocks. His companion was in his early twenties, a scrawny specimen with long, thin fingers, one of which was missing. He wore gold earrings in both ears, clearly visible where his unwashed hair was swept back. As Lausard watched, the sailor climbed into the rigging and made his way swiftly up it, moving as surefootedly as a chimp until he was thirty or forty feet above the deck. A number of his fellow sailors already moved around up there, scurrying back and forth with an assurance Lausard found it difficult not to admire.

'That's landsmen for you,' Marek said, pointing upwards at the men in the rigging. 'They work the yards. I say they're the most skilled men on the ship.'

'Why do you call them landsmen?' Lausard asked. 'They're sailors like you.'

'No they aren't.' Marek snorted disdainfully. 'I'm a professional. I have a rank. They're untrained. They couldn't work a cannon or plot map co-ordinates. You need a brain for that.'

'Then what are *you* doing here, you glorified fisherman?' Rocheteau said.

Some of the other men laughed, but once again their amusement was stifled by a jolt to the frigate, which caused it to lurch uncomfortably in the churning water.

'Have you got any idea what our final destination is, Marek?' Lausard asked.

'If I had why should I tell *you*?' The seaman smiled.

'All we want to do is get off this stinking boat,' said Lausard. 'We don't want to be on here any more than you and your men want us aboard. Besides, *you* might be used to smelling like a pig but *I'm* not. I haven't even been able to change my uniform for weeks.'

'That's the trouble with you soldier boys, you're pampered,' the gunnery sergeant jibed. 'Too much soft living. When it comes to *real* hardship you start crying.'

'We fought our way across most of Italy,' Rocheteau told him. 'We sent the Austrians running before us. We've seen things you couldn't even dream of.'

'Don't try to impress me with your tales of war,' Marek sneered. 'I fight in darkness, down there.' He pointed towards the main deck below. 'Choked by smoke, blinded by fire and with enemy guns only feet away from me. That's *real* war. And out here there's nowhere to run. We can't just turn and flee when things turn against us. Not like you.'

'Considering how many times the navy has been beaten, perhaps you'd have been better off running,' Lausard retaliated, glaring at Marek.

There was more laughter from the other dragoons.

Marek opened his mouth to say something but thought better of it, and simply raised a hand and stalked off across the deck in the direction of a group of sailors manhandling a twelve-pounder into position.

Lausard watched the retreating figure, then turned

back to the choppy water to watch the other ships. The powerful wind billowed in their sails, sending them speeding along, cutting through the choppy water with ease, but the smaller craft, *L'Esperance* included, seemed to feel every single bump and swell of surf.

'You're a friend of the Almighty,' Roussard said, nudging Moreau. 'Can't you have a word with him and get him to calm the sea?'

Moreau glared at his companion.

'Better still,' Rocheteau added, 'ask him if he knows where we're going.'

Some of the men laughed, but Moreau was unamused. He continued to clutch the side of the deck barrier, his face milk white.

'I wonder how the horses are doing,' Tabor murmured.

All the animals, pack mules and cavalry mounts alike, were on separate transport further back in the great armada. They had been herded into stalls below deck, around twenty animals to each ship. The farriers travelled with them, fed them their meagre rations and tended to them as best they could. For the animals the voyage was even more arduous than it was for the troops. Stuck in the holds in perpetual darkness, many of them died of thirst, and were either hurled overboard or, in some cases, eaten by the starving crews.

'To hell with the horses,' Delacor rasped. 'What about *us*?'

'I wonder what our new captain thinks of all this?' Lausard mused aloud.

'I think he's enjoying himself,' Rocheteau said. 'Captain Milliere is a dedicated gambler it seems. Which is just as well because the only things to do on this ship are gamble or be sick.'

'You should know about the gambling,' Lausard reminded him. 'You organized it.'

The men laughed.

'Perhaps it's a good job we haven't had any pay for so long,' Rostov offered. 'If we had we'd all be broke by now.'

'I wonder what old Deschamps would make of this?' Giresse said.

'He was a good officer.' Lausard looked around at the men. 'I hope he's well.'

'Where *are* all the officers, anyway?' Roussard enquired.

'Below deck, gambling or trying to sleep,' Rocheteau informed him.

'A boat took some of them over to *L'Orient* this morning; Desaix went with them, I saw him,' Bonet observed.

'It would be difficult to miss someone as tall as General Desaix,' Charvet noted.

'He was wearing that old blue jacket of his,' Bonet continued. 'Without the lace. You'd never know he was a general.'

'Perhaps *he* knows where we're going,' Giresse wondered aloud.

'Him and Bonaparte,' Delacor said. 'You can be sure that *they'll* both have enough to buy more than six acres of land when all this business is over. I heard that most of the generals were feathering their own nests during the Italian campaign.'

'Like some others I could mention?' Rocheteau chuckled.

'What did we get out of that?' Delacor challenged. 'A few pieces of gold and silver. Some officers had enough to buy houses, entire estates. The Bourbons were removed because they had too much wealth and now they've been replaced by men even more greedy.

Even the Directory are no better. They are only rulers under another name.'

'Every country must have rulers,' Lausard said. 'Whatever shape they take.'

'I thought we fought to free people from their rulers,' Delacor continued.

'We fight because we are ordered to,' Lausard told him. 'Nothing more, nothing less.'

'So who will we fight if we ever get off these stinking ships?' Roussard wanted to know.

Lausard merely gazed out to sea, at the huge armada of vessels as far as the eye could see. He wished he knew. He wished he could answer Roussard's question, but as yet, like everyone else in the army, he was clueless. He had already spilled Austrian, Piedmontese and Italian blood. But whose blood he would spill next, he couldn't begin to imagine.

Two

As Lausard descended the narrow wooden stairway that led down into the Stygian depths of the main deck, he gripped the handrail tightly. Buffeted by a wave, the frigate rocked uncertainly for a moment and Lausard feared he would be hurled off the narrow walkway, but the tremor passed and he continued on his way, struck, as ever, by the foul stench that permeated this nether region. Exactly how many men inhabited this part of the ship he didn't know. He guessed two or three hundred: a combination of the sailors who normally called this their home and the men of his own unit who had been assigned this black hell-hole as living quarters for the duration of the voyage.

The troops slept on the bare boards of the deck while most of the naval personnel had hammocks slung from the beams, many of them above the cannon. The crews slept around their guns as if the bond between them was unbreakable. Six to a crew, they were, almost without exception, squat, powerful men who spoke little, even to each other.

Among the crew was a number of young boys, some in their teens, some even younger. Lausard had learned that during a battle these boys would rush from gun to gun carrying powder where it was needed and, in some cases, even tending to the wounded as best they could. Life at sea seemed unpleasant enough for grown men, thought the dragoon, but what it must be like for these children he could only imagine. One of them, a boy of about twelve, dressed only in a pair of threadbare knee-length *culottes*, was scooping water into a ladle from one of the barrels at the foot of the wooden steps. Lausard watched as the boy rinsed out his mouth with the rancid fluid then spat it out on to the deck close to the dragoon's boots. The boy looked at him then ambled off back towards a nearby twelve-pounder.

Lausard stuck his hand into the water and scooped some on to his face, washing away the sweat. The water was slightly warm and smelled rancid. But it was all they had. There were two barrels at either end of the deck, for drinking, washing and cooking. It was rumoured that there was fresh water in the hold but they had received nothing resembling fresh water for more than a week now.

Lausard made his way slowly along the deck, stepping over sleeping men, ducking to avoid hammocks where he had to. He could see barely two feet in front of him in the gloom. At various points on the deck candles were burning, offering tiny islands of illumination in this sea of blackness, but for the most part the deck was funereal. Occasionally the gunports would be opened to allow in some much needed fresh air and some natural light, but on the whole the main deck was lit just by these few candle flames and it became impossible to tell day from night.

There was a number of cabins towards the rear of the ship where the officers of both the army and the navy had their quarters. These, so it was rumoured, were well lit and comfortable, but Lausard found it difficult to believe that anywhere on *L'Esperance* offered much in the way of respite from the hideous day-to-day existence he and his colleagues endured. Like most, this was his first time at sea and he hoped it would be his last.

He tripped over the outstretched legs of a sleeping dragoon but the man didn't even stir. He was lying with his head on his saddle, his face hidden by the blackness, only his low breathing indicating that he was still alive. His tunic was undone and open, his hands clasped on his chest. Many of the men had divested themselves of their uniforms because of the stifling heat but also because the material was in such an appalling state. Without the benefit of sanitation, many men, crammed together in such restricted conditions for so long, found the stench of their own clothes, never mind those of their comrades, intolerable. Dried sweat, urine and vomit were the overpowering odours that filled the foul air. As oppressive as the darkness, their combined smell hung like an invisible cloud over the men.

Many of the men had retreated to the dank, reeking abyss of the main deck over an hour before in an attempt to get some sleep. It seemed that only when sleep claimed them were they free of the ravages of hunger, thirst and seasickness.

Lausard had stayed topside for a little longer, looking out over the churning sea, watching the seamen at work and thinking. His thoughts had turned to France. He didn't doubt for a moment that there was purpose in this mission but what it was he could not comprehend. Why had the men not been told their destination? Where could Bonaparte be taking them that would hold so much fear? Had that been the reason for the secrecy? he pondered. And yet, most of this army, dubbed 'The Legions of Rome' by its commander, were veterans of the Italian campaign. Men who would not show fear easily. Men, like himself, who had fought their way through battles like Mondovi, Lodi, Arcola, Rivoli and Castiglione. But Lausard had no fear of the final destination, wherever it may be. Whatever awaited them had to be better than the hell they were living aboard ship.

The frigate listed again and Lausard cursed as he almost overbalanced. A candle was burning just ahead of him and he could see some of his comrades gathered around it, heads bowed in some cases.

Joubert was lying on his back, his face slick with sweat, his belly spilling over the top of his breeches. He had removed his tunic, as had Tabor, who was lying curled up in a foetal position, his head resting on the jacket.

Sonnier lay on his side, one hand clamped across his mouth, the other ineffectually clutching his stomach. Lying against his legs was Gaston. The young trumpeter had suffered a little less violently from seasickness than his older colleagues and now, as he saw Lausard approaching, a smile creased his youthful features. The private tried to return the gesture but it faded as he became aware of his stomach contracting and thought that he was going to be sick again. To his relief, the tremor passed and he sat down, cross-legged, next to Rocheteau, who was chewing cautiously on a piece of salt biscuit he'd found in his pocket. He offered a chunk to Lausard, who shook his head.

'No water,' Lausard muttered, 'and yet all they give us

to eat is salt beef and salt biscuits. Salt makes you thirsty.' He shrugged.

'Bonaparte might know how to organize an army,' Delacor said indignantly, 'but he doesn't know how to feed one.'

'It isn't his fault,' Lausard argued. 'It's the contractors who supply us. They're a bunch of crooks looking to make a fast profit.'

'So they sit on their fat backsides in France, while we starve to death on this stinking ship,' Roussard hissed.

'Us and everyone else in the army,' Sonnier echoed.

'I don't care about anyone else,' Delacor told him, 'I care about *me*.'

'We'd noticed,' Rostov responded, rubbing both hands across his sweat-drenched face.

Bonet seemed oblivious to the bickering of his companions; he was looking fixedly at a copy of *Le Moniteur*.

Lausard could just make out the date of the newspaper in the odorous blackness of the main deck. 19th May, 1798. 'The news in there will be a little out of date, Bonet,' he said.

Bonet smiled. 'I bought it just before we sailed. As a kind of keepsake. There are reports in here about the fleet leaving Toulon. But they have no idea where we're heading either.'

Lausard held out his hand and Bonet passed him the paper.

'"Officers and soldiers,"' Lausard read aloud. '"Two years ago I came to take command of you. At that time you were on the Ligurian coast, in the greatest want, lacking everything, having sold even your watches to provide for your needs. I promised to put an end to your privations. I led you into Italy. There all was given you in abundance. Have I not kept my word?"'

'Who said that?' Tabor asked vaguely.

'Bonaparte, you half-wit,' Delacor snapped.

'According to the newspaper, we all answered with a single shout of "Yes",' Lausard continued.

'What he said is true, isn't it?' Sonnier offered. 'Napoleon *did* lead us into Italy.'

'And nearly got us all killed,' Delacor qualified.

'Napoleon?' Giresse said, smiling at Sonnier. 'Are you on first-name terms with our commander now, Sonnier?'

The men chuckled.

Lausard held up a hand for silence then continued reading.

'"Well, let me tell you that you have not done enough yet for the fatherland, nor the fatherland for you. I shall now lead you into a country where by your future deeds you will surpass even those that now are astonishing your admirers, and you will render to the Republic such services as she has a right to expect from an invincible army. I promise every soldier that upon his return to France, he shall have enough to buy himself six acres of land."'

'Is that why you kept the paper, schoolmaster?' Rocheteau wanted to know. 'So that you could show that to Bonaparte in case he tried to cheat any of us?'

'It says here the speech was followed by shouts of "Long Live the Immortal Republic" and by patriotic hymns,' Lausard said, flicking the newspaper with his finger. He passed it back to Bonet. 'It seems it is easier to be patriotic on dry land.'

'Have you stopped believing in Bonaparte then, Alain?' Rocheteau questioned. 'I thought you were the patriot amongst us.'

Lausard shrugged. 'I've never had the monopoly on

patriotism. But you tell me, would a speech like that have been as well received by this army had Bonaparte given it two days ago?'

Rocheteau shook his head. 'I for one would not have applauded it.'

'And yet, when we land, we will fight if he tells us to fight,' Lausard said. 'We will charge if he tells us to charge, and we will do it because we are soldiers, not because we are patriots.'

'I fight for God.' Moreau's voice came from the gloom.

'Then I hope he takes care of you,' Delacor said. 'Me, I'll trust myself, no one else – and certainly not your God.'

Moreau crossed himself.

'Is that what you would build on your six acres, Moreau? A church?' Carbonne prompted his colleague.

'I would build a fitting monument to His majesty, to His power and goodness,' Moreau said.

'I'd build a bakery like my father's, and every day I'd awake to the smell of freshly baked bread, just like I did when I was a child,' Charvet said wistfully.

'Do you have to mention food when I'm so hungry?' Joubert complained.

'We're all hungry, Joubert, not just you,' Delacor snapped.

'I'd build a farm in the Urals where I was born,' Rostov declared.

'I'd build a brothel and fill it with the most beautiful women in France.' Giresse chuckled. 'Then I'd make sure the only customer they ever had was me.'

A wave of laughter came from the men. The sound was subdued; swallowed and stifled by the impenetrable blackness.

'Shut up!' shouted an anonymous voice.

Lausard turned and tried to peer into the umbra, attempting to pick out the source of the shout.

'Can't you shut up and go to sleep,' the voice said again, more insistently this time.

'Are you such a coward that you shout at us from the darkness?' Lausard called back. 'Show yourself.'

'Be quiet, soldier boy,' a voice called from much closer.

Several of the dragoons could see one of the sailors sitting up in his hammock smoking a pipe, thick smoke billowing around him.

The man was huge. Fully six feet tall and sporting thick muscular arms and a torso that looked like granite. His face was almost hidden by the gloom, only portions of it illuminated by the sickly candle light. Lausard could make out a thick moustache and beard but that was about all.

'The sooner we reach land the better,' the huge sailor said. 'Then we can all be rid of you. You don't belong here.'

'Do you think we *want* to be here, you idiot?' Delacor snarled.

There was a loud thud as the sailor slid from his hammock and dropped to the deck floor. He rose to his full impressive height and took a step towards the dragoons. Several other seamen joined him as he advanced towards the troops.

Lausard got to his feet, Charvet and Rocheteau flanking him.

Rocheteau's hand fell to his belt, his fingers touching the hilt of the small knife jammed there.

All around the deck men were moving, voices rising in volume. Curses and threats were exchanged.

Delacor stood close to the gigantic sailor, forced to look up into his face.

'What's going on?' a familiar voice asked, and both soldiers and sailors saw Marek approaching through the darkness.

'I think these little men need to be taught a lesson,' the big seaman said.

'Ah, so you've met Legros?' Marek chuckled. 'You should stay away from him. You might upset him.'

'What will he do?' Lausard remained unimpressed. 'Suffocate us with his stench?'

Legros took a step forward, lunging at Lausard, who stood his ground.

Marek stepped in front of the sailor. Charvet blocked Lausard's path.

'The time will come, soldier boy,' Legros snarled. 'You and all of your babies will be food for the fish. I'll kill you.'

'You're welcome to try,' Lausard said calmly.

Charvet raised his hands into his boxer's stance, his eyes boring into those of Legros.

'A fighter,' Marek said. 'You would dare to fight Legros?'

'I'll fight all of you,' Charvet said.

Marek looked at Rocheteau, who nodded.

'There could be money in a fight like that,' Marek observed.

Rocheteau smiled. He pushed the last piece of salt biscuit into his mouth and chewed.

Three

Napoleon Bonaparte raised the glass of red wine in salute, looked around at the other men who had joined him in his cabin, then drank. Those who surrounded him did likewise, some against their better judgement. Despite the relative comfort enjoyed by the higher-ranking officers on the voyage, many of these fighting men were still experiencing their first taste of sea travel, and the seasickness that afflicted so many of their troops had also struck them.

Bonaparte himself had escaped the worst ravages of the long voyage. He sat on the edge of his bed, which had been fitted with gimbals to counteract the effects of the repeated dips and rises of tide, and looked around at those who had been summoned to his cabin aboard *L'Orient*.

'Gentlemen, we dock at Malta tomorrow. The first part of our great adventure. The first chapter in a catalogue of deeds that men will talk about for years to come.'

'Why Malta?' a quizzical voice from close by asked and Bonaparte looked up to see General Dumas looking down at him. Dumas was a giant of a man, a mulatto who towered over most of his colleagues.

'The island has strategic value,' Bonaparte informed him. 'But at present it is necessary for us to take it to replenish our supplies. Especially water. Orders have already been sent to the Grand Master of the island informing him that we wish to dock to take on water. Whether or not that permission is given we will land troops to the north and south of the capital, Valetta, and also on Gozo, the neighbouring island. We will then encircle Valetta, and wait for the knights to surrender.' He took another sip of his wine, satisfied that his explanation was clear enough.

'This Grand Master of whom you speak,' Dumas continued, 'who is he? Grand Master of what? And who are these knights?'

Bonaparte chuckled but Dumas frowned in bewilderment.

'His name is Baron Von Hompesch,' the cavalry general was told. The answer came from Louis Alexandre Berthier, Bonaparte's chief of staff. 'A German. He is Grand Master of the Order of the Knights of St John of Jerusalem. The Knights Templars. It is an ancient order.'

'An outdated order,' Bonaparte added. 'It no longer serves a purpose and it will fall because it *has* to fall.'

'The knights rule the island,' Berthier continued, 'and the island rules the Mediterranean. The English, the Austrians and the Russians all wish to acquire it. The Russians in particular. It would give them a foothold here. The Tsar has publicly declared himself to be a protector of the Order.'

'If we do not take it then our enemies will,' Bonaparte said.

'If not the Russians, then the Austrians. Von Hompesch is sympathetic to their cause.'

'These knights, will they fight?' The question came from General Caffarelli. He was a lean, thin-faced man who had lost a leg in Germany fighting for the Republic. As he moved slowly about the cabin, his wooden leg bumped loudly against the floor.

'Some of them might,' Berthier replied. 'More than half of them have always been French but our intelligence tells us that many have somewhat conflicting attitudes towards the Republic.'

'If they will not accept us then they should be destroyed,' Caffarelli stated.

Bonaparte smiled. 'Your loyalty to the Republic is admirable, Max,' he said. 'But, at times, perhaps a little over-zealous.'

Some of the other officers laughed but the engineer general turned and glared furiously at them. 'All who oppose the Republic should be destroyed,' he hissed. 'As were those Bourbon leeches we carried to the guillotine.'

'I agree with Caffarelli.' General Desaix sipped at his wine. 'If these knights oppose us then let us eradicate them.'

'There *are* Republicans among them,' Berthier said. 'Intelligence reports have revealed as much.'

'What intelligence reports?' Desaix demanded.

'In December of last year, I myself despatched two emissaries to Malta,' Bonaparte informed the other man. 'One of them was sent as a spy, the other, Citizen Poussielgue, on official business. One of his cousins is Guardian of the port of Valetta. He remained for four months and he spoke to many of the French knights. He found Republican sympathizers. Among them Bosredon de Ransijat, the Treasurer of the Order, and also a man called Fay, the Commissioner of Fortifications. The other knights said that they would resist any invasion unless they were assured of compensation.'

'It would seem that diplomacy rather than force is what is required,' Berthier added.

'You would have us held to ransom by these dogs?' Caffarelli snapped. 'Why pay them when we can simply destroy them?'

'Do you think I doubt my own men?' Bonaparte hissed. 'Men who have subdued and conquered half of Europe will take this island without weapons if they have to.'

'Even if they do decide to fight there should be little problem,' Berthier said. 'There are enough supplies in Valetta to withstand a siege for four months but the defences are poor. There are nearly a thousand guns but they have not been used for a century. The powder supplies, according to our reports, are rotten and unusable.'

'What about troops?' Desaix enquired. 'How many are there on the island?'

'About ten thousand Maltese militia, poorly armed and not eager to fight. There is a native garrison of about fifteen hundred men and three hundred and thirty-two Knights Templars, fifty of whom are either too old or too sick to fight. The others have no heart for it.'

The officers listened to the news in silence, occasionally swapping glances with each other.

'We know that our men will fight,' said Desaix. 'But what of these "pekinese" you have brought along with you? These architects, surveyors, chemists, studiers of animals and rocks. What place have they on a military mission?'

'Ask Caffarelli, he helped to pick them,' Bonaparte said, smiling.

The engineer turned on his colleague, looking up at Desaix. 'These civilians are men of great knowledge,' Caffarelli said earnestly. 'All have their purpose.'

'I heard that there were singers and poets among them,' Dumas commented. 'How will *they* help us?'

'They will all be needed when the time is right,' Caffarelli insisted. 'There is a need for brains as well as brute force on this mission, Dumas.'

The cavalry general snorted dismissively and reached for the decanter of wine, refilling his glass.

Bonaparte looked around the room at one of the men who had not yet spoken. He was dressed in a dark blue, long-tailed tunic, dark blue breeches and short leather boots. The bicorn he held sported a huge white feather plume. Admiral Brueys sipped his wine and listened distractedly to the conversations of the army officers, his mind seemingly elsewhere.

'What are your views on this landing, Brueys?' Bonaparte asked finally.

'I have no view, General,' said the admiral. 'The business of which you speak is military. My concerns are for my ships.'

'What concerns do you have?' Bonaparte wanted to know. 'Have you no faith in your men or in your own abilities?'

'I don't doubt my own abilities, General,' said the admiral. 'Just as I don't underestimate the abilities of my opponent. Nelson has ships in the Mediterranean. We only avoided him leaving Toulon by luck.'

Bonaparte waved a hand dismissively. 'That one-eyed, one-armed Englishman,' he snorted. 'Don't try to frighten me with tales of Nelson.'

'It is not fear that I feel for him, but respect,' Brueys responded. 'A respect you would do well to share, General.'

Bonaparte glared at the seaman. 'You were assigned this force because of your ability, you *and* your colleagues. You have in your charge over forty thousand of my men but you also have something else. You have the destiny of France in your hands. That destiny, like my men, must be protected. Against Nelson or whoever else comes against us.'

'If he catches us in open water he will destroy us,' Brueys said flatly. 'The British ships are faster. They will move through a fleet of this size like a knife through butter.'

'It is your job to see that they don't.'

'That may be easier said than done if he catches us.'

Bonaparte poured himself another glass of wine and returned to his bed, even though the ship was relatively stable as it moved through the night-shrouded ocean.

The uneasy silence was interrupted by a knock on the door of the stateroom and Berthier crossed to open it.

He found himself confronted by an aide-de-camp, dressed in an immaculate uniform, who saluted smartly and handed the chief of staff a piece of paper. Berthier scanned it, returned the salute, then closed the door, listening to the ADC's receding footsteps. Finally he walked back towards Bonaparte, the piece of paper held before him.

'From Grand Master Von Hompesch himself,' Berthier

said. 'No more than four ships at a time are to be admitted to Valetta harbour.'

Bonaparte's expression darkened. 'Send a communication back to the Grand Master now. Take this down. General Bonaparte will secure by force that which should have been accorded to him freely.'

Berthier crossed to the small writing desk in one corner of the room and hastily scribbled down the message, the quill scratching noisily across the paper as he wrote.

Caffarelli smiled.

Desaix finished his wine.

'We land tomorrow, gentlemen,' Bonaparte declared.

'And after Malta?' Desaix asked. 'Where then?'

The Corsican smiled. 'The place where Alexander found his greatness. The place where all men of destiny are drawn. Egypt.'

Four

It was a beautiful day in Paris. The kind of day that made men and women want to feel the sun on their faces. The kind of day that made them feel glad to be alive. The sun was high in the sky, a burning circlet in a blue firmament barely trimmed with wisps of white cloud. In the gardens of the Tuileries the smell of roses was strong in the air. A heady aroma that symbolized summer as much as the buzzing of bees that floated on the calm breeze collecting pollen. Flowers throughout the huge gardens were in full bloom, each, it seemed, competing with the others to display the most brilliant colours and tempting scents. A network of wide gravel paths twisted and turned through the gardens, passing ornamental fountains, rockeries and flower beds.

Charles Maurice de Talleyrand paused beside one of the rose bushes, snapped off a bloom just below the head and sniffed it approvingly before attaching it to the lapel of his long frockcoat.

'A day like this makes a man appreciate God and all his works, don't you think, gentlemen?' he said, smiling, looking round at his companions.

'What chance do I have?' Paul Barras sighed. 'I am surrounded by priests.'

He looked first at Talleyrand then at the older, taller man who accompanied them. Emmanuel Joseph Sieyès was in his late forties but appeared older, the ravages of so much childhood illness having wrought its damage on his features.

'You discredit me, Barras,' Talleyrand said. 'Sieyès was formerly a priest. *I* was Bishop of Autun.'

'Eventually defrocked,' Sieyès reminded him triumphantly.

'This is true,' the younger man conceded. 'But I like to think that God's loss has been France's gain.' He chuckled.

They continued walking, their feet crunching the gravel beneath. Seated ahead of them on one of the ornamental benches that were dotted around the impressive gardens was Gohier, another member of the Directory. He was gazing at the massive edifice of the palace itself, his eyes narrowed.

'When the Bourbons were executed we should have destroyed this place,' he said, nodding towards the building. 'As long as it stands it remains a monument to their corruption. To the obscenity of born rulers.'

'What are we if we are not rulers?' Sieyès challenged.

'We were not born to these positions,' Gohier retorted. 'We gained them by our ability, not by our breeding.'

'You cannot judge a man by his breeding. We have already proved that talent, sensitivity and character were not the property of the so-called upper class. Did it help them to survive? No. *We* are the ones who survived.'

'Men of the people,' Talleyrand said, a smile touching his features.

'You find that description amusing?' Barras snapped.

'Come, my friends, you have the privilege and wealth of those born to fortune. Are you any better than those you replaced?' Talleyrand asked.

'For a minister of state, Talleyrand, you speak with the words of sedition,' Barras told him.

'I thought this country was one of free speech now. Am I not entitled to voice my opinions? My position as Minister of Foreign Affairs doesn't prevent me from having my own thoughts, even about those whom I serve.'

'We are not here to discuss the workings of this government.' Gohier's tone was dismissive. 'We are here to discuss General Bonaparte and his latest venture.'

'His latest folly would perhaps be more appropriate,' Barras said sardonically. 'This Oriental expedition is doomed to failure.'

'Then why was it sanctioned in the first place?' Talleyrand demanded. 'You all know that if it succeeds it will yield vast dividends. It will swell France's coffers even more than the Italian campaign did and it also has untold strategic value.'

'What is to be gained by seizing a country so far away?' Gohier wanted to know.

'The policy of any country should be expansion,' Talleyrand informed him. 'Preferably into territories it can colonize and use for its own benefit, whether those benefits be military or economic. The colonization of Egypt offers both.'

'We already have merchants there,' Sieyès reminded his colleagues.

'And a consul general in Cairo as well as consulates in Alexandria and Rosetta, the two principal ports,'

Talleyrand added. 'We have a larger interest in Egypt than any other country in Europe has.'

'French trade with Egypt amounts to less than six million livres a year,' Barras said. 'It isn't a very impressive figure.'

'But that is from only fifty or sixty merchants dealing in coffee, rice, sugar or cotton,' Talleyrand said. 'And they are constantly harassed by the Mamelukes, the rulers of the province. I think they would welcome outright *seizure* of the country.'

'What do you know of these Mamelukes?' Barras enquired.

'They are a warlike people,' Talleyrand said. 'When they are not fighting amongst themselves they battle the Turks, our allies. They are little more than thieves but very successful ones and their horsemanship is legendary. They live in luxury at the expense of those they rule.'

'Like any monarchs,' Gohier interjected.

'The current rulers, Ibrahim and Murad Bey, have signed a trade treaty with the British,' Talleyrand informed the other men. 'If they gain a foothold there then our problems will multiply ten-fold. In short, gentlemen, if *we* do not take Egypt, someone else will. The Ottoman Empire is the "sick man of Europe". I think it is up to us to administer the cure.'

Sieyès nodded sagely. 'I agree. The loss of our colonies in West India would be lessened by the acquisition of Egypt and its surrounding lands.'

'Egypt is the link joining Africa, Asia and Europe. If General Bonaparte can take it then the possibilities are endless. Trade routes to Arabia and India would become ours. We could deal a crushing blow against England's Asian trade. For, after all, is England not the real enemy?'

'I fear we are throwing away money that would have been better spent elsewhere,' Barras said.

'An invasion of England would be far more expensive than what it has cost to send General Bonaparte and his men to Egypt,' Talleyrand explained. 'By establishing France in Africa, we shall guarantee the peace of Europe.'

'Should we not consider another reason too?' Sieyès broke in. 'The freeing of the captive people of Egypt. If we can restore to them some measure of self-rule then we will be following the ideals of the Republic.'

'An admirable sentiment,' Barras commented. 'But I think there is a reason for us to rejoice in this expedition – a reason that exceeds any financial or cultural considerations.'

The other men looked at him in bewilderment.

'It frees us of the presence of Bonaparte,' Barras explained. 'How long will he be gone? Six months? Longer? It gives us time to consolidate our power against him.'

'The man is a hero,' Gohier snapped. 'He conquered Italy for us. Why should we fear him?'

'Because there is nothing more dangerous than an idle hero,' Barras said quietly. 'Especially when he has control of the army. He is an ambitious man. How long do you think it would be before his ambition extended to the Directory? To us. I tell you now, he would have settled for nothing less than that.'

'You may be right,' Sieyès agreed. 'I fear he would as easily turn against us. Without an enemy to confront he would seek one out.'

'This expedition gives him the chance to pursue his own dreams of glory while helping the Republic,' Barras said.

'Your suspicions, it seems, have no end where our General is concerned,' Talleyrand offered. 'Perhaps it would be better for all of you if he simply did not return.'

'We wish no harm against him,' Sieyès assured him.

Talleyrand shrugged.

'He is a very able general,' Sieyès continued. 'But make no mistake, he wanted to lead this expedition. With the Austrians subdued he has no war to fight. He is merely another general kicking his heels waiting for action, waiting for the chance to be a hero again. We allowed him that chance.'

'You try to hide fear with nobility now,' Talleyrand countered. 'But I myself know how keen he was to set sail. General Bonaparte seeks Egypt for as many complicated reasons as we ourselves.'

'He thinks he's on some kind of mission of liberation and education,' Barras said. 'That's why he's taken so many civilians with him. He has a hundred and sixty-seven members of the Commission of the Sciences and Arts with him. Astronomers, botanists, antiquarians, mathematicians, chemists. He even has a poet with him, Parseval-Grandmaison. What does he hope to do, conquer Egypt or educate it?'

'A little of both,' Talleyrand said.

'He will soon tire of these *savants*,' Barras snapped. 'Bonaparte knows only battle, he will not be interested in their teaching when the time comes.' There was a note of scorn in the Director's voice that Talleyrand found distasteful.

'You seem to harbour a strong dislike of the General, Citizen Barras. Could it be because he stole your mistress?'

Barras shot Talleyrand a vicious glance, aware that the eyes of the other men were also upon him.

The look turned to a sneer. 'He took nothing that I was unwilling to release.'

Talleyrand smiled and began walking along one of the other paths, followed by Gohier and Sieyès.

Barras glared at the statesman's back for a moment longer then strode up alongside him.

'When Alexander conquered Egypt he took thinkers as well as soldiers with him,' Talleyrand said. 'Forty centuries later our own conqueror does the same. Bonaparte and Alexander are very alike in nature.'

'Then I hope our General remembers that Alexander died during his time in the Far East,' Barras chided.

'I'm sure he knows that,' Talleyrand said. 'And much, much more.'

Five

'Tell me I'm not seeing things,' Joubert murmured. 'I'm so weak from lack of food that what I see is not real, is it?'

'It's there, fat man,' Delacor assured him, gazing out across the water, a wan smile on his sallow features.

Lausard too was beginning to wonder if the sight before them was imagined. The result of too long at sea, of too little food. Had the ravages of their terrible journey finally caused them all to begin seeing things, imagining what they *wished* would be there? He felt his stomach contract slightly as *L'Esperance* was rocked by a large wave, but the sight before him – a sight he had begun to doubt he would ever see again – seemed to make even the misery of seasickness dissipate slightly.

Land.

The arrival of the leading ships in the armada had been presaged by a swarm of activity amongst the sailors aboard the frigate and, no doubt, aboard many other ships of the fleet. Up to an hour earlier they had been rushing about above and below deck, for the first time during the voyage seemingly unconcerned by the presence of their unwanted passengers. Intent only on completing the duties assigned to them prior to dropping anchor.

At first Lausard and the other dragoons who had been on deck had watched, bemused, as the sailors had set about their tasks wondering what had precipitated such furious industry. Others were languishing below, either unable or unwilling to drag themselves up, but as the ferocious actions of the sailors grew ever more intense, nearly all of Lausard's unit had managed to find their way up on to the quarterdeck, into the hot sunshine that bathed the fleet, where they now surveyed the glorious sight before them. Even the officers had left the relative comfort of their cabins to watch the flurry of activity.

Lausard found himself standing beside Lieutenant Royere, who was gazing around him at the sailors, at the land and at the other ships that lay anchored a few hundred yards offshore. Men clambered with incredible speed and purpose through the maze of rigging above them, tying and untying ropes, securing or releasing sails. Some of the watching troops didn't know what was more amazing, the *sight* of land or the preparations necessary to reach it. Sails were furled, pennants fluttered from mizzen masts, each carrying a different message, but what those messages were Lausard had no idea. Men high up in the crows' nests of ships signalled to each other with flags. To the army it was another silent and foreign language, but all that they cared about was the sight of land. Their journey was over. At last they would be able to leave the ships that had carried them so far and caused them so much suffering. Wherever they were, whichever foe they were to face had to be preferable to the hell they had experienced since leaving Toulon.

'I had an uncle in the navy,' Royere muttered, watching the dizzying array of flags that streamed from the leading ships. 'He used to tell me about sea voyages when I was a child.'

'Did he tell you how uncomfortable they were?' Lausard wanted to know.

Royere grinned. 'Somehow he neglected to mention that.'

'Do you know where we are, Lieutenant?' Lausard turned to Royere.

'I have no idea.'

'Weren't even the officers told of our destination? Is it *that* important? I don't understand the need for mystery.'

'Perhaps if we'd have known where we were going before we sailed, we'd have all deserted,' Sonnier offered.

'Well, you'd know all about deserting, wouldn't you?' Delacor riled him.

Sonnier turned away.

'Do the naval officers know our destination?' Lausard pressed.

'We have had little contact with them, Lausard. We occasionally eat our meals together but they tend to keep to themselves, as do we. There is no love lost between the army and the navy.'

'We've noticed.'

'They see us as unwanted baggage,' Royere continued. 'Nothing more. If they could cast us all overboard I have no doubt they would.'

Lausard looked around and saw Captain Milliere making his way slowly along the deck, peering towards the outcrop of land that so many of the French ships were anchoring close to.

Milliere was in his early thirties. He was a slim but powerfully built man who sported a thick moustache and a swarthy complexion, giving him the appearance of having some Italian or Spanish blood in him. The most striking thing about him were his eyes. Emerald green, they seemed to glow as if lit from within by a searing iridescence.

He joined Royere and Lausard and gazed out at the land.

It was inhospitable. A tiny stretch of beach was abruptly halted by towering cliffs that seemed to form a sheer face, lowering down at the French as if challenging them.

'How do we get horses up there?' Royere contemplated.

'We don't,' Milliere told him. 'I received orders this morning that we are to stay aboard ship. Cavalry will not be needed for this landing.'

Those men within earshot groaned audibly.

'So we're to be left on these stinking ships while the infantry take all the glory?' Charvet bemoaned.

'*And* all the booty?' Delacor hissed. 'By the time those bastards have finished, there'll be nothing left for us. No gold or silver, no food or water.'

'Two hundred of General Bonaparte's guides will be going ashore,' Milliere continued. 'Apart from that, it's an infantry job according to orders.'

'Orders from whom?' Lausard demanded.

'General Dumas himself,' Milliere explained. 'Believe me, *he's* not too happy about it. He always was impatient. I served under him back in 'ninety-three.' The captain smiled wistfully. 'The first thing he did when he took over as General was to tell his staff officers to strip off their gold and silver rank badges. He said they smacked of luxury and corruption.' Milliere chuckled. 'He said they should replace them with wooden items.'

'So, when do *we* get off these stinking ships?' Roussard wanted to know.

'When we reach our final destination,' Bonet offered. 'This obviously isn't it.'

'So where the hell are we?' Delacor insisted.

Milliere looked up towards the forecastle of the ship and saw a group of blue-uniformed naval officers poring over a map.

'That's the captain.' Milliere pointed to a small man in a long frock coat. 'Verdoux. He would know where we are.'

'Could you ask him, sir?' Lausard enquired.

'Does it matter? We're stuck on this ship until General Bonaparte says otherwise.'

'But if we know where we are, why we are anchored here, we might have some idea of *why*?' Lausard persisted.

'To take on fresh rations and fresh water, I should think. We can do nothing, men, except wait.'

'And suffer,' added Royere.

'Look,' Rocheteau said, grabbing Lausard's arm and pointing towards one of the other anchored ships.

As they watched, a rowing boat was lowered over the side of the ship into the water below. The small vessel rose on a wave then seemed to settle momentarily, and the men watched as the sailors in the boat retrieved oars and pushed them into the water. Next rope ladders were hurled over the side of the ship and, as the dragoons looked on, blue-jacketed infantrymen began to make the unsteady descent into the waiting boats. Elsewhere, lengths of thick hemp were tossed over and the foot soldiers climbed down as best they could, gripping on to the rope for dear life, afraid to look down at the sea for fear of falling into it.

The sailors tried to keep the boats steady as the first of the infantry reached the bottom of the ladders, but the surf was choppy and it was an almost impossible task. The first two men reached the boat with relative ease, the third jumped from the bottom rung of the ladder and landed heavily, but a fourth man misjudged his footing and toppled into the water. Sailors dragged him from the water and left him gasping in the bottom of the boat. Another man fell in, losing his musket in the process. He too was dragged aboard after a struggle.

Those climbing down the lengths of rope seemed to be having even less luck.

Lausard watched as a man inched his way down the thick hemp only to lose his handhold. He plummeted fully twenty feet into the dark sea, his shriek of terror rapidly silenced by the watery embrace of the ocean. He did not resurface.

More and more men were beginning to clamber uncertainly into the waiting boat and, elsewhere, other ships were disgorging their terrified cargoes into similar transports. Each of the boats took about thirty men and the dragoons watched as the first of them struck off for land, the sailors forcing the oars through the churning surf towards the shore. More boats gradually filled with infantry and followed the leading vessel until a flotilla of about a dozen of the small craft was heading through the choppy waters to the beach. Only by Herculean effort did the sailors manage to prevent some of the craft from overturning in the savage waves, and Lausard could see the infantrymen clinging desperately to the sides of the rowing boats to prevent themselves falling out.

More men were pouring down the rope ladders, other unfortunates sliding down the ropes with varying degrees of success.

Another man went under but was pulled to safety.

An officer, trying to climb one-handed while he held his sword scabbard away from his leg to prevent it entangling in the rope ladder, slipped close to the bottom and fell into the water, knocking a sailor in with him. Both men disappeared beneath the water.

Efforts were made to rescue them but only the sailor emerged from the dark water, coughing and spluttering, helped aboard by his comrades.

Gaston shuddered as he spotted several pieces of equipment floating on the sea, but noticing the boy's reaction, Roussard put a reassuring hand on his shoulder.

'You're lighter than us,' he told him. 'You'll float.'

Gaston didn't seem particularly cheered by the thought and continued to watch the parade of infantry clambering uncertainly down the side of the ships into the rowing boats, which ferried them ashore, turned around and repeated their task.

The disembarkation of infantry continued for what seemed like an eternity, watched by the solemn dragoons.

'Why the hell are we standing here?' Carbonne asked. 'If we're not landing, what's the point?'

'What else shall we do, then?' Giresse said. 'Go below and sing songs of victory? Count our back-pay? Cook ourselves a meal? What else *have* we to do?'

'I wish we *could* cook ourselves a meal,' Joubert complained.

'Do you think they'll bring back fresh water, Alain?' Rocheteau asked.

'Fresh water *and* food, I hope,' Lausard said, still gazing fixedly at the boatsful of infantry being buffeted by the waves as they were rowed ashore.

'They don't care about us; they're not going to bring us anything back,' Delacor whined. 'They'll be too concerned with their own well-being.'

'General Bonaparte will have sent commissaries ashore,' Bonet said. 'They'll take care of our food.'

'To hell with that,' Delacor said angrily. 'I want to go ashore.'

'Don't be ridiculous,' Giresse snapped.

'What's so ridiculous about wanting to get off this hulk?' Delacor challenged. 'What's so insane about wanting to find fresh water and food? Am I the only one who is sick of being on this floating dung-heap?'

A number of the other men shook their heads.

'We can't go ashore, it's against orders,' Tabor said. 'We have to do as we're told, don't we?'

'You half-wit,' snarled Delacor.

'You heard Milliere,' Rocheteau insisted. 'This is an infantry operation.'

'I heard him say that we weren't needed,' Delacor said. 'He didn't say we *couldn't* go ashore.'

'Then you'd better start swimming now.' Rocheteau's comment was accompanied by a burst of laughter from the other men.

'What kind of riches do you think are there?' Delacor motioned towards the mountains. 'We have no idea what country that is or what we might find there. We could find fortunes for ourselves if we went ashore.'

'We could also find death,' Roussard countered. 'We

don't even know where we are. We could be on the other side of the world for all we know.'

'I don't think we've been sailing *that* long,' Lausard observed, amidst a chorus of chuckles. 'But Delacor does have a point. We don't know how long the infantry are going to be ashore. We don't know how long we're going to be stuck here waiting.'

'What are you getting at, Alain?' Rocheteau pressed.

'Just thinking aloud.' Lausard looked around to see the dragoon captain climbing a narrow flight of steps towards the forecastle, followed by Royere.

The two cavalrymen were greeted with frosty stares from Captain Verdoux and his staff and Lausard watched the men gesturing over the map then towards the craggy outcrops of land, towards the cliffs rising from the sea like towering monoliths. After a moment or two the cavalry officers made their way back, Royere pausing against the guardrail as the ship lurched violently. Then he and Milliere rejoined their men.

'That,' said Milliere, gesturing towards the cliffs, 'is the island of Malta.'

'Where the hell is that?' Delacor wanted to know.

Bonet stepped forward. 'So, we're still in the Mediterranean,' he said. 'I thought we were.'

'Thanks for the georgraphy lesson, schoolmaster,' Delacor chided, 'but that doesn't mean anything to me.'

'Gozo and Malta,' Bonet continued, 'they're islands about fifty miles south of Sicily.'

'That's right,' Milliere told him. 'We saw them on Verdoux's map.'

'Does *he* know what's going on?' Lausard asked.

'If he does he isn't saying,' Royere elaborated. 'Troops are landing on both islands. We're here to capture them.'

'Not *us*,' Delacor hissed, 'just the stinking infantry.'

'Malta,' Lausard murmured under his breath.

As he watched, another of the rowing boats reached land, its occupants scrambling gratefully from it.

After another hour there were nearly two hundred men ashore. And still the ferrying of infantrymen continued.

'So, if Malta isn't our final destination, where is Bonaparte taking us?' Carbonne asked.

'Just shut up and throw the dice,' Rocheteau urged.

The men were seated in a wide circle on the quarterdeck of *L'Esperance*. Some had removed their tunics in the heat and were using them as makeshift seats. Carbonne had tied his shirt around his bald head to protect his shiny pate from the ravages of the sun, which was beating down mercilessly on the anchored French armada.

Lausard glanced overboard every now and then to see rowing boats still taking infantrymen ashore. He consulted his watch and noted that the French had been landing on Malta for over three hours now. The first men to land had long since disappeared into the interior of the island, not up the sheer face of the cliffs as Lausard had expected, but through deep ravines that cut through the granite façades like natural passageways. The actual journey inland appeared fairly easy, at least from the quarterdeck of the frigate. Lausard wished that he and his unit had been ordered ashore, not merely so that they could feel solid ground beneath their feet, but because anything, even the prospect of battle and possibly death, was preferable to the endless waiting he and his comrades had been sentenced to. He was also overcome by a feeling of worthlessness, as if he was superfluous to this operation. The blow dealt to his pride was almost as keenly felt as the ravages of seasickness and, in both cases, he was powerless to alter the situation.

The other men of his unit seemed to have faced the prospect of remaining ship-bound with varied attitudes. Some were relieved that they would not have to fight too soon, while others longed for the opportunity to vent their frustration on their opponents at having been cooped up for so long. Others coveted landing so that they could feel firm ground again and possibly find fresh food and water. But, as hordes of infantrymen were ferried ashore, all the dragoons could do was watch helplessly.

There wasn't much to bet with. What little pay the men had received before leaving Toulon had long ago been gambled away, won back and gambled away again. In fact, the money never left the ship. A man might lose his money and his watch one day and win the whole lot back the next, only to have it taken from him once more in another bout of boredom-banishing gambling. However, after twenty-three days, even the gambling had become monotonous. The men could muster little enthusiasm for the odd roll of dice, especially when the stakes they were playing for were so meagre. As Carbonne rolled, the kitty comprised two half-eaten salt biscuits, a gold earring, two buttons and a battered clay pipe that had no tobacco in it. It was hardly a prize to set men's pulses racing.

'Where did Milliere and Royere go?' Giresse asked, noticing that the officers weren't present on deck.

'Back to their cabins probably,' Delacor grunted. 'To sit in comfort while we all fry out here like fish drying in the sun.'

'So, even they don't know where we're going,' Rostov observed. 'I wonder why Bonaparte hasn't even told his officers what our final destination is?'

'Perhaps he doesn't trust them. I know *I* don't,' Delacor said. 'I don't trust any of these officers.'

'They probably feel the same about you,' Lausard told him. 'After all, it isn't easy to trust a rapist, is it?'

Delacor glared at Lausard menacingly, but Lausard held his gaze defiantly.

'Coming from a thief that's a bold statement,' Delacor snapped.

'I stole out of necessity,' Lausard countered. 'It wasn't necessary for you to rape a woman, was it?'

A heavy silence had descended over the circle of men, all eyes turned towards the two arguing troopers.

'That's all in the past now,' Delacor hissed. 'What does it matter? We're all criminals. No man here is better than any other.'

'Are we going to gamble or fight?' Rostov prompted.

Finally, Delacor waved his hand in Lausard's direction, aware that the younger man's gaze was still fixed on him. 'Give me the dice,' he demanded.

'This is a waste of time,' Sonnier grunted. 'Why are we gambling over biscuits and buttons?'

'Because we've got nothing else to gamble with,' Rocheteau reminded him.

'You can bet the infantry will have plenty to gamble with by the time these islands are taken,' Giresse observed.

'That's what I told you.' Delacor hurled the dice. 'They'll be able to take what they like and we sit here rotting and penniless.'

'Valetta has a higher percentage of prostitutes than any other city in Europe you know,' Bonet offered. 'Valetta is the capital of Malta.'

'More prostitutes than Paris?' Giresse's eyes lit up.

Bonet nodded.

'Even more reason to go ashore then.' Giresse chuckled. Some of the other men laughed too.

'You can bet the infantry will be having their fill of the women too,' Delacor said.

'And the food,' Joubert added, rubbing his huge stomach.

'Then perhaps we *should* go ashore,' Lausard said quietly.

The other men looked at him.

'When? You heard Milliere, we're under orders to stay aboard ship,' Bonet said.

'He said that he had received orders that the cavalry were not needed for this operation,' Lausard reminded his companion. 'He didn't say we *had* to stay on this ship.'

'But how do we get ashore?' Roussard enquired.

'The same way as the infantry. By rowing boat.'

'When?' Delacor asked.

'Tonight. We take a boat and we go ashore. We explore this place for ourselves. We find our own food, our own water, our own plunder and our women.'

'We'll be court-martialled if we're caught,' Sonnier said.

'I don't intend to be caught,' Lausard said flatly, his eyes scanning the ring of troops around him. 'Who is with me?'

Six

As Napoleon Bonaparte sat on the edge of his bed in his stateroom aboard *L'Orient*, he listened to the creaking of the massive flagship as it bobbed gently in the waters. Outside he could see the blackness of the night occasionally disturbed by lights aboard some of the other moored vessels. They twinkled like fireflies in the seemingly palpable gloom beyond. He cradled a glass of water in one hand and sat, head bowed, blinking hard, his room lit only by a few candles.

Major Jean Andoche Junot stood gazing down at his superior. He thought how small the General looked, sitting there in just a shirt, breeches and boots that looked two sizes too small for him. This wiry Corsican didn't look like the conqueror of Italy, the scourge of the Austrian army and the man who intended to subjugate Egypt. To Junot, a powerfully built man in his twenty-eighth year, he looked more like the man Paris society had so cruelly nicknamed 'Puss in Boots'. And yet, Junot, who had served with Bonaparte as his secretary at Toulon back in 1793, then as his aide-de-camp in Italy, knew that the

General had the demeanour not of a gentle cat but of a great predator.

Bonaparte's eyes darted around the room as he looked up, and Junot saw that familiar radiance and vitality in them. Junot had woken the General just minutes earlier, and the two men had since been joined by Berthier, who now stood close to the writing desk in one corner of the room, furiously scribbling on a piece of paper, the quill scratching loudly in the stillness of the room.

Junot had been ashore that day along with the infantry and his commander and he had been surprised at how easily the two islands had fallen. Gozo without a shot being fired, and then, but for a few half-hearted volleys from the local militia, Malta itself had been overrun. The major had felt something akin to disgust at how easily the Maltese had surrendered their homeland. He himself had been wounded three times in the service of France during the last nine years, the last time in August of 1796 when he'd been seriously injured but had managed to despatch six of the enemy during the engagement. He had no time for cowardice or for the men who sought refuge in white flags and raised arms. His dislike of the Maltese, therefore, had been instant and deep-seated. Two of them now waited outside the stateroom, patiently preparing themselves to be summoned before the leader of their conquerors. Junot hadn't liked the look of the men who had arrived at *L'Orient* seeking a truce. They looked like men whose only desire was to please their invaders. They came seeking peace not with resentment and bitterness in their hearts but with relief. For that he despised them.

Bonaparte got to his feet and buttoned his shirt. He looked at his two companions. 'What of these warrior knights, Junot? What do they want here?'

'They want peace, General,' the major told his commander. 'But they are not warriors. They are cowards. They didn't stand against our men today. They sought only to surrender. They have no hearts.'

'Did you expect them to stand against the army that conquered Italy so easily?' Bonaparte asked. 'Against the men who brushed aside the military might of Austria like so much dust? Perhaps you judge them too harshly.'

'They embraced our men as liberators, not as conquerors,' the major offered finally, a note of distaste in his tone.

'Surely that showed sense.'

'It showed cowardice.'

Bonaparte slapped him on the shoulder.

'The two men who are here were instrumental in helping us take these islands so easily,' Berthier interjected. 'But for their influence we might have faced stiffer opposition. They are Republicans, both of them. They told many of their colleagues how futile it would be to resist us.'

'So, they are traitors too?' Junot sneered.

'If that is the word you choose to use,' Berthier said. 'Their deceit proved to be a powerful weapon.'

'We do not need the help of traitors,' Junot snapped.

'Do not underestimate the value of deceit, Junot,' Bonaparte said, smiling. 'Sometimes deceit can be as powerful as fifty cannon.'

'We should thank them, not despise them,' Berthier observed. 'If the Maltese had resisted then we might have lost many men today. Men we cannot afford to lose.'

Junot remained unimpressed.

'Best show these men in,' Bonaparte said finally, watching as the major crossed to the door and opened it.

He ushered in two figures whose faces looked deathly

pale in the dull glow of the candles in the stateroom. They both stood sheepishly at the threshold, heads bowed, hands clasped before them like naughty children facing the wrath of an angry teacher.

'Come in.' Bonaparte watched as the men entered, Junot closing the door behind them. 'Would you care for some wine?'

Both men shook their heads.

'Which of you is de Ransijat?'

The shorter of the two men looked up. 'The Treasurer of the Knights of St John,' he said.

'We are aware of the position you held,' Bonaparte informed him. 'And of the history of your order. You have a noble tradition but you and your kind have no place in this modern world. You are relics of the past.' He sipped at his water. 'Where is your Grand Master?'

'He awaits you on the island,' de Ransijat said, 'to welcome you.'

'So you are his messengers. His errand boys. Well, then take some news back for your leader.'

'Grand Master Von Hompesch desires peace, General Bonaparte.' The other man, taller and more sturdily built than his companion, with a white moustache, spoke.

'And who are you?'

'My name is Fay. Commissioner of Fortifications for the Order.'

'All we ever wanted was peace,' de Ransijat added. 'We have no quarrel with France or with the Republic. We are Frenchmen ourselves.'

'And yet you ruled this island like monarchs. Like the Bourbons who ruled France. You are aware of *their* fate?'

Both men nodded.

'You shall have your peace,' Bonaparte continued. 'France and I would gain nothing by destroying you but we gain much by your allegiance. I am also aware of your efforts and those of some of your comrades in the months leading up to our arrival and I will not overlook your contribution.'

'What is to happen to the Order?' Fay wanted to know.

'It will be disbanded. All knights under the age of sixty will leave the island within three days. They may take money with them for travel expenses but no more than two hundred and forty francs.'

Berthier sat down at the writing desk, dipped his quill into ink and began writing.

'What of the Grand Master?'

'A principality will be obtained for him in Germany,' Bonaparte said. 'He should be happy to return to his homeland. He will be paid a pension of three hundred thousand francs a year. That is more than generous compensation.'

'And the other knights?' de Ransijat enquired.

Bonaparte shrugged. 'They will receive pensions dependent upon their age. Between seven hundred and one thousand francs. As for Malta itself, the island is to become part of the French Republic. A commission, headed by one of my men, will act as the government of this province. I will also expect a number of knights to join my expedition.'

'To where?' Fay asked.

'That need not concern you now. During the next few days I will detail men to make an inventory of your treasures. We will take what we need from you.'

'We have possessions beyond value, General,' de Ransijat

said, his expression darkening. 'I beg you not to touch those.'

'What are these things you value so highly?' Bonaparte demanded. 'Everything has a price.'

'We have a splinter of the True Cross,' de Ransijat said. 'The symbol of our Lord's death. I beseech you, do not deprive us of such a priceless gift. If you steal that you steal not just from us but from God himself.'

'I am no thief,' Bonaparte said sternly. 'I have no need of pieces of wood. They cannot buy me provisions. Keep your splinter.'

The Knights' treasurer bowed his head gratefully. 'May God smile upon you,' he said.

'God may wear whichever expression he pleases. It matters little to me.'

The only sound inside the stateroom was the scratching of quill on parchment as Berthier continued to write. Bonaparte stood in the dimly lit room eyeing his visitors, aware that Junot was also running an appraising, if somewhat scornful eye over the two men. Berthier finally finished writing, blew on the ink and handed the paper to Bonaparte, who scanned it quickly before passing it to de Ransijat. The knight bowed low and took it.

'Take that to your Grand Master. Tell him I will come ashore in Valetta tomorrow. Remind him how lucky he is that I do not come carrying a sword.'

The two knights again bowed then turned to leave the room as Junot ushered them out.

'There is still much to be done here, Berthier,' Bonaparte said. 'Only then can the true purpose of this expedition be fulfilled. Only then will we find our destiny.'

'And what of Nelson?' Berthier asked.

'He will not stop us. He has too few ships and is too far away.'

'How can you be sure? Admiral Brueys is convinced that—'

'Admiral Brueys is afraid of this one-eyed Englishman,' Bonaparte snapped, cutting his companion short.

'Perhaps with good reason.'

'Nelson and the entire English fleet will not prevent us from reaching Egypt. Nothing will stop me from treading in the footsteps of Alexander.'

Seven

The rowing boat was about fifteen feet long, suspended from a hemp cradle just above the quarterdeck of *L'Esperance*. Like the six others dotted around the ship it represented the only means of escape for the occupants of the frigate should it sink. It swung gently to and fro with the swell of the sea. The strength of the waves seemed to have grown with the coming of night and now, as the blackness covered the ocean in the early hours of the morning, the sea and the sky appeared to have merged into one impenetrable umbra. The smell of salt water, noticeable all through the heat of day, seemed, strangely, to be even more prominent in the stillness of night.

Lausard, Rocheteau and Delacor took hold of one of the ropes holding the rowing boat in position while, at the other end, Giresse, Carbonne and Rostov mirrored their movements.

Sonnier stood close by, eyes scanning the gloom, peering around for any signs of movement.

Gaston too was present on the quarterdeck, watching

and listening for any who might interrupt this *sojourn* by the men in the unit.

The lines were released and the men braced themselves, the boat heading for the churning waves that seemed to be slamming into the side of the frigate with unpleasant ferocity. Lausard looked over, down towards the black ocean, and saw the white crests of waves breaking against the hull. Every so often a drizzle of spray would fly up like a salty curtain. He wiped sea water from his face and nodded towards the thick lengths of rope the men had secured to the central mast.

These were guarded by Moreau and Tabor who looked on with a combination of bemusement and nervousness, watching as their six colleagues began their descent towards the rowing boat with nothing but their grip on the rope preventing them from falling twenty feet into the sea.

Lausard was the first to descend, moving hand over powerful hand down the rope towards the bobbing rowing boat. He could hear the sea churning beneath him, felt the tilts and sways of the frigate as it was left to the mercy of the tide. With infinite care he continued his climb down, looking below only when he was sure he was within sight of the rowing boat. It was ten feet below now, he guessed. He continued to climb down. With less than six feet to go he paused, wondering if it would be safe to jump this final distance, but somewhere at the back of his mind the thought nagged that the bottom of the rowing boat might give way beneath him. He may well plunge straight through the flimsy wood into the black water.

Above him, the other men were climbing down. He heard Delacor cursing as he eased himself down the rope. Rocheteau kept looking down and shaking his head. Giresse made the entire descent with his eyes closed, gripping the rope until his knuckles turned white. Like green-clad monkeys, the dragoons eased themselves carefully down the side of *L'Esperance*, past the closed gun-ports and the sailors inside who neither suspected nor cared for the antics of these troublesome soldiers. If they had known, they would probably have hoped that all of them ended up dead in the water.

Lausard saw that he was about three feet from the rowing boat. He let go of the rope and fell the short distance into the small craft, grunting as he hit the bottom, relieved when he didn't hear the sound of splintering wood. He looked up to see Rocheteau about to join him, the corporal also dropping the last couple of feet into the boat. Both men grabbed oars, steadying the vessel as their companions cautiously made their way down the ropes to join them. Carbonne hesitated as he dangled helplessly against the side of the frigate, afraid to let go of the rope.

The other men urged him to let go, to jump the final few feet as they had but the former executioner kept a strong grip on the rope, terrified to release himself to the forces of gravity or, more particularly, to the hungry sea. A wave struck the side of the ship, splashing water up and over him, causing the rowing boat to rise several feet into the air.

'Jump or you'll get us all drowned,' Rocheteau snarled.

'I can't let go.' Carbonne's huge hands were locked on the hemp as surely as if someone had sewn them to it.

'Come on, or we'll leave you there,' Delacor threatened.

'Let go, Carbonne,' Lausard said. 'Do it now.' As he spoke he raised the oar he was holding and prodded the big man hard in the ribs. The shock made Carbonne lose his grip and he fell from the rope, tumbling the last three feet into the rowing boat and landing with a thud.

'You could have got us all killed, you fool,' Delacor hissed.

'Shut up and row,' Rocheteau commanded, forcing another oar into Delacor's hand.

Each of the men took hold of a shaft and, on a signal from Rocheteau, they began to force the blades of the oars deep into the water. Waves rocked the boat and drenched the men with spray but they continued rowing, forcing their way through the surf towards the towering cliffs, which seemed to have thrust their way up from the sea like accusatory fingers. But beneath those cliffs was land, and it was the thought of reaching that land that gave the men the added strength to drive the boat on, fighting back that ever present feeling of nausea. Lausard fought back the all-too-familiar feeling, and soon, as he peered through the gloom he saw that the shore was mere yards away. He tapped Rochteau's shoulder and the corporal also saw the welcoming sight of dry land.

With renewed vigour the men worked the oars, their need to be free of the clutches of the sea reaching a state of near desperation now.

The rowing boat finally hit the beach with a thud, the impact causing Rostov and Giresse to topple from the stationary craft. The Russian fell on to the sand, a smile spreading across his grizzled features as he felt the grains between his fingers. Water lapped against his legs but it didn't appear to bother him. Carbonne too seemed oblivious to the tide washing ashore, drenching his already sodden uniform. He was crawling on all fours up the beach, squeezing the sand beneath his large fingers.

Lausard and the others leaped clear of the boat and dragged it up the beach, aware of an incredible dizziness sweeping over them. Lausard felt as if his legs might buckle at any second. He realized it was because they had not walked on firm ground for so long. He dropped down into the sand, a combination of relief and joy enveloping him. Twenty-three days had passed since any of them had been on solid ground and no one knew how many more days would elapse before they would be again. But at that moment, all that mattered was they were ashore.

Giresse rolled over and over in the sand, like a child freed of restraints for the first time in its life.

Delacor picked up a handful of the sand and kissed it.

The men hauled the boat further up the beach, noticing some bushes growing close to the base of one of the cliffs. Beyond that natural curtain of flora, Lausard could see one of the many narrow paths that cut through the cliffs. He glanced down at his watch, squinting in the gloom. It was just after one.

'It'll be light in less than five hours,' he said. 'Let's not waste any time. We have to be back aboard before dawn.'

'Let's find what we came ashore for,' Giresse said, smiling. 'Women.'

'And food.'

'And drink.'

'And booty.'

'Come on,' Lausard ordered heading towards the path. 'Let's move.'

The dragoons headed off towards the interior of the island.

The smell of oranges was overpowering and quite magnificent. Lausard was the first to detect the wonderful aroma, which seemed all the more intense in the stillness of the night. He realized that it was coming from a low-walled garden surrounding a house up ahead. The fragrance caused his mouth to water and, within seconds, all six men were running towards the low wall. They climbed over it with ease and found themselves surrounded by dozens of small trees, each bearing scores of the ripe fruit. Delacor pulled several of the oranges from a branch and bit into the first without even removing the skin.

Lausard tore open some of the fruit and sank his teeth into it, savouring the flavour, allowing the sweet juice to run down his chin. He ate one after another, gorging himself on this first taste of fresh food for almost a month. His companions were doing the same, stuffing the fruit they couldn't eat into their pockets.

It seemed as though succulent fruit trees stretched for miles, and as the men walked on they felt as if they were in heaven. The foul taste of salt biscuits and salt beef was forgotten, even the horrors of their voyage were momentarily pushed to the backs of their minds.

The grass that carpeted the tree-lined area was covered in a heavy dew and Lausard suddenly pulled off his jacket and shirt and rolled in the moisture, enjoying the cooling caress of the wet grass. It was the closest he had come to a wash since leaving Toulon and it was an opportunity he didn't intend to miss. Giresse copied him, smearing the dew over his torso and face. He even knelt to sniff the earth beneath, the familiar musky scent so welcoming after the constant stench of vomit, sea water and unwashed companions.

'I think we've landed in heaven,' he said, smiling. 'All I need now is a woman and my life will be complete.

I could die here and now and I would be a happy man.'

'I'm just glad to be off that stinking ship.' Delacor was nibbling at yet another orange.

'It's so beautiful here,' Carbonne commented, looking around him at the trees and blossoms.

About two hundred yards further on, half hidden by the thickly planted orange trees, was a house. A white-stone dwelling with a slate roof and olive vines entwined around it.

'Let's see if they've got anything worth taking,' Delacor said, getting to his feet. 'I'll bet the infantry have scraped everything clean on this island. I told you they would.'

Lausard finally got to his feet, slung his jacket over his shoulder and wandered after his companions, his pace unhurried. He wanted to enjoy the peacefulness and beauty of this place for as long as he could. He pulled a blossom from a low branch and sniffed it.

Up ahead, Delacor and the others had reached the house, where they could see that its back door was open.

'No sentries,' Rocheteau observed.

'They'll have pushed on into the interior by now,' Lausard said.

'How can you be sure?' Delacor questioned.

'Our troops were landed here to capture arms and supplies, not farms.' Lausard pushed past Delacor and strode through the door into the kitchen. There was bread on the table. Even a half-empty bottle of wine.

'Giresse was right,' Rocheteau said, joining his companion inside the kitchen. 'We *have* landed in heaven.' He snatched up the loaf and bit off a piece of it.

The other men entered the kitchen, their eyes widening with delight at the sight of the food and drink.

Rocheteau handed a piece of the bread to Rostov, who ate heartily, while Delacor snatched up the wine and downed several great gulps before handing the bottle to Carbonne.

Giresse began pulling cupboards open. He found flour, maize, biscuits and even cheese. The smell of the food was overpoweringly welcoming and he grabbed as much as he could.

'It's strange,' Lausard said, accepting a piece of bread from Rocheteau. 'There are no signs of a struggle. No evidence of fighting.'

'Who cares?' Delacor said, pulling open drawers with one hand while gripping a lump of cheese with the other.

'It looks as if the inhabitants fled,' Lausard said, wandering through into the other part of the house, noticing how immaculately kept it was. 'Let's move on, see if we can find our way to a village or a town, perhaps we can find out what happened.'

'What about the food?' Rostov wanted to know.

'We'll carry as much as we can. We should take some back for the others on the ship.'

'To hell with them,' Delacor growled. 'They should have come ashore themselves, let them go without.'

Lausard threw him a disdainful look then headed back into the kitchen. He pulled the cloth from the table and began stacking fruit, bread and other provisions upon it.

When he'd finished he pulled the four corners together and tied them, forming a makeshift sack. This he fastened to his belt.

Delacor had moved into the other part of the house and was searching for valuables. Unable to find anything he stormed upstairs and the other men heard him clumping about angrily. They heard a couple of muffled oaths and then he thudded back downstairs to rejoin his companions.

'I told you those bastards in the infantry would take everything,' he snapped. 'There's nothing to be had in this place.'

'Why didn't they take the food?' Rocheteau questioned. 'That would have been more important than riches.'

'Nothing is more important than riches,' Delacor said.

'Money's no good when you're starving,' Lausard reminded him. 'You can't eat gold, can you?'

'Joubert could.' Giresse chuckled. 'That fat man could eat anything. I've got some bread for him. It should stop him grumbling for a few minutes.'

'To hell with him,' Delacor hissed. 'To hell with all of them. They're not sharing any of *my* food.'

'Remember that when *you* want something of *theirs*, Delacor,' Lausard warned him. 'We are all comrades now, we share everything within the unit.'

'Not I.'

'There will come a time when you need the help of others.' Lausard took a step towards him. 'And when that time comes think back to this day.'

The two men glared at each other, until Lausard pushed past his colleague. The other dragoons followed, striding through the house until they reached the small front garden. Beyond it was a narrow road, little more than a dirt track. Lausard saw the marks of many boots in the dust and realized that the infantry had come this way earlier in the day. The road sloped up sharply towards a range of low hills, and above those hills he could see the reflection of many lights illuminating the night sky. The other men also noticed them as they walked along unhurriedly, passing more houses on either side of the road. All the dwellings were as untouched as the first one, and Lausard's suspicion that the inhabitants had fled without any resistance seemed to be correct.

'That must be Valetta up ahead,' he said, pointing towards the crest of the hill and the lights beyond. 'The capital.'

'I hope Bonet was right about it having so many prostitutes,' Giresse said excitedly.

'I hope there's a decent inn,' Rostov pondered. 'I want a drink.'

They were close to the top of the ridge now and they heard voices on the reverse slope. French voices.

The men crested the ridge and found themselves confronted by blue-clad infantrymen. They were sitting in a circle, some lying on the dewy grass, others sitting cross-legged, passing a bottle of wine among them. One man was smoking a pipe; two others were munching contentedly on pieces of bread. They were gathered around the dying embers of a camp fire that seemed scarcely necessary in the heat of the night. Beyond, the dragoons could clearly see down into the heart of Valetta, its streets well lit and swamped with French troops.

'Where did you lot come from?' a tall corporal asked, getting to his feet and running appraising eyes over the dragoons. 'I thought all the troops were landed this morning.'

'That's just like the cavalry,' another man shouted. 'They arrive only when the fighting is over.'

A chorus of laughter rang around the infantrymen.

'And what use would these have been?' another observed. 'They haven't even got any horses.'

'I see no horse but I see a horse's arse,' Lausard said, looking at the infantryman.

It was the dragoons' turn to laugh.

'Was the fighting so fierce you needed us, then?' Rocheteau asked.

'They hardly fired a shot, these Maltese,' the corporal informed him. 'Those that didn't turn and run got on their knees to greet us. Just as their women did.'

'Only most of them got on their backs to show their gratitude,' a soldier nearby called and more raucous laughter filled the air. 'There are some rare beauties here. Dark eyed and mysterious, like sirens.'

'Where are they?' Giresse wanted to know.

'In Valetta.' The corporal gestured towards the town beyond. 'You'd better hurry though, they've been busy.'

As the dragoons passed the infantry they heard more laughter.

'Is that why you've left your horses behind, boys?' called an infantryman. 'Do you plan to ride something else tonight?'

The closer they got to the outskirts of the town, the more troops they saw. Infantrymen were walking about, cooking, sitting talking, smoking and generally enjoying being back on dry land, however short their stay might be. Lausard saw one man sitting with his back against a house darning his socks. He nodded amicably towards the dragoons as they passed. Close by, five men were gambling and Delacor heard the unmistakable chink of coin on coin.

He turned around, looking longingly at the pile of gold coins in the middle of the men.

'See, I told you they'd have taken plunder,' he said. 'They must have got it here; they can't be using their own pay.'

'That's for sure,' Giresse echoed. 'I haven't had any pay since we left Italy.'

There was a church up ahead to their right, the doors open wide. Men were ambling in and out as if they were on some kind of pilgrimage. Lausard noticed that many were carrying bundles, which on closer inspection he could see ranged from candlesticks to pieces of altar cloth. Delacor quickened his pace, walking ahead of his companions.

'Those thieving bastards. They've even robbed the church.'

'Damn them for doing it before *we* got here,' Rocheteau said, also walking ahead.

'Alain, look.' Giresse was pointing towards a two-storey building with balconies outside its upper windows. A woman with flowing dark hair, dressed only in a diaphanous white robe, was leaning over the rail, looking down at the scores of French troops moving through the streets below.

As Giresse looked on longingly, the woman was joined by another, slightly younger woman who was holding a sheet around her slender body. She too gazed down at the Frenchmen, even waving to Giresse, who returned the gesture frantically.

'I'm going in,' he said, grinning. 'These women have obviously been waiting for a man of my charms, a man who knows how to treat them.'

Lausard smiled, watching as Carbonne joined his companion, wiping a hand over his bald head as he approached the door of the building.

'It looks as if it's just you and I, Rostov,' Lausard said to the Russian. 'Let's get a drink.'

Opposite the church was a large tavern, the pavement

cluttered with infantry either about to enter or in the process of leaving. Lausard could hear the sound of raucous singing and laughing coming from inside. He and Rostov entered, surprised to find the tavern less crowded than they'd expected. There were a dozen tables, eight of them occupied, the main one by a group of infantry from the Fortieth Demi-Brigade. It was they who were singing, led and conducted by a large man with a grey moustache and pitted skin. He was stripped to the waist to reveal a white, undernourished body. The result, Lausard reasoned, of so long a sea voyage and insufficient food. He would not, the dragoon thought, be the only one in that condition.

Dozens of bottles of wine stood on a table at one end of the room and Lausard and Rostov took one each and retired to a table in a corner, where they watched the drunken escapades of the other men, two of whom were dancing in the middle of the floor to the great amusement of their colleagues. On the far side of the room, Lausard could see the raven-haired Maltese women sitting with the French troops, quite prepared it seemed to put up with their drunken fumblings. Other women moved from table to table, grabbed intermittently by the drunken infantry and held like prizes.

'Do you ever wonder what our purpose here is, Alain?' Rostov was gazing at a particularly beautiful young woman in her early twenties, who was sitting on the knee of a corporal, kissing him.

Lausard looked puzzled for a moment. 'On these islands?'

'No, on earth. What is our purpose as men? What were we all born to do?'

'Has the sea turned you into a philosopher, Rostov?'

Lausard grinned. 'It's a strange time to be questioning the purpose of life.'

'We are born, we struggle through life and we die, few of us ever making a mark.'

'Then perhaps we should thank the army for giving us the chance to make that mark. If not for the army we'd all still be rotting in jail cells now.'

'Instead of facing death in battles? I'm not sure which I'd rather choose.'

'When my family was killed, I lost everything. Honour, pride, self-respect. I felt as if I'd lost my soul. At least the army has given me the chance to regain some honour, even if it does come with death.'

'Are death and honour not separate things to you?'

Lausard could only shrug. He sipped at his wine. 'If the two exist together, then so be it. If my death *is* the only honour then I accept that. Life has nothing to offer me any more apart from that chance to regain some of my pride and self-respect.'

'What did life offer you before? You were a thief living in the gutters of Paris. That was hardly fulfilment, was it?'

'So, what do *you* want from life, my friend?' Lausard was anxious to guide his colleague on to a different topic. He knew only too well what life had offered *him* before the deaths of his family. He had lost so much more than the men whom he now called comrades. None of them knew his true background: his rich and privileged upbringing, his wealth, the love of his family. It had all vanished beneath the bloody blade of the guillotine. The lives of those he loved extinguished as surely as his would have been. He shared a uniform with these men, he shared his food, risked his life with them and sometimes *for* them, but beneath the surface he was as different from them as chalk from cheese. He had been an aristocrat; they had been peasants. He had been educated; few of them could even read. He had known little hardship prior to the death of his family; they had known nothing but deprivation.

And yet he had slipped with frightening ease into their midst, had been accepted readily into a class he had never expected to encounter let alone live amongst. He did not see them as beneath him; he felt no contempt for these men he called comrades because now he was no different from them. They all wore the same uniform; they all fought for the Republic. They were united by their circumstances. Lausard noted the irony of the situation: these same men would probably, five years earlier, have helped carry him to the guillotine.

The Russian's voice interrupted his reverie. 'All I ever wanted from life was my own farm, a wife and children. Is that too much to ask?'

Lausard shook his head. 'All I ever wanted was to be a soldier. And now I am. Perhaps I should be grateful. Perhaps we should all be grateful to Bonaparte. It is *his* ambition, *his* purpose in life that has brought us to where we are now. We are merely the tools of his intent. Puppets in his hands to be used as he wishes. And I am content to let him lead.'

'But lead us where?'

'Your guess is as good as mine,' Lausard replied, downing more wine.

Two women approached the table, both in their early twenties. They were slim, dark haired and clad in simple dresses of green and brown muslin. The taller of the two smiled at Lausard, and he returned the gesture, his eyes fixed on her, taking in every detail of her face.

'You remind me of someone,' he said quietly, as she sat down beside him.

'Your wife?'

'My sister. How old are you?'

'Twenty-two.'

Lausard reached out a hand and gently stroked her cheek, relishing the softness of her flesh.

'Have you come to keep us company?' Rostov asked the girl sitting close by him.

'We have come for whatever you wish. My name is Louisa, this is Marie.' She nodded towards the other, slightly younger girl.

Lausard was still staring at her, apparently mesmerized by her darkly beautiful looks and her slate grey eyes.

One of the infantrymen at a nearby table had pulled a small whistle from his tunic and was furiously blowing a jaunty little tune that had several of the drunken infantrymen on their feet, dragging their Maltese companions and even their own fellow soldiers up to the centre of the room. They danced without grace but made up for that with their exuberance.

'Will you dance with me?' Rostov asked Louisa, getting to his feet. 'It's a pleasure I've long forgotten.'

She smiled and allowed herself to be led into the mêlée.

Lausard watched his companion for a second then turned his attention back to Marie.

'Do you want to dance?' she asked.

He shook his head.

'I will do whatever you wish,' she said, placing one hand on his thigh and leaning closer to him.

'Just drink with me, talk with me, that's all I ask,' he told her, gazing into her face.

'Most of the men who I've met today have asked me for much more than that. What makes you so different?'

'Does it bother you that I want you for something other than your body?'

She looked down a little shyly. 'I'm grateful,' she said softly. 'You said I reminded you of your sister. Where is she?'

'Dead.'

She reached out and touched his hand, a gesture of tenderness he had not experienced for longer than he cared to remember.

'Her name was Nicole,' Lausard said quietly. 'She was the same age as you when she died. Such a waste of life.'

Lausard felt her squeezing his hand more insistently now, and he looked into her eyes.

'Come upstairs with me. I want you to.'

'Why, because you have a living to earn and I am your next source of income?'

'No. So we can speak in peace. It's too noisy down here.'

Lausard looked across and saw Rostov merrily twirling his companion around the dance-floor, a smile fixed across his grizzled features.

Lausard got to his feet, his hand still held by Marie. He allowed himself to be led towards a staircase at the far end of the room. There was a table close to it where several infantrymen were seated. As they drew nearer, one of the men, a corporal, snaked out an arm and grabbed Marie around the waist, pulling her on to his lap.

She shook loose of him and tried to step away but he got to his feet.

'Come on, pretty rabbit, don't hide from me,' he said, slurring his words.

'Leave her alone,' Lausard said, stepping between the drunken corporal and Marie.

'This is none of your business. This is between me and the whore,' rasped the corporal, lunging forward.

Lausard grabbed the man by the lapels and pulled him closer so that their foreheads were almost pressed together.

'I said leave her,' the dragoon hissed then flung the corporal backwards. He crashed into a table, overbalanced and went sprawling, upsetting several bottles of wine that promptly shattered on the wooden floor. As the corporal staggered to his feet, he grabbed at one of the broken bottles, gripping the neck so that the jagged shards were pointing at Lausard.

'I'm going to gut you like a fish,' the corporal snarled.

'Try.' Lausard didn't flinch. Even as he watched three other infantrymen rise and surround their corporal his expression never changed from one of steely determination.

The corporal took a step forward, jabbing the broken bottle in the dragoon's direction. One of the other men picked up a chair and hefted it before him.

'Let's at least make this a fair fight.'

Lausard recognized the voice without looking round.

Rostov had joined him and the big Russian stood eyeing the opposition. 'Four against two seems fair enough to me.'

'Four against four is even fairer,' came a shout from close to the doorway of the tavern.

Out of his eye corner, Lausard noticed that two more green-jacketed men had entered.

Rocheteau and Delacor strode across to their companions and stood on either side of them, glaring at the infantrymen.

'Come on then,' Lausard said to the corporal. 'You and I, now.'

The corporal looked at the other dragoons then at his own men.

No one moved.

Every eye in the place was trained on the confrontation.

'It's just as well the Maltese *did* run,' Lausard said, his eyes never leaving the corporal. 'If you were the best that France had to offer they would have probably stood firm.'

With a shout of rage, the corporal lunged forward, the broken glass aimed at Lausard's face.

The dragoon side-stepped the clumsy movement, grabbed the corporal's wrist and snapped it sharply upwards, the sudden pain forcing the infantryman to drop the bottle. Lausard drove a fist into his stomach, watching as his opponent doubled up in pain.

One of the other infantrymen reached for his bayonet but stopped as he felt the needle-sharp tip of a blade against his throat. 'Leave it,' Rocheteau instructed quietly.

Lausard struck the corporal twice in the face, the second blow splitting the man's bottom lip. He fell backwards, crashing first into his men then into a table behind.

As the dragoon watched, the infantryman rose but only as far as his knees, blood spilling down his chin.

Lausard motioned towards the exit, and Rostov and Delacor began moving steadily through the watching infantrymen.

'I'll remember you,' the corporal hissed, wiping his mouth with the back of his hand. 'There'll be another time.'

'Perhaps,' Lausard said, a faint smile on his lips.

He took a step towards Marie and kissed her tenderly on one cheek.

'Take care,' he whispered, gently touching her face. Then he and Rocheteau spun round and headed for the door of the tavern.

'I'll find you somewhere and we'll finish this,' the corporal shouted after him.

Lausard ignored the bellow of rage.

'You should have killed him,' Delacor said as Lausard and Rocheteau emerged from the tavern.

'There'll be enough time for killing in the days to come,' Lausard said. 'Now, let's get what we need and head back to the ship. It'll be light in an hour.'

Eight

Paul Barras sipped at his glass of wine and shook his head slowly

'What does Bonaparte think he is?' he said irritably. 'A politician? We sent him on this expedition as a soldier and he attempts to mediate and govern as a politician.'

'Is that so wrong?' Gohier demanded. 'And, as you so rightly said, it was we who sent him on this expedition with orders to capture Malta. He has succeeded. Why do these despatches trouble you so, Barras? He has been successful in the first part of our orders.'

'I feel you supported General Bonaparte in his expedition rather than sending him on it,' Talleyrand interjected, moving to the large picture window in Barras's office. He looked out into the gardens beyond, tiring of his position before the large table that accommodated the Directory members.

'What do you mean?' Barras demanded. 'We commanded Bonaparte to take Malta and Egypt.'

'Bonaparte would have done that anyway,' Talleyrand insisted. 'You know that he intended to leave for Egypt whether or not you and the other members of the Directory had backed him. There was no way you could have stopped him. Our General is on a mission of his own. To achieve spirtual as well as military control over this land he is so drawn to.'

'I can see nothing wrong in these reports,' Sieyès offered. 'Bonaparte has done nothing but good, for himself, for France and for the Directory.'

'I agree,' Gohier echoed. 'The measures he has implemented since his capture of Malta are further proof of his ambition and his ability.'

'I don't think any of us doubt his ambition,' Barras said. 'It is just a matter of how far that ambition takes him. What will satisfy it? Taking power from us?'

'Bonaparte is a soldier,' Sieyès insisted. 'He seeks glory on a battlefield, not in the political arena.'

'It seems to me we should be grateful to him for the amount of money he has secured for the Republic.' As he spoke Gohier looked at another of the pieces of paper before him. 'He confiscated almost seven million francs worth of treasure from the Order of St John.'

'And most of that has been transferred to the paymaster and taken on to Egypt,' Barras protested. 'This expedition has already cost over three million francs.'

'Money that came from the Vatican and from Switzerland,' Talleyrand reminded the other man. 'Not from the Republic.'

'And for the work he has done in Malta I feel he is to be applauded not villified,' Sieyès said. 'You only have to look at the action he has taken. He placed the island under the control of a nine-man governmental commission, eight of them native Maltese. By doing that he prevents the risk of revolt by the locals.'

'I think leaving General Vaubois behind with four thousand men to act as a garrison should help to prevent revolt too,' Gohier chuckled.

'He abolished slavery,' Sieyès continued. 'He freed nearly two thousand Turkish and Moorish slaves, isn't that the true code of the Republic? To free those who are oppressed?'

Barras nodded almost imperceptibly. 'I can read his list of achievements as well as the rest of you,' he said irritably. 'He has ordered that all Maltese men wear the French tricolour cockade, set up a military hospital, reorganized the island's postal service, reduced the number of monasteries and the number of priests ordained. As I said, I can read these and all the other schemes he has initiated. But why has he ordered that sixty boys from the wealthiest families on Malta be sent to Paris and educated here? And at the expense of the Republic, I might add.'

'He has also requested the Directory to send graduates of the École Polytechnique to Malta to teach mathematics, mechanics and physics,' Gohier added. 'I see nothing wrong with the children of Malta learning from the country that liberated them. Bonaparte has set up a new primary and secondary school system too and prescribed a new curriculum.'

'With emphasis on the sciences, French and the principles and morality of the French Constitution,' Sieyès added. 'It is an admirable piece of thinking in my opinion. In less than a week he has liquidated a state centuries old, out of touch with our modern world, and transformed it into a more worthwhile and vital part of the Republic.'

'What is your view on this, Talleyrand?' Barras turned to his colleague.

'As Minister for Foreign Affairs I see the expansion of the Republic as a good thing.'

'Bonaparte wishes *you* to travel to Constantinople; he is anxious to bolster our alliance with the Turks.'

'Our alliance with Turkey is strong enough without me undertaking such a journey. They will support General Bonaparte when the time comes.'

'Bonaparte has ordered you to go,' Barras insisted.

'As you constantly remind me, Barras, General Bonaparte does not rule the country, he commands the army of the Orient,' Talleyrand said. 'He has *requested* that I liaise with the Turks. It is a request I feel to be irrelevant. I am not answerable to our General.'

'Perhaps he fears the Turks will not offer their support when the time comes,' Gohier interjected.

'Turkey has nothing to gain by siding with the Arabs against us,' Talleyrand reminded him. 'They have suffered as much as any during the rule of the Beys.'

'Do the Turks know of General Bonaparte's expedition?' Sieyès asked.

'They have known about it since before he sailed,' Talleyrand said. 'I myself assured their ambassador here in Paris, in April, that France had no hostile intentions towards them.'

'I understood that they were concerned that Moslem territory should be occupied by a non-Moslem power,' Barras said. 'If Bonaparte conquers Egypt that is precisely what will happen. They may decide to fight our army on Holy grounds.'

'There is an old Turkish proverb,' Talleyrand began. '"An Ottoman hunter, if he wants to chase a hare, goes by oxcart."'

'Meaning what, Talleyrand?' snapped Barras. 'We haven't the time for games.'

'Meaning that the Turks will be in no hurry to break

their alliance with France and fight General Bonaparte. They will not side with the Mamelukes. They would be joining their own sworn enemies if they did that. However, even if such a thing *should* happen, I feel we must maintain our position, both military and political. All trade in the Mediterranean *must* pass into French hands and Egypt *must* belong to the Republic.'

'If Bonaparte performs as well in Egypt as he did in Malta then it is surely just a matter of time,' Gohier said, smiling. 'How long is it since he left Malta?'

'The fleet sailed five days ago,' Talleyrand informed him. 'He should reach Egypt in five or six weeks dependent upon the conditions.'

'And Nelson,' Barras added.

'Is Bonaparte aware of Nelson's presence in the Mediterranean?' Sieyès asked. 'He makes no mention of it in these despatches.'

'The Englishman's presence will not have escaped him,' said Talleyrand. 'But he is well ahead of the English fleet. For now.' The words hung ominously in the air.

'He has very able men commanding the fleet,' Sieyès said. 'Our ships are a match for anything the English have.'

Talleyrand scratched his chin thoughtfully.

'I wish I could agree with you,' he said cryptically. 'Let us hope, for everyone's sake, that assumption is not put to the test.'

Nine

It was getting hotter. There was no doubt about it. The men were all agreed that, aboard *L'Esperance* and every other ship in the massive French armada, the temperature was climbing, as it had been ever since they had left Malta. Each successive day at sea saw an increasingly oppressive rise in the level of heat, and men who had found the twenty-three-day voyage to Malta difficult were beginning to find life aboard ship close to intolerable.

Lausard noticed, through bouts of persistent seasickness, that the swarms of seagulls which had followed the fleet from the outset seemed to have thinned – as if the birds themselves could not stand the heat. Even the breeze that filled the sails of the ships and sped them through the water was warm. The air itself had turned stagnant, along with most of the water aboard.

There was little food left. That which the dragoons had retrieved from the island themselves was all but used up, supplemented now only by the usual ration of salt beef which, as before, only increased the men's raging thirsts.

The main deck of *L'Esperance* was like a huge coffin. Dark, airless and fetid it was a miserable place for the dragoons but offered their only respite from the sweltering sun. They could either spend time on deck retching miserably over the sides, seared by the blistering rays, or retreat to the reeking gloom of the main deck. Some of the men, those suffering most acutely from seasickness, were up on the quarterdeck, while Lausard and about twenty of the other men in the unit remained in the subterranean darkness below.

Lausard had hauled a bucket of sea water aboard and was attempting to wash his tunic. The stench of the green wool had become so overpowering that even *he* could barely stand it, and the salt water did little to help. All it did was make him feel sick when he smelled it.

'Why bother cleaning it?' Joubert's voice was low and gravelly, his breathing laboured. 'You'll probably be dead before you get the chance to wear it again. Dead from hunger, thirst or that infernal sun.'

Lausard ran a hand through his soaking hair, the long strands sticking to the back of his neck and his shoulders.

'If you're wounded wearing a filthy tunic then the dirt will get into your blood stream.' The big man suddenly looked concerned about the appalling state of his own jacket. Lausard grinned.

'I can't stand much more of this heat,' Moreau said, lying on his side on the wooden deck, perspiration running in rivulets from his body.

'Why not ask your God for a cool breeze?' Lausard enquired.

Gaston was also lying down, trying to sleep in order to find at least some temporary relief.

'Any ideas where we might be going, schoolmaster?' Rocheteau said, nudging Bonet.

'As far as I can tell, we're still travelling East. But for how much longer I don't know.'

'East,' Rocheteau grunted. 'Where will that take us?'

'Morea, Candia, Anatolia, Cyprus. Or Egypt.'

Lausard looked quizzically at the schoolmaster.

'I think we're sailing in circles,' Roussard offered.

'I'd give my soul for a bath,' Bonet said. 'Sinking into cool water up to my neck then—'

'Shut up, schoolmaster,' Rocheteau snapped. 'Aren't we suffering enough?'

'Still complaining?' The voice seemed muffled in the darkness, as if the rancid air was acting as an invisible blanket.

'What do *you* want?' Rocheteau said, realizing that the voice belonged to gunnery sergeant Marek.

'I was looking for you. I didn't know if you might be topside spewing blood with the rest of your babies.'

'Tell me what you want then leave me alone,' Rocheteau snapped.

'I want to talk about a wager.'

'We've done nothing but gamble since we got on board this hulk,' Joubert said. 'We're all bored with it.'

'I'm not talking about rolling dice or turning cards. I'm talking about sport.'

'What kind of sport?' Rocheteau took up the bait. 'What can we do on a ship?'

'You know how much we hate you land babies,' Marek chided. 'I think it's time to settle our differences once and for all and make some money at the same time.'

Rocheteau looked at the sailor expectantly.

'Boxing,' Marek said. 'A series of fights. Your best against our best. Bets to be taken on each contest.'

'What will the officers say?' Rocheteau asked. 'They'll find out where the fights are to take place. There's nowhere to hide on this thing.'

'The officers are as bored and in need of distraction as you. Don't worry about them. If you can find five men with the guts to face five of mine then we've got a contest,' Marek challenged.

'If they're to fight *you* the men will be queuing up,' Rocheteau said and a chorus of chuckles rose from the dragoons.

'I have no intention of fighting. I just need your help to organize this. What do you say?'

'I say yes,' snapped Rocheteau.

Marek smiled crookedly.

'We'll hold the fights here, on the main deck,' he said.

'Go and see if you can find five of your fishermen then,' Rocheteau chided. 'Let's begin as soon as we can. I'm looking forward to taking your money.'

Marek spun and disappeared into the gloom.

Lausard also got to his feet.

'Alain, where are you going?' Rocheteau wanted to know.

'To find Charvet,' Lausard told him. 'Remember what they locked him up for?'

The other men looked blank.

'Gambling in a church,' Lausard said, grinning. 'Gambling on fights that *he* was taking part in. We don't need five men. We *have* our boxer.'

Rocheteau wiped blood and perspiration from his companion's face using a cloth soaked in filthy water. He watched as the crimson fluid dripped from the material as he wrung it out into a bucket. He then wet the cloth once again and laid it across the back of Charvet's neck.

If the atmosphere in the main deck of *L'Esperance* had been appalling earlier in the day, the night had brought fresh discomfort. There were more than a hundred men, dragoons, sailors and marines all crowded into an area little more than ten yards square at the bow of the deck. It was a little better lit than usual, lamps having been ignited to give those watching – and those participating – a better chance to see. Most of the men had discarded their shirts and tunics and stood around, sweat pouring from them, watching this latest and riveting diversion from the rigours of the voyage.

Charvet dabbed at a cut on his bottom lip and spat blood into the makeshift fighting area – a portion of deck, now spattered with water and blood, and surrounded by men anxious to watch the bouts and even more anxious to bet on the outcome. Lausard had already won a purse full of gold coins from a disgruntled marine, who had handed over the money reluctantly as the sailor involved in the first bout was helped away, his face a bloody ruin from the pummelling Charvet had given it. The sailor had been game, perhaps even a little stupid, Lausard thought, refusing to admit defeat until Charvet had broken his jaw with a piledriver of a right hand that had also sent two teeth flying from his mouth.

The second sailor had fared no better. A lucky swing had cut Charvet's bottom lip, but other than that his blows had landed only on the dragoon's powerful arms or shoulders, and he had finally resorted to grabbing and holding on to Charvet as best he could to prevent himself being struck. He hadn't managed it for very long before a series of powerful blows had split his lip, his cheek and finally broken his nose.

The second casualty was being doused with water as the dragoons, gathered on one side of the designated fighting area, clapped and cheered happily, inspecting their winnings. So far the noise had not attracted the attention of any officers who, Lausard reasoned, were probably more content to stay in the comfort of their cabins than to investigate its source.

The stench of sweat and unwashed bodies, so prevalent throughout the journey, seemed to have intensified a hundred-fold and it was tainted now by the coppery odour of blood.

Marek stepped into the centre of the fighting area, oblivious to the puddle of blood he was standing in. He looked irritably towards the dragoons, then back at his own men and at the newest challenger to Charvet. The sailor was already stripped to the waist, and as he stepped forward Lausard noticed a number of scars on his torso. He was also heavily tattooed. Like most of the sailors he was a squat, powerfully built man with an abundance of muscles in his shoulders and upper body.

Charvet eyed his latest opponent with indifference and flexed his considerable muscles, punching the air three or four times as if warning the seaman what was to come. Cheers rose from the watching sailors and marines, matched by shouts of encouragement from the dragoons as Charvet stepped forward.

Marek raised his arms to silence both sides. He waited until the sound had died down, then pointed at the sailor.

'Leonardo,' he shouted, watching as the seaman raised both arms, fists clenched, accepting the adulation of his colleagues.

Charvet hawked and spat, a glob of mucus landing close to the sailor's foot. The man glared at the dragoon but Charvet was undaunted.

Men fumbled for their money or whatever else they were going to bet with, and Marek passed among the sailors, and Rocheteau amongst the dragoons to collect their stake. After the first bout, it had been agreed that the stake wagered on the winner would be divided amongst those who had selected him. It had taken too long for individual bets to be settled at the beginning and both sides were agreeable to this fairer and quicker alternative.

The fighters eyed each other malevolently, standing only a foot or so apart, waiting for Marek to give the signal. Leonardo sneered at the dragoon but Charvet took the gesture as one of bravado rather than confidence.

Marek looked at the two fighters then, taking a step back, called out, 'Fight!'

Charvet struck immediately: a thunderous right-hand punch that slammed into Leonardo's face and sent him reeling. Stepping forward, the dragoon followed up his advantage, catching the sailor with a left cross that snapped his opponent's head to one side and opened a cut over his left eye. Leonardo shook his head, then suddenly he launched himself at the dragoon, managing to avoid another punch and locking Charvet's head in a vice-like grip. He bit deeply into the dragoon's left ear and clung on like a terrier to a rat. Charvet howled in pain and tried to shake the seaman free, but he clung on, blood spilling down the side of Charvet's face. A great cheer erupted from the audience as Leonardo began raining blows into Charvet's face, his teeth still embedded in the dragoon's ear.

Charvet, trying to reason through the wave of excruciating pain, could think of only one course of action. He reached behind him and closed his huge hand on Leonardo's testicles, gripping them, then squeezing with as much power as he could muster.

The sailor opened his mouth to scream his pain, releasing his grip on Charvet's ear.

Taking the advantage, the dragoon spun round, his hand still crushing the sailor's testicles. Finally, he relinquished his hold and watched as Leonardo sank to his knees in agony. Charvet took a step forward and drove one foot into the sailor's face, then before Leonardo could recover, Charvet slammed his right fist into his opponent's face three times. The sound of cracking bone was audible as the sailor's nose splintered, fresh blood spurting on to Charvet and inflaming him further. He struck again. And again. Finally, a powerful left hander sent Leonardo crashing to the floor, where he lay burbling incoherently on the reeking wood of the deck. Charvet raised his arms in triumph and walked back towards the cheering dragoons, touching his savaged ear with the tips of his fingers, and wincing when he realized that a chunk was missing.

'Look what that animal did to me,' he snarled at Rocheteau, who was already wiping blood from the bitten ear.

'Is that the best you've got to offer, Marek,' Lausard taunted. 'A little dog?'

'If you don't like the way my men fight then you are free to withdraw – if you haven't the courage to face them.'

'That wasn't courage. He was too frightened to fight fairly.'

'Fighting does not always follow the same rules. Weren't

you taught to be prepared for anything?' Marek looked at
Charvet who was standing with one hand clapped to his
torn ear, blood pouring through his fingers. 'It looks like
your boy cannot carry on. Perhaps he should forfeit the
next contest.'

'I will fight in his place,' Lausard snapped, stepping
forward.

'No, Alain, I am fine,' Charvet insisted, shooting out
a hand to restrain his companion.

'You need to rest,' Lausard told him. 'Let Rocheteau
work on that ear. I know what I'm doing.'

Lausard stepped into the fighting area and strode
towards Marek.

'*You* fight me, *now*,' he hissed, pushing the gunnery
sergeant.

Marek almost overbalanced and another sailor watching in the front row leaped to his feet and ran at Lausard,
who easily side-stepped the clumsy charge and tripped the
man as he passed. The sailor went sprawling, but rolled
over and came at Lausard again.

Men on both sides were shouting their encouragement
as the fighters clashed again.

Lausard drove a fist into his attacker's stomach, wind-
ing him. The sailor dropped to his knees but lunged at
Lausard, closing his arms around the dragoon's legs and
knocking him off balance.

The two men fell to the ground, the sailor trying to
strike at Lausard's face. But the dragoon brought his knee
up into the other man's side, knocking the breath from
him. As the sailor scrambled back, Lausard jumped to
his feet and punched him hard in the face. Another blow
landed against the side of the sailor's face and sent him
crashing to the ground. He struggled upright in time to

be met by a blow that sent him back to the deck, his head lolling limply on one side, blood dribbling from his mouth.

Lausard watched as his unconscious opponent was dragged away.

'Now you,' he snarled at Marek.

'Meet your next opponent,' the gunnery sergeant said, grinning, and motioned to the watching sailors, whose cheers seemed to grow in volume. A mountain of a man emerged from their midst. Lausard recognized the thick beard and moustache of the man who now glared at him with a murderous look in his hooded eyes.

'Meet Legros.' Marek smiled.

Lausard felt hands tugging at him and turned to see Charvet standing there, a dirty bandage fashioned from a strip of muslin wrapped around his ear to protect it. Blood was already seeping through the thin covering.

'Let me fight him, Alain.'

Lausard hesitated, glancing at the blood dribbling down his companion's face. 'He knows you're at a disadvantage.'

'He *thinks* I am,' Charvet said, grinning.

Still Lausard would not step aside.

'Hurry up and decide which of you land babies is going to be the first to fall, will you?' Marek goaded.

'Let me fight him,' Charvet repeated.

Reluctantly, Lausard stepped aside and Charvet faced his newest, and largest, opponent.

'I have been waiting,' Legros snarled.

'Then your wait is over at last,' Charvet told him, leaning closer.

Marek raised his hands for silence.

'Officer!' The shout came from the other end of the deck and all the men froze.

'One of ours or one of theirs,' Lausard murmured quietly.

'We'll all be hanged now,' Sonnier said.

Lausard squinted through the gloom and finally caught sight of a familiar figure.

Captain Milliere made his way along the reeking, black-shrouded lower deck to where the throng of sailors and dragoons waited.

'What's going on here?' he demanded, looking around at the men then down at the blood-flecked floor.

'A little diversion from the journey, sir,' Lausard told him. 'A contest between ourselves and the navy.'

Milliere smiled. 'Boxing, eh? A fine sport.' He looked at the sailors. 'I'm not sure your captain would approve though.' He glanced at Charvet and saw the bloody bandage and the slicks of crimson on his face. 'You realize that all sport is more interesting when there is a wager behind it?' Silence greeted his remark. 'Are *you* gambling men?'

Still no one answered.

'Is this bout due to begin?' Milliere asked, inspecting Legros and Charvet.

The dragoon nodded.

Milliere fumbled in the pocket of his breeches and pulled out three gold coins. He held them in his fist for a moment then looked at Lausard.

'Who else will bet with me?' the officer asked, looking around. His gaze was met by men who thought they were being tricked into revealing the purpose of the fights. They all knew that gambling could carry a stiff penalty. Lausard looked at Rocheteau who nodded curtly.

'Where would you place your money, Captain?' Rocheteau asked.

'On my own man, of course,' he said, slapping Charvet jovially on the shoulder. 'I'd back one of my dragoons to beat one of Captain Verdoux's men any time.'

A great cheer went up from the dragoons.

'Will no one else join me in wagering on this contest?' Milliere persisted. He looked at the sailors. 'Have you so little faith in your man that you will not support him with a few francs?'

Marek stepped forward. 'I will bet against you.'

Milliere smiled. 'At last.'

It was as if a switch had been thrown. The lower deck suddenly erupted in a frenzy of shouts and cheers. Bets were placed and collected and Milliere took up position between Carbonne and Delacor so that he had a clear view of the fight.

At a signal from Marek, it began.

The fighters swayed from one foot to the other, moving around in a circle, looking for the best opening. It was Legros who struck first, aiming a blow at Charvet's face, but the dragoon blocked it and struck back, catching his opponent in the side of the face. Despite the power of the blow, Legros never wavered. Instead he struck low at Charvet, driving his fist up into the dragoon's stomach, trying to wind him. Luckily, Charvet had anticipated the blow and tensed his muscles. He hit back and opened a cut on the sailor's cheek. Immediately Legros struck at his ribs, ducking his head and buffeting the dragoon. The two men crashed into one another like bull buffalo, slamming countless punches into each other's bodies with seemingly little effect. Sweat poured from them as they increased their efforts and the men watching realized that this contest was to be unlike those they had previously witnessed. Each punch sounded like the thump of wood on wood, a dull slapping sound followed by the occasional grunt from either fighter. Toe to toe they traded punches, displaying incredible strength and resilience.

Then Legros struck low, smashing his fist into Charvet's genitals, the sudden agonizing pain causing the dragoon to drop his guard. Legros took advantage and smashed two blows into Charvet's face. The dragoon backed off in pain, and he was off balance when Legros advanced upon him, striking him in the face once again.

The seamen shouted their approval as Charvet almost lost his footing on the slippery deck. He ducked beneath another blow and caught Legros with an uppercut, a punch of such terrific force it staggered the sailor. Now it was the turn of the dragoons to cheer, Milliere amongst them.

Charvet caught him again with a left cross, shattering two front teeth and cutting a lip. Blood ran into Legros' thick beard, spraying outwards in a wide arc as Charvet hit him again, driving him backwards until he was almost among the sailors cheering him on. Those nearest pushed the big man back towards the dragoon. But even as Charvet scented victory, Legros managed to summon up some reserves of strength, and as Charvet came at him again, he blocked one blow with his forearm and smashed his other fist into the dragoon's face, roaring his defiance. Charvet reeled back from the impact but then, shaking his head to clear his senses, he stood ready as Legros advanced. The men faced each other, hands raised, preparing to either block or deliver the next blow. Spattered with blood, they were both breathing heavily, trying to suck in lungsful of the stale air. Gazes locked, they watched for the slightest sign of attack from their opponent. Charvet could see that Legros' breathing was becoming more laboured, and he winced with each intake of breath. He guessed that the sailor was injured around the ribs, possibly even internally. Bruises were already beginning to darken around Legros' sides and chest and several large swellings had risen above and around his eyes and cheeks.

Charvet himself was still feeling pain from the blow he'd sustained in his groin and he could taste blood in his mouth. The wild cheering of the men had died down as both seamen and dragoons watched for the first sign of renewed aggression from their chosen man.

Legros blinked hard as sweat ran into his eyes.

It was the split second that Charvet had been waiting for.

He lunged forward and struck twice, catching his opponent in the stomach then the face. Legros' nose seemed to crumble beneath the impact and blood spattered those nearby as well as spraying Charvet. Another powerful left hook opened one of the swellings over the sailor's eye. Charvet moved in to finish the fight, hitting his opponent squarely beneath the chin, a blow that almost lifted the big man off his feet. As he staggered backwards, Charvet caught him with a final blow that smacked into his temple.

Legros went down like a puppet with its strings cut, slamming face first into the deck, his arms motionless at his sides.

The dragoons roared their victory.

Marek kicked at the limp body of Legros. 'Come on, you fool, get up!' he shouted angrily.

One of the other sailors hurled a bucket of bloody

water over the downed fighter, but to no avail; he didn't stir.

'Pay up,' Rocheteau said, grinning. 'It's all over.'

Marek was kneeling beside Legros now and Lausard watched as the gunnery sergeant pressed two fingers to the big man's neck.

'You're right,' Marek said. 'It *is* all over. Legros is dead.' He glared at Charvet. 'You murdered him.'

'He knew the risks,' Lausard said, stepping forward alongside Charvet and Rocheteau.

'They killed Legros,' Marek roared to his watching companions.

A number of the sailors advanced towards the dragoons and Lausard saw more than one of them slide knives from their belts. Lausard himself reached for his sword, pulling it from the scabbard. He was surprised to see Milliere beside him, sword also drawn. The two sets of men stood only a few feet apart, Legros' body lying between them like some kind of bleeding demarcation line. The silence that descended was ominous, as the men glared at each other, each waiting for the other side to move.

The sound that finally galvanized the sailors into action came not from inside the frigate but outside.

Marek raised a hand to his ear. 'Get to your positions now!' he shouted at his men, then he turned to the dragoons. 'We'll settle this later.'

'What's going on?' Lausard demanded as the dull clanging of bells drifted on the still night air.

'Those aren't *our* watch bells,' Marek said. 'They're English. That one-eyed bastard Nelson has found us.'

Ten

The fog was so thick Lausard couldn't see more than ten feet in any direction. It was as though someone had draped the sea and the entire French fleet in a gauze shroud. Coupled with the unearthly silence that had fallen over the armada it was as if the men aboard *L'Esperance* were suddenly the only people alive in the entire world. Only the creaking of the hull and the occasional flapping of a sail in the light breeze broke the overpowering stillness, and every so often the sound of bells drifted across the clouded air. It was difficult to judge how close the English ships actually were. Lausard could not distinguish the difference between French and English bells, but he appreciated Marek's fear meant the enemy must be close.

The fog continued to swirl around the frigate and all the other vessels, masking their occupants' view of both each other *and* their enemy. Sailors waited at their posts in silence, concern etched on their faces, perspiration running down their bodies. Many of them dreaded an attack by the English Navy for fear that *L'Esperance* might be sunk. Lausard didn't even care to contemplate the carnage that might ensue if the English warships actually sighted their prey and opened fire. If indeed it *was* the English who were out there.

'They don't sound very close,' Tabor said quietly, as more bells sounded.

'They might be miles away,' Lausard said. 'Sound carries at night.'

'And if they're not?' Delacor asked.

'This fight is out of our hands,' Lausard told him.

'Well I don't like having to leave my life in the safe-keeping of these sailors,' Delacor snapped. 'I don't trust them. How do we know they'll fight?'

'Because it's their lives too, you idiot,' Rocheteau hissed, looking nervously around him.

'I don't like having to rely on other people,' Giresse said.

'Me neither,' Lausard agreed. 'But this time we've got no choice.'

Moreau closed his eyes and crossed himself.

'God will protect us,' he said softly.

'What's he going to do?' Rocheteau was scornful. 'Steer our ships past the English?'

There were one or two muted chuckles.

'Shut up!' Rocheteau snapped and silence descended once more.

The sound of bells once again drifted through the shrouded night.

On the forecastle of *L'Orient*, Napoleon Bonaparte paced slowly back and forth, occasionally glancing into the thick fog as if he expected it suddenly to part and reveal his enemy.

'Thank God for this fog,' Admiral Brueys said, stroking his chin thoughtfully. 'Let us pray that it remains. While we are hidden from the English we are safe.'

'There are fourteen ships of the line out there,' Bonaparte said angrily. 'We have over four *hundred* ships to oppose them.'

'Most of them overloaded with men and supplies,' Brueys reminded him. 'If the English attack we will have no chance. *Ten* warships would do us untold damage if they manage to find us. All we can do is keep sailing on our present course and pray that we miss them.'

'Can you be sure that the intelligence reports you received are correct?'

'I have no reason to doubt them. The reports said that the squadron was sailing eastward moving at twice the speed we ourselves are. If they *have* got in front of us then they could be waiting when we reach Egypt.'

'How could that be possible?' Bonaparte snapped. 'Nelson doesn't know our destination.'

'I have tried to tell you, General, this man is no fool. He knows which direction we are sailing. He will know that there are only a limited number of destinations we *could* be heading for. Egypt is the most logical.'

Bonaparte waved a hand dismissively in the foggy air. 'I fear you overestimate our English foe.'

Brueys didn't answer. He saw little point in prolonging the conversation when Bonaparte was so set in his own opinion. The General continued his slow pacing back and forth, watched by Junot and Berthier.

'Why not send some ships to the north?' Berthier offered. 'Perhaps Nelson will follow them and we will be able to slip away unnoticed.'

'I will not divide my force,' Brueys said with an air of finality.

'It is not *your* force, Admiral,' Bonaparte reminded him sharply. 'They are your ships but they carry *my* men and *my* equipment.'

'You are reliant on myself and my colleagues to get you to your destination, General,' Brueys retorted angrily. 'If not for the skill of my sailors we would not have come this far.'

'If your sailors and your subordinates are so skilled why are we still being pursued by Nelson?' Bonaparte demanded. 'Why hasn't he been destroyed by now? You run when you would perhaps be better to engage him.'

'War at sea is different to the kind of war you know, General. Kindly allow me to conduct myself in the ways of the sea and to suggest that you reserve your expertise for the land.'

'Should we ever reach it,' Junot offered. 'If you do not avoid or defeat the English then none of us will ever walk on firm ground again.'

'Junot, I'm surprised at your lack of faith. Has luck not smiled upon us so far? Why should we rely on the negative instincts of our admiral here? Better to trust to luck.' There was scorn in Bonaparte's tone that Brueys deigned not to rise to.

'How long before you know whether or not we've outrrun them?' Berthier asked.

'They are moving quicker than we are,' the admiral told the chief of staff. 'We cannot outrun them. We can only hope to bypass them. There are four hours until sun-up. If they keep sailing in a northerly direction then we will be safe.'

'And if not?' Berthier pressed.

'Then God help us all,' Brueys murmured.

The unearthly silence continued, every sound cloaked even more densely by the ever-present fog. Lausard remained on the quarterdeck, peering out towards where he imagined the other French ships to be. Finally he turned and headed back down to the main deck. Rocheteau and a number of the other dragoons followed, clambering down the wooden steps into the frigate, to be enveloped immediately by the overpowering stench of sweat, blood, salt water and excrement. The lamps and candles were still burning towards the bow of the ship, and bathed in the lazy light was Legros' body, still in the position they had left it. As Lausard drew closer he saw that the dead sailor's eyes were still open, glazed like those of a fish on a slab. The blood that stained his face and torso had begun to congeal, and looked black in the dismal half-light of the main deck.

'There'll be hell to pay when word of this gets around,' Roussard said nervously. 'Organizing the fights and betting on them was bad enough, but killing one of their men . . .' He allowed the sentence to trail off.

'I didn't *mean* to kill him,' Charvet protested.

'Who cares?' Delacor said. 'At least we got to pick up our winnings before the English arrived.'

'It was an accident,' Lausard said, looking down at the body. 'It might just as easily be Charvet lying there.' He prodded the corpse with the toe of his boot.

'You'll hang for this.' The voice came from the gloom, from a member of a twelve-pounder crew kneeling close by. The sailor was almost invisible in the blackness. 'It was murder.'

'Shut up, fisherman,' Rocheteau ordered. 'No one had

better try to hang our friend here or there *will* be trouble.'
He patted Charvet on the shoulder.

'It was a fair fight,' Lausard insisted. 'Legros was just
unlucky.'

From the other end of the ship, the dragoons heard
the sound of footsteps growing closer. Even through the
gloom they could see a group of blue-uniformed marines
marching towards them, muskets sloped and bayonets
fixed. Marek was with them.

'That's him.' The gunnery sergeant pointed at Charvet
and the marine officer stepped forward, pulling his sword.

'What's going on here?' Captain Milliere asked.

'This man is under arrest,' said the marine officer, a
slender man with a thick moustache. 'By order of Captain
Verdoux.'

'Captain Verdoux has no right to give such an order,'
Milliere protested. 'This man is under *my* command,
not his.'

'And you are all on Captain Verdoux's ship,' the marine
officer persisted, stepping towards Charvet. 'The charge
is murder.'

The waiting marines lowered their muskets, swinging
them up to their shoulders. Lausard heard the sound of
half a dozen hammers being pulled back. He looked at
Milliere then at the other dragoons. No one moved.

'Go with them,' the captain said to Charvet finally.

The dragoon stepped forward reluctantly.

'You can't let them take him, Captain,' Carbonne
protested, but Milliere raised a hand to silence him and
all the men watched as the marines formed up around
Charvet. He was marched away towards the stern and
into the enveloping blackness.

'You can't let them hang him, Captain,' Lausard insisted.

'I don't intend to,' Milliere said. 'We'll wait until morning, until Verdoux announces his plan.'

Lausard looked on angrily.

'Diplomacy might be called for,' Milliere continued.

'And if diplomacy fails?' Lausard persisted. 'If they condemn Charvet? I for one will not stand idly by while they hang him. I will not let that happen, Captain, and I don't care who I have to kill to prevent it.'

Eleven

The searing early-morning sun seemed to have driven off the English as effectively as it had driven away the sea fog of the previous night. High in the cloudless sky, it bathed the sea and the French fleet in its blistering rays, the temperature rising ever higher as the French continued eastward. It was like sailing into the mouth of hell, Lausard thought, glad to be able, albeit momentarily, to focus on something other than the scene being played out on the quarterdeck of *L'Esperance*.

The dragoons were drawn up in three lines, Milliere and Lieutenant Royere at their head. They were facing two lines of marines who had their Charleville muskets shouldered. Behind them, standing on the forecastle, were Captain Verdoux and his staff. For the first time in weeks, the dragoons were wearing full uniform, and although they had been allowed to remove their brass helmets they were increasingly suffering as the blazing sun burned into the thick wool of their green tunics and leather breeches. Each one of them wore his sword and carried his carbine. Loaded and ready. This was no parade as far as the soldiers were concerned. It was a show of strength. Verdoux knew it too and was grateful for the marines standing before him. The heat in the air was matched only by the tension on the frigate. Tension that he felt may well spill over into something much worse.

For more than thirty minutes the dragoons had remained facing him and his marines. All around them sailors went about their duty, although every now and again one or two of those up in the rigging paused to look down upon the tableau unfolding on the deck below them.

'What do you want?' Verdoux asked finally.

'I want my trooper returned to me,' Milliere said flatly. 'You had him arrested last night on a false charge.'

'I had him arrested on a charge of murder. He killed one of my men.'

'It was an accident.'

'That doesn't alter the fact that one of my men was killed by one of your men,' Verdoux persisted. 'Killed I might add while engaged in an illegal pursuit.'

'You cannot stop men fighting, especially in these conditions,' Royere offered. 'I doubt if this is the only ship on which there have been confrontations.'

'These fights of which you speak were organized for the purpose of gambling. My man was killed because of a petty wager.'

'So what do you propose to do?' Milliere wanted to know.

'I want to see that justice is done.'

'Then release Charvet. He didn't set out to kill your man. I will not have one of my troopers made an example of.'

'And how do you propose to stop me?'

'Present arms,' Milliere shouted and as one man, the dragoons raised their carbines.

The marine officer looked up at Verdoux, waiting for orders.

'You would turn this ship into a slaughterhouse for the sake of one man?' Verdoux said.

'Why not? *You* would assume the role of executioner for the sake of an accident.'

Lausard had his carbine pressed tight to his shoulder, squinting down the barrel at the waiting marines.

'Tell your men to stand at ease,' Verdoux instructed. 'Or you leave me no choice.'

The dragoons did not move.

'Present arms!' Verdoux shouted, and the marines raised their muskets. Both sets of troops now faced each other, weapons primed and ready. One shaky finger, one false move and the quarterdeck of *L'Esperance* would be transformed into a floating battlefield. Lausard felt a bead of sweat trickle down the side of his face. He was standing directly opposite a marine corporal who was blinking nervously, gripping his weapon tightly. Lausard felt surprised at his calm; how at ease with himself he would be to open fire on his own countrymen if the order was given. Obviously the marine corporal did not feel the same. For what seemed like an eternity, the two sets of troops faced each other.

'What is your answer, Captain?' Milliere asked. 'Do I get my man back? Or do I take him?'

Verdoux looked at his staff with something akin to disbelief. 'You would risk so many lives for the sake of one trooper?'

Milliere nodded.

'This is senseless,' Verdoux exclaimed. 'Lower arms,' he called and the marines obeyed.

Still the dragoons remained at the ready.

'My trooper, Captain Verdoux.'

'There must be *some* punishment,' Verdoux said. 'If he is to avoid hanging then he should think himself lucky to escape with a flogging.'

'There will be no flogging,' Milliere insisted.

'That kind of punishment has been banned under army regulations since 'ninety-four,' Royere reminded the naval officer.

'This is not the army,' Verdoux said. 'You are on my vessel, you will abide by my rules. The trooper will be flogged.'

'They're not going to let him go, Alain,' Rocheteau whispered.

'Then a lot of men are going to die,' Lausard said, his aim still fixed on the marine corporal ahead of him.

'You talk about punishment,' Milliere said. 'Don't you think we've suffered enough on this ship since we left Toulon? All of us have been punished by our very presence for the last six weeks.'

'Then blame your General, not my ship,' Verdoux protested. 'None of my men wanted you aboard. The sooner you leave the better and, thank God, that day will soon be here.'

'You know our final destination?'

'We are less than a day's sail from it. Doesn't your General trust you enough to tell you?' Verdoux taunted. 'You will disembark in Egypt.'

A collective sigh escaped the men on deck.

'What are we going to do in Egypt?' Rocheteau murmured.

'That's the other side of the world,' Roussard added.

'We'll never see France again,' Sonnier bemoaned.

If Milliere was surprised by the disclosure, he didn't allow the bemusement to show in his expression. 'Then when we land I will take with me a full complement of troops. All unharmed,' he said. 'Give me my trooper.'

Verdoux smiled wanly. 'Very well. Have him back. Any punishment I could inflict upon him will be nothing to the agonies he will suffer once you land.'

Milliere waved a hand for the dragoons to lower their carbines. They did so almost reluctantly and stood to attention on the quarterdeck, watching as two marines disappeared below. They returned a few minutes later with Charvet between them, and as Lausard watched one of them untied the rope around the dragoon's wrists. He immediately marched across to his companions and took up position between Lausard and Bonet.

'Be grateful,' Lausard said quietly. 'All this is for you.'

Charvet smiled and stood to attention.

Up on the forecastle one of Verdoux's staff was trying to attract his captain's attention, gesturing over the side of the ship towards something. Verdoux finally looked and saw a rowing boat containing six sailors and two blue-uniformed men, who were clinging to the side of the rowing boat, troubled by the buffeting it was taking from the waves. As the captain looked he could see dozens of similar craft being rowed throughout the length and breadth of the fleet. Some were already mooring precariously next to the frigates, brigs and ships of the line and he watched as rope ladders were lowered into the waiting rowing boats. Even as he looked on, such an operation was being performed aboard *L'Esperance*, and a sallow-looking messenger, his uniform stained with salt water, clambered over the side and almost fell on to the quarterdeck. Sailors and dragoons looked on quizzically as the messenger made his way towards the forecastle and Verdoux.

Lausard watched the two men chatting animatedly for a moment, then he saw Verdoux snap an order to a subordinate, who hurried off towards the bow of the frigate. Moments later a stream of different coloured flags and pennants was raised into the rigging of the ship and displayed. It was followed by another line, then another. Lausard had no idea what the flags signified but he guessed they formed some kind of communication, and as he looked around, he saw that other ships in the armada were now also showing pennants. Whatever the message *was* fluttering from the rigging of the ships, it was being passed on with speed and efficiency throughout the entire fleet.

The messenger who had come aboard was dressed in the uniform of Bonaparte's personal guides and, Lausard noticed, he was carrying a rolled parchment in his hand. He took up position on the forecastle and surveyed the men on the quarterdeck, his own gaze met by the puzzled glances of troops and sailors alike as they moved closer to hear what he had to say. He unfurled the parchment and cleared his throat.

'I have a proclamation from General Bonaparte.' He looked around at the men, who seemed largely unimpressed by his announcement.

Lausard looked on indifferently, noticing how pale the messenger looked. He wondered if the man was going to be able to read the proclamation before he succumbed to seasickness. The boat rocked violently as a wave struck it and a number of men, including the watching dragoons, felt their stomachs contract. It was a feeling they had come to know with unpleasant, monotonous familiarity. However, the messenger recovered his composure and began to read.

'"Soldiers, you are about to undertake a conquest whose effects on the world's civilization and trade are incalculable. You will inflict upon England a blow that is certain to wound her in her most sensitive spot, while waiting for the day when you can deal her the death blow."'

He looked around, as if for approval of the words.

'England,' Tabor whispered in confusion. 'I thought we were going to Egypt.'

'We are, you half-wit, now shut up and listen,' snapped Delacor.

'"We shall make some wearisome marches,"' the messenger's voice rang out. '"We shall fight a few battles; we shall succeed in all our enterprises; destiny is for us . . ."'

'Death is for us more likely,' Roussard whispered.

'"The Mameluke beys, who exclusively favour English trade, who have oppressed our merchants with vexations and who are tyrannizing over the unhappy people of the Nile Valley, will cease to exist a few days after our landing,"' the messenger continued, his words ringing with a pride as deep as if he had composed them himself. '"The people with whom we shall live are Mohammedans. Their chief creed is this: 'There is no God but God and Mohammed is His prophet' . . ."'

'That's blasphemy!' Moreau declared. 'There is only one God.'

'Is God a Frenchman?' Rocheteau murmured to his companion.

'I sometimes think the devil is a Frenchman,' Rostov offered.

'"Do not contradict them,"' the Messenger read, swaying slightly as the frigate passed through some particularly venomous surf. '"Act towards them as in the past you have acted towards the Jews and the Italians."'

'What does he mean by that?' Bonet queried. 'That we should slaughter them?'

The messenger paused, looked at the watching men, then went on.

'"Show the same tolerance towards the ceremonies prescribed by the Koran and towards the mosques as you have shown towards convents and synagogues, towards the religions of Moses and of Jesus Christ. The Roman legions used to protect all religions. You will find here customs quite different from those of Europe; you must become used to them. The people of the countries where we are going treat their women differently from the way we do . . ."'

'I am sure that with the correct treatment they will blossom as surely as any European woman,' Giresse sighed wistfully. 'How fortunate for them to experience *my* expertise.'

'"But",' the Messenger's voice was more stern, '"in all countries, the man who rapes is a monster . . ."'

Lausard looked at Delacor who shuffled uncomfortably, aware of other eyes upon him.

'"Looting enriches but a few . . ."'

'Yes, me, hopefully,' Rocheteau said and the men around him were forced to suppress chuckles.

'"It dishonours us, it destroys our resources, and it turns the people whom we want to befriend into our enemies. The first city we shall see was built by Alexander.

At every step we shall find traces of deeds worthy of being emulated by the French."' The messenger studied his audience a moment longer then took off his shako and raised it into the air. '*Vive La Republique, Vive Bonaparte!*'

The troops and sailors matched the shout with a somewhat half-hearted reply.

'A plea to the godless, eh?' Milliere mused. 'For tolerance towards believers. A plea I fear that will fall on deaf ears.'

'Some men choose to be deaf when it suits them, Captain,' Lausard said. 'As for emulating the feats of Alexander, I think that seasick and starving men have little concern for the feats of ancient heroes.'

Milliere could only nod in agreement, watching as the guide hurriedly nailed the proclamation to the main mast of *L'Esperance* then clambered back over the side, easing himself down the rope ladder towards the waiting rowing boat.

Lausard crossed to the starboard side of the ship and looked out across the water. 'Egypt,' he said softly, gazing eastward. 'In one day we at last set foot on dry land.'

'The land of the pharoahs,' Bonet mused.

'And the Mamelukes,' Rostov added.

'Do you think they will see us as liberators?' Lieutenant Royere asked. 'This is part of our duty as Republicans, isn't it? To free those who are held captive. The Egyptian peasants are held captive by the Mamelukes. Perhaps they at least will welcome our arrival.'

'With respect, Lieutenant,' said Lausard. 'I doubt if the Egyptians *or* those who rule them will see us as anything other than what we truly are. We come to this country not as liberators but as invaders.'

'Allow me at least a little of my idealism, Lausard. You and I fight for different reasons.'

'We all fight because we are ordered to.'

'Perhaps,' Royere said. 'One more day at sea. Thank God. May it pass quickly.'

Lausard gave a curt nod. 'I agree. However, we *know* what miseries we are expected to endure aboard ship. None of us can even guess at what awaits us when we land.'

Twelve

'How can you argue with these reports, General?' Admiral Brueys said agitatedly. 'You ordered the reconnoitre of Alexandria's defences yourself.'

'I am not arguing with the reports, Admiral,' Bonaparte said, still gazing at the maps laid out on the table before him. 'I argue about the hysteria surrounding Nelson. Am I never to be free of others' fears about this cursed Englishman?'

'The reports say that the English fleet left Alexandria less than twenty-four hours ago,' Brueys persisted. 'That means there is every chance Nelson is still close by.'

Bonaparte appeared unmoved by this revelation. 'I am well aware of what the reports mean. I know that this means the landing of the troops must take place perhaps a little sooner than I had planned. The weather changing has not helped matters either.'

As if to reinforce his statement, *L'Orient* was suddenly rocked by the choppy sea and the powerful wind that had sprung up during the past few hours. What had been calm, perfect weather for a landing, had rapidly degenerated into something approaching a full-scale storm.

'The problem of *where* to land them remains also,' Bonaparte mused. 'A landing in Alexandria itself is out of the question. The fortifications may be ancient but our enemies will be waiting. We cannot land there without a battle.'

'Also, the approaches to the harbours are narrow, and in this heavy weather there is a danger the battleships might run aground. You would be better off landing here.' Brueys jabbed a finger at the map. 'Aboukir Bay. The water is deeper, it would be safer for my ships.'

Bonaparte shook his head. 'It would waste time,' he said dismissively. 'Aboukir is fifteen miles east. I would have thought, with your terror of Nelson, Admiral, that you would be anxious to allow my troops to disembark as quickly as possible, not to loiter in these waters waiting for him to turn up. No, Aboukir Bay is out of the question.'

'I fear the enemy would expect us to land there too,' Berthier added.

'Precisely,' Bonaparte agreed. 'This fishing village here at Marabout, only eight miles to the west – it would seem to be a good spot.'

'The coast and coastal waters around there are uncharted,' Brueys protested. 'The sea is ugly enough without the extra risk. Why not wait until the weather changes? It would make the landing much easier. There are better spots along the coast that—'

'You speak to me incessantly about the need to avoid Nelson and now you tell me to wait for a change in the weather,' Bonaparte snapped. 'Admiral, we have no time to waste. Luck grants me three days, no more. If I don't take advantage of them, we're lost.' He continued staring at the maps. 'This decision has been forced upon me.'

'Also, the longer we wait, the more time the enemy has to amass his forces against us,' Berthier offered.

'Quite so,' Bonaparte said. 'I will issue orders that the landing is to begin at noon. The troops commanded by Desaix, Menou and Reynier are less than three miles from shore. They will go ashore first. Then those of Kléber and Bon.'

'I still say you are taking a chance landing your men at such a point,' Brueys persisted. 'In calm seas it would be hazardous enough but in weather such as this it is even more of a problem.'

'Not to you, Admiral,' Bonaparte snapped. 'As you told me once before, the army is my concern. Let *me* worry about this landing. I am not plagued by your indecision and caution. If all goes well, I should have two divisions ashore by nightfall.'

'That may be an optimistic estimate,' Berthier interjected.

'Not you too,' Bonaparte said, waving a hand in the air dismissively. 'Is this fear and uncertainty like some kind of plague? Does it spread from man to man?' He looked at Brueys. 'I fear you have infected my chief of staff with your malaise, Admiral. The sea could not stop us. Nelson could not stop us. We have reached our first objective. It is going well for us.'

It felt as if the rowing boat had been lifted into the air by some huge invisible hand. It rose on a wave, seemed to hover in space for a moment, then slammed back down into the choppy sea. The dragoons gripped on to the sides of the rowing boat, on to the wooden seats, some even lay in the bottom of the small craft – anything to prevent them being tossed overboard by the increasingly violent swell of surf. Lausard gripped his seat with one hand and held on to Rocheteau's belt with the other while the corporal retched over the side of the vessel. Spray exploded over the boat in a stinging white curtain, showering the men, drenching uniforms that were already heavy with sweat.

Three rowing boats had left *L'Esperance* carrying the dragoon unit and Lausard could see similar movement from other ships anchored nearby. More green-coated dragoons belonging to their regiment were being ferried ashore from their own transport about five hundred yards to the left. Dozens of small vessels carrying blue-coated infantrymen were heading for shore, streaming away from the ships with as much speed as those sailors rowing could muster. Lausard also noticed that some of the vessels had overturned in the furious surf. A group of infantrymen and sailors were clinging to the overturned boat not that far from them, trying to keep their heads above water, occasionally screaming for help. Equipment was floating on the choppy water. Packs, shoes, gaiters, headgear. Lausard even saw a pair of trousers bobbing about in the surf.

The cavalrymen had the extra disadvantage of having to carry with them their saddles and the shabraques that lay beneath – or at least it would become a major disadvantage once they reached the shore. Lausard could see the dirty sand that awaited them, sloping sharply down towards the sea. A hastily abandoned fishing boat had been left close to the beach and it was being buffeted with each fresh flood of surf on to the beach. How he longed to reach that sand, to be free of the grip of the sea once and for all but, at the moment, it looked a thousand miles away.

They were rowed past the towering edifice of *L'Orient*, some of the men gazing up in awe at the huge battleship. Dozens of rowing boats crammed with men were being guided away from the flagship. Lausard wondered when Bonaparte himself would go ashore. He was still pondering this when a huge wave struck the rowing boat and caused it to list violently to one side. He heard a yell from behind him and saw that Carbonne had toppled into the churning water. Lausard spun round and noticed the former executioner's bald head disappearing beneath the water. But before Lausard could act, Tabor shot out a huge hand and grabbed his companion by the collar, hauling him back into the boat with relative ease. Carbonne coughed and spluttered, emptying his lungs and his stomach of salt water while Tabor looked on indifferently. Lausard smiled at the big man, steadying himself as another large wave lifted the boat then sent it hurtling back down with such force that it seemed everyone aboard would end up in the water. But the craft held and the sailors dug the oars deep into the surf, powering the vessel along as best they could, sweating and cursing from the exertion.

Lausard wiped the stinging water from his eyes. He blinked in an effort to clear his vision, his stomach contracting with appalling regularity. Gaston was huddled in the bottom of the boat, curled into a foetal position, his arms clasped over his head, his eyes tightly shut. The red dye from his trumpeter's tunic had run in one or two places and stained the top of his breeches, and to Lausard looked uncomfortably like blood.

Away to the left there was an enormous crash,

accompanied by the sound of splintering wood and screams of panic that managed even to eclipse the pounding waves. A boat carrying some infantrymen had struck a rock, a hole like some terrible wound having been torn in the hull of the vessel. The craft was sinking rapidly, its occupants either tipped or jumping into the water to escape the stricken boat. Oars and other pieces of timber were quickly tossed skyward by the erupting sea and the air was once more filled with the terrified shrieks of men.

Most of the sailors struck out for shore, swimming as best they could in the strong current and savage surf, but the infantry were helpless, a number of them trying to cling to the sinking craft. Two men clung together but Lausard and the others watched as they simply sank together, arms aloft in the vain hope of rescue.

'Can't we do something?' Bonet grabbed at a sailor close to him. 'Row towards them, help them.'

The sailor shook loose and glared at him.

'They're our own men, we can't leave them to drown,' the ex-schoolmaster continued frantically.

'If we try to help them, we'll end up the same way,' Lausard reasoned.

One of the desperate men had managed, somehow, to paddle his way towards the boat and he was shouting for help, water filling his mouth each time.

'We've got to help him,' Bonet persisted.

'His extra weight will unbalance us,' a sailor snapped. 'He's lost.'

'Do you think he'd help *you*?' Lausard grabbed his companion by the arm and stared into his eyes. 'Worry about your own life.'

Reluctantly Bonet took his seat on the wooden bench next to Lausard. When he looked across at the stricken infantryman again, all he saw was a hand disappearing beneath the waves.

'There's some more of our men.' Tabor gestured towards another rowing boat a little further back, as he spotted the green tunics of dragoons.

'I can see that bastard Delpierre,' Rocheteau said. 'It's a pity *he* doesn't fall in. I'd personally hold him under until he drowned.'

Lausard glanced around and caught sight of the sergeant Rocheteau referred to. 'Never mind him. We've got other problems to think about.' He nodded ahead.

As the surf dipped, the men caught sight of a long line of jagged rocks about fifty yards in front of them. The points were jutting menacingly above the water like filthy teeth. However, there was no other way for the boat to go and the sailors continued to row manfully against the crashing waves. An oar snapped against an underwater rock. The hull of the boat scraped noisily against another protrusion, and Lausard looked down with concern as if expecting the jagged stone to rip its way through the hull at any moment. Fortunately for the dragoons, a powerful wave caught the boat and lifted it clear of the jutting rocks, slamming it down again fifteen feet further on, the impact again spilling the troops into the bottom of the vessel. As the men struggled to regain their seats they were soaked as another wave washed over the boat, threatening to pitch them into the sea. Blinded by spray, racked by seasickness, soaked to the skin and baking beneath the blistering sun, the dragoons held on desperately as the shore approached.

A number of other boats were already unloading their human cargo, men falling gratefully on to the sand, ignoring the incoming tide that swept over them. Their relief at being ashore knew no bounds. The rowing boats immediately turned around and headed back to the waiting ships, ready to ferry more troops ashore. Lausard could only guess at how long the entire landing was going to take. But for the moment his only concern was that he and his companions were about to reach dry land.

The sailors raised their oars and the boat glided the final few yards. Unable to stand another second in the vessel Rostov leaped free and waded through the surf. Charvet joined him, both men holding their carbines above their heads with one hand, dragging their saddles through the water. As the boat touched land, Joubert scrambled out, losing his footing and falling face down in the water. Delacor hauled him up then strode on himself, feeling his own knees begin to sag. The other dragoons were suffering similarly: so long at sea had affected their balance. Sonnier felt drunk and dropped to his knees, his head spinning. Moreau was also on his knees, his head bowed. Roussard fought his way clear of the pounding surf and staggered several yards up the beach before falling on to the sand, a look of relief etched on his haggard features.

Lausard, his arm around Rocheteau's shoulder to steady the corporal, also advanced several yards up the sharply sloping beach, immediately aware of the newest intrusion.

Flies.

There were hundreds of them. Like living cinders they filled the baking air, landing on the men, crawling over their skin and their uniforms, driven away only momentarily by flailing hands. Their buzzing was incessant and loud. The air was also filled with a rancid, vile odour, which Lausard recognized as rotting fish. A number of abandoned half-full nets littered the beach, the catch now at the mercy of the flies and the scorching sun. The combination of flies, the stench of rotten fish, the all-too-familiar odour of salt water and the increasing heat would at any other time have been unbearable for the incoming troops, but they were so happy to be free of the ships that even these discomforts were endured.

All along the beach, troops were spilling gratefully from their transports and Lausard watched as some kissed the ground. Many of the men didn't appear to be carrying any weapons and Lausard could only assume that they had been lost during the hazardous three-mile trip from ship to shore.

Without weapons, their uniforms incomplete and reeking, the men staggering ashore looked more like an army of scarecrows than a force of invaders. They stood in unsteady groups or flopped helplessly on the sand, surrounded by clouds of black flies, their throats parched, their stomachs longing for food, waiting for their officers to give them orders, wondering how they could find shelter from the scorching sun. Those who had lost their head gear were in even more dire straits and some were already pulling their tunics over their heads in an effort to protect themselves. Even the sand burned beneath their feet.

Lausard reached up and momentarily removed his helmet, feeling how hot the brass had become. His entire body was sheathed in sweat, his head swimming from the journey and lack of food or water. When he moved it was on unsteady legs. A legacy of the six-week voyage. Some of the men were even worse. Joubert could barely take two steps before falling to the sand, his head spinning. He blinked hard to try to cure the double vision he temporarily had to contend with. Roussard took off his helmet and looked up at the cloudless sky.

'Don't do that, you fool,' Milliere snapped, suddenly approaching. 'The sun will blind you if you look directly at it.'

'And keep your helmet on,' Lausard added.

Rochctcau swatted away another fly, aware he was fighting a losing battle. The insects swarmed around all the soldiers like a black cloud, landing on any piece of exposed flesh, and crawling across faces, hands and shirtless bodies. Gaston spat as one crawled into his mouth.

'What about our horses, Captain?' Lausard asked.

Milliere could only shrug.

'Your guess is as good as mine. I have no idea which transport they are on or when they are likely to be brought ashore. Until they arrive, we are infantry.'

'Complaining again, *Private*?'

Lausard recognized the voice immediately.

Sergeant Delpierre was striding towards him, smoothing the moustache that grew beneath his hooked nose.

'Private,' he said, grinning. 'There is such a wonderfully ironic sound to that word when I address *you*, Lausard. You and all this scum like you.' He glanced around at the other dragoons. 'How does it feel to be a mere private again? How humiliating was it to lose your rank?'

'I lost it in a good cause,' Lausard told his fellow dragoon.

'In a good cause, *Sergeant*,' Delpierre reminded him.

Lausard glared at the other man.

'Well don't expect to regain it in a hurry,' Delpierre said. 'You are again what you will always be. A common soldier.'

'Rank means nothing. A man is generally what he feels himself to be.'

'And what do you feel *you* are?' Delpierre sneered. 'What kind of inflated opinion of yourself do you have? Do you think yourself better than me? Better than Sergeant Legier over there.' He motioned to the stockily built NCO with his right ear missing, who was busily forming some newly landed dragoons into line on the sand.

'I have no thoughts about *you*, Sergeant,' Lausard told him. 'What I think of you or any other man is my business.'

Delpierre was about to retaliate when Milliere stepped close to him.

'Get on with rallying the men, Sergeant,' the officer ordered curtly. 'I want all of us prepared before nightfall.'

'I can't make the boats hurry, sir,' the sergeant protested. 'Some of the regiment are still being brought ashore.'

'Then help Sergeant Legier organize those who have already landed,' Milliere told him, and Delpierre stalked off across the sand. The captain turned to Lausard. 'I didn't know you were once a sergeant, Lausard. What happened? How did you lose your rank?'

'I had a disagreement with your predecessor, sir,' Lausard told him and a number of the men nearby chuckled, Royere included.

'Nearly *everyone* had a disagreement with Captain Cezar,' the lieutenant said, smiling.

Milliere nodded. 'If you lost your rank it is up to you to regain it,' the captain offered. 'I'm sure there will be ample opportunity during this campaign.'

'Ample opportunity to get killed,' Roussard murmured, brushing a fly from his cheek.

'Steer clear of that bastard Delpierre, Alain,' Rocheteau advised.

'I have nothing to fear from him,' Lausard assured his companion. 'Perhaps it is *he* who should fear *me*.' He looked at the sergeant's broad back, watching as he shouted orders to another group of dragoons still struggling to find their land feet.

Stretching in both directions along the beach, infantry, artillery and cavalry were beginning to form into units, the latter two arms of the service being somewhat at a disadvantage as they were without their equipment. The artillery in particular seemed disconsolate about having no guns. The gunners carried a pistol each but other than that their only weapons for the time being were the short swords they possessed. Many of them sat around on the sun-baked sand merely watching as other troops formed up, and the sound of bellowing officers and NCOs began to fill the air as surely as the clouds of flies. Out to sea, the small armada of rowing boats continued to ferry men ashore and the number of troops steadily grew. High above them all, like a massive floating furnace, the sun continued to beat down with unceasing ferocity.

Thirteen

Lausard looked up at the night sky, gazing at the moon as if hypnotized by it. He, like his companions and the other French troops who had landed, had hoped that the onset of night would bring a respite from the unbearable heat, but the temperature had dropped only a few degrees. The raw heat of the sun had been replaced by a cloying humidity that made it difficult to draw breath. Men sat huddled around in groups silently cleaning their equipment as best they could. There was no food and no water and, despite the darkness, dozens of flies still flitted through the gloom and surrounded the troops. Those who tried to sleep found that the sand was still uncomfortably warm from its daytime baking, and if they removed their shirts to seek a little comfort, the irritating grains stuck to their skin and made conditions even more insufferable.

An order had been issued that no fires were to be lit, which struck Lausard as a little ridiculous even though he knew the primary reason was so that enemy troops would not discover their position. Firstly, there was no wood with which to build a fire; secondly, who in such sweltering temperatures would want to sit close to flames; above all, they had neither food nor water to heat over a blaze. From the map that Bonet had taken from his pack, Lausard could see that the French were now about two miles inland, away from the beach where he could still hear troops arriving in the darkness. The journey from the ships had been hazardous enough in daylight, what it would be like in the pitch blackness he could only begin to imagine.

'We're about five miles from Alexandria,' Bonet said, pointing at the map. 'Where we are now used to be a lake. We're in the dry lake bed of Mareotis.'

'It's a pity it's dry,' Joubert commented. 'We might be able to get a drink.'

'It seems a question of whether we starve to death or die of thirst,' Sonnier added.

'Perhaps we should eat Joubert,' Rocheteau teased, prodding his portly companion. 'There's enough meat on him to feed us all.'

The other men laughed, the sound echoing through the night.

'This isn't funny,' Delacor rasped. 'We haven't eaten or drunk for two days. It's no laughing matter.'

'We're all in the same position,' Lausard reminded him. 'There's no point in crying about it.'

'I bet the officers have got food and drink,' Delacor persisted. 'Those bastards aren't suffering like we are.'

'Everyone's suffering,' Lausard insisted, pulling his sword free of its scabbard. He took a piece of rag from his portmanteau and began cleaning the straight-bladed, three-foot-long steel, ensuring it wasn't damp. If it was replaced in its scabbard with moisture on the blade, the weapon would rust. When he'd finished he did the same with the fifteen-inch bayonet that could be fitted to his carbine.

Sonnier was busily cleaning his Charleville carbine, using a rag to dry the frizzen and the priming pan. He had already laid a number of his cartridges on the sand to dry the black powder inside. Damp powder was no good to any man.

'I lost some ammunition in that stinking boat,' Rocheteau said, counting the cartridges from his cartouche. 'I'm down to twenty-three and we haven't even *seen* any enemy troops yet.'

'Perhaps they've all run away,' Roussard offered hopefully. 'When they saw our ships, perhaps they decided it would be better to flee.'

'I doubt it.' Lausard ran a hand through his hair. 'They've probably been watching us since we came ashore. They're more than likely waiting to attack *us*.'

Roussard looked around nervously in the moonlight but was met by the sight of only French troops, mostly infantry. There were other dragoons, men from the same regiment, and a few artillerymen, but no sign of any hostile opponents as yet. Just as there was still no sign of any cannon or horses.

'How are we supposed to fight without horses?' Charvet wanted to know. 'We're meant to be cavalry, aren't we?'

'I haven't seen any of the other cavalry yet,' Bonet offered. 'No hussars and only a handful of Bonaparte's guides.'

'This terrain is no good for cavalry.' Rocheteau picked up a handful of sand and let it drain through his fingers.

'Let's hope we get the chance to find out,' Lausard said.

'Our enemies must have cavalry,' Rostov mused.

'The Mamelukes are legendary horsemen,' Bonet told him. 'They are reckoned to be the finest in the world.'

'And we're supposed to face them on foot?' Rostov muttered.

'They'll do no damage against infantry squares,' Charvet insisted.

'But where will *we* be?' Giresse asked.

'Hiding in those squares, if we've got any sense,' Roussard said.

'There'll be no need to hide,' Lausard responded. 'I don't intend to hide from anyone.'

'Always the hero, Lausard,' Delacor chided. 'Why are you always so keen to fight? Always so eager to face death? What are you trying to prove?'

'I have nothing to prove. I am in this army to fight, just like we all are. We are all soldiers, fighting is our business.'

'But you revel in it. You seek it out. Why?'

'That is *my* business,' Lausard said, glaring at his companion. 'If you are too much of a coward to face death then do not condemn me for your own shortcomings.'

Delacor scrambled to his feet. 'I could kill you for that.'

'You could try,' Lausard told him coldly, his eyes unblinking. He allowed one hand to drop to the hilt of his sword.

Delacor hesitated a moment then sat down again on the hot sand, looking across at Lausard. He finally lowered his gaze and began cleaning his carbine.

'Egypt,' Rocheteau sighed. 'What are we doing here?'

'We are spreading the culture of France throughout a desperate world,' Lausard replied and the other men laughed loudly. 'Freeing those who suffer the shackles of tyranny. Bringing to them what we have.'

'And what is that?' asked Rocheteau, a grin consuming his face.

'Empty bellies and a desperate need for water.' Lausard's remark was greeted by another wave of laughter from the men gathered around.

'We have freedom,' Bonet said. 'France has freedom. All those years of bloodshed, of upheaval, they must have given us something.'

'They gave *us* a place in a jail cell,' Lausard reminded him.

'We are not criminals any longer,' Charvet said.

'That's ironic coming from a man who killed someone during a fight and was nearly hanged for it,' Rocheteau chuckled.

'That was a fair fight . . .' Charvet began but allowed the sentence to trail off.

'No, seriously, Alain,' Bonet continued, 'what do *you* think France achieved by destroying the Bourbons?'

'One set of rulers was merely replaced by another. The Directory are as corrupt as any monarchy, probably worse. We do not fight for *them*, we fight for France and for ourselves. Are any of us better off under the Directory than we were under the Bourbons? No.'

'You sound like a Royalist,' Giresse chuckled.

'A realist.' Lausard smiled.

'We should all thank God we are still alive,' Moreau interjected. 'It was He who saved us from the guillotine, He who saved us from the sea and delivered us here safely.'

'I wouldn't thank him for bringing us *here*,' Roussard said.

'I'd thank him for some food,' Joubert said, rubbing his stomach.

'I'd thank him for the company of a woman,' Giresse added.

'You wouldn't have the strength for a woman after what we've been through,' Carbonne tried to convince him.

'I *always* have the strength for a woman,' Giresse assured his companion. 'I wonder what manner of delightful creature awaits my attention here.'

'According to that proclamation, the women here are treated with more reverence than back in France,' Bonet reminded him. 'They are held in high esteem.'

'I hold *all* women in high esteem. And *they* hold *me* in high esteem after they've experienced my touch and kindness.'

The other men laughed.

'As long as their men have something worth taking,' Delacor snapped irritably. 'I don't plan to leave this place empty handed.'

'And what are you going to steal?' Lausard pressed. 'Sand? There seems to be little else on offer at the moment.' He felt his stomach rumble, the cramps tightening a little more. 'Let's hope there's plenty of food in Alexandria; looking at this map there aren't any other cities of any size for miles. It's all desert.'

'When do you think Bonaparte will order the attack?' Rostov asked.

Lausard could only shrug. 'My guess would be as soon as possible. The quicker the city is taken, the less time there is for the Egyptians to reinforce it.'

'Attacking a fortified city after two days with no food, what does he think we are?' Delacor groaned. 'I bet he's enjoying a meal now. Chicken, bread, cheese, wine.'

'Shut up!' Rocheteau said, hurling some sand at his companion.

'It looks like we've got company,' Rostov said, looking out over the dry lake bed.

The men turned to see a group of officers trudging slowly across the sand, each unit they approached getting to its feet and drawing itself stiffly to attention. Shouted orders began to fill the night and the dragoons also raised themselves from the hot sand, eyes still fixed to the small group of men who moved in and out of the rapidly formed units of infantry. Under the white glow of the moon, they were able to make out at least one of the figures.

'It's Bonaparte,' Lausard said. 'It looks as if he's making an inspection.'

'Isn't that Kléber with him?' Rocheteau was pointing to the tall grey-haired general who strode alongside the Corsican.

As the officers drew nearer, they could also make out the features of Generals Bon and Menou, both sweating in their blue uniforms, Menou carrying his bicorn, the feather dangling from the cockade unmoved in the stillness of the air. Bonaparte himself was dressed in a Grenadier uniform. The top button of his tunic was undone but, unlike those around him, he seemed unaffected by the heat and strode along briskly through the shifting sand, glancing at each soldier, trooper and gunner he came to, running swiftly appraising eyes over them all. The dragoons drew themselves to attention as he reached them, saluting as one man when their commander raised his hand in their direction. He passed by rapidly, on to the next unit, and Lausard looked round to see that Captain Milliere had slipped away from the group of officers and rejoined his regiment.

'We march on Alexandria in one hour,' Milliere informed them.

'Is there still no sign of our horses, sir?' Lausard pressed.

'General Bonaparte will not wait for them to arrive, he says we are well equipped without them, that it would waste time to wait,' Milliere told him. 'We also have no artillery pieces. And yet the plan is to take a walled, fortified city.' The captain raised his eyebrows.

'How many men have we?' Lausard asked.

'Fewer than five thousand,' the officer informed him. 'All starving, all thirsty and all exhausted.' He turned to Rocheteau. 'What odds would you give me on a victory, Corporal?'

'Even money, sir,' Rocheteau said, smiling.

'If I told you there was food and water inside Alexandria would you change those odds?' Milliere grinned.

'I would say that the outcome is not even worth betting on, sir,' Rocheteau continued. 'I would say that the city is as good as ours.'

'That is what General Bonaparte thinks. Let's all hope he's right.'

'These men are in good enough condition,' Bonaparte observed as he continued with his inspection, his fellow officers struggling to keep up with him.

'The promise of food and water should be enough for them,' Berthier commented. 'A full belly is a bigger incentive sometimes than glory.'

Bonaparte laughed. 'There is *no* bigger incentive than glory, my friend.'

They passed more men, all drawn up in lines, standing to attention.

'How many of Desaix's and Reynier's men are ashore?' Bonaparte demanded.

'No more than three or four hundred of Reynier's troops have landed, General,' Berthier informed him. 'They did have further to come than the others, their transport was moored almost six miles from shore.'

'They've had enough time. I want the landing area well protected before we set off to attack Alexandria.' Bonaparte waved a hand in front of his face to drive away an irritatingly persistent fly. 'The artillery should have been in the forward transports too, as well as some horses. If we had just *one* squadron of cavalry able to function properly they could act as a screen for our advance.'

'I would have thought our intentions were fairly obvious to our enemies by now,' Dumas commented haughtily. 'And if you are so worried about a lack of cavalry then wait for the horses to arrive.' The huge mulatto cavalry commander wiped sweat from his face. 'I for one did not come to this infernal country to walk.'

'You have little choice, Dumas,' Bonaparte told him. 'I will not delay the advance any longer. There is no way of knowing how long it will be before the horses are brought ashore. We can always take mounts from the locals.'

'I thought we came as liberators and already you talk of stealing from these people.'

'They will be reimbursed,' Bonaparte snapped. 'We are bringing them freedom. What greater payment is there than that?'

'I don't care one way or the other where my men get their mounts,' Dumas persisted, 'only that they do.'

Bonaparte chose to ignore the comment and continued walking, passing more troops, casting an almost cursory glance over them. Bedraggled was the best word he could think of to describe them. Over two years ago, when he had taken command of the Army of Italy, he had seen men in a similar condition: shoeless, without weapons, many without uniforms; starving, penniless and resigned to the fact that defeat and possibly death was all they had to look forward to. Morale at rock bottom. He had taken command of an army of scarecrows and turned them into an invincible fighting machine. The bulk of that fighting machine was with him here in Egypt but, as he walked briskly among them, he could not help but feel that they had left that air of invincibility behind them on the rough seas between here and their homeland. The rigours of exhaustion, hunger and thirst were etched deeply into the features of nearly every soldier he surveyed as they stood obediently beneath the moonlight awaiting his order to begin their advance on Alexandria.

Standing on a ridge looking out over the dry lake bed of Mareotis, Bonaparte knew that the rest of his army was still coming ashore at Marabout but it was towards the north-east that his gaze was drawn, towards Alexandria. He felt as though some kind of invisible magnetic force was pulling him towards its spires and minarets, towards the city named after and founded by the conqueror he sought so desperately to emulate and eventually eclipse. He wondered if all those many hundreds of years ago Alexander had stood here in this same spot, anticipating his own coming conquests, aware of his own destiny and so eager to fulfil it. He was aware of the questioning gazes of his companions, of a certain restlessness among them, but even that could not disturb his meditative attitude and an unshakeable belief that what he had already embarked upon would bring him even greater glory.

It was another ten minutes before he spoke and gave the order for the advance to begin, watching as the commanders dispersed. Despite the cloying heat, Bonaparte felt a shiver at the back of his neck. The troops were beginning to form into a large column, ready for the journey. He smiled to himself. The time had come.

Fourteen

As he marched, Lausard was surprised at the varying consistency of the sand. In places it was soft and he sank as deep as his ankles whereas in others it was firmer and much easier to walk on. Unfortunately the majority was soft, making the troops' passage even more strength sapping. There was no road leading to the city, only an endless sea of sand, featureless and barren. No trees, no grass – and certainly no water.

Lausard looked up at the sky and saw that the moon had sunk almost out of sight; he guessed that dawn could not be more than thirty minutes away. The air was already warm and the day threatened increased temperatures. He, like the other dragoons, marched as best he could; all were weighed down by saddles and shabraques, their swords trailing in the sand or bumping against their dust-covered boots, their carbines held in their free hand. Lausard could already feel sweat pouring down his face, soaking through his woollen tunic and covering his legs, encased, as they were, in leather breeches. In contrast, up ahead the infantry marched with just their packs, bulging with what few personal belongings they had brought from the ships, and muskets sloped.

Lausard could see Bonaparte at the head of the column, striding determinedly through the sand. He was surrounded by a collection of officers, including Caffarelli, who seemed to be having the most difficulty negotiating the landscape. His wooden leg sank into the soft sand, and more than once Lausard saw the huge figure of Dumas physically lift the engineer clear. Dommartin also trudged along disconsolately, glancing up at the sky as if dreading the arrival of dawn and the onslaught of heat it would bring. The generals looked curiously out of place, the commander of cavalry having no horses at his disposal, while Dommartin, the artillery general, was equally lacking cannon. Berthier and Junot trailed along in the wake of Bonaparte, both trying to keep pace with him.

The endless dunes sloped up and down, the incline sometimes gentle, sometimes precipitous, and the men had trouble retaining their footing as they descended some of the sharper ones. Joubert overbalanced but a hand hauled him upright.

'God, I'd give my soul for a drink,' the big man said, wiping sweat from his face.

'Do not take our Lord's name in vain,' Moreau ordered irritably.

'Why can't God make it rain?' Joubert continued.

'God has no control over *this* country,' Bonet offered. 'It is a law unto itself.'

'It's a hell-hole,' Delacor added, glancing up at the sky.

The clouds were tinged with a bright orange hue, signalling the imminent arrival of dawn. And with dawn would come the unforgiving heat. Rocheteau checked his timepiece as the sun began to rise higher into the cloudless heavens. As it beat down on the marching men, Lausard wondered if he was the only one to notice the pace of the march change. It slowed to a walk as the men were blanketed in a heatwave unlike anything they had ever experienced before. Yet still they pressed on, aware now of a hot wind that had sprung up from the south, which sent particles whipping into their faces, adding to their misery. Sand stuck to their sweat-stained faces and hands. Those who opened their mouths to speak found their tongues were immediately covered by sand and they were forced to spit to clear it. But with no saliva this was a difficult task. Thirst that had seemed unbearable even as the march began was now growing intolerable. Lausard reached into his pocket, pulled out a handkerchief and tied it swiftly and expertly around his mouth and nose, giving himself at least some respite from the stinging grains. He wondered how long it would be before weapons were clogged by the fine clouds.

Up ahead two infantrymen toppled over, one of them rolling on to his back. Companions tried to haul them to their feet but neither of the men could move. The column continued.

Lausard felt his own legs trembling, the breath catching in his throat, but he drove himself on, putting out a hand to steady Giresse when he threatened to fall.

'How much further?' Sonnier gasped, feeling the heat from the sand even through the soles of his boots.

No one could tell him.

Lausard saw men pulling off their tunics in an effort to relieve some of the incredible discomfort caused by the heat. One or two even hurled the garments aside to lighten their load. He and the men around him were faced with a difficult decision: they could either remove their brass helmets and risk sunstroke or retain them and suffer even more acutely from the ravages of the sun. The metal itself was heating up. Lausard could feel his hair plastered to his head and neck, and when he blinked salty sweat ran into his eyes; however, at least it helped to keep his vision clear as it washed away the grains of sand. And through it all there were the flies. Black clouds of them swarmed around the troops and crawled over them in such numbers that, after a time, the men didn't even bother to swat them away.

It was Rocheteau who spotted the four figures on the crest of the ridge to the north. He tugged at Lausard's sleeve and pointed in the direction of the horsemen.

Through the swirling sand and the shimmering heat it was difficult to make out their features or even if they wore uniforms. They sat motionless on small white ponies and Lausard squinted in an effort to pick them out. He could see that two of them were carrying long spears, their bodies wrapped in white robes.

'Give me your telescope,' he said to Rocheteau, who handed him the implement. Lausard put it to his eyes and adjusted the focus, gazing at the watching horsemen, who were pointing at the column of French troops.

'What do you make of that, Bonet?' Lausard said, handing the telescope to the former schoolmaster.

'Bedouins,' Bonet said without hesitation, studying the horsemen. 'Local tribesmen.'

'Hostile?' Rocheteau asked.

'I should think so,' Bonet murmured.

As Lausard watched, the four horsemen disappeared

behind the sand dune as if they had melted into the desert itself. Others in the column had spotted them too and many men were pointing in the direction in which the tribesmen had disappeared. But the march continued, fairly large gaps now opening up between the units despite the efforts of officers to retain the closeness of the marching men. Lausard trudged on, glancing up at the hills every so often as if expecting to see the watching Bedouins again. Nothing moved on the ridge.

The shouts that came from the front of the column suddenly dragged his attention away from any thoughts of Arab horsemen. He looked round to see dozens of men racing from their formation towards a deep cleft in the sand that was surrounded by coarse grass.

'My God, it's a waterhole,' Bonet declared, suddenly pulling away from the rest of his companions and joining the headlong race for the source of water.

Officers and NCOs made no attempt to stop the men's frantic dash towards the waterhole; most had joined the charge, troops crashing into one another in their eagerness to get at the precious fluid. Delacor was the next dragoon to run off, then Joubert and a dozen more of the green-coated troopers. It took Lausard only a moment or two to follow them, he and Rocheteau wandering across to join the rapidly growing throng. They pushed their way through the heaving mass to see that the waterhole was in fact a makeshift well. At least it had *once* been a well. The source of possible moisture was filled with sand and rocks almost to the top.

'Those bastards!' Delacor stared at the polluted, useless well.

Other men were turning miserably to rejoin their units, realizing that the promise of water was now as remote as any chance of respite from the blistering heat and the swarms of flies.

'There'll be food and water in Alexandria,' Lausard said.

'If any of us get there alive.' With this, Delacor turned and followed his colleagues back into their formation.

Many of the men had sat down on the burning sand when the dash towards the well had begun, too exhausted to join the rush. Some now rose and began marching again; others could not drag themselves upright and simply sat watching, seemingly unconcerned, as the column moved on. Indeed, several men lay stretched out in the sun, ignoring the rays burning their flesh. Infantrymen, even a few of the dragoons, could march no longer. They would catch up later, they told themselves, when they had time to regain their strength. They would not, *could* not move another step and few of their NCOs made any attempt to force them. Even Delpierre stalked past two dragoons lying spreadeagled on the sand, making no effort to rouse the men. He marched on as efficiently as he could, his own throat parched, his own belly rumbling and crying out for water. Sand grains stung his eyes and made them tear, the moisture rolling down his already reddened cheeks. He licked at the salty droplets when they trickled to his mouth.

Lausard's helmet was like a small oven on his head, the brass absorbing the incredible heat. He removed it, but as soon as he felt the searing heat on his scalp, he quickly replaced it. He felt light headed; the heat, lack of food and water, combined with exhaustion, gradually wearing him down, as it was every man in the column. He looked back and saw dozens of men lying or sitting on the hot sand. Most had taken off their uniforms, some had even stripped as they tried to counter the sweltering effects of the sun. Close to Lausard Gaston stumbled, dropping to his knees momentarily. Lausard picked up the young trumpeter, hoisting him back on to his feet.

'Keep moving,' he told the boy. 'You must keep moving.'

At the head of the dragoons Captain Milliere and Lieutenant Royere were stumbling through the sand. Royere looked particularly badly affected by the heat and was dragging his saddle, the leather now coated by a thin film of sand and dust. He seemed to be moving as if in a trance, each step an effort, every yard a battle.

Rostov walked with his head bowed, staring down at the sand, cursing it and the heat.

'Alain, look.' Again Rocheteau was gesturing towards the hills, towards the figures silhouetted against the clear blue sky.

Bedouins.

Lausard counted twelve this time. They were still watching the column, perhaps counting its numbers, calculating its condition, satisfied that their sabotage of the well had deprived these invaders of some much needed water. As Lausard watched, another dozen joined the band of onlookers. Then even more. Their number had swelled to almost fifty now, many of them carrying long spears, clearly visible as they sat astride their sleek ponies.

To the south, Lausard counted another thirty of the Arabs, and even as he watched their numbers swelled alarmingly.

'Do you think they'll attack?' Rocheteau asked.

Lausard didn't answer, and simply watched as yet more

of the tribesmen came into view on both sides of the dunes. He guessed that they must be about five or six hundred yards away. Waiting.

'How many do you think there are?' Roussard was unable to keep the anxiety out of his voice.

'Well over a hundred,' Lausard replied. 'And that's only what we can *see*.'

The Bedouins remained motionless, seemingly content with watching the bedraggled French troops.

Then, suddenly, they began to move. The leading horsemen turned their mounts and began riding parallel with the column.

'They're tracking us,' Lausard said, aware that the number of tribesmen continued to grow. He looked to his right and left and guessed that there must be over two hundred Arab horsemen by now. They were moving at the same pace as the column, and as awareness of their presence spread through the French, so too did fear. Was there to be an attack? If so, when?

Even more tribesmen joined the slowly moving sentinels, and it seemed to Lausard as if they were emerging from the sand itself. Still the steady procession continued, the Bedouin guiding their horses along patiently, level with the increasingly nervous troops. Some of the men who had stayed behind on the scorching sand scrambled to their feet and attempted to catch up with their comrades, eager not to be left to the mercy of these desert dwellers. But many found their strength had left them, and they could only crawl in vain pursuit of the safety offered by their respective unit.

With each torturous yard the French marched, more Arabs appeared, and Lausard was now convinced that well over three hundred Bedouin flanked them.

'Perhaps they're some kind of escort,' Tabor offered, looking at the Bedouin.

'They're not an escort, idiot.' The nervousness was apparent in Delacor's voice. 'Why don't they attack?'

'They're trying to frighten us,' Charvet surmised.

'Well they're doing a good job,' Sonnier assured him. 'Delacor's right, why don't they attack and get it over with?'

Lausard looked to his right and left and saw that both groups of Bedouin had brought their horses to a halt and were forming up in untidy groups. 'It looks as if you're about to get your wish.'

Up on the hills, the groups of Bedouin to the north and south were now still, gathered together in large groups about one hundred and fifty strong on each flank. They sat motionless for agonizing seconds, watching the marching Frenchmen impassively.

Lausard was looking from right to left constantly, watching for some sign of movement from the tribesmen, waiting for both groups to come hurtling at the column. Then he heard a high-pitched shriek, followed quickly by another then another until both ridges echoed with the screams of the Bedouin. He watched as the long spears were raised into the air and felt his heart beat faster.

The first of the horses from the group on the northern ridge suddenly lurched forward, its rider holding his spear in his left hand, screaming something in Arabic as he hurtled towards the startled French.

Another horse burst from the group on the opposite ridge and also began galloping across the sand.

But that was it. Two men. No more.

From either side of the stunned Frenchmen, they raced forward.

'Hold your fire!' shouted an infantry officer whose men had formed two lines about fifty yards from the dragoons. Totally puzzled, they watched as the Bedouin warriors drew closer, waving their spears madly in the air while their tribesmen sat in silence again on either ridge.

Lausard's hand slipped to the hilt of his sword as the tribesmen drew closer. Rocheteau had raised his carbine to his shoulder. They could now see the faces of the Bedouin, contorted as they screamed their defiance and hurtled on towards the French column or, Lausard noted, the gaps in it.

The tribesmen hurtled through a gap between units of about twenty yards, passing within touching distance of the French and of one another. Then they swept on up the respective slopes and rejoined their fellow tribesmen. Almost immediately, more of the Bedouin sped their mounts forward and Lausard counted six from each group gathering this time, all shrieking madly and waving their spears.

Fifty yards from the French column, they split up, three or four sweeping through one gap in the bemused Frenchmen, half a dozen others riding into and beyond another breech in the lines. As with their predecessors they galloped up the hills to join their waiting companions.

'What kind of game is this?' Rocheteau snarled. 'Do they mean to attack us or not?'

'I would imagine they realize we cannot chase them with no cavalry,' Lausard said. 'They are trying to see what we do next.'

More horsemen detached themselves from the Bedouin hordes and followed the same routine as their companions, sweeping through the gaps with blood-curdling screams and little else. One of them spat at Milliere as he passed but that was the extent of the aggressive activity. The French infantry had lowered its weapons and were watching warily as yet another group of Bedouin came charging down the slopes, shrieking madly. This time some rode off towards the rear of the column, towards the stragglers. Lausard watched as an infantryman, dressed only in a pair of ripped pantaloons, was grabbed by one of the larger Bedouin and hauled up across the saddle, carried off like some kind of trophy. This happened three or four more times, the starving, exhausted Frenchmen powerless to fight back.

More Bedouin swept down towards the French, who now watched them more carefully. One of them slowed his horse as he drew near, adjusted the position of his spear and, as he rode through, drove the long weapon towards a watching infantryman.

The sharp point caught the man in the throat and he keeled over, blood spurting from the wound, staining the sand.

Angry shouts now rose from the French ranks.

Sonnier swung his carbine up to his shoulder and fired at the fleeing Bedouin, watching with satisfaction as the man toppled from his horse and lay still in the sand.

With the sound of the single shot still reverberating over the dunes, a number of the tribesmen turned and rode away, taking their captives with them. A dozen others, however, made one last charge towards the French.

Lausard drew his sword, ducked beneath the jabbing spear of a tribesman, and struck out with a powerful back-hand slash that caught the Arab across the chest, tearing through his flimsy garments and scything into his chest. The tribesman toppled backwards from his horse and fell at Lausard's feet. Rocheteau used his pistol on the Bedouin nearest to him, waiting until the man was no more than two yards away before firing at his attacker's face.

Tabor grabbed his assailant by the arm and, using his massive strength, pulled both him and his horse to the ground. The horse scrabbled wildly to regain its footing, one hoof slamming into the cheekbone of its rider, effortlessly shattering the bone. The Bedouin staggered to his feet as the horse galloped away, but before he could turn and run, Delacor had finished him with his sword. The other Bedouin turned their mounts and rode off, disappearing over the hills as quickly as they had come. By the time Lausard looked up, the ridges were empty again. The Arabs had vanished like ghosts. All that remained of their presence were the pony tracks in the sand and half a dozen bodies over which flies were already swarming.

'If that's the stiffest resistance we come up against we should conquer this country in a week,' Rocheteau said, smiling.

Lausard didn't answer. He wiped his bloodied sword blade with a piece of cloth then slid it back into the scabbard.

'What horsemen,' Bonet enthused. 'They didn't have any saddles. The horses didn't even have proper bridles, just reins in their mouths.'

'We should have tried to capture some of the horses, it would have saved us walking,' Delacor observed.

'They weren't shod either,' Bonet added. 'I suppose that's so they get a better grip in the sand.'

'Why did they take those men prisoner?' Tabor wanted to know.

'God knows,' Lausard murmured. 'I don't even want to think about what they might do to them.'

'It will discourage stragglers from now on,' Rocheteau chuckled, looking up at the dunes once more, his tone turning reflective. 'What kind of men fight like that?'

'Or ride like that? I'd back one of them against any one of us in a race,' Charvet said.

'Do you think they'll be back, Alain?' Rocheteau asked.

Lausard wiped sweat from his face, his eyes still scanning the dunes. 'It isn't a matter of if, it's a matter of *when* and how many.'

Ahead of the column was a steep slope. Men toiled up it in the blistering heat, scarcely able to force their shattered bodies along in the sucking sand. Lausard watched as many of them paused as they reached the top; he assumed it was from exhaustion, but as the dragoons crested the ridge he saw why so many had slowed their pace. It was the sight before them that caused them to pause. The bleached stone walls swarming with frantic defenders, the ancient cannon barrels protruding through the embrasures and, beyond these outer walls, a number of minarets and spires.

'Alexandria,' Lausard murmured.

Fifteen

Lausard guessed that the stone monument about five hundred yards away, poking upwards into the cloudless sky like an accusatory finger, was close to seventy feet tall. It was towards this monument that he saw Bonaparte and his generals moving, the Corsican gesturing all about him as he walked.

The shouts of officers and NCOs filled the air and Lausard saw that the troops were moving into position in preparation for attack. Exhausted, starving and racked by thirst as they were, the French troops were to be given no rest before the city was assaulted. The bulk of the infantry was marching to the north, in the direction of a smaller, triangular fort that guarded the approaches to the city. Lausard's weary unit formed up behind a demi-brigade and marched towards one of the main gates to the north of the fort. Lausard could see the tall, grey-haired figure of General Kléber issuing orders to his subordinates, who scurried off to complete them.

'What time is it?' Lausard asked Rocheteau, his eyes never leaving the silhouette of the city.

'Eight.'

'I don't think I can take another step without food,' Joubert insisted.

Lausard was about to answer him when the early-morning air was suddenly filled with an unearthly screeching.

'What the hell is that?' Delacor demanded, looking towards the city.

It took the men just a few seconds to realize that the defenders lining the walls were shrieking uncontrollably, either in fear or in an attempt to frighten off their attackers.

A moment later there was a thunderous roar of cannon fire as the guns on the walls of the fort opened up and the projectiles could be heard whistling through the scorching air. They landed in the soft sand about twenty yards ahead of the waiting French troops, sending up geysers of dust and sand.

'Forward!'

No one was quite sure where the order had come from but, as one man, the French advanced, carbines sloped uniformly. Lausard looked across and saw that the troops commanded by Menou and Bon were also moving forward. The shrieking that had greeted their initial arrival seemed to double in volume but it served only to aggravate rather than deter the attackers.

As they drew nearer to the cracked walls the first popping of muskets began to fill the air, but there was no uniformity to the fire. Lausard could see men leaning over the walls firing down on him and his companions.

The infantry, carrying ladders to scale the walls, had already reached the fortifications and were beginning to climb.

Sonnier raised his carbine and aimed at one of the defenders on the parapet, smiling as he saw his quarry struck by the ball. The Arab tottered uncertainly for a second then toppled over the battlements, his scream cut short as he struck the sand below. Sonnier was reloading when he was struck on the shoulder by something heavy, something that had been hurled from above. He went down clutching at his arm and Lausard saw that a sharp rock the size of a man's fist had caught his companion, causing him to drop his weapon. Another smaller projectile slammed against Lausard's helmet, the impact staggering him momentarily. Suddenly the air seemed to be filled with stones, all hurled with great power and desperation from the battlements. The hail of rocks struck the attacking French and more than a dozen infantrymen toppled from the scaling ladders, one with his forehead laid open practically to the bone. Men at the foot of the walls were now firing up at the defenders and the air began to fill with the stench of acrid smoke that was rolling across the sand like man-made fog, adding to the already foul quality of the air. As the firing intensified, the morning air seemed to turn red hot. It was like taking lungsful of air directly from a furnace.

Roussard was hit by a rock that cracked one of his fingers.

Tabor staggered as another thudded into his chest.

Only the occasional musket was fired from above and Lausard heard a bullet whistle past his ear and bury itself in the sand. Ahead of him several infantrymen had succeeded in clambering to the top of a ladder and were swinging themselves over on to the parapet. More swarmed up after them and the dragoons followed.

As he pulled himself over the battlements, Lausard

drew his sword in time to meet the charge of an Arab, who swung what looked like an axe at him. Lausard ducked beneath the clumsy attack and drove his sword into the man's stomach, pulling him on to the blade then wrenching it free. There were nearly two dozen Frenchmen on the ramparts now and the numbers were growing by the second as more and more climbed the ladders. Many of the defenders jumped down into the fort, anxious to escape the battle, but others fought on. Lausard was struck in the face by a rock. He tasted blood on his lip and lurched towards his attacker, catching him by the throat and hurling him off the parapet.

Further along, Rocheteau had flattened one attacker by slamming the butt of his carbine into the Arab's face and was about to bayonet another of the terrified men but before he could strike the Arab leaped from the rampart, crashing through the roof of a stable below as he fell.

Lausard saw Captain Milliere and Lieutenant Royere both using their swords against the hapless defenders. Royere was suddenly struck by a rock and went down heavily, bleeding from a cut behind one ear. Milliere turned on his companion's assailant and drove his sword into the Arab's chest. However, the blade stuck between the man's ribs and, as he fell back, the sword was pulled from Milliere's grasp, leaving him momentarily defence-less against another, much larger assailant, armed with a wickedly curved sword.

The officer ducked under the first vicious swing but Lausard could see that the crush of men fighting left little room for manoeuvre on the ramparts. He pushed his way through the mêlée and stepped in front of Milliere's attacker, blocking the devastating downward stroke, then driving his fist into the Arab's face. The impact drove the man back and Lausard struck out with his sword, driving the blade through the Arab's throat, ignoring the blood that spattered him.

Milliere pulled his weapon from the body of the man he had killed and slapped Lausard on the shoulder in a gesture of thanks.

They both helped Royere to his feet, the lieutenant wincing as he touched the cut behind his ear, but he nodded that he was all right and the three men pressed on, aware that the ramparts were now almost exclusively occupied by blue- and green-jacketed troops. The defenders who weren't already dead were fleeing. Rostov shot one down as he tried to climb down a ladder, watching with satisfaction as the body hurtled to the ground.

Lausard looked down over the battlements and saw that hundreds of French troops were advancing towards the outer walls of Alexandria, tricolours flying high above them. These men, like himself, were, he thought, not fighting for pride or honour; they were attacking with such fury because they were all too aware of the provisions that awaited them within the walls of the ancient city. Food and water. Men ran at the walls with little regard for their lives, propping the ladders and scrambling up like monkeys, roaring oaths, seemingly oblivious to the shower of rocks and the desultory volleys of musket fire that greeted their assault.

The triangular fort was empty now, home to only the dead and wounded of both sides. French troops ran through the buildings looking for any scraps of food or traces of water; when they found none, they rejoined their comrades in the assault on the outer walls of Alexandria.

Lausard scrambled down a ladder and joined the rest of his unit, many of whom were firing upwards at the walls. Smoke was drifting across the battlefield making it difficult to see more than ten yards in front, the noxious clouds swirling around the men like reeking fog. Lausard heard cheers, screams, curses. He heard voices bellowing in Arabic, many of those screaming.

Carbonne lurched towards him out of the smoke, his face bleeding, his cheeks smeared with powder. He was gasping for breath, finding it difficult to draw in air that was red hot and seared the lungs.

'The main gates have given way,' he declared triumphantly. 'The infantry have broken through.'

The exhaustion the men had felt an hour earlier was forgotten, all other considerations replaced by the desire for victory, the desire to storm the city and get at its supplies. Lausard heard bugles sounding the advance, heard officers bellowing orders and, above it all, the constant crack of musket fire.

He followed Carbonne through the thick smoke, a light wind suddenly blowing away the black pall to reveal the open gates, now battered by the ferocious attacks on it. French troops were flooding in, waving their swords and muskets above their heads, firing on anything that came within range.

Rocheteau appeared at Lausard's side, his face blackened by the smoke but his expression cheerful. 'We have them. And we have their city.'

As Lausard followed his companion he glanced to his left and saw several soldiers gathered around a grey-haired officer, whom he recognized immediately as Kléber. The general was bleeding heavily from a wound above his eye, blood soaking through the bandages as quickly as the surgeon could tie them.

Lausard ran on, into the city itself. Immediately, several

musket balls hit the ground close to his feet, and he and Rocheteau dived for cover behind some barrels. The shots had come from a nearby house, and infantry were retaliating, pouring fire back into the buildings. The narrow streets were awash with choking fumes that stung Lausard's eyes and scorched his throat. He coughed and spat, then reached for a cartridge from his cartouche; he bit off the ball and, holding it in his mouth and tasting the black powder as he did so, he poured powder down the barrel, pulled the ramrod free and spat the ball down the carbine, ramming the remains of the cartridge down after it. He tapped the weapon gently against the ground to allow more powder to spill out into the priming pan, then he swung the weapon up.

Rocheteau, like most of the infantry and the dismounted dragoons, had fixed his bayonet, the fifteen inches of needle-sharp steel gleaming on the end of the weapon.

The two men moved off down a street, finding it difficult to walk side by side as the thoroughfare was so narrow. From all around them they heard screams, the constant crackling of fire, orders shouted in French, and oaths roared in many languages. Lausard heard a child crying and a woman weeping, but he could not tell where these sounds came from or how close they were. The interior of the city was bedlam. Men, women and children ran back and forth in the smoke and flames, some fighting, some trying to escape, some trying to hide and, through it all, the French forged on through the labyrinthine streets shooting, bayoneting or sabring anyone who crossed their path.

The coppery smell of blood began to mingle with the cloying gunpowder.

A loud bang sounded to Lausard's left, which he recognized instantly as the discharge of a pistol and he heard a ball whistle past his ear. Spinning round he swung his carbine up to his shoulder and, in one fluid movement, sighted and fired at the Arab who had shot at them from a doorway. The carbine spat out its deadly load, the bullet finding its target. The Arab went down like a rock, blood spewing from the wound in his chest. Rocheteau crossed to the body and ran his bayonet into the man's face angrily.

'Bastard!' he hissed under his breath and, for the first time, Lausard saw that his companion had been struck by the pistol shot. A piece of flesh the size of a thumbnail had been blown from Rocheteau's left ear, and blood was coursing down the side of his face, mingling with powder stains.

The two men moved on, finding that they'd been joined in the narrow street by half a dozen infantrymen, who were moving in and out of the houses looking for any of the enemy who might be hiding, and also for any food or water they could find. They emerged empty handed, the discovery only serving to galvanize them further.

Lausard and Rocheteau emerged into a large square already filled with troops, some gathered around a trough in the centre. Any water in it had been drunk by the time the dragoons reached it and several men lay around on the bleached cobblestones burbling incoherently, as intoxicated as if they had drunk a gallon of wine. A large building filled the skyline directly opposite, and from its shining dome Lausard guessed it was a mosque. A dozen or more infantry were approaching the main doors, muskets lowered, more than one of them admiring the jewels that festooned the heavy wooden partitions.

Several dead bodies, most of them Arabs', their robes torn and bloodied, littered the square. Some had already been stripped, their silken garments taken as souvenirs by the French. Lausard saw several men from his own unit wandering about the square. He recognized Charnier, a corporal from the third squadron, busily ripping gold earrings from a couple of dead natives before slipping them into his cartouche. He waved amiably at Lausard, ignoring the occasional bangs and cracks of pistols and muskets still exploding periodically from the houses that overlooked the square. But only a handful of the city's residents had chosen to fight on and the firing was sporadic; most had surrendered or fled.

Like Lausard and Rocheteau, a number of infantry-men were heading towards the mosque, admiring its bejewelled doors.

'Easy pickings.' Rocheteau smiled.

Suddenly the doors of the mosque burst open and the men froze. Standing inside the holy building were more than twenty Arabs, men and women, all armed with muskets and pistols.

For what seemed like an eternity no one moved, then the Arabs opened fire.

A savage volley of bullets raked the advancing French and a number went down in the hail of lead, one man clutching his face, another screaming madly as he held up a hand that had been holed by a ball. A sergeant grunted as his knee was shattered by a shot.

A rolling bank of smoke filled the doorway to the mosque and screams immediately replaced the roar of fire as the enraged troops rushed towards the building, crashing into the doors and forcing them open, driving the defenders back inside. Lausard saw an officer raise his sword above his head and charge in with the infantry. 'Kill them all!' he roared, his face contorted with rage.

Rocheteau drew his sword and dashed in after the infantry, closely followed by Lausard. Inside the mosque every sound was amplified; every shot was deafening, every scream of pain or desperation magnified, every curse or prayer intensified.

Those who carried weapons were cut down first, their bodies trampled as the soldiers sought to reach those beyond.

A child of no more than five clung to its mother, and Lausard watched as one infantryman shot the woman while another drove his bayonet through the child, lifting it into the air like some kind of obscene trophy.

An old man raised a hand to surrender, only to have it hacked off by a sword blade.

A woman threw herself to the floor, prostrate before a large sergeant, who merely brought his foot down on the back of her head with all the power he could muster. He repeated the action a number of times before finally running his bayonet into the motionless body, then charging on to skewer a man who was on his knees praying.

Rocheteau struck an Arab across the face, laying the flesh open to the bone with his sword. The man dropped to his knees, head bowed as if seeking mercy. Rocheteau had none to spare and struck again, a powerful blow that practically severed the man's head. He toppled sideways on to a dead child.

Most of the Arabs who remained alive had retreated to the rear of the mosque where, without exception, they prayed, their voices amplified by the hollow interior. The floor was awash with blood, and Lausard strode through it towards the officer who had ordered the attack, who was aiming his pistol at the head of a terrified child, clinging desperately to its mother.

'Enough!' Lausard shouted, grabbing the officer's arm.

The man shook loose of the dragoon's grip and glared at him with blank eyes. It was an expression Lausard had witnessed before; a trance-like stare that consumed men who had killed to excess. The air reeked of blood and excrement, the cries of the Arabs echoed loudly around the confined space.

'They fired upon us, they deserve to die,' the officer said, his pistol still pointed at the child.

'Look how many have,' Lausard said, motioning around him at the carpet of bloodied corpses covering the floor of the mosque. 'It is time to stop.'

Something flickered behind the officer's eyes; Lausard couldn't be sure what. Realization? Pity? Humanity? He blinked hard and nodded, as if emerging from his hypnotic state.

'They fired on us.' His voice was barely above a whisper.

'I know,' Lausard told him.

The officer turned and ordered his men from the mosque, the infantry wandering out back into the blistering heat of the noon sunshine. Lausard watched them go, then he turned to look at the Arabs still gathered in prayer at the rear of the mosque. Their heads were bowed, all apart from an old man with a long grey beard who got to his feet, walked across to the dragoon and kissed his hand. He babbled something in Arabic and dropped to his knees at Lausard's feet.

'Why did you stop them, Alain?' Rocheteau asked. 'You once said that there were no innocents in war. Besides, they *did* fire on us, that officer was right.'

Lausard drew his sword suddenly and held the hilt towards his companion.

'Take it,' he said angrily. 'Finish what you started. Is that what you want, Rocheteau? They are all helpless now. It shouldn't take more than a few minutes to slaughter the rest of them.'

Rocheteau looked at him warily, the sword only inches away from him.

'We've killed civilians before,' the corporal reminded him. 'What's the difference now?'

'Perhaps you're right,' said Lausard, and he turned his sword, gripping the hilt, drawing it back so that the point was pressing against the throat of the old man. 'Let's kill them all.'

The old man shrieked something unintelligible and tried to back away but Lausard held him by the shoulder.

Rocheteau jumped to his feet and grabbed Lausard's sword arm. 'All right, Alain,' he said. 'You've made your point. They live.'

Lausard slowly withdrew his sword and sheathed it. 'We might be killers, but we aren't yet murderers.'

The two dragoons turned and headed out of the mosque, the prayers and cries of the surviving Arabs echoing inside their heads.

Sixteen

'It isn't how I'd imagined it,' Bonet said, looking around. 'I'd been expecting something more imposing. Something magnificent. Not this.'

The former schoolmaster stood in the centre of one of Alexandria's main squares gazing around him sadly. Lausard, too, was less than impressed by the city founded by Alexander so many centuries earlier. The tall stone monument he'd seen prior to the attack on the city was, Bonet had informed him, named Pompey's Pillar, but other than that there was little to suggest a place of awe and splendour – only one of filth and squalor. The streets were unpaved and filthy, the buildings a jumble of hovels constructed from unbaked clay bricks, wood and dirt – the only buildings that looked even remotely impressive were the mosques, of which there were many. And what struck Lausard particularly was the absence of trees: other than a few date palms, there were none.

'I don't care what it looks like now I've eaten.' Joubert was munching on a flat cake he'd purchased at one of the bazaar stalls moments earlier.

The bazaar itself was a kaleidoscopic collection of soldiers, Arabs and traders, some of whom had come from the desert to sell their wares. Lausard noticed stalls selling pigeons, sheep, lentils, watermelons and tobacco. The men had eaten and drunk their fill within hours of the capture of the city, and ever since had been anxious to stock up with food in case of another shortage. Most of the infantrymen wandering about had their packs stuffed with all kinds of provisions. Water was the most expensive commodity as, even in the city itself, it seemed to be in relatively short supply. However, a number of Bedouin groups had been sent out into the desert to lead Caffarelli's engineers to nearby wells, and water was being ferried back to the city for the benefit of both the French and their new-found allies.

'I don't think much to their women,' Giresse commented as a girl in her early twenties passed by. She was wearing a dirty blue shirt and nothing else. He looked down at her filthy bare feet and noticed that her toenails were painted red. She was followed by two young children, both naked, who were jabbering in Arabic to each other and looking curiously at the French as they passed them.

'What's so different about here to Paris?' Rostov said. 'The streets there are filthy; we were no better than these people, living in filth.'

'At least we had some dignity and didn't walk around in rags or allow our children to roam the streets naked,' Delacor protested indignantly.

'And what fine suit of clothes were *you* wearing when you were arrested?' Lausard asked.

The other men laughed.

'I was dirty for a reason. I couldn't help it.'

'Perhaps it is the same with these people,' Lausard responded.

'Five hundred years of slavery has crushed their spirits,' Bonet offered.

'And what were we but slaves to the Bourbons?' Delacor retaliated. 'Now slaves to Bonaparte and the Directory instead.'

'Better slaves than dead men,' Roussard interjected.

'We are not slaves, we are soldiers,' Lausard said sternly.

'What's the difference?' Delacor demanded.

'You used the word dignity,' Lausard reminded him. 'Perhaps we still have some of that left. As long as we retain it we will also retain our humanity.'

Rocheteau raised one eyebrow as he looked at Lausard. Something unspoken passed between the two men. Rocheteau remembered how Lausard had acted in the mosque and wondered if that was the humanity his colleague spoke of.

Up ahead a small crowd had gathered, comprised almost entirely of French troops, among them many green-jacketed dragoons. Lausard and the others pushed their way to the front of the throng, anxious to see the object of interest. On the cobbles of the square Charnier, from the third squadron, sat cross-legged and behind him a huge Arab, stripped to the waist, was sharpening a razor against a flat stone.

'I thought I needed a shave,' Charnier said, smiling. 'I don't know why everyone wants to watch.'

Lausard looked down at his companion then up at the Arab barber, and a slight grin creased his features. 'You have more faith than I, my friend.'

'He's only a barber,' Charnier said dismissively. 'What harm can he do to me?'

Lausard saw the barber being guided into position by an assistant and the grin broadened on his face.

'*I* wouldn't trust a blind man with a razor,' Lausard told him, laughing aloud as the smile faded rapidly from Charnier's face. As it did the big Arab suddenly clamped both knees around the Frenchman's head, one against each ear, tilting the dragoon's chin upwards. He then set to work, moving the razor with devastating speed and skill, shaving off the thick growth of bristles that covered the Frenchman's cheeks, chin and neck.

'Blind?' Charnier shrieked, unable to move as the barber continued his work.

The watching men were convulsed with laughter.

'If you want to keep your nose, I'd keep still.' Rocheteau chuckled.

Lausard watched as the steel was wielded with such skill and precision that Charnier barely felt it against his flesh. The barber finished with a flourish and released Charnier from his grip to a loud chorus of applause from those watching.

'I don't think you'll ever be called upon to show your courage in any other way, my friend,' Lausard called, laughing, but Charnier was unable to reply. He simply pushed a couple of coins into the barber's sweaty hand, staring at the milky cataracts that discoloured the man's eyes.

'Blind,' he mumbled as two of his colleagues helped him to his feet, the laughter of the other troopers echoing in his ears.

'I wouldn't have trusted that bastard to shave *me*,' Delacor said. 'I don't trust any of these pigs.' He looked disdainfully at a group of Arabs sitting close by.

'They probably don't trust us either,' Bonet reminded him. 'After all, we have invaded their country.'

'Not *invaded*, Bonet,' Lausard corrected him sardonically. 'Liberated. Isn't that our mission as soldiers of the Republic? Some of the idealists in the army think so and doesn't it say so in this proclamation from Bonaparte himself?' He reached across and pulled a large piece of paper from a nearby wall, surveying carefully the words printed on it. Hundreds of them had been read aloud to the inhabitants of the city and also posted throughout Alexandria the previous day. Lausard read aloud. '"In the name of the French Republic, founded on liberty and equality, the commander in chief of the French armies, Bonaparte, lets it be known to the whole population of Egypt that the beys who govern Egypt have insulted the French nation and oppressed French merchants long enough: the hour of their punishment has come. For too many years that gang of slaves, purchased in Georgia and the Caucasus, has tyrannized the most beautiful region of the world. But Almighty God, who rules the universe, has decreed that their reign shall come to an end."'

'God has decreed nothing concerning this country,' Moreau interjected. 'This invasion was decreed by civilians, by men, not by God.' He crossed himself.

'I agree,' Delacor added. 'His holiness here is right. This entire expedition was dreamed up by the Directory.'

'What makes you think that?' Rocheteau wanted to know. 'Since when did you become a politician?'

Some of the other men laughed.

Deep in thought, Lausard stroked his chin. 'You could have a point, Delacor,' he mused. 'A strong army is a threat to the Directory, especially when it has a leader as powerful as Bonaparte.'

'Perhaps that's why there are so many civilians on the expedition,' Roussard offered. 'They're probably spies, sent by the Directory.'

'That's ridiculous,' Bonet told him. 'They are learned men. Historians, architects, artists and writers. They are here to chronicle the culture of this country, not to spy on *us*.'

'How do you know that?' Roussard persisted. 'Those preening "pekinese", I don't trust any of them. All they do is complain about their conditions.'

'Like some others I could mention?' Lausard quipped and the men laughed.

'I heard from someone in the second squadron that all of them had been put on privates' rations and in quarters fit for privates,' Joubert said.

'Good. Let them suffer as we suffer. What use are they to us anyway? They are only any good if they can use one of these.' Delacor patted the hilt of his sword.

'There is always a need for brains as well as brute force,' Bonet said.

'And what was it that took this city?' Delacor challenged. 'I didn't see too many of your thinkers and painters up to their ankles in blood yesterday. They were probably busy hiding or they didn't want to dirty their precious hands with Arab blood.'

'What else does the proclamation say, Alain?' Rocheteau asked.

Lausard scanned the paper, his lips moving silently for a moment, then he began to read again, loud enough for all the men to hear.

'"Once you had great cities, large canals, a prosperous trade. What has destroyed all this if not the greed, the iniquity and the tyranny of the Mamelukes?"' He glanced over another portion of the proclamation. '"Tell the people that the French are also true Moslems,"' Lausard read.

'I don't wish to be classed with these heathen.' Moreau was indignant.

Lausard ignored him and read on. '"The proof is that they have been to Rome the great and have destroyed the throne of the Pope who always incited the Christians to make war on the Moslems, and that they went to the island of Malta and expelled the knights, who fancied that God wanted them to make war on the Moslems."'

'This is heresy,' said Moreau, trying to snatch the proclamation from Lausard.

'No it isn't,' Lausard told him. 'It's propaganda. Bonaparte is trying to convince the Arabs we're their friends, not their conquerors.'

'I hope it works,' Rostov added.

'"All villages that take up arms against the army will be burned to the ground,"' Lausard read on.

'So, we are to kill more civilians if we are ordered,' Rocheteau observed.

Lausard nodded.

'Bonaparte calls the Mamelukes tyrants and then tells us we will have to kill women and children,' Bonet commented.

'It wouldn't be the first time, would it?' Lausard said quietly.

'To hell with them,' Delacor rasped. 'I don't care *who* I have to kill.'

'"May God curse the Mamelukes and bestow happiness on the Egyptian nation,"' Lausard read mockingly.

'There you have it. We are now bringers of happiness as well as liberators.' He balled up the proclamation and threw it into the gutter.

The men made their way back through the narrow streets and crowded bazaars and it seemed as if every house and building inside Alexandria had been used to billet French troops. Even the houses of the rich had been used by officers. Some of these dwellings had gardens, but other than that and gold ornamentation adorning some doors and windows there was little to distinguish them from the hovels inhabited by other residents of the city. Rumours about bubonic plague were circulating, of how the yearly epidemic had only just run its course, and it struck fear into the French.

'Perhaps Delacor is right, perhaps the Directory really *are* trying to get rid of us,' Rocheteau observed as they neared their billets close to the Rosetta Gate. 'First they nearly starve us to death during the sea voyage, we arrive in a country that doesn't want us and then we find out we could all catch the plague.'

'A man could be forgiven for thinking the odds were against him,' Giresse added.

'It's all a gamble, isn't it?' Lausard said. '*Life* is a gamble. It seems that *our* odds are shortening though.'

The conversation died as they saw Captain Milliere advancing towards them, forage cap protecting his head from the blistering sunshine. Like his men he was dressed in the single-breasted *surtout* and grey overalls the dragoons wore on campaign.

'You are cavalry again,' he informed them, smiling. 'The horses arrived from the landing site an hour ago. They are being inspected by the farriers now, but I warn you – they are in a bad way.'

'How bad, sir?' Lausard asked.

'Like us, they were hungry, thirsty and sick,' Milliere told him. 'At least forty from this regiment alone died during the journey. I'm surprised it wasn't more.'

The dragoons hurried off in the direction indicated by Milliere, who held up a hand to halt Lausard.

'A word,' he said quietly, snaking one arm around Lausard's shoulder. 'I have already received orders from General Bonaparte himself that the first columns of infantry are to leave here tomorrow. He does not want them advancing into terrain that has not been scouted. Now that our horses have arrived I can send out patrols. I want you in one of those patrols. Lieutenant Royere will command and he will need good NCOs to back him up. I know that you lost your rank in Italy.'

'General Bonaparte himself took it from me, sir,' Lausard said, a wan smile on his lips.

'Well, *I* am returning it. I have watched you, Lausard. During the voyage here and during the fighting you conducted yourself with honour. That honour should be rewarded. As from now, you are a sergeant again. General Bonaparte has approved the promotion.'

Lausard smiled.

'Go and find your horse, *Sergeant*,' said Milliere. 'Tell your companions.'

'I'm sure some of them will be delighted, sir,' said Lausard, saluting sharply. 'Thank you.'

'Perhaps you shouldn't thank me for sending you out into the desert,' the officer mused. 'God knows what you'll find.'

'I doubt if even God knows what we'll find out there, sir, and I still thank you.'

'And if you find death?'

Lausard didn't answer. He simply headed off to look for his horse.

Napoleon Bonaparte pointed at one of the many maps spread out on the table in the room then looked around at the officers who stood with him.

'Cairo,' the Corsican said. 'By marching upon it we will force the Mamelukes into a battle and that, gentlemen, is precisely what we must do. They would be content to avoid us until the conditions favour them. They would fight us on ground of their own choosing if we let them. We must force their hand. Marching on Cairo will do this. It will ensure that they confront us and, when they do, we will destroy them.'

'You seem very certain they will oppose us so quickly,' General Kléber said, his head still heavily bandaged from the wound he'd received the previous day.

'They will not allow us to take their capital city without a fight,' Bonaparte said assuredly. 'But that fight must come sooner rather than later. If we delay too long the Nile will flood, it will make troop movement difficult.'

'This desert makes most things difficult,' Dumas declared, brushing a fly from his cheek. Even in the relative stillness of the night the insects continued to fill the air in unwanted abundance.

'You shouldn't complain, Dumas.' Bonaparte smiled. 'At least you and your cavalry have horses now.'

'Most of them. Some will still have to fight on foot. The supply trains and the horse-drawn artillery are still without animals.'

'That is the concern of Caffarelli and Dommartin, not you,' Bonaparte reminded him. 'Just ensure that *your* men perform the tasks I assign them. They will be used mainly in a scouting role until other mounts can be acquired.'

'And how do you propose to *acquire* these additional mounts?' the cavalry general asked, a note of doubt in his tone. 'I have seen few horses of any quality here since we landed.'

'I have already met with thirteen Bedouin sheiks,' Bonaparte told him. 'For a cash payment they will supply us with three hundred horses and five hundred camels. In addition, they have also agreed to supply us with a further one thousand camels and camel drivers who we may hire for a negotiated price.'

'Camels?' Dumas said incredulously. 'You would use camels to draw artillery and supply trains?'

'I would use oxen if I thought it would help our cause here. Besides, camels are perfect. They are stronger and they will cope with the terrain better than our own horses.'

'Do you trust these Arabs enough to trade with them?' Dumas wanted to know.

'It isn't a matter of trust, it's a matter of necessity,' Bonaparte informed the mulatto. 'I need troops on the move as soon as possible. This entire campaign, as in Italy, relies on speed and on the concentration of our troops against the Mamelukes as quickly as possible.'

'What is your plan?' Kléber moved closer to the profusion of maps as he spoke.

'You, Kléber, will remain here with two thousand men to garrison the city,' Bonaparte instructed, his words spoken with enthusiasm. 'Desaix's division will march out tonight; they will be followed tomorrow by Bon's division, then by Reynier and Vial. Murat and Dugua will march on Rosetta in the north; they will then be supported on their march south by a flotilla that will patrol the Nile itself. The entire army will rendezvous at El Rahmaniya.'

'A march across open desert,' Dumas commented, looking at the maps.

'The distances are minimal,' Bonaparte protested. 'Desaix, Bon, Reynier and Vial's divisions will pass by way of Damanhur, just forty-five miles from here. It is another fifteen miles from Damanhur to El Rahmaniya. Three days' march at most.'

'I must confess, I share Dumas' concern about the terrain and the conditions,' Berthier offered. 'A three-day march across such hostile country is not an enticing prospect.'

'There are many places where the troops can stop en route,' Bonaparte said sternly. 'Such as Beydah or El Karioun. They can stock up on provisions and water there, I'm sure the locals will be only too happy to co-operate. They will see us as their saviours, why should they make our progress difficult? Furthermore, I do not want the local population antagonized during these marches. All supplies purchased and any labour performed will be paid for by cash, in local currency. Some of the gold and silver we brought from Malta has already been exchanged to facilitate this.'

'At a greatly disadvantageous rate, I might remind you,' Berthier said.

'What else were we to do? There was no mint in Alexandria and the loans we raised were insufficient for our needs. These people we go amongst are hostile, fanatical, distrustful and excitable. I want them to know that we French come as friends and liberators and as respectors of their culture and their country. Not as thieves and murderers like the Mamelukes who have oppressed them for so long. I swore to free them and that is what I shall do. The *fellahin* will be grateful to me. They will welcome us all with open arms once we have destroyed the Mamelukes.'

'Since when do invaded nations welcome their would-be conquerors?' Dumas demanded. 'They see through our intentions.'

'What they see is not important,' Bonaparte said. 'Perhaps they *do* fear us as conquerors but that fear is nothing compared to what we offer them. We offer them freedom from a yoke of tyranny they have worn for hundreds of years. If they distrust us now they will grow to respect us once the beys are removed from power. As I said, this must be done with utmost speed. The Mamelukes must be destroyed and Cairo must be taken within four weeks.'

'And what if that is impossible?' Kléber pressed.

The Corsican smiled. 'The word impossible has no place in my vocabulary. Nor should it have in yours. We have already pushed back the limits of human capability and this campaign has yet to begin in earnest. Glory awaits us. I suggest we do not keep it waiting.'

Seventeen

Lausard reined in his horse and patted its neck. Although the animal had been ridden for less than twenty minutes, a combination of the almost intolerable heat and the horse's poor condition meant that it was already well lathered. Lausard looked down and saw that the animal's tongue was lolling from its mouth and it was panting heavily, as desperate for water and food as were most of the men. Before leaving the outskirts of Alexandria at dawn the horse had eaten half a bag of oats and drunk a little, but none of the French mounts were on anything like normal rations and hadn't been since they'd first left Toulon.

Lausard tried to think back to the voyage, the storming of Malta and the constant fear of attack by Nelson's warships, but the entire episode seemed to have blurred in his mind. It felt like centuries since he had left his homeland. It crossed his mind that it must feel the same way for his horse. Struggling under the weight of its rider and his saddle and shabraque and equipment, thirsty and woefully short of sustenance, it was a miracle the animal could even walk let alone break into a trot, something he had urged it to do frequently during the journey from Alexandria. Lieutenant Royere, who was commanding the patrol, had given orders that the horses were not to be worked too hard because of their condition, an order the other eleven men in the patrol had been only too happy to comply with. Their mounts were in a similar, sometimes worse state. The animals ridden by Charvet and a tall Gascon named Tigana had suffered so badly that their ribs were showing, pushing against their normally sleek coats. But, like their riders, they fought their way through the sand and the heat, able to do nothing other than endure the discomfort.

It was Tigana who now drew his mount to a halt alongside Lausard, removing his helmet briefly to wipe sweat from his already sodden face. He was a thin-faced individual with sad eyes but his horsemanship was almost legendary within the regiment. He'd been raised on a farm on the outskirts of Paris, his parents having died in an outbreak of typhus in Gascony. Taken in by an older brother he had worked with horses on the farm for most of his life until they were seized by the Republican army, so desperately in need of remounts and food. Tigana had refused to let any horses be slaughtered for meat and had ended up in prison for 'wilfully obstructing the aims of the Republic'. When the army found itself in need of troops two years later, he had been taken from his cell in Bicetre and forced to fight, just as Lausard and most of the remainder of the regiment had been.

Lausard nodded a greeting to the trooper then looked out over the forbidding terrain.

The plains of Beheira formed an unending carpet of inhospitality to all who crossed them. Lausard failed to see how even the Bedouin warriors who called them home could exist in such an arid and desolate environment. All he could see was sand, great shifting expanses that seemed to shimmer in the haze. There were no roads, no recognized routes across this wilderness. He had no doubt that the Bedouin used trails, but how, he could only imagine. With the constant hot wind the sand covered anything stationary within hours, blowing around like stinging grains of hot shrapnel. Lausard brushed some from his nose and the corners of his mouth just as his horse snorted to clear its own nostrils of both sand and flies. The sergeant could feel the sweat soaking through his tunic, staining the material in a huge dark smear all across his shoulders and down to his kidneys. He had a little water left in his canteen but decided to wait a while before drinking it. He knew that a sip would not suffice; he would have to drain the entire contents to even come close to slaking his raging thirst.

'Have you found anything?' Lausard asked finally.

'Some camel droppings, a few tracks,' Tigana told him. 'But if you mean water . . .' He shook his head.

'Any sign of Bedouin?'

Again Tigana shook his head. 'Just the tracks. They were probably around but I didn't see them, though God knows where they could hide in the middle of this.' He waved a hand in the direction of the featureless sand. 'What about you, Sergeant, any luck?'

'There's supposed to be a village about a mile or two ahead,' Lausard informed him, pulling a map from his pocket and unfolding it a little. 'El Tantara. Perhaps there'll be food there for us *and* our horses.' Again he patted the neck of his mount. 'If there is, Desaix will want it for his men so we'd better get what we need first.' He folded up the map once more and flicked his reins, coaxing his horse forward.

The patrol was spread out across a frontage of about three to four miles, some thirty minutes' ride from General Desaix's marching troops, who were making their way even more slowly and tortuously across the burning sand. Other patrols of varying size had been sent further south, and some north towards Lake Idku and Aboukir, while the bulk of the dragoon regiment crossed the desert as part of Desaix's division. If anyone in Lieutenant Royere's patrol found provisions, water or caught sight of the enemy, they were to ride back to the column immediately with the information. But, Lausard thought, while the possibility of finding food and water in this barren wilderness was remote enough, the chance of finding any Mamelukes was even slimmer. They had no reason to attack when they could simply lure the French deeper and deeper into the desert. Indeed, the sergeant wondered if this campaign might even be settled *without* a battle. The sun and sand were probably as capable of destroying any army as were the Mamelukes. Why should they risk their lives in combat when the elements would do their work for them?

The sand dunes rose steeply and the two dragoons found their mounts were having difficulty making the climb. Lausard resisted the temptation to put spurs to his horse and the animal finally reached the top of the ridge, panting even more heavily. He wiped sweat from his eyes and looked down, shaking his head as he gazed at what lay before him.

'What's that?' asked Tigana, similarly perplexed by the sight.

'The village of El Tantara,' Lausard replied, his voice low.

There were fewer than a dozen small huts constructed of mud and straw, all deserted. Abandoned. Two or three palm trees grew close to one of them and there was what appeared to be a well, but not by any stretch of the imagination could this be called a village. Lausard and Tigana rode forward slowly, their eyes focusing on the well. When they reached it they both dismounted.

The wind seemed to have dropped a little and it was replaced instead by the loud, insistent buzzing of flies. Great, corpulent black ones that swarmed around the lip of the well as if it were an open wound. Lausard crossed to it as Tigana wandered into the nearest of the hovels. As Lausard drew nearer he recoiled from a particularly foul smell. A putrid odour that clogged in his nostrils and forced him to raise a hand to his face. He peered down into the well.

It was half filled with rocks and dirt but it also housed the remains of a camel. Lumps of rancid meat had been tossed down into the water with the other debris, ensuring that even if some fluid was extracted from the dirt it would be tainted and undrinkable.

Lausard stepped away from the poisoned well and glanced over to see Tigana walking from hut to hut. His inspection didn't take long. As he walked back towards Lausard he paused beside several piles of horse droppings, picking up one of the dung balls in his hand. He broke it open and glanced at the inside.

'Still moist. Whoever was here couldn't have left more than thirty minutes ago. This stuff dries quickly in the sun.'

'Bedouin,' Lausard murmured, noticing some camel

tracks nearby. 'I would ask you if you're sure but I usually make it a point of honour never to argue with a man about horseshit.'

Tigana chuckled.

Lausard pulled the map from his pocket once again and studied it.

'There are dozens of places marked on here between Alexandria and Beydah,' he mused. ''Towns and villages. But who's to say they're any bigger than this?' He glanced around at the crumbling mud huts.

'And there's the Bedouin to worry about,' Tigana said, his colour draining slightly. 'I heard what they did to some of those they took prisoner. They raped them, as men would rape women.'

'Who knows what goes through the minds of men who live on camels' milk all year round?' Lausard said, wandering back towards his horse. 'Come on, we'd better move. We're supposed to rendezvous in an hour with the rest of the patrol at Barada.'

'Let's hope they've had more luck than we have,' Tigana said, swinging himself into the saddle.

'I wouldn't bet on it,' Lausard said quietly. 'I really wouldn't.'

The village of Barada lay in a hollow, although, Lausard thought, it looked more like a collection of hovels. Even though the dunes on all four sides sheltered the dwellings from the hot wind, they also acted as a heat trap, snaring the rays of the blistering sun, reflecting them off the steep slopes of the dunes. It was difficult to breathe the air was so warm, and as Lausard and Tigana guided their horses down the steep slope towards the village, they both felt the air temperature increase. Tigana removed his helmet but the ferocity of the sun soon persuaded him to replace it. His exposed skin was already seared red – he didn't want to risk sunstroke as well.

Lausard heard voices, one of which he recognized as Rocheteau's. A second later he saw the corporal's horse tethered to a nearby palm tree, the animal pawing the sand with its hoof, shaking its head as the flies constantly buzzed around it.

The other voices, he soon saw, belonged to Delacor, Moreau and Fornac. They were gathered around one of the huts and, as he and Tigana drew nearer, he saw that they were standing before a wiry-looking Arab, who seemed relatively undisturbed by their threatening gestures and tone. He merely looked at each of their faces in turn as if trying to memorize some detail of their features.

'What's going on?' Lausard called and Rocheteau spun round, a smile flickering on his face.

'Alain, did you get lost?' he said. 'Come and see what we found here.' He nodded towards the Arab, who observed Lausard with the same cool indifference with which he regarded the other dragoons.

Lausard dismounted and wandered across to the little group.

'He saw us coming,' Rocheteau said, motioning towards the Arab. 'But he never attempted to run.'

'He's up to something,' Delacor hissed.

'Have you searched the village?' Lausard asked, glancing away from their captive for a second to run appraising eyes over Barada itself: fifteen or sixteen huts, clumps of palm trees and a well. It could have been any village anywhere in Egypt. There was nothing to distinguish it from any other.

'There's a little grain,' Rocheteau told him. 'That's it.'

'What about water?' Lausard pressed.

'The Bedouin have filled the well with camel shit and sand,' Rocheteau told his companion. 'We'll get nothing out of that.'

Delacor took a step towards the Arab and raised his hand as if to strike him, but the man remained defiant, standing motionless.

'Every well or cistern we found has been contaminated,' Delacor rasped. 'There's no water.'

'All the other villages we found were deserted too.' Fornac brushed a fly from his face as he spoke. 'They've all run off into the desert to hide.'

'Or prepare themselves,' Lausard murmured, looking once again at the captive Arab. 'So why didn't this one run?'

'Riders coming in,' Moreau called, pointing to the south of the village, and the dragoons turned to see six more horsemen, led by Lieutenant Royere, making their way towards Barada.

'A prisoner?' Royere mused, dismounting.

'We should shoot him here and now,' Delacor suggested.

'We have no reason to kill him,' the officer said. 'Besides, he may be of use to us. We found tracks to the south-west, camels and horses. Hundreds of them. It's a Bedouin raiding party but much larger than any of us could have expected, and they've got between us and the main column. We're cut off.'

'What do we do?' Sonnier said worriedly. 'They'll destroy us.'

'We could try to make it back to the column, but if they catch us out in the open they will destroy us.'

'Which direction were they moving?' Lausard wanted to know. 'They might have been moving *towards* the army, away from us.'

'They were heading straight for here,' Charvet told the sergeant.

'So do we try to outrun them, stand and fight, or surrender? Perhaps our friend here could act as a go-between.' Royere motioned towards the Arab.

'I'm not giving myself up to those animals,' Tigana said. 'I'd rather die fighting.'

'We should take a chance and try to rejoin the column,' Sonnier offered. 'Some of us will make it.'

'If we surrender they might spare us,' Chatillo said. 'Prisoners have already been traded. Some of the other men who were captured were returned for ransom.'

'And what if the army won't pay a ransom?' Delacor snapped. 'What then? I say we fight the bastards.'

'I'll kill myself rather than be taken prisoner,' Tigana added.

'We haven't got a chance, we don't even know how many of them there are,' Chatillo persisted.

'We have to make a run for it, they won't get us all,' Sonnier persisted.

'I will not be responsible for the deaths of these men if I can avoid it,' Royere said. 'Running across the desert on tired horses is a sure enough way of getting us all killed. What do you say, Lausard?'

'Stand and fight them, Lieutenant. I for one would rather die with a sword in my hand than running from men such as this.'

'And I,' Rocheteau echoed.

'If only we knew their strength,' Royere mused.

'There are about two hundred of them.'

The men looked round in bewilderment at the source of the words. The Arab stood unflinchingly before them, amused at their reaction.

'They passed close to here about an hour ago,' he continued.

'You speak our language,' Royere exclaimed.

'I speak many languages. Yours, English, Arabic and my own.'

'What is your name?' Royere pressed.

'Karim.'

'Why are you not with your people?'

'I *have* no people any more. I am not a true Egyptian. I am Circassian, brought to this country by the Mamelukes when I was ten. Taught to ride and to fight by them, educated by them but enslaved by them until I escaped when I was eighteen. I have lived in the desert for the past four years, an outcast among people who think of me as one of their own. But I do not belong among them; I will not be a slave to any man.'

'Whom do you owe your loyalty to?' Lausard wanted to know.

'To myself and my beliefs. I owe no loyalty to *any* man.'

'He's dangerous,' Delacor said sharply. 'I say we should kill him. How do we know any of what he's saying is true?'

'If it were lies what would it matter?' Karim said. 'There was no need for me to speak at all and yet I chose to tell you the strength of the Bedouin who will come to attack you. I don't ask you to trust me, simply to listen to me.'

'What makes you think the Bedouin will attack us?' Royere asked.

'If you found *their* tracks then you can be sure they will

have found *yours*. They will destroy you because you are trespassers on their lands and because they have been commanded to fight you.'

'Commanded by whom?' Royere pressed. 'I heard that many tribes were to help us. They were supposed to be our allies.'

'The ulemas and sheiks of Cairo have sent word to the tribes to fight you. They have been called to wage a holy war against you invaders and they will,' Karim informed the men. 'If they can destroy you in ones or twos, twenties or thirties, in hundreds or thousands, they will.'

'And when the time comes, who will you fight with?' Lausard asked.

'You and your leader came to liberate Egypt, to free it from the rule of the Mamelukes. I have nothing but hatred for the Mamelukes and I feel no allegiance to the Bedouin. I will fight with you against whoever opposes you.'

'You can't trust this bastard, Lieutenant,' Delacor persisted. 'As soon as our backs are turned he'll either run or stick a knife in us.'

Royere regarded Karim evenly then looked at Lausard.

'I think we need all the help we can get,' said the sergeant.

'I agree. Arm yourself, Karim. You fight with us now.'

Eighteen

In the burning heat of the afternoon sun the dragoons worked furiously, pausing every thirty minutes to sip at water that had been carefully rationed to one cup per man. The desire to gulp down the precious fluid was overwhelming but they knew that they must try to control the raging thirst that tormented them, to concentrate on their labours in the hope that they might forget their discomfort. It did little to help. Toiling in just their breeches they felt the sun scorching their flesh, burning them with its fiercesome heat and sucking the very breath from their lungs.

Karim had found a few tools: an axe, a couple of large knives, a scythe and some rudimentary chisels. Tabor had been given the axe, his prodigious strength having been employed to chop down several of the palm trees growing around the village. As he brought each one crashing down, Tigana and Carbonne dragged it to its appointed place where it was split several more times into long shafts; both ends were sharpened and driven into the sand with about three or four feet of wickedly pointed wood sticking menacingly out.

Lengths of rope were tied around other palm trees, the ends loose and trailing back into the collection of hovels.

Fornac was carefully loading carbines and sharing out ammunition, the prepared weapons laid upon a shabraque to prevent them clogging with sand.

Moreau was minding the horses, ensuring that they were tethered in the centre of the village. He fed them what little grain had been found in Barada then, that done, he helped Sonnier, who was busy sharpening swords and bayonets against a stone.

Rocheteau and Lausard dragged a wagon into position and, with Chatillo's help, overturned it, placing bags of sand behind it to act as a firing platform.

Charvet was sharpening smaller, thinner lengths of wood to be used as additional weapons if the fighting became too desperate or if the dragoons' bayonets weren't up to the task. Made from easily malleable metal, Charvet had seen them bent easily by strong men. As he whittled points he tried not to think about the possibility of hand-to-hand fighting, although if it came to if he would be ready. Karim joined him and began sharpening pieces of wood using a short knife he took from his belt. Also attached to the thin strip of leather was a curved scabbard containing, Charvet assumed, a matching sword, the angle of the blade from hilt to tip even more pronounced than that of a light cavalryman. Karim finally noticed the Frenchman's interest and drew the weapon.

The blade was wafer thin and looked as if it would break at the slightest contact with anything solid. Karim offered it to Charvet, who was surprised at its lightness.

'How do you cut anything with this?' he asked, hefting the blade.

'It is the sharpness of the blade that matters, not its weight. A sharp sword will cut in any hands.'

'Is that the kind of sword the Bedouin use?'

The question came from Lieutenant Royere, who was strolling towards the two men accompanied by Lausard and Rocheteau.

'They are not skilled fighters,' Karim told him. 'This weapon is the weapon of the Mamelukes. One of their leaders is said to be able to decapitate an ox with one blow of a sword like this.'

Lausard took the weapon from Charvet and inspected it, touching his fingertip to the blade. He applied no pressure and yet the skin on the pad of his middle finger still split, although not deeply enough to draw blood.

'And you know how to use this?' he asked, returning the blade to Karim.

'I was taught from the age of ten. The men who taught me were masters of the sword.'

'Your admiration for them is commendable,' Royere noted. 'I trust it will not interfere with your ability to fight them.'

'The men who are coming here to destroy us now are not the men who taught me,' Karim reminded him. 'Those who will come here are the true people of this country who despise the Mamelukes as surely as I do, but they would destroy me as well as you. Do not fear for my loyalty.'

'Why will they want to kill you when you're one of them?' Lausard queried.

'*Like* them, but not one of them,' Karim corrected him. 'Now, do you wish to continue arguing with me or would you perhaps be better employed readying yourselves for the Bedouin attack?'

Lausard smiled and slapped the Circassian's shoulder.

'The traps are set at the approaches to the village,' said Rocheteau, turning to look at Royere. 'And all the weapons are ready.'

'How will the Bedouin come at us?' Royere addressed Karim.

'They will try to ride you down. It is all they know.' Karim looked around at the dunes that rose on all four sides of Barada. 'They may come from just one direction, they may attack from all four sides at once. It is impossible to say what they will do.'

'The stakes and ropes will slow them down,' Lausard mused. 'We need concentrated fire against them on those parts of the village that are not protected.'

'Concentrated fire,' murmured Fornac, who had joined them. 'From twelve men? We haven't got a chance.'

'Enough of that talk,' snapped Royere. 'We don't know how far away the rest of the army is. General Desaix and his men might even reach us before we are attacked.'

Lausard caught the officer's eye and saw the lack of conviction in his expression.

'What's that?' Rocheteau murmured.

It sounded like the sea breaking on the beach. A low rolling rumble growing steadily in volume. It was coming from the north.

'Can you feel it?' the corporal continued. 'The ground is shaking.'

'Take your positions,' shouted Royere and the dragoons rushed to retrieve their weapons, five or six of them scurrying to the firing platform behind the overturned wagon. Sonnier took up position on the roof of one of the mud huts, his carbine trained in the direction of the steadily growing noise.

Lausard and Rocheteau were close to the wagon, sheltering behind more sandbags. Nearby, Tabor held one end of the thick rope strung between two palm trees about fifty yards from the makeshift rampart. In his other hand he held his sword.

Royere checked his pistols, jamming both into his belt.

The rumbling grew louder and now the men could also hear yelling, the snorting of camels and the neighing of horses. All eyes turned towards the crest of the northern dunes.

Moreau crossed himself.

Lausard felt his heart thudding heavily against his ribs.

Rocheteau swallowed hard, a bead of perspiration trickling down the side of his face.

Tigana gripped his carbine more tightly, whispering softly to himself as he squinted down the sight.

Carbonne pressed one palm to the sand, feeling the heat but also the incredible vibrations that shuddered all the way up his arm. He closed his eyes tightly for a second, trying to control his breathing, although it was difficult to suck any air from the scorching heat that surrounded him.

Lausard watched the crest, saw dust clouds rising, heard the thundering of hooves growing ever louder, then, finally, he saw them. The full mass of the Bedouin seemed to reach the crest at once. A great seething swarm of men and animals, the leading riders roaring at the tops of their voices, both to urge on their mounts and also to frighten their enemies. The Bedouin were an impressive sight, pouring up and over the crest like a tide, some of them waving spears, others brandishing swords and even pistols. He pulled his carbine more tightly into his shoulder and waited for the order.

Royere was pacing slowly back and forth, watching as the Arabs flooded down the reverse slope and galloped towards the collection of hovels that formed Barada. They were five hundred yards away and closing rapidly, spear points gleaming in the sun, their tightly packed group spreading out into several ragged lines. But there was no order to the charge and Royere wondered if the horses and camels might even be blown by the time they reached the French.

Four hundred yards. And they came with the same frenzied speed.

One group had veered off to the left slightly and Lausard wondered if they were going to try to hit the French in the flank. He nudged Rocheteau and Tigana and they joined him as he scuttled to a position about twenty yards to the right of a clump of palm trees. It was then that he realized the riders were heading for the rope strung between the trees, at present hidden from their view as they charged.

'Tabor,' the sergeant called out. 'The rope. Tie it off. Now.'

The big man obeyed, hurrying to wind the thick hemp around a tree near him to secure it.

With the Arabs dashing towards the palm trees the now-tightened rope suddenly sprung up, only feet from their speeding horses. Unable to stop, they went crashing into it, the rope taking the animals around the forelock. It was enough to bring a dozen of them down in a flailing heap, and Lausard looked on in satisfaction as two of the Arabs were crushed beneath their mounts and another smashed in the face by a wildly kicking horse's hooves.

'Fire!' Lausard shouted, and he and his two comrades brought down another horse and two Arabs.

The rest jumped to their feet and ran.

The blast of muskets caused both Frenchmen and Arabs alike to glance in the direction of the first contact, but the howling Bedouin continued charging towards the rest of the dragoons.

From his perch up on the roof of one of the houses, Sonnier took aim and fixed a tall Arab riding a camel in his sights. The man was still two hundred yards away but he would make a good target once in range.

Lausard pulled another cartridge from his cartouche, bit off the end, held the ball in his mouth, dropped powder in, spat the ball after it then rammed down wadding. The taste of powder filled his mouth as he swung the carbine up to his shoulder and waited as the enemy came within one hundred yards.

They were nearing the wooden stakes. Covered carefully with palm leaves, the vicious spikes were invisible to the onrushing riders as they hurtled closer and closer.

'Ready!' Royere shouted, raising his voice above the rampaging Arabs.

Those at the front had reached the spikes.

Too late, they realized what lay beneath the concealing leaves.

The razor-sharp points seemed to erupt upwards from the sand, as if pushed from beneath by invisible hands.

The leading riders tried to turn their mounts to avoid the trap but the sheer momentum of those behind pushed them forward on to the deadly spears.

Lausard watched as the leading horses were impaled on the wooden stakes and their agonized shrieks began to fill the air. Men, unhorsed as their mounts were skewered, fell beneath the churning hooves of those following. One man tried to pull his mount around, away from the points, but the animal pulled up sharply and sent the rider spinning from its back. He screamed loudly as the stake pierced his body. Others shared the same fate, catapulted over their horses' necks to be impaled on the stakes. The sand all around began to turn red and those Arabs behind were held up by the crush of dying men and horses, frozen in one place, unable to either attack or retreat.

'Fire!' Royere bellowed and the dragoons opened up.

A loud explosion of musket fire rolled over the scene, the pan-flashes and muzzle bursts followed immediately by choking clouds of sulphurous smoke.

More Arabs went down, struck by the lead balls and the dragoons frantically began to re-load, spitting bullets down barrels, ramming them home with wadding, then preparing to fire again, choking on the stench of their own gunpowder, spitting the black grains as they tasted charcoal and saltpetre. By now, some of the Bedouin had managed to either bypass the confusion or extricate themselves from the bloodied mess, and they were now hurtling towards the hovels where the French sheltered. Another volley of fire brought more crashing down, horses rolling on riders, wounded men trying to crawl away bleeding their life into the scorching sand.

Then the first riders reached the French. Lausard swung his carbine like a club, slamming it into an Arab and knocking him from his horse. As the man struggled to his feet, Lausard drove his bayonet into the man's chest twice, then turned to face another Bedouin, who was coming at him with a large, flat-bladed sword. Lausard pulled free his own sword and blocked the Bedouin's first strike, then he shot out a hand and pulled at the horse's bridle, the sudden shock causing the animal to rear. It flung its rider to the sand, and as he tried to get up, Lausard thrust his sword into the man's throat.

Royere fired both his pistols simultaneously at an attacking Arab, both balls striking the man in the chest. He toppled from his horse, the terrified animal sweeping past.

Fornac turned to deal with one Bedouin, exposing his back to another. The Frenchman shrieked as the second Arab drove a long spear into his kidney, forcing the weapon on with such force that it erupted from the Frenchman's stomach. He dropped to his knees clutching at the bloodied point. Lausard saw that the Arab was now defenceless and stabbed him in the side, hauling him from his horse, then driving the blade into his face to finish the job.

Karim stood firm as a Bedouin bore down on him. He ducked under the Arab's swipe then spun round and, with one savage blow, hacked off the Bedouin's hand. The appendage spun into the air, spurting blood, and the Arab rode off shrieking. Sonnier shot him as he swept past, the body landing with a thud on the sand.

Lausard ducked as he heard a bullet whistle past his ear. It struck the wagon close to him.

He turned to see three Arabs firing at him from horseback.

'Those are Charlevilles.' Rocheteau was beside him. 'They're shooting at us with our own guns.'

'They must have taken them from prisoners,' Lausard observed, keeping low as another shot smacked into the wood close to him.

Royere was reloading his pistols when he shouted in pain and went down in an untidy heap, clutching his leg.

Lausard and Karim rushed across to him, seeing immediately that the officer was bleeding from a wound just above his knee. Lausard checked the entry wound and was relieved to see a larger, more ragged hole at the back of Royere's thigh.

'You're lucky, it went straight through.' The sergeant began ripping at the officer's breeches, exposing the wound more fully, pulling small pieces of material from the ragged edges with his fingers, waving away the flies that buzzed round the bloodied hole. Karim saw that one of the Bedouin had dismounted from his limping horse and was running straight at Lausard and the wounded officer, sword brandished above his head, yelling insanely. The Circassian stepped into the Bedouin's path, swinging his scimitar up to parry the blow. As the Arab prepared to strike, Karim lashed out. With a blow combining devastating power and effortless expertise, he caught the attacker just below the chin. The razor-sharp steel of the scimitar sheared through bone and flesh with ease and the Arab's severed head spun into the air, propelled by a geyser of blood. The body remained upright for a moment then hit the ground with a thud.

Royere began crawling towards one of the hovels, leaving a trail of blood behind him. Lausard snatched up one of his pistols, handing the other one to the officer, who was gesturing towards three Bedouin riding towards the village at break-neck speed.

'Rocheteau!' Lausard shouted, drawing the corporal's attention to the onrushing horsemen.

The corporal tore the end off his cartridge, poured in powder, spat the ball in, rammed the wadding and raised his carbine, desperate to get a shot off in time. So eager that he realized he'd forgotten to remove his ramrod from the barrel. As he fired, the metal stave was shot out of the barrel like a spear. It embedded itself in the leading Arab's chest and he screamed, clutching at the metal rod as he toppled from his horse. The other two wheeled their horses and turned away, one of them struck in the back by a bullet.

The men saw that all the Bedouin were turning, fleeing, riding back over the bodies of their own dead and wounded, leaving their comrades impaled on the wooden spikes, on the blood-drenched sand or slumped beneath the bodies of their dead mounts.

Lausard helped Royere to the shade offered by one of the mud hovels.

'You take command,' Royere said breathlessly, hastily wrapping a piece of cloth around his injured leg.

'You're going to be fine, you've just lost some blood,' Lausard assured him.

Royere smiled and raised hands covered by the crimson fluid. 'I can see that,' he said quietly. 'I'm giving you an order, Lausard. Take command. Do whatever you have to do to save these men and, if you have to get out of here and leave the wounded behind, then do it.' He gripped the sergeant's arm tightly. 'And I mean *all* the wounded.'

Lausard looked down at the officer's bullet-torn leg.

'Alain, they've gone,' Rocheteau shouted. 'All of them.'

'But they'll be back, won't they?' Lausard looked at Karim.

The Circassian nodded slowly.

'One dead, five wounded including the lieutenant,' Rocheteau reported. 'I've told Sonnier and Tigana to bury Fornac.'

'How bad are the wounded?' Lausard asked, glancing

across to where Sonnier and Tigana were scrabbling in the sand, creating a makeshift grave for their dead companion.

Rocheteau shrugged. 'Moreau was kicked by a horse. Charvet has a cut across the arm, Chatillo has a bullet wound in the side and Carbonne lost the top of a finger. They'll live. They can fight on. What about Lieutenant Royere?'

'We have to get him out of here before infection sets in,' Lausard said, walking slowly across the sand. 'Karim stopped the bleeding and patched him up well enough, but he won't last too long without proper attention and food and water.'

'That goes for all of us, Alain,' the corporal reminded him. 'None of us have drunk anything for over fifteen hours.' He looked up at the sky. 'This stinking weather. This stinking desert.'

'The Bedouin know our strength now, they'll attack again. Karim is sure of it.'

'Do you trust him, Alain?'

'Why shouldn't I?'

'He's one of them.'

'He's no more one of them than any of us, besides, you saw the way he fought. He knows this desert and its ways, Rocheteau. He may yet be our saviour.'

Rocheteau looked puzzled.

'If we sit and wait for the Bedouin to attack again we could all die of heatstroke, hunger or thirst,' Lausard explained. 'We can't outrun them in open desert, they'll cut us to pieces. There'll be no relief from Desaix's column because no one even knows we're here. As far as Desaix is concerned we're still scouting, or perhaps he thinks we've run off to find water or food for ourselves, or just been killed by the Arabs. Who knows? What I'm trying to tell you is we have to reach the column. Someone has to ride back to Desaix and bring help here, to relieve us. Someone has to ride across the desert and return with reinforcements. I'm going to send Karim and two other men. The column can't be more than half a day's ride from here.'

'That Arab bastard will run off and join the Bedouin,' Delacor said, who had overheard part of the conversation.

'No he won't,' Lausard said. 'You'll be there to make sure he doesn't. I'm sending you with him. You and Tigana.'

'And what do *we* do?' Rocheteau wanted to know.

'We hold the Bedouin here until they return with extra men; I doubt if they'll attack at night. As soon as the sun goes down, Delacor, you, Karim and Tigana will ride for the column. Understood?'

Delacor nodded slowly.

Lausard and Rocheteau continued walking.

'Do you think they'll make it?' the corporal said.

'Bonaparte promised us all six acres of land, didn't he?' Lausard mused. 'Well, if they don't bring help then you and I won't get six acres, we'll get six *feet* of Egyptian sand.'

Nineteen

The night was pitch black and other than one small fire in the centre of Burada, the dragoons were without light. Hemmed in on all sides by a sea of gloom they surrounded the dull yellow light of the fire as if seeking refuge in its dancing flames. They certainly didn't need the heat; the raging temperatures of the daylight hours scarcely dropped with the onset of night and the air was still humid and stifling.

Lausard walked to the rim of the dunes and peered out into the desert. Beyond he saw what at first looked like hundreds of fireflies but which he then realized were the fires of the Bedouin tribesmen, waiting until morning to relaunch their attack. Lausard had no idea how many of them there were but every so often, when the wind was blowing in the right direction, he could hear excited chatter and the guttural sounds of camels.

Judging by the number of fires it appeared that more tribesmen had joined those who had attacked. Lausard wondered how many of the desert warriors would come at them the following day.

'How will you get through?' he asked Karim, as he approached the Circassian. 'It looks as if they're everywhere.'

Karim nodded gently and swung himself on to his horse's back, Delacor and Tigana following his example.

'Give me one of your bullets.' Karim held out his hand to Lausard.

The sergeant looked puzzled but reached into his cartouche and did as he was asked, watching as Karim bit off the ball and threw away the remains.

'Do as I do,' Karim said, showing that he still had the ball in his mouth. 'Chew it. This will stimulate saliva, it will help your thirst a little.'

'You have six hours before first light,' Lausard told them.

'Then so have you,' Karim echoed. 'The Bedouin will not attack before dawn.'

The three horsemen led their mounts down the reverse slope of the dunes and within seconds they were lost in the almost palpable blackness of the night. Lausard turned and headed back towards Barada, walking past the corpses of dead Arabs that had already swelled like overripe melons in the blistering heat. The stench of death hung heavy in the air and, all around, the flies swarmed over the banquet: men, horses, puddles of dried blood. Come first light, Lausard knew that there would be much more for them to feast on.

Six hours. Would it be enough?

'We'll never make it to Desaix's column if we have to walk the horses the whole way,' Delacor said irritably.

'Keep your voice down,' Tigana ordered, looking around him in the darkness.

Karim remained silent, guiding his horse across the sand, occasionally glancing at the myriad camp fires of the Bedouin. In places they seemed only a few hundred yards away, in others it appeared as if they were way off in the distance, thousands of miles across the black desert like grounded stars.

'When do we start to ride?' Delacor persisted.

'When I say it is safe,' Karim told him. 'Are you so eager to die? If we begin hurrying the horses now the Bedouin will hear their harnesses, they will be upon us in seconds.'

'How do we know you're not leading us into a trap, anyway? You're just like them.'

'I am nothing like them, do you find it so hard to understand?' Karim snapped at Delacor. 'I told you, I am Circassian. My home is in the Caucasus. I was brought here, like many of my countrymen, by the Mamelukes. Every Mameluke has two man-servants, *serradji*, and I was to be raised as one. I was educated, instructed in the fighting arts, taught to ride but I was still a slave. I ran away when I was sixteen and I've been living in the desert ever since.'

'Why don't the Mamelukes just train the Egyptians to be their slaves?' Tigana wanted to know.

'They use the *fellahin*, the local peasants, as infantry but they afford them none of the honour that goes with their own caste,' Karim explained. 'They have harems full of Egyptian, Nubian, Abyssinian, Georgian, Armenian or Circassian women but they rarely have children by them and marry only their own kind. Mameluke wives often cause themselves to abort to preserve their youthful looks and keep their hold over their husbands, so the Mamelukes buy boys from the Caucasus and train them as warriors and *serradji*. I would not be a slave to those men.'

'Very noble,' Delacor said acidly. 'These Mamelukes, do they fight alongside the Bedouin?'

'The Mamelukes look down on all except their own,' Karim said. 'The Bedouin are ungovernable, their fighting abilities are limited and of little use to the Mamelukes.'

'If these Mamelukes are such great fighters, why don't they confront us?' Delacor asked. 'Why are they still running from us? Why haven't we even *seen* one of them yet?'

'They are waiting for the right moment,' Karim said. 'They know that the longer your army is in Egypt, the greater the likelihood it will crumble to thirst, hunger and disease. Three useful allies. When you and the rest of your army are on your knees, they will attack then.'

Tigana was still chewing the bullet as he'd been ordered, the taste of lead strong in his mouth. However, it seemed to be having the desired effect and for the first time in more than a day his mouth wasn't intolerably dry.

'Don't you know of any water holes around here, Karim?' he asked. 'You've lived here long enough.'

'There are usually one or two wells or cisterns to each village. The Bedouin have poisoned most of them, as you know. The closest are at Beydah and El Karioun, in the opposite direction to that in which we travel.'

'There must be some nearby,' Delacor pressed. 'We can't—'

Karim raised a hand to silence him.

Immediately, all three men halted their horses.

About twenty yards to their left they heard voices babbling excitedly in Arabic.

The men remained motionless in the saddle. Delacor stroked his horse's neck gently as the animal tossed its head from side to side, worried the sound of the bridle buckles would be heard in the stillness.

The voices seemed to be growing closer. Then, suddenly, they were gone.

Karim sat motionless for a moment longer then dug his heels into his pony and the animal began moving across the sand once again, followed by the two dragoons. Even though they could barely see where they were going, the men were aware they were descending a slope, the dunes closing around them.

'We follow this dry river bed for another two miles,' Karim informed them. 'Then we ride like the devil to find your general.'

The four Bedouin suddenly loomed up towards the trio of men as if they'd risen from the sand itself. Large men armed with swords and spears, they flung themselves at the dragoons and their escort, one of them knocking Delacor from his saddle. As Delacor hit the sand he saw more of the tribesmen emerging from the blackness, then suddenly he felt a crashing impact against the back of his head and he slipped into unconsciousness.

Karim and Tigana were also taken by surprise, neither man having the chance to draw his sword before the Bedouin overran them. As Karim was pulled from his horse, fists and feet raining down on him, he had one brief, terrifying thought: the Bedouin wanted them alive. He could see Delacor's unconscious form being dragged by three of the tribesmen and Tigana trying to fend off blows until his resistance was ended by a blow across the forehead. Karim watched as one of the Bedouin lifted the dragoon's discarded brass helmet like a trophy and tried to put it on over his own headdress, but another Arab snatched it off and ran away into the desert pursued by the first man. Some of the tribesmen were already pulling at the buttons on the dragoons' tunics, cutting them free with knives when they couldn't tear them off. Two more were trying to pull off Delacor's boots, squabbling as they wrenched at the leather, one of them eventually freeing the right boot and whooping triumphantly as he held it aloft.

Karim saw faces close to his own, smelled rancid breath and heard curses. He felt hands against his skin as the Bedouin inspected its roughness compared to that of the captured Frenchmen. Threats were shouted at him in Arabic and a globule of mucus hit him just below the left eye, running down his cheek like a sticky tear. He felt the point of a dagger being pressed against his side, another slashing open his silk robe.

Karim was dragged along and soon he noticed the night was illuminated by the glow of dozens of camp fires. He saw dozens of Bedouin rising from their positions around these fires, all eager to inspect the captives as they were dragged towards a large tent in the centre of the camp.

Both of Tigana's boots had been taken by now, as had his tunic, the buttons from his shirt and his helmet. Delacor was naked but for his torn breeches, and even these were being tugged from him as the Bedouin hurled him, unconscious, into the tent. Karim watched as three or four of their captors rolled the dragoon on to his stomach, one laughing as he caressed his buttocks. The Arabs nearby were beginning to pull their robes open to reveal their nakedness beneath.

Karim had known what was to happen from the moment they were captured but only now did he attempt to fight, suddenly wriggling free of the three men who held him. He struck one hard in the face, splitting his lip, a final act of defiance. The stock of a musket was slammed into his temple and he went down heavily, enveloped by the merciful oblivion of unconsciousness.

All three men were naked when they awoke. Arms bound behind their backs they lay on the hot sand inside the tent, emerging one by one from their own private darkness.

Delacor was the first to awake, the throbbing in his head matched only by an even more excruciating pain around his groin and anus. He winced as he tried to roll over, looking across at the lifeless forms of Karim and Tigana. He gritted his teeth and tried to twist his hands free of the rope that had been bound so tightly around his wrists that it shaved away skin at every movement. He cursed under his breath, aware not only of his pain but of the musky, sickly stench inside the tent. He managed to shuffle, worm-like, towards Karim and butted the Circassian's shoulder in an attempt to rouse him. After a second or two Karim slowly opened his eyes and glanced across at the Frenchman. Delacor grunted in pain again as he moved.

Tigana was beginning to stir and he too felt the same searing pain around his groin and buttocks. He moaned as he tried to sit up, his stomach contracting. For a second he thought he was going to be sick, but the feeling passed.

It was still dark outside the tent, the interior lit only by a battered oil lamp. Tigana could see what remained of their uniforms lying in an untidy heap near the exit. All the buttons had been ripped off, the collars torn away. They were little more than rags.

'They're going to kill us, aren't they?' he said, his voice a low guttural rasp.

'Eventually,' Karim told him. 'We have to get away.'

'And how do you propose we do that?' Delacor said. 'We're miles from help, they'd ride us down even if we managed to get out of this stinking tent. And if we did get away, where do we go? Further into the desert? Back to Barada to be slaughtered?'

'Sergeant Lausard sent us out to find the main army,' Tigana reminded his colleague.

'I know that, you idiot, but would you mind telling me how we're going to do that trussed up here like turkeys. And I bet those bastards haven't finished with us yet, have they?'

Karim shook his head. 'That might be our chance,' he said, looking towards the flap of the tent. 'If we can be ready for them when they come back we might be able to get away.'

'If we can get free of these ropes,' Delacor reminded him. 'But even then we have no weapons, no horses. It's impossible.'

Karim ignored him, concentrating instead on flexing his wrists within the tight bonds. He winced as the rope chafed his skin, drawing blood in several places. Tigana offered his bound wrists to Delacor, who shuffled closer and clamped his teeth around the rope, chewing frenziedly. His mouth, already parched, grew even drier as he chewed at the rope and he made little headway. But then he spotted a loose length of the knot and began pulling at it frenziedly, ignoring the blood that streamed from his gums, almost grateful for the lubrication it allowed him. Grunting, he tugged harder and the rope began to give. Tigana twisted his wrists and the tightly fastened bonds gave way slightly. The gap grew wider until, finally, he could slip one hand free. He held it up triumphantly, blood staining his wrist.

'Untie me.' Delacor rolled on to his stomach.

Tigana undid the rope with relative ease.

Karim had also freed himself.

'Come on, let's get out of here,' Delacor urged.

'No, we must wait for the Bedouin to return,' Karim instructed.

'Return and do what? Kill us? Or even worse? I have learned that there are some things worse than death.'

Karim heard the sound of excited chattering outside the tent and he signalled to his companions to be silent. All three men slid their hands back into their bonds, ensuring that they could free themselves easily when the time came. They sat up, watching as three Bedouin entered the tent, led by a large man with a bushy beard who walked straight across to Karim and spat in his face, snarling something at him. The Circassian looked on impassively as the Arab drew a long jewelled dagger from his belt and held it beneath his chin, the point digging into the soft flesh there. He rasped something in Arabic and gestured towards the two Frenchmen.

'What did he say?' Tigana demanded.

'He asked me why I ride with Infidels,' Karim answered, never taking his eyes from the bearded Arab. He spoke quickly in Arabic, his expression never changing. The Bedouin all looked at him angrily, another of them taking a step towards him, also drawing a dagger. Delacor and Tigana looked on in horror and Tigana slid one hand from his loosened restraints.

Karim and the Bedouin were still speaking to each

other, their voices occasionally rising in volume and the two Frenchmen could only guess at what was being said. The bearded Arab was gesturing towards them now even though his fiercesome gaze was fixed on Karim. Another Bedouin moved towards the Frenchmen, kicking out at Delacor with his foot, rolling him over so that his face was in the sand. He ran a hand over Delacor's buttocks and shouted something at Karim.

'What are you saying to them?' Delacor shouted as he felt the Arab's hands on him. 'I won't let these bastards touch me again.'

Delacor smelled fetid breath close to his face. 'Karim!' he bellowed.

'Strike now,' the Circassian ordered.

Delacor slipped his hands free and grabbed the Arab by the throat, forcing him down on to the sand, the sheer speed of the attack taking the Bedouin by surprise. Delacor grabbed the back of his enemy's head with one hand and his chin with the other and, with one expert movement, wrenched the Arab's head hard to one side, the sound of his breaking neck reverberating inside the tent. He immediately pulled a dagger from the dead man's belt and turned on the next Arab, catching him by the hair and sliding the blade into his neck just below his ear.

Karim brought his foot up into the groin of the bearded Arab, the impact forcing the breath from the Bedouin. He fell forward and Karim slipped the rope around his neck, tugging on both ends with all his strength. He straddled the Arab, feeling his body shudder as the life was throttled from him.

Meanwhile, Tigana caught the other Bedouin by the arm and wrestled him to the ground, his hand closing around a sharp stone just beneath the surface of the sand. The Gascon gripped it in his fist, held the Bedouin's head down and rained blows into his face, pounding away with the stone until the Arab's visage was reduced to a bloody pulp. Tigana finally fell forward, exhausted, lying on the sand next to his dead foe, the rock still in his now crimson fist.

'Put on their clothes,' Karim instructed, already tugging the dead Arabs' garments from them.

Delacor seemed not to hear, kicking frenziedly at the body of one of the dead Bedouin, snarling incoherently with each savage impact. Karim watched him for a second or two then gently touched his arm.

'We have to get out of here before others come.'

Delacor turned to him with blank eyes.

'Now,' Karim persisted. 'There isn't much time.'

Delacor drove one last angry kick into the face of one of the dead Bedouin. Breathing heavily from the exertion, he tore off the Arab's clothes and wrapped them around himself as Karim instructed.

'We'll never get out of here alive, they'll see our faces,' Tigana said, pulling a sash around his waist.

'You saw how dark it is. They won't be expecting us to have escaped, they're not going to question us. They won't even see our faces in the night,' Karim said with more assurance than the Frenchmen enjoyed.

'What were you saying to them to make them so angry?' Delacor wanted to know. 'Were you trying to get us killed?'

'They were going to kill us anyway,' Karim told him. 'I told them they were all cowards and sons of camels who would be blown to the four winds like the sand in a storm.'

'What about these bastards?' Delacor pointed to the bodies.

'Leave them. We have to go now,' Karim said, watching as Tigana gathered up their ravaged uniforms and what remained of their equipment. Karim was surprised to see his scimitar on the sand beneath the green jackets. Tigana passed it to him and he hefted it before him proudly.

'Why did they take our swords but leave yours?' the Gascon asked.

'They have seen weapons like mine before, your swords are unusual to them. Now let's get out of here before it's too late. And when we get outside both of you keep quiet, no matter what. I will speak for all of us.'

Delacor gripped his arm. 'I'm still not sure we can trust you.'

'You had better hope you can,' Karim stated simply and stepped out into the night.

A camp fire was burning about thirty yards from the tent, the Bedouin around it sleeping, one propped against the side of his camel. The animal snorted in the direction of the three men but few of the Arabs themselves even glanced at the figures emerging from the tent. They made their way to where twenty or thirty horses were tied together by their bridles. Karim walked calmly but the two Frenchmen found the urge to run to the horses, leap on to one and ride away as fast as possible almost overwhelming. When they finally reached them they found two tribesmen standing talking. Karim greeted the men in perfect Arabic and one even laughed, slapping him on the shoulder and gesturing towards the horses. The Circassian signalled for Delacor and Tigana to mount up, which they did with difficulty, struggling with the unsaddled ponies. Both teetered precariously on their mounts' backs momentarily, Tigana silently praying that his horse wouldn't rear up and throw him, then they steadied themselves and gripped the thin leather reins favoured by the Bedouin.

Karim was still standing talking to the two guards, not wanting to make their exit seem overly hurried, but the combined effect of not knowing what was being said and the feeling that the Arabs somehow knew that the men beneath these clothes were not like themselves was driving Delacor insane with worry. Worry that was seconds from becoming full-scale panic. He knew he had no choice. He would have to dig his heels into the pony and run for it. He looked down at Karim then straight ahead. Still the Circassian was talking, patting the neck of one animal as he did so. Delacor gripped his reins more tightly, preparing himself. Tigana also felt the growing sense of terror, the unshakeable belief that they were about to be discovered or that someone was going to stumble on the dead bodies in the tent and raise the alarm.

Karim finally swung himself on to the back of a pony and flicked the reins, urging the animal on. It set off across the sand followed by the two relieved Frenchmen.

Tigana could not resist a look behind him but the two Bedouin were already invisible in the darkness.

'Now we must reach the column,' Karim said. 'It'll be dawn in less than two hours. When the Bedouin attack again they will not give up until they have destroyed Barada and all the men in it.'

The horses and their riders sped across the sand aware that even the speed of the sleek Arab ponies might not be enough.

All three had the unshakeable feeling that they would

return to the village to find only the corpses of their comrades.

Two hours.

They rode on.

Twenty

'We're all going to die, aren't we?' said Charvet, glancing up from cleaning his carbine, his eyes peering in the direction of the dunes that surrounded Barada. 'Delacor and the others aren't going to reach Desaix's column in time. We haven't got a chance.'

Lausard was sharpening his sword against a stone, testing the edge with the pad of his thumb every so often.

'Does it really matter that much to you where you die, Charvet?' the sergeant asked. 'Here, Italy, France, Prussia, Austria. What's the difference? Bullet, sword or guillotine. Death is death however it comes.'

'Aren't you afraid of dying, Alain?' Rocheteau said.

'Men who have nothing to live for usually don't fear death,' Lausard told him. 'Sometimes death becomes the most attractive option when compared to a life that offers so little.'

'Well, I'd rather have any kind of life than die here today.' Rocheteau was defiant.

'A life lived in gutters and sewers, starving, fighting

for the next sous, the next piece of bread. Is that kind of existence so difficult to leave behind?'

'I don't fear death because I know that it will unite me with God,' Moreau offered.

'Death will unite you with six feet of earth, nothing more,' Lausard said dismissively. 'Do you think any God of yours would have put you in this position? What kind of God do you worship, Moreau? One who throws away the lives of men the way fools throw away fortunes?'

'There are no fortunes in France any more,' said Charvet. 'All those who had them are dead.' He chuckled.

'Do you honestly believe that?' Lausard said. 'Do you think there are no rich men in France? What about the Directory? What about our own generals? They made fortunes during the Italian campaign. I thought the Republic was created to make men equal. What was all the misery for if it failed?'

'It didn't fail,' said Lieutenant Royere, hobbling out of the darkness, using a carbine as a makeshift crutch. His injured leg was heavily bandaged with pieces of cloth torn from garments found in the abandoned hovels of the village. 'The Bourbons were destroyed. The rich were removed from power and their wealth redistributed.'

'Your idealism is showing again, Lieutenant,' Lausard said, smiling.

The officer sat down next to him.

'As is your cynicism, Sergeant,' he said, patting Lausard on the shoulder. 'But I must say I agree that the wealth wasn't redistributed with quite the fairness embodied by Republican ethics.'

'We've had none of it,' Charvet said. 'When was the last time we were paid?'

'There isn't anything to spend your money on out here,' Tabor offered.

'That's not the point,' Charvet told him. 'We never get what we're promised.'

'Bonaparte promised us nothing but hardship and he's given us that,' Rocheteau said. 'Perhaps he *has* kept his word.'

'A man's word should be as valuable as gold,' Lausard murmured. 'Any man who gives his word and then breaks it has no honour.'

'It isn't what he says that matters, it's who he says it *to*,' Rocheteau added. 'It's the same as responsibility. Mine is to this unit; not to the whole army or even to France but to men who fight alongside me.'

'So, you are not a patriot then, Corporal?' said Royere.

'I love France but I don't want to die for her,' Rocheteau told the officer.

'So what beliefs are worth dying for?' Royere continued.

'No belief is worth dying for,' Lausard interjected. 'A belief is something worth *killing* for, not dying for. If I die for a belief, who does it benefit? Others perhaps less worthy than myself?'

'For a thief, Lausard, you have a remarkable faith in your own worth.' Royere smiled. 'I respect that.'

'There is nothing in *me* to respect, Lieutenant, believe me,' Lausard told him, getting to his feet.

'Where are you going, Alain?' Rocheteau wanted to know.

'To check on Sonnier,' the sergeant replied, disappearing off into the gloom, heading towards the dragoon who stood sentry about a hundred yards away. Royere scrambled to his feet and hobbled away after the sergeant. He caught him after a few strides.

'What did you mean when you said others less worthy than yourself?' the officer enquired.

Lausard glanced at him warily. 'Does it matter, Lieutenant?'

'I was curious. You are full of contradictions, my friend. You claim not to value your own life and yet you fight like the devil to preserve it. You say you belong in the gutter and yet you have a nobility about you most men would kill for. You care nothing for the Republic and yet you are one of its finest products. The embodiment of what that struggle was about. You claim to be as ignorant as some of the men you fight alongside and yet it is clear to anyone that you have an intellect far superior to any of them. As I said, contradictions.'

'What is *your* background, Lieutenant? Are you a product of the Republic too? Did years of hardship shape your resentment for the upper classes and the rich? Did you despise them enough to see them slaughtered? Did *you* stand in the Place de la Revolution and cheer each Aristocrat's death?'

'I was too busy enjoying the sun in Navarre, helping my father with his mill,' Royere said, smiling. 'I didn't suffer any undue hardship and I never despised the upper classes. But I could see that what was happening in France then was wrong. Whether the slaughter of the privileged was a way to right that wrong, to this day I don't know.'

'What does it matter now?' Lausard said dismissively, slowing his pace to allow the wounded officer to keep up with him. 'All those bodies in unmarked graves. Rich *and* poor. And for what? So that we could follow Bonaparte halfway around the world to die in some hellhole like Barada? Is that our legacy from your Republic, Lieutenant? Ten unmarked graves in the desert?'

'It needn't be. The sun will rise in less than thirty minutes. If you leave now, you have a chance of reaching the column. Leave me behind, I can't ride like this.' He motioned to his injured leg. 'I told you to get out if you could. I and the rest of the wounded will stay. We will not hold you back. Not all lives here need be wasted.'

Lausard shook his head.

'I will order you to leave if I have to,' Royere insisted.

'And if I choose to ignore that order, Lieutenant? What will you do? Have me shot? No. We *all* stay. One way or another we remain together. Even if that unity brings death. Unity, Lieutenant. Wasn't that one of the doctrines of your Republic? It is the one lesson worth learning. When the sun rises we will see that lesson put into practice. How many of us live to praise it remains to be seen.'

It was a long time since Lausard had watched the sun rise. He wiped sweat from his forehead and squinted as the shimmering perimeter of the blood red orb poked its way over the horizon, splitting the thick blanket of night and sending scarlet gashes tearing across it. With the coming of light, the heat grew in intensity until it sucked the breath from the men's lungs and scorched the air itself. Rising higher in the sky, the sun drove back the vestiges of night and began to claim the land for itself, spreading its pall of blistering heat across the sand as it took command of the heavens. It glinted on the weapons of the waiting dragoons, who stood in position watching the dunes, waiting for the inevitable onslaught.

Lausard walked back and forth, his sword bumping against his boot, his carbine slung over his shoulder by its strap. Both his pistols were jammed into his belt, loaded and ready. He glanced at each of his companions in turn.

At Lieutenant Royere, his leg heavily bandaged, propped against one side of the overturned wagon watching the crest patiently.

Charvet kept lifting his carbine to his shoulder, lowering it then raising it again. When he tired of that he tapped the hilt of his sword agitatedly.

Tabor stood motionless, occasionally looking up at the cloudless sky, his huge frame dwarfing that of Chatillo who was kneeling on the hot sand, his jacket removed to reveal the bandages wrapped around his torso. There was blood on the makeshift dressing from the wound in his side and Lausard noticed how pale the dragoon's face was despite the heat.

Moreau had his head slightly bowed and his lips were moving silently.

A few yards further back, Sonnier had again taken up a position on top of one of Barada's mud huts, his pistols and carbine close at hand.

In the hovel across from him, Carbonne stood in the doorway, either inspecting the stump where the top of his little finger used to be or kicking impatiently at the sand.

Rocheteau was crouched behind two fallen palm trees, cartridges laid out on a piece of rag beside him for easy access. As Lausard approached he turned and shrugged his shoulders in the sergeant's direction.

'Alain, why us?' he said wearily. 'Out of all the men in the French army who could have been here, why did it have to be us? Stinking luck, eh?'

Lausard nodded and joined him. 'You should be used to it by now, you've had bad luck all your life.' He smiled.

'I suppose you're right. Moreau would probably say it was the will of God.'

'It was no God who put us where we are now.'

'No. It was a Corsican.' Rocheteau chuckled at his own wit.

'I wouldn't change places with any man,' Lausard stated flatly. 'What do you want? To be sitting back in Paris in some prison cell waiting for them to carry you to the guillotine? At least here we're free.'

'Free to do what? Die? What *are* we doing here, Alain?'

Lausard smiled crookedly. 'We are spreading the Revolutionary culture, throughout a desperate world. Don't you feel honoured?'

Beneath them, the ground began to shake.

The initial shudder grew steadily into a wave that seemed to roll across the entire desert.

'This is it,' said Lausard, running back across the village, checking on the men once more, his heart thudding hard against his ribs, the heat momentarily forgotten. He was surprised at how focused he was, his vision, his mind all clear and prepared for what may come. And if it was death that came then he was ready for that too.

The shaking of the ground was now accompanied by a steadily rising rumble of sound. Horses' hooves ploughing through sand, the distant neighing of animals being urged on by their riders. A dust cloud rose above the northern dunes, signalling the approach of many horsemen and the dragoons looked in that direction, filled with either fear, desperation or resignation. Lausard felt a curious exhilaration, as if fire was running through his veins. It was a feeling akin to semi-drunkenness, a raising of his spirit. He felt sweat trickle down his face and he looked up into the clear blue sky, marvelling at the purity of the heavens. It was as though all his senses had been heightened. As he pulled his carbine into his shoulder the smell of the black powder seemed even more pungent than usual, the feel of the metal trimmings on the barrel caused his skin to tingle.

Now he turned his attention to that growing dust cloud, to the increasing volume of the horses' hooves. Again he looked around at his companions and, whatever emotions possessed them, there was a grim determination etched on each of their features. If they were to meet their deaths this blistering morning then it would be with passion and courage, battling to their last breath, taking as many of their enemies with them as they could. Lausard swore an oath to himself that if he was to die he would leave the sand around him piled high with the bodies of Bedouin, thick with their blood.

From the sound of the approaching horde the men realized that the onrushing horses on the other side of the dunes were no more than two hundred yards away by now. The bodies of dead animals from the previous day's fighting still littered the approaches to Barada. Like their riders they had been ravaged by the heat and by flies and ants, their stench filling the air like a noxious cloud. Many more would soon join them today, Lausard thought.

He moved closer towards Lieutenant Royere as the riders prepared to crest the ridge.

'You should have run while you had the chance,' Royere said, thumbing back the hammers on both his pistols.

'We started together, we'll end it together,' Lausard murmured.

'Do you think they will call us heroes?'

'I will be content for them to call us soldiers.'

The first line of horsemen was about to sweep over the dunes.

'Ready!' shouted Royere.

'What do you think heaven is like?' Tabor asked, his eyes never leaving the ridge.

'You'll know in a few minutes,' Charvet told him.

'Let us hope that God will judge us kindly,' Moreau commented. 'After some of the things we have done He would be entitled to turn his back on us.'

'He already has,' Charvet retorted.

'You put your trust in God, I'll put mine in this,' said Lausard, tapping the barrel of the Charleville.

The horsemen swept over the ridge and hurtled down the slope towards Barada.

'My God!' murmured Royere.

Lausard didn't speak, lowering his carbine slightly.

'Tell me I'm not dreaming,' Charvet said.

'It's a miracle,' Moreau whispered. 'A miracle sent by God.'

The horsemen riding towards them were dressed in the green jackets of dragoons. The horsehair manes on their helmets streamed out behind them as they cantered towards Barada, towards the incredulous troops who looked on in disbelief.

It was Lausard who recognized Captain Milliere riding

at the head of the men, flanked by Delacor, Tigana and Karim. He also spotted Bonet, Rostov and Joubert amongst the leading riders.

'They got through,' Rocheteau said, appearing at his side. 'They actually got through.'

'Did you think they wouldn't?' Lausard managed a smile.

Rocheteau patted his companion on the shoulder and sighed in relief.

Lausard saluted as Milliere reined in his mount before him.

Behind him there must have been close to one hundred men; it looked as if an entire company was present. Sweating men on lathered horses looking uncomfortable beneath the now blazing sun, but Lausard welcomed the stench of unwashed bodies. Gaston smiled at the sergeant and waved his trumpet in triumph. A number of the dragoons, including Milliere, dismounted, glancing at the corpses of the Bedouin that littered the area around Barada.

Delacor, Karim and Tigana were crossing the sand behind Milliere, and Lausard saw that the Circassian was wearing the green jacket of a dragoon. He was walking a little uncertainly in the boots but apart from that he looked comfortable in his new attire. He reached the sergeant and extended his right hand, which Lausard shook warmly.

'It seems I am one of you now.'

'God help you,' Rocheteau chuckled.

Lausard noticed that the Circassian still wore his scimitar, the curved blade attached to his belt by two straps. 'You did well,' he said. 'All of you.' He shook hands with Delacor and Tigana too.

'It seems you had some trouble here,' Milliere observed, nodding towards the Bedouin corpses.

'A little. We weren't expecting you, Captain. How close is the main column?'

'Two or three miles behind,' the officer told Lausard. 'We are to push on to Damanhur. Some say there is water there and God knows we need it.'

'What about the Bedouin?'

'They have fled,' Karim announced. 'They would not stand against other horsemen. We passed through what was left of their camp about an hour ago.'

'What now, Captain?' Lausard asked.

'We rejoin the main army. We continue across the desert as General Bonaparte ordered. Cavalry units will continue to act as scouts and intelligence. The General is still eager to find the Mamelukes.' Milliere looked up at the cloudless sky. 'I would be just as grateful to find some water and some food, for ourselves *and* the horses.'

Lausard nodded his agreement, glancing around at the dead bodies scattered across the sand.

'God was with us,' said Moreau, wandering past him. 'We have Him to thank for our lives.'

'You've got *us* to thank for your lives, your holiness,' snapped Delacor, pointing first at his own chest then at Karim and Tigana. 'We brought the help and you should pray to your God that you never have to go through what we went through to save your miserable skin.'

'We were lucky, Alain,' Rocheteau added, wiping sweat from his face.

'Luck had nothing to do with it,' the sergeant said, watching as Lieutenant Royere was helped on to his horse. The officer looked across and waved at Lausard, who returned the gesture.

'I say it was a miracle,' Rocheteau insisted.

Lausard held up his carbine. 'A miracle of men and weapons. Bravery and honour. We owe our lives to our own abilities. It is as simple as that.' He walked off to find his horse.

The man was in his late twenties, Lausard guessed, although it was difficult to tell because of his haggard appearance. Also virtually impossible to distinguish was his unit. Cavalry, infantry or artillery? The dragoon sergeant had no idea. The man was sitting on the burning sand dressed in nothing more than a pair of filthy undershorts. The skin on his back and chest was blistered and red from the sun, the soles of his bare feet raw and bloody from the march across hot sand. He sat cross-legged, the pistol pressed to his temple, his lips moving soundlessly. As he pulled the trigger, Lausard looked away, the sound reverberating over the dunes.

When Lausard looked back, the man was lying on his back, blank eyes staring at the sky, a spreading pool of blood seeping into the sand around his head. There were bodies on either side of the slowly moving column, most of them almost naked. Soldiers who still marched had discarded their packs, their tunics and in some cases even their weapons. Officers and NCOs made little or no attempt to stop them. Indeed, a number of the higher ranks had done the same. Anything to bring temporary relief on a march that was killing them.

Lausard had no idea how long he and his companions had been in the saddle. He thought perhaps twelve hours. Since rejoining the main column they had been moving steadily across the endless sand with little idea of where they were going. Men and horses had been falling with appalling regularity throughout the march. Some men had staggered away from the column screaming for water and Lausard had lost count how many had taken their own lives. Many others had simply collapsed on to the hot sand and waited for death to take them, unable or unwilling to take another step in this living hell. No trees, no shade, no food, no water, no respite from the sun. Lausard himself rode with his head down, his horse stumbling a number of times, its own strength pushed to the limit. Like most of his regiment he rode a large, powerful animal bred in Normandy; renowned for their strength, even these magnificent creatures were helpless beneath the intolerable heat. Somewhere behind him he heard a plaintive whinny and one of the animals crashed to the ground. Neither it nor its rider rose again, preferring death to the misery of the march.

Large numbers of troops staggered along with bandages wrapped around their eyes, blinded by the rays of the sun, the damage done to their sight further exacerbated by the burning dust of the khamsin, the red hot southerly wind that swept across the dunes like airbound fire. Lausard and a number of others had tried tying cloths around their faces and the muzzles of their horses to prevent their and their animals' nostrils clogging with the foul dust, but it did little to help. The route of Desaix's men could easily be followed by the trail of bodies, discarded uniforms and weapons, and dying horses.

Every now and then half a dozen Bedouin would appear on the dunes, watching the painfully slow progress of the French, but the troops paid them little heed. It was as if they *wanted* the tribesmen to attack. At least a fight would take their minds off their terrible predicament and, if they were lucky, it might bring a quick death rather than the long, lingering death from thirst, hunger and exhaustion that seemed to be their fate.

Lausard looked across at Rocheteau who had his head bowed and his eyes closed. Lausard reached out and tugged on the corporal's arm, rousing him from his stupor. Rocheteau looked blankly to the left and right, his eyes wide and staring, then he came to his senses, shook himself from his lethargy, nodded at Lausard and shifted slightly in his saddle.

Joubert had slumped forward virtually on to his horse's neck. Rostov rode with his eyes closed, protecting them from the sun and the dust. Roussard was whispering silently to himself as his horse struggled along, barely able to find the strength to transport itself never mind its rider through the shifting sand.

Bonet and Giresse had dismounted and were stumbling ahead of their exhausted mounts, tugging the animals along by the reins, the temporary removal of their extra weight giving the stricken horses something of a respite. But the men could barely drag one foot in front of the other and after another thirty minutes they both climbed wearily back into the saddle. Lieutenant Royere appeared to be riding with less difficulty than his men, despite his wound. Like so many men in the column, he was more concerned with the horrendous heat and his raging thirst than with his injured knee.

The only man who seemed in control of the situation was Karim. His pony stepped enthusiastically through the sand, the Circassian himself still chewing on a piece of leather to stop his mouth drying up. But despite his outward assurance, Lausard could see in the Circassian's face that he too was suffering, and Lausard reasoned that even one who is used to living in such a hostile environment must still occasionally suffer its torments. For his own part he had never experienced anything like this in his life and doubted, if he survived, if he ever would again. The pure, unadulterated misery and hopelessness of their situation was crushingly reinforced as each new dune was surmounted and all that greeted the men upon reaching its crest was further expanses of unforgiving sand, baked by the constant scorching heat of the sun.

Lausard was beginning to wonder if this would be the first campaign where an entire army was wiped out without ever encountering its enemy. Other than the Bedouin, they had seen nothing of their true opponents. The Mamelukes. He assumed they were massing their forces somewhere, preparing to strike. A quick glance around at the demoralized troops made him fear for their fate should the enemy strike in any reasonable numbers. As well as the suffering, Lausard was aware of a senselessness to this entire episode. He wondered why Bonaparte had sent close to eighteen thousand men into the middle of a waterless wasteland, knowing how inappropriately they were equipped. What was he thinking of?

Lausard was still trying to work it out when he felt a hand tugging at his arm and he turned to see Tabor staring at him. On closer inspection Lausard noticed that the big man wasn't looking *at* him but past him, into the distance. He was pointing fixedly and Lausard now saw what had caught his attention. About five hundred yards to the north was a massive expanse of clear, blue water. Lausard wondered what it was. A lake? The tributary of the Nile? Had their journey taken them that far already?

Whatever it was it shimmered beneath the baking sun, a teasing, tempting oasis amid the oceans of dry sand. Salvation. Life.

Dozens of infantrymen had already broken rank and were running towards the shimmering blue expanse, some screaming joyfully, others already pulling off what remained of their uniforms, ready to throw themselves into the beckoning blueness. Ahead of Lausard, half a dozen dragoons urged strength from their shattered mounts and rode towards the shimmering vision, and despite himself Lausard joined them, eager to taste the water, to feel the liquid on his flesh, to drink until he was full. Perhaps they were to be spared after all.

Karim followed at a leisurely pace, watching as officers and men alike joined the mad rush towards the shimmering expanse.

Delacor leaped from his horse close to the water and ran on, followed by dozens of infantrymen. They ran on towards the water. And into it. Yet there was no cooling moisture, no relieving feel of water on their baked flesh. One of the infantrymen raised a hand to drink and spat as he felt sand in his mouth.

Lausard was by now standing where the shore of the lake had appeared to be. He dropped to his knees and plunged his hands not into cooling water but into hot sand.

'What witchcraft is this?' shrieked Delacor, holding up his hands, watching the sand pour through his clenched fingers. 'Where is the water? I *saw* it. I saw water. We all did, didn't we?'

Two of the infantrymen were crawling around on their bellies licking at the sand, coughing and spluttering. Another was sitting on the sand sobbing.

Lausard dug his hand into the sand and held the burning particles in his fist.

'A mirage,' said Karim, appearing beside him. 'I have seen them myself. There is no water. It is a trick of the eye.'

Lausard got to his feet, staring at what, moments earlier, had looked like a vast blue lake. It was only sand. It had only *ever* been sand. The sergeant was breathing heavily, his eyes screwed tightly together. He could hear the wails of anguish coming from the hundreds of other men gathered around, many crying like children. Others simply turned and trudged back towards the column, which had continued to move on at its slow, faltering pace.

Karim dismounted and took Lausard by the arm, handing him the reins of his horse. Lausard nodded slowly and remounted, looking around at the frantic troops still sifting through the sand for any trace of the water they were certain they had seen. More than a dozen lay on the sand, refusing to move, content to await death in this arid, unforgiving wilderness.

Tabor was stumbling around, arms outstretched, occasionally dropping to his knees.

'Come on,' Lausard said. 'There is nothing for us here.'

'I cannot *see*, Sergeant. I am blind.'

Bonet heard Tabor's words and hurried across to the big man, leading him back towards his horse, helping him on it. He pulled free Tabor's belt and fastened it around the big man's eyes, then he took the reins and led the horse back towards the column. Lausard watched him go.

'Blind or dead, what difference does it make?' Delacor snarled.

'Come on, we're leaving,' Lausard said.

'I can't go any further,' Delacor said wearily, the anger suddenly leaving his voice. 'I've had enough. What's the point in carrying on? We're all going to die. You know that too. Just leave me.'

'Get on your horse, Delacor,' Lausard ordered.

'And what if I don't? Are you going to shoot me? You'd be easing my suffering if you did. Don't threaten me with death when death is the best option I have. Shoot me now. I'm *asking* you to do it.' He extended both arms.

'Get on your horse,' Lausard repeated. 'I won't leave you here to die.'

'Then stay and die with me,' Delacor said quietly.

Lausard dismounted and walked across to the trooper.

'Death is all there is for us now,' Delacor said, resigned to his fate. 'I haven't the strength to fight it any longer.'

Lausard looked at his comrade for a second then, with lightning speed, he drove a powerful punch into the right side of Delacor's jaw. The blow took the dragoon by surprise and he was unconscious before he hit the sand. Lausard dragged the dragoon's body across to his horse and, with Karim's help, lifted him across the saddle, then the two men remounted and headed back towards the column, Lausard leading Delacor's horse.

'He wanted to die, why didn't you let him?' Karim asked.

'Because he's *my* responsibility. He's one of *my* men. As I said before, we started this together, we'll end it together. No matter what.'

'Do you still believe in what your General Bonaparte says? He uses you like pawns in a chess game.'

'Pawns are sometimes sacrificed for the advancement of the king,' Lausard replied. 'Bonaparte still has eighteen thousand pawns left. I fear this game is far from over.'

Twenty-One

Time no longer had any meaning for Lausard. Hours, minutes, seconds, even days and weeks had all become just words. All that he and his companions were aware of were thirst, heat and exhaustion. How long they had been riding through the desert had no relevance; as far as Lausard was concerned, they would be riding for ever, never seeing anything but a few miles of parched, lifeless sand in all directions. More men would die, go blind or kill themselves and their bodies would be covered by the khamsin-driven sand. In time, the entire column would simply cease to exist, buried by the sands of Egypt as surely as a sunken galleon is covered by the raging sea.

Other than the cries of dying men and the pathetic exhortations of those begging for help that could not possibly arrive, the column moved in virtual silence, men dragging themselves through the sand, some on their knees, although most of those gave up after a few hundred yards. Of those men who went down, few got up again, and their comrades could not find the strength to support them. Not that they wanted help; they were resigned to a death from hunger, thirst or heat, and they wanted nothing more than to be left alone to await it. The same was true of many of the horses. Lausard had counted at least two dozen of the stricken beasts crash to the ground, unable to continue, as desperate for water as their riders. They lay still on the sand, just their heads rising occasionally in a useless gesture of anguish. The corpses of man and beast were covered almost instantly by swarms of the black, bloated flies that seemed to appear from nowhere to feast on those who had fallen.

Since the mirage, Lausard had been reluctant to trust even his own eyes. The same false hope had been experienced more than once during the journey and men had still rushed towards those shimmering illusions in the hope that what they saw was real, only to find nothing but sand. After each crushing disappointment, at least one man had ended his own life, tired of the suffering, and Lausard was now sure that the number of suicides must be close to fifty. How many had been claimed by the heat, thirst and hunger he couldn't begin to imagine.

Throughout their horrendous trek, Bedouin tribesmen would appear on the hills, sometimes in ones and twos, sometimes in groups of up to a dozen, seemingly satisfied with picking off the many stragglers. Some they killed there and then, riding past and cutting them down with their swords, running them through with their spears. Those less fortunate were hauled up on to the sleek Arab ponies and carried off into the desert shrieking, collected by these desert warriors as if they were trophies. Hardly any of the men even bothered to shoot at the marauders any more.

Lausard looked around him at the men of his unit.

Their uniforms were covered by a fine sheen of sand, their faces scorched by the sun, their equipment filthy. At least what remained of it. Many had tied their jackets across the backs of their shabraques. Some had even removed the saddle-cloths in an effort to spare their horses some discomfort, but this attempt at kindliness had backfired as the persistent rubbing of the saddle against the horses' backs had produced appalling saddle-sores.

As Lausard looked in to the distance he wondered if the minarets and cupolas, the palm trees and the greenery he saw rising about half a mile before him were figments of his tortured imagination as the phantom expanses of water had been. He decided that they weren't and slapped Rocheteau on the arm. The corporal, who had been dozing in the saddle, looked up, his gaze following Lausard's pointing finger.

'Am I still dreaming?' Rocheteau pleaded.

'If you are then so am I,' Lausard told him. 'And so is the rest of the column.'

All eyes now seemed fixed on the buildings and palm trees ahead and many men began to cheer.

'It is the city of Damanhur,' said Karim. 'The seat of a bey, one of the centres of the cotton trade.'

'To hell with that,' snapped Delacor. 'Will they have food and water there?'

Karim nodded.

'And who will we have to kill to get it?' Lausard murmured.

The entire column moved forward with a haste and organization that had seemed impossible an hour earlier. Officers and NCOs shouted orders and the entire motley crew of troops formed up into their units as they marched with surprising efficiency towards the waiting city. To the starving, thirst-crazed troops of Desaix's division, Damanhur looked like the most beautiful place on earth. Even Lausard managed a smile.

Napoleon Bonaparte paced agitatedly back and forth inside the large barn-like building, stopping occasionally to chew on the plate of wheat cakes standing on the table along with a jug of milk. The small but very welcome meal had been presented to him a few hours earlier upon his arrival in Damanhur. He and his headquarters staff had ridden from Alexandria the previous evening through the darkness of the desert, a journey that had brought them to the city in just ten hours. The troops of Desaix and Reynier, who now occupied Damanhur, had taken four days to cover the same distance.

Bonaparte peered quickly at the pile of papers on the table. He looked at each requisition order, each report, each despatch with the same casual expression, but the two other men present knew that the speed with which he read and digested these pieces of information was not born of indifference but of a burning energy. His chief of staff, Berthier, sat at another table scribbling notes, while the General's aide-de-camp, Sulkowski, looked on, his eyes never leaving his commander.

Sulkowski was dressed in the uniform of a hussar, the red pelisse slung over his left shoulder, the buttons of his dolman jacket undone – his only concession to the heat that filled the room. His right hand was bandaged, the legacy of the French attack on Alexandria more than a week ago now. It felt as if it had been longer. Sulkowski felt as if he had been away from his homeland for an eternity. First the privations of the long sea voyage and now the inhospitality of Egypt had combined to make him long to see France but, above all, his native Poland. In fact, the surroundings he now found himself in made him want to see *anywhere* other than this endless hell of sand, flies, disease and thirst, and Arab tribesmen. He, like so many other men, officers and private soldiers alike, was already disillusioned with the country, even with the motives their General had for bringing them here. The arrival at Damanhur had done little to alter that feeling. What had been professed to be a city of some size and importance had turned out to be little more than an agglomeration of mud and straw hovels, interspersed by a series of less than impressive mosques. The city had not been the paradise the French had hoped for but, Sulkowski thought, it was better than the desert. *Anything* was better than the desert.

Bonaparte finished reading the last of the papers on the table and turned towards Berthier, regarding his chief of staff silently for a moment. Then he switched his piercing gaze to Sulkowski, who noticed that his commander's brow was furrowed slightly, as if he battled with a troubling thought.

'In every one of these reports there is mention of disquiet within the ranks,' Bonaparte said eventually. '*All* ranks. It seems everyone is infected with the same discontent. I have generals complaining to me that they haven't enough food or drink for their men. Where do they expect me to get it? Do they expect me to pull it from empty air?'

'Your men expect much of you because they are accustomed to you delivering much,' Berthier told him. 'The French army are born grumblers.'

'These are not grumblings, Berthier,' Bonaparte said holding up a handful of the despatches. 'In these I read not just of discontent but of the threat of mutiny from some units.'

'In times of suffering thoughts can become extreme. And it has been hard on them.'

'It has been hard on *all* of us. War is never easy, Berthier. You know that. I expected my men to know it. These men we have here are the men who conquered Italy, the men who destroyed the finest armies Austria could send against them. They were scarecrows when I took command of them. Their officers were timid and unadventurous. I transformed them all. I *made* them what they are and now all I get as thanks is talk of mutiny.' He hurled the papers aside angrily.

'It will pass, General,' said Sulkowski. 'Once the men have eaten their fill and gathered some loot they will be more amenable to their situation.'

'Will they? Food and drink may satisfy private soldiers but they are not the only ones complaining, are they? This spleen has infected those of the highest rank. Despair is an epidemic that must be treated.' Bonaparte nodded towards the main door that led into his room and Sulkowski crossed to it, lifting the locking bar and ushering in those who waited outside.

Bonaparte watched as the men filed into the room, hats in hand: cavalry generals Mireur and Dumas, divisional commanders Desaix and Reynier. They formed a line before him, their expressions as grim as that of their commander.

'I have read your reports,' Bonaparte addressed them, 'and I am disappointed in you. That is one of the reasons I called you here. It seems that not only can you not control your men, you cannot control your own emotions either. These reports have a hint of hysteria about them. Where is your pride? Where is your belief?'

'Back in France where *we* should be,' Mireur said sharply. 'We should never have come to this place to begin with. This entire expedition is a hopeless and irresponsible adventure that can only end in failure.'

'I agree with Mireur.' Dumas spoke. 'Surely not enough thought went into the planning of this invasion or we would not all be suffering as we are now.'

'This is no invasion,' Bonaparte retorted. 'It is a logical and necessary progression in the expansion of the Republic, of great strategic and political importance.'

'My men care nothing for these matters, all they care about is that they have no food,' Desaix said. 'Time and time again during my march across the desert I requested provisions from you and received nothing. No rations have been distributed since we landed nearly two weeks ago. This negligence has cost me fifteen hundred men.'

'My division, too, has suffered,' Reynier added. 'I asked for help and was given none. I have seen men die in agony for want of a mouthful of water. More than forty men were trampled to death at El Beydah so desperate were they for water. I watched comrades fighting over a cupful of dirty water, men suffocating in the rush, others killing themselves when they could not drink.'

'You think I do not realize this?' Bonaparte shouted. 'These are *my* men you speak of. Each one of them like a son to me.'

'You do not see their suffering at such close quarters,' Dumas insisted. 'You do not know them as we do. Your nerves may be of steel but ours are not. To stand by helplessly while the men who we command lose their minds in despair is more than any man can take. We have to experience that every day. You do not. You are above it. Cocooned by your staff and your *savants*, those "pekinese" who would march into the mouth of a lion if you ordered them too. They have no minds of their own. They are fit only to live as puppets with you pulling their strings.'

Sulkowski took an angry step forward but Bonaparte raised a hand to halt him.

'Be careful who you insult, General.' Sulkowski glared at Dumas. 'Or I will show you how puppets fight duels.'

'My remarks were not addressed to you. I know of your bravery.'

'Then know too that these men of science and learning whom you despise so much are also capable of reason,' Bonaparte snapped. 'They have their place here as much as any fighting man. And do not presume to tell me about my own army. I know my men suffer and if there was any way to allay that suffering I would, but sacrifices must be made. If some small parts must be lost for the good of a whole machine then so be it. Eighteen thousand men have crossed the desert to this point, if a few hundred have been lost it is a regrettable but very small price to pay to achieve our ultimate goal.'

'*Your* goal, General,' Dumas corrected. 'The longer this sorry mess continues, the more convinced I am that it is personal glory at stake here, not the advancement of the Republic. It is the advancement of Napoleon Bonaparte that we suffer and die for.'

'You are talking sedition,' Bonaparte said vehemently. 'Be careful or I will do my duty. Your five foot ten inches would not save you from being shot by a firing squad two hours from now.' He ran a furious gaze along all the faces before him. 'Perhaps you have all grown soft. Is this kind of warfare so much harder on you? Do you miss the comforts of the Italian palazzi and casinos so much? You all grew fat on the spoils of *that* war, didn't you? Where is your strength now?'

'It is not just the physical hardship that is causing these problems,' Desaix said evenly. 'It is the sense of isolation that we and the men feel, a loathing for the country and its people. It is impossible to convey in words the disgust, the discontent, the melancholy and the despair of this army. When men would rather take their own lives than march another mile, what does that tell you? Not about the men but about this country, about this entire expedition. Some feel that what they are being put through is inhuman.'

'To make men do what *I* make them do requires a strength of character you cannot begin to imagine. You accuse me of inhumanity. Well, let me tell you, if I had been the least bit more human this entire army, and all of you, would have perished. The worst is over. I know that morale is low and there is but one way to raise it. A victorious battle. And that is what I will give this army.'

'A victory against whom?' Mireur asked the question on all of their lips. 'An enemy we have not even encountered yet? Where *are* the Mamelukes? How are we to defeat them if we cannot even find them? Are we to spend the rest of our lives marching across sand searching for them?'

'We are less than sixty miles from Cairo,' Bonaparte said. 'The Mamelukes will not allow their capital to be threatened, that was what I said from the beginning of this campaign. All we have to do is continue our march and *they* will come to *us*. Trust me in this.' He turned his back on the other generals. 'This meeting is adjourned. You have spoken, I have listened and I have listened enough. Leave me.'

The generals filed out slowly, Sulkowski closing the door behind them.

Bonaparte returned to the plate of wheat cakes and ate one.

'These are dangerous times,' Berthier commented. 'An enemy massing before us and the threat of mutiny within our own army.'

'There will be no mutiny. If there is I will crush it with the same swiftness and fury with which I will crush the Mamelukes. This expedition cannot be allowed to fail, least of all by the men I brought here to carry it through. I will show no mercy to such men. Even if they *are* my own.'

The market was crowded with soldiers from all units. All, it seemed to Lausard, intent upon one thing: the purchase of as much food as they could possibly carry. None of them knew when they would come across civilization again – or what passed for civilization. Lausard crossed to a stall where wheat cakes were baking on hot ashes. The smell was appealing and he took one, chewing it quickly, ignoring the protestations of the stall owner who babbled at him in Arabic.

'What is he saying?' Lausard asked Karim and the Circassian smiled.

'He says that you are welcome to his wares. He says that you do not look like the demon he expected.'

'Demon?' Lausard chuckled. 'What does he mean?'

'Ibrahim Bey posted notices in every town and city telling the locals that you French, you Infidels, had fingernails a foot long, enormous mouths and ferocious eyes.' Karim grinned. 'He said you were savages possessed of the devil and that you went into battle linked together with chains.'

Lausard smiled then looked across to another of the stalls where Joubert and Roussard were arguing furiously with an Arab trader, pointing at his goods and then at him, while the Arab himself was pulling at their tunics. Lausard and Karim, now joined by Rostov, wandered across towards the mêlée.

'I'm trying to pay him but he won't take the money,' said Joubert, trying to push away the Arab who was still tugging at his jacket. 'One goose, one chicken, one bag of beans and one bag of lentils. Thirty-five paras each for the goose and the chicken, one para each for the lentils and beans. As set out in the orders of the day and *he* won't take the money.' Joubert pointed towards the trader, who was still babbling frantically and indicating Joubert's tunic. Joubert pushed him away. 'What does he want?'

Karim spoke to the Arab in his native language, the dragoons looking on as he pointed at them. Karim nodded as he listened to the trader.

'He wants the buttons for payment. He says for two buttons you can take everything.'

'What does he want with buttons?' Rostov asked. 'Surely the money is of more use to him. Why won't he take coins?'

'Because if the Mamelukes find anyone in possession of foreign currency, they will accuse them of having dealt with the Infidels,' Karim explained. 'At the very least they will confiscate the coins.'

'So he thinks the Mamelukes are going to beat us?' Lausard observed. 'He's no fool, is he?'

'He is being cautious,' Karim continued. 'If he takes your buttons as payment and the Mamelukes *do* win, should they find them on him he can always claim that he acquired them honourably by killing and robbing an Infidel. If *you* win, the buttons will be worth more than the current price of the merchandise.'

'So either way *he* wins,' Lausard murmured.

The Arab said something excitedly and pointed at Lausard.

'He says he will sell you a horse for six buttons.'

'Tell him to go to hell,' Lausard muttered.

'As for the food, he will not sell it to you unless you pay with your buttons. It is as simple as that.'

Without hesitation Joubert tore two of the pewter buttons from his tunic and thrust them into the eager hand of the excited Arab, snatching up his purchases. As the men made their way back towards the houses where they were billeted, they saw many other troops walking around minus a few buttons. One corporal of the Twenty-fifth Demi-Brigade had just two left on his jacket but he was weighed down with provisions. Lausard wondered how long his purchases would last him. He or any of the men who were milling around the streets and squares of Damanhur carrying everything from bags of dried dates to live chickens. A few men had bought water bottles but it seemed a little late for that. If more had been equipped with drinking vessels before leaving Alexandria, thought Lausard, then perhaps that part of the march would have been slightly less tortuous. He wondered how much further they would be forced to march at the whim of their commander. Supposedly, the Nile itself was less than fifteen miles away. Perhaps there they would all be able finally to quench thirsts that had built up to intolerable levels.

As they returned to their billets, they saw Delacor, Tigana and Carbonne sitting outside the huts smoking from a clay pipe they had purchased for a tunic button at another market. The tobacco had cost another two buttons. Some of the other dragoons paused to share the smoke but Lausard headed inside the hovel to where he knew Tabor and Bonet waited.

The big man was lying on the ground, his eyes bandaged. Bonet sat beside him.

'Is he any better?' Lausard asked.

'I took the bandages off for a while earlier on.'

'I could see better, Sergeant,' said Tabor. 'I can't see clearly yet but it doesn't hurt.'

Lausard patted his arm. 'Your sight will return soon,' the sergeant assured him. 'Keep your eyes protected from the sun for the time being.'

'Any news, Alain?' Bonet wanted to know.

'We march out tonight for El Rahmaniya.'

'We've only been here a day,' Bonet protested. 'Bonaparte could have given us longer to rest.'

Lausard shrugged. 'Perhaps he wants to hurry us to our deaths.'

'Do you think we will win, Alain?'

'Yes, I think we will beat the Mamelukes. I think Bonaparte will have his victory, he will probably even conquer this country and subjugate its people in the name of his Republic. Whether or not any of *us* ever survive to tell about it is a different question.'

'I don't want to die here,' Bonet said. 'Not in this godless country.'

'I have seen no evidence of a God in *any* part of the world and that includes France. What kind of God looks on while countrymen slaughter each other? While innocent women and children are dragged to the guillotine just because they are fortunate enough to have money or to possess different political views to those in power? If there ever was a God he turned his back on *our* world a long time ago.' Lausard got to his feet. 'We face another march across the desert, Bonet. How many of us will even manage to survive *that*? If you are looking for a God, don't look for him in the sands here. In fact, save yourself the trouble of looking anywhere. You would have more chance finding water in this dried-up land than of finding a God.'

He turned and headed towards the doorway, out into the blistering heat.

Twenty-Two

The men who refused to march belonged to the Twenty-third Demi-Brigade. As if by some prearranged signal, virtually an entire battalion of the infantry had moved, en masse, away from the slowly moving column. Many had discarded their tunics before they had even sat down on the hot sand; others had hurled away their bicorns, trampling them angrily. One officer had pulled his sword from its scabbard and snapped it across his thigh, hurling the two broken segments away in disgust.

As he looked on, Lausard wiped his face and tried to suck in some air, but it felt like passing through an enormous oven. The heat was incredible, even by the standards they had become all too used to. Lausard counted more than seventy men now sitting on the sand, showing no intention of moving. He wondered how many other men in the column felt the same way, how many in his own unit would join them if they had the chance?

The remainder of the men of the Twenty-third slowed their pace, finally coming to a halt as the shouts of officers echoed back and forth in the searing heat. Some of those who had left the column had stretched out on the sand, looking incapable of further movement no matter what their officers and NCOs bellowed at them.

As the column came to a halt, Lausard and the dragoons found themselves little more than twenty yards from the immobile infantrymen, who continued to ignore the furious shouts of their superiors. Lausard was aware that this was far more than a simple mass expression of exhaustion. The other troops looked on, some with bewilderment and others with admiration, even envy. Five or six men at a time might leave the column – Lausard had seen it happen all the way from Alexandria – but seventy or more at once . . . This was something far more insidious than weariness or discontent.

'What the hell are they doing?' Rocheteau murmured.

'They're doing what we should all do,' Delacor interjected. 'They're giving up. They've had enough. It's called common sense.'

'It's called mutiny,' Lausard responded, watching keenly. 'Look.'

Thirty or forty infantrymen from another battalion were also leaving the column, ignoring the shouts of their officers and NCOs. They trudged away from the column and sat down on the sand, heads bowed.

Captain Milliere rode up and down the length of the dragoon units as if daring any man to follow the actions of the infantry. Sergeant Delpierre rode close to Lausard and paused momentarily.

'Aren't any of your bastards going to leave?' he hissed. 'It seems this is the time for cowards.'

Lausard glared at him, at his ravaged features and

sweat-covered face. 'Why don't *you* leave? No one would miss you anyway, you whore's son.'

Delpierre tugged on his horse's bridle and rode back down the column, snarling at a dragoon who could not keep his mount still.

'What happens now?' Rocheteau asked, his eyes never leaving the large group of infantrymen, who seemed unconcerned that two lines of their comrades were marching towards them with fixed bayonets. From the head of the column, surrounded by half a dozen staff officers and guides, General Desaix was leading his horse towards the scene. He waved a hand in the air to halt the advancing troops, then approached the tall officer who had broken his sword.

Desaix saluted the man. 'What is your name?'

'Captain Noiret, Twenty-third, sir.' The officer returned the salute sharply.

'I gave no orders for a halt. Get back to your positions now. General Bonaparte ordered us to march on El Rahminaya and we can afford to waste no time.'

'I will not march, sir, and neither will my men. Not until we have had the water and provisions we've been promised.'

'I cannot give you something I do not have.'

'Then we will remain here, sir.'

'I cannot allow that, I cannot allow disorder within the ranks.'

'But you have it, General,' Noiret said angrily. 'I would not do this unless I had to. I would not betray my comrades without good reason. I love this army, I would die for General Bonaparte or you, sir – but in battle, not from hunger and thirst. Where is the honour in that?'

'I understand how you feel,' Desaix told him. 'But we all suffer in the same way. If there was anything I could do about your predicament, don't you think I would?'

'I do not *blame* you, sir,' Noiret told him. 'And I realize that we are all in a similar position, but I will not, I cannot, take this any longer, and neither can these men.' He gestured towards the dispirited, lost souls squatting or lying on the burning sand. They seemed oblivious to what was going on around them. 'We will not march on.'

'General Bonaparte has ordered that any mutiny or sedition is to be dealt with summarily,' said Desaix. 'I will not ignore his orders. While I understand your grievance, I cannot support it and I cannot tolerate it. Orders dictate that I must act, so I ask you once again to lead your men on to El Rahminaya.'

'And if I refuse, sir?'

'I will have no choice but to have you shot.' Desaix turned to one of his ADCs. 'Select twenty-four men for a firing squad now.' The ADC nodded and guided his horse towards the nearest infantry unit, relaying Desaix's orders to their officer. The general looked intently at Noiret, who seemed unfazed by this latest development, even as he saw the soldiers sloping towards where he and his exhausted men waited.

'Do not make me do this, Captain,' Desaix said. 'Believe me, I take no pleasure in it.'

'You must do your duty, sir. The prospect of being shot, even by my fellow countrymen, is not something to be feared. At least not in this vile country. Instead of a slow, lingering death from thirst and starvation, you offer me a quick death. I welcome that. If you shoot me you do not punish me, you reward me by ending my suffering. But no matter what you choose to threaten me with, I will not march another foot.'

'Then you leave me no choice. As an example, you and twelve of your men will be shot.'

'Is that the way to restore morale, sir?'

'I am ordering this because I too am following orders,' Desaix snapped, watching as an ADC moved among the rebelling men, pulling them to their feet until twelve stood close to Noiret.

'I thought Desaix was supposed to be a more understanding man,' said Bonet, watching with the other dragoons.

'What do you expect him to do?' Lausard challenged, his gaze never leaving the twenty-four-man firing squad as it readied itself under the watchful eye of a large sergeant. 'This mutiny could spread throughout the entire army if it isn't checked.'

'So you agree with our own men being executed do you, Alain?' Rocheteau pressed him.

'Those men have gone through no more than we have. They have suffered no more than us, they have not been deprived of anything we ourselves have not gone without. Why is their situation worse than ours? They complain of no food and water. So does most of the army, ourselves included. But we march on. We don't give up.'

'Perhaps we are bigger fools than they,' Delacor suggested. 'Perhaps we would be better off seeking death before a firing squad than suffering the torments of the desert and this stinking country.'

'Then join them,' Lausard said. 'If you are so keen to end your life then take your horse and join them. Perhaps I should have left you back in the desert when you wanted me to.'

Delacor did not speak. He was too busy watching the first four of Noiret's men being bundled in front of the firing squad, who already had their Charlevilles shouldered and were taking aim at the hapless men. When the order was given to fire, the sound of two dozen muskets tore through the air, a great choking cloud of smoke rolling towards the dragoons. When it finally cleared, driven away by the hot wind, the dragoons saw the four bodies sprawled on the sand, surrounded by spreading pools of blood. Lausard watched as the next four men were shoved in front of the busily reloading firing squad. Then, when they had been despatched, the last group, led by Noiret, moved into position to await death. Noiret looked defiantly at the hovering gun barrels. A fraction of a second before the order to fire was given he looked at Desaix, then back at the yawning muzzles. As they breathed fire and lead, Moreau lowered his head in prayer. When the smoke cleared again, five more bodies lay on the already drenched sand.

Desaix wheeled his horse and rode back towards the front of the column, not looking back to see how many of the would-be deserters had rejoined the division. Very few wandered back to their comrades as the column moved on, preferring to remain beneath the mighty flare of the sun.

Lausard had been impressed at the fortitude with which the men had faced the firing squad, but their courage, he mused, had been worthless. It had gained them nothing. It had been only a minor diversion. If three hundred men or even a thousand had been shot for refusing to march on, he reasoned, it would have made no difference to Bonaparte. The Corsican obviously intended seeing this campaign through to the bitter end no matter what the toll of misery and suffering. He glanced across at the bullet-blasted bodies as the dragoons rode slowly past.

Delpierre rode past him and spat in their direction. 'Cowardly scum.' He looked directly at Lausard, who ignored him.

'Why does that man hate you?' Karim asked, as Delpierre rode back towards the rear of the dragoons.

Lausard smiled. 'Ask *him*'

'It does not concern you that one of your comrades despises you?'

'He's no comrade of mine. He's in the same regiment that's all. But even if he *was* in this unit, why should I be troubled by his hatred? He means nothing to me. I don't ask *any* man to like me. I appreciate their respect but I care nothing for their feelings towards me.'

'But you would risk your life for them?' Karim persisted.

Lausard nodded. 'As if they were my brothers. Is that so hard to understand, Karim? Perhaps that is why the Mamelukes think we are possessed by demons. Sometimes we don't even understand our own actions, let alone those of others.'

'So you would fight alongside men you hate or who hated you? You would risk your life for those you have nothing in common with?'

'Yes. Because in the end it isn't a matter of belief, it's a matter of honour. And honour is the one thing I have left that I value. And I will take it to my grave. Wherever that may be.'

The column moved on.

Lausard had been expecting a majestic, awe-inspiring

blue and green expanse of water cutting through the sand like a sword through silk. What he saw was a dirty brown ribbon of water meandering between sand dunes. There was very little majesty about the Nile at its lowest level. Nevertheless, it was a sight to cheer any man. Water. No matter how filthy, how polluted by mud.

On both sides of the sloping banks palm trees grew abundantly and, amidst the patches of greenery covering the land around the river, the men found large round objects bigger than cannonballs, which some of them recognized as water melons. Dotted close to the westerly bank were two or three dozen of the mud and straw hovels now so familiar to the French, and a couple of abandoned camels roamed amongst the crumbling buildings.

The town of El Rahmaniya was even less impressive than Damanhur had been, but Lausard, like most of the men in the column, was more interested in the sight of the Nile and the water melons than in the town itself. Even as he watched, men began to break ranks and run towards the river, officers among them. No attempt was made to check the stampede of troops, who seemed to have discovered new strength in their frenzied race to be the first to reach the cooling waters. Several dragoons broke away, urging on their horses at a gallop, such was their eagerness to reach the Nile. They passed the infantrymen who struggled through the sand, desperate to reach the river before it disappeared like one of the all-too-familiar mirages. Lausard saw Captain Milliere raise his hand in an effort to halt some of the dragoons but, realizing the futility of trying to stop the men, he gave up and joined them himself. Even Lausard spurred his mount and joined the headlong rush.

The leading troops crashed through the patches of

water melons, crushing some beneath their feet. Many of the men fell on the fruit as if it was a kind of heaven-sent manna, ripping it open and gorging themselves on the red pulp within. They stuffed chunks of it into their mouths, savouring the moisture, screaming their delight and relief. Some were so ravenous they even ate the skin.

Most, Lausard included, hurtled on towards the banks of the Nile and into the water itself. Even the horses seemed to be seized by the same maniacal joy as their riders and threw themselves full length into the muddy depths, tossing their riders from the saddles. Many of the men didn't bother to remove their uniforms, and plunged into the muddy flow, mouths open, drinking down the soothing liquid with an unbridled ecstasy.

Lausard launched himself from his saddle and landed with a loud splash. He swallowed great gulps of the muddy water, hardly aware of the sand grains it contained. He felt his belly swelling as he continued to drink, noticing that Rocheteau, Moreau, Delacor and even Milliere and Lieutenant Royere had joined him in the muddy river.

On the shore, more men were tearing off their clothes, running naked into the water, their shouts of delight mingling with those of the men already slaking their thirsts. Having satisfied their immediate needs some were contentedly floating on their backs or swimming back and forth slowly, enjoying the coolness of the water on their skin.

As men and horses alike drank until their stomachs were full, Lausard looked up and noticed Karim sipping slowly from a metal cup. The Circassian raised the cup in salute and Lausard smiled.

Charvet, Bonet and Joubert were sitting surrounded

by melons, cutting them open with their bayonets and feasting on them without even bothering to spit out the pips. Joubert devoured three of the large fruit in minutes and rubbed his belly.

Even General Desaix was standing in the water, up to his boot tops, scooping the dirty fluid into his hands, splashing his face and drinking too.

To Lausard it seemed as if the entire river was filled with troops, drinking and washing, swimming or floating and relaxing. Even the sun beating mercilessly down upon them could not quell their joy. When it became too unbearable, the men simply ducked their heads beneath the surface. Lausard saw horses cavorting about in the water like spring lambs, as delighted to be drinking as their riders.

The sergeant had no idea how long he spent in the river, but finally, his stomach distended, he walked up the shore, where he joined Karim and Carbonne, who handed him a piece of water melon. Lausard ate hungrily. He stood on the bank with some of his men watching others thrashing about in the water. Delpierre scooping water into his mouth, Chatillo and Tigana washing their tunics in the muddy river, Charnier from number two squadron lifting a gourd full of water over his head and pouring it down to cool his sun-baked scalp. An air of happiness and relief that had not been witnessed for many months had overtaken the men, and it was an infectious joy, one which even Lausard felt. It was as if all the toil and torture of the desert marches had been worthwhile for just this moment.

Momentarily the men forgot everything: the agony of the blistering sun, the heat that sucked air from their lungs, the searing sunlight that blinded them, the khamsin that scorched their skin and peppered them with hot sand grains. Even the agonies of thirst and hunger were pushed to the back of their minds.

Lausard accepted another piece of water melon from Carbonne and ate it with relish, juice running down his face. As he looked on he noticed amongst the banks littered with discarded uniforms and weapons a number of soldiers lying motionless, some half in, some half out of the water. He crossed to one, an infantry sergeant, and prodded the man with the toe of his boot. The soldier's head fell to one side and Lausard saw that his eyes were staring blindly. The man's belly was swollen up as if he was pregnant, his tongue lolling from one corner of his mouth, and Lausard realized he was dead. There were others in the same condition. To drink so much after having gone without for so long had taken the ultimate toll on these men.

Elsewhere, others, bloated with the amount they had drunk, were crawling out of the water like wriggling, swollen worms, making their way up the bank where the scorching sun rapidly dried their uniforms and once again tortured their flesh. Those who had eaten their fill of water melons were now feeling the painfully uncomfortable beginnings of stomach cramps, but many ignored the pain and continued to gorge themselves. The effects of excessive eating and drinking were as dangerous as the discomfort of thirst and hunger, but as they had flocked towards the Nile and its bounty, none of the men had given a second thought to how their stomachs, deprived of food and water over the past weeks, had shrunk. All they saw was the chance to relieve their suffering and they took it.

Those men who had water bottles were eagerly filling

them with the muddy water, determined not to have to go without fluid again for as long as they had during the desert marches. A canteen full of dirt, it seemed, was preferable to nothing at all. Now that the dragoons had quenched their own thirst, those whose horses hadn't charged into the river of their own accord now led their animals to the Nile to drink. Many of the animals, Lausard noticed, drank with the same abandon as their riders – and many also paid the price. As he strolled up and down the bank Lausard saw more than a dozen of the stricken animals collapsed on the soggy sand or in the water itself. He also saw many of them urinating or defecating into the water, while, all around them, troops still not satiated continued to drink.

Food, water and rest. The three things they had craved so badly for so long were theirs for the time being and Lausard, like so many of the other men in the division, was determined to enjoy this brief respite from suffering. He had no idea how long it would last.

It began with agonizing stomach pains.

To Lausard it felt as if someone had pierced his belly with red-hot hooks and was trying to yank out his insides. The pain was excruciating. It spread slowly to his lower back and his bowels, and as it did he felt a new sensation. Not pain but an unavoidable relaxing of the muscles there.

Others were suffering too. Joubert and Moreau were experiencing the same symptoms, and from the groans rising into the night air Lausard was convinced that most of the army was suffering exactly as he and his companions were. The vile odour of human excrement seemed to clog his nostrils. He saw Gaston doubled up, the young trumpeter vomiting Nile water and water melon on to the sand. And he was not alone. Throughout the division, men were in the grip of this insidious torment – the latest torture they had been forced to endure since arriving in a land with nothing but hardship to offer.

'What curse is this?' Delacor clutched his stomach, feeling his bowels loosen. He looked at Karim accusingly.

'The fruit and the water. You drank too much and you ate more than you needed.'

'How do we stop it?' Lausard asked through clenched teeth.

'Cooked rice or bread usually works – or at least helps.'

'Did the Mamelukes teach you medicine as well as swordplay and horsemanship?' Rocheteau wanted to know, feeling his own stomach contract.

'They taught me many things. I learned the ways of the desert myself for the most part.'

'Bread,' Lausard said, looking around at the hovels of El Rahminaya. 'There is plenty of wheat around here but no flour mills or baking ovens.' He turned to Rocheteau. 'Give me that bag of wheat you took.'

The corporal handed it over without hesitation.

'Fetch me some flat stones,' Lausard instructed. 'And some kindling. We need to build a fire.'

Half a dozen of the dragoons scurried off to fetch what the sergeant had requested, pulling branches from nearby palm trees and stripping them. Sonnier and Gaston returned with five or six large, flat rocks and watched as Lausard poured some of the wheat on to one and began pounding it with another until he had a large quantity of brownish yellow powder. To this he added some water from his canteen, and used a stick to stir the mixture around in a small clay pot Roussard had found in one of the abandoned hovels. Meanwhile, Rocheteau and Giresse lit a fire, using two spare flints the corporal took from his cartouche. When it was ablaze, Lausard poured quantities of the thick wheat and water mixture on to some flat stones and placed them in the fire. After a few minutes a glorious aroma spread from the blaze, and even though the loaves were charred, the men found their mouths watering. Troops nearby also detected the heavenly scent and some wandered over to check it out. But the dragoons stood and faced them, guarding their meal jealously, the pain that racked them making them even more fearsome. The stones were glowing red and Lausard used his bayonet to pick one from the fire, flipping it out, taking the flat, blackened creation baked upon it in his hand. He broke it into several pieces and handed it around to the men closest to him, who ate ravenously.

He did the same with each of the six delicacies as and when they were ready for consumption.

'Glorious!' Joubert declared, chewing on the seared wheat that looked more like a blackened pancake than a loaf, but it was a welcome change from water melon.

'My father would have been proud of you, Alain,' Charvet said, pushing a piece of the bread into his mouth. 'He was a master baker. If I close my eyes I can still imagine the smell of his shop and those loaves he cooked.'

'And a good red wine to go with it,' Giresse added. 'With some onions cooked in oil.'

'And an omelette.' Bonet wiped his mouth with the back of his hand. 'I can't remember the last time I ate eggs. Mind you, I can't remember the last time I ate bread.'

'I haven't eaten any bread since before we left Toulon,' Lausard exclaimed. 'How long ago is that? Time seems to have lost its meaning here.' He rubbed his stomach as he ate, his belly rumbling ominously. He hoped this remedy worked.

'Water melons can be cooked,' Karim informed them. 'If they are, they should be safe.'

Lausard nodded.

'How come you're not afflicted with this disease as we are?' Roussard asked Karim.

'Your stomachs are not used to this kind of diet. That is why you suffer. You have known only pampering for too long.'

'Pampering?' Delacor snarled. 'Fighting for crumbs in the gutters of Paris. Do you call that pampering?'

'It seems you have lost your sense of humour along with the contents of your stomach.' Karim's reply was accompanied by laughter.

'When is this all going to end?' Joubert asked mournfully, his stomach contracting painfully yet again. He groaned.

'The rest of the army is gathered here or close by,' Lausard said. 'The time is near.'

'For what?' Roussard demanded. 'Our deaths at the hands of the Mamelukes?'

'Better a death in battle than to disease, thirst or hunger,' Lausard retorted.

'I don't want death from any*one* or any*thing*,' Roussard announced.

'We could all pray to God to protect us,' Moreau offered.

'The way he's protected us so far?' Lausard sneered. 'Go ahead, you pray if that's what you want, but leave me out of it.'

'Do you believe in God, Karim?' Bonet addressed the Circassian.

'I believe in Allah, all praise to him. That is what I was brought up to believe. That is why the Mamelukes and the Bedouin will resist you. To them this is a holy war. You represent not just a threat to their country but a threat to their religion too. They will not allow that.'

'We'll see,' murmured Lausard, pushing more of the charred bread into his mouth. 'They may not have any choice.'

Twenty-Three

The tent was small compared to Bonaparte's usual dwelling. He had chosen to spend the night in a subaltern's tent rather than his usual 'Marquis' tent, forsaking the hundredweight of canvas and seven-foot supporting ridgepoles for a bivouac usually shared by up to three men. The size of the enclosure didn't bother him though. His mind was on more pressing matters as he pored over the maps laid out before him. Berthier sat at a small table, quill in hand, watching his commander, while Sulkowski and Junot hovered close by the entrance should they be called upon to deliver orders to any of the five divisional commanders.

'Are you sure the information is correct?' Berthier asked, finally breaking a lengthy silence.

Bonaparte looked around at him and smiled. 'The spies who acquired it were well paid. Even now Murad Bey approaches the town of Shubra Khit. Less than eight miles south of here. He has under his command three to four thousand horsemen, several thousand foot soldiers and a flotilla of gunboats. It is the moment I have waited for, Berthier. The chance to confront the *true* enemy. The Mamelukes.'

'What are your orders?'

Bonaparte got to his feet and began pacing back and forth slowly, gazing off into the distance, as if looking through the material of the tent.

'You will instruct Generals Desaix, Reynier, Bon, Dugua and Vial to march on Shubra Khit,' the Corsican began. 'They are to march through the night if necessary and they will manoeuvre by way of the town of Minyet Salama.'

The scratching of quill on parchment became clearly audible inside the tent as Berthier transcribed his commander's words.

'Captain Perrée's flotilla will also converge on that point,' Bonaparte continued. 'Send an order to General Andréossy that he is to go aboard *Le Cerf*, Perrée's flagship, and direct the supporting action from the river. Instruct General Dumas that all non-mounted cavalry are also to board the flotilla. Those men with mounts will take shelter inside each divisional square unless otherwise instructed. The baggage trains will also remain inside the squares. Each division will fight in squares six ranks deep on all four sides, the artillery to be placed at the corners of the squares. It is imperative these orders are followed. The strictest discipline must be maintained during the battle. There is but one way to defeat the Mamelukes and that is to face them with an orderly, immovable front. That is exactly what I intend to do.'

Berthier scribbled away. 'What is the strength of the Moslem flotilla?' he asked.

'As far as my spies could tell they have seven ships. Mostly manned by Greeks and Turks.'

'Seven to our five.'

'The combat will be on the land, not the water. That is merely a diversion.' Bonaparte clapped his hands together and smiled broadly. 'The time has come, Berthier. In a few hours from now we will destroy the Mamelukes once and for all. Our destiny awaits us.'

Lausard sat motionless on his horse and watched as the six horsemen cantered around the perimeter of the square. All of them were large men, their stature increased further by the sheer volume of clothing they wore and the array of weapons they carried. The early-morning sun glinted on their weapons and gilded helmets, the rays accentuating the dizzying variety of colours worn by each of the Mamelukes. Over muslin shirts they wore layers of bright and brilliant silken vests and caftans, more often than not criss-crossed by belts inlaid with jewels, and the entire dazzling ensemble was highlighted by voluminous silken trousers, one leg of which would have comfortably wrapped a man. Their horses too were richly harnessed, some wearing saddle cloths inlaid with gold and precious stones. Even the flat, Oriental stirrups they used were gilt. But these were deadly too, the outer and inner edges sharpened to act as an extra weapon during close-quarters combat. Infantry could be kicked in the face, enemy horses slashed or opposing cavalry cut with one expert kick of those scythe-edged stirrups.

Lausard was mesmerized by the brilliance of these horsemen but also puzzled by their tactics. For more than three hours now, ever since dawn, small detachments of Mameluke horsemen had left their seething lines to the south of Shubra Khit, galloped towards the French, then slowed their magnificent mounts and cantered in and around the network of divisional squares looking at their enemy. They made no attempt to attack but rode past repeatedly as if on some kind of bizarre parade, occasionally speaking to each other and pointing at the squares.

The squares were six deep, as Bonaparte had ordered. The first two lines formed an impenetrable hedge of steel, some of the soldiers kneeling and resting the butts of their muskets on the sand so that the razor-sharp metal pointed upwards towards the Mamelukes. Behind, four more rows of muskets waited to fire at the given order. Two four-pounders had been left at the corner of each square, the gunners sheltering inside until told to man their pieces. They had loaded with case shot in preparation for the Mameluke attack which, at present, didn't seem to be materializing.

The Mameluke battle-line extended in a sickle shape from the Nile at Shubra Khit to the south and west of the French squares. Lausard noticed that although the line didn't move forward it was certainly not stationary. Every now and then, apart from horsemen who rode to inspect the French squares, men would dash forward and gallop at incredible speed from one end of the line to the other, as if to display to their comrades their finery and the majesty of their mount.

Lausard fumbled in his pocket for his telescope and peered more closely at the enemy troops. Behind the cavorting Mamelukes was a mass of foot soldiers, some, he noticed, armed with nothing more than wooden clubs. They were in no particular formation but stood beneath the blazing early-morning sun waiting for the order to advance, while their horsemen continued to display their riding skills in front of each other, apparently oblivious to the waiting French.

Lausard pocketed the telescope again and noticed that another small group of Mamelukes was cantering towards the square. It rode within ten yards of the bristling bayonets, peering curiously at the motionless French and the impenetrable squares. The French troops looked on with a mixture of bewilderment and something close to amusement. They continued to hold their fire.

'What the hell are they doing?' Rocheteau asked Karim.

'Looking for a weakness. This is all new to them. They are not yet sure how to attack.'

'Who are the infantry?' Lausard nodded towards the foot soldiers.

'Mostly Mameluke servants. The rest are Egyptian *fellahin*. They want to be here even less than you do,' Karim smiled.

'I doubt that,' Roussard said, watching as the enemy mass seethed, the sun glinting on all manner of weapons, jewels and precious metals.

'Will the servants fight?' Lausard pressed. 'They don't seem very well equipped.'

'Their only job is to help their masters,' Karim observed. 'The Mamelukes always fight in the same way. They will fire their carbines first then slide them under their thighs. Then they will fire their pistols; some carry up to three pairs. Those they will throw over their shoulders to be collected by their servants. Then they will throw their *djerids* – javelins made from stripped and sharpened palm branches – and, finally, they will charge with their scimitars. Some carry two; they grip the reins in their teeth and slash to right *and* left. And they will take off heads with one blow given the chance.'

Lausard nodded gravely as he listened.

'They know no fear,' the Circassian added. 'And they are rarely captured. For them there is either death or victory. If they are forced to flee they will do so with the same speed with which they attack. They will not allow you to take possession of their riches if they can help it.'

'Riches?' said Delacor, sitting up in his saddle.

'Each Mameluke carries his personal fortune on him, in money belts. Sometimes in the form of coins, sometimes as jewels.'

'Now that *is* interesting,' Delacor mused, rubbing his aching stomach.

'Perhaps we *will* go home rich men if we can get our hands on some of that.' Rocheteau chuckled.

'I wish to God they'd just attack and get it over with,' said Roussard.

'What's your problem?' Carbonne asked. 'We're safe in here.' He gestured around him at the six-rank walls of the square. 'It's the dog-faces who are going to get the worst of it.' He looked at the infantry and grinned.

A corporal in the rear rank heard him and looked round. 'We usually do. You bastards only ride in when the *real* work's been done. You should be thanking us for saving your miserable asses.'

Carbonne ignored him and, like his comrades, continued to gaze at both the detachments of Mamelukes still riding around the squares and the main force of Oriental horsemen, who continued to sway back and forth but made no attempt to advance.

'Perhaps they're waiting for the infantry to break ranks,' Bonet suggested.

'Then they'll be waiting a long time,' Lausard mused.

'Well at least they're prettier than the Austrians,' Rocheteau commented and several men within earshot laughed.

The sound was eclipsed by the sudden and thunderous retort of cannon fire.

All eyes turned in the direction of the blasts, to see that the French and Moslem flotillas on the Nile were exchanging fire. Within minutes, banks of thick smoke enveloped the vessels and began rolling across the water towards the land. It was as though a signal had been given. Lausard looked towards the Mameluke masses as he heard a chorus of high-pitched shrieks and screams. For brief seconds everything seemed to freeze. The horsemen, swords held up high in the air appeared motionless in full gallop, their horses rearing and kicking their hooves. Then the second passed. The full, teeming horde of Mameluke horsemen, screaming oaths and brandishing their glittering weapons, bore down on the French like a tidal wave. Dust from so many churning hooves sent a thick cloud into the air as the horsemen thundered forward. Trailing in their wake came the servants and the *fellahin*, dashing along as fast as they could behind their masters, who were now closing to within one hundred yards of the waiting French. Artillerymen slipped out from the squares to man their pieces and Lausard watched as corporals checked the sights and elevations of the barrels. Portfires were lit and ready. Around every square orders were bellowed to the infantry to hold their fire until told otherwise. Some of the words were lost amid the rumbling caused by the onrushing Mameluke horde, the churning hooves causing the ground to shake.

Lausard noticed there was no formation, no organization to the charge. The sharpened stirrups the Mamelukes used prevented them from riding in close order for fear of injuring each other. The entire frantic advance was nothing more than a disordered dash accompanied by blood-curdling shouts designed to strike terror into the enemy. But the French remained steady, awaiting the order to open fire. Some of the dragoons pulled their carbines to their shoulders, prepared to add their own firepower to that of the infantry.

The Mamelukes were less than one hundred yards away now and Lausard could see all manner of weapons being brandished by some of the leading riders.

Eighty yards.

Bullets sliced through the air as some of the Mamelukes opened fire.

Seventy yards.

Lausard could see battleaxes, maces, spears, swords and pikes being held aloft as the massive wave of horsemen drew ever nearer.

Sixty yards.

'Ready!' roared NCOs.

Fifty yards.

'Fire.'

The sound of so many muskets being discharged at once was deafening. And with that eruption came the fury of the cannon, spewing out their case shot into the onrushing Mamelukes. The volleys of fire and the salvoes from the cannon were devastating at such close range. Men and horses went down in bloodied heaps, riders' magnificent costumes transformed into bloody rags as bullets tore into them, the superb Arab ponies turning crimson. The entire battlefield was immediately shrouded in noxious, sulphurous smoke, and the Mamelukes appeared from the choking clouds shouting their defiance and milling around the squares, seeking some way in.

More volleys of fire, executed with perfect precision by the French, sent more of the enemy crashing to the ground. Some of those who had lost their horses charged the squares on foot, but they were shot down before they could get within twenty yards.

Despite the deafening crackle of musket fire, Lausard could hear an unceasing cannonade coming from the vessels on the Nile. He could also see smoke rising from more than one of them. The ships of the two flotillas were jammed together, some so close that men were fighting hand to hand aboard the flimsy craft. Then a choking cloud of smoke rolled across the square to once more hide the ships from view.

In many places, the Mamelukes withdrew a hundred or so yards and contented themselves with riding around the squares. Other groups charged at opposite sides of the same formation, hoping to find a weakness. More were brought down by the well-drilled fire. Lausard noticed how infantry in squares not under attack would peer across to watch their comrades firing endlessly into the mass of horsemen. Then, as the last of the Mamelukes withdrew to a safe distance, Lausard heard orders being shouted to cease fire.

Smoke drifted thickly across the battlefield as the French waited for the next wave of attack, but the only place where combat seemed to be truly taking place was on the Nile itself. Two of the ships from the French flotilla were now ablaze, thick black smoke rising into the cloudless sky, momentarily blotting out the sunlight over the vessels. Lausard wished that it would do the same inside the square. The temperature seemed to have risen, driven up by the fire from so many muskets. Infantrymen reloaded, their already dry mouths further parched by the coarse black powder from their cartridges and foul smoke that seared their throats.

Officers and NCOs strode around the inside of the formation checking for any gaps, but they found none. Those dragoons who had used their carbines against the Mamelukes were also busy reloading in anticipation of the next attack. But once again the Mamelukes seemed more intent on displaying their magnificent costumes and consummate horsemanship than on renewing combat. Lausard watched one of them riding back and forth waving his scimitar above his head, occasionally hurling it into the air, catching it by the hilt as it fell. He continued doing this for some time and Lausard could not resist a wry smile at the Moslem's theatrics. Sonnier lifted his carbine and prepared to take a shot at the dashing Mameluke, but Lausard raised his hand and pushed the barrel down, giving his companion a disdainful look.

Artillery men were busily preparing their cannon for the next onslaught, their attention distracted occasionally by the thunderous exchange coming from the Nile-bound flotillas. The ships were barely visible now, such was the thickness of smoke pouring from the burning vessels.

'There's some hot work going on there,' Lieutenant Royere commented, gazing across at the battle. 'Most of Bonaparte's *savants* are aboard those ships.'

'Let's see how those preening "pekinese" enjoy some fighting. Perhaps they'll use their brains to work out a way to defeat the Arabs. After all they're all so clever, aren't they? What good will their brains do them when they're blown out of their heads?' Delacor laughed at his own wit, as did a number of the other men.

'They have suffered hardships as we have,' Bonet said. 'And why do you decry them for their intellect? Just because you are an idiot.'

'Watch it, schoolmaster, or I'll spill *your* brains.'

'At least I have some to spill.'

'Shut up, both of you!' Lausard snapped, watching as the battle on the Nile became more frenzied.

The gunfire was incessant and through the swirling, choking smoke, Lausard could see that batteries on both sides of the Nile – French and Moslem – were being brought to bear on the ships. Protected by infantry, the French gunners poured shot into any Moslem ship within range while, from the far bank, more Greek and Turkish troops added their firepower to that already devastating the French flotilla.

'Look,' Moreau said, grabbing Lausard's arm. 'They're withdrawing.' He was pointing to the Mameluke cavalry, who had wheeled away from the French and started retreating in the direction they had come, towards Shubra Khit. Almost immediately, a series of orders was barked out and the squares broke, the infantry hastily forming columns. Captain Milliere and Lieutenant Royere galloped between squares, gathering their men, forming them into small detachments which moved off slightly behind the infantry.

'What about the bodies?' Delacor said, looking down at a dead Mameluke riddled with bullet wounds. 'If they're all carrying money like Karim said . . .'

'This isn't over yet,' Lausard told him, noticing in the distance that the Mameluke cavalry were rapidly re-forming.

'This is no battle,' Rostov said disdainfully. 'They have no stomach for it.'

Lausard didn't answer, but kept his eyes on the glittering horde, aware also of the increasing volume of noise to his left where the water-borne battle continued. Smoke seemed to have virtually consumed the French fleet and Lausard glanced across to see flames leaping from within the choking blanket. Every now and then he could just make out bodies falling into the water, some pushed, some toppling from wounds, others jumping to avoid the hand-to-hand combat that had spilled over on to the decks.

Meanwhile, the advancing infantry had raised standards, as if this show of martial pride might goad the reassembling Mamelukes into another charge, but still the Moslem horsemen seemed content to career about with apparently no purpose, seemingly unconcerned that their enemy was now advancing towards them. A series of demi-brigades was marching towards the Nile with the intention of bringing their own firepower to bear on the attacking enemy flotilla. From somewhere Lausard could hear the familiar strains of 'La Marseillaise', but the continuous cannon fire and the smoke and the dust being raised by so many marching feet made it impossible to detect its source.

Lausard looked towards the Nile once more.

The explosion was enormous.

A thunderous detonation that deafened even those several hundred yards away and sent a concussion blast rolling across both water and sand.

Lausard watched as the Moslem flagship disappeared in a scorching ball of red and yellow fire, lumps of wood, metal, canvas and men flung into the air by the ferocity of the blast. The ship, he reasoned, had to be carrying extra ammunition. No conventional shell hit could cause such incredible destruction. Several secondary blasts confirmed his suspicions, and he looked on as the ship continued to explode even as it was sinking. Those on board who had survived the initial series of blasts were now hurling themselves into the murky waters of the Nile to escape the fury of the inferno.

'Jesus!' Rocheteau murmured, peering through the rolling smoke at the remains of the vessel.

Lausard continued to watch the blazing wreckage until Rostov grabbed his arm to draw his attention to the Mamelukes. They had wheeled their horses and were galloping away from the advancing French, the dust cloud they left behind almost as thick as the belching smoke drifting across from the burning flagship.

'I said they had no stomach for this,' Rostov said, grinning, and several of the men around him began to shout obscenities at the fleeing Moslems. Even the infantry were bellowing abuse at their fleeing foes, some even laughing hysterically as they watched the remains of the flagship being engulfed by flames.

'Look, there's Bonaparte.' Giresse pointed to the commander in chief riding past on a grey horse, accompanied by Berthier, Junot, Sulkowski and several guides.

'He doesn't look too happy for a man who has just won a battle,' Carbonne commented.

'Rostov was right,' Lausard observed. 'This was no battle. Not the victory Bonaparte wanted. This was just a skirmish. All it has proved is that the Mamelukes don't know how to defeat well-trained, disciplined men.'

'Even if half of them *are* blind and suffering from diarrhoea,' Bonet added and a number of the men laughed.

'Let's hope they run as easily *every* time we meet them,' Sonnier said.

'And let's hope we all get a rest now we've beaten them.' Joubert wiped sweat from his face.

'I wouldn't count on it,' Lausard said. 'And perhaps we should be more disappointed they *didn't* fight. Because the longer they run, the further we have to chase them across this stinking desert. I disagree with you, Rostov. I don't think they flee because they have no stomach for a fight. I fear they flee because they know that this country is as much an enemy to us as they are. How long will it be before they stand against us again? Or before we even *see* them? I suspect that is why Bonaparte looks so angry. He is thinking the same thing. We need to *crush* them, not play cat and mouse with them. They are drawing us deeper into *their* land, where we must fight them on *their* terms, on *their* terrain. They are not cowards and they are not fools. Half the army is sick now. Who knows what state we'll all be in by the time we face them again.'

Twenty-Four

'What is the name of this place?' Napoleon Bonaparte asked, looking down from the dunes that surrounded the village.

'Nekleh,' Sulkowski informed him, his eyes riveted to the pandemonium before him.

The village was ablaze. Every single dwelling had been torched by the marauding French troops, who Bonaparte and his staff now watched dashing through it, some on foot, some on horseback. Bodies littered the narrow streets and small squares. Men, women and children had been butchered by the French as their commander in chief looked on, undisturbed by the sight.

'What do you hope to gain by allowing such atrocities?' Berthier asked, looking on with disgust.

'Atrocities?' Bonaparte's eyes never left the burning village. 'This is war, Berthier, and it calls for drastic action. This village had promised to sell us provisions. It would not. I cannot allow that kind of insolence. It has already spread to many other places during our journey. Would you rather I allowed these savages to treat our men as they wish? To deprive them of food and water? Would you prefer our men to die in their place?'

'But these are women and children whose deaths you ordered,' Berthier argued. 'This village has no tactical worth, its inhabitants offer no threat.'

'They offer a threat to order by their treachery. And their determination *not* to sell us provisions indicates to me that they are our enemies, that they would see us starve or die for want of water. What they suffer they bring upon themselves. They and others like them. This army has always survived by foraging, it will continue to do so here.'

'Foraging, not *butchering*,' Berthier challenged. 'We are meant to be winning over the local people by our presence, by our role as liberators from the tyranny of the Mamelukes, and instead we bring them death and torture. Where are the principles of the Republic? Where are *our* principles?'

'Lost in the desert sand. We have pursued the Mamelukes for four days now since Shubra Khit. I have twenty-five thousand men with which to defeat them. Intelligence reports tell me that they await me with almost forty thousand. They are fresh, rested and fighting on ground of *their* choosing. My army is sick, hungry, thirsty and exhausted, and yet still they march because they believe in *me*. They have no doubt that they will be victorious. They know I will give them the victory they need.'

'Is the massacre of innocents what they need in order to?' Berthier persisted, glancing down at the smoking ruins of Nekleh.

'The village was hostile. Do not presume to question me, Berthier. I know what I must do and I am prepared to do it. For the greater glory of France and the Republic, incidents like this, although regrettable, must occur. I will tolerate no resistance.'

'You speak like a conqueror, not a liberator.'

'The two are very similar,' Bonaparte told him. 'Those who welcome us need have no fear. I have tried to be fair throughout this campaign but I am repaid with treachery. I will not stand for that. What some see as kindliness others see as weakness. I cannot allow myself to appear weak before these people. Similarly, what some see as brutal, others view as strength. It is strength that we must show if we are to prevail. Let the name of this village stand as an example to those who would oppose us, but if this example is not sufficient then I will not hesitate to order more action against the locals. They must be taught a lesson. They must learn to welcome us, not oppose us, and if it is by fear that we rule then so be it.'

Lausard sat on the damp sand, gazing into the flames of the camp fire as they flickered and danced in the stillness of the night. The mouth-watering aroma of roasting pigeon, skewered on the ramrod of a carbine and suspended on the makeshift spit over the fire, reached him, although it was accompanied by a number of other less savoury odours. The smell of many unwashed bodies, of excrement – human, horse and camel – also washed over him. The entire army seemed to have been crushed into the smallest area possible, and were crowded all around. And this mêlée of men and animals did not respect rank because officers, even colonels and generals, were hemmed in as comprehensively as ordinary soldiers. The sick, the able-bodied and those somewhere in between were all gathered together unceremoniously.

There were other camp fires close by, men from other units eagerly cooking everything from lentils to water melon. Even though the fruit had caused such ferocious dysentery among the men, they had continued to feast on it during the four-day march from Shubra Khit, mainly because there was little else to fill their bellies or quench their raging thirsts, but an order from Bonaparte himself instructed that provided the fruit was cooked it was safe to consume.

Elsewhere, those who had scavenged through the pitiful provisions of some villages on the march were enjoying meat, rice and even some of the local bread. Lausard himself had taken two sacks of rice from a village only that morning, and some of his haul was now bubbling away over the same fire in a metal bowl Delacor had stolen, along with a chicken now dangling from his saddle. Giresse had taken some cashmere shawls from one of the villages and stuffed them in his portmanteau, assuring his companions that he would trade them for food when he had the chance, but Lausard doubted anyone in the army would swap something edible for a few shawls, regardless of their value. The only things that had *real* worth in the desert were food and drink.

He watched Rocheteau turning the pigeon, his stomach rumbling from both hunger and the ever-present dysentery. The men sitting around the fire seemed subdued, wearied beyond endurance by the rigours of the campaign. Lausard thought particularly of the massacre at Nekleh. His unit had ridden through shortly after the leading infantry units had begun their eradication of the village. Bodies had littered the streets; men, women and children shot, bayoneted or burned to death. All of the men had seen death before, Lausard thought, all of them had killed and would kill again, but the slaughter at Nekleh was different in its ferocity, and the apparent relish with which it was carried out. Someone had told him that over nine hundred Egyptians had been killed in less than an hour. He marvelled at how men who were so exhausted and drained by hunger and fatigue could suddenly find the energy to commit such acts. But they had, and Lausard had no doubt they would again before this campaign was over.

Gaston, Roussard and Tigana were busy feeding the horses with what little they had collected from various villages during the march. While most of the officers of other units, cavalry *and* infantry, had allowed their men to scavenge at will, Milliere had detailed his men to fetch fodder for the horses along with provisions for themselves.

Finally, Rocheteau took the cooked pigeon from the ramrod and set about cutting it up.

'About time,' Joubert said, rubbing his stomach. 'I'm starving.'

'You're always starving, fat man,' Rocheteau told him.

Lausard accepted his portion and some of the rice and chewed thoughtfully.

'Save some for the others,' he instructed, nodding towards the men feeding the horses. 'They'll need it.'

'We all need it,' Delacor complained.

'Shall I give some to Lieutenant Royere? He's over there.' Rocheteau gestured towards the officer, who was stretched out on some straw, his head resting on a rolled-up blanket.

'I'll take it,' Lausard said, getting to his feet, taking the food and heading off towards the officer.

As Lausard sat down beside the lieutenant and pushed the pigeon and rice towards him, he saw that the officer was studying a map. Several crosses had been drawn on it.

'The Mamelukes await us outside Cairo,' Royere said, chewing a piece of meat. 'Captain Milliere has already been given orders that we move out at two this morning.' He consulted his time piece. 'Less than an hour.'

'To where? To march across more of this desert? To chase the Mamelukes? To try to fight men who do not *want* to fight?'

'If it is any consolation, Lausard, the entire army shares your feelings. There isn't a man here, and that includes some of the officers, who knows what the hell Bonaparte is doing. Perhaps he isn't even sure himself.' The officer exhaled wearily. 'Once it was a new adventure, but I have a feeling that one day this land will swallow us up. Is that sedition?' He smiled. 'Am I betraying the ethics of the Republic?'

'Don't ask *me* about the ethics of the Republic, Lieutenant,' Lausard snapped. 'I know nothing of its ideals and I *care* nothing for them. Perhaps *that* is sedition.'

'What about the ideals of the ordinary soldier?'

'The French soldier no longer has any ideals. Even if he had to begin with. He is not fighting for the culture of the west, or for one form of government which he wants, and not for the Republic. He's fighting for his life.'

Royere shrugged. 'You may be right. But as a soldier, I feel it is my duty to subordinate my own ideals to the principles and ideals of my country, of the Republic.'

'Right or wrong?'

'Possibly. I believe what Bonaparte is trying to do here is right. Don't you?'

'Does my opinion really matter, Lieutenant? To you? To anyone? It certainly doesn't matter to Bonaparte. How many men have we already left back in that desert? How many have died since we first landed here? Thousands? And for what? Are we any closer to subduing the Mamelukes? Are we any nearer taking control of this country? No. Instead we march and we starve and we die.'

'Other men refused to march on. Why didn't you if you feel so strongly about the futility of this campaign?'

'Those men would not do their duty. As soldiers they should. I am bound by something more powerful than duty. I am bound by honour. That is why I will march and fight and obey orders, even if I do find some of them both ridiculous *and* distasteful.'

'You mean Nekleh?'

'That was *one* order, Lieutenant. One idiotic order among hundreds that have been given since we landed, and both of us know there will be more.' He got to his feet, preparing to rejoin his companions.

'And will you obey them, Lausard?'

The sergeant smiled, then disappeared back into the gloom.

Throughout the night march, Lausard could hear the waters of the Nile lapping against its shores. The army rarely moved more than a mile away from its flowing current, keeping the river on its left flank as it trudged through the sand and water melon patches. Palm trees grew in relative abundance along the river bank and the gentle breeze rustled their fronds as the French passed beneath them. The jingle of harnesses and the rattle of equipment also filled the ears of the marching men, who found, to their relief, that the terrain was fairly level.

As dawn broke and the sun rose into the cloudless sky, the heat Lausard and the rest of the army had come to know and detest began to intensify. Flies swarmed around the men with even more frenzy than usual; dressed as most of them were in filthy uniforms, they made even more tempting targets for the bloated insects. Horses flicked their tails to drive away the troublesome pests while many of the men seemed resigned to the flies' presence and allowed them to crawl over their flesh.

Every few yards men broke rank and scuttled off towards the nearest sand dune or clump of trees as their dysentery tormented them. Some didn't even bother to break ranks and merely defecated as they marched.

A strange, subdued air had overtaken the entire army as it moved relentlessly across the sand. A combination, Lausard thought, of weary resignation and dogged determination. The men were clearly exhausted and moved like automatons, some supported by equally weary colleagues, some still suffering from ophthalmia; all still hungry and thirsty. But it was as if, because they had come this far, they were determined not to give up now.

As the day dragged mercilessly on, the sun rose higher in the sky, the heat growing unbearable. At least half a dozen cavalry mounts collapsed and were shot to put them out of their misery. The animals that drew the artillery fared even worse and the gunners had a difficult task guiding their cannon over the numerous dry streams and irrigation canals. Wheels and axles on both guns and their limbers broke with despairing regularity and a number of units were left to repair the equipment on the spot.

Through the shimmering heat, Lausard saw something moving.

It took him only a second to realize that it was a large body of troops, the sun dancing on their bright costumes and numerous weapons. On both sides of the Nile they swarmed back and forth, and Lausard guessed they were less than a mile from the advancing French. As at Shubra Khit, the Mamelukes rode madly about on their magnificent horses, glorying in their opulent appearance, as if that alone would be enough to make the French turn back. Lausard looked on with admiration: they had exhibited great bravery at Shubra Khit and he wondered how effective they would be if that bravery was ever harnessed to correct military discipline and tactics.

He kept his eyes on the seething, threatening mass, glancing occasionally across to the left, at the glittering skyline of domes and minarets that rose above Cairo itself. And beyond the Mameluke battle line to the outlines of the great pyramids, the huge and mysterious objects clearly visible even at ten miles' distance. Bonet too had seen them and seemed to forget momentarily the Arab horsemen before him, so intent was he in gazing at the ancient monuments. Lausard handed him his telescope, allowing the former schoolmaster to see the massive edifices more clearly.

'Magnificent!' Bonet breathed, his voice full of awe. 'Just look at them. A wondrous sight to behold.'

'What are they?' Tabor asked.

'The great pyramids, my friend,' Bonet said, still gazing through the telescope. 'The final resting place of the pharoahs.'

'And who were the pharoahs?' Delacor pressed. 'Are they our enemies like the Mamelukes and every other bastard in this stinking country?'

Bonet chuckled. 'I don't think we have anything to fear from *them*. They have been buried inside the pyramids for thousands of years.'

'You mean those things are graves?'

'Hundreds of feet high,' Bonet said, still marvelling at the sight. 'Built by thousands of slaves as monuments to the greatness of their kings.'

'The Bourbons didn't get anything like that after we'd finished with them, did they?' Delacor cackled. 'All they got was a hole in the ground.'

Some of the other men laughed.

'The pharoahs were buried with all their personal belongings and fortunes,' Bonet continued.

'You mean those things are full of gold?' Delacor suddenly had a new interest in the ancient monuments. 'If we could get inside them we'd be rich.'

Bonet laughed. 'Some of the slaves who helped to build them were killed afterwards so they couldn't tell what kind of treasure was inside.'

'Who cares?' Roussard said agitatedly. 'We're about to be ridden down by those madmen over there and all you're concerned about is some piles of stone.'

'Piles of stone?' Bonet blurted indignantly. 'They are one of the seven wonders of the world, not some fairground side-show.'

'I still think they're too big for gravestones,' said Rocheteau, smiling.

Lausard also grinned and took back the telescope from Bonet, using it himself to sweep the Mameluke battle line.

He turned to Karim. 'Will they attack us as they did at Shubra Khit?'

'They will because they know no other way.'

Lausard looked up and saw Captain Milliere galloping across the sand towards them. He reined in his horse and looked at Lausard.

'Your squadron is to occupy that village,' he pointed to a collection of buildings away to their right. 'General Desaix has ordered it to be held. He is sending some grenadiers to support you.'

'What about the rest of the regiment, sir?'

'They will take up shelter within General Desaix's divisional square as before.'

Lausard looked past the captain and saw that the infantry was no longer in columns. Indeed, across the entire five-mile front, the troops were in the process of forming their squares, the artillery being positioned at each corner as it had been at Shubra Khit. Led by Milliere, Lausard and his squadron cantered across the burning sand towards the collection of buildings that made up the village of Biktil. Behind them, a detachment of grenadiers followed, some glancing worriedly towards the Mamelukes, anxious to reach the relative safety of the houses they were to defend.

Lausard and his unit drove their horses into the small dwellings, then immediately began preparing their carbines in readiness for the attack. Lausard chose a window and pressed his weapon hard into his shoulder, his cartouche open, ready to pull more cartridges free. Sonnier looked up at the flat roof of the house and decided that it would make a better firing platform. With Rostov's help, he scrambled up.

'How do we know they won't run again?' Lausard did

not take his eyes from the Moslem horsemen even as he addressed Karim.

'There is nowhere else *for* them to run.' Karim was carefully wiping the blade of his scimitar with a cloth. 'They are fighting outside the very gates of their capital city. They will destroy you or die in the attempt.'

'Then let them come,' Lausard said through gritted teeth.

Bonaparte swept the battle lines with his telescope, a smile touching his thin lips.

'They hold the upper hand as far as numbers are concerned,' Berthier said, as he too studied the enemy troops. From the relative safety of General Dugua's divisional square, the commander in chief and his staff took careful note of the Mameluke disposition.

'Intelligence has their numbers at over seventy thousand,' Sulkowski said, trying to calm his skittish horse.

'That may be,' Bonaparte murmured. 'That may be. And we are twenty-five thousand, but the Mamelukes have divided their forces.' He pointed towards the right bank of the Nile. 'Over there, Ibrahim Bey is encamped at Bulaq, perhaps because they feared we would try to cross the Nile before attacking them. On this side of the river, Murad Bey has the remainder of their forces.'

'They also have a flotilla on the river itself,' Berthier added.

'Much good it did them at Shubra Khit,' Bonaparte said, still surveying the Moslem troops. 'They are exactly where we would have wished. If they had chosen to await us on the far bank they would have enjoyed an advantage. As it is, they have played into our hands.'

'What about that village?' Berthier motioned towards

the fortified stronghold of Embabeh, which backed on to the Nile. 'They have artillery there. A frontal assault will cost many troops.'

'Intelligence leads me to believe that the guns are on fixed carriages. Once Vial and Bon's men have passed through the initial barrage they should encounter little trouble. We will penetrate through the centre of their line and cut off their retreat.'

'And what if the Mameluke troops on the far bank attempt to cross, to join with their comrades?' Berthier mused.

'Our own flotilla will prevent that and artillery has already been positioned to cover the main landing points should they attempt it.' Bonaparte took the telescope from his eye and snapped it together, looking around at his staff, his eyes blazing. It was as if his entire being was quickened, his veins filled with fire. 'From those monuments yonder,' he gestured towards the pyramids in the distance, 'forty centuries look down upon you.'

Sulkowski glanced at his pocket watch.

'What time is it?' Bonaparte wanted to know.

'Half past three, sir,' Sulkowski told him, looking across towards the right of the French line, where the first wave of Mameluke horsemen was sweeping with incredible speed towards Desaix's division, the torrent of horsemen bearing down with such ferocious haste that it seemed the French would be engulfed before they could form squares.

'What the hell are they playing at?' Berthier said, a note of concern in his voice. 'What is Desaix doing? Hasn't he seen them?'

Bonaparte smiled. 'Where is your faith, Berthier? Desaix is no fool. He will have seen the attack coming. The

Mamelukes will not break through there or anywhere else.' He watched as they galloped madly across the blazing desert, a magnificent, glistening multitude. 'Gentlemen, it begins.'

Twenty-Five

Lausard had never seen cavalry move so fast. He had marvelled at the Mamelukes' horsemanship at Shubra Khit, but the speed with which they now advanced was amazing. The charge was carried out with such incredible speed and impetuousness that it looked as if it might be successful by its sheer audacity. The ground shook beneath his feet as over five thousand Moslem horsemen swept across the desert like a shimmering tide. The brilliant sunlight glinted on their upraised swords and the thunderous pounding of so many hooves was matched by a chorus of blood-curdling yells and oaths. A huge dust cloud chased them, rising skyward, threatening to blot out the sun.

Lausard wiped sweat from his face and pulled his carbine more tightly into his shoulder, watching as the leading riders began to draw perilously close both to the village and also to General Desaix's men, who were hastily forming a square. Lausard knew that if the infantry was caught in open order by the onrushing cavalry, it would be cut to pieces, and it seemed as if the entire division was moving in slow motion as it formed its ranks ten deep to meet this tide of men and horses. But considering their weakened condition, the French troops completed the manoeuvre with great efficiency, and as the Mamelukes drew nearer, they saw that several rows of bayonets and muskets awaited them. Lausard couldn't hear the order to fire, the noise of the churning hooves drowing it out; all he saw was a great flash of fire as the first volley was fired into the Mamelukes, the dull boom of cannon fire accompanying it. Then a second volley from another rank as the square spat flames and lead again and again.

Dozens of horsemen were sent crashing to the ground, some already dead, others badly wounded. Many were killed by the pounding hooves of oncoming horses. After three volleys the square was hidden from view by clouds of black smoke, but the soldiers kept on firing and Lausard could see the man-made fog being periodically ripped asunder by fresh volleys of fire. The Mamelukes couldn't even get close enough to swipe at the infantry with their swords, the impenetrable rows of bayonets ensuring that the men firing were protected as they constantly loaded and reloaded.

The Moslem horsemen divided into three columns, snaking around Desaix's square and coming under fire from Reynier's men. Lausard could see that the ground between Biktil and Desaix's square was already strewn with corpses; dead men and horses lay in untidy heaps close to the tightly packed formations. Elsewhere, wounded men crawled aimlessly on the bloody sand, one or two actually crawling towards the French troops, intent on inflicting damage on them even in the hour of their death. Lausard watched as two Mamelukes staggered to within feet of the hedge of bayonets before three or four grenadiers inside the square shot them down. A riderless horse galloped past, leaping and cavorting wildly. Another charged past dragging its lifeless rider with it, his foot still stuck in the stirrup.

In addition to the thundering of hooves, Lausard now heard the booming of cannon fire from further across the line, and pulling out his telescope he could see that French troops were moving forward towards the village of Embabeh. Moslem cannon fired at them as they advanced and, to the rear of the French positions, mortars hurled shells into the Mameluke mass. Explosions sent more of the enemy flying into the air, and sand and earth were sent spiralling upwards towards the cloudless sky. Smoke and dust rolled across the battlefield.

'They're not going to touch us,' Roussard said excitedly.

'What makes you think that?' Lausard asked.

'They rode past the village,' Roussard continued. 'They could have attacked us but they rode past.'

The Mamelukes had splintered into dozens of smaller groups by now, each flinging itself at a chosen square with little effect. The ocean of horsemen had floundered on the rocks of the French formations. The infantry kept up a steady fire and the rumble of musketry replaced the thunder of hooves as wave after wave of fire poured into the furious horsemen.

'Alain!'

Lausard looked up as he heard his name shouted and he stepped out of the house in which he was sheltering to where he could see Sonnier sitting on the roof. Using a water barrel beside the building, Lausard clambered up.

'Look,' Sonnier said, pointing.

'I see them,' Lausard murmured.

He guessed there must be close to five hundred Mamelukes hurtling towards Biktil, possibly more. They were charging towards the village with the same suicidal fury with which their comrades were flinging themselves against the squares. Lausard looked down into the village and realized that both his own men and the grenadiers would be overrun by this charge. More horsemen were converging from the western side, close to a thousand men intent on slaughtering the defenders of Biktil, eager to vent their rage and frustration on any French troops they could.

'Everyone up on the roofs,' Lausard ordered, glancing around him. 'Hurry!'

Men all over the village scurried to comply with the order, scrambling to haul themselves up. Lausard saw Tabor lifting first Gaston then Bonet up on to the roof of the building next door, then the two men helped the big man heave his massive frame up alongside them.

Moreau and Rostov used their carbines as a makeshift step, allowing Carbonne to put his foot on the weapons before hoisting him up. Everywhere, dragoons and infantry were dragging themselves up on to the roofs, aware from the thundering of hooves that the Mamelukes were drawing closer by the second.

The first dozen or so riders swept into the narrow streets and rode along hurling their *djerids* up towards the Frenchmen, swinging scimitars at them. The French shot down with pistols, carbines and muskets into the growing tide of horsemen.

More and more of the Moslem horsemen poured into the village, others swarming around it, ensuring that none of the French escaped. Lausard watched as a tall Mameluke on a white horse rose in his stirrups and slashed with his scimitar at a grenadier who was still climbing on to a roof. The razor-sharp steel cut easily through the man's leg just below the knee, the severed limb dropping to the ground, the grenadier screaming and losing his grip. As he fell, another devastating blow practically shaved away half his head.

Lausard swung his carbine up to his shoulder and shot the Mameluke in the face.

Sonnier brought another man crashing down, his horse also toppling as it was hit by bullets fired from another roof. The animal brought down several riders following and French troops nearby poured fire into the mêlée of struggling animals and riders. Horses reared, enabling their riders to slash at the French troops who were sheltering a mere twelve or thirteen feet above the furious horsemen. Lausard stepped back as a bullet struck the roof close to his foot, and for a brief moment, he thought it had come from one of the other roofs. A second bullet convinced him that the Mamelukes swarming around the village were firing at the French with their pistols.

Using his horse as a step, one of the Mamelukes tried to scramble up on to the roof. Lausard drove his bayonet forward and skewered the Moslem through the chest, kicking him away, watching as the man fell back into the street. Others were now following suit, and all over the village, the defenders found that their enemies were climbing up to face them hand to hand.

Karim parried a blow with his scimitar then struck at the stomach of his opponent, disembowelling the Mameluke with one blow.

Rocheteau slammed the butt of his carbine into the

face of another attacker, watching as the man reeled backwards, blood and shattered teeth falling from his mouth. As the Mameluke struggled to regain his senses, Rocheteau drove his bayonet into his chest and kicked him off the roof.

Carbonne shouted in pain as a scimitar blow laid open his forearm. He managed to grab the Mameluke by the wrist, pull him towards him, and drive his head hard against the Moslem's nose. He then grabbed the man in a bear hug and held him while Moreau stabbed the Arab repeatedly with his bayonet.

Below them the Mamelukes still swarmed around the buildings and Lausard wondered how long they would continue their attack. It was a non-stop assault and as soon as one group rode off another would come hurtling into the village. All the time, those Moslems outside the village continued to ride around as if waiting their turn to attack.

The narrow streets of Biktil were choked with dead riders. Wounded men crawled into the houses seeking either shelter or somewhere to die. Riderless horses careened back and forth, slamming into the Mamelukes who already rampaged around the dwellings. The stink of black powder and blood was overpowering, and there was so much smoke billowing up from the continual fire of the French troops that it appeared as if the village was ablaze. The pounding of horses' hooves was accompanied by the clanging of metal on metal as swords and scimitars clashed with bayonets.

Lausard knelt on the roof, picking his targets and firing. He repeated the process continuously until his throat was parched, his mouth filled with grains of black powder and his eyes watering from the fumes. He bit the tops from cartridges, poured powder, rammed ball and wadding down the barrel and fired, then did the same again. And again. Nine or ten Mamelukes lay dead or dying around the house, and as Lausard looked down, he saw and smelled burning. Many of the Moslem corpses were now ablaze. The layers of silken clothing were so fine that the blazing wads from French carbines and muskets had ignited the rich garments as the bullets penetrated them. The stench of burning clothing soon gave way to that of burning flesh. Yet still these furious riders swarmed in and around the village.

Lausard saw that a few of the houses had been taken. Mamelukes were on the roof tops, some clutching pistols with which they were now firing at the French. He looked towards one house where three grenadiers had been sheltering and noticed angrily that all three men had been killed, their conquerors each triumphantly holding the severed heads of the infantrymen in one hand and their blood-laced swords in the other. Lausard swung his carbine to bear on the nearest of them and fired, watching with satisfaction as the man toppled backwards. Sonnier added his own fire and shot another in the stomach. The third leaped to the ground, still gripping the severed head. He disappeared amongst the tangle of dead and wounded.

Lausard blinked away sweat from his eyes and looked out across the rest of the battlefield. He could see that groups of Mamelukes were still defiantly attacking the French divisional squares despite the bodies of their dead companions littering the areas around each face of the impenetrable formations. Dead horses were piled like bloodied barricades around the squares. Some Mamelukes whose horses had been killed were running at the squares on foot, while others sought a fresh mount before resuming their suicidal assault.

'They're insane.' Sonnier was also watching the Moslems' fanatical displays of aggression. 'Don't they realize they're beaten?'

Even as he spoke, one of the guns positioned at a corner of Desaix's square let loose with another charge of canister shot, the eruption of sixty-three metal balls weighing between one and two ounces each ripping through the charging horsemen with devastating effect. An entire line went down as if tripped by some invisible wire. Those following became entangled in the bloodied mess and were promptly fired on by the infantry. All over the battlefield the scene was repeated.

Lausard's appraisal of the battle was interrupted when a bullet whizzed past his ear, missing him by inches. He spun round and saw that a Mameluke had fired a pistol at him and was now clambering up on to the roof top. Realizing he had no time to reload, Lausard dropped his carbine and pulled his sword, facing the scimitar-wielding Moslem. Lausard ducked beneath the first sweeping cut, meeting the second with his own sword. A loud clang reverberated as the two weapons smashed together and Lausard felt the power in his opponent's attack. The sergeant took a step back and thrust at his foe.

The size of the Mameluke belied his agility and he neatly side-stepped the probing blade and struck out with his own weapon, catching Lausard a glancing blow with the tip that split the sergeant's left cheek. In anger as much as pain, Lausard struck out with a shuddering back-hand stroke, which the Mameluke parried but could not hold back. Lausard's momentum carried him forward, and as he fell on to his opponent, he drove a fist into the Moslem's face, splitting the man's lip. The two men rolled towards the edge of the roof, the Mameluke clambering to his feet first, raising his scimitar high above his head. Lausard struck out and drove his sword into the big man's genitals, forcing the blade upwards until he had pushed it almost half the length of the three-foot blade. The Mameluke shrieked, dropped his own sword and grabbed at his punctured groin, blood spilling over his lips. Lausard wrenched his sword free as the Mameluke toppled over the edge.

Lausard looked down at the discarded sword of his enemy. It was a magnificent weapon. The pommel was inlaid with gold, the handle had been carved from some kind of animal horn and the blade itself was black steel. Lausard wiped his own sword and sheathed it, then he slid the scimitar into his belt and went to retrieve his carbine.

The fighting in the village seemed to be abating somewhat and Lausard noticed a number of the Mamelukes fleeing. When he looked to his right he saw why. Several hundred infantrymen had taken advantage of a lull in the fighting and, led by an officer and a trumpeter, they were moving towards Biktil, formed into a smaller but just as effective square. A burst of flame erupted from one side as they fired, downing several enemy horsemen. More and more of the Mamelukes now turned and fled, only a handful charging towards the square. The others hurtled off in the opposite direction, leaving a dust cloud in their wake.

Lausard looked across to the house nearest him where Karim and Rocheteau were crouching on the roof, their faces blackened with smoke. Karim raised a hand in the sergeant's direction and Lausard nodded gently.

Looking beyond, he could see that the Mameluke attack had broken. Many were galloping in the direction of Embabeh, itself ablaze. The blazing muzzle flashes of cannon occasionally illuminated a battlefield still shrouded in smoke and dust.

From the rooftops of several houses a number of the grenadiers began singing 'La Marseillaise' and Lausard looked round to see that Moreau, Giresse and Joubert had joined in, the latter waving his carbine triumphantly in the air, watching with delight as the beaten Mamelukes fled towards the Nile.

'There's nowhere for them to run,' Sonnier said, the sweat pouring down his face cutting swathes through his blackened cheeks. 'They cannot cross the river.'

Lausard didn't answer. He touched a hand to the cut on his cheek, looking down at the blood glistening on his fingertips.

'Are you all right, Alain?'

The sergeant looked towards the rapidly flowing river, seeing that many of the Moslem horsemen were plunging desperately into the water while still astride their mounts. Men and horses thrashed helplessly in the water, the Mamelukes weighed down by their equipment and clothes. From the bank, French infantrymen were already shooting into the terrified mass and, in places, the river was turning red.

'Bonaparte has his victory at last,' Lausard said, observing the scene of carnage. 'I hope he's happy.'

For the first time since arriving in Egypt, Lausard noticed that men did not seem to care too much about the appalling conditions. The heat of the day had given way to the miserable dew-soaked night but there were few complaints. The troops had other things on their minds. Lausard had heard that over two thousand Mamelukes had been killed that afternoon, their bodies either scattered over the battlefield or floating in the waters of the Nile.

As Lausard wandered through the scene of devastation, he saw that not one of the corpses had been left untouched. Even as he passed, men were tearing the clothes from those corpses that hadn't already been stripped. Several grenadiers were arguing over a pair of yellow leather boots they had taken from one rider. Two dragoons from his own regiment were struggling back to their squadron carrying a sack of coins so heavy it needed their combined strength to lift it.

Lausard paused beside a dead, half-naked Mameluke and noticed a gold earring that had gone unnoticed by the other pillagers. He pulled it free and dropped it into his pocket before walking on.

The smell of powder and smoke had been replaced by the stench of rotting flesh. The blazing sun had accelerated the decomposition of the dead and everywhere the all-too-familiar swarms of flies feasted. Lausard passed more troops squabbling over some gold-inlaid horse bridles. One of them was wearing a turban he'd taken from a dead Mameluke, the silk wrapped awkwardly around his head so that it looked more like a bandage.

'Not joining them, my friend?'

The voice startled him and he spun round to see Lieutenant Royere wandering across the sand towards him.

'The money they are collecting from the dead Mamelukes may well buy the six acres General Bonaparte promised us,' Royere said and both men laughed. They continued walking across the body-strewn battlefield.

'Captain Milliere has already collected his own booty. Two cashmere shawls, a skull cap inlaid with fifty gold pieces and some ivory-handled daggers.'

'And you, Lieutenant?' asked Lausard. 'What have you taken? I know that thieving is not confined to us so-called common men.'

'Hardly thieving, Lausard. See it as a redistribution of wealth. One of the purest principles of the Republic.' They both grinned. 'I must confess to having liberated some fine china, a number of rugs and some rather fine silverware from the Mamelukes' baggage train. How much of it I will ever manage to transport home to France is a different matter. I doubt if I will have enough left to make me a rich man.'

'Then perhaps you should be grateful for that, Lieutenant. Rich man and Republic do not sit very comfortably together, do they?'

'We are speaking of riches acquired through personal effort not through birthright,' Royere insisted.

'What is the difference? Wealth is wealth, whether acquired or inherited. It is strange how easily the principles of the Republic have been forgotten here tonight. How many men who fought for liberty, to rid France of the rich and privileged do you see on this battlefield now? These men care only for their own wealth.' He watched as a dragoon, unable to remove a large gold ring from a corpse's finger, sliced off the entire digit with a knife then scuttled off into the gloom in search of more riches.

'Would you care for one of these?' Royere held out a handful of sugar-dusted sweets. 'They are very good. Stolen too I might add but that does not diminish their flavour.'

Lausard took two and pushed them into his mouth.

'It is my sensibilities that are affronted,' he said, grinning, 'not my taste buds.'

Royere chuckled and gestured towards the brilliant orange hue that coloured the sky above Cairo.

'Word has it that the Mamelukes set light to three hundred Egyptian vessels in the port before fleeing,' the officer said.

'Perhaps we should be grateful they didn't set fire to the city itself,' Lausard observed, stepping over a naked corpse as he walked. 'Capturing Cairo was Bonaparte's goal, wasn't it? Enough men have died to achieve it.'

'I fear it is just the first of many objectives. He will not rest until he has subdued the entire country.'

'And then what? Where do we follow him after he has conquered Egypt? To India? Or beyond? Do you really think there is a limit to his ambition, Lieutenant?'

'Like you, Lausard, I do as I am ordered and my orders do not include speculation on the motives of our commander in chief. Although I suspect that for most of the men in this army, the only place they wish to follow him to is France. I must confess I share their longing. Don't you?'

'There is nothing for me in France. There hasn't been since I lost my family. Why should I be so eager to return to a land that took from me what I loved most?'

'France is your home.'

'I have no home. Not any more. The army is the only home I know, wherever it goes.'

'Where it goes next I can only guess. General Bonaparte has sent three companies of infantry under General Dupuy to occupy Cairo. I suspect that he will continue to pursue the Mamelukes. They were beaten today, not destroyed.'

'So we continue to march across the desert in pursuit of them? What has this campaign been other than march and fight, march and fight. I realize that is the way in war but at least in Italy it seemed to serve some purpose. Here, all the suffering has so far been for nothing. The Mamelukes' capital is in our hands, we have beaten them in battles and yet they still remain the rulers of this land. The local people resent us as much as they do the Mamelukes and yet we came supposedly as liberators. Does Bonaparte think that presenting a few tricolours to local tribesmen will make these people accept us? They will rejoice with us only when we leave or when we are all dead. Whichever comes first.'

Twenty-Six

For Lausard and the men of his unit life in Cairo gradually undertook a tedious monotony. As soldiers, their purpose was to fight and they soon grew tired of a life without purpose.

Lausard reflected on the conflicting feelings tormenting the men ever since they had left Toulon over five months earlier. During the long voyage from France to Egypt they had wanted nothing more than to feel solid ground under their feet and face their enemy – to use the skills they had been taught and had used to such devastating effect a year earlier in Italy. But upon arriving in Egypt, they had been overcome by its desolation. The desert marches had seen many die – from the effects of thirst and sun, by their own hand and from other ailments peculiar to a country the men found exceptionally hostile. The battles with the Bedouin or the Mamelukes had served to take their minds off their suffering, but they also presented the men with the possibility that they might lose their lives. And yet now, having been billeted in the European quarter of Cairo for more than a month, they craved action once again, even though it might end their lives. They needed combat as a hungry man needs food.

News that the Mamelukes had been fought and beaten at a place called Salalieh had circulated, but the dragoons had not been involved. Cavalry, it seemed, were superfluous to requirements on this campaign. So Lausard and his regiment, like many other troops, had been left to fester in the capital city, surrounded by squalor they could barely have dreamed of. Even as he sat sipping his coffee, Lausard looked around the square of Birket-el-Fil and yet again ran his eyes over the filth. He had long since decided that it was a city which did not deserve its great reputation. Narrow, unpaved, filthy streets, dark houses that appeared to be falling to pieces, public buildings that looked like dungeons, shops that resembled stables; the entire city was redolent of dust and garbage. Blind and half-blind men, and people dressed in rags pressed together in the streets or squatted in the squares or cowered in the entrances of buildings smoking their pipes. For the most part the women were filthy too, their faces covered but their pendulous breasts clearly visible through their torn gowns. Many were accompanied by yellow, skinny children, who were covered with suppuration and devoured by flies. And everywhere there was an unbearable stench – a combination of the dirt, dust and smell of food being fried in rancid oil. Sanitation was virtually unknown, and in most places raw sewage ran through the streets.

At night, the streets were largely impassable, unlit and in places overrun with packs of wild dogs. Even the houses of the rich lacked certain elementary comforts, and the buildings where Lausard and the other men of the squadron were billeted were even more basic. At times, Lausard thought that the stables where the horses were kept were no more uncomfortable.

The days had become almost indistinguishable from each other. Each day dawned with monotonous, scorching regularity and Lausard and his companions found themselves with nothing to do to alleviate their boredom. They had sampled the so-called delights of this city early on. It seemed that its entertainment ran to belly-dancing and snake-charming. Even the prostitutes were old, wizened and, for the most part, horribly diseased.

Lausard took another sip of his coffee and thought, not for the first time, that his time in Cairo had, so far, been one of the most pointless and soul-destroying episodes in his life.

Beside him, Rocheteau was also cradling a cup of coffee, inhaling the aroma. Delacor was sipping a glass of date wine, looking across the table at Joubert, who was chewing hungrily on a pastry. Giresse, using a piece of charcoal, was busily sketching two old Arabs squatting in the middle of the square, oblivious to those who passed them by on either side. Tabor and Gaston sat watching their companion's creation take shape, fascinated by the swift, assured strokes he applied and the image forming on the paper. Bonet was engrossed in the latest edition of the *Courrier de l'Egypte*, one of two newspapers printed in the capital by the members of Bonaparte's Scientific Commission. Karim also glanced at the paper occasionally, between sips of his coffee. He was the only one who still wore his *surtout* buttoned to the neck, the other men having either unbuttoned their top three or four buttons or opened theirs fully. The heat didn't seem to bother Karim. But then again, Lausard had noticed, not much did.

The café where the dragoons had gathered was like many that had sprung up during the French occupation. Some owned and run by merchants, others by members of the more enterprising elements of the army. One man had traded gold he'd confiscated at the battle of the pyramids in exchange for ownership of one of the cafés, which served not just coffee but also wine, rum and brandy, and pastries freshly cooked on the premises. It offered the men a reminder of home, as did the libraries, reading rooms and billiard halls they frequented. But, as Lausard reasoned, the more that was done to make the men feel at home, the more they were reminded how much they missed it.

'It says in here that General Desaix is chasing the Mamelukes all the way into Syria,' Bonet said, jabbing a finger at the newspaper. 'It says that it is only a matter of time before they are completely destroyed.'

'And you believe that, do you, schoolmaster?' Delacor said scathingly.

'And if they *are* destroyed? What then?' Rocheteau wanted to know. 'Does that mean we can go home?'

'I hope so,' Joubert intoned. 'I'm sick of this filthy country and its people. They'd slit our throats if they had the chance.'

'Do you blame them?' Lausard said. 'We have stolen their country from them. How would you feel if it had been they who had invaded France? Would you not have wanted to kill them?'

'We saved them from the Mamelukes, didn't we?' Delacor said.

'You have replaced one form of tyranny with another,' Karim countered, sipping his coffee.

'We have freed them,' Delacor protested.

'We have tried to change Cairo into Paris,' Lausard said. 'Renaming streets after our own, taking over their businesses. I'm not surprised they resent us.'

'This isn't like the Paris *I* can remember,' Rocheteau said, looking round.

'How good is your memory, my friend?' Lausard asked. 'We live in filth here, we lived in filth back in Paris. What's the difference?'

'I'll tell you the difference,' Giresse interjected, still sketching. 'We had women back home.'

The men laughed.

'There are women here,' Joubert offered.

'Not if you are as selective as I am, fat man. I prefer beauty and gentleness in a woman. The women *I* knew back in France were always beautiful. Not like these creatures here. I would not soil myself by lying with them.'

'Nor I,' Delacor insisted.

'When did *you* acquire standards when it comes to women?' Lausard wanted to know.

'You can marry an Egyptian woman if you wish,' Bonet said. 'I know men who have. All you have to do is become a Moslem, speak their words of faith. "There is no God but God and Mohammed is his Prophet." And that is it, you have a wife.'

'If Paris is worth a mass, then eleven words is the worth of a bed mate here.' Lausard grinned.

'It's blasphemy,' Moreau said. 'We are not Moslems, we cannot become Moslems. They worship a different God. Not *our* God.'

'Shut up, your holiness,' Delacor snapped. 'If I thought that speaking eleven words would get me a woman for the night I might just do it.'

'I would speak twenty-two words and have two women,' Giresse added, and once again the men laughed.

'There is an old Turkish proverb,' Karim told them. 'Take a white woman for the eyes and an Egyptian woman for pleasure. Perhaps you should bear that in mind.'

Giresse finished his sketch and held it up for his companions to see.

'Very good.' Bonet admired it. 'You have excellent natural talent, Giresse.'

'There is magic in these fingers,' Giresse said, grinning. 'Ask any of the women I've slept with.'

The men chuckled loudly.

'Perhaps Bonaparte will invite you to join the Scientific and Artistic Commission,' Lausard suggested. 'You can run around drawing these ruins he seems so obsessed with. I'm sure they'll find you a job somewhere. There seems to be more work for civilians out here than soldiers.'

'Those "pekinese" are no use to us.' Delacor's tone was dismissive. 'I don't know why Bonaparte brought them. All they do is get in the way and eat the food *we* should have.'

'There are some brilliant men amongst them,' Bonet confirmed.

'But why are they *here*?' Tabor enquired.

'To study the country and its history,' Bonet told him. 'There is much to be learned from this country.'

'Yes,' Rocheteau rasped. 'Look at what this country has offered us. Dysentery, blindness, thirst, madness, suicide, fever and all manner of other suffering.'

Lausard slapped him on the shoulder. 'Order some more drinks. We cannot change our fate, we can only endure it. All the ills this country and its people throw at us will not break us.'

'I wish I could believe you, Alain,' Giresse said.

'You only need look at what our commander in chief offers us to pass our time,' Lausard said, a wispish smile on his lips. 'How can you doubt his concern for us? Theatrical shows with men playing women's parts. Jugglers. Puppet shows. I even heard that a club is to be opened and balls organized. And if we tire of those diversions, we can always visit the pyramids again or go ostrich hunting. How can you miss France when you have such a wealth of activities at your disposal?' There was a strong note of scorn in his voice. 'Perhaps one day, Bonaparte will remember we are soldiers, perhaps he will let us fight again.' Lausard raised his cup in salute. 'To that day, my friends.'

Other receptacles were raised in salute.

'What is the toast?' Rocheteau asked.

'Women,' Giresse said.

'Food,' Joubert offered.

'Home,' Rocheteau added.

'Survival,' Lausard concluded.

The men drank.

Napoleon Bonaparte walked around like a man in a trance, passing from one room to another in the sumptuous surroundings of the palace of Mohammed Bey el-Elfi. He had taken up residence in the magnificent building in Esbekiya Square upon entering Cairo, struck by its opulence, impressed that the building – unlike many of those owned by the upper classes of the Moslem caste – was truly fit for a conqueror like himself. The windows boasted glass panes, the staircases were of marble, alabaster and polished granite from Aswan, the floors covered by mosaics. There was a bath on every floor and, to complete the vision, the main reception room boasted a monumental ornamental fountain.

But at this moment the Corsican cared nothing for this show of wealth. He cared nothing for his victories or anything to do with this country. He paced back and forth in one of the smaller state rooms, hands clasped behind his back, his head bowed.

'Your generals are waiting,' Berthier told him, his voice gentle, almost consoling.

'Let them wait.' Bonaparte continued pacing.

'I can send them away if you wish. The meeting can be held—'

'Just let them wait,' Bonaparte repeated, finally stopping his relentless march back and forth. He looked directly at Berthier, something close to bewilderment in his eyes. 'Why did she betray me? She was the world to me. Could she not see that? Did she not realize the spell she cast upon me?' He crossed to a nearby chaise-longue and sat down heavily. 'It is the end of my world, Berthier. Without Josephine there is nothing for me. All I have achieved here is meaningless. My whole *life* is meaningless.' He sat back, gently stroking his forehead with his fingers.

Major Junot cleared his throat somewhat theatrically and took a step forward.

'Sir, I feel that *I* am to blame for your melancholy,' the aide-de-camp said. 'Had I not let it slip out that your wife had been indiscreet then—'

'Indiscreet! The word barely captures the nature of her treachery. And as for keeping this news from me, you would have done me no favours, Junot. Josephine is *my* wife. Don't you feel I have a right to know what the whole of Paris society has known for some time? If I am to be a cuckold then I want no whispered indignities behind my back. This was no indiscretion, this was betrayal – and for what? The attentions of some common soldier? This dog is nothing more than a dandified hussar, and yet his charms, it would appear, rank more highly in the eyes of my wife than do my own achievements. To conquer countries, to destroy armies, to extend the boundaries of the Republic is not enough for her. She seeks more in a husband perhaps. And yet, if this is so, why should she content herself with a mere hussar?' His voice had risen both in volume and vehemence. He exhaled deeply, the weariness returning to his tone. 'I am weary of humanity,' he said quietly. 'I need solitude and isolation. Greatness bores me. My feelings are dried up. Glory is stale when one is twenty-nine. I have exhausted everything, there is nothing left for me but to become really and completely selfish.'

He got to his feet and crossed to the nearest window, looking out over the city.

'Have you ever loved someone with such consuming energy, Berthier?'

'My young Mistress Visconti. Not a minute passes that I don't think of her.'

'But she has not betrayed you. It is a sad thing to concentrate all one's feelings on a single person, in a single heart. Especially when that love is not returned.' Bonaparte shrugged. 'It is nearly two months since I discovered this betrayal and yet still it tortures me. I fear it will never end, this pain I feel, and yet how can I dwell on my own disappointments when the army relies on me?'

'It is only natural you are still affected,' Berthier consoled him. 'Love does unspeakable things to men. As cruel as anything a battlefield can offer. But at least in combat a wound to the heart means certain death; in love a wound to the heart means a lifetime of suffering.'

Bonaparte nodded sagely, his entire demeanour changing from self-pity to grim determination.

'Send in the others,' he ordered, watching as Junot opened the doors leading to the state room. A number of officers walked in, led by General Dupuy. Behind him came Murat, a huge white ostrich feather in his bicorn and his feet adorned by yellow leather boots. General Caffarelli stomped in behind him, his wooden leg thumping loudly on the marble floor. Bonaparte waited until the men were settled, then he looked at each one in turn.

'Where do I begin, gentlemen?' he said. 'We came to this country as liberators, prepared to accept the ways of those we encountered. Tolerant of their religion and their ways – and how do they repay us? By rising against us. In nearly every town and village we have occupied the populace has risen against us. *That* is their thanks to us for bringing them freedom. In the Menzala region of the Nile we are faced with what amounts to guerilla war. The leader of those guerillas, Hassan Tubar, is in constant contact with Ibrahim Bey who, even as we speak, is being pursued by General Desaix and his men. The population massacred the garrison at El Mansura and, every day, fresh reports reach me of more risings, all of which I have given orders should be dealt with summarily. Even here in Cairo itself there is still resistance. I order five or six people beheaded every day in this city.' He exhaled deeply.

'What news from Desaix?' Murat asked.

'He pursues the Mamelukes into Syria. When he catches them he fights and beats them, but his men are suffering from sickness, as are the men all over Egypt.'

'I heard that fifteen per cent of the troops were in hospital,' Caffarelli said.

'That is true,' Bonaparte agreed. 'Men who cannot be replaced. Not since that cursed Englishman Nelson destroyed our fleet at Aboukir bay. We have been separated from our homeland, we are in a hostile country that fights us either openly or behind our backs while we still chase an enemy whose only concern is to run. Our men are sick and dying. And on top of all that, the Sultan of Turkey has declared war on us. But, I promise you, we will still prevail.'

'I hope your optimism is well founded,' Murat remarked. 'How are we to stand against a Turkish army when we cannot even control the Egyptian peasants?'

'I thought the Turks were our allies,' Dupuy said.

'The Sultan has issued a *firman*, declaring a holy war against us. I have already devised plans for the defence of Egypt.'

'We are to defend a country that isn't even ours yet.' Murat snorted.

'The Turks plan a pincer movement. According to my intelligence, one pincer will be formed by the Army of Rhodes. This is to be transported by sea, with the assistance of the English.'

'Always the English,' Berthier murmured.

'Just so,' Bonaparte said, smiling. 'But they will not influence the outcome of this venture. The second pincer is formed by the Army of Damascus, who will advance by way of Palestine and the Sinai desert.'

'So how do you propose to stop them?' Murat wanted to know.

'I intend to leave ten thousand French troops, supported by local militia, to control Egypt. I will lead the remainder of the army across the desert into Palestine, defeat the Army of Damascus then double back to meet the Army of Rhodes and crush *them*.'

The other officers listened in silence.

It was Murat who finally spoke. 'We cannot control Egypt with *thirty* thousand men. How do you propose to do it with just ten thousand? This entire country has risen against us.'

'Then each revolt must be met with sterner punishment,' Bonaparte snarled. 'For every Frenchman killed, I want ten Arabs executed. I have shown them mercy and they have thrown it back in my face. They will not be allowed to do that again.'

'If it is reprisals you wish to see, then put your chief of police in command,' Dupuy said. 'The man is a maniac.'

'Would you prefer the lawlessness we found when we first arrived here?' Bonaparte challenged. 'The Janissary companies work well.'

'They are supposed to be highly trained,' Dupuy protested. 'They are riff-raff. Turks, Greeks, Moors, and commanded by that butcher Bartholomew they are little better than those they seek to subdue. He presented me with a sackful of severed Bedouin heads less than a week ago as I was about to eat dinner. Am I to assume that he is also responsible for the slaughter of those prostitutes who were beheaded and tossed into the Nile?'

'The problem was out of hand,' Bonaparte said

dismissively. 'Every one of them was infected with syphilis. I could not allow such a plague to spread through the troops.'

'Four hundred were killed and disposed of,' Dupuy persisted.

'We have more pressing problems than dead prostitutes, Dupuy.'

'Have you heard any news from the Directory?' Caffarelli questioned Bonaparte. 'Do they know of our predicament? They should be sending us food, supplies and reinforcements or are they content to let us rot here in this godforsaken hole?'

'The English Navy is blockading the approaches to Alexandria,' Bonaparte said. 'Nelson and his ships control the seas. We are forced to deal with our problems in our own way.'

'So the Directory has abandoned us?' Caffarelli continued. 'I always suspected they would. I told you they were no better than the Bourbons they replaced. They care nothing for this army now, or for what becomes of it. They only supported you because they felt that this country was rich pickings. That is why they instigated this invasion.'

'This was, from first to last, *my* idea,' Bonaparte snarled. 'I did not need some fool in the Directory to tell me the advantages of conquering Egypt. *I* saw its worth. I made *them* see. We came to this country because *I* decreed it, not the Directory.'

'So, should the men blame *you* for their predicament here?'

Bonaparte put an arm around Caffarelli's shoulder. 'Max,' he said quietly, 'we have been alone ever since we landed here with nothing but our wits and our courage to sustain us. They have been good enough so far, they will see us through whatever else is to come. We do not *need* the Directory. We never have.'

'When was the last time you received any communication from them?' Murat wanted to know.

'As I said, the English fleet has blockaded the harbours,' Bonaparte stalled. 'This has prevented the exchanging of information, but this very day I received word that the ship *L'Anemone* was beached at Marabout. There is a courier on board carrying despatches from the Directory.'

'Then where is he?' Caffarelli demanded.

'He and twenty-five other passengers were taken prisoner by Bedouin tribesmen. They are demanding a ransom for their release. I want those prisoners back. I want those despatches. But I will not pay these savages one sous.'

'The hostages are probably dead already,' Murat said dismissively.

'I cannot take that chance. I must have the despatches the courier is holding.'

'So what do you propose to do, send another army back to Marabout to free these men? To fragment an army that is already in pieces?'

'Sometimes stealth is to be preferred to force,' Bonaparte told him. 'This matter requires the services not of an army but of a small unit of troops. A detachment of your cavalry, Murat. That should be sufficient.'

Berthier stepped forward. 'General, I thought your policy was to pacify the local population. To win them over. If you send troops against them you will defeat your own objectives.'

'Berthier, no one has gone farther than I in attempting to appease these savages,' Bonaparte said bitterly. 'I have tried to coax them on to my side. I assured them that we came not to destroy their religion but to preserve it. But that religion has been the chief obstacle to unity here. I could tell these people three times a day that neither myself nor my men are Christians. That we had imprisoned the Pope and closed the churches and that we respected Islam. But it would not matter. All the rhetoric and charlatanry in the world will not change the fact that to these people we are Infidels and we always will be. Why do you think they have risen against us in so many places? Against forces who seek to bring only order to a disordered land.' He exhaled loudly. 'I never wished to destroy their religion, only their apathy, their submissiveness to a fate they believed could not be altered. I have tried to drag them from their feudalism into our modern world and they have repaid me with treachery and disrespect. I will play their games no longer. I have tried mercy, perhaps they will respond better to tyranny.'

Berthier nodded slowly.

'Now these hostages.' Bonaparte addressed Murat. 'I want them freed as soon as possible.'

'And what of their captors?'

'If they can be bargained with, so be it. If not, destroy them.'

'It is a dangerous mission,' Murat observed.

Bonaparte took a step towards him, his piercing eyes looking deeply into those of the cavalry general.

'Then make sure you pick the right men.'

Twenty-Seven

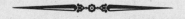

'This is like retreating,' Delacor complained. 'How long did it take us to cross this stinking desert in the first place? And now, we are retracing our own footsteps just for the sake of some bastard "pekinese".'

'It isn't the same route,' Bonet observed. 'We didn't follow the path of the Nile when we first landed.'

'Who cares? We're still going back to where we started, aren't we?' Delacor glanced up at the cloudless sky. 'Three days in this godforsaken desert already and for what?'

Lausard, riding a couple of lengths ahead, turned briefly in his saddle.

'Delacor, why don't you shut up? Save your energy. You're going to need it. You were bored in Cairo, now's your chance to do something.'

'Like what?' Roussard wanted to know. 'Get killed by the Arabs. I'd rather be in Cairo.'

Lausard turned back in his saddle, his eyes fixed on Captain Milliere, Lieutenant Royere and four other troopers who rode about thirty or forty yards ahead of the column of dragoons. The squadron had made good time since leaving Cairo, stopping just twice for water and food. They carried sufficient hard rations for a week and there was enough fodder for the horses at each outpost they stopped at. The length of the Nile was patrolled by French troops garrisoned in places like Wardan and El Rahmaniya. In fact, Lausard had noticed, the troops in these more distant outposts seemed much more cheerful than the men stationed in the larger towns and cities. They seemed to get on better with the local population, those who hadn't fled into the desert, and at Wardan the French troops had taught the Arabs how to use the baking ovens they had been supplied with. Lausard and his men had picked up loaves as well as supplies of wine and brandy made with dates.

'From what I hear, we're better off out of Cairo at the moment,' Rocheteau remarked. 'I was talking to a grenadier back in Wardan and he said they'd heard that the locals had risen against Bonaparte. Over two hundred of our men were killed in the city and nearly three thousand of theirs.'

'You can't trust these bastards, I always said that,' Delacor said.

'A revolt in Cairo will be followed by more elsewhere,' Lausard commented. 'This whole country will explode one of these days.'

'And we'll be right in the middle of it,' Roussard said uneasily. 'It's because of men like *him*.'

His words were directed at the silver-haired individual riding alongside Lausard. The man tried to ignore Roussard's comments but Lausard could see him shift uncomfortably in his saddle.

'It's your friends we're supposed to rescue, isn't it?'

Roussard continued. 'Risk our lives for a bunch of chemists.'

Citizen Gustav Caminarro glanced at his critic and considered retaliating, but the fierce look in the eyes of Roussard and those who flanked him told him that silence was the better option.

Caminarro was in his early thirties. A thin-faced, distinguished-looking man who had been all too eager to join the expedition to Egypt and more than happy to accept Caffarelli's invitation when the gathering of scientists and other thinkers had begun. He had experienced the same hardship and privations as the troops, but his arrival in Egypt had not, as it had for most of the army, been the beginning of another chapter of suffering – it had been the fulfilment of his dream and his duty.

'So, what do you do here?' Lausard asked him. 'Why did you come on this expedition?'

'I am a geologist. I have been working under the supervision of Berthollet to find a way of purifying Nile water, but I have also been studying the rocks and minerals of this region.'

'A rock is a rock, isn't it?' Rocheteau said and some of the other men laughed.

'The geological features of this country are unlike those I've seen anywhere else. They are quite fascinating.'

'So while we've been dying of thirst and hunger, fighting the Mamelukes and trying to subdue the Arabs, you've been crawling around collecting stones?' Delacor's tone was dismissive.

'I would imagine that the work has been very interesting,' Bonet said. 'I myself went to look at the pyramids and I was amazed by them. It is the history of this country that I find so fascinating.'

'Shut up, schoolmaster,' said Delacor. 'Perhaps you should join Bonaparte's "pekinese" if you're so impressed with this stinking place.'

'I wouldn't expect you to appreciate the beauties of this land. Only educated men like Citizen Caminarro and myself are capable of that.'

'The only things I want to appreciate are a good woman and some good wine,' Giresse said, smiling.

'Or some good food,' Joubert added.

'What could you find here that you couldn't find anywhere else?' Lausard asked.

'This country is rich in treasures,' Caminarro told him. 'All kinds of natural treasures. Their study will benefit all of mankind eventually.'

Delacor hawked and spat. 'Who cares?'

'Why do you hate men of learning like myself?' Caminarro enquired. 'We have done you no harm and yet you insult us constantly. You show us no respect.'

'Respect has to be earned,' Rocheteau reminded him. 'If you could use a sword and a pistol, men like Delacor would be more likely to accept you.'

'I am not a fighting man. Not unless I have to be. But I fought at Shubra Khit. I and many of my colleagues were on the ships the Moslems attacked. A number of them were killed. And now more will die unless you rescue them from the Bedouin who hold them captive."

'Are all the hostages from the Scientific Commission?' Lausard pressed.

'Most of them, but I believe that there are a handful of men who are representatives of the Directory.'

'Even more reason to let them die then,' Carbonne grunted.

'How will you free them?' Caminarro asked.

Lausard shrugged. 'Captain Milliere said that we were to bargain with them if possible. If not, we are to destroy them. They are Bonaparte's orders. Remember, citizen, we do not have the luxury of choice here. We do as we are ordered and we were ordered to recover the hostages.'

'You must have been chosen for your abilities, for your bravery.'

Lausard smiled wanly. 'The reason we were chosen is because we are expendable.'

'That's right,' Rocheteau added. 'No one cares about a few ex-prisoners.'

'You are criminals?' Caminarro's expression darkened.

'Not all of us,' Karim said, grinning.

'No, not our Circassian here,' Lausard said. 'He is not like us. He fights for revenge, don't you, Karim? And Lieutenant Royere up ahead, he is driven by idealism. We all have different motives, citizen, but that need not concern you. All you need to worry about is whether or not we can free your companions.'

'And can you?'

Lausard did not answer the geologist. His attention had been caught by the sight of two riders approaching the column from the north-west. Even from a distance he knew that they were Rostov and Moreau. Captain Milliere had despatched them in the direction of Marabout nearly an hour earlier.

'Why the hell couldn't Kléber have sent some of his men to rescue these "pekinese"?' Roussard demanded. 'Why drag *us* halfway across this stinking desert?'

'I told you,' Lausard reminded him. 'We're expendable.'

'What is the name of the place we are going?' Tabor asked.

'What does it matter?' Delacor snapped. 'Every stinking place in this whole filthy country looks and smells the same.'

'Marabout is where we landed, isn't it?' Rocheteau said.

Lausard nodded. 'All these months of marching, fighting, suffering and dying, and we're back where we started.'

Milliere lowered the telescope then looked across at Lausard who, from his vantage point up on the ridge, was also peering at the Bedouin encampment. He could see twenty or thirty tents, dozens of horses, camels and donkeys wandering unhindered through the encampment, and well over a hundred tribesmen. The sinking sun cast long shadows over the camp and tinged everything that moved with the crimson hue of fresh blood. Even the sea beyond looked as if someone had dyed it the same vivid colour. Some of the Bedouin were lighting fires as the night crept across the land, still an hour or two away but announcing its approach by the discoloration of the sky. Lausard held his horse by its bridle, the animal tossing its head skittishly every now and then, finally calmed by a soothing pat on its neck.

Caminarro had also dismounted, his backside and legs sore from the long journey, and he accepted the telescope that Milliere handed him, squinting through the eyepiece at the Arab encampment. He could see no sign of the hostages, only the bustle of animals and Bedouin. He handed the telescope back to Milliere.

'What are you supposed to bargain *with*, citizen?' Milliere asked. 'How much will it take to keep your comrades alive?'

'I have a bag of fifty gold pieces with me.'

'Don't say that too loudly or you'll be robbed by the squadron before you can free the hostages,' Lausard advised. 'Why should the Bedouin be interested in gold anyway? They have no need of money.'

'They will take it,' Karim said. 'They will see it as a sign that they have the power to force the Infidel to do their will.'

'You're very sure of that, Karim?' Milliere said.

'I know how their minds work.'

Milliere nodded. 'Very well. Citizen Caminarro, myself, you Lausard, Rocheteau and Gaston will ride into the village and meet with their leaders. Karim will act as interpreter.'

'Captain, I do not think that taking the boy with us will help,' Karim offered. 'The Bedouin may wish to keep him. You all know too well their fondness for youth. The boy will be safer if he remains with the squadron. The Mamelukes have fought battles over the possession of young boys, the Bedouin are the same.'

'Let Joubert come with us then,' Milliere said. 'Surely even the most depraved mind could not find *him* a worthy prize.'

The men laughed.

Lausard mounted his horse and motioned to Rocheteau and Joubert to join him. Milliere turned to Lieutenant Royere.

'If they will not bargain,' he instructed, 'if they try to kill us on the way into the camp, while we are in it or during our exit, then attack. And spare no one.'

Royere nodded, watching as the small procession set off down the sandy ridge towards the Bedouin camp.

As they drew nearer, Lausard could hear the sound of

voices raised excitedly. He could hear the neighing of horses, the snorting of camels, the braying of donkeys, even the sounds of sheep and goats. A light breeze had sprung up and one of the Bedouin tents flapped gently, the noise adding to the overall cacophony. As well as the aural assault, a profusion of smells accosted them. The stench of excrement, human and animal, was prevalent, as was the odour of unwashed bodies.

The small party of Frenchmen was now no more than fifty yards from the outer perimeter of the camp and Lausard saw several Arabs watching them intently as they drew closer. Eventually, one turned and sprinted off into the heart of the camp.

Caminarro shifted uncomfortably in his saddle, the sweat running down his face not just the product of the early-evening heat. He could feel his heart thudding ever faster and he found it increasingly more difficult to control his breathing as he saw more and more Bedouin stop to watch the approach of the dragoons.

A mounted Arab rode towards them slowly, circling them with his pony. The troops did their best to ignore him but Caminarro could barely contain his fear and watched the Arab's every movement with mounting terror. He fumbled beneath his saddle cloth, one hand hovering over his pistol.

'Leave it alone,' Lausard ordered without looking at him.

They were past the outer perimeter now, heading towards the very centre of the camp. It seemed that every Arab present had turned to watch their steady progress. One stepped towards the horse ridden by Karim and ran a hand along its hindquarters, muttering something in Arabic. Karim ignored the remark, even the cackling laugh that followed. Another Bedouin spat in the path of Lausard's horse, barking something angrily. The sergeant glared at the Bedouin from beneath the peak of his brass helmet and the look was enough to make the man step back a pace.

Caminarro glanced behind him and saw that the other Bedouin had formed a tight circle around the dragoons. He paused momentarily, his heart hammering against his ribs.

'Keep going,' Lausard murmured through gritted teeth.

Another Arab pulled his robe aside and exposed his genitals to Rocheteau, who edged his horse sideways slightly and almost knocked the man to the ground.

He shouted something in his anger.

Rocheteau turned to Karim. 'What did he say?'

'He called you a jackal.'

'He must know you,' Joubert commented.

'Shut up!' Milliere snapped, also looking around at the gathering of tribesmen.

Lausard was sure that there were well over two hundred Bedouin gathered around, looking on with curiosity as the dragoons reached a particularly large tent in the centre of their camp. But it was what stood before the tent that caught the attention of Lausard and his companions.

'Oh my God!' Caminarro gasped, his hand across his mouth. He felt his stomach contract.

Three long stakes were embedded in the sand outside the largest tent. On top of each was a severed head. The eyes of the one in the centre were still open and Caminarro swallowed hard, transfixed by the lifeless orbs. Lausard saw him pull more tightly on his reins, and for a second the sergeant feared that Caminarro might try to gallop away. He edged his horse closer to the geologist. The horde of Arabs had drawn in even more tightly around the dragoons and one of them was tugging at Lausard's shabraque. The sergeant glared down at him, flicking out one boot to push the man back. Rocheteau rested one hand on the hilt of his sword but Lausard noticed and shook his head.

Two Arabs emerged from the tent. Big men, one sporting a large growth of beard. The remainder of his face was pitted and swarthy, and he regarded the dragoons with a mixture of distaste and amusement.

'Tell him I want to see the hostages,' Milliere said to Karim. 'Tell him we have his ransom.' The dragoons looked on as the Circassian translated.

The bearded Arab shouted something towards the tent and the flap opened.

Lausard and the others saw half a dozen naked figures being pushed out into the blazing sunshine. Their Bedouin guards were pushing them, kicking those who lost their footing, herding them towards the waiting dragoons. The men looked terrified and, Lausard noticed, many bore bruises on most parts of their bodies. The tribesmen nearby were spitting and shouting at them, some grabbing the men as they passed.

'Please God, help us,' said the leading Frenchman, looking up imploringly at the dragoons. 'They will kill us all. Get us out of here.' He pointed towards the three severed heads. 'We will all end up like that if you do not save us.'

'When did they do that?' Milliere asked.

'This morning. They will kill us all.'

'Which of you is the courier from the Directory?'

'It is I.' One of the men stepped forward. 'My name

is Lesimple. I carry despatches for General Bonaparte from the Directory. It is vital that he gets them.'

'Do you still have them?' Milliere pressed. 'These savages haven't stolen them, have they?'

'They took everything else of value,' Lesimple said. 'Our clothes, shoes, personal belongings, but they didn't seem interested in the papers I carried.'

'Where are the other hostages?'

'Inside that tent,' Lesimple told Milliere, gesturing behind to the canvas cover.

One of the Arabs suddenly stepped between Lesimple and Milliere and began raving, gesturing wildly at the tent, Lesimple and also at the dragoons.

'He says they want the ransom now,' Karim informed Milliere. 'Otherwise they will kill the hostages and us too.'

'Let them try,' Rocheteau hissed, glaring at the bearded Arab.

'Not yet,' Lausard murmured.

'Shall I give him the gold?' Caminarro wanted to know.

'How many hostages are left?' Milliere asked Lesimple.

'Including myself, twenty-two. They killed three, as you can see. Another man was wounded when we beached; he died last night.'

The leading Arab was still speaking excitedly in his native tongue.

'He says that unless you pay now, the rest of the hostages will be executed immediately,' Karim said, without taking his eyes from the Arab, who suddenly drew his sword and pressed it against the throat of the hostage standing closest to him. The man yelped in fear, his face draining of colour.

'For the love of God give him what he wants,' Lesimple urged.

'Tell him to release the hostages and we'll pay,' Milliere instructed Karim.

Karim relayed the instructions, nodding as the Arab snarled back at him angrily.

'No gold, no hostages,' the Circassian informed his officer.

'If we give them the gold they'll kill the hostages anyway,' Lausard said.

'Then what do you suggest, Sergeant?'

'Give him half now,' Lausard advised Milliere. 'Tell them to release half the hostages and that he'll get the rest of the gold when *we've* got the other hostages.'

'I don't think we're in a position to bargain,' Milliere said, looking around at the large number of Arabs surrounding them.

'Please get us out,' Lesimple begged.

'You have to give them the gold,' Caminarro insisted.

'Tell them that unless they release the hostages we'll kill them all,' Lausard said, looking first at Karim then at Milliere.

'There are six of you,' Caminarro blurted. 'How can you hope to fight this many? Are you insane?'

'Tell him, Karim,' Lausard insisted.

The Circassian looked at Milliere for confirmation.

'They don't know our strength, Captain,' Lausard persisted. 'They won't stand against organized troops, we saw that at Barada.'

'But in the time it takes us to bring the rest of the squadron back, they could have killed all the hostages,' the officer said.

'They're going to kill them anyway, you know that.'

'We have to retrieve those papers from the Directory.'

'What about us?' Lesimple protested. 'Do not speak of us as if we were not here. How dare you play with our lives?'

'You will *have* no life without our help,' Lausard reminded him.

'Offer him half,' Milliere said. 'Half now and the other half when the rest of the hostages are released.' He nodded towards Karim who translated.

The Arab spat on the sand in front of Milliere's horse. He then babbled something that Karim listened to intently before turning again to Milliere.

'He says they will release ten of the hostages now for half the gold. They will release five more tomorrow for the other half. They will keep seven for themselves.'

'You cannot let them do that,' Lesimple said, his face turning white with terror. 'You don't know what foul torments these heathens have put us through already.'

'Tell them they must release *all* the hostages,' Milliere said.

Karim repeated the instructions and received a tirade in return.

'He says they will keep seven.'

'Any ideas, Lausard?' Milliere turned to the sergeant. 'If we return to Cairo without hostages *and* despatches I don't think General Bonaparte will be the happiest man in Egypt.'

'They have no idea of our strength, Captain . . .' Lausard began.

'But they hold the trump card, Lausard. We must get those despatches back.'

'And these men,' Caminarro protested.

'We can get both,' Lausard suggested, 'if we attack in the right way. You forget, Captain, you command a squadron of criminals. Men of cunning as well as courage. I think both will be needed here.'

Milliere nodded.

'Give him half the gold now, tell him we'll be back to pick up the other hostages in the morning.'

'All of them?' Milliere asked.

'All they will release. Fifteen is better than none.'

'You cannot play with our lives this way,' Lesimple said, tugging at the bridle of Lausard's horse.

'Get away from me, you fool,' Lausard snapped. 'If you trust us you might *all* get away from here with your lives.'

'Give him half,' Milliere instructed Caminarro and he watched as the engineer counted out twenty-five pieces of gold and handed them to the Arab. 'The rest tomorrow.'

The officer wheeled his horse and raised a hand, beckoning his troops to follow him.

'We go,' he said. 'There is nothing more we can do here.'

'You can't leave these men,' Caminarro shouted.

'If you want to come with us you ride out now,' Lausard said simply. 'If not, then stay with your friends.'

'Don't leave us,' Lesimple wailed, his mournful cry echoed by some of the other hostages.

The dragoons guided their horses through the wall of Arabs, determinedly looking straight ahead, refusing to be distracted by the shouts and jeers of the leering Bedouin. Behind them they could still hear the terrified yells of the hostages, shrieks of despair and cries for help, but none looked back, not even Caminarro. Gradually those mournful shrieks were drowned by the raucous laughter of the Arabs, who gathered around their captives once more.

As the group reached the perimeter of the camp, a Bedouin ran across towards Rocheteau's horse and shouted something at the corporal.

'He called us cowards,' Karim explained as the Arab repeated the words and made an expansive gesture with his arm designed to encompass all the riders.

'I find it hard to disagree with him,' Caminarro snapped. 'You have abandoned those men to God knows what fate. You were sent here to free them and yet you give them gold and for what? They will all die because of you—'

Lausard grabbed his arm. 'We've abandoned no one. It is just a matter of time.'

'Time before what? Before they are all butchered?'

'This is *our* business now. I suggest you leave it to us.'

Behind them, the laughter of the Bedouin grew louder.

Twenty-Eight

Lausard felt uncomfortably exposed beneath the dull white glow of the full moon. The impenetrable blackness that normally covered the desert at night existed only in the shadows. Elsewhere, the landscape was illuminated by a silvery sheen. Every now and then the sergeant glanced up towards the sky, hoping that the wisps of cloud driven by the easterly breeze would grow and form thicker banks to envelop the moon and give him the darkness he wanted. In the meantime, he continued to crawl across the sand like some nocturnal hunter, his eyes fixed on the low range of sand dunes fifty feet ahead. Beyond them was the Bedouin camp.

Lausard could see the tips of the closest tents poking upwards as if thrusting out of the sand itself. Ten yards to his right, Rocheteau was also hauling himself across the sand, a knife gripped in one hand. To Lausard's left, Giresse crawled a few more feet, then raised himself up on to his haunches and sprinted for the nearest dune, throwing himself down behind it. He crouched nervously, waiting for Lausard and Rocheteau to join him. Behind them, moving with a little more ease, came Gaston. He crawled with surprising speed, his red trumpeter's tunic looking black in the cold light of the moon. He carried a pistol and his sword but he also carried his trumpet, slung around one shoulder by its braided strap. If Lausard's plan was to work, the instrument would be as integral a part of events as any blade or bullet.

The dragoons reached the dunes and paused, Lausard edging up to the rim of the sandy ridge, peering over. The nearest Bedouin tent was about ten yards away, the others dotted across the sand in no particular formation. Many had ponies or camels tethered outside but the bulk of the horses were gathered together away to the left, about fifty yards from where the dragoons now sheltered. Between the dragoons and the animals were five or six tents, two of which had small fires burning outside them, one still bearing the remains of a charred goose on a makeshift spit. The fires had died down, glowing dimly in the night, but for Lausard and his companions that would be sufficient.

Lausard ducked down as he saw an Arab emerge from one of the tents and peer around in the gloom. Lausard wondered if the Bedouin could possibly have heard their approach but reasoned that it was impossible. The dragoons had used stealth of which the tribesmen themselves would have been proud. Lausard's thoughts were confirmed when he saw the Arab pull up his robe and squat down, his back to the dragoons. He grunted and began to defecate. The sergeant nudged Rocheteau and indicated towards the Arab. He watched as the corporal scurried across the sand, caught the Arab around the jaw and, with one swift, skilful movement, drew the knife across his throat. Rocheteau held on to his victim to prevent any sound escaping the man's lips, and finally released the body, allowing it to slump back on the sand, blood jetting darkly from the gashed throat.

Lausard and the other two dragoons hurried over to join him, the sergeant using his sword to slice off several lengths of canvas from the dead Bedouin's tent. Then, closely followed by Giresse and Gaston who were mimicking his actions, he hurried towards the nearest fire. All three men placed the ends of the canvas in the dying embers, watching as the material caught fire, then they swiftly yanked the burning streamers free. A number of the horses begin to whinny, alerted and alarmed by the activity going on so close by. Lausard knew that their frightened reaction would soon stir the Bedouin; he and his men had to act quickly. Each of them ran towards the tents and dropped two lengths of burning canvas on to them. The flames erupted quickly, devouring the dry material with relish. Three of the makeshift shelters caught fire within moments, and shouts of alarm began to rise from inside.

Lausard wrapped one of the burning streamers swiftly around the end of his sword and ran towards the horses, touching the flame to the flanks of several mounts. They reacted with the fury he'd expected, kicking out and whinnying in pain and fear. More than fifty horses began to move away from the source of the fire, anxious to escape it. They swung right, crashing into several more tents whose occupants were now stumbling out to see what was happening. Two were ridden down immediately by the terrified horses. Another drew his sword and ran at Lausard, who ducked beneath the clumsy swing and drove his sword into the Bedouin's back, the blazing canvas still attached to the point. The steel pierced his kidneys and the cloth ignited the robe he wore, rapidly transforming the tribesman into a human torch. He shrieked in agony as he rolled on the sand in an attempt to snuff out the flames that devoured him.

Elsewhere Rocheteau had ignited other tents. More and more Arabs were spilling out into the night, aware that they were under attack but unsure of the source. They saw their horses stampeding away, other tents burning, the occupants of some staggering about as fire enveloped them. Figures dashed to and fro in the flame-lit hell, the dragoons able to move easily amongst their bewildered enemies. Lausard struck down two more tribesmen with his sword. Giresse dispatched another with a blow to the skull that practically split the man's cranium. Even Gaston drove his blade into the belly of an Arab, forcing the sword so deep he had to kick the Arab away to free the bloodied steel.

Moving with speed and purpose, the dragoons made their way towards the centre of the camp, setting other tents ablaze, leaving more fires in their wake. Many of the Bedouin seemed more concerned with regaining their horses or camels than with the attackers in their midst, and a large number had dashed off into the desert in pursuit of their mounts. Others had simply fled, thinking that such a venomous assault must be the work of many foes. If they had known there were just four Frenchmen among them they may well have stayed and fought.

The camp had been transformed into a scene of utter chaos. Men rushed back and forth, some seeking their enemies, others trying to retrieve belongings or animals, most dazzled by the leaping flames from the burning tents, many more swept away by the stampeding or terrified horses. Very few even saw the dragoons making their way towards the tent that housed the hostages. The four men were further hidden by the dense smoke. Lausard felt the heat from the flames on his cheeks and the smoke stung his eyes, but he raced on. As he reached the large tent he pulled a pistol from his belt and forced his way inside. The Arab who confronted him froze momentarily, transfixed by the sight of the dragoon. Lausard raised his pistol and fired at point-blank range, shooting the man in the face and ignoring the blood that spurted on to him.

Giresse met one of the other Arabs in the tent with a powerful back-hand swipe that caught the man across the shoulder, shattering his collar bone. As he dropped to his knees, blood flowing from the savage wound, Giresse drove his sword through the Bedouin's throat.

Rocheteau grabbed the third man by the hair, simultaneously bringing his knife upwards, driving it through the Arab's bottom jaw and on into the roof of his mouth.

'Take them out the back way,' Lausard instructed, and Gaston began hacking at the canvas of the tent with his sword. 'Move!' Lausard shouted at the terrified hostages, who rushed towards the hole that Gaston had hacked in the rear of the tent.

'Alain, look,' Giresse said, peering out through the tent flap into the camp, which was now illuminated by fire.

Lausard saw half a dozen Arabs running towards the large tent.

He nodded to Giresse and Rocheteau to follow the hostages and Gaston out into the night. Then he pulled a cartridge from his cartouche, bit off the end, spat the ball down the pistol barrel, rammed down the wadding and thumbed back the hammer. He fired off the shot then turned and scurried after his men.

As they spilled out into the night, Giresse and Rocheteau guided the terrified hostages towards a sand dune about thirty yards away. They urged them on, occasionally pushing the frightened men to speed their escape. Fortunately for the Frenchmen, the majority of the Bedouin were too preoccupied with saving their possessions to give chase, but the Arabs Giresse had spotted running towards the large tent continued to give chase. Lausard faced them, joined by Rocheteau.

The sergeant killed the first of the attackers with a single thrust to the chest, his sword passing cleanly between ribs as he drove the steel in deep. He slid the blade free and spun round to face the next man. Rocheteau, meanwhile, drove a boot into the groin of his first opponent, the man doubling up in agony. The corporal brought his sword down on to the back of the Arab's neck and he sprawled in the sand at his feet, blood spreading around him. Another of the Bedouin turned and fled. Of the two who remained, one tugged a pistol from inside his robe and shoved the barrel to within inches of Lausard's face. Everything seemed to freeze for the sergeant. Then the Bedouin pulled the trigger and the hammer slammed down. Nothing happened. Instantly Lausard realized that either the powder was damp or the flint had worn smooth. The smile the Arab had been wearing vanished and he stood motionless, unable to believe his bad luck. Lausard reacted with devastating speed, striking so powerfully with his sword that he severed the Arab's arm just below the elbow. The tribesman dropped to his knees, shrieking in agony until Lausard caught him with another back-hand swipe that shattered his jaw and sent several teeth flying across the sand. The remaining Arab turned to flee, but before he had taken two paces, Rocheteau skewered him twice in the back.

Lausard turned to Gaston and nodded.

'Now!' he shouted.

Gaston raised the trumpet to his lips, knowing what he had to do. Summoning every ounce of strength, mustering every breath in his body, he began to blow the notes that signalled the charge. Among the hostages, Lesimple heard the familiar sound and looked on with bewilderment. Then, suddenly, they began to feel the ground shake beneath them. The accompanying sound originated from the eastern edge of the Bedouin camp and it grew like rolling thunder.

To the ridge away to the east, illuminated by the cold brilliance of the moon, first one, then two lines of horsemen appeared, followed by a third, all with swords raised, all driving on their mounts with ferocious speed. Lausard could make out the figure of Captain Milliere leading the charge, Lieutenant Royere close behind him, urging the men on, and as the horsemen hurtled towards the already panic-stricken Arabs, Gaston continued to blow the charge. It was as if the notes he delivered spurred the charging dragoons on to even greater speeds. They crashed through the outer perimeter of the encampment, riding through the remains of tents, hacking down Bedouins as they tried to flee. Those not killed by sword cuts were trampled beneath the churning hooves of the big Breton horses. Few tried to fight back. Their only objective was escape, many dashing off into the desert on foot. Some of the men in the third line of dragoons broke off to pursue them, but for the most part they were allowed to run.

Lesimple and the other hostages watched in awe as the dragoons crashed through what remained of the camp. Many of them were now reining in their mounts, some slipping from their saddles to inspect what the Arabs had left behind.

Milliere and Royere rode towards Lausard, who raised his sword in salute.

Rocheteau patted Gaston on the back and the youth smiled.

As the two officers drew nearer, Lausard could see that they were closely followed by Caminarro, who nodded towards the sergeant.

'Forgive me for doubting you,' he said flatly. 'Are *all* the hostages safe?'

Lausard nodded. 'All they've lost are their clothes and a little pride.'

He was aware of someone standing close to him and turned to see Lesimple clutching a sheaf of papers close to his chest.

'These are the despatches sent by the Directory,' he said, holding them out towards Caminarro. 'I must get them to General Bonaparte. I have guarded these with my life.'

'We'll camp here for the night,' Milliere told the courier. 'At first light we set out for Cairo.' He dismounted and crossed to Lausard, shaking the sergeant's hand. 'You did well.' He looked at Rocheteau, Gaston and Giresse. 'All of you did. Well done. I suggest you join your colleagues. They are busy trying to find anything of value the Arabs might have left behind.'

Rocheteau, Giresse and Gaston scuttled off, while Lausard wiped his sword with a piece of cloth and sheathed it.

'And when we return to Cairo, Captain, what then?' Lausard asked.

'Who knows?' the officer said. 'Your guess is as good as mine. All we can do is await orders.'

'And find out where our General decides to send us next? What mission will he have for us, I wonder?'

'There may be some instructions in those despatches,' Royere mused.

'I doubt it,' Lesimple said. 'I know what these despatches contain. When the Directory entrusted me to deliver them they also informed me of their contents.'

Lausard and Milliere exchanged glances.

'Is that usual procedure when urgent political documents are involved?' Lausard queried.

'It wasn't a matter of procedure. I am a close friend of Citizen Sicyès who occupies a position on the Directory. It was he who told me of the contents of these despatches. Since you risked your lives to save my life *and* the despatches, I feel you have a right to know what they contain.'

'Are we to march on India after conquering Egypt?' Lausard demanded, his voice thick with scorn. 'Are the despatches instructions for the further expansion of the Republic?'

'They contain congratulations on the capture of Malta.' Lesimple was almost apologetic. 'Nothing more.'

The dragoons looked disbelievingly at the courier for a second then at each other.

'Bonaparte sent us halfway across Egypt for nothing,' Milliere said.

'I felt you had a right to know,' Lesimple continued.

Lausard laughed but it had a hollow ring.

Royere kicked out angrily at a small mound of sand.

'I suspect that General Bonaparte will be as disheartened as you when he receives the despatches,' Lesimple said quietly.

Milliere nodded his agreement.

'They care nothing for us,' Lausard said. 'The Directory has more pressing issues, such as lining its own pockets. It has left us here to rot, but if the truth is told, did we ever really expect anything else?' He turned and began walking away towards what remained of the Bedouin camp.

'Where are you going, Lausard?' Milliere called after him.

Lausard turned briefly, a crooked smile on his lips. 'The same place as you and everyone else in the French army, Captain. Hell, eventually.'

The darkness swallowed him up.

Twenty-Nine

During the campaign Lausard had thought often how time can play tricks with a man's mind. The sheer monotony of a long march, coupled with lack of food and water and searing heat caused even the most level-headed soldier to lose track of time. Hours passed like days, and days themselves seemed to stretch out indefinitely. But at least the four-day return trip to Cairo from Marabout was more favourable than the outbound journey. The provisions he and his companions had taken from the Bedouin camp had been plentiful, more than enough to sustain them during the trek across the desert, and he reasoned that the sensation of time elongating affected him less with a full belly. But even with the relative wealth of supplies, several horses had died from exhaustion and two or three dragoons had been struck down. The freed *savants* seemed to have endured with remarkable strength, Lausard thought, but compared to the horrors they had been subjected to at the hands of their Bedouin captors, a desert march was a favourable alternative.

The squadron had kept the Nile in sight on its left

during the entire return journey. The odd patrol from French-occupied towns had been encountered along the way, but other than that the men had seen no one. Certainly no roving Bedouins. As they crested another ridge of sand, Lausard saw the spires and minarets of Cairo glinting in the searing midday sun. He also spotted something else.

Three large white tents were set up outside the walls of Cairo, each one about fifty feet long and fifteen feet high. Above each one an imposing black flag fluttered.

'Hospital tents,' Lausard murmured, spotting the black standards.

'But why *outside* the city?' Rocheteau questioned.

He was not the only one to notice several sentries with fixed bayonets gathered twenty or thirty yards from the tents. As the squadron drew nearer, the infantrymen lowered their weapons as if the dragoons were enemies, musket barrels aimed at them, bayonet points sparkling in the sunlight.

'Ride on,' a tall corporal ordered, waving the dragoons past.

'What's happening here?' Milliere demanded.

'If you've got any sense you'll ride on,' the corporal repeated. 'The men inside are all infected.'

Milliere looked puzzled.

'Oh my God,' Karim muttered. 'It's the plague.'

The corporal nodded.

'Bubonic plague,' Karim said quietly. 'It kills more Egyptians a year than starvation and thirst combined.'

'The men in these tents are dying,' the corporal told them. 'More than fifteen a day, inside *and* outside the city. General Bonaparte has set up these quarantine measures to prevent it spreading any further. Some of the officers won't leave their houses in the city. They give orders through hatches cut in the doors and they won't receive any paper unless it is soaked in vinegar first. They think that helps.' He smiled wanly. 'Any man complaining of a fever is sent to one of these tents and not allowed within four hundred yards of his comrades. Their rations are placed one hundred yards from their tents, those well enough to reach them usually live, those who can't die anyway.' He sighed wearily. 'Like I said, I'd ride on if I were you. We're here only because we're on a punishment detail. We stole from one of the mosques. The officers don't care if we live or die, they're too busy trying to keep on the right side of these stinking Moslems.' He hooked a thumb over his shoulder in the direction of Cairo. 'This plague has broken out in Alexandria and Damietta too. It'll probably kill the whole army in a matter of weeks.'

'What treatment is there?' Lausard asked.

'How the hell do I know? You're welcome to come inside and ask one of the surgeons if you like.'

'There is no cure,' Karim told the sergeant. 'I have seen this plague before, many times. It begins with a fever then growths form under the arms or in the groin. Sometimes it takes less than twenty-four hours to kill a man.'

'You have seen it, you have survived it,' Lausard said. 'How?'

'No one knows what causes it so no one knows who is more likely to catch it. I have seen men survive it, but not often. If they live beyond four days then they have a chance, but it isn't usual.'

'Everyone's panicking,' the corporal interjected. 'Some surgeons are refusing to treat those who are infected.

There is talk that those wounded in skirmishes with the Bedouin are put into beds previously occupied by plague victims, that orderlies are selling the clothes of the dead instead of burning them. No one knows what to do to survive. Some of the bodies were buried so shallow the dogs in the city dug them up and devoured them. The whole city is falling apart and yet still Bonaparte talks of conquest. He is marching into Syria even now. Those who have gone with him are lucky. The rest of us sit around with our thumbs stuck up our backsides waiting to die.'

Milliere jerked on the reins of his horse and turned the horse away, Lausard and the rest of the dragoons following him.

'I don't want to die of some terrible disease,' said Joubert. 'If I have to die I'd sooner it was on a battle-field.'

'I don't want to die at *all*,' Roussard commented.

'Nor I,' Sonnier added.

'*Vive Bonaparte*,' Delacor said cynically.

'You can't blame him for *this*,' Bonet admonished.

'He brought us here, didn't he? I'll blame him if I want to.' Delacor rounded on Moreau. 'Where is your God now when we need him?'

'It won't be a God, *anyone's* God, who decides whether you live or die now,' Lausard said.

'I've always been lucky, I hope my luck holds out.' Rocheteau looked at Lausard. 'You always said we were better off away from Paris, Alain, better off away from a life in the gutter or in prison. Do you still believe that?'

Lausard didn't answer.

* * *

An unearthly stillness filled the house where the dragoons were billeted; a silence that came with fear and
foreboding. Those who could slept. Others sat on their
makeshift pallets of straw-stuffed rags staring into the
gloom or talking quietly, almost reverentially.

Lausard sat on his mattress, using an oily rag to clean
the blade of his sword, a single candle providing an island
of light in an ocean of blackness. Beside him, Rocheteau
lay on his back, arms crossed behind his head.

'If I was to return to France now and sell all the
gold, silver and precious stones I've collected since we
got here,' the corporal pointed out, 'I could be a very
rich man.'

'Then perhaps you should be thankful you are here,'
Lausard told him. 'Being a rich man in France hasn't
been much of a pastime these past ten years, has it?
You should know, you saw enough people go to the
guillotine.'

'No, you're missing the point,' Rocheteau insisted.
'What I'm trying to say is that I could have anything
I wanted now and yet I'll probably end up dying here of
plague, or even if I don't, I can't see how any of us will
ever get back home. What with the English blockading
the ports and everything else that's going on.'

'So all your gold and jewels are no good to you then?
Do you want me to take them for you?'

Rocheteau smiled. 'I think I'll take my chances.'

Lausard finished cleaning his sword and slid it back
into the scabbard.

'We *are* going to die, aren't we, Alain?'

'Every man dies,' Lausard said. 'It's just a matter of
when and how. But not every man truly lives.'

'And you think *we* have?'

'We have been more alive during the past two years than we ever were stealing and scraping a living in the gutters of Paris. At least the army gave us something. A reason to go on. A chance to die as free men. That is more valuable than all the gold and jewels in the world.'

Lausard glanced up to see a figure in the doorway at the far end of the room. A man dressed, like himself, in the dragoon uniform. The trooper was looking around the billet, squinting into the gloom. He finally took a few faltering steps inside, passing men who glanced quizzically at him. He looked at each puzzled face, his gaze finally alighting on Lausard's. The private crossed to the sergeant and drew himself to attention.

'You are Sergeant Lausard,' he said and it sounded more like a statement than a question. 'I was sent to find you.'

'Who sent you? What's the charge this time?'

The private looked perplexed. 'I have something for you.' He reached into his pocket.

Lausard watched as the man withdrew a gleaming object and held it out to him. It glinted dully in the light cast by the candle and the sergeant could make out that it was a snuff box.

'Who is sending me gifts?'

'It is from Corporal Charnier of the third squadron. He asked me to bring it to you. He said he wanted you to have it as he would have no further use for it himself. He said you were a man of honour, that you would appreciate this gift.'

'Where is Charnier?' Lausard demanded.

'He is in one of the hospital tents outside the city. He's been there for the last four days. He has the plague.'

Lausard was on his feet in an instant. 'Take me to him,' he instructed.

'Alain, don't be a fool.' Rocheteau grabbed his companion's arm. 'You'll end up the same way as the others. You heard what he said. Plague. This isn't something you can stand up and fight like you would one of the enemy. Charnier knows that too.'

Lausard shook his arm free. 'Charnier is a good man. I'm not going to leave him to rot in that plague tent. Would you leave *me* to die like some miserable dog?'

Rocheteau shook his head.

'Karim said that if a man survived beyond four days then he might recover,' Lausard reminded the corporal. 'If there is a chance that Charnier can be saved by taking him out of that place then I will do it.'

'And what about your own life?' Rocheteau asked. 'By going there you risk catching the plague yourself.'

'Why should I worry about losing my life?' the sergeant snapped, then he turned to the private. 'Take me to him. Now!'

'I will not go back inside that place again. Charnier gave me that snuff box when he first caught the fever. I promised to give it to you but that was all I promised. I will not risk my life again.'

Lausard snatched the snuff box from him. 'Which tent is he in?'

The private told him and Lausard was already striding towards the door.

'Alain,' Rocheteau called after him but the sergeant didn't stop.

'He's a fool,' the private said dismissively.

'Better a fool than a coward,' Rocheteau said scathingly.

*   *   *

As Lausard rode he was surprised at how quiet and dark the city was. Very little light filtered into the narrow streets from the buildings on either side and some of the men he passed were barely visible in the blackness. Only as he reached the outer walls did the night seem to come alive. He heard the barking of wild dogs, the rustling of a breeze through the branches of palm trees; even the low mutterings of sentries seemed to echo in the stillness as he passed through the main gate and out into the desert. He rode at a steady pace, eyes fixed ahead, his horse cantering evenly as he guided it across the sand. Up ahead, looming white like phantoms in some fevered dream, he could make out the shapes of the hospital tents.

'Halt.'

He obeyed the order and saw an infantryman advancing towards him, Charleville pressed to his shoulder.

'Turn back,' the private instructed. 'No one is allowed beyond this point, by order of General Bonaparte.'

'I must get through,' Lausard told him.

'You know what lies beyond? In those tents? The men inside are dying of plague. Do you wish to join them?'

'Step aside,' Lausard persisted.

'I have orders to shoot anyone who tries to pass this point,' the private said, aiming the musket at Lausard's chest.

The dragoon edged his horse a couple of steps nearer, his eyes fixed on those of the sentry.

'Then shoot,' the sergeant challenged.

The private thumbed back the hammer on his musket, the sound echoing in the stillness. Lausard extended his arms on either side, pushing out his chest as if to give the infantryman a clearer target. For long moments the two men faced each other, the musket wavering slightly. Lausard remained in the saddle like a statue, his expression fixed, his eyes boring into the private. One slip of the man's finger and Lausard knew that the Charleville would blast him from point-blank range. With only a couple of feet between the two men, the private couldn't miss. The only sound to punctuate the delicate impasse was the occasional snorting of Lausard's horse as it pawed at the sand with its hoof.

Then, without a word, the infantryman lowered his musket and stepped aside, allowing Lausard to ride on.

Another minute and Lausard was outside the tent housing Charnier. He glanced up at the black flag of warning, flapping wildly in the breeze.

Lausard dismounted, leaving his horse watching patiently, sniffing the air. Like Lausard it could smell the foul odour emanating from the hospital tent, an odour that became almost intolerable as Lausard pulled aside the flap and entered the makeshift hospital. The place reeked of death and disease. The stench of excrement mingled with a more cloying, nauseating smell of pus, all exacerbated by the heat. Very little sound came from inside and many of the men who lay on the rough beds did not move.

Lausard passed among them, peering at the dimly lit faces on either side of him as he made his grim trek through the seemingly endless lines of wretches. Here and there bodies were covered with rags to hide their faces, a last attempt at dignity in a world that had stripped men of their humanity. Bowls beside some of the beds were filled with water, blood or vomit dependent upon the stage of the disease the occupant had reached. The water was usually brackish and stank as much as the blood.

Lausard moved slowly through the hall of suffering, wondering what kind of care these men were receiving. It seemed to be very little. One man was lying half in and half out of his bed, burbling incoherently. Lausard crossed to him, ready to help him back in. He studied the man's features. The milk white complexion, the dark rings beneath the eyes, the sweat that slicked the man's face and most of his upper body. And, beneath both arms, he saw three swollen, purulent growths. Almost as big as eggs. The man opened his eyes and, for precious seconds, looked directly into Lausard's. Whether the man realized he was being helped Lausard had no idea but, briefly, a smile touched the man's lips. He tried to speak as Lausard laid him back on his bed but he could not manage to get any words out. Instead he gripped the sergeant's hand and squeezed with a strength Lausard would have thought impossible. He knelt beside the man for a moment longer, watching him attempting to mouth something. Lausard could smell the rancid breath and the awful putrescent stench that rose from the body; it was as if the man was beginning to decompose before death had even taken him.

As Lausard rose, the man gripped his hand even more tightly, and the sergeant understood. He nodded gently and extended one hand, touching it to the man's fevered brow, stroking his hair gently. He would not leave this poor wretch now. Not at the point of death. The man looked at him once more and his eyes seemed to clear. There seemed to be an instant of incredible clarity and the smile that Lausard had felt sure he'd seen grew wider. A single tear rolled from the man's eye and trickled down his cheek, and Lausard felt the grip on his hand slowly released. The man's eyes remained open and Lausard waited for long moments before carefully closing them. He pulled the filthy sheet that covered the soldier over his head and stepped away.

Lausard had no idea how many men the hospital tent was home to but he kept walking, looking at each tortured face. Some had found the oblivion of sleep, some the even greater release of death. Flies buzzed around the bodies of dead and living alike, crawling over them gleefully. They welcomed the corpulence, the open wounds and the weeping sores. To his right someone moaned softly in their sleep. He looked round and saw that it was a boy in his late teens, his body wasted and ravaged by plague.

In the bed next to him was Charnier.

Lausard knelt beside him and gently shook him, allowing the corporal time to wake from his troubled slumber. He opened his eyes slowly and, it seemed, with difficulty.

'Charnier. It's me, Lausard. I came to return your gift.'

Charnier tried to sit up but the effort was too much. He pressed a hand to his head and sucked in a deep, polluted breath.

'Alain,' he said, clearing his throat. 'How did you get here?'

'I'm taking you out of here. I will not let you die in this place.' He reached into his pocket and pulled out the snuff box, holding it up for Charnier to see. 'I want to return this. You will have need of it. Not I.'

'I fear I will have need of *nothing* any more. The surgeons told me they could do nothing for me.'

'You're still alive.'

'God knows how. I've seen enough poor devils die of

this stinking plague during the last four days. Perhaps it's just as well I didn't trust those surgeons. Look.' He lifted up the shirt he wore and revealed the bloodied mess beneath one arm. 'I had two growths there, they call them buboes. Another in my groin. The doctors said it would do no good to lance them. Perhaps I was wrong, but I opened them myself. That was two days ago. There have been no more. I thought that if I released the poison I would feel better. Perhaps *I* should have been a doctor.' He managed a smile.

'Can you stand?' Lausard asked.

With Lausard's help, Charnier struggled to his feet, swaying uncertainly for a second, then he nodded.

'My uniform is under the bed. Unless those damned orderlies have sold it. That is what they do with most of the clothes around here.'

'Where *are* the orderlies and the doctors?'

'They ride back into the city every night at sun-down and return at daybreak. They care nothing for our suffering because they can do nothing to help us.'

Lausard helped him dress quickly then supported him as they made their way towards the far end of the tent, out into the night air.

'Alain, I can't ride.'

'Get up.' Lausard indicated his horse. He held the animal still while Charnier hauled himself up into the saddle, then Lausard climbed up behind him, gripping the reins with one hand and snaking his arm around his companion with the other, holding him tightly. Charnier gripped the mane of the horse as Lausard put spurs to it and headed back towards the city.

The sentries they passed paid them little heed, even those at the main gates of Cairo simply nodded as

Lausard rode past with his companion slumped across the pommel of his saddle. Once inside the city both men dismounted, the sergeant helping Charnier, who smiled and stamped his feet on the rough cobbled street.

'Do you think I will die, Alain?'

'I don't think there has been a bullet, blade or shot made that will snuff out your worthless life, you old pirate. Certainly not a disease.' He handed the snuff box to Charnier, who took it and dropped it into his pocket.

'Alain,' he began, 'you saved my life. If I had remained in that tent I . . .'

'Return to your squadron, my friend,' Lausard said, preparing to remount his horse. He extended his right hand and Charnier shook it warmly.

'I owe you my life,' the corporal repeated.

'You owe me nothing. You saved yourself. Besides, many years ago I abandoned some people I should have protected. I allowed them to die to save my own life. I hid like a snivelling dog while my own family was slaughtered. I can never wipe out the memory of my failings, of my cowardice. What I *can* ensure is that it never happens again. It is I who should thank you, my friend.' Lausard saluted and rode off, the sound of his horse's hooves echoing on the road. They gradually disappeared, dying away in the darkness like forgotten dreams.

Thirty

'Can a man lose time as easily as he loses money?'

Lausard looked up, puzzled by the comment, amused slightly at its source.

He and a dozen of his companions were watering their horses in the muddy water of the Nile, the animals lathered and weary after the ride. Lausard guessed that the patrol had been out for close to an hour. The sun was beating down with its customary ferocity and most of the dragoons had undone their tunics in an attempt at relief from the sweltering temperature. But, after so long in such a hostile and unforgiving land they should, Lausard reasoned, have all known better.

'What the hell are you going on about?' Delacor looked across at Tabor, who was gazing out towards the endless desert. 'How can you *lose* time, you idiot?'

'I think we've all lost time since we came to this country,' Rostov commented. 'How long have we been here now? Fourteen months? And for what?'

'I heard that Bonaparte himself is thinking of returning

371

to France,' Bonet said. 'War with Austria has begun again. The Directory needs him.'

'Who told you that?' Delacor demanded.

'A private of hussars I spoke to the other day. He was with Bonaparte right through Syria and Palestine. He was at the siege of El Arish and at Acre. He said that at the siege of Acre the artillery were so short of shells that they had to collect those fired by the enemy. They were paid for each ball they retrieved. Twelve sous for a twenty-four-pound ball, nine sous for an eighteen-pound ball and—'

'Is he the same one who told you Bonaparte is leaving Egypt?' Lausard interrupted.

'I have no reason to doubt him, he is a good man.'

'And when he leaves, how many of *us* leave with him? Certainly not those he ordered poisoned at Jaffa. Did your hussar tell you *that* story?'

'Bonaparte ordered our own men poisoned?' Rocheteau was aghast.

'Plague victims who couldn't be moved,' Lausard continued. 'Rather than let them fall into the hands of the Turks he ordered them killed. Perhaps there was mercy behind his thinking.'

'I wish he'd show some mercy to us and let us go home,' Roussard said mournfully.

'If there is war against Austria he will have need of troops,' Bonet offered. 'Let us just hope that we are among those he needs. He knows of our abilities.'

'There'll be no room for us when he leaves,' Delacor hissed, 'but you can be sure that he'll take his "pekinese" with him. His poets, his artists and his writers. He values them more than he does his soldiers.'

'I wonder how much France has changed since we left?' Rostov mused.

'You mean how much the Directory has changed it,' Lausard corrected. 'They will not be eager to see Bonaparte return, war or no war. Here he is no threat to them. Back in France they fear him.'

'Do you think the people here will ever forgive us for what we have done, or forget us?' Tabor asked.

'In a year they will not even remember you were here,' Karim said, smiling.

'And when we return, Karim, will you return with us?' Lausard asked.

'I am one of you now. As long as I wear the same uniform I fight at your side.'

'And when we return, do we get our six acres of land that Bonaparte promised us?' Rocheteau muttered.

Lausard smiled and swung himself into his saddle, followed rapidly by the other men.

'Your six acres, Rocheteau,' he said, pointing out towards the desert. 'There they are. Yours, mine and every man's in this whole disease-riddled, hungry, exhausted army. Bonaparte promised us land and wealth but all *he* ever wanted was glory. The problem is that the pursuit of glory is a meaningless chase.' He wheeled his horse and rode off, watched for a second by the other men, his broad back silhouetted against the horizon, the heat haze hanging like a shimmering blanket over the scorched land. Rocheteau spurred his horse and followed the sergeant, as did the other men, dust rising behind them.

Lausard looked at his pocket watch and noted that it was approaching noon. They would stop for food, what little they had, in another hour and try to find shelter from the searing sun just as they did every day and would continue to do until otherwise ordered. The patrols usually lasted three or four hours. Any longer was unbearable for both men and horses. Lausard glanced again at his watch and shook it. It had stopped. Dust had probably clogged the delicate inner workings, he thought. The timepiece was useless now, the hands frozen for ever. Perhaps this was final confirmation that time truly had no relevance in this land. He dropped the watch, allowing it to fall into the soft sand. The horses following galloped over it.

The patrol rode on.

High above them in the cloudless sky the sun blazed.